Soldiers' Daughters

Fiona Field joined the army at eighteen, married a bomb disposal expert at twenty-one and then, at twenty-six, got thrown out for getting pregnant. Her youngest child is a soldier recently returned from Afghanistan. She is also the author of *Soldiers' Wives* (Head of Zeus, 2014).

Also by Fiona Field

Soldiers' Wives

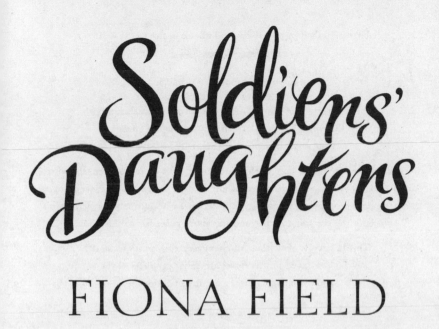

Soldiers' Daughters

FIONA FIELD

HEAD
of ZEUS

First published in paperback and eBook in the UK in 2015
by Head of Zeus Ltd

9 7 5 3 1 2 4 6 8

A catalogue record for this book is available from the British Library.

Paperback ISBN: 9781781857762
eBook ISBN: 97817818577755

Typeset by e-type, Aintree, Liverpool
Printed and bound by Clays Ltd, St Ives PLC

Head of Zeus Ltd
Clerkenwell House
45-47 Clerkenwell Green
London EC1R 0HT

WWW.HEADOFZEUS.COM

To Ian.

For being patient.

Chapter One

As her father's car drew up in front of Old College, Sandhurst, Samantha Lewis felt a surge of fear, raw, primal fear, and for a moment she thought she might actually be sick, as the adrenalin squirted into her bloodstream. She swallowed, shut her eyes and breathed deeply. When she opened them again after a couple of seconds she glanced across at her father, who was staring back at her. As usual his face was expressionless; no reassuring wink, no flicker of understanding, just an emotionless stare.

It wasn't unexpected, that was how he was and she was used to it now, and over the years she'd come to accept the reason why, but the lack of empathy and sympathy shown by her father stiffened Sam's spine. Determination replaced the fear. She'd show him. She'd prove to him she could do this. She'd make it, she'd get through the next year and she hoped when he came to her commissioning ceremony he would be proud of her. Maybe, if she succeeded, she'd finally crack the shell he'd developed to protect himself but which had also kept her at arm's length for twenty-two years.

A warrant officer in immaculate number two dress and Sam Browne approached the car. Her father, Colonel Tim Lewis, wound the window down and turned his attention to the sergeant major.

The senior NCO glanced into the car, past the driver to Sam and said to her father, 'If you'd like to park your car over there, sir.' He waved his pace stick at the end of a line of already neatly parked vehicles. 'And then, if the young lady would like to proceed into the building, she'll be given further instructions.'

'Thank you,' said her father. Then he said, over his shoulder, 'Get that, Sam?'

Sam sighed. The instructions were hardly difficult. She'd passed the army officers' selection board, she had a first-class degree in electrical engineering and her father still treated her as if she was at prep school.

Her father parked the car as directed and Sam got out.

'I'll wait for you here,' said her father, leaning across to talk to her through the still-open door.

Sam smoothed down the skirt of her dark suit and took a deep breath.

'Get on with it, girl. We haven't got all day.'

Around them, other cars were also disgorging new cadets and Sam glanced at her fellow inmates and tried to size them up. They all looked bright and eager but Sam wondered if they were putting on as much of a front as she was, trying to convince themselves, as much as anyone else, that they weren't actually bricking it about what the next weeks and months held for them. She slammed the passenger door and headed for the steps to the main door. A colour sergeant was directing the new arrivals into the building so they could register, find their accommodation and then start the process of unloading all the kit they would need to survive in this environment.

A female staff sergeant took Sam's name and details, handed her a map of the building, marked in pencil, of how to get to the back of it, where her father would be able to park and they could start the process of unloading.

'When you've finished, Miss Lewis, if you could ask your father to re-park his car back out at the front and then if you could all report to the Memorial Chapel at two o'clock sharp for the Commandant's welcome.' Again the map was marked in pencil to show Sam where she needed to be. She suspected that finding her way without asking for further directions was one of her first tests here.

Sam returned to her dad and told him where they needed to go.

'I'm having flashbacks,' he remarked as he slipped the car into gear. Well, bully for you, she thought, nerves making her grumpy.

He drove off the huge parade square at the front of the beautiful neo-classical building that was to be Sam's home for the next year – assuming the army didn't have other ideas and chuck her out. Not that being chucked out was an option. She knew she had to have the moral fibre and courage to take everything the army might throw at her and get on with it. She had to get through this course. It was only a year. Surely anything was bearable for a year? To fail was unthinkable. She knew if she did she'd disappoint her father and she couldn't bear to give him more heartache.

While her relationship with her father might be troubled, she hadn't lacked for affection from other sources. Her grandparents and the succession of three nannies who had looked after her had all told her she was loved and cherished even though her father had never managed it. Now Sam was an adult she understood why, but her earlier bewilderment had left its indelible mark. Back then she'd been sure that he blamed her for the tragedy that had struck his family. Maybe if she'd not been born first everything would have been all right. It was William, her twin, who had died at birth, along with their mother, when the emergency C-section had gone horribly wrong. Sam's birth had gone well but then William had got stuck and when his heart rate had dipped alarmingly they'd been forced to operate and that was when the placenta had been severed. In the desperate chaotic minutes following this, the team hadn't been able to save either her mother or her brother. When she'd been old enough her granny had told her what had happened and had assured her that it had been no one's fault, least of all hers. A terrible accident, 'one of those things'. But for years Sam had been sure she'd known differently – it was her fault. Her fault for being first.

Now she was older she understood that her father was probably terrified of going through the hurt of loving someone again in case they got ripped out of his life, like his wife and baby had been. Keep everyone at arm's length, don't get involved, that way you can't be hurt again. No wonder her father hadn't ever been able to love her properly, although for all his shortcomings as a parent she still loved him. And she hoped that maybe one day she'd make him so proud he *would* love her back.

Michelle Flowers's father drew his car up on the parade square about ten minutes after the Lewises' car had been driven off round the back of Old College.

Major Henry Flowers shook his head. 'You know, I still can't get my head round the fact that you passed selection.'

'Get over it, Dad. The army sees my potential, that's all.'

'Hmm.' Her father was far from convinced. 'Mind you, it's one thing, pulling the wool over their eyes at the selection board. It'll be another thing entirely, convincing them for the best part of a year that you've got the makings of an officer.'

'I've got everything they're looking for,' said Michelle confidently. 'Brains, courage, spirit…'

Henry snorted. 'I didn't hear obedience in that list.'

'That's because I've got a mind of my own.'

Henry snorted again. 'There's a difference between being able to think independently and being wilfully rebellious.'

'So I don't behave like a sheep. Baa,' she added, insolently. 'I was only obeying orders? Yeah, right. Like those are words which have gone down well in history.'

Henry gave up arguing. 'Still, it's made you get rid of those awful dreadlocks and the nose stud so that's something to be grateful for.'

'Dad, a couple of piercings and a hairstyle don't make you a dead loss to society.'

'No, but a drug habit does. In my day, any hint of drugs or anything like that and the army wouldn't have had anything to do with you.'

Michelle shook her head in disbelief at her father's attitude. 'They're more enlightened now, as long as you're clean when you join.'

'And are you?' her father shot at her.

'Chill. Of course I am.'

Her father muttered something about she'd better be and Michelle got out of the car to collect her instructions about accommodation and what she needed to do, as Sam had done just before her.

Sam was on another trip to the car to ferry yet more belongings to her new room. She pulled the ironing board off the top of the pile, one of many items of 'suggested' kit on the list that had accompanied the letter formally requesting that she make arrangements to swear the oath of allegiance prior to her arrival at Sandhurst. Also included on the kit list had been shoe-polishing equipment, ten wooden hangers, black court shoes, spray starch, foot powder, padlocks, a steam iron, worn-in trainers, swimming costume, bedding, towels, toiletries, a smart suit, an alarm clock, plus a mass of personal documentation to prove she was who she claimed to be, including passport, birth certificate, P45, national insurance card and her educational certificates. It was like going back to boarding school, Sam had mused as she'd labelled everything and packed it in suitcases which were put in a pile in the hall together with the rest of her kit. Boarding school with guns...

'Bloody hell!' exclaimed her father as he turned into the bleak corridor that led to Sam's room.

Sam jumped and assumed she'd done something wrong. But her father wasn't looking at her. There, coming in the opposite direction, was an old friend of her father's, a fellow army officer and the father of a girl she'd shared a room with at prep school.

Sam felt her eyes widen in stunned shock. So if Major Flowers was here that meant Michelle...

And there she was, behind him. OK, she was a lot older than when Sam had last seen her but she was still completely recognisable and still incredibly tall. Only now she wasn't lanky but elegant and slender, like a gazelle. Sam propped her ironing board against a cream-painted wall and thundered down the corridor.

'No running,' bawled a stentorian voice behind her. But Sam had reached her goal and was hugging Michelle. And like their last hug, years previously, Sam still only came up to Michelle's shoulders.

Both girls were laughing and staring at each other in amazement. And in her absolutely joy at seeing a familiar face, Sam forgot that being friends with Michelle hadn't always been plain sailing.

'I can't believe it,' said Sam. 'This is such a surprise. I mean you. You of all people.'

'I can't say I'm so surprised about you, following in your father's footsteps and everything.'

On the other hand, Sam was stunned that Michelle had joined up. She had always been so madcap and impulsive. Maybe she'd calmed down now she was older.

'Which is your room?' asked Michelle.

Sam pointed down the corridor. 'That one.'

Michelle looked at the piece of paper in her hand. 'I'm twenty-six F.'

The pair scanned the corridor.

'There,' said Sam. 'Almost opposite. Perfect.' Then she added, 'Oh, this is so fantastic. I know that everyone says the first five weeks are hell on earth but anything's bearable with a buddy.'

Michelle nodded. 'Oh, God. And I thought getting here was fucking brilliant, but now you're here too...'

Sam suppressed a grin at the look on both fathers' faces caused by Michelle's swearing. Maybe she hadn't changed. Sam wondered how the hell her old friend was going to manage, here at the RMAS, given her past, uneasy relationship with authority.

The beginning of that first day was wonderfully civilised. After all the cars had been unloaded everyone made their way to the memorial chapel, which was across the square at the back of the college, behind Sam's and Michelle's rooms. There, surrounded by the names of officers who had trained at Sandhurst and then made the ultimate sacrifice in the mud and blood of the Flanders trenches, the cadets' parents were assured by the Commandant that the Royal Military Academy would mould their offspring to be leaders, give them an unswerving moral compass to distinguish between right and wrong, just and unjust, how their pastoral care would always be a priority and how they would become valuable members of society. It was sobering and uplifting in equal measure.

Then it was tea and cake in the officers' mess while their company commanders and the civilian teaching staff, collectively known as the directing staff (or the DS, Sam's father told her), circulated, making polite chit-chat. But once the parents were off the premises there was a distinct shift in mood and tempo.

The cadets returned to their rooms where they took off their smart suits and donned their issue, one-size-fits-all, green coveralls, which actually fitted no one but would be their everyday garb until they could be issued with everything else they'd need, from PE kit to parade uniforms. Now dressed uniformly, they were directed to stand outside their respective bedroom doors.

And that was when the shouting started. Suddenly they weren't civilians but the lowest of the low as far as the army was concerned. Pond life ranked higher than they did and, it seemed, was certainly considered more intelligent and was held in higher esteem by the entire army. They *knew* nothing, they *were* nothing and if they knew what was good for them they would *do* nothing but obey orders from their superiors, and it seemed that everyone else at Sandhurst – probably including the stable-yard cat, thought Sam – was superior. Talk about being at the bottom of the food chain.

It was over supper that Michelle and Sam finally got to catch up on what had happened in the intervening years since they'd been sent off to different boarding schools when they were eleven.

'So you did electrical engineering at uni?' said Michelle. 'Bloody hell. You're a bit of a clever clogs, then, aren't you? Mind you, your dad always gave you weird presents for birthdays and everything, didn't he? You must have been the only girl at St Martin's with a Meccano set and a model railway. At least my step-mum made sure Dad's presents were more appropriate. She might be a cow and I still hate her but at least she made Dad choose girlie pressies,' said Michelle.

And your family life probably explains why you're a bit bonkers, thought Sam, fondly. But, then, she wasn't in much of a position to cast aspersions on Michelle's family hang-ups when she had her own to contend with. It suddenly seemed obvious to her that she and Michelle were both desperate for their fathers' attention, only they tried to get it in different ways: Michelle through her outrageous behaviour and shock tactics, and she by being good and trying only to please.

'So what about you? What did you read at uni?'

Michelle snorted. 'Sore subject. I did English but failed my first-year exams. It didn't help that I had a bit of a fling with my tutor before it all turned sour.' She sighed. 'Mind you, he didn't have to threaten to get a restraining order slapped on me.'

Sam's eyes widened. 'What?'

'He was a total drama queen, if you ask me,' said Michelle, shrugging off the enormity of what she'd disclosed. 'I only wanted to get him to see my side of the argument, but he said I was harassing him. If he'd only stopped and listened to me...' She sighed again. 'Anyway, Dad went off on one so, what with one thing and another, I fucked off to Aus.'

'Really?' Sam barely knew what to say. Restraining order? Although Michelle said he'd only threatened her with one so maybe it had been a scare tactic, nothing more. Even so... sheesh. But she'd made it through selection so what the heck.

'Yeah. And I had a great time in Aus,' continued Michelle, unaware of how stunned her old friend was. 'It's such a blinding place. So laid back and friendly. At least the people are; their government is a bunch of bastards.'

So she'd managed to cross the Australian authorities as well as her uni tutor? 'What did you do?' said Sam.

'I over-stayed my visa by a few weeks and they got really arsey.'

'Michelle! Of course they would. There are rules. And how long was a few weeks?'

'Nine months.' Sam gasped and Michelle shrugged. 'Anyway, I was up shit creek because my open return air ticket had run out and I couldn't work because of my visa – which they refused to renew – so I couldn't earn enough to buy another ticket…' She gave Sam a look as if to suggest it had all been a conspiracy against her rather than a total cock-up on her part.

'Bloody hell. What did you do?'

'I had to get Dad to bail me out. And of course as soon as I got back he went off on one again. Honestly, Sam, it was only a few hundred quid for the ticket – well, maybe five, but he could afford it.'

Sam didn't think that was the point but kept quiet.

'Anyway, as he was being a pain to live with, I decided I'd better get a job that came with living accommodation. So here I am. From making the decision to getting here it's all been a bit of a roller-coaster, so if I find it's complete pants I can easily get out. All I need to do is tell them I'm back on the dope and that'll be me home free. Not that I really want to do that because I really, really do think, for once in my life, I've made the right decision. But it's nice to know I've got an exit strategy handy, you know, just in case…'

Sam grinned. Michelle really hadn't changed. Still nuts, still incorrigible.

'Dad is utterly convinced,' continued Michelle, 'I won't make it through to Sovereign's Parade and I really want to prove him wrong. Honestly, if anything is going to keep me going his lack of faith in me will.'

Once again it seemed that she and Michelle had a lot in common – they were army brats, they'd both been sent to boarding school and neither of them had their birth mother around, but now it seemed both of them wanted to prove to their fathers they had what it took to get a commission.

Sam might have thought she was fit, she thought she knew how to look after her kit, she thought she knew how to bull her drill shoes and she thought she knew how to march because she'd been in the Officer Training Corps at uni. How wrong she was. In a matter of hours she discovered that she knew nothing. Zero. Zilch. Not a single thing that she did was remotely up to the standard deemed acceptable by the colour sergeant in charge of her platoon of thirty women. But if she thought she was faring badly, it was even worse for Michelle. Michelle might also be the daughter of an officer but she hadn't a clue about the army or what was expected. Maybe backpacking round Aus hadn't been the greatest preparation.

After a few days Michelle really began to struggle. She took almost twice as long as Sam to get her kit up to scratch or arrange all of her issue kit ready for inspection, or any damn task they were set, but her worst failing was her total inability to bring her drill shoes up to snuff. Bulling boots was a skill she couldn't master. Luckily Sam could and had, so as soon as she'd sorted out her own stuff she rocked across the corridor to sit on Michelle's bed with a duster, the boot polish and Michelle's drill shoes. And while Sam's duster-encased finger traced minute circles all over Michelle's toecaps, her friend got on with ironing her shirts, or de-fluffing her beret with sticky tape, or cleaning the skirting board of her room with a toothbrush.

'You don't need to do this,' protested Michelle as it approached midnight and Sam was still working on her mate's boots.

'I do, I owe you. You got me through the first weeks of prep school. What goes around comes around.'

When they'd first run into each other, back when they were both seven-going-on-eight, her initial impression of Michelle had been far from favourable. Sam had been sitting on her bed in her two-bed dorm at boarding school on the first day, feeling abandoned and bereft after her father's perfunctory departure, when a tall, skinny and noisy girl had thundered in.

'But I wanted that bed,' she said by way of greeting, glaring at Sam.

Sam felt irked. She'd got here first, this was her bed and she wasn't going to be pushed about. But even though she made her mind up to stay put she also felt intimidated.

Then the girl's father arrived. 'Now, now, Michelle, I'm sure the other bed is as nice.'

'But it's not by the window.'

'Honestly, Michelle,' said her mother, who entered the room a second after her father, 'does it really matter?'

To Sam's amazement Michelle turned, gave her mother a vile look and then said, 'Of course it matters,' in such a withering tone that Sam felt a surge of embarrassment at having witnessed the scene. She pushed herself further up her bed and as far into the corner as she could, clutching her teddy like a shield in front of her. How could this girl treat her mother like that? thought Sam, who, not having a mum, longed for one more than anything in the world.

After this they barely spoke to each other for a couple of days; Sam thinking Michelle over-confident, brash and annoying, and Michelle categorising Sam as wet, shy and a waste of oxygen. But then, when Michelle caught Sam crying with homesickness even her, rather stony, heart softened and tentatively she gave her room-mate a hug.

'Listen,' she said, 'I'm sure you're the normal one here, missing your folks and everything, unlike me. Isn't that a good thing?'

'I suppose.' Sam sniffed and tried to dry her eyes. 'Don't you like yours, then?'

'Dad's all right.'

'What about your mum?'

'She's not my mum. My mum ran away a few years ago and left me with Dad.'

Sam didn't know what to say. She wondered if being left behind – not wanted – was worse than having a mum who'd died.

'But even so, don't you mind being away from home?' Sam sniffed.

'Nah,' Michelle said robustly. 'Can't stand my step-mother so I'm thankful I don't have to see her, the mean cow.'

The idea that Michelle had a step-mother, and one who seemed to be wicked to boot, was somewhat thrilling. And it explained the exchange between Michelle and Mrs Flowers that first day.

'What about your folks?' Michelle asked.

'Dad's always busy working and Mum's dead.'

There was a short silence that followed that announcement. Then, 'Sorry. Do you miss her?'

'Never knew her, but I know I'd have liked to have had a mother.'

'I miss mine. I wish I knew why she walked out.'

'You've no idea why?'

Michelle shook her head. 'Dad won't talk about it but maybe, if he hadn't married Janine, Mum might have come back.'

'Do you see her?'

'Who, my real mum?'

'Yes.'

'No.'

'That's sad.' Sam reckoned that was really sad; sadder than having a dead mum. Poor Michelle.

From then on loud, brash, brave Michelle took Sam into her protective care and stuck with her through prep school; making her laugh, making her face her fears and frequently making her late. Oh, and getting them both into trouble when Michelle's pranks went a bit too far, but Sam also knew that without Michelle her experience at prep school might have been very different and a lot less happy. Now it was pay-back time and just as Michelle had kept her head above water at St Martin's, at Sandhurst it was Sam's turn to be Michelle's life-saver.

Chapter Two

Despite their best efforts, despite the fact that they always thought they had brought their rooms and uniforms to a state of perfection, they still got shouted at. They got shouted at for being scruffy, shouted at for being late, shouted at for breathing loudly and yet, because everyone was always getting shouted at for the same things, it was, bizarrely, almost funny.

After the first few weeks they were all so exhausted neither Sam nor Michelle knew how they managed to function at all, but function they did. Everyone in their intake at Sandhurst had been turned into zombies by the relentless pressure. And it wasn't just the endless inspections – there were route marches, PT sessions, lectures to listen to, essays to write, and the transition between any of these activities invariably involved a change of clothes and sometimes yet another snap room inspection to check that, having changed uniforms at lightning speed, your room was still a showpiece. Sleep was a luxury and, like every other cadet, Sam got used to managing with five hours a night, often less, so staying awake in lectures, which took place in warm, cosy classrooms, was a complete mission.

'Whatthehelldoyouthinkyou'redoingLewis?'

Sam was so startled her bum actually left the hard plastic seat she was sitting on.

'Sir?' she gasped, her heart hammering with horror at being caught sound asleep in a lecture on military law. A dry subject and a warm room had proved a fatal combination. She stared at the angry face of the instructor, inches from her own. She could smell mint on his breath and a bubble of crazy hysterical laugher threatened to escape.

'You were sleeping, Lewis,' he snapped.

'Yes, sir.'

'Is my lecture boring you?'

It had been. Tedious was the only word to describe it but Sam knew a big fat lie was in order. 'No, sir, of course not. I'm a bit tired, that's all.'

'Not getting your beauty sleep,' he sneered.

Sam knew that her kit might be immaculate, as was her personal hygiene, but other than that she looked a complete mess. A comment Michelle had made a couple of days before leapt into her head.

'It's all very well being as fit as a butcher's dog but I wish I didn't look like one as well.' Which, considering how pretty Michelle was with her fine bone structure and clear skin, had begged the question that if Michelle thought she looked rough, how bad did the rest of them look?

She couldn't remember the last time she'd worn a hint of make-up or moisturised her skin. Her hands were calloused and her nails broken and chipped. Her hair, too long to be off her collar, was scraped back into an unbecoming knot, and her lip was swollen and split from when she'd slipped on the assault course earlier in the week and hit her face. Beauty sleep? Who was Captain Philips kidding?

'So,' he said, not waiting for her answer, 'to make sure you don't drop off again, maybe you'd better stand at the front here. Don't want you missing any more of my lecture. I didn't spend hours preparing it for it to be wasted.'

'Yes, sir.'

The other cadets all sent Sam looks of support and sympathy as she made her way to the front of the classroom and stood next to the whiteboard, swaying with exhaustion. Of course, standing out in front of the class also meant she couldn't take notes so she'd have extra work to do, copying up somebody else's.

'Bastard,' said Michelle, as they ran back to their accommodation to change into PT kit for the endurance run that was next on the agenda. 'You can copy my notes. I did them extra carefully so you can read them. Best handwriting and everything.'

'Thanks, hon.' Michelle was a good friend.

Their first term at Sandhurst edged towards Christmas and a fortnight's leave. Before they all departed there was a dinner night for their intake where the officer instructors all arrived in myriads of different regimental mess kits, turning the evening into a parade of peacocks. And then the final event of each and every term – Sovereign's Parade – the commissioning parade for the senior term. As Sam stood on the parade square in front of Old College, immaculate in her number one dress uniform, a high-necked, navy-blue suit with white collar tabs, gleaming white belt, white gloves and black drill shoes bulled to a mirror finish, and watched the top intake march past the saluting base before going up the steps and through the doors of Old College, she knew she wanted to be commissioned more than anything in the world. Sod how tough it all was, stuff the sleep deprivation, and bollocks to the hard work, it would all be worth it for that moment.

'What you doing for the Christmas leave?' asked Michelle. 'Going to your gran's as usual?'

Sam nodded. 'Now I've left school and I'm grown up, Dad isn't entitled to a quarter any more so he lives in the mess. I can't really go and stay with him there, can I? Anyway, I think he's going skiing with some friends.'

'Can't you go too?'

'I think I'd rather be with Gran and Grandpa. It'll be more normal. And after a term at Sandhurst I could do with a dose of normal.'

Not, thought Sam, that holidays had ever been really normal, not since she could remember. When they'd lived in Germany, she'd been palmed off on other families on the patch. It had been OK but she'd always been conscious that she was a guest in someone else's house so it had been difficult to really relax, not like you could in your own place with your own toys and belongings. Then they'd moved back to England and shortly after that she'd been sent to boarding school. Sometimes she went to stay with her maternal grandparents but sometimes her father took leave and she'd go and stay with him in his quarter for a week or so. But, of course, with him being posted on a regular basis, on several occasions 'home' wasn't the same 'home' as it had been on the previous visit, so she'd arrive at a strange house, on a strange patch with strange neighbours and unknown children in the play-park. Her belongings might have been unpacked into this new bedroom but it never felt like her room; *her* room was the one she shared with Michelle at boarding school and then later the one at her public school. That was the constant that didn't change in her life, that was home. The place she stayed with her father was just a house.

Right now, the calm normality of her grandparents' cottage held far more appeal than a skiing holiday with her father. It might be in a village in the back of beyond, where the only social life took place in the local pub and where the average age of the customers had to be topping fifty, but the thought of having two weeks during which she could eat, sleep and relax and not be shouted at seemed heaven on earth. Besides, her grandparents would smother her in love and cuddles – and she could do with a dose of that too.

*

From the first day of her second term, Sam knew there was a distinct but subtle change in her intake's training. For a start, they were no longer the junior term. The new intake's cadets were the ones who were the focus of the opprobrium of all the directing staff. Sam's intake was treated a smidge more like grown-ups. There were slightly fewer pointless changes of uniform every day, they had more time to themselves, there were fewer show parades, fewer inspections. And they could only feel sorry for the new cadets who were being put through what they had survived. Sorry, but also a little smug. After all, they had survived it... well, *they* had but some hadn't.

At the end of their first term there had been casualties: the cadets who had been told they were never going to make the grade; not committed enough; not clever enough; not fit enough... And the outstanding cadets were already being promoted. OK, the promotions were to meaningless unpaid cadet ranks but these promotions did bestow kudos because it meant the DS had recognised and acknowledged who was ahead of their peers. Sam was amongst the chosen ones and was now an officer cadet lance corporal along with two other colleagues. At the other end of the scale, Michelle was on a warning.

'What's that all about?' asked Sam when Michelle had exited her company commander's interview ashen and close to tears.

'He said I don't pay enough attention to detail.'

'Oh, hon.' Sam gave her a hug.

'And he said I question authority.'

'Well...'

'But some of the stuff we have to do is bonkers. Pointless.'

'I know, but it's the way it's done here. Once we get commissioned it'll all be different. Just suck it up for the next few months and stop asking why.'

'I suppose,' said Michelle, despondently.

'When will your warning be reviewed?'

'Four weeks.'

'You can do it,' said Sam. 'Head down, work hard and don't question orders.'

'But this is what I said to my dad. *I was only obeying orders* isn't a good argument.'

Sam laughed. 'The DS aren't asking you to shoot unarmed civilians – they're seeing how far they can push you.'

'Maybe.'

'And why not take some initiative? The DS like that. They want to see us being proactive – you know, leading from the front.'

'Doing what?'

'I dunno.' Sam scratched her head. 'Look, Arnhem Company ran that talent night. How about doing something like that?'

'The talent night was pants.'

It had been embarrassingly awful but it wasn't the point: the point was that Arnhem Company's cadets had taken it upon themselves to try to entertain everyone else. 'So organise something that isn't. Look,' said Sam, 'if you sink your father will have been proved right. And if that happens you'll have to go home and live with him and your step-mother and eat humble pie.'

'You're right.' Michelle leaned over and gave Sam a big hug. 'OK, Dettingen Company is going to have a party. And it's going to be the best ever.'

'Sounds good to me,' said Sam.

'When?' said Sarah, the cadet most likely to win the sash of honour. 'When are we going to do this?'

She, like the rest of Michelle's colleagues, was lounging around in one of the battered leather armchairs in the cadet mess anteroom.

'This party has got to be on a weekend when everyone's here,' said Kim. 'We don't want it to be a flop because half the others are away on exercise. Hang on, I'll get the programme.' She shot out of the room to the noticeboard, which had the copies of Academy orders and company daily detail which together mapped out their daily, weekly and termly routines.

A minute later she was back with the green A4 sheets. She flopped back into the chair and began leafing through the pages.

'Nope, nope, nope,' she said as she scanned the weekly programmes and saw which platoons were being sent off on adventurous training or on exercise. 'Eureka. Got it. Oh, and it'll be Valentine's weekend.'

'It's written in the stars,' said Michelle. 'So what's the theme to be? Vamps and Tramps? Shipwreck?'

There was a chorus of catcalls.

'You think of better,' she said, sulking.

'Films?' suggested Sam.

'That's rubbish,' said Michelle. 'All the lads'll pick characters from *The Bridge on the River Kwai* or *The Longest Day* or *A Bridge Too Far*. Honestly, they'll all turn up in uniform and what's the point in that?'

'But that's exactly the point,' said Sam. 'You know what men are like when it comes to stuff like dressing up: they'll only do it if they can do it easily. If we make it too difficult they'll bail out.'

The others agreed. 'And anyway,' said Sarah, 'we can all glam up. We can be film stars. Sam can come as Scarlett Johansson. She's little and blonde with enviable knockers.'

'Oi,' protested Sam, throwing a cushion across the room, despite the fact that what Sarah said about her tits was true. Even in a top-of-the-range sports bra, running was always uncomfortable because of her boobs and army uniforms had never been designed with an hourglass figure like hers in mind.

Everyone else laughed but then the cadets began to discuss who they would come dressed as.

Michelle realised she was completely outnumbered in her objection to the theme and joined in. 'On that basis I shall come as Nicole Kidman. Isn't she hugely tall?'

'Good shout,' said Kim. 'Tall and gorgeous. She's yours.' Michelle preened.

'Well, I'm going to use a year's supply of cam cream and come as Princess Fiona in ogre mode,' said Sarah.

There were hoots of derision but there was a definite air of excitement in the mess as the cadets discussed the arrangements.

'Hang on,' said Sam. She grabbed a notebook. 'We need a committee. Michelle, as it was your idea, I vote you to be chairman. All agreed?' She looked around the anteroom. 'Carried. And I'll take the minutes.' She began to write notes as the cadets came up with ideas thick and fast.

Later, when they were returning to their rooms, Michelle turned to Sam.

'We don't really need a committee, do we?'

'No, probably not. But now we've got one, and you are chairman, it makes it all rather official. And it has the added bonus that if I'm going to do my job properly the minutes need to be published. And that way the DS will know exactly who is responsible for the idea. If not, someone like Sarah is bound to get the credit just because she's Sarah.'

Michelle stopped in her tracks. 'God, you are such a genius, Sam. Respect.'

The plan worked and shortly after the party, which was a roaring success, Michelle's warning was removed.

'I'm back in the game,' she announced, skipping into Sam's room without knocking.

'Phew. Just make sure it stays that way,' said Sam. 'It's all about survival and doing what it takes to get to the end.'

She had a vested interest in Michelle's survival – when Michelle got into trouble she sometimes caused a lot of collateral damage, and Sam had no desire to be caught up in the fall-out if Michelle screwed up. Michelle was huge fun, wonderfully generous and kindness itself, but she was wild and impetuous and often acted before she'd considered the consequences – and with Michelle, Sam knew, the consequences could be serious, unforeseen and far-reaching.

In the meantime, they had the rest of their second term to get through, although with regard to their skills, experience and ability they'd come a zillion miles from their starting point the previous September. Sam felt as if they had been climbing a mountain, concentrating on plodding upwards, one foot in front of the other, eyes only on the path ahead, and now they were allowed to turn around and look at the view. And to see how far they'd come was stunning. She knew that, as a result, they all stood a little taller, their backs were a little straighter, and they held their chins an inch higher.

Their progress through the Sandhurst mill continued, punctuated by days of real fun, like when they were taken for a week's adventurous training, to times of utter torment, when they were on a field exercise for days in one of the coldest and wettest Februaries on record. But they survived and, with each challenge they overcame, their own Sovereign's Parade came closer. The lectures, the fitness training, the drill, the fieldcraft and all the other military skills they would one day need continued and then suddenly they were allowed another two weeks' leave and on their return they were the senior intake. Wide-eyed juniors looked up to them with real respect, and even the attitude of the training officers was friendlier. Now, instead of being knocked into shape, they were being polished to a final, shimmering finish. Military tailors arrived at the Academy to fit them for their uniforms and the various corps and regiments of the army sent representatives to interview the cadets, to see which ones they wanted to select to join their ranks.

It was with trepidation that Sam waited to be called for her interview with the Royal Electrical and Mechanical Engineers to see if they thought her worthy of becoming a REME officer. And if they didn't...?

Michelle's goal of becoming a helicopter pilot had taken a huge knock as she'd failed the aptitude test. Sam had wondered privately if Michelle's ambition hadn't been a bit of a stretch – given the fact she couldn't even drive a car, having twice failed her test – but it didn't make Michelle's disappointment any less devastating.

'So, what are you going to do now?'

'Stick pins in models of helicopters.'

'Seriously?'

Michelle sighed. 'I don't know. Join some outfit that'll have me and have another go later. Maybe I'll take some private flying lessons.'

Sam didn't state the obvious – that maybe Michelle ought to have done that before. But that was Michelle all over – wise, after the event. 'So what appeals?'

Michelle sighed yet again and slumped back in the armchair in her bedroom. 'If there's one thing all these field exercises here have taught me it's that I am not a fan of being wet, cold and miserable—'

'Who is?' interrupted Sam with feeling.

'Hence wanting to be a pilot; all cocooned in a nice little Plexiglas bubble with climate control, no yomping across moors, no lugging one's own body weight in kit... I suppose if I can't do that I need to look at something office-based. Admin-fodder, I suppose.'

'You'd be great at that. You're so good at that HR and personnel stuff.'

'You mean I'm crap at everything else?'

'You said it,' said Sam with a grin.

Michelle reached behind her for a cushion, which she threw at Sam. 'At least I won't be a garage mechanic.'

'Maybe I won't either.' After all, her best mate had failed at what she wanted to do, so there was no guarantee that she would be granted her wish.

Sam needn't have worried, although for a fortnight, until she heard, she'd felt sick with apprehension every time she'd considered the possibility that the REME mightn't think her good enough. But when she finally got the news that she could join the corps of her choice it made her feel floppy with relief.

The day of Sovereign's Parade was overcast and cool but it was better that way. Who wanted to be standing in blazing sun for the duration? She and Michelle checked each other's appearance before they were inspected by their colour sergeant, then their platoon commander and finally the company commander. From windows at the front of Old College they could see the stands on the far side of the parade ground filling up with the friends and relatives of those about to receive their commissions. Somewhere in amongst the smart business suits, uniforms, dresses and hats was Sam's father.

And then the moment came to march onto the parade ground, the band playing jaunty tunes, and Sam knew that the past forty-eight weeks of near hell had been more than worth it. The sense of achievement was overwhelming and when she and her peers finally marched up the steps and through the double doors, followed by the Academy Adjutant on his white horse, she was thankful she had her back to the crowds as tears of relief and pride streamed down her face, making her mascara run in a trickle of black smears.

Once through the door and in the gloom of the main hall, she and Michelle hugged and cried. They'd done it.

And later her father told her he was proud. He mightn't have told her he loved her, but it was a start.

Chapter Three

The consequence of their success was that Sam and Michelle would be separated again. After a fortnight's leave Sam was going off to the army School of Electrical and Mechanical Engineering to complete her platoon commander's course and Michelle was going to Winchester to, as she put it, 'learn how to fill in forms'.

'But we can see each other at weekends,' said Sam.

'Every weekend,' said Michelle.

Possibly not, thought Sam. They'd have work to do. Just because they'd made it through Sandhurst it didn't mean they were home and dry. And in her case, if she didn't pass her young officers' course for the REME, her career plans could yet go horribly wrong. This was no time to start slacking and thinking that every weekend for the next few months was going to be free.

'We may have to work,' she said tentatively.

The two girls were sitting side by side on Sam's stripped bed in her now-empty bedroom. The walls, which had been covered with posters and pictures, were bare, the ironing board had gone, folded flat and stowed in the boot of her dad's car, along with suitcases, bulging with the rest of her civvy and army kit, and her uniforms, in their suit carriers, laid carefully on top. Her father and Henry Flowers had gone on a tour of Sandhurst, a trip down memory lane for both of them, leaving their daughters to say their farewells and gather their last bits and pieces together.

'I am so going to miss this,' said Sam.

'Bet you never thought you'd be saying that last September,' said Michelle.

'Shit, no. That first month was so awful.' The pair lapsed into silence as they considered it.

'God, I got some bollockings,' said Michelle.

Yes, you did, thought Sam. But then they all did.

'Do you remember the time I had that negligent discharge?' said Michelle.

'How could I forget?' said Sam. Firing a gun by accident was about the worst thing a soldier could do. 'Shit, if the sergeant major had twigged you really had had an ND can you imagine the bawling out?'

'I'd have been on a charge, for sure. I still don't know how I had the presence of mind to loose off a whole magazine and yell for everyone to "stand to".'

'Listen,' said Sam, 'doing that covered it up. Not that the sergeant major was convinced. He didn't half give you a hard stare but he couldn't prove otherwise.'

'No, he couldn't,' said Michelle, with a giggle. 'Sandhurst has taught me a zillion things but thinking on my feet is the main one.'

'Except in this instance you were lying on your stomach in a puddle.'

'With my elbow in cow poo.'

'And people think army officers are glamorous.'

'They do? Bonkers,' said Michelle, giggling more.

Sam's father stuck his head into the room. 'You girls aren't still gassing, are you? I don't want to get stuck on the M25.'

'Yeah,' said Sam. She gazed about her room. 'Time to go, I suppose. End of an era.'

'Nah,' said Michelle. 'Start of a journey.'

*

Sam's faint hope that her father's slight unbuttoning might be the start of a change in their relationship faded almost instantly. When she'd suggested it would be nice if he came with her to her grandparents' place in Devon he'd insisted it would be impossible to get leave. Sam supposed she ought to be grateful he'd taken time off to see her get her commission. Not that she minded about spending time with her grandparents; as always, as soon as she'd stepped through the door, she'd been almost swamped by a virtual comfort-blanket of love, spoiling and home-made scones and jam. From the instant she'd arrived, her granny and grandpa had wanted to know everything about the course and her plans, so she'd given them the expurgated version of life at Sandhurst, omitting the awfulness of some of the exercises and having to shit in the woods like a bear, and the new words and phrases she'd learned from the NCOs who had been less than impressed with her performance with a bayonet. On the positive side she'd been able to tell them all about the parties, the commissioning ball and about the new focus in her life, the REME, and what working for them would entail.

'Your dad must be so proud,' said her gran. She looked up from the saffron cake she was making for their tea.

Sam nodded. Well, he had been, for a minute or two, but she didn't want to tell her gran that, even after twenty-three years, life with her father could still be pretty bleak. 'Yes,' she said. 'Yes, I think he is.'

Her gran wasn't a fool and picked up on the momentary hesitation. 'I know you never got to meet your dad's folks but they were much the same; not a family to show emotions. You'd think they imagined the world would end if anyone even thought of wearing their heart on their sleeve. And a life spent in the army can't have helped your father in that respect either.'

'Not much hope for me, then,' said Sam. 'Same genes, same career choice.' She said it as a joke but there was a niggle of worry at the heart of the glib sentence.

'Ach, don't be daft. You're your mother's child through and through. It was a shame she was taken so young. If anyone could have softened up your dad it was her.' She stared at the mixing bowl for a second, deep in thought. Sam's father might have lost his wife but Gran had buried her own child. Then, falsely brightly, 'And how's your little friend Michelle?' She began to beat some eggs into the sugar and butter.

'She's not little. She huge, almost six foot.'

'She'll always be little to me.' Which was rich as Sam's gran wasn't more than five two at the most. 'I haven't seen her for…' Gran did the sum. 'Ooh, it must be over ten years. She was a cheeky little madam.'

'She hasn't changed much. She's still thin, she's still got big brown eyes and amazingly thick dark hair, only now she's not all gangly, now she's more like a super-model. She is so pretty. If I didn't love her so much I'd hate her.'

Gran began to pour the cake mixture into the loaf tin. 'She always had the makings of a beauty, that one. Is she getting on any better with her step-mum? You know, I never thought there was much wrong with her father's second wife. Why Michelle took against her I never really understood. Of course, I never knew her birth mother so maybe I'm talking out of turn.' Gran scraped the very last of the mixture into the tins and then gave the bowl to Sam. 'I suppose you'll want to lick this out.'

Sam took the bowl and ran her finger around then sucked off the goo while she wondered if maybe she wasn't in agreement with her gran about Michelle's antipathy to her step-mother. She remembered the first time she'd gone to stay with Michelle, back when she'd been about eight. Michelle had filled her head with stories about the WSM – the wicked step-mother – and Sam was honestly expecting to meet some fairy-tale horror like Cinders's or Snow White's awful ones. Instead she found a perfectly pleasant woman who seemed to want to make Sam's stay as nice as possible.

'She's not so bad,' she'd remarked to Michelle after the first day.

'You are joking,' Michelle had screeched. 'Can't you see it's an act? She's only being nice to you because you're an outsider. You don't know anything about her. It's all because of her that Dad keeps having a go at me. She puts him up to it, I know.'

Sam had been a bit shocked at Michelle's reaction and hadn't dared say anything again since. But she's always had a niggling feeling that maybe Michelle had made up her mind from the get-go that the second Mrs Flowers was the Bitch-Queen from Hell and, having done so, couldn't ever be seen to change her mind.

Maybe, just maybe, it was Michelle who was so unreasonable and her father's exasperation at the situation was the reason he got so irritated by Michelle. But then, thought Sam, no one really knew what went on in other people's families so she might have completely misjudged the situation. Anyway, it was none of her business.

After their leave the two women had to attend special-to-arm training courses before finding out where their first postings as commissioned officers would be.

'Where are you off to?' said Michelle over the telephone the evening after she'd been informed of the army's plans.

'The Light Aid Detachment of 1 Herts – it's the repair centre in the battalion for all their vehicles and kit.'

'And aren't they based somewhere in Kent?'

'They were. Apparently they're being arms-plotted to Salisbury Plain. Warminster, to be precise.'

'You happy about that?'

'Very. I'll have command of my own little unit. It'll be bloody brilliant. How about you?'

'Remember what I said my worst posting could be?'

'What, training recruits?'

'Exactly. So guess where I'm being sent?'

'No.'

'Oh, yes. I'm going to the training regiment at Pirbright. I'm going to be a platoon commander.'

'Get away.'

'It's going to be awful. You have to be perfect all of the time – always setting an example, always toeing the line. It's a punishment posting.'

'I'm sure it isn't.'

'Huh,' said Michelle, gloomily.

'You'll be fine,' said Sam, stoutly. 'You'll be a great example to the recruits. Honest.' But in her heart she knew that maybe Michelle was right; maybe she had been sent there as a punishment, to a place where she would have to shape up and where there were lots more senior officers to keep an eye on her, to stop her careering off course.

Chapter Four

It wasn't just Michelle and Sam who were on the move. The whole of 1 Herts was packing up to go, lock, stock and a whole armoury full of barrels. There was, of course, a certain amount of grumbling, especially from the soldiers. Infantry soldiers' default setting is griping and bitching, and anything which annoys them sets them off; being uprooted and sent across the country to a new barracks for no apparent reason was more than enough to start them ticking like clocks. And it wasn't only the soldiers who were belly-aching; the wives were pissed off too. They had thought they were going to be in Kent for the duration, well, the foreseeable future anyway, and so the news that they were having to up-sticks and traipse across the country to Wiltshire hadn't been greeted with enthusiasm. And as it wasn't just the families moving quarters but every office, every department, every scrap of military kit too, the planning was eye-watering and had involved hours of overtime for all the military, leaving their spouses to sort out the domestic arrangements single-handedly. For days the married patches had been full of removal vans as the families had, one after the other, been marched out of their quarters and then trailed westwards like some modern-day wagon train of settlers – or refugees.

Maddy Fanshaw had been one of the first wives to go and now she was in her new quarter. In, but not unpacked. Once again she surveyed the mountain of boxes, tried to raise the energy to make a start on getting straight, failed and sighed. She thought she'd got her life back on track, and now the army had thrown a spanner in the works. Actually, not a spanner – the whole sodding tool box. She'd managed to get herself back in full-time employment after having a baby when, only weeks later, Seb, her infantry captain husband, had come home one evening and told her about the move.

'What? Everyone?' said Maddy, sitting down on the sofa.

Seb nodded. 'Yup, every last man-jack of us.'

'When?'

'Four months' time.'

Maddy had stared out the window, willing herself not to cry. After months of dealing with the boredom of being unemployed, sleepless nights and a colicky baby, everything in her life had seemed to be almost perfect, and then, *wham!* Thanks very much.

So here she was again surrounded by packing cases, waiting to be emptied. At least, she thought, trying desperately to look on the bright side, this move wasn't as ghastly as the last one; Seb was around to help, Nate wasn't too badly behaved for a one-year-old and this house, on first impressions, was nicer than the previous one. But moving still meant upheaval and that she was, yet again, unemployed.

On top of that, her best friend Caro (who also acted as Nate's childminder) and her husband Will hadn't been posted down to Wiltshire along with the rest of the battalion – instead, Will had been sent off to London to some position at the MOD, so now Maddy had lost her job and her favourite neighbour and her lovely childminder too. Looking for employment was going to be a mission – and it wasn't going to be made easier by having to find childcare too. Did she find a job and then look for childcare, or vice versa?

Maddy sat down on an armchair, suddenly feeling overwhelmed with tiredness. What was the matter? she wondered.

No doubt the fact that she felt rather less than 'well' was down to the stress of the move. With every single family and all the soldiers having to pack up and relocate in one monstrous game of musical chairs, the wives weren't in much of a position to help each other out. With everyone up to their eyeballs cleaning their quarters, getting the removal companies in to pack, and the menfolk frantically organising the move of all the kit, weapons and vehicles, no one had any spare capacity to lend a hand to anyone else.

Maddy shut her eyes. She felt utterly wiped out. Instantly Nathan crawled over to her and clambered onto her lap, thrusting his favourite stuffed rabbit at her.

'Hello, Bun,' said Maddy, wearily giving the toy a waggle. Nathan leaned against her and sucked contentedly on his thumb.

'Well, this isn't going to get the house straight,' said Seb, bouncing into the room.

'I need tea before I can start to tackle this,' said Maddy.

Seb looked at her expectantly and then the penny dropped. 'Oh, you want me to find the kettle and make it, do you?'

Maddy suppressed a sigh. Well done, Einstein. 'There's a box in the boot of the car with everything in.'

After Seb had left, Maddy let her eyes droop again. Five minutes' peace, that's all she wanted. She shut her mind to the clattering and huffing that Seb was generating in the kitchen. Why did he have to make such a performance about any sort of domestic duties? She felt herself start to drift...

'Wake up, sleepy.'

Maddy yawned and tipped Nathan off her lap before accepting a mug of tea. Nathan shuffled across the carpet and then plopped down on his nappy-clad bottom before rolling onto his back and waving his chubby legs in the air. God, thought Maddy, how wonderful it would be to lie down like that without a care in the world. She took a sip of her tea. Her stomach lurched.

Carefully she put the mug down on a nearby box. Not just tired, but now ropey as well. What was wrong with her? She didn't have time to be ill. There were beds to be made up and the kitchen to start on or they wouldn't be able to eat and sleep.

Her stomach griped again. Uh-oh. She left her tea and dashed from the room to the downstairs loo, which she remembered being by the front door. She just made it before she retched, bringing up that sip of tea and precious little else.

Seb appeared at the still-open door. 'You all right, Mads?' He sounded worried.

She couldn't answer him as she was retching again, but with nothing to bring up all it did was make her feel as if her body was trying to turn itself inside out. Wrung out, she slumped down on the cold lino and leaned against the wall.

Seb pushed open the door further. 'Mads?'

She shook her head. 'Go and look after Nate. My tea…' She worried he might be able to reach it from the top of the box.

'It's all right, I put it on the mantelshelf. What's wrong? My tea-making isn't that bad surely?'

Maddy looked up at her husband and gave him a wan smile. 'No idea. I've been feeling a bit off colour all day, to be honest.'

'You should have said.'

Maddy shut her eyes. And if she had? Would the move have been postponed? Not a chance. 'Give me a minute. I'll be OK in a mo. Honest.'

Seb didn't look convinced.

There was a wail from the sitting room. 'Go on, Seb,' insisted Maddy. He left and she felt a slight sense of relief not to have him fussing over her. She loved him to bits but she knew there was nothing he could do. She wasn't operating at a full hundred per cent, that was for sure, but with Seb flapping the percentage fell way down the scale. Wearily she pushed herself off the floor and clambered back on her feet. Her knees felt so shaky she sat on the loo for a second to steady herself while her head stopped swimming. The ringing in her ears slowly faded and the waves of nausea became ripples. Whatever it was seemed to have passed – sort of.

'You all right now?' asked Seb as she returned to the sitting room.

'Yeah, fine,' she lied. She glanced at her tea, longing for the drink but not sure that she dared risk another sip. She gave a brisk exhalation of breath. 'Right, well, this isn't getting the unpacking done. I'm going to make a start on making up the beds. There's an army-issue playpen in the hall. Can you put it together, please, so Nate isn't on the loose, then find some toys to keep him amused, and then maybe make a start in here?'

Seb nodded. 'Anything else, ma'am?'

'Not for the time being.' Maddy trotted up the stairs with a false show of strength and bravado and collapsed in a heap on the double bed when she made it into the main bedroom. Her head was spinning again. For the second time in a few minutes she waited for the dizziness and nausea to pass. Maybe she needed to eat, maybe that was the problem. She hadn't had much since she'd got up at dawn to get herself and Nathan washed and dressed before the removal men came to collect the boxes. Seb had spent the night down in Wiltshire, having taken over their new quarter the night before, but had come back first thing to help hand over the old one and then drive them to their new home. Maddy had managed a Ryvita while she'd fed Nathan his mashed banana and rusk but since then it had all been go-go-go. Yes, she decided, that was probably the trouble.

The next morning she was awoken, as usual, by Nathan squawking in his cot in the nursery, which was, in effect, the little box room, opposite their bedroom. As Maddy swung her feet out of bed she felt her head start to spin again and the feeling of nausea from the day before thundered back. She ran to the washbasin in the corner of their bedroom and heaved.

'Mads?' said Seb.

Between body-racking waves of retching Maddy told him that he'd have to see to their son. And as she did the penny began to drop that this queasiness might have more significance than a passing bug. With obvious bad grace Seb lumbered out of bed and stomped across the landing.

An anguished yell came from the nursery. 'Mads, you'll have to come and help. Nathan's done a poo. I can't cope, I might be sick.'

'Sod off, Seb, you'll have to. I am actually *being* sick.' Honestly, thought Maddy, sometimes she could cry.

Sam showed her ID card at the guardroom of 1 Herts' new barracks and then drove her nifty little red sports car up the hill towards the battalion HQ, where she would report to the CO. When she'd done that she'd be free to move into the officers' mess and make a start on turning her allocated room into something more like home. Actually, not like home. She wanted her room to be comfortable and cosy and not functional and austere, which was how their quarters had always felt. No woman's touch to soften the edges. She wanted scatter cushions on her bed and armchairs, photos on the walls, bright rugs on the floor, and shelves full of books; all the things her father called dust-traps. His only concession to photos was the one of her mother he kept in his study, a duplicate of the one Sam had. The only difference was that Sam looked at hers.

But thinking about how she might arrange her possessions in her room wasn't the priority right now; her priority was to make sure she made a good first impression on her new boss.

She swung her Mazda into the visitors' car park at the battalion HQ, checked her appearance in the rear-view mirror – yup, she'd do – before grabbing her beret and settling it on her blonde curls. As she slammed the car door, she clocked a couple of soldiers giving her an appreciative once-over before they snapped her a salute. She returned it with a 'Carry on, lads' as she pushed open the door to the office block and made her way to the chief clerk's office, passing piles of boxes of stationery in the corridor, a slew of map cases and a couple of filing cabinets. Sam knew the battalion had recently been arms-plotted to this barracks and they were obviously still trying to get straight. A pretty brunette female clerk sitting at a desk near the door stood up respectfully when she saw Sam enter. Sam read the fabric name label stitched to her combats and noticed the stripe next to it.

'Corporal Cooper, do sit down again. I'm Captain Lewis and I'm reporting for duty – the new OC of the Light Aid Detachment. Could you direct me to the adjutant so I can introduce myself to him and the CO?'

'Yes, ma'am. Of course.'

Sam stood to one side to let Cooper past so she could follow her. 'Sorry about the mess ma'am. The move means we're all at sixes and sevens. Should be straight again soon, though. And if I may say so, ma'am, it's nice to see another woman join 1 Herts. There's only about a dozen of us here so your arrival is very welcome. Carry on at this rate and we might make the infantry almost civilised.' Sam grinned at Corporal Cooper and took an instant liking to her. If Cooper was representative of the other members of the battalion, Sam felt she was going to get on just fine.

Cooper stopped outside an office near the other end of the corridor from the clerk's office and knocked.

'Sir, this is Captain Lewis. She's the new OC LAD.'

Cooper stood back to let Sam into the office. Sam entered

and saluted. Andy Bailey, the adjutant, stared at her slack-jawed from behind his desk before remembering his manners and leaping to his feet.

Sam was a tiny bit taken aback. Something obviously wasn't right, but she couldn't work out what the hell it was.

'Sorry,' said Andy, 'this is a bit of a shock. I assumed Captain Sam Lewis was going to be a man.'

Sam gave him a wry smile. 'Well, I hope that the fact I've turned out to be a woman isn't too much of a disappointment.'

'No, well...' Andy stopped. 'My fault for assuming. It's, well... 1 Herts has never had a female officer who has lived in the mess before. I'm Andy, Andy Bailey.' He stuck out his hand for Sam to shake before he gestured to her to take a seat.

'What, never?' she exclaimed as she took her beret off and sat down. 'Then it's probably about time.' Sam tried to sound casual and upbeat but she hadn't expected not only to be the sole woman to be living in but also the first.

'Of course, we've had a fair few female soldiers serve with us – got a few right now, as a matter of fact – and a while back we had a female medical officer, but she was married and lived out.'

'So, me being here isn't going to be a problem,' said Sam.

'Of course not,' said Andy, swiftly. Then he grinned. 'A novelty maybe, a problem, no.'

But Sam wasn't entirely convinced.

'Anyway, we need to tell the colonel you're here.' Andy Bailey pressed a buzzer on his intercom. 'Sam Lewis is here, Colonel.'

'Send him in,' came the reply.

There was a pause before Andy took his finger off the intercom button. Sam looked at him and raised her eyebrow.

'The CO's in for a surprise too, isn't he?' she said.

'He'll get over it.'

Andy stood up, walked round his desk and opened the

interconnecting door to the next office. Sam shoved her beret on her head again, pulling it down automatically to make it mould into the correct shape, and followed the adjutant.

'Sir,' she said as she saluted on the threshold.

'Come in...'

Sam saw Colonel Notley's eyes widen before he smoothly recovered himself.

'Come in,' he repeated. 'Shut the door.'

Sam did as she was ordered and then approached his desk. The CO's office was perfect with a mass of regimental group photos on the freshly painted walls, the trophy cabinet filled with gleaming cups, and all the office furniture neatly arranged. Chaos might still be the order of the day for much of the battalion, but not in here. The privileges of rank and all that.

'Take a seat,' the CO instructed. 'Tea? Coffee?'

Sam declined. 'I'm fine, thanks, sir.'

'So...' The CO stared at her. 'This is a bit of a turn-up. The postings branch didn't explain that Sam was short for Samantha. It is, isn't it?'

She nodded. 'Sir, the adjutant tells me you haven't had a woman living in the mess before.'

'No, well, it'll be a new experience for the men. No doubt you'll bring a civilising influence to bear. Of course, we've always welcomed the fair sex with open arms – wives, girl-friends – but being an infantry regiment, well, there aren't many roles for female officers.'

'Andy thought I'd be a bit of a novelty,' said Sam.

'And a very welcome one.'

She hoped he was right.

The interview continued, with Colonel Notley questioning her about sports and activities she liked, the way he hoped she'd soon become a fully integrated member of the unit and, very interestingly, the news that the following February the whole of the battalion, the LAD included, would be off to Kenya on exercise.

Kenya! thought Sam. That's a bonus. There was she thinking that all she'd get to see over the next couple of years was a lot of Salisbury Plain and now, suddenly, the future looked vastly more exciting.

As she left battalion HQ and drove across to the officers' mess she wondered how the lads in the mess would take to having a woman in their midst. Would she be embraced or shunned? She suspected it would all very much come down to how well she made the effort to fit in. She'd managed it on her REME troop commander's course but this was a whole other issue.

She found the mess without difficulty – a long, two-storey, neo-Georgian, red-brick building with a sandstone portico. She parked her car and then made her way to the front door to find the mess manager and then her room.

She pushed open the heavy oak front door and went up the two steps into the large entrance hall, her footsteps deadened by the thick maroon carpet. In the middle of the hall was a circular pedestal table with a bowl of flowers in the middle, the scent of the roses just discernible over the smell of damp dogs, Brasso and wax polish. The mess was silent, all the livers-in being at work and the staff, having cleaned and tidied the place, were now, she imagined, in the kitchens, preparing the next meal.

She followed the sound of faint clattering and finally found signs of life behind heavy, double swing doors that issued a gust of delicious-smelling warm air as she pushed them open. Silence fell amongst the chefs and stewards as she poked her head into the kitchen.

'Sorry,' she apologised, 'but I've been posted in and I'm looking for the mess manager. I heard voices and was hoping one of you would be able to tell me where to find him.'

The silence continued for a second longer, then a man in chef's whites stepped forward and said with an East London accent, 'Posted in? 'ere? You sure? This is 1 'Erts' mess.'

As Sam nodded she saw the guys exchange looks.

'Yes, 1 Herts. I'm the new OC LAD.'

'Ah,' said a mess waiter in a white bum-freezer jacket, 'you're REME.'

Sam nodded. 'That's right,' she reassured him. 'Women aren't planning on trying their luck in the infantry yet!'

The mess staff laughed.

'If you'd like to follow me, ma'am,' said the mess waiter.

'Thank you,' said Sam.

Behind her she heard one of the staff say, '... and thank God for that. Can you imagine what women would be like in the trenches – demanding we all wipe our boots before we entered the dug-outs.' A louder burst of laughter followed that remark, cut off suddenly as the heavy kitchen door finally closed.

In silence she followed the waiter along the thickly carpeted corridor to a door off the main hall, tucked under the big staircase that led to the upper floor.

The waiter opened the door and stood to one side to let Sam pass. The office was almost filled by a large partner's desk and a filing cabinet. A sergeant, sitting behind the desk, stood as Sam entered and cast her a puzzled look.

'I'm Captain Lewis,' she explained. 'New posting. Could you show me to my room, please?'

The sergeant's mouth opened slightly, before he caught himself and shut it quickly. Hadn't anyone thought that Captain Lewis, REME, might be a woman? They did exist in the REME – had done for years, now.

'Yes, of course, ma'am. I'm Sergeant McManners, the mess manager. Welcome to 1 Herts.'

'Thank you, Sergeant.'

They made their way up the wide, shallow stairs to the first floor, where McManners paused. He appeared to be thinking.

'To be honest, ma'am, seeing as you're a captain I was going to put you on this corridor with the other junior officers, but given that you're also a lady I think you might be more comfortable in a field officer's suite.'

'But I'm only a captain. And I really don't think that making special allowances because I'm not a man is the best way to help me integrate, do you?'

'But, ma'am, if you have a suite, you'll have your own sitting room. Some of the lads have been known to get quite...' he paused '...rowdy.'

Ah, he thinks I might be some sort of shrinking violet. 'Honestly, I'll be fine.' Sam considered quoting Queen Elizabeth I's speech about being weak and feeble but having the stomach and the heart of a king. No, a bit too much at this early stage. 'Please, Sergeant McManners, if I find it's a dreadful mistake we can re-think at a later date, but, in the meantime, treat me like any other officer.'

'You'll never guess,' said Seb, when he got home that night.

'Guess what?' asked Maddy. She put a china ornament she'd unwrapped on the sitting room mantelpiece.

'Old Ian Abbott's replacement is a woman. Very young, very pretty and very curvy, according to the mess gossip. That's going to set the cat among the pigeons. I can't see some of the old hands in the workshop taking kindly to being bossed about by a woman.'

Maddy raised her eyebrows. 'Then they'll have to get used to it. It's about time some of the army dragged itself into the twenty-first century and realised women are just as capable as men.'

'It's still bound to cause trouble.'

'Why?' Maddy couldn't see what the problem might be.

'Well, stands to reason. Apart from anything else, there's going to be a single woman living in the mess with all those testosterone-fuelled men.'

Maddy walked across the sitting room, scooped Nathan out of his playpen and carried him into the kitchen, where she posted him into his high chair. Deftly she handed him a bread-stick to chew on while she got a glass down for Seb and mixed him a gin and tonic.

'You not having one?' he asked as she passed him his drink.

Maddy shook her head.

'Still feeling under the weather?'

'Sort of. Sit down, Seb.'

Seb's eyes widened momentarily as he hooked out a chair from the kitchen table. 'You're not ill, are you?'

'Not ill, Seb. Pregnant.'

'Pregnant!'

Maddy nodded.

'But we weren't trying...'

Maddy shook her head. 'No, sweetie, we weren't. But if you remember I fell pregnant with Nate in a heartbeat. We're obviously super-fertile.'

'Oh.'

'Is that it? Oh?'

'Sorry, sorry, Maddy.' Seb put down his drink, jumped up and gave Maddy a hug. 'You're a clever girl and I love you.'

'But...' Since Maddy had done the test after Seb had gone to work she'd worried about how they'd cope financially with two tiny children, and how she'd cope, full stop. Seb hadn't been exactly hands-on with Nate, and she didn't think he was about to have a Damascene moment about fatherhood now. She adored him for lots of reasons, but not for his parenting skills.

'No, no buts.' He kissed the top of her head. 'I am so thrilled.' And he really sounded it.

Maddy put her doubts to one side and snuggled against him. 'What do you fancy, a boy or a girl?'

'I really don't care.' Seb kissed Maddy's head again and then returned to his seat, looking rather pleased with himself.

'At least we can be sure we won't be moving from here for a while,' he said, taking a slug of gin. 'That's a good thing, isn't it? As things stand, by the time we have to move again, this next little one will be almost old enough to go to prep school.'

Maddy nodded. She'd long since accepted that she'd be sending her children off to boarding school. 'Considering this is Nate's third house and he's not even a year old, I think not moving for ages is a very good thing.'

'So,' said Seb, 'I was thinking… it might be nice if we invited this new girl over for supper one evening. She might appreciate a bit of female company.'

'You think?' said Maddy. 'Of course, it might be her idea of bliss to have all those blokes to herself.'

'Maybe.' Seb didn't sound convinced. 'But if she doesn't, you and she must be about the same age and I can't see her wanting to hang out with Mrs Notley. From a personal point of view, I don't think I'd want to be the only bloke living with a couple of dozen women.'

'So you're not thinking of indulging in a bit of polygamy and having your own personal harem?'

'Never. You're the only woman for me, Mads.'

Maddy smiled at him and blew a kiss towards him. 'Love you too, hon.' And she did. Seb might have his faults but she was still besotted by him and couldn't believe her luck that she was Mrs Seb Fanshaw and had been for almost two years.

Chapter Five

Artificer Sergeant Major Williams, Sam's number two in her little unit, stood in front of her desk. He didn't look happy.

'Look,' said Sam, in what she hoped was a conciliatory tone, 'Captain Abbott might have had his way of doing things, but I have mine.'

'With all due respect, ma'am, there was nothing wrong with Captain Abbott's methods.'

Sam counted to three. 'Probably. But I am in charge now.'

The ASM stared at her, obviously wishing she wasn't. 'I just don't see how making the men down tools and listen to a speech from you is going to help anyone.'

Sam could feel her shoulders rising up from the tension in her neck. Honestly, he couldn't be more difficult about her request if she'd told him she expected all of the soldiers to donate a kidney. She forced herself to relax. 'It's only going to take five minutes, if that. I want to have a word with them, I want to introduce myself to them, I want to start to get to know them.' She stared back at him. Why was he being so bloody unreasonable about this? All she wanted to do was have the men under her command gathered together so she could make a short introductory speech just to break the ice. She knew that having a woman as the boss might not sit well with some of the older soldiers, but she hadn't imagined her right-hand man to take against the concept quite so obviously from the get-go.

The ASM sighed heavily. 'If you say so, ma'am.'

'I do.'

He turned and left her office and Sam exhaled slowly. What was his problem? She gathered her notes together and made her way out of her office in the corner of the workshop to where her troops were being gathered together in a rough semi-circle by a bad-tempered Mr Williams.

'Hello,' said Sam to the group once they'd all settled down. 'You all know who I am – that's the advantage of being the old hands here – but I want to say how much I am looking forward to working with you over the coming months. Mr Williams has spent this morning telling me about the standards you've set and the glowing reports achieved in the last few annual inspections. You ought to be justifiably proud of yourselves.' As she said this she saw a few backs straighten, a few chins lift, and she knew she'd said the right thing. So suck on that, Mr Williams. 'That tells me that my predecessor, Captain Abbott, ran a really sound operation, and I've got my work cut out if things aren't going to slide. I'd like to think all of you will do your best to help me maintain that benchmark of excellence.' There were a few nods of assent from her soldiers. She hoped she was making a favourable impression. If Mr Williams was going to continue to make life tricky she didn't want the rest of the troops automatically siding with him and not her. Sam wasn't planning on altering anything for some while, or indeed *ever*, if it wasn't necessary. None of that new-broom malarkey to make a point that this was *her* workshop, tempting though it was given Mr Williams' attitude. No, she had every intention of watching to see how her team of soldiers meshed together and then tweak, if necessary, in due course – assuming the ASM didn't stop her.

'So,' she finished off, 'over the next couple of weeks I'd like to have a quick chat with each of you in turn, so I get to know who you all are and so I can put names to faces, but until then I'll try and leave you in peace to get on with your job. Of course, if any of you want to have a word with me then my office door is always open. Thanks for listening.'

The ASM brought all her soldiers to attention, and Sam nodded her acknowledgement of the courtesy as she returned to her office. After the ASM had dismissed the troops back to their posts he followed her.

'So,' said Sam, as she sat down in her office chair, 'I told you I'd be brief.'

'Hmm.' He was obviously still sore about her getting her way.

'Take a seat. I'd like you to give me the low-down on the men.' The ASM looked quizzical as he drew up a chair and sat down. 'Have we got any troublemakers, any problem cases?' she elucidated.

'Not problem soldiers as such,' said Mr Williams.

Sam raised her eyebrows. 'There's a *but* coming, isn't there?'

Mr Williams nodded. 'Sergeant Armstrong.'

'Ye-e-es. Want to tell me about him?'

Mr Williams sucked his teeth. 'His partner, Jenna, is a bit of a minx by all accounts. She was married to a soldier – another one – who picked up an injury in Afghan but when the authorities came to give her the bad news they found Sergeant Armstrong in her bed. So he got posted here to Warminster at the speed of light, but she left her husband and followed.'

Sam managed to keep a straight face at the story, which seemed to come straight out of a soap opera or a French farce. Then she said, 'Well, no one died and I don't suppose her ex was too keen to keep her after that.'

'Ah,' said Mr Williams, 'but her ex-husband was with 1 Herts. And now they're here too.'

'Oops.'

'Oops indeed, ma'am.'

'Does her ex know she's here?'

'I have no idea. I've checked out who he is and it turns out he's currently posted to the Catterick training regiment, but a lot of his old mates are still with the regiment and, of course, their wives, who will remember her from the patch. I thought you should be aware of the situation.'

Sam nodded. 'Do we know what Armstrong thinks of 1 Herts pitching up?'

'He told me it isn't a problem. He and his partner don't live in quarters – they've got a flat in town.'

'Well, if he thinks it'll be OK, I probably needn't worry.'

'No, ma'am.'

'But thanks for the heads-up. Is that it?' There was a pause. 'That's a "no", then.'

'Corporal Blake.'

Sam nodded encouragingly. 'What's he done?'

'That's the odd thing, ma'am. He's a model soldier, perfect.'

Sam cocked her head.

'He's not like any soldier I've worked with before. He's got a stack of GCSEs, he should have A levels to go with them but he hasn't.'

'So? Maybe he wanted to join up because he hated his school.'

'So why didn't he join at sixteen? He could have gone to the apprentice college.'

'Have you asked him why he didn't?'

'Oh, yes, ma'am.'

'And?'

'It's like talking to a brick wall. He's perfectly polite but... I don't know, he clams up or gives evasive answers that tell you nothing. And none of the other soldiers get close to him. He's an oddball. A real loner. Not unpopular or anything, utterly trustworthy, a hard worker, but odd.' Then the ASM added, 'He reads.'

Sam had to suppress a giggle. 'Well, there's nothing in Queen's Regs that says a soldier can't be odd – or read.'

'Indeed there isn't, ma'am. All the same...'

Sam began to put some files back in the cabinet by her desk.

'One other thing about him,' said the ASM.

'Yes.'

'His next of kin is a friend – a male friend, not a relation.'

'So he's an orphan? Or he's gay? That's not against Queen's Regs either.'

'No, I know.' There was another pause. 'I don't know, ma'am, you wait till you meet him, you'll see what I mean.'

'Thank you, Mr Williams.'

After he'd returned to the workshop and Sam was taking a break from reading the stack of files on her desk and trying to get her head around her new job, she glanced through the office window to where her men were working. Mr Williams was surrounded by a group of soldiers. He was, she judged from his gestures and body language, regaling them with some sort of story; obviously a funny one because everyone was laughing. And then Mr Williams glanced in her direction and saw she was watching him. Even at this distance she could see the look of guilt on his face. Was he feeling guilty at being caught slacking? Or had he been taking the piss out of her? She looked away again.

The truth was, being the only female officer was a tougher call than she'd expected. OK, she hadn't for a moment imagined that she would be welcomed with open arms, that everyone in an almost exclusively all-male regiment would think she was the best thing to happen to 1 Herts in the battalion's history, but she hadn't expected such awkwardness. It was almost as if no one had the least idea how to treat her.

Didn't the blokes, her fellow officers, have girlfriends or mothers or sisters? Did they behave with such stand-offishness with other female companions? Their girlfriends?

Her first night in the mess had been a case in point. Although her fellow mess-mates had been perfectly polite and gentle-manly, she'd felt a bit like an act in a freak show. The conversation had been predictable – where had she been to uni, who had been her company commander at Sandhurst, did she know this officer or that? She'd answered and the conversa-tional ball had been batted around the table, but it had all been fairly dull and banal. For some reason Sam had got the definite impression that everyone was on their best behaviour. She had wanted to tell them that they weren't to stand on ceremony because of her but she decided against it. It was best, she reck-oned, to let them get used to her. Once the novelty of having a woman in the place wore off, things would revert to normal; no point in trying to force the issue. In the meantime, maybe she should give them some space, let them get used to her by degrees. She'd excused herself from the table as soon as she'd finished her meal, telling the other livers-in she had to finish her unpacking, and was halfway up the stairs when a huge gust of raucous laughter billowed out of the dining room. Was it in response to a general joke or was she the butt of it?

A week later Maddy was wheeling a sleeping Nathan in his buggy through the main street in Warminster when the sight of a familiar face stopped her dead in her tracks. Even though the person she recognised was on the other side of the road there was no mistaking the silvery blonde hair or the endlessly long legs. Jenna. Jenna, who had been her hairdresser back in the old barracks. Jenna, who had been married to Private Perkins, who had been injured while on duty in Afghanistan. Jenna, who Seb, when he'd called round to break the bad news about her husband, had pretty much caught in flagrante delecto with a REME sergeant. Jenna, who had buggered off with her new man, right away from 1 Herts and the mess she'd created. So what the hell was she doing here?

Well, thought Maddy, everyone had to be somewhere. And, of course, Jenna's new man had been another soldier, and this was a garrison town so it wasn't so completely unreasonable that she should be here too. But it was going to be Jenna's bad luck that the battalion she'd tried to escape from had now moved into her new back yard.

Maddy was about to call hello to her when a bus thundered past, and when her line of sight was clear again Jenna had gone. Had she imagined it? She blinked and stared at the spot where Jenna had been standing. Pregnancy might be turning her brain to mush again but her eyesight was still twenty-twenty.

Seeing her made Maddy remember the wonderful haircuts Jenna had given her in the past. And, dear God, didn't her hair need doing now? It had been months since she'd had it done. In fact, no one had gone near it since Jenna had so precipitously crashed out. For some time Maddy had been scraping it back into a tatty ponytail each morning to have done with it – out of sight, out of mind. She looked at her reflection in the shop window beside her – and saw someone who might be mistaken for Rosa Klebb. But without the fun-loving personality and fashion sense, she thought. Shit, she looked rough.

She pulled her phone from her pocket and spun the list of contacts, her thumb hovering over the names as they whizzed past. J. She pressed down. Jack, James... Jenna. Then she pressed the telephone symbol.

'Maddy?' There was no mistaking the stunned surprise in Jenna's voice.

'Er... hello, Jenna.' There was a silence. 'Jenna, you still there?'

'Yes, yes, I am. What do you want?'

Not the most gracious start to a conversation. 'Jenna, are you in Warminster?'

'Why d'you want to know?'

'Because I'm in Warminster and I think I've just seen you.'

There was another silence. 'Really?' Jenna sounded mightily unimpressed.

'So... did I?'

'Yeah. You did.'

'Fancy a coffee?'

There was a sigh, then, 'Why not?'

Maddy looked about her. 'What about Costa? Five minutes.'

'See you there.'

Maddy disconnected and turned the buggy towards the coffee shop in the marketplace. She was queuing for a cappuccino when she heard her name being called. She spun around.

'Jenna. Lovely to see you,' she said brightly. 'You bag a table, I'll get the drinks. What would you like? Here,' and she pushed the buggy towards Jenna. 'Park Nathan up for me so I can carry the coffees.'

'OK, thanks. Skinny latte, please.'

A couple of minutes later Maddy made her way through the other customers over to the sofa Jenna had bagged.

'So,' said Maddy, as she deposited the two cups and saucers. 'What have you been up to?'

'What? Apart from getting a divorce, you mean?'

'Well...' Maddy shrugged.

''S'all right. Water under the bridge. Or it was until you lot rocked up. I mean, I never thought that 1 Herts would turn up here. I couldn't believe it when Dan – he's my partner now – told me what was going on because he's REME and works in the LAD. I mean, what are the chances that I get away from 1 Herts only to find that they come chasing after me.'

'That's going to be tricky,' said Maddy.

'Tell me about it. I thought I'd put all that baggage well behind me. Although my spies tell me my ex is up in Catterick so that's something to be grateful for. Can you imagine how tricky it would've been if him and his new missus had been here too?'

'I suppose,' said Maddy noncommittally.

'But I don't think I'll be going to any more sergeants' mess dos. Don't want to show my face there only to have some of the old biddies spit in it. And they would.' Jenna shrugged. 'Not that I care because, in my limited experience, those army dos are usually pretty shit, so no great loss.'

Maddy didn't contradict her, even though she thought the army's social life could be bloody good fun.

'What about you?' Jenna asked.

Maddy shrugged. 'Nothing much to tell. I thought about trying to find a job here but then... well, I'm pregnant again.'

'Blimey,' said Jenna. 'You're not wasting any time are you? How old is Nathan?'

'He'll be almost eighteen months when the baby arrives.'

'Good luck. And you're going to need it. Bloody hell, two under two.'

That wasn't what she wanted to hear, thought Maddy disconsolately. She sipped at the froth on the top of her drink. 'Do you still do hair?'

Jenna nodded. 'Not that I work in a salon. That bitch Zoë wouldn't give me a reference and anyway there doesn't seem to be anything going in that line around here. I still work from home when any business comes my way.'

Maddy's eyebrows shot up. She knew the chaos caused by Jenna's last foray into working from home.

Jenna rolled her eyes. 'I haven't done any alterations to my new place. Not that it'd matter as Dan and I don't live in a quarter. Thank God,' she added with feeling. 'I've had enough of the army ordering me around. Just as well really when you think about it. Can you imagine what my life would have been like if I lived on the patch when all my old neighbours pitched up?'

Maddy thought she could. The furore that had been caused by Jenna's behaviour back when she'd been married to Private Perkins had been the talk of the patch for weeks and weeks. Maddy could imagine the reception Jenna would get if she showed her face around the 1 Herts' wives again.

'Your hair needs doing,' said Jenna, changing the subject. 'If you don't mind me saying so, Maddy, it looks like shit.'

Maddy smiled. 'Get off the fence and say what you really mean.'

'Well, it does,' said Jenna, unrepentant. 'I'm not being mean, but it is in serious need of a bloody good cut. I'll do it for you, if you'd like. I haven't forgotten that you were kind to me when all the other wives were ganging up against me.'

Maddy shrugged. 'I didn't do much.'

'Maybe not, but it was more than anyone else did. And you didn't have to. I didn't deserve anything – not after what I did.'

'You didn't do anything so terribly dreadful. What you did wasn't a crime or anything.'

'That's not how the other wives saw it. I mean,' said Jenna, 'it's not like I'm the first person ever to have a bit of a fling. I read somewhere the other day that almost every married person has at some stage. And I heard on the grapevine that Lee's happier with his new wife.' Jenna laughed and flicked her hair over her shoulder. 'I probably did him a good turn in the long run. Anyway, how about I do your hair for you? As a favour, for old times' sake.'

'Would you?' Maddy felt pathetically grateful for the offer. And maybe a smart cut would give her some of her old mojo back.

''Course. Only would you mind coming to mine? I don't

think I can face running into any of my other old customers. I don't want to have my past raked up again. It was bad enough what happened the first time round.'

For all Jenna's outward brash devil-may-care attitude, Maddy reckoned it was a front and underneath she was just as vulnerable as everyone else.

Sam was slowly working her way through the list of soldiers in her Light Aid Detachment. She'd interviewed more than half and now it was the turn of Sergeant Armstrong. He came into her office looking slightly wary. 'Sit down, do,' she said as he stood in the doorway and saluted her. 'And take your beret off.' Sam gave the senior NCO a smile to put him at his ease as she watched him pull the chair towards him and sit down. 'So, tell me a bit about yourself.'

'Like what, ma'am?'

'Like what motivated you to join the army. Like where you would like to be in ten years' time.' She smiled again. 'That sort of thing.'

Dan Armstrong blew his cheeks out. 'I joined because employment prospects around where I lived were shit... sorry, ma'am... rubbish. I got into the apprentice college and I've never looked back. The life is all right, the pay is decent and I've got to see a bit of the world. And in ten years' time I rather hope I might be an ASM like Mr Williams.'

'No reason why you shouldn't. I've had a look at your records and you've got the skills and most of the qualifications. You just need to keep going as you are.'

Armstrong nodded. 'I'm hoping that other business...'

Sam shook her head. 'Other business?'

'Come off it, ma'am. The ASM will have told you about what happened at my last posting.'

'Oh, that.'

'Yes, that. I'm hoping that won't scupper my chances.'

'Why should it? It doesn't make you a bad engineer all of a sudden.'

'I thought the army took a dim view of behaviour like that.'

'Well, it doesn't encourage it but as long as you don't make a habit of it...'

'I'm not planning to, no. Jenna – that's my partner – she's a clever lass. She's the one for me, she'll keep me on the straight and narrow now.'

'I'm glad to hear it. Does she have a career?'

'She's a hairdresser. A good one. She once worked for Marky Markham.' There was real pride in Armstrong's voice.

'Really?' Even Sam was impressed. 'Which salon does she work in?'

'She works from home. I'll give you her number if you'd like.'

'Actually, I'd really like that. I need to get a trim. Thanks.' Sam pushed a pad of paper and a pencil across to Armstrong and he scribbled the number down. 'Now, anything you want to ask me before you go?'

Armstrong shook his head.

'I mean what I say about my door always being open. Any worries about your career or anything like that, it's my job to help you as best as I can.' Although Sam knew that a guy, several years her senior, would probably go to almost anyone in the battalion before he asked a woman for advice.

After Sergeant Armstrong left she made a couple of notes on his file and then took the next one off the pile. Blake. But the phone rang at that point and there was a problem on the workshop floor with a vehicle repair; by the time everything had been resolved it was almost time for the troops to go off and get their evening meal. Blake would have to wait.

Chapter Six

Michelle stared around the anteroom of the officers' mess at Pirbright. Honestly, she thought, there were probably morgues with more life in them. The silence was oppressive. Even the faint chink of teaspoons in post-lunch cups of coffee, or the rustle of newspapers, seemed intrusive and loud. Sandhurst had been full of life and chatter and laughter, and the mess at Winchester, where she'd done her junior officers' course, had been fun and lively, but this...

She got up and left the room. As she reached the door she noticed that no one had looked up from their paper. Perversely, she wanted to do something loud and disruptive; strip off her uniform top, or shout *Long live the revolution*, or dance on a table. That'd shake up the place. But instead she went to her room, switched on Radio 1 and turned the volume up as loud as she dared. The more senior officers lived on the floor above and they complained and handed out extras at the least excuse – as Michelle had already discovered.

Two years of this, she thought. How was she going to bear it? She felt insanely envious of Sam and her posting to an infantry regiment. All those hunky young subalterns to knock around with. And what did she have here? A whole heap of passed-over majors, time-serving till their pensions kicked in, with no sense of humour, who found endless fault in the junior officers who were, themselves, cowed into submission.

She flopped onto her bed and stared at the ceiling. Surely there had to be more to life that what she had right now? Surely there had to be some way of shaking up this joint? Maybe she'd ring Sam and see if she fancied coming down to Surrey and helping her do a bit of hell-raising. It seemed to Michelle that all her contemporaries in the mess were so wet they needed to be wrung out – or was that just because all the old fogeys had made them that way? She pulled her phone out of her pocket and pressed the buttons to get Sam.

'Hiya, hon,' she said when Sam picked up. 'I can't tell you how envious of you I am right now.'

'Of me?' replied Sam.

'Of course. It's beyond dreary here, the job sucks, the pressure is insane, the mess is dead and at weekends it's empty. So, come on, tell me, what are all those fit young men like?'

A heavy sigh breezed over the airwaves. 'I don't know. They barely talk to me.'

'You what?'

'You heard. I've kind of given up and I spend half my free time in my room. Over and above that my ASM hates me and I'm beginning to have real doubts as to whether I'm cut out for this.'

'No-o-o... but you're the perfect officer. Shit, if anyone is destined to whoosh up the ranks it's you. Why the self-doubt?'

'I dunno. Maybe it's just a bad patch. Maybe I need to man up, get used to it.' There was another sigh.

'That's it, then, we need to get together. You need to get your butt down to Surrey. We need to have a weekend on the lash, go clubbing, experience hangovers again, what do you say?'

'God, yes, Michelle. Yes! When?'

'Well, not this weekend, I'm on duty, but maybe one soon.'

'You got spammed for a weekend duty early. You've only just arrived there.'

'Sort of. I picked up an extra or two.'

'Michelle!'

'I was late on parade. My alarm didn't go off.'

'Oh, Michelle. You are a numpty.'

'Never mind. I'll ring next week. We can firm up some proper plans.'

'Brilliant.'

'Hello, Sam.'

Sam put down the copy of *The Times* she was reading while enjoying a quiet post-work cup of tea in the mess anteroom. As she looked up she saw James Rosser, one of the platoon commanders of 1 Herts. 'Hello, James.'

'Mind if I join you?'

Sam glanced around the anteroom of the mess. The groups of armchairs gathered around low coffee tables were mostly unoccupied. There were a couple of the other platoon commanders across the room, reading the papers, but the majority of the livers-in had already downed a swift cuppa and shot off to their rooms to grab a bag, before racing off for the weekend. The mess this weekend, like the last one, was going to be very quiet.

'Please do,' she said. 'But don't feel you have to keep me company if you've got something you'd rather do.' She quite liked James. He seemed very old-fashioned, which was faintly endearing, and even more endearing, in Sam's opinion, was his distinct resemblance to a young Hugh Grant, complete with floppy fringe, smiley blue eyes and slightly diffident and shy manner.

James gave her a lopsided grin and put his own cup of tea down on the table before he slumped into the chair opposite her. 'Like my laundry, you mean?'

'Hey, for all I know, you might think that ironing is the best fun you can have with your clothes on.'

'As long as you don't iron your clothes while you are wearing them.'

'Ouch, no. As the battalion health and safety officer I would have to advise against that.'

'You're all right, that's not something I indulge in.' James took a gulp of tea. 'You going away for the weekend?'

Sam shook her head. 'Nope. You?'

'Duty officer.'

'Ah, hard luck.'

'Only for tonight. I'm free tomorrow.'

'That's nice.' Sam picked up the paper, folded it and put it on the table in front of her.

'Sorry,' said James. 'I'm disturbing you. You were perfectly happily reading the paper and I come along and interrupt you.'

'No, honestly. I was only glancing at it for want of anything better to do. Really.' She paused. 'Do you think anyone would mind if I nicked it and took it to my room?'

'*The Times*? You're joking, aren't you?' He called across the room to their fellow officers. 'Hey, Will, Ben, either of you want to fight Sam for *The Times*?'

Will waved his copy of the *Sun*. 'Not enough pictures for my taste.'

Ben laughed. 'I'm with Will.'

'There you go,' said James. 'The paper is yours.'

'Good.'

'So, you going to spend the evening in your room – like you usually do?'

Sam shrugged.

'We don't bite, you know,' said James.

Sam looked at her lap. 'I don't know... I feel a bit of an interloper. You guys all know each other so well.'

'Well, you won't get to know us by avoiding us.'

'No.'

'I mean, when you did your platoon commander's course you must have been in a minority.'

'Yes, but that was different.'

'How come?'

Sam thought about it. 'I don't know, it just was. I think the REME are more used to having women around.'

James laughed. 'Frankly, there are monasteries more used to having women around than some infantry regiments.'

Sam laughed.

'Well, how about you don't disappear tonight after supper?' said James. 'Stay and keep me company. I expect Will and Ben'll bugger off to a pub or something so I'll be on my tod. I'd appreciate the company. Come on – take a chance.'

Sam smiled. 'OK, why not. That'd be nice.' And she realised it would be. Maybe it was time to try and integrate a little more.

Maddy put down her toast and marmalade. 'Seb, darling, could you look after Nathan for a couple of hours this afternoon?'

Seb sighed, and lowered the paper. 'Why?'

Because he's your son, thought Maddy. 'Because I want to see if I can get my hair done. I need a cut, badly.'

'Does it have to be today?'

'Why? Have you got plans?'

'But it's Saturday,' said Seb. 'I've been working my socks off all week. Aren't I entitled to a day off?'

And I'm not, thought Maddy. Obviously housework and childcare don't count as work. No, she told herself, she was being unfair. She worked nothing like as hard as Seb but she was only asking for a couple of hours of his time. She said as much.

'I was going to go to the gym to do some training. I've not had the chance to get a proper workout all week.'

'You're not planning on working out all day, though, are you? Can't you go this morning?'

'I suppose. Have you actually made an appointment?'

'Not yet. I was going to ring up on spec.'

'So, you could get it cut next week.'

'Yes, I could, but then I'd have to beg a favour from Susie or pay for childminding.' Maddy felt exasperated. Was it so much to ask Seb to look after his own son for a few hours? Honestly, it would be easier to get blood out of a stone.

'All right, then,' said Seb, grudgingly.

'Good,' said Maddy. She bounced out of the kitchen to find her mobile and ring Jenna before Seb could have second thoughts. And she wasn't going to tell Seb who she was making an appointment with. She could imagine the row if he found out.

Sam wandered into the mess dining room, grabbed a paper, which she tucked under her arm, before she poured herself a glass of orange juice and a cup of tea and carried all three over to the huge wide, mahogany dining table. A mess waiter appeared from behind the kitchen door.

'Cooked breakfast, ma'am?'

'Mmm, please. Poached egg, bacon and tomato and some brown toast.'

'Certainly, ma'am.'

'Hello, Sam.' James bounced in looking remarkably chipper.

'Quiet duty?'

'Mostly. There was a bit of a ruckus down at the soldiers' bar after you went to bed – but that's hardly unexpected on a Friday night, it was nothing the regimental police and the duty sergeant couldn't handle. I almost got my full quota of beauty sleep.'

'Glad to hear it.'

James grinned as he too got tea and orange and brought it over to the table. 'Are you implying I need as much as I can get?'

Sam shrugged and smiled back. 'If the cap fits.'

The mess waiter reappeared and took James's breakfast order. Once he'd asked for a full English 'with mushrooms if there are any' he turned back to Sam.

'What are your plans today?'

'Nothing much. I think the main excitement might consist of trying to make an appointment to get my hair cut.'

'Blimey, life in the fast lane.'

Sam nodded. 'Oh, yes.'

'Look, yesterday Ben and Will and I made some vague plans about high-tailing it off to the seaside for the day; the forecast is brilliant. Just a drive down to Bournemouth or somewhere like that, a walk along the beach, a fish and chip lunch or maybe a pie and a pint and then back here for tea and medals. How about you join us?'

'You don't want me along. I'd only cramp your style.'

'In what way? We're only going to the seaside. We're not planning on trying our hand at world domination or anything like that.'

Sam laughed. 'OK, but only if you think the others won't mind. And as long as you all promise not to get silly and chivalrous and not let me pay my way.'

'I can only speak for myself but if the other two have bank balances anything like mine you will be perfectly safe in that department.'

'Then it's a deal.'

'Right, the plan is to meet at ten o'clock in the anteroom.'

Sam's breakfast arrived and she tucked in with gusto, feeling ridiculously pleased at the prospect of the day ahead. After she'd finished, she returned to her room to ring Sergeant Armstrong's partner to make an appointment for the next weekend, sort her kit out for the following week before meeting the others at the agreed time.

'All set?' said James.

'Certainly am. Seaside here we come!'

What with the sunshine and the roof of James's Audi being down, the four young officers were slightly wind- and sunburned by the time they arrived at the Dorset coast. They were also happy and laughing and at ease with each other.

'This is grand,' said James, as he hauled on the handbrake in a parking spot, right by the beach. 'A day by the sea and the sun is shining.'

Sam got out of the car and stretched. She sniffed the air, savouring the smell of seaweed and ozone. 'I do love the sea.'

Will and Ben, who had insisted that Sam, despite being the smallest of the four, had ridden in the front seat, uncurled themselves from the rear of the car and eased their shoulders. 'That's better,' said Ben. He walked round to the boot and opened it. He reached in and brought out a couple of travelling rugs and a football.

'Let's hit the beach,' he said, and chucked the ball to Will, who caught it neatly and then bounced it several times as they waited for James to lock up his vehicle.

'Oh, the sea,' said James. 'It brings out the kid in me. Makes me want to dig holes, build sandcastles and paddle.'

'Well, what are we waiting for?' said Sam. She ran down the beach to the water's edge, where she hopped on first one foot then the other as she pulled off her trainers and socks, abandoning them any old where as she dashed into the water, sending up a spray of water droplets that caught the sun and turned into an instant, ephemeral rainbow.

Ben and Will spread out the rugs and then began to have a kick-about with the ball while James stood by the water and watched Sam.

'Come on, slowcoach,' she yelled at him over the subdued thump of the small waves that broke rhythmically on the shore.

'Too cold. Don't want to get my trousers wet,' he said as a larger wave broke, and surged threateningly towards him.

Sam had no such inhibitions and her jeans were soaked from the knees down. She made her way back out of the water.

'Stick-in-the-mud,' she said.

She gathered up her shoes and socks and wandered back up the pebbly sand to the rugs, where she sat down and brushed off as much sand as she could and dried her feet on her socks before slipping them into her trainers.

'Ooh, gritty feet,' she complained.

'Well if you will get as wet as that with no change of clothes...' said James.

'You sound like a mother.'

'Really? What's she like – your mother?'

'I never knew her.'

'Shit, I am so sorry.'

So Sam told James about her odd upbringing, the endless moves, some of the places they lived, being sent off to boarding school at an early age and all the rest of the baggage that went with being a soldier's daughter.

'Still, it taught me to be independent,' she said as she finished.

'You don't sound as if you enjoyed it much.'

'It's difficult to judge, isn't it? I mean, it's the only childhood I know about.'

'Poor you.'

'I wouldn't worry about it. I don't.' Sam's stomach rumbled loudly. 'Excuse me,' she said, giggling. She glanced at her watch. 'Oi! Oi, you two,' she yelled to the other two. 'It's lunchtime. Let's go and find some scoff.'

The other two wandered over, puffing and panting from their exercise, while James got to his feet and held out his hand to help Sam to hers. She took it and pulled herself upright, then dusted more sand off the seat and the upper part of her trousers, giving up when she got to her knees. 'Yuck,' she said. 'Cold, wet jeans. Still, it was worth it.'

The four of them picked up the rugs, shaking them out before folding them up, and then the group wandered companionably up the beach, discussing what they fancied eating. They strolled along the promenade, past the beach huts and the seaside residences, the smell of frying and vinegar leading them by their noses until they found a mobile catering van.

They each ordered a portion of cod and chips and took their hot parcels of food to a nearby sheltered bench, where they tucked in and basked in the warm October sun in silence till they'd finished.

'I am stuffed,' said Sam, finally admitting defeat and laying her little wooden chip fork back on the newspaper. 'Full to busting.'

'Me too.' James scrumpled up his paper and the remains of his meal and took Sam's leftovers too. He shoved them in a nearby bin, watched beadily by an opportunist seagull, which took flight with an angry cry when it realised it was out of luck.

'Now what?' said Sam. She pulled her fleece on. A sudden veiling of cloud had encroached over the sun and while it was still glorious the temperature had fallen by a degree or two.

'Home, I suppose,' said Ben. 'It's getting too nippy for my taste.'

Sam nodded. 'It was lovely, but the weather's on the turn, isn't it?'

They began to walk back to the car.

Sam sighed contentedly. 'That was a lovely way to spend a Saturday.'

'I bet it beat sitting in your room.'

'It did. Maybe I'll try hanging around downstairs a bit more in the future.'

'You should. As I said yesterday, we don't bite.'

Sam shrieked with laughter as Ben suddenly pounced in front of her with a snarl and a growl. 'Except then the moon is full.'

'You're nuts!'

As Sam and her friends were driving back from the coast Maddy was heading over to Jenna's flat and trying to ignore any feelings of guilt about abandoning Seb and Nate.

'Come in, come in,' said Jenna as she opened the door to Maddy.

'Hey, this is nice.' Maddy had forgotten that Jenna had such good taste. She'd transformed her quarter back at the old barracks – although some of the transformations had been completely against army housing regulations. Jenna's flat was light and airy, with a blond wood floor and some stunning prints on the walls.

'Thanks,' said Jenna. 'Better than a crappy quarter, eh?' She led Maddy through to the bathroom.

'This is really kind of you to fit me in today. I felt a bit bad about interrupting your weekend but I haven't found a childminder yet for Nathan.'

'It doesn't matter. I'm glad of the business, to be honest. And Dan's out playing footie for the battalion so I've nothing better to do.' She held out a gown for Maddy to slip into and then pushed a stool across the bathroom floor. 'What do you want done?'

'A bloody good cut, please. Work your magic on it.'

Jenna lifted a clump of Maddy's hair. 'I'll do my best. Right, then, lean over the basin.' She tucked a towel around Maddy's neck and attached a shower head to the taps. 'Tell me if the water's too hot,' she said as she drenched Maddy's head.

'Perfect,' said Maddy with her eyes squeezed shut to stop water running into them. She mightn't have approved of the backwash unit Jenna had had installed in her bathroom in her old quarter but it made for a more comfortable hair wash.

'I had that new captain ring me today,' said Jenna, conversationally, as she dolloped on the shampoo and began to bring it to a lather.

'Which new captain's that?' mumbled Maddy, clutching the towel tight around her neck to keep the water from running down it.

'Dan's new boss. The REME girl.'

'Oh, her. Is she nice?'

'Dunno about nice; Dan says she's a bit of a looker. I asked him what he meant by that and he said she's got big tits.'

'Really?'

'Well, not that big, but he said she's very curvy. Typical bloke, isn't he, to notice something like that?'

Maddy nodded. 'Good luck to her, I say. It must be tough to be in such a minority.'

'Dan said she looks like a much younger Kylie, with short hair and bigger boobs. It's got to help that she's pretty, though.'

'I suppose,' said Maddy.

'Although Dan also says Mr Williams – he's the warrant officer in the workshop – is giving her a hard time. Obviously her looks cut no ice with him.'

And why should they? thought Maddy, but she didn't say so. However pretty Sam Lewis was, Maddy didn't think Jenna would have to worry about Sergeant Armstrong's eye wandering.

'Bet she has a blinding social life, though.'

'How do you work that out?'

'Stands to reason – being the only woman officer in the mess.'

'You think?'

'Of course. They'll all be falling over themselves trying to get her to go out on dates so they can get into her knickers.'

Which didn't sound like an ideal social life to Maddy. 'I think a lot of the livers-in already have girlfriends,' she said carefully.

Jenna snorted dismissively. 'Like that means anything when there's totty on tap. Trust me,' said Jenna, 'I know exactly what soldiers are like.'

Maddy didn't doubt it.

'They're all the same,' continued Jenna. 'If they think they can have a crafty shag, and not get caught, they will.'

'Seb's not like that,' said Maddy staunchly. Of course he wasn't.

'Maybe it'd be nice if you made friends with her,' said Jenna. 'Dan says she's only young – your age-ish, I think. You ought to have her round one evening, maybe when your old man goes rowing training. He's always doing that, isn't he?'

'Well, not so much in the evenings. Weekends, usually.'

'But he's not training this weekend.'

'No – I think it was because of the hiatus of all the move here.'

'She's coming to have her hair cut next Saturday.'

'Who?'

Jenna began to rinse Maddy's hair. 'That new officer.'

'Then give her my number. I'd like a bit of company if she fancies an escape from the mess.'

'Will do. Mind you, I'll check her out first before I hand it over. If I think she's a right cow I won't bother.'

Chapter Seven

'Come in, Corporal Blake.' Sam'd made up her mind, as she'd set out to work on Monday morning, that she'd get through the rest of the initial interviews this week, come hell or high water. She was determined to know the names of every single one of the men under her command by Wednesday at the latest. Corporal Luke Blake was next on the list and, after what the ASM had told her about him, she was intrigued to meet him.

She studied the NCO as he approached her desk. He didn't look odd, despite what the ASM had said. He looked far from odd with his thick, dark, wavy hair, very blue eyes, tanned skin and unfairly long eyelashes. He was also wearing just a khaki T-shirt with his multicam trousers and she could see his muscles under the stretchy fabric. The only thing that spoilt the image was the way he glowered at her from under his level eyebrows and the angry set of his mouth. Sam tried a tentative smile but he stared back impassively, his intensely blue eyes unwavering, as if he was analysing her. Sizing her up. The cheek. But there was one thing about him Sam was certain of: despite Corporal Blake choosing to nominate a male friend as his next of kin, he wasn't gay.

'Have a seat.' She waited while he took his beret off and settled himself. 'I've been looking at your records.' She smiled at him.

'Yes, ma'am.'

Even that short sentence told her he had a surprisingly educated accent. Which tied in with what the ASM had told her. 'That's quite a clutch of GCSEs you've got there.'

'Yes, ma'am.'

'But you didn't do A levels?'

'No, ma'am.'

'Any reason?'

'Several.'

'Which were?' She tapped her pencil on the desk.

'Leaving school was pretty instrumental, ma'am.'

'But you could have gone to college with those results.'

'Could… but didn't.'

She sighed and put her pencil down before she broke it. 'So, what about hobbies?'

'I ski a bit.'

'Did you learn through the army?'

'No, ma'am.'

'School trip?'

'Not really.'

She leaned forward. 'So *how* did you learn?'

'With the Ecole du Ski Français.'

She took a long, deep breath before she continued. 'Any other hobbies? Sports?'

'A bit of swimming and cycling and I run.'

'How much is *a bit*?'

'Ironman triathlons.'

Sam kept her face impassive. She reckoned he was baiting her and she was *not* going to rise. She changed tack. 'Where do you see yourself in ten years?' she asked.

'Depends where I get posted to.'

'Rank-wise?' she snapped.

'Warrant officer, I hope.'

'You could go for a commission.'

'No!'

His vehement reaction wrong-footed Sam. 'It was just a suggestion.'

'A suggestion I would prefer to ignore...' A pause, then, 'Ma'am.'

'May I ask why?'

Blake looked her directly in the eye and said, 'No.'

Sam's irritation with him was now morphing into real, cold anger. 'Well,' she said, trying to keep her voice steady, 'I mustn't keep you. I am sure you have plenty to be getting on with.'

'Thank you... ma'am.' Blake put his beret on his head and gave her a salute and a look that stopped just short of being insolent.

After he'd shut the door of her office Sam flopped back in her chair. First the ASM and now Blake. What had she done to deserve that pair in her workshop?

At lunchtime, after a long tedious morning cross-checking documents, Lance Corporal Immi Cooper strolled into the corporals' club, which was above the newly re-located Tommy's Bar. As she pushed open the door she once again thought that there were distinct advantages to having moved up from being a private soldier. For a start, she was now entitled to a single, en suite bunk and didn't have to share the ablutions with the other women in the barracks. Not that there were many, but it was nice not to have to queue for the shower. The other advantage of having a stripe was automatic membership of the corporals' club, which, unlike Tommy's Bar, had carpet rather than lino on the floor, softer, plusher seating and was, mostly, far less rowdy and noisy. Immi, despite enjoying men's company, did like being able to get away from the rough and tumble and casual sexual harassment that went with being one of only a dozen women in an otherwise all-male environment.

Immi liked blokes, but on her own terms and not twenty-four seven.

Immi was looking as smart as she could in barrack dress and her web belt was cinched in as tightly as possible to emphasise her tiny waist. Her platinum hair – she'd got fed up with being brunette and had reverted to a previous favourite over the weekend – was in an immaculate chignon, which she knew made her rear view almost as eye-catching as the front one. She made her way to the bar to order a lemonade and lime and a sandwich, aware, as she did so, of a number of pairs of eyes following her. She patted the bun on the nape of her neck as she placed her order and then she leaned against the bar to survey who was already there, who she might fancy chatting up. There were only a handful of blokes present; not a lot of talent to choose from. Then she saw Corporal Blake, sitting on his own in a corner, mucking about with his iPad. He had to be the most fanciable bloke in the entire battalion, but he was an oddball – everyone said so. She watched him for a few seconds, taking in his dark, curly hair and very blue eyes framed by thick black lashes a supermodel would covet. Sod the fact he was an oddball, maybe he'd like some company, she thought. Nonchalantly she wandered over in his direction and put her drink and sandwich down on the table.

'Mind if I join you?' she asked.

Luke gestured to the half dozen empty chairs before he said, 'Be my guest.'

As Immi settled herself down, Luke returned to his iPad.

'What'ya doing?' she asked.

'Reading.' He didn't look up.

Immi spluttered her drink. 'Reading! Why?'

This time Luke did look up. 'Because I can. I can even do it without pointing at the words with my finger and saying them out loud.' He then gave Immi a look which seemed to imply that he didn't reckon she could.

'It's a bit boring,' she countered.

'Depends on what you read.' Luke pointedly turned his attention back to his iPad.

Immi stared at him with narrowed eyes. Oddball or no, there was no need to be a right arsey git.

Could she be bothered to sit here and be ignored by him or would she be better off cutting her losses and heading off to her room to watch a bit of daytime TV before going back to work? She stared at Luke, noticing how his lashes curved onto his cheekbones, taking in his tanned skin and his muscled shoulders. She willed him to look at her and see how interested she was in him, but nothing. Zip. Diddly-squat. She necked her drink and stood up. Luke carried on ignoring her. That's it, she thought. Anything was going to be more fun than staying here if he was going to be like that. She grabbed her snack, swept out of the room and headed towards her block, already planning how she might make him notice her.

She was crossing the main road that led through the barracks when she had to step back onto the pavement as a little red sports car zipped past. Immi instantly recognised the driver: the new REME officer. A little buzz of jealousy pulsed through her. She would love a snazzy car like that, but she knew her salary wouldn't allow it. And it wasn't fair that this new officer looked so glam. Then Immi shrugged. So what? It wasn't as if they'd be fishing in the same pond – not with Captain Lewis being an officer and everything.

'Maddy, I'm home. What's for lunch?' Seb slammed the front door behind him. No answer. 'Mads?' called Seb, again as he chucked his beret onto the hall table.

Maddy called back a greeting, rather wanly, he thought,

from the sitting room. God, was she still feeling sick? How long was this going to go on for? It had been almost a fortnight since she'd told him she was pregnant. Wasn't it time she got a grip and stopped making a meal of it?

Seb went to find his wife. She was lying on the sofa, white as a sheet – maybe she wasn't feeling a hundred per cent, thought Seb a little grudgingly – while Nathan amused himself in his playpen with a stack of plastic toys.

Seb dropped a kiss on her forehead. 'What's for lunch?'

Maddy groaned. 'Dunno. Have a look in the fridge.'

'But I'm famished,' he protested, 'and I haven't got long.'

Maddy gazed up at him. 'Seb, I feel like I'm dying here. I honestly think I'm getting worse, not better. Today I haven't even been able to keep dry bread and water down, and you want me to cook lunch?'

'Oh,' said Seb. 'So haven't you made anything for Nate?'

'Nate's had some finger food and as soon as he goes down for his afternoon nap, I'm going to be joining him. Why don't you go to the mess and get a sandwich there and save me the bother? If I get a rest this afternoon I'll probably be able to raise the energy to make supper.'

Seb hoped she was right. He didn't want to come home after a tough day in the office and have to rally round in the kitchen. But what Maddy said about eating in the mess made sense – and at least he wouldn't have to listen to her banging on about how sick she felt. Odd that she'd been perfectly all right when it came to going out to get her hair done. Now he wanted a bite of lunch she was at death's door. Well, she couldn't have it both ways.

Not, if he was honest, that he minded all that much about lunching in the mess. The prospect of chatting with his old muckers, rather than discussing Nate's teething or the state of his nappies, was attractive. Best he didn't look too enthusiastic, though – Maddy was bound to misinterpret it and get all frosty. He put on his sympathetic face.

'Maybe your idea is best, Maddy. I don't want to put you out, especially if you're feeling a bit ropey. How about I book into the mess for lunch for the next couple of weeks – till you're back on your feet? Then you don't have to worry about me at all during the day.'

'Good idea,' said Maddy, listlessly. 'You do that.'

As Seb made his way back to the mess from the officers' patch, despite the fact he had a pink chit giving him complete freedom not to go home for lunch for the foreseeable future, he still felt a wee bit put out. Yeah, lunch in the mess wasn't a problem, far from it, but it wasn't just lunch that Maddy had ceased to bother with. Sex had been off limits since they'd moved, too. He and Maddy had barely got their sex life back on track following the horribly difficult and sleepless months after Nate's birth, and now it had ground to a halt again. It was all right for her, he thought rather selfishly. She was feeling so poorly she obviously didn't fancy it – but he bloody well did.

He walked past a couple of houses where the occupants were moving in. This had to be the last of the rear party arriving. The chaos of arms-plotting an entire battalion across the country to a new location was almost at an end, and soon everything would be back to normal. On the plus side the battalion was going to be spared going on an autumn field training exercise; on the minus side they'd all have to up-sticks and fly out to Kenya for training in February instead. Or maybe that was a plus too, thought Seb. Six weeks in the sunshine might be rather pleasant. It was bound to be hard work but he could put up with that for a bit of extra summer. And by the time he got back, Maddy's pregnancy would be almost over and frankly, the way it was going, missing a chunk of it might be no bad thing.

He made his way into the mess, dumped his beret on the big round table along with everyone else's and then made his way to the bar, where he ordered an orange juice and a round of cheese and ham toasted sandwiches.

Andy Bailey was sitting at a table at the side of the bar. When he saw Seb, he called him over.

'Just the chap,' he said.

Seb stifled a groan. The adjutant wanting to talk to you always meant work.

Seb feigned cheerfulness. 'What can I do for you, Andy?'

'Got a job for you.'

Knew it. 'Really?'

'I had a call today from Army HQ. They want to bring on more army rowers.'

'I'm not going to complain about that,' said Seb. 'In my opinion, you can never have too many rowers.'

'Good, because they want you to identify soldiers with potential and then train them. They've put out a call to all units for volunteers to come forward for an initial assessment weekend and then they want you to pick a dozen or so each from the men and women for a fortnight's training.'

'OK,' said Seb. 'When?'

'Soon. I've got the dates in my office. Drop over after lunch and I'll give you all the gen.'

Seb nodded.

'Maddy'll be all right with that, won't she?' continued Andy.

Seb rather thought she'd be more than happy not to have to worry about him, given the state she was in. It didn't cross his mind that she might like him there to pick up some of the slack in the evenings and at the weekends, especially as she was feeling so lousy.

*

Sam looked at the battalion orders which had been delivered to her in-tray. The sheets of paper detailed the guard rota for the next twenty-four hours, notice of a block inspection for A Company, and various other events affecting any, or all, of the soldiers. But nothing that Sam herself needed to worry about, she thought. She took the orders, left her office and began to pin them up on the main LAD noticeboard for the soldiers to read. She was turning back towards her office when one of the notices at the bottom of the orders caught her eye.

'Inter-company handball competition.' She looked at the details and then went to find the ASM.

'How about it?' she said when she'd given him a quick résumé of competition rules.

'You can ask for volunteers,' said Mr Williams. His tone implied that he didn't think she'd have any luck.

'I'll get Sergeant Armstrong to put something on daily detail,' said Sam, briskly. She knew the soldiers were more likely to read daily detail than battalion orders as the information on daily detail was only relevant to the LAD. 'And we'll see, won't we?' She eyeballed her second-in-command, daring him to make a snide remark.

But, rather to her surprise, a whole sheaf of the guys in the LAD volunteered.

'We're going to have to run trials,' Sergeant Armstrong told her, 'to pick the best. We only need seven and we've had sixteen guys sign up.'

'Seventeen,' said Sam.

'Oh, have I missed someone?'

'Me. I'm rather partial to handball.'

Sergeant Armstrong nodded. 'Nothing to say you couldn't play for the team...'

'If I'm good enough.'

The ASM joined the conversation. 'Is that wise, ma'am? It's a rough old sport. Lots of body contact.'

'I know, I've played it before.'

'But you're a woman.'

'Really? Look, Mr Williams, I'm an adult and I know what I'm doing.'

'If you say so... ma'am.'

Sam turned on her heel and walked to her office. Bloody man!

Dan Armstrong organised the trial in the battalion gym the following morning before work. Sam was faintly surprised to see that Blake had turned up. She'd had a bet with herself that he would have thought he was far too superior to demean himself by having to go through a selection process.

'Right,' said Sergeant Armstrong. 'I'm going to call out two lists of names. I'm afraid three of you will have to sit things out for the time being, but I'll sub you in when we change ends. I couldn't get hold of any bibs so to differentiate the two teams we're going to have shirts versus skins.' The lads all looked at Sam and someone wolf-whistled. 'And let me say that we're not drawing lots to see which team is which. Ma'am's team will be shirts, always.'

A rumble of laughter echoed through the cavernous gym, although Blake didn't join in. Instead, he stared at her, his face expressionless. Self-consciously she tugged her shirt down.

Armstrong sorted out the two teams and then one half of the lads stripped off their tops. Most of the opposing team were either stark white or had farmers' tans. But Blake... Blake, Sam noticed, looked like a poster boy for Ambre Solaire. Armstrong blew a whistle to get the game under way. It was fast and furious and Sam soon found that being an officer and a woman made no difference to the way the lads treated her. She got tackled as hard and as ruthlessly as any of the players on the court, but she'd been a star shooter in her school's netball team and managed to score a couple of goals, which she knew gave her a tiny bit of kudos with the men. And then she was lunging to intercept a pass between two opposing team members when she was barged. She crashed to the ground, banging her head hard on the floor. Pain exploded and then momentary darkness.

'You all right, ma'am?' The voice sounded distant and tinny.

What the hell had happened? she wondered vaguely. Groping through the woolliness in her mind, she thought she must have blacked out for a second or two.

'Ma'am?' The voice was clearer now.

Sam forced her eyes open. Above her were several worried faces, peering down at her.

'You all right, ma'am?'

Sam swivelled her gaze to the speaker, Sergeant Armstrong. She tried to rally. 'What happened?' she mumbled.

'You hit the deck,' said another voice. She moved her eyes to see who else was speaking. Blake. Even in her woozy state she heard him add, 'Told you a woman shouldn't have played. She was bound to get injured.'

Sam lay still, trying to work out how bad she felt. She certainly had a belter of a headache. Even lying flat on the floor, her head was spinning. But it wouldn't do to make a meal of it in front of the troops – confirm to the likes of Blake that she was weak and feeble.

'Help me up,' she said. She propped herself up onto an elbow and regretted it. She shut her eyes again as the entire handball court seemed to lurch like a raft on the sea.

'She ought to go to the med centre,' she heard Blake say. 'You heard the crack when her head hit the floor. She's probably got concussion.'

'You'd better take her, then,' said Armstrong. 'Stay with her till you know she's all right.'

Sam managed to open her eyes again.

'Ma'am,' said Armstrong. 'We think you ought to go to the medical centre. Blake'll go with you and look after you. We think you ought to get checked over.'

Part of Sam wanted to insist she was fine, that if she sat out for a few minutes she'd recover, but another bit of her knew Armstrong was right. And that knowledge was compounded by the fact she felt most odd. Maybe going to the medical centre was the best course of action.

'I'll carry you,' said Blake.

'No! No, I'll be fine. I can walk.' She hoped she could.

'OK, then.'

With Armstrong's help she managed to stagger to her knees and then she leaned on Blake as he helped cart her towards the door of the gym. For a second or two her slight feeling of queasiness and a banging headache made her regret turning down Blake's offer.

'Put your shirt on before we go outside,' she muttered. 'You'll catch your death.'

'Don't worry about me, ma'am.'

It wasn't him she was worrying about. 'Do as you're told,' she snapped.

Blake stopped dead. Swiftly and with barely concealed irritation he plonked Sam on a nearby bench before spinning on his heel and fetching his top as ordered.

Their slow, hobbling journey to the medical centre was completed in silence and, although Blake stayed with her till she'd been checked over and given painkillers for her headache, the atmosphere was chilly.

'I'll see you to the mess,' he said when the MO told her to take the rest of the day off and lie down.

'I'll be fine.'

'You're not well, you've had a bang on the head and Sergeant Armstrong told me to look after you.'

'And I'm telling you I'm all right.' She glared at Blake.

He stopped walking. 'Oh yes? If you're so *all right* why did the MO stand you down for the rest of the day? I'm sorry, but I am going to see you to the mess and make sure the staff there look after you properly and you're in no position to stop me. Ma'am.'

Sam felt too shit and too tired to argue. If he wanted to trail along after her it was no skin off her nose, although she was quite surprised by his chivalry – if that's what it was.

Chapter Eight

'Maddy.' Seb's voice permeated Maddy's brain. Then he called her name again, louder. She was jolted awake. Shit, she must have dropped off.

'Hello, Seb. You home already?' she called. She rubbed her eyes and tried to look bright and breezy.

Seb walked into the sitting room. At the sight of his father, Nathan hauled himself upright using the bars of the playpen that contained him, and held his arms up to be carried. Seb lifted his son out and then instantly dumped him on Maddy's lap.

'Yuck, he's soaking. Poor little mite,' Seb admonished. 'How long have you been asleep and ignoring him?'

Maddy scrambled to her feet. 'Just a couple of minutes, honest,' she lied.

Seb rolled his eyes. Maddy took Nathan and shot upstairs to change him.

'You know, she said to her son, kissing the top of his head, 'it wouldn't have done your daddy any harm to change you for once, now, would it?' Nathan gurgled and gave her a gummy smile.

When she got back downstairs with a clean and dry baby, Seb was happily reading the paper. She plopped Nathan back in his playpen.

'God, that child spends his life in there,' said Seb.

'He does not,' said Maddy. 'He and I spent ages at the

swings today and we went for a walk, but I can't cope with him rushing around when I'm doing other things.'

'Like sleeping.' said Seb.

She decided to ignore the comment. 'And now I am going to make you a cup of tea and cook Nate's supper. But,' said Maddy, picking Nathan out of his pen, 'since you are here, you can take over.' She plonked the toddler on Seb's lap.

'But I was reading the paper.'

'Read it later,' said Maddy, disappearing to the kitchen. Honestly, she'd like to see Seb cope with a baby and house-work and cooking with Nathan underfoot. Besides, he had all his toys in his playpen so he was hardly having a deprived childhood. She made up a plate of finger food for Nathan's supper and then buttered some bread to go with it. When she returned to the sitting room to get him she found he was back in his playpen and Seb was, once more, immersed behind the paper.

Huh, she thought, do as I say, not as I do... It was nearly eight by the time she'd got Nathan bathed and ready for bed and then cooked supper for Seb and herself. She reckoned she might make it as far as the ten o'clock news before she collapsed. She was knackered.

'By the way, before I forget, I won't be around this weekend,' announced Seb as he tucked into his pasta bake.

'Really? Rowing?'

'Kind of. That assessment weekend for potential rowers that I've been spammed to run – it's this weekend.'

'Oh. Will you be away for all of it?'

'I'm going to leave before lunch on Friday. There's going to be tented accommodation set up for the participants and I need to make sure that's all sorted before the rowers arrive. And I can't see myself getting away till the evening on Sunday so there's no way I'll be back till late. Sorry, hon.'

Maddy tried to look suitably disappointed but the truth was, with Seb away, she and Nathan could do some world-class loafing. She wouldn't have to make proper meals; she could eat cold beans out of the tin if the fancy took her. She could even have Nathan in bed with her after his early morning feed and have a lovely lie-in. Seb would never allow Nathan in their bed – said it was a sign of lazy parenting and that it was the sort of way drunks and junkies behaved. Like he knew anything about parenting, or drunks and junkies for that matter, but Seb had very set views about a lot of things and didn't like them to be challenged, even if he was completely wrong.

'Oh well, can't be helped,' said Maddy, trying to sound suitably disappointed.

'Thanks for being so understanding, Maddy,' said Seb. He sighed heavily. 'It's not my idea of a fun weekend but there's no getting out of it.'

You fibber! thought Maddy. Like he'd ever passed up an opportunity to get out on the water in a boat, and even if he was training other rowers, rather than doing his own training, he'd still be in his element.

'Fancy jumping in your car after work tomorrow and coming down here to the sticks?' said Sam over the phone to Michelle. It was Thursday evening and Sam was facing another weekend in the mess with precious little company and even less to do. 'I'm supposed to be getting a haircut on Saturday but, if you come over, I'll rearrange it for another time.'

'Sam, I'd love to, but your hair appointment is safe. I've been dicked to run a sodding work detail starting tomorrow.'

'What? Over the whole weekend.'

'I know, I know. Shit, isn't it? Honestly Sam, some of the officers here have got it in for me. It doesn't matter what I do, I always seem to piss someone off.'

Sam groaned. 'What have you done now?'

'I didn't do the weekly stock check of the mess bar.'

'Michelle! You're the mess wines member. It's your job to do that. It's like not turning up for staff parade when you're duty officer.'

'Look, I forgot, that's all. It's not like anyone died, is it?' Michelle sounded defensive; she always did that when she knew in her heart she was in the wrong.

'No, it isn't. But you can't forget stuff it's your responsibility to do. No wonder someone got pissed off.' How could Michelle be so utterly hopeless and drop herself in it yet again?

Over on the married patch Maddy was watching Seb pack, ready to go away to Dorney Lake in the morning. He wanted to be there before the wannabes arrived, to check all the kit, the boats, the arrangements, the tentage and everything else that would make the weekend a success.

'So you'll be back late Sunday, is that what you said?' she asked.

'That's the plan,' said Seb as he threw some underpants into a case. 'Get everyone out on the lake on Saturday morning to learn the basic technique, then more advanced training Saturday afternoon, followed by trials all day on Sunday to see who's got the most potential. After that I pick the best of the bunch to go forward for further training for a whole fortnight, after which we should have some who might be capable of joining the army team.'

'Do you know how many people have applied?' Not that Maddy cared. It didn't really make any odds if Seb was dealing with two or two hundred, she knew he'd be as happy as Larry to be back on the water, doing what he loved best.

'Not a clue,' said Seb. 'The only criteria, as far as I could gather, was a minimum height requirement and another one for fitness. How the hell applicants were screened after that is anyone's guess.' He fished his Lycra all-in-ones out of the cupboard and stuffed them on top of his other clothes. 'Let's hope the weather isn't too bad. I think I'm getting soft in my old age. The thought of training in driving rain has no appeal at all.'

'And you call yourself a soldier,' said Maddy, snuggling up against him. She was going to miss him, she really was. It was the other stuff – the cooking and the tidying up and the rest of it – that she needed a break from.

Seb zipped up his holdall. 'There, all done. Remind me to put my washing and shaving gear in first thing.'

'I'll do my best,' said Maddy, 'but you know what my brain's like at the mo.' She yawned hugely. 'Shit, I'm knackered. If you've finished, I think I might turn in.'

'An early night?' Seb waggled his eyebrows suggestively.

Maddy felt herself sag. Oh, please God, no. 'Seb,' she said, 'I'm really tired. I want a proper early night – you know – sleep.'

Seb sighed crossly. 'Like there's anything else you want to do in bed these days.'

'Don't be like that. It isn't *just* my fault I'm pregnant. I can't help feeling shitty. I'm not being sick on purpose.'

But the look on Seb's face didn't seem to suggest he agreed with her.

Miserably Maddy went to bed and when Seb came up later she feigned sleep. She knew if he thought he had a chance of a bit of rumpy-pumpy and she rejected him again he'd only get snarky. She didn't have the strength to cope with one of his sulks so it was best avoided completely. However, even in the silent darkness she was aware of his simmering resentment.

Seb took the car into the barracks the next morning with his holdall shoved on the back seat. He had some paperwork that needed seeing to before he could get away from the office. And away from all that moaning about feeling a bit queasy. God, he thought, as he drove into work, Maddy was only pregnant, not ill. She hadn't been like this with Nathan but now... now she was going about like a wet weekend, with a face on her that could stop traffic. It was just a bit of nausea when all was said and done, and yet she seemed to be using it as a stick to beat him with at every turn. Shit, he'd even had to iron a shirt this morning because she'd said she wasn't up to it. It was like she was using morning sickness to get out of anything she didn't fancy doing. It'd been all right before, when she'd been expecting Nathan. Then she'd managed to cope with that and a full-time job – but she'd liked that job. Now she was a full-time wife and mother it was a different story. *Now* she seemed to resent having a bit of childcare and housework to do. Was it so much to ask that she did the support role at home while he was filling up the bank account every month? And what happened to shagging? He could barely remember the last time he and Maddy had made love. A quick one off the wrist in the shower really wasn't what a man needed.

Seb was still mulling over the state of his marriage as he got back in his car and set off for the rowing lake. By the time he was approaching Eton Dorney he had calmed down, although he was completely convinced that he was being perfectly reasonable and that whatever was going wrong with their marriage at the moment it was all Maddy's fault. Well, hers and the unborn baby's.

Seb left the motorway with the massive pile of Windsor Castle looming on the skyline and then wiggled his way along the country roads of Berkshire till he came to the sign that announced he'd arrived at his destination. He turned into the grounds surrounding the Olympic rowing venue and onto the road that led down alongside the two-kilometre lake, past the

Olympic rings and towards the big boathouse at the far end. Before he reached that, he veered left and into the car park beside the campsite used by visiting crews.

He stretched when he got out of the car and glanced at his watch. Eleven – he'd made cracking time. Slamming the car door, he wandered through to the campsite to see if the tentage he'd ordered had not only arrived but was being put up by a work detail from the nearby barracks. As he rounded the hedge that separated the two areas he could see it was all going to plan. Furthermore, the trailer loads of boats from the Army Rowing Club had also been delivered. Better and better. He might even have time to get out on the lake himself before nightfall.

He cast about to find whoever was in charge to introduce himself to. He spotted a tall, uniformed woman, with her back to him, who was issuing orders to the squaddies and who was very obviously in charge of the work detail. Seb wandered over.

'Hello,' he said.

She spun round and Seb stopped in his tracks. Stunning was the word that sprang to mind. Wow! He'd heard the phrase fine-boned but this was the epitome of what those words actually represented. She was tall and elegantly slim, like a model, with huge brown eyes and a mass of thick dark hair that she'd tied back in a ponytail. Then she smiled at him and a dimple appeared in each cheek. Maddy was pretty, of course she was, but not in this league.

Clearing his throat and trying to get his thoughts in order, he introduced himself. 'Sebastian Fanshaw.' As he said his first name a combination of a gust of wind, a crack and flap of canvas and a bout of heavy-duty swearing from a nearby soldier meant the first syllable of his name was lost.

'Bastion?' said the vision. 'Like the camp in Afghanistan?'

Quite why Seb didn't put her right in that instant he couldn't explain – not even to himself. 'Bastian – with an 'a'.'

'And I'm Michelle Flowers. Pleased to meet you. Can I call you Bas for short?'

Again Seb didn't even stop to think. 'Of course.' He smiled at her. Shit, she was gorgeous. 'So, are you the boss here?'

Michelle nodded. 'Something like that. Whip-cracker in chief, that's me.'

Seb grinned. 'So, Miss Whiplash, are you staying for the rowing?'

Michelle shook her head. 'Hey, I don't think we know each other nearly well enough for you to use that name. Only special friends are allowed to do that.'

Funny, flirty *and* gorgeous, thought Seb.

'No,' continued Michelle, 'I'm here to supervise this lot and see the tents get put up properly.'

'You don't know what you might be missing out on.'

'I don't think rowing's my style.'

'Really? I mean you're tall enough and it stands to reason you're fit. And given the fact that you've got long limbs you might be very good at it.'

Michelle wrinkled her nose in a way that made Seb's heart miss a beat. 'Yeah, well, whatever, but I've heard what some of those Olympic rowers said about the pain. I might be in the army and I might be whip-cracker in chief but I'm not into masochism.'

'Shame,' said Seb.

Michelle let out a very unladylike guffaw. 'Do I look like I want to visit the Red Room of Pain?'

'The what?'

Michelle shook her head. 'Look, if you don't know about the Red Room of Pain, I don't think I ought to be the one to tell you about it. Google it when you get a chance. Nuff said.' She shot Seb another naughty smile, which he found completely disconcerting.

'Anyway,' he said, 'why don't you give rowing a whirl? What are you doing this weekend?'

'Stuck here mostly. Well, that's not exactly true but I don't think I'll be finished here till late and then I've got to be back with the guys on Sunday morning to take it all down again.'

'There you go. Your weekend seems to be a bit of a car crash as you've been lemoned to sort stuff out for me and the rowers, so why not hang around on Saturday and give it a go? What have you got to lose? And you never know, you might even enjoy it. If you're hopeless—'

'Thanks for the vote of confidence.'

'If you're hopeless, we'll call it quits and I'll never make you get in a boat again. But you never know, you might be the new Katherine Grainger.'

'Yeah, right.'

'Don't knock it till you've tried it.'

'Well, as my mother said, try everything once except Morris dancing and incest.'

'Exactly. So on that basis you'll give it a go?'

'OK.' She gave him a wide smile. 'Why not? You've persuaded me. So as soon as we've got the camp sorted I'll pop back to barracks and get my sports kit and see you back here on Saturday morning.'

'Or you could come back later today. There a double scull on that trailer. I could take you out on the water – give you a head start. Then there's a cracking pub down the road. If you do well enough I'll buy you supper.'

'Deal,' said Michelle.

'Deal indeed.'

Sam was lying on her bed reading her Kindle in a desultory way for want of anything better to do. Later she was going to get her hair cut but right now she was killing time. Her laundry was done and hanging up in the drying room, she'd been for a run, she'd bulled her parade shoes and tidied her room. And now she was bored, very bored. Her mobile rang. Idly she picked it off the duvet. Ooh, Michelle; she hoped her friend was ringing for some full-on girly gossip and not a quick call.

'Hi, hon, how's the work detail going? Is it as grim as you thought it would be?' Sam flopped back against the pillows propped up against the headboard and winced; she'd forgotten again about the lump on her head. And the fact that she'd bashed it earlier that morning when she'd brushed her hair hadn't helped matters either.

'Oh, Sam, I've got to share this with someone. I've met this man.'

'You lucky thing.' Sam rubbed her head to try and minimise the throbbing. 'More than I've done.'

There was a splort down the phone. 'Pull the other one, Sam, you're in an all-male battalion. You're surrounded by men.'

'Yeah, well…' Sam dickered with the idea of telling Michelle that there was a bloke she half fancied but it was a bit early for that. Just good friends was really the only appropriate description of her and James. 'Anyway, tell me about this bloke. Who is he, where did you meet? I want every detail.'

'Well… where do I start? We met yesterday and he's gorgeous and fit. And fit in the old sense too. Honestly, even his muscles have muscles, and he's tall and did I say he was gorgeous?'

Sam laughed. 'You might have mentioned that.'

'And he's called Bas and he rows and he's teaching me how to row.'

'You? Rowing?' Sam couldn't contain her amusement.

'Yeah. And your point is? Just 'cos I usually avoid team sports… Anyway, Bas says I am perfectly built for it. Long limbs,' added Michelle, smugly.

'I suppose,' conceded Sam.

'And he's clever and funny.'

'Well, lucky old you, he sounds a catch.'

'Well, I haven't actually caught him yet, but, Sam, I really hope I do. He is gorgeous. Did I say that, because he really, really is.'

'So, this gorgeous Bas bloke, what does he do?'

'He's a soldier. In fact, you probably know him; he's with the Hertfordshire Regiment.'

'Officer?'

'Of course.'

Sam racked her brains. 'Nope, no Bas. We don't have a Bas in the battalion.'

'You sure?'

'Pretty positive.'

'He must be with one of the other battalions or off doing a staff job somewhere.'

'That's probably it.'

'Honestly, Sam, there I was in charge of all these hairy-arsed squaddies putting up tents and then this full-on Adonis pitches up and I thought I'd died and gone to heaven when I saw him. And we had a bit of a chat and then he bribed me with a promise of dinner if I had a go at rowing – and, well… I mean, what sane girl would turn down an offer like that?'

'And your mental health has never been an issue,' said Sam, dryly.

'Indeedy. And then, well, let's say I don't mind being stuck here this weekend after all. Things are looking up.' Michelle sighed, contentedly.

'So all is rosy in Michelle-world.'

'Well, things are certainly better than they were. I'm hoping now I'm going to make the squad of rowers so I get to see a lot more of him. And I mean a *lot* more of him.' There was a pause. Sam suspected Michelle was busy imagining her new flame in the buff. 'Oh, Sam, he is so wonderful. Honestly, if he'd invited me to spend last night in his tent at the lake I'd have been there like the proverbial rat up a drainpipe.' There was another pause. 'I've got it bad, haven't I?'

Sam laughed. 'Considering you probably haven't even known him for a whole twenty-four hours, you certainly have! But I'm pleased for you, really I am. He sounds lovely... and gorgeous.'

'He is, he is! And I know you'd agree with me if you met him too.'

'Then we'll have to fix something up. Try and stay out of trouble so you don't pick up any more extras—'

'Hey, that's unfair... well, thinking about it, maybe not.'

'And tell me when Bas can make it too and we'll sort something out. Maybe, you never know, I might have found someone nice and we can have a double date.'

'Ace idea. It sounds like a plan to me.'

Chapter Nine

Sam wasn't the only person in the battalion feeling a little bored. Immi Cooper was also kicking her heels and wondering what on earth she could do. Unusually for her she was without a current boyfriend, which was why she was stuck on camp for the weekend. She had her elbows on the windowsill of her bunk and was staring at the view across the parade square. She supposed she could catch the bus into Warminster and go shopping, but she was finding it hard to raise the enthusiasm to do even that. She was about to fling herself down on her bed and read a magazine when she saw someone walking around the edge of the square. She recognised who it was. Luke! So he was stuck here too. Maybe the weekend wasn't a dead loss after all. Maybe she could engineer a chance meeting... she'd take a trip to the corporals' club later on and see if he popped in. It was time to put Operation Luke into action.

At lunchtime Immi strolled into the corporals' club, bought herself a glass of red wine – ignoring the startled look the barman gave her – and carried it over to a quiet corner, away from the bar. There she extracted a pair of glasses and a book from her handbag and began to read. She'd Googled the top classic books of all time and had found the second on the list – *Pride and Prejudice* – in the garrison library. Surely Luke would be impressed. He ought to be, it had some fucking long words in it. Prejudice for starters. Who wanted to read a book where you had to eat a sodding dictionary before you could get a handle on it? On the other hand, she'd got the DVD up in her room so she didn't have to read that much of it to find out what happened. But while she waited for Luke to turn up she'd have to make a stab at the opening pages.

God, it was dull. Where was the sex, the action, the plot? Her mind drifted away from the page. How long would she give it before she threw in the towel and returned to her room? She glanced at her watch and decided that if he hadn't arrived by one o'clock she'd give up. She forced her attention back to her book. Come on, Luke, get a move on. This is as boring as fuck, she thought as she struggled through a few more pages. And reading it wasn't made any easier by her glasses. They might have been the weakest easy-readers in the shop but they still made the words a bit blurry. She sipped her wine, pretending she was enjoying her sophisticated drink, while she tried to make sense of her book and kept a vague eye on the comings and goings in the bar to be sure she didn't miss Luke.

'Wotcha, Ims.'

Immi glanced up and whipped her glasses off. Des from B Company. Where had he sprung from? He was all right – good company and everything but not the man she was waiting for.

'Hi, Des.' She shoved her book into her lap. She knew Des – he'd rip the piss if he saw what she was reading.

'Can I?' he asked, looking at the spare seats at her table, and before she could answer he'd hooked a chair out with his free hand and plonked his beer on the table.

Immi gave him a look which she hoped he'd take as a hint he wasn't welcome.

Des ignored it. 'What's with the face furniture, Ims? Didn't know you wore glasses.'

'I don't.' She corrected herself. 'I mean, I don't as a rule.'

'Oh, contacts, then.'

Immi nodded.

'Ever thought of having your eyes lasered?'

She shuddered. 'Yuck.'

'Honest, it's brilliant. I had mine done. What they do is, they shove some drops in and then when your eye is numb, they laser open the cornea, flip it back—'

Immi held her hand up. 'Stop! If you want to see what I had for my breakfast you're going the right way about it.'

'Squeamish?'

'Des,' said Immi sternly, 'if I was into that sort of stuff, do you think I'd have chosen to be a clerk? I like sitting in a nice warm office, I like shuffling paper, I do not like getting wet, cold or muddy and I don't like anything medical. Got it?'

'Sorry,' said Des, grinning at Immi's rant. 'I'll get you a drink to make it up. What's that?'

'Red wine.'

Des started to laugh. 'Red wine? You're kidding me, right? And did I see you reading when I came in?' He shot a hand across the table and fished the book off Immi's knees before she could stop him. He glanced at the title and his eyebrows hit his hairline. '*Pride and Prejudice*? Red wine? Glasses? Come on, Ims, what's your game?'

'I don't know what you mean.'

Des laughed harder. 'Ims, don't lie to Uncle Des. Who are you trying to impress?'

'No one,' she countered primly. 'Why shouldn't I read *Pride and… and…* whatever,' she finished lamely. Des turned towards the others in the bar, brandishing the book, but Immi grabbed his arm and hauled it down to his side. 'Shh, Des. Please.'

Des turned back and put the book on the table. 'OK, I'll keep quiet but only if you spill the beans.'

'OK.' She took a deep breath. She was beaten, she knew it. 'It's Luke, Luke Blake.'

Des made a face of complete disbelief. 'You fancy Blake?'

Immi shrugged. 'And? Why not?' She stared at Des.

'Because he's weird, that's why.'

'Just because he's got more brains than your average grunt doesn't make him weird.'

'And he's always got his nose in a book, he doesn't go out on the lash, he doesn't get in fights, he doesn't play *Call of Duty*...'

'And your point is?' said Immi.

'He's a soldier, in case you haven't noticed, Ims. That's what soldiers do. All of them. Except Blake. That's why he's weird.'

'Well, I disagree,' said Immi, firmly. 'I think that makes him a bit more interesting, that's all.'

Des shook his head. 'Trust me, Immi, he's not for you. Stick with guys like me.' He blew her a kiss. 'You know you want to really.'

Immi picked up her book and stuffed it back in her bag, drained the last drops of her wine and handed her empty glass to Des. At least if he was going to keep her company she was spared from reading Jane Austen. 'Now, about that drink you offered me...'

She had to hope that Des would have the good sense, or the good manners, to bugger off if and when Luke did turn up.

'That's it, Michelle. Watch the angle of your blades.' Bas was puttering along in a motor launch in the wake of the double scull that Michelle was rowing in with another female soldier. 'And drive with your legs. Now, remember to pull your elbows through as you start to extract the oar from the water. Feather the blade, slide forward, catch and drive. Brilliant. Feather, recover, catch, drive.' Bas repeated the mantra time and time again to keep the two girls in perfect rhythm as they swept along the rowing lake, their sculls dipping in and out of the water with the elegance of a swan in flight, leaving little puddles of ripples at perfectly evenly spaced intervals. 'You're doing fabulously,' he called. 'Keep it up and keep practising for another k or two while I go and help a couple of the other crews.'

'He's a slave driver,' panted Michelle's rowing companion, Katie.

Michelle could hear how laboured her breathing was and was heartened by the realisation that Katie was finding this as hard as she was. To take her mind off her thundering heart rate and her aching lungs she gazed across a few yards of water to Bas's boat and fantasised, for a moment, about being seduced by him. God, what would it be like to feel his mouth on hers?

'Hey,' shouted Katie, a second before one of Michelle's sculls clattered into her partner's. The little boat lurched dangerously as Michelle almost overbalanced. 'Watch it!' shrieked Katie, afraid they were both going to end up in the icy water. They both let go of their sculls and clutched the sides of the tiny craft until the violent rocking settled and they recovered their equilibrium.

'Sorry,' puffed Michelle, half-collapsing with exhaustion. 'I don't know what happened there.' She heaved in another lungful of air. 'Lost my concentration for a second.' She was glad that she was in the bow and thus Katie couldn't see her face. Mind you, she thought, Katie would be hard pressed to spot a flush caused by embarrassment given that she knew she was sweating like the proverbial pig from all this thundering up and down Eton Dorney Lake. Rowing might look almost effortless if you were watching it but the reality of being a participant was somewhat different. The muscles in her legs were trembling with fatigue and her shoulders and upper arms were burning.

'Let's take a breather for a minute,' gasped Michelle, slumping forward over her oars.

'Good shout... A couple of minutes... and we can... go again.' Katie's words came out in groups of two or three between heavy breaths.

The boat lay still on the water as the two girls recovered, but after about thirty seconds the light breeze began to chill them down.

Michelle shivered. 'Let's go before we freeze,' she said. 'But let's take it steady; concentrate on technique, not speed.'

They pushed their hands forward so their blades were in the water as close to the bow of the boat as they could get them, their knees hauled up against their chests, then Katie, as stroke, said, 'And drive...'

They pulled on the oars, their sliding seats rolling backwards as their feet pushed as hard as possible against a metal plate, and the boat shot forward. Michelle followed Katie's movements as closely as she could, extracting and feathering her blades in unison with her team mate.

'And drive,' called Katie again. The pace was slower than when Bas had been spurring them on, but Michelle reckoned their style was tidier.

They completed another kilometre along the lake and wound up back at the boathouse end feeling completely knackered.

Bas was standing on the pontoon ready to greet them as they pushed their oars onto the jetty and began to climb shakily out of the little craft, which rocked wildly.

'Here,' said Bas, leaning down and holding out his hand to Michelle.

She took it and felt a bolt of something powerful – electricity? Lust? Animal magnetism? – course right through her. Involuntarily, she glanced up at his face; had he felt it too? Given the way he was staring at her with wide, dark-eyed intensity, she was sure he had. She thought of the Michelangelo painting in the Sistine Chapel where God's finger points at Adam's and brings him to life, and suddenly understood how Adam must have felt at that moment. Bloody hell... she felt rocked to the core.

'How are you settling in?' asked Jenna as she held out a gown for Sam to slip on.

'Yeah, fine, I suppose.'

'Dan says you had a bit of an accident the other day. Wound up in the medical centre.'

Sam nodded and touched her head. 'Yeah, and I've still got a bloody great bruise. Just here...' she indicated the spot '...so if you could go carefully round it, I'd be grateful.'

Very gently Jenna parted Sam's hair and had a look at the injury. 'Nasty.'

'Luckily, I only got a really mild bout of concussion. I was fighting fit again in a few hours.'

'Lucky you indeed. Mind you, you'd have been even luckier if you hadn't been injured in the first place.' Sam couldn't fault Jenna's logic. 'So, what do you want done?'

Sam explained she wanted a good trim, 'so it lasts for a couple of months.'

Jenna got busy with the shampoo, being very gentle around the bruised area, as she chatted to Sam about this and that – the weather, holidays, the usual hairdresser to client chit-chat. Then, 'So what's it like, being the only woman in the mess?'

'It's OK, I'm finding my feet and they're mostly pretty friendly. I think they're working it out that I don't faint if I overhear the odd swear word or dirty joke.'

Jenna chuckled. 'You don't? Ooh, I am shocked! Talk about letting the side down.'

'Exactly. No, to be honest, I'm finding it tougher at the LAD.'

'Really?'

Sam nodded. 'Don't repeat this, but I don't think the ASM likes me.'

'Oh, *him*. I wouldn't worry about Graham Williams. He and your predecessor, Ian Abbott, went way back. Abbott was commissioned from the ranks and I think he and Williams knew each other from apprentice college. Or that's what I heard. There's no way he's going to like anyone who follows on from his best buddy.'

'Honest?'

'Cross my heart. I mean, it probably doesn't help that you're a woman, but that's blokes in the army for you. I really don't think it's personal.'

Sam snorted. Indeed. The army might be outwardly all about equal opportunities but there was still a lot of casual sexism amongst some of its male soldiers.

Jenna finished rinsing out the first application of shampoo and began the second wash.

'Jenna?' said Sam.

'Yes.'

'What do you know about Corporal Blake?'

Jenna's hand stilled as she considered the question, then, after a few seconds, she said, 'Apart from him being odd, you mean?'

Sam nodded her head and felt water trickle down the back of her neck and under her T-shirt. Odd. That was the adjective everyone used. 'Yes, apart from that.'

'I met him at the LAD summer barbecue a few months ago. Apart from the fact he's got a bloody great plum in his mouth I thought he was nice – the weather was fuck-awful and he gave me his jacket. And I could see the goose-bumps all over his arms, so he must have been freezing his knackers off, but he wouldn't take it back.'

'The perfect gentleman,' said Sam wryly.

'Nothing wrong with that,' said Jenna, starting to rinse the suds out a second time.

No, there wasn't, thought Sam. She remembered, despite his apparent irritation at being asked to look after her following her accident, he had been pretty solicitous. Well, once he'd got over being told to put his shirt back on.

'Anyway, for all his brains and superiority and oddness, I reckon he's got a kind heart in there somewhere.'

Maybe, thought Sam, but if there was, it was bloody deeply buried. Whenever she looked at him he seemed to be brooding about something.

Jenna started to towel-dry Sam's blonde curls. 'You met many of the wives yet?'

Sam shook her head from inside the confines of the fluffy towel. 'Not really. Put it this way, at weekends I have observed them from a distance and decided that we probably don't have that much in common. Of course, my dad was a soldier so I grew up on a patch but I looked at my friends' mums as just that – mums.'

Jenna laughed. 'Well, thankfully I'm not a proper army wife. I mean, me and Dan aren't married for starters and I don't live in a quarter. I did once and that was enough. Don't you think the proper variety are all a bit Stepford?'

'Stepford?'

'You know, like the thriller, where the wives are like robots, designed to be perfect and help their husbands' careers. No minds of their own, doing as they're told, obeying regulations and not rocking the boat.'

Sam laughed, because, looking back at all her friends' mums and then at the wives of the Sandhurst directing staff, she knew exactly what Jenna meant. 'You may have a point,' she agreed drily.

'You'd like my friend Maddy, though.' Jenna led Sam back into the kitchen and sat her down on a stool in front of a large mirror on the counter, propped up against the bread bin.

'Maddy?'

'I've been doing her hair for ages, since before 1 Herts got moved here, when they were at their last barracks. She's nice.' Jenna ran a comb through Sam's hair to get out any tangles. 'Officer's wife, got a kid, but don't let that put you off. She's not all coochey-coo and baby-talk.' Jenna started to snip. 'And she's been known to have a good bitch about the sort of shit the army flings at you, which is a lot if you're a wife... or partner. In fact, when I told her I was going to be doing your hair she said I was to give you her number, in case you fancy a bit of female company now and again. Her husband is some sort of athlete; always away training, especially at weekends. I think you'd be doing her a favour too, if I'm honest. Remind me to get you her number before you go.'

Sam thanked Jenna but wasn't sure about Maddy's offer. Life as the only female in the mess mightn't be ideal but she wasn't convinced Maddy's motives for friendship were entirely altruistic – was she just after someone to fill in the gap when her husband was away? And, furthermore, Sam wasn't struck on kids. But even if she took the number, she didn't have to ring it.

'Love the hair,' said James, when Sam returned to the mess later that afternoon.

Sam patted her newly cut curls. 'I didn't think men noticed stuff like that,' she retorted, although she was inwardly pleased with the compliment.

'Well, we do sometimes.' James gave her a grin. 'It's a bit novel to have a mess member with a hairstyle as opposed to a number two buzz cut.'

'Anyway, what are you doing back here? I thought you'd gone off to see your folks this weekend.'

'I did and I have, and now I'm back.'

'Oh, OK.' Why, if he had the option to be somewhere else, would he want to come back to the mess early, which, at the weekends, had less life going on in it than a sterile Petri dish. Still, it was his decision. 'Can't keep away from the place, is that it?'

'You mean, the lure of joining the pads for Sunday drinkies and chatting about nappy rash and marks on their carpets was too strong for me to resist?'

Sam giggled. James had absolutely nailed Sunday lunchtime conversation in the mess bar. Which was why Sam tended to stay in her room at weekends and which was also why she hadn't yet really met any of the married officers' wives. And that reminded her... she fingered the scrap of paper in her pocket that Jenna had given her.

'Hey, James, do you know Maddy Fanshaw?'

'Maddy? Of course I do. Lovely lady and married to Seb Fanshaw. Why do you ask?'

Sam shrugged. 'We share a hairdresser and she said she thought we'd get on.'

'You would. There's nothing not to get on with where Maddy's concerned. She's a real star. Funny, pretty... I think half the single officers in the battalion are secretly in love with her.' James laughed. 'Maybe some of the married ones too, for all I know. Some of the guys are married to real dragons. I bet they'd swap what they've got for Maddy in a heartbeat, if the chance came up.'

'Are you? In love with her, that is?'

'No. No, not at all, she's not really my type.' He laughed then said, 'Anyway, Seb's twice my size and would probably knock down anyone who tried anything on with her at the drop of the proverbial hat.'

'Well, since you seem to think so highly of her, maybe I'll give her a ring.'

'Do that. I'm sure the pair of you would hit it off.' James smiled at her. Sam began to turn, ready to head to her room.

'By the way,' said James. 'Um…' He sounded a bit diffident. 'I don't suppose you fancy going out to supper tonight? Foolishly I booked out for all meals over the whole weekend so the staff won't be catering for me tonight. I thought I'd go over to that nice pub – you know, the one on the road to Westbury – for sups. I'd love it if you'd join me, then I won't look like Billy-No-Mates.'

This was a no-brainer – supper out with James or on her own in a lifeless mess? She didn't even have to think about it for a second. 'James, I'd love to. But let's make it a Dutch treat, eh?'

'It goes against the grain, but…' He cocked an ear. 'Yes, I can definitely hear the sound of my bank manager starting to breathe again. And you're sure you don't mind?'

'No, I'd feel so much more comfortable about it. But if you want to make it a real treat you can drive, then I can have a drink.'

'Deal!'

'I'll see you back here at…' Sam looked at her watch '…half six? Or is that too early?'

'Nope, perfect. See you then.'

Sam took the stairs two at a time back to her room, feeling strangely cheerful about the prospect of spending an evening with James. It was nice to have a friend in the mess and especially nice to have a friend who seemed to want to be just that – no other agenda. If it wasn't for blooming Williams at the LAD she'd swear she'd almost been accepted by the battalion.

Chapter Ten

On hearing the bell, Maddy dragged herself to the front door. So much for being able to do some industrial-grade loafing while Seb was away for the weekend. Somehow, between the household jobs that really couldn't be avoided, Nathan having a bad night, running out of milk and butter so she'd had to go shopping, and feeling absolutely bloody awful, there'd been no way she'd been able to chill out like she'd hoped. Maybe tomorrow, Sunday, would go more like she'd planned. Behind her, in the sitting room, Nathan was banging a wooden spoon noisily on his toy box, and that wasn't helping things either, but Nate was happy, which was what mattered. Maddy opened the door and there, on the doorstep, was her husband's boss's wife, and good friend, Susie Collins. They'd been neighbours on the last patch, before the move, but Maddy and Susie had both been so busy getting their respective houses straight they hadn't seen much of each other since arriving in their new location. Despite how crap she felt, Maddy felt a tiny little tweak of pleasure at seeing her old mate. She smiled, albeit weakly.

'Hello, Susie.'

Susie stared at Maddy, her brow furrowed with worry. 'Sweetie! You look terrible. Are you all right?'

'Not really,' admitted Maddy.

'What can I do?' said Susie, briskly. 'I actually came round to see if you had any spare tea bags and I can see now it was a bloody good job that I ran out and had to make the call. It was obviously meant to be!' She pushed past Maddy into the house. 'So what's the matter? Has the move completely knackered you, have you been overdoing things?'

'Nothing like that, honest.'

Susie gave her a hard stare. 'You don't fool me, Maddy, something's wrong. You sit down. I'm going to make you a cup of tea – assuming you haven't run out of tea bags too.' She saw Nathan begin to crawl towards them from the sitting room. 'And don't worry, I'll see to the baby.'

Maddy gave in and allowed herself to be propelled to the sofa where she collapsed, while Susie scooped up Nathan and took him with her into the kitchen. She lay back against the cushions and her eyes shut. She heard Susie bustling about in the kitchen, opening and shutting cupboards, cooing at Nate, filling the kettle, putting it on... Oh, the bliss of being looked after. She relaxed, enjoying the moment.

'Here's your tea.' Maddy opened her eyes again as Susie put a mug on the table in front of her. 'I took the liberty of putting sugar in it. I think you need some energy, you look wiped out. Now, what's the matter, Maddy? You look awful, like you're going down with something dire.' She looked so concerned Maddy felt she owed it to Susie to explain the situation.

'I'm not ill, just pregnant. I was going to wait a few more weeks before going public... well, now you know.'

'Ah...' Susie nodded. 'That would explain it. But congratulations. You must be thrilled.'

'I know I should be...' Maddy sighed, dejectedly. 'But the sickness is awful this time. When I was expecting Nate it wasn't half as bad.'

'And back then you didn't have someone waking you up early and needing constant attention.'

Maddy gave Susie a wan smile. 'No, I didn't. And Nate doesn't give me much peace either.'

Susie grinned at her. 'You should have told me before, though; I can help. With the twins back at boarding school I'm hardly pushed for time and things to do, am I?'

Maddy shrugged. 'I know but I didn't want to make a fuss. Other people manage.'

Susie shook her head in mild reproach before she sat down on the chair opposite Maddy. 'Well, you don't have to manage tonight; I'm here. How about you tell me what you were planning on cooking for Nathan's supper and I'll do it while you put your feet up.'

'You don't have to. Honest. Seb's away for the weekend and Nate and I were going to have scrambled eggs on toast.'

'I can do scrambled eggs on toast. And then when you've had that I'm going to give Nathan his bath and put him to bed. And when I've done that I suggest you go to bed too. You look done in, my dear, if you don't mind me saying so.'

'Oh, Susie, you don't have to bath Nathan.'

'Yes, I do. Don't argue, and do as you're told. Before I get started, though, I'm going to pop back over to Mike and tell him where I am, so he doesn't send out a search party. And if I could nick those tea bags...'

'Of course.'

'Back in a mo.'

Nathan, safely corralled, picked up his wooden spoon again and banged on his toy box till Susie returned and took him into the kitchen, whereupon relative peace descended. Maddy could hear her making a fuss of her son, who was obviously lapping up the attention, judging by the gurgles and giggles, while she allowed her mind to drift. Thank goodness for the wonderfulness of her army-wife neighbours.

*

At tea-time on the last day of Bas's selection weekend, all the rowers were lined up in front of the Eton College boathouse, waiting to hear the news before they dispersed back to their units. Had they, or hadn't they, made the grade to go forward for further training? Katie, Michelle noticed, looked pretty indifferent, and maybe she was. However, Michelle herself had butterflies the size of eagles battering her ribcage with their wings and she hoped it wasn't obvious to everyone that she was bricking it. She hadn't felt this jittery since Sandhurst and she'd been waiting outside her company commander's office for her final interview. Back then, she'd known she was going to be told one of two things: either she hadn't made the grade and was going to be back-squadded, or she had made it and so she would be getting commissioned alongside all her peers. Then, like today, her knees had shaken so much she'd barely been able to stand.

Man up, she told herself, sternly. If you don't make the grade there may be a way you can see him outside of rowing. But, her alter ego argued, as he was obviously a complete rowing nut, she'd be so much more attractive in his eyes if she showed she had a real talent for his chosen sport.

Bas came out of the boathouse with a sheaf of papers in his hand. Michelle's heart rate and stress levels went ballistic.

'Right,' said Bas when he got to the front of the group. 'The people whose names I call out first I want to stand on my right, the others stay where you are.'

Oh, fuck, why does he have to make a production out of it? This isn't an *X Factor* audition and you're not Simon Cowell, thought Michelle, her anxiety making her cross. Yes or no would do it.

Bas ran through a list of names and the relevant people shuffled forward. Michelle's name wasn't called. She looked at the line of men and women standing beside Bas and tried to work out if they were the no-hopers or if it was her group that was. Surely Katie, in the other group, was better than her? And that guy from the Royal Tank Regiment had been a real powerhouse... Michelle's stomach lurched with nerves. Oh, get on with it, she implored silently.

Bas gestured to Michelle's group. 'Sorry, guys,' he said.

Michelle's body sagged. That was it then. She'd failed.

'Sorry, guys, but you'll be back here for more training.'

For a second or two what Bas was saying didn't compute. She stared at him. What was he on about? Then the penny dropped and the relief was insane. For a second she thought she might cry but then she pulled herself together. Don't be wet, she told herself sternly.

The others, those who hadn't made the grade, were being thanked by Bas for the effort they'd put in, but Michelle wasn't listening. All she could think about was that she was going to be seeing more of Bas. A lot more, she hoped. The trembling in her knees morphed from nerves to nervous energy. All she wanted to do was ring Sam and tell her the good news.

It was over an hour later when she was able to. Before then Bas had given his new recruits the personal training schedule he expected them all to stick to over the intervening weeks in order to build up some essential muscles. He also gave them a suggested diet plan so they would have the energy for the extra training, and finally he'd given them the dates of the future training weekends that they would be expected to commit to, if they were going to be on his team.

Michelle was feeling shell-shocked at what she was suddenly expected to undertake, but if it brought her to Bas's attention, if it made her irresistible, then it was going to be so worth it.

Before the successful rowers went their separate ways everyone swapped contact details with Bas, 'so,' he told them, 'I can keep you in the loop about kit requirements, any alterations in training dates, shit like that.'

As Seb drove home he found himself obsessing about Michelle. What the hell was wrong with him – apart from the fact he was a red-blooded bloke and she was incredibly attractive, single and very available, to judge by the signals she'd transmitted over supper on the Friday night. He could hardly remember the last time he'd wanted a woman as much as he wanted her. He thought about ripping her clothes off, about having hot, sweaty sex with her… he stopped and adjusted his trousers. He told himself he should be thinking about his driving, not getting a raging hard-on from fantasising about Michelle. Besides, he was pretty certain that when he got home, Maddy wasn't going to want to have her clothes ripped off or indulge in hot, sweaty sex – or any sort of sex. He sighed. And when had she? The last time they'd had wild sex must have been about a year and a half ago; before she'd been pregnant with Nathan, at any rate.

He switched on the radio – anything to stop himself from thinking about Michelle, because he knew he shouldn't. Although, was thinking about another woman so wrong? It wasn't as if he was going to be unfaithful to Maddy. No way. The words on the radio didn't stop his mind drifting back to Michelle and that supper they'd shared. It had only been a pub meal, hardly a romantic dinner for two, but it had been such a terrific evening. She'd made him laugh – which made a change as there was precious little to laugh about at home right now, what with Maddy complaining about feeling sick all the time. And the way she'd looked at him across the table – like she was saying fuck me now. Seb shook his head. No, she wasn't, of course she wasn't, although he would have liked it to be so.

He heard his phone chirrup to tell him a text message had

come in. He glanced across to the passenger seat. Could he risk reading the message while he was hurtling along the A303? Possibly not the best idea while he was topping seventy-five, so maybe he'd better pull over first. Besides, he could do with a piss. He decided to stop at the next filling station, have a leg-stretch and a pee and pick up the text then. It was probably Maddy, wanting to know what time to expect him back. He drove on for another mile or so until he spotted a sign directing him to 'services'. He took the slip road to the garage and pulled the car into a parking space. He stretched before picking up his phone. A number, no name – so not Maddy, then. It was probably spam, he thought, but curiosity made him open it.

Hi Bas thx 4 a fab w/e. Had a gr8 time. Promise 2 train hard. Can't w8 4 next training session Michelle xx

Seb stared at the text, mesmerised by the words and trying to work out if there was any significance in the fact she couldn't wait for the next training session, or whether it was just a polite thank-you note. He slipped the phone into his pocket before getting out of the car, locking it and wandering across the garage concourse to find the gents. On his way back he bought himself a coffee and then he sat in the car as he read and re-read the text. Then he saved the number under MF, her initials, before he texted back.

Well done. Looking forward to more training too.

He pressed send thinking, as he did so, that she didn't know just how much he was looking forward to it too.

He got home about an hour later and was greeted effusively by Maddy. It was lovely to have such a welcome. He smiled at her fondly.

'Hi, hon,' he responded as, encumbered by Maddy, hanging on one arm, he lugged in his kit bag and pushed the door shut behind him. 'How was your weekend?'

'Quiet,' said Maddy. 'Yours?'

'Busy.'

'Worth the effort? Did you find the next super-star rower?'

'No, not really.'

'Then did you find anyone to make the trip worth it?'

Seb smiled. Oh, yes – yes, he had. 'Let's say it wasn't a complete waste of time.'

October was moving rapidly towards November. The shops in Warminster were decorated in orange and black ready for Halloween and there were signs up all over the place advertising fireworks for sale, but everyone knew that as soon as Guy Fawkes' Night was over everything would be cleared out and replaced with fake snow and tinsel. The knowledge that Christmas was now a matter of weeks away meant that planning Christmas parties had shot to the top of a lot of agendas. And that included the corporals' club committee of 1 Herts. Not that Immi was on the committee, but she'd spent the past few days bending the ear of the OiC of the corporals' club, Captain Rosser, with ideas for Christmas parties that she'd pinched from the magazines she liked to read.

'Look, Corporal Cooper,' he'd said after she'd cornered him for the third time in as many days, 'why don't you come along to the next meeting and put your ideas to the committee yourself? I mean, I'd be happy to do it for you, but you know that old thing about send three and fourpence we're going to a dance...'

Immi didn't have a clue what the hell he was on about and neither did she care because she'd got exactly what she wanted. Luke was on the committee, and if she was there too, and given the floor in order to put some bloody brilliant ideas about decor and food to them, then Luke couldn't help but notice her.

So, on the last Friday in October Immi got the chief clerk to give her an hour off work so she could attend the meeting and, looking her very best with her hair and make-up absolutely immaculate, she entered the corporals' club, trying to look cool and efficient.

'Wotcha, Ims,' said Des, as he saw her walk across the floor to where a table and chairs had been set up ready for the meeting. He and half a dozen guys were already there. 'Didn't know you'd been elected on to the corporals' club committee.'

Immi flopped down into one of the still-vacant chairs and placed the file she was carrying in front of her.

'Not elected, Des. Co-opted.'

'Why's that?'

''Cos I've got lots of good ideas about the Christmas bash.'

'Like?'

'That'd be telling.'

Des put his head on one side. 'And you getting on the committee hasn't got anything to do with Luke Blake being on it?'

'Is he? Well, there's a thing,' said Immi, trying to look innocent.

Captain Rosser, the officer in charge of the corporals' club, entered the room. Des and Immi leapt to their feet.

'At ease,' said Rosser, taking off his beret and also putting a stack of files on the table. 'Who are we missing?'

Des named a half dozen people who were absent. 'And Corporal Blake,' he added.

Rosser looked at his watch. 'We've still got a few minutes till we're due to kick off. Let's wait for the others, shall we?'

Just then the door opened again and the remaining committee members, including Luke, barrelled into the room.

'Sorry, sir,' they said as they took their seats. Luke sat down opposite Immi. She would have preferred it if he'd been next to her but, hey, it was a half-decent result. She smiled winningly at him but Luke didn't respond. She sighed inwardly. What the hell did she have to do to get his attention?

'You're all right,' said Rosser, 'I haven't started. But I will now, if that's everyone?' He flicked open a file.

'Yup, sir,' said Des. 'All present and correct.'

'First of all, I'd like to welcome Corporal Cooper,' said Rosser. 'I've invited her along as she's brimming with ideas for the Christmas party and I thought it would be easier for her to talk to you rather than for me to try and pass on the ideas second hand. But before we get to that we've got the rest of the agenda to get through. I trust you've all seen the agenda?' He looked around the table. The men opened their files and produced their copies, took pens out of their combat jacket pockets and tried to look businesslike. Immi sat up straight and tried to look as if she was interested.

The meeting droned on, with discussions about what guest beers the bar should stock, the problem of graffiti in the loos, and other matters involving the minutiae of running the club. Finally the topic of the ball was reached. At last, thought Immi, but even then she wasn't called to speak. Immi shifted on her uncomfortable chair, trying to look alert and interested and intelligent despite the fact she barely understood a word about the funding of the event, though she did manage to pick up that the PRI – the battalion's welfare fund – was going to stump up several hundred pounds towards raffle prizes, subsidising the ticket price and, most importantly as far as Immi was concerned, replacing some of their stock of decorations. She hadn't actually said anything to Captain Rosser about decorations in her chats to him but she had ideas on this subject too.

She stuck her hand up and then felt totally foolish. She wasn't at school like a kid, now, was she? 'I'd like to say something about the decorations and stuff, sir. If that's all right with you.'

'Yes, Cooper.'

'I mean, I know I'm here because I had some ideas that I told you about... anyway, I thought it would be good to go with a red and white theme this year and try and deck this joint out a bit like an Alpine ski hut – you know, lots of red and white gingham tablecloths, and maybe we could ask people if they could lend us skis and sleds and kit like that. And I thought we could serve beer and glühwein and brat-wurst and stuff...' Her voice petered out again as she saw them all staring at her in silence. It didn't look as though there was any enthusiasm for her plan at all. Instead of looking bright and intelligent in front of Luke, she was looking like a prat. She could feel her face starting to flare. Maybe she should get her coat and go. 'Sorry, it's obviously a crap idea. Forget it.'

'No,' said Luke. 'No, I really like it.'

'It's great,' said Captain Rosser. 'And you're right, Cooper, the Germans really know how to do Christmas.'

'The Germans,' said Luke, 'are great, aren't they – Wein-achtsmarkts, Christkindlmarkts, real candles on Christmas trees...'

Immi gazed at him in gratitude. He – Luke – liked her idea. Coo! She felt a warm glow of pride take the place of the burn of embarrassment from sticking up her hand.

'You can forget the candles,' said Captain Rosser. 'Can you imagine what health and safety would have to say on the subject? But apart from that, what does everyone else think?'

There was a rumble of assent and some nods around the table.

'I don't suppose,' said Luke, 'there's any chance of hiring a snow blower so when everyone arrives they get snowed on?'

Immi squealed, 'Oh, fab,' and then coloured and shut up. Not cool, Immi, she told herself. Not cool at all.

'Glad someone likes the idea,' said Luke, smiling at her. Immi glowed.

'I suggest you make enquiries,' said Rosser, 'if you think the idea is worth going with.' He looked around the table and saw nods of assent from the committee members. 'OK, Blake. I'll leave that with you. But please remember that there is only a limited budget.'

Immi whispered across the table to Luke, 'I so hope it's affordable. It would be so totally ace.'

Luke grinned at her. 'Wouldn't it just.'

It wasn't long after that the meeting broke up and everyone made their way out of the club. Immi fell into step beside Luke. 'So how come you know so much about German Christmases?'

'I don't know any more than you do,' replied Luke.

Immi raised her eyebrows. 'No? From the way you spoke it sounded as though you had first-hand experience. Have you lived there? Were your folks in the army?' It wasn't an unreasonable assumption, lots of kids followed in their parents' footsteps.

But Luke stared at her and then strode away.

Immi stamped her foot. 'Fuck, shit, bollocks,' she muttered.

'Oops,' said Des, directly behind her, making her jump. 'That wasn't part of your plan, now, was it.'

'Fuck off, Des,' snapped Immi, as she stormed off too. 'And mind your own sodding business.'

Things were going better at Eton Dorney, and Michelle, despite having a dislike of wet and cold conditions, was so thrilled to be in Bas's presence again that she was even prepared to overlook the fact that for the whole week the weather had been far from ideal. For the past five days she'd been training with the other potential rowers and had come on, in ability, vastly in the time. Over and above the improvement in her technique, her fitness – which hadn't been too bad to start with – was on a different level entirely. She knew that her leg and arm muscles were in a whole other league from when she'd done the original trial a fortnight earlier, and although she was just as knackered at the end of a one-kilometre time trial it was because she was rowing considerably faster. She was now rowing in a single scull, which she rather liked. She didn't have to worry about anyone but herself and she knew that if her performance time improved it was entirely down to her; no one else could take any of the credit.

The only fly in the ointment was that, living as close as she did to Dorney Lake, the Army Rowing Club hadn't bothered to book her into the Aldershot garrison mess with all the others and so she dipped out on the evening socialising. She'd rung the mess herself in an effort to rectify the situation but had been told there were no spare rooms left. Oh well, shit happens.

'Well done,' said Bas, as Michelle sculled her tiny craft up to the pontoon at the end of the lake and prepared to get out. She was even finding that much easier and was able to get into and out of the fragile, narrow and hugely unstable little boat with hardly any rocking or danger of capsizing at all – a change from her first few attempts, which had all almost ended up with a dip in the lake. 'You looked really good out there.'

She beamed up at him as he crouched down so he didn't tower above her so much.

'Thank you,' she panted. She was bushed. It had been a tough session and she'd pushed herself as hard as she could to impress Bas. His opinion mattered a ridiculous amount to her and she was determined that he would be proud of her.

'No, I mean it. You've worked the hardest of anyone here.'

Michelle felt herself glow, despite the nippy breeze that was ruffling the calm water. 'Aw,' she said. 'You're really good at motivating us.'

She used one of her sculls to steady the boat against the pontoon and then levered herself out onto dry land.

'I'll give you a hand with that,' said Bas, as Michelle bent down again ready to lift the boat out of the water.

'It's all right. I can manage.'

But Bas leaned over too and the pair collided. Michelle wobbled dangerously, teetering, as she was, at the edge of the landing stage. He put his hand on Michelle's shoulder to steady her and once again she experienced the same reaction. Some powerful surge shot through her and she didn't know what had caused it – chemistry, magnetism, biology? All she did know was that it made everything shift, like she'd been over the epicentre of a tiny localised earthquake. She jumped and stepped away from the edge, staring at Bas. He was still kneeling, looking at the water, and then slowly he turned his face towards her.

Out on the lake, his other protégés were still practising; the pair were alone on the pontoon and the noise of the other rowers and crews, the creak of their blades on the riggers, their shouts of encouragement to each other, the splash of the water all faded and drifted into silence as the pair stared at each other, both of them with dark, dilated pupils.

Suddenly Bas seemed to return to his senses and broke the spell.

'Right,' he said, shaking his head. 'Let's get this thing out of the water.' With a fluid movement he reached out, grabbed the riggers with both hands and swung the little craft up, out of the water and on to the staging.

Michelle longed to ask him if he'd felt what she'd felt but she knew it didn't need confirming verbally. She knew instinctively that he had. Now what? she wondered.

She carried her oars over to the boat shed, to the racks that Eton College was allowing them to borrow for the fortnight, and stowed them. She was about to turn to go out again when the light in the shed changed and she saw Bas enter, carrying her boat. Carefully he stashed it and then turned to her.

'How about dinner tonight?' he said.

'Well... yes, I'd love to.'

'And I could book you into the mess. Save you having to drive back to Pirbright.'

'But I'm commuting because I was told there was no room.'

'Maybe not during the week, but there's always spare capacity at the weekends – trust me.'

Michelle stared at him, wide-eyed. Was he suggesting what she thought he was suggesting? No, she was being daft. He was trying to make life easier for her.

'Um, I suppose...' she said. What she really wanted to say was please do it now, before the staff at the garrison mess say the mess is fully booked, that it's too late, or find some other damned excuse to scupper the plan – but to say that might look a bit desperate. Instead she replied, 'If you want.'

'OK,' said Bas. 'I'll ring the mess.' He gave her another long stare. Michelle wondered if he was thinking about kissing her; she was certainly considering kissing him.

There was a clatter from outside the door and some loud swearing.

'Careful,' shouted one of the male rowers.

Bas moved away and busied himself with making sure the scull was firmly on its rack. Michelle sighed. Another time – maybe later today.

Chapter Eleven

Once again, Sam was sitting in an empty anteroom in the officers' mess, on a Friday tea-time, reading the paper. At the end of a long week she was feeling tired and more than a bit fed up, and she was whiling away an hour or so before dragging herself up to her room and working out how she could fill the weekend. Her mobile began to play 'Lillibullero', the REME regimental march, which also doubled as her ringtone. She glanced at the screen: Michelle. There were rules about taking mobile calls in the mess's public rooms but, frankly, seeing she was the sole mess member around to enforce them, she felt she could make an exception in this case.

'Hiya, 'Chelle. How's the rowing?'

'Good, thanks.'

'How's the rowing coach?'

'Sen-fucking-sational.'

'Still gorgeous, then?'

'Uhuh.'

'And you're rowing all weekend?'

'I certainly am.' There was no mistaking the smug note in her friend's voice. 'What about you? What have you got planned?'

'Nothing much. Most of the livers-in seem to bugger off to see relies or girlfriends at the weekends so, once again, I'm Norma No-mates.' This wasn't strictly true because James, Will and Ben often stuck around at weekends but Sam was very wary of hanging around looking lonely and thus making them feel beholden to ask her to join in with their plans. If they had bloke-ish things to do it was more than likely they didn't want a woman tagging along and cramping their style. 'Are you sure you'd rather be rowing with Bas than spending the weekend here with me?' she wheedled, hopefully.

'Erm, how can I answer this… yes!'

'Cow.'

'Because Bas has not only invited me out to dinner and but he's also booked me into his mess so I don't have to drive after-wards and you know what that might mean.'

Sam did. And she was happy for her friend, although there was a bit of her that was more than a tad jealous.

James, Will and Ben barrelled in to the room, chatting and laughing, and Sam had an instant rush of guilt at being caught, red-handed, breaking mess rules.

'Listen, Michelle. I can't talk. I'm in the anteroom and I shouldn't be on my mobile.'

She saw James and the others gesticulating wildly that it was OK, and mouthing that they didn't care, but somehow Sam felt she'd heard enough about Michelle's love life and would like to change the record. 'Bye, hon,' she said, and pressed the 'end call' button before Michelle could lodge any objections.

'You didn't have to do that,' said James.

'Listen, I'm a REME officer, not an agony aunt, which was what my mate wanted me to be. And, besides, I'd heard quite enough about my bessie's love life. In fact, I don't want to hear about anyone's love life or problems or hang-ups… If people want to talk to me I'd really prefer it if they just want a bit of a gossip or an exchange of views on the weather.'

The three guys exchanged a significant look.

'Who rattled your cage?' said Ben.

'Sorry,' said Sam, knowing she'd gone a bit far. 'Sorry,' she repeated, and shrugged. 'Long week,' she offered by way of explanation.

Will and Ben both grabbed a cup of tea and a slice of cake and headed for their rooms, muttering about personal admin, leaving James and Sam on their own.

'Want to talk about it?' said James.

Sam sighed heavily. 'You don't need to hear my problems.'

'A problem shared and all that crap.'

Sam put her cup and saucer on the table. 'It's just…'

'Just?'

'It's a guy at work.' She paused. 'I may be imagining it, but he seems to chuck spanners in the works at every opportunity. Whatever I suggest, whatever I say, he argues against me.'

'That's not good,' said James. 'Who is it?'

'It's the ASM. But then there's Corporal Blake, who seems to resent me and despise me in equal measure. Every time I look up and see Blake, he's staring right back at me. I mean, does he do that *all* the time?'

'So, how often do you look at Blake, if you think he's *always* staring at you?'

Sam frowned and wrinkled her nose. 'I don't get you.'

'It's not unreasonable that you *would* look at Blake. I mean, I'm not a woman, but I'd say he was very good looking.'

'Is he?'

James gave her a disbelieving look.

'OK, maybe he is, but I'm surprised you've noticed – or even know who he is come to that.'

'He and I are on the corporals' club committee,' said James in explanation.

'Oh. But his looks do nothing to alter the fact that, between them, Williams and Blake are getting right on my tits.'

James smiled.

'Yeah, I know…' said Sam ruefully, glancing down at her boobs. 'You don't have to say it. We all know they're big enough.'

James sucked in his cheeks. 'Sam, I wouldn't have dreamed of making a comment.'

'You thought it, though.' She grinned.

'No comment.'

'I'm being a wuss, aren't I?'

'Well…'

'That's a *yes*.'

'You've got to grip them. You're the boss. You've got to deal with this: haul Williams into your office and say if he isn't prepared to work with you, you'll be happy to arrange a posting for him so he doesn't have to. I bet that'd do it. I can't imagine Mrs Williams would be happy if her old man got short-toured and she'll give him a much harder time than ever you could.'

'You think?'

'It's extreme but it'd work. And as for Blake, tell him to stop bugging you or he'll be packing up his belongings too.'

Sam felt her eyes widen. Could she really be that confrontational? It certainly went against her people-pleasing tendencies.

'It's up to you,' said James.

She nodded. He had a point about getting a grip and she needed to think about how to handle it. Maybe she'd run a bath and mull over the problem while she had a long hot soak.

She grabbed the paper and stood up.

'Thanks for the pep talk.' She meant it. 'See you at dinner,' she said.

James looked a bit disconsolate. 'You off?'

'I need to think about your suggestion, and I'm going to do it in the bath. It's a good place to address problems.'

Fifteen minutes later she was semi-submerged in Crabtree & Evelyn bubbles, trying to think of an alternative way of dealing with Williams and Blake while controlling the temperature of the bath with her toe on the hot tap. OK, so being stuck in the mess over a weekend might have its downsides, but an endless supply of hot water and an uninterrupted soak went some way to compensate. Sam sighed and turned her attention back to how confrontational she dared to be with her ASM. Blake was a different matter. What was it with him? she wondered, yet again. He simmered, he brooded, he had this air of total superiority to everyone, even herself, and yet...

No, there was no *and yet*. He was a corporal and a pain in the arse, full stop. And he was a pain in the arse because whenever she asked him to do anything, issued him with any sort of order, his attitude implied that he was obeying her as a favour, that he was patronising her, that he was helping her out before she made the most almighty fool of herself. Arrgghh.

There was a thunderous bang on the bathroom door. She jumped and water sploshed over the side of the over-full bath

'Oi, Sam, you in there?' It was James's voice.

What now? She called back, 'Yes, what is it? I'm in the bath.'

'It's me, James.'

Yes, she knew that.

'Will and Ben and me are going to the flicks in Salisbury. There's that new spy spoof on and there's a showing at eight. We could have a quick pizza first. But don't feel you have to join us. It's just we'd like it if you've nothing better on.'

It was a *much* better option than a solitary dinner in the mess and then mouldering in her room for the evening. She felt a surge of happiness that she was really beginning to feel included. OK, she might not have a boyfriend like Michelle, but she had friends. Lovely friends. It went a long way in making up for feeling undermined by her ASM and Blake

– she'd think about them tomorrow. 'Give me five minutes,' she yelled back. 'I'm definitely up for that!'

Immi stood at the door to the guardroom, in the queue of soldiers waiting to book out for the weekend, and watched Luke, the duty guard commander, sitting behind the desk. She didn't think she'd seen anyone look quite so bored in her life. He was tapping a tattoo on the desk with a pencil, staring at the screen of his iPad and yawning intermittently. Immi grinned to herself. He might think he was a cut above all the other grunts in the battalion but he still had to do the same crap duties as the rest of them. All those GCSEs didn't bestow on him any special favours now, did they? And then, at the end of the evening, just like everyone else who did guard duty, he'd have to deal with all the sozzled soldiers returning from a night on the piss. There were bound to be a few lairy ones who would try and throw a punch because the guy on the gate had looked at them oddly, or they'd misinterpreted a comment, or they just felt like it because that was what drunk infantry soldiers tended to do. Immi had been in the company of enough of them to know what the score was. She edged nearer to the booking-out sheet. Ahead of her were a couple of guys who obviously intended one heck of a night to judge by their plans for a pub crawl. More than likely they'd return on the verge of being dead drunk; the ones who would vomit on the RSM's parade ground or the guardroom steps, and Luke would have to clean it up. Well, not him personally – he'd dick a subordinate to do that – but he'd still have to oversee the job, make sure it was done properly. Yeah, like you really need a physics GCSE to do that, thought Immi as she reached the desk.

'Wotcha, Luke.'

He looked up. 'Immi. Come to book out?'

'Yeah. Thought I'd go into Warminster.'

'Off you go, then.' He returned to his iPad.

Immi sighed. She did not like to be ignored. She hadn't dolled herself up to the nines to have blokes fail to notice her, especially not Luke.

'Aren't you going to ask me what I'm planning to do this evening?'

Luke kept his eyes on his book. 'No.'

Immi tapped her foot and stared over his head and out the window as she thought of a way to grab his attention. Driving past the guardroom was Luke's boss, Captain Lewis, in a car with Captain Rosser. 'Who'd have thought it?' she said out loud.

This time Luke did look up and followed Immi's gaze to the car waiting for the barrier to be lifted.

'Do you think they're an item?' said Immi. 'That's the second time I've seen them together.'

'Really?' said Luke.

'I think it's rather sweet.'

Luke stared at her. 'Rosser and Lewis? Sweet? Get a grip, Immi. Captain Lewis could do so much better than that twat Rosser.'

'Rosser's not a twat, he's nice.'

Luke shrugged.

Shit, Blake might be gorgeous but he was insufferable. Slyly, she said, 'Just because you fancy her.'

For a second Luke looked thunderous then he said, 'Really, Immi, don't be stupider than you can help.'

She couldn't resist goading him further. 'Fibber.'

'Well, if that's what you want to believe,' he said coldly.

She'd thought she was joking – now she wasn't so sure.

Chapter Twelve

Michelle's evening with Bas was not going according to her plan. Talk about taking a horse to water and making it drink, she thought as she stared at Bas across the table of the little curry house near the Aldershot garrison mess.

'Good curry, isn't it?' she said, as she broke off another piece of naan bread and dipped it in the delicious sauce that accompanied her chicken dish.

Bas nodded as he chewed. 'Lovely.'

Getting him to throw the conversational ball back was proving to be uphill work. It was almost as if he was regretting asking her out and he looked as if he had the cares of the world on his shoulders. Where was the light-hearted, flirty Bas who had taken her out to dinner that very first weekend?

'So,' she said, making yet another effort to get him to chat, 'what got you into rowing?'

'Basically it boiled down to the school I attended. As simple as that.'

'Yes, but I did hockey at school but I didn't carry on after I left.'

Bas shrugged. 'Well, I wasn't really planning on making a career out of being a rower but when you wind up at Oxford... Well, first my college wanted me to row and then I got spotted as having some potential. Anyway, I almost made the blue boat.'

Michelle had learnt enough about rowing over the previous

few days to know the significance of what Bas had said. 'Blimey. How almost?'

'To be honest, I'm not sure. I picked up a stupid injury, broke my collar bone a couple of months before the race so I couldn't train. Maybe I wouldn't have been selected anyway, but I'll never know.'

'That's tough.'

'That's life.' Bas chewed on some more lamb pasanda. 'Anyway, no one died.'

But Michelle could tell from the tone of his voice that though a person may not have died, his ambition had.

'But didn't all that commitment mean you never had a social life? Let's face it, we've all been training this week and the others are bitching about not having a day off over the weekend and being completely knackered already, and we're only halfway through.' She smiled at Bas. 'And we're beginners – so not doing anything like the training you must have done. I can't imagine how it would have been at Oxford with rowing and your studies. Your only spare time must have been spent sleeping.'

'Depends whether you date another rower,' said Bas. 'If your partner rows then you tend to spend a certain amount of time together.'

'And did you? Date another rower, that is?'

There was a bit of a pause. 'I did while I was up at Oxford.'

'And are you still seeing her?' God, she was being nosy but she had to know where she stood.

Bas looked at his plate. 'Things change.'

Ooh, hopeful. It sounded as if she'd left the scene. She poured some wine into Bas's glass.

'You have some, too,' he said.

She poured herself a half-glass. 'So,' said Michelle, 'what are your rowing ambitions now?'

'I once hoped to make the Olympics. I thought I was in with a real shot because I rowed at Oxford with two guys that did make it. Remember Lyndon-Forster and Quantick…?'

'Oh, God, yes. Gold medallists at London 2012.'

'Well, I rowed with them. I wasn't in their league, though.'

'And you'd broken your collar bone.'

Bas nodded. 'Yes, there was that, but that was in 2011 so theoretically I was fit for the trials for 2012, but then I did Op Herrick 14… I went out to Afghan at the start of the Olympic year so that was my chances stuffed, really.'

'You really didn't get the luck of the draw, then, did you?'

Bas shook his head. 'But you still ask yourself whether you would have made it. I like to think I would but… well, I'll never know, will I?'

'Hang on,' said Michelle a bit indistinctly, owing to a mouthful of murgh chicken. She swallowed before she continued. 'You can't give up. What about 2016?'

'I suppose. It's a big commitment when you decide to aim for a goal as high as that.'

'But wouldn't the army support you? And, you know, if you haven't got any other commitments or relationships to hold you back…' She let the sentence linger.

But all Bas did was shrug.

Michelle concentrated on clearing her plate and wondered how, short of asking him straight out, she could find out if she had any competition? With her plate empty and her stomach full she leaned back in her chair.

'Pud?' said Bas.

'You have to be kidding. I am stuffed.'

'Coffee?'

'Tell you what, why don't we go back to the mess and get one there? I could do with a walk to help me digest this lot.'

'Good shout,' said Bas.

Bas caught the waiter's eye and signalled for the bill. The waiter came over with it on a salver. Bas glanced at it, extracted a couple of notes from his wallet and told him to keep the change.

'Ready?'

Michelle nodded and felt an anticipatory thrill about what might happen next zing through her.

They pulled on their coats and headed out into the autumnal evening where a brisk wind was swirling some dead leaves around on the pavement. Despite her jacket, Michelle shivered.

'Cold?'

'I've been warmer,' she admitted. She walked close to Bas and linked her arm through his. He didn't object. She snuggled closer. 'That's better,' she said. 'Shared body heat is the best way to keep warm, or so I've been told.'

'It's more convivial than a thermal blanket,' said Bas.

Michelle laughed. 'And you don't look like an oven-ready turkey.'

They strolled towards the turning that would lead back to the officers' mess. Michelle kept the pace as slow as possible, enjoying the moment. She felt ridiculously happy to be in his company. It felt so completely right and there was nothing about him that she didn't like. She stared up at him. Because she was five feet eleven it wasn't often that she could go out with a man and wear heels and still be shorter than her escort, but Bas, at nearly six feet six, certainly made that possible.

Bas must have been aware of her stare because he turned his face towards her. Was it desire or the fact that it was dark that made his pupils so dilated? And was he going to kiss her…? Michelle waited, her heart hammering, willing him to make the move.

Oh, sod that. She took the initiative. She stood on tiptoe and raised her mouth to his, terrified that he might recoil or rebuff her. And he didn't. Their lips met and then suddenly he was holding her tight against him and she felt the vibration of a groan escape. She parted her lips and let him explore her mouth. She lost track of time as they stood there, on the main road, oblivious to the traffic passing them, to the curious stares of passers-by, to the chill wind that played around their ankles, she was so wrapped up in the moment.

Finally, when they drew apart, Michelle's legs felt wobbly so she remained clinging to him.

'Wow,' she sighed, half to herself.

'Wow, indeed,' said Bas.

Michelle felt steady enough to disentangle herself from him. 'Well,' she said lightly, 'this isn't getting us that coffee, is it?'

'Coffee's the last thing on my mind right now,' said Bas, his voice thick with emotion. He gazed at Michelle with undisguised longing.

'What is on your mind?'

Bas smiled at her lazily. 'You don't want to know.'

Michelle raised her eyebrows. 'I think I do.'

They arrived at the mess. Bas opened the door and held it for Michelle to go through first. The entrance hall, starkly lit, was empty, and the mess was silent. For some reason Michelle was rather glad, because she couldn't help but feel faintly furtive and guilty about making her way to Bas's room. They crept up the thickly carpeted stairs and along the corridor. Still no one. When they got through the door to his room Michelle found herself giggling stupidly.

'What's the matter? What's so funny? What have I done?' Bas looked bemused.

Michelle brought herself under control. 'It's just...' She hiccupped as she swallowed another burst of giggles. 'It's as if we're behaving like we've got a huge guilty secret, creeping around like this. And it's mad, because it isn't as if we aren't both free and single.'

Bas stared at her.

Michelle felt her heart plummet; she'd ruined the mood. 'Aw, come here.' She stepped towards Bas.

'Michelle...' He hesitated. 'I don't think...'

She drew even closer. 'You don't think you can resist me?' She slipped off her jacket and began to unbutton her shirt.

Bas watched her hands, mesmerised. Then Michelle shrugged her shoulders and let the garment fall to the floor, revealing her tiny, lacy bra.

Bas groaned. 'Oh, God, Michelle.' Then it was like someone had flicked a switch. He seemed to come to his senses and his eyes focussed instead of having a hazy, dreamy look. 'No, Michelle,' he said with sudden determination. 'No, stop. I mustn't. It... it's... it wouldn't be appropriate.'

'Appropriate? Who are you kidding?'

'But I'm your instructor.'

Michelle grinned. 'At rowing, yes. However, given what we're about to do, I reckon I could teach you a thing or two.' She moved her hand forward and rubbed his crotch. 'And don't lie, Bas. You want me as much as I want you.' Slowly she began to draw the zip of his fly downwards and as Bas's erection stiffened, Michelle knew that any doubts he had were crumbling.

Seb found it hard to concentrate on the way home. What had he done? he asked himself, over and over. He'd tried to resist Michelle but she'd hypnotised him, she'd bewitched him and then, ultimately, she'd seduced him. He was just a man, when all was said and done, and what man, offered sex with a gorgeous woman, would have the resolve to refuse? Not that it was going to happen again. Ever. He'd made his mind up; it had been a one-off, an aberration and, as long as he didn't tell Maddy, she'd never be any the wiser.

Only it hadn't been a one-off, had it? Michelle had returned to his room in the garrison mess on three subsequent nights. In fact, it would have probably been every night but their love-making had been so passionate and energetic that they'd agreed that they needed time apart to get some much-needed sleep or the rowing would have been utterly useless.

Seb felt his heart pound as he remembered their nights together. God, she was a minx. Maddy could be pretty good in bed but Michelle... A whole different league. It was a bit like comparing a Vauxhall Conference football team with Real Madrid. He felt his cock stiffen at the memory and had to adjust his trousers as he drove. He was going to sleep like a log tonight. Never had the expression 'shagged-out' been more appropriate. Anyway, he didn't think Maddy would mind; Michelle had probably done her a favour, he thought, disloyally.

Ah, Maddy... His feeling of arousal turned to guilt. He'd committed adultery. He'd betrayed the mother of his child... worse, children. Whichever way he cut it, he was massively in the wrong. It would be fine, he kept telling himself. If he ignored the issue it would eventually go away. And when he and Michelle met at the next training weekend he would tell Michelle the truth – he would tell her that he was married and that what had happened had been a mistake and that it couldn't happen again.

Maddy heard the car draw up in their drive and raced to the door.

'Seb, you're back,' she called to him from the doorstep as he got out of the car and stretched. 'I've missed you.'

'Have you?'

Maddy nodded. 'It's been a fortnight. That's a long time. Little Nate has got another ten words.'

'Has he? That's brilliant. And has he missed me?' Seb collected his stuff from the boot and walked over to Maddy and planted a big kiss on her forehead.

'I expect so. His conversation isn't up to discussing his emotions yet. If it isn't to do with his toys and food then I'm afraid you're out of luck.' Maddy snuggled up next to him. 'Hmm, you smell nice.'

'Do I?'

'It's not like you to use aftershave.'

'Aftershave?' Then there was a second or two hesitation. 'Oh, I know what it must be. It's probably the poncy shower gel I found in the boathouse. Yes, that'd be it.'

'That's all right, then. You smell like a girl so I was almost worried there.' Maddy giggled. 'Come in. All the heat is escaping.'

'And how are you?' Seb dumped his holdall in the hall.

'Quite a bit better,' said Maddy. 'Still throwing up in the morning but it's not so bad during the day. I think I'm over the worst.'

'I am so pleased.'

Maddy looked at him. She knew he was glad that she was better – of course he was, but she knew her husband. He was pleased because her being better would let him off the hook regarding any household chores. Oh, well, she'd never even pretended to herself that she'd married him for his domestic skills. She heard his mobile signal an incoming text.

'Who can that be?' she said grumpily. God, she'd just got her husband home and she didn't want to start sharing him. Hadn't the army had enough of him?

Seb pulled his phone from a pocket and glanced at the screen. 'Just one of the new team confirming contact details.' He stuffed his phone away again.

'You've given them your mobile number? What's wrong with your work number? I hope they're not going to be calling you at all hours of the day and night.'

'I doubt it. What's for supper? I'm starved. And where's Nathan?'

'To address all of those points: one, good, or they'll have me to answer to; two, supper is sticky chops and rice; three, when aren't you; and, four, Nate's in bed.'

Seb flicked the end of Maddy's nose with his finger. 'Silly goose!'

Maddy giggled. Goodness, it was nice to have Seb home, even if he did smell a bit like a tart. 'Gin?'

Seb eased his shoulders, still stiff from the drive. 'I'd love one, really I would.'

Maddy pottered into the kitchen to pour his drink and as soon as her back was turned Seb got his phone out and re-read the last text. Keeping one eye on the kitchen door, he texted back an answer to the message.

Missing you 2 can't w8 for next weekend xx

As he hit send he remembered his very recent resolution to keep Michelle at arm's length but, as he hit another button to delete the record of messages, he told himself that if he hadn't replied she'd have texted again. Better that he did this than risk Maddy wanting to know who was contacting him. Yes, this was the only course of action possible. He stuffed his phone back in his pocket as Maddy returned with his drinks.

She handed him his gin and sipped at an orange juice before she plonked herself in an armchair.

'I was thinking of inviting that new officer round to have supper with us, you know, the female REME officer.'

'Sam Lewis?'

'That's the one. She rang me the other day. It seems we've got a mutual friend.'

'Oh? Who's that?'

'One of the wives.' No way was Maddy going to tell Seb it was Jenna. 'Anyway, she seems really nice. You wouldn't mind that, would you?'

'Not if you're feeling up to it.'

'I told you, I'm much better.'

Seb slurped his gin. 'Just a thought, but if you feel like doing a bit of entertaining would it be an idea to pay back some of the other people we owe hospitality to as well? And then Sam could meet some other people socially. That'd kill lots and lots of birds with one stone.'

Maddy considered the idea. 'I was planning a sort of kitchen supper but I suppose we could have a bit of a party. Maybe if we left it a few weeks so I was sure of being better... It's an idea. I'll think about it. In the meantime, if I don't put the rice on, you're not going to eat.'

Even though Maddy was feeling better, tiredness was still an issue and it wasn't long after they'd eaten that she felt her eyes beginning to droop.

She glanced at her watch. Would Seb think he was in with a chance if she suggested she fancied an early night? She considered this as a possibility and decided that if he did, it would be rather nice. She really was feeling a lot better.

She yawned expansively. 'I think I'll turn in.' She gave Seb an encouraging smile.

'Off you go, then. I'll try not to wake you when I come up.'

Oh, so not his normal, frustrated reaction. Maddy wasn't sure if she was glad or not.

Chapter Thirteen

'Hi, Sam,' said Michelle after a single ring.

Sam laughed. 'You must have been sitting on your phone.'

'I was. Waiting for a call.'

'And I take it you weren't waiting for mine.' There was the merest hesitation. 'That'll be a "yes", then, will it? And I imagine it's Bas you were expecting to ring.'

'Sorry.'

'Don't be. Listen, I'll be quick – I don't want to be responsible for ruining your love life... When I ring off I want you to get your diary out and text me weekends that you're going to be free between now and Christmas. We haven't seen each other for an age and I really need a girly weekend.'

'That's going to be tricky.'

'Oh, come on, 'Chelle. You can't be seeing Bas every weekend.'

'No, not as such. But the rowing training is full on.'

'So, you are.'

'Not like that. Well... OK, I'll come clean, a bit like that. But we will be rowing as well. Honest.'

'Bloody hell, Michelle, you must have it bad for Bas. I mean, you usually only do sport when you have to. What's come over you? And if you answer "Bas" to that last question I shall vomit.'

Sam heard a dirty laugh down the phone. 'All right, I won't. And I'll send you those dates. Promise.'

'You see that you do. Bye, hon.'

'Bye.'

*

Michelle's text came through the next morning when Sam was at her desk.

'One date? One poxy date!' She chucked her phone back on to her desk in disgust and flipped open her own diary. Unsurprisingly, that date was free. She wrote in that she and Michelle would spend it together and was about to shut it up when her phone rang. She picked it up.

'Captain Lewis,' she said.

'Oh, hello,' said a woman's voice she didn't immediately recognise. 'It's Maddy. Maddy Fanshaw.'

Sam felt a ping of guilt.

'Oh, Maddy. I am so sorry.'

Maddy laughed. 'Why on earth?'

'Because I said we ought to arrange a date to meet and I haven't got back to you.'

'Never mind. Truly it doesn't matter. But that is sort of why I am ringing. I thought I'd have a bit of a lunch party and I wondered if you'd like to come along. That way we can get to know each other and you could meet some of the wives too.'

'Oh.'

'I promise we won't talk about babies.'

Sam laughed. 'I expect I could cope even if you did.'

'I wouldn't blame you if the thought of all that domesticity made you want to run a mile. That's how I felt when I first gave up work and became a proper army wife. I kept thinking the other wives didn't have a life because they seemed to obsess about their homes and families, but when you keep moving and your career goes tits-up it's hard to focus on the bigger picture.'

Sam knew she was going to like Maddy. She sounded very grounded. 'So what date are you looking at?'

'Three weeks on Sunday. I hope it's clear, I'd love you to come.'

Sam glanced at her diary but she already knew the answer. 'Oh, Maddy, you'll never believe it but I have just got off the phone from arranging to spend that weekend with an old friend. How rotten is that? I've got endless free weekends, just not that one.'

'Oh, that's a real shame. Well... unless you're spending the weekend here with your friend. In which case why not bring him – her – along too? The more the merrier.'

'It's her... and are you sure? I mean, it's a bit cheeky.'

'Look, when you're cooking for loads, one more mouth isn't an issue, honest. Check with your friend that she doesn't think it is the worst idea in the world to be landed with lunch with a bunch of pads. If I don't hear to the contrary I'll expect to see you both.'

'OK.'

'Twelve o'clock. Oh, and is there anything either of you don't eat?'

'No, nothing. Even compo rations!'

'I promise faithfully not to serve up that.'

'See you then, and looking forward to meeting you.'

'It'll be fun. Bye.'

Sam replaced the receiver and then texted Michelle with news of the arrangement.

Cool, was the response from Michelle. So that was all right, then.

November had gone out with a series of dreary days, mostly bringing lashing rain, gales and bitter cold, and December had rolled in as if it were trying to make amends. The first week had consisted of bright, gin-clear weather with cloudless blue skies and sharp overnight frosts. The battalion's countdown to

Christmas had begun and plans for the various unit and sub-unit parties were in differing stages of advancement. Not only was it now imperative for people to roll their sleeves up and start turning plans into practical arrangements, it had also reached the stage when those attending the events had to find partners to take.

James Rosser, as OiC of the corporals' club, had been issued an invitation by the committee for him 'plus one'. Both he and the committee knew he wouldn't really be welcome, but for form's sake he needed to show his face and stay for at least a couple of hours. And if he didn't want to spend most of his time sitting on his own with no one to talk to then he needed to find someone to fill the role of the 'plus one'. With just over a week to go till the bash James decided that he couldn't put off addressing the problem any longer.

He left his cosy office in his company lines and, pulling his combat jacket zip up firmly against the chill air, he made his way across the parade square to the far side where the Q stores could be found, along with the vehicle garages and the LAD.

The huge double doors of the workshop were open but despite that almost half of the craftsmen seemed to be working in shirtsleeves, although, given the hard graft that was going on, they were all probably burning enough energy to keep the cold at bay. He wandered past the inspection pits and ramps, past the lathes and the workbenches to the office in the corner. He could see Sam's head bent over a mound of paperwork, her face lit by the glow of a computer screen and her brow furrowed in concentration. For a few seconds he wondered if he ought to interrupt her. As he hesitated, the phone on her desk rang. She looked up as she picked up the receiver and caught sight of him. As she began speaking to the caller, she raised her right hand and enthusiastically beckoned him in.

James opened the door and a gust of warm air billowed out.

Come in, mouthed Sam, and gestured to a chair in the corner before she began taking notes.

James shut the door behind him and sank into the tatty old office chair by her desk. He let his mind drift while Sam dealt with whatever problem was being thrown at her. Finally the receiver was back on the cradle.

'Sorry about that,' she said cheerily. 'What can I do for you? And while we discuss that, would you like a cuppa? I'm parched.'

James noticed a shelf above a sink in the corner, with tea-making paraphernalia on it. 'If you're having one, I wouldn't say no.'

Sam got up, filled the kettle and plugged it in. 'Tea or coffee?'

'Tea, please.'

'So what's dragged you across here?' she asked as she dropped tea bags into a couple of mugs.

'I'm after a huge favour.'

'Are you, now?'

'I am.'

'How huge?'

James held his arms at full stretch. 'That big.'

'Blimey. I think that size of favour needs to be indented for. You can't just requisition that sort of stuff.'

'That's what I was afraid of.'

The kettle boiled and there was silence as Sam made the tea. She handed James his mug.

James thanked her before saying, 'So where do I get the forms asking for the battalion's only female officer to accompany the OiC of the corporals' club to their Christmas party?'

Sam took a sip of her tea. 'Not sure I've got the relevant form for that, here in the workshop.'

'That's a shame.'

'But we could always live dangerously and see if we could get away with it, without the right paperwork.'

'You think? I don't want to end up being court-martialled for not going through proper channels.'

'I won't report you, if you don't report me. How about risking it?' Sam put her mug down on her desk and flipped open her diary. 'It's next weekend, right?'

James nodded.

'Spookily, it's free.'

'Are all your weekends like that?'

Sam shrugged. 'Seems like it. Although this weekend I've got a friend coming to stay and we've both been invited to Maddy Fanshaw's for a buffet lunch party.'

'You too? Ace. I've got an invite to that, and a bunch of the others have as well. It should be a good do. Seb and Maddy are fun. I'll see you chez Fanshaw, then, on Sunday.'

Sam laughed. 'If you're not planning on being out of the mess on Saturday I've no doubt we'll see each other before then. Michelle and I aren't doing much other than hanging out and catching up with each other.'

'Michelle?'

'We were at Sandhurst together, and before that at the same prep school. You'll like her, she's good news. Bonkers but good company.'

'I look forward to meeting her, then.'

In the corporals' club Immi was standing at the top of a step-ladder, leaning precariously to one side clasping a length of red and white gingham in one hand and a box of drawing pins in the other.

'Immi!'

She looked round cautiously. 'Oh, it's you.' She smiled at Luke. 'What can I do for you?'

'You can get down off that ladder and move it closer to where you want to be. You can't lean like that – you'll fall off.'

'I'm all right,' said Immi.

Luke sighed. 'No, you're not. And you won't be any good to anyone if you fall off and break your neck.'

Immi felt a little whoosh of pleasure. Maybe Luke cared about her.

'And if that happened the party would have to be cancelled,' he added. 'And what a waste of work that'd be.'

Oh, maybe he didn't. Bollocks.

'Now get down,' he said sternly.

'Catch me?' asked Immi with a hopeful smile.

Luke frowned as he looked at her but held his hand out to steady her as she came down the steps.

Petulantly, Immi pushed the stepladder a couple of feet so it was directly under the place she was about to festoon with gingham and climbed back up.

'This place is starting to look quite good,' said Luke, staring at the decorations Immi had put up so far. The corporals' club now had the distinct look of a German bier keller, with little vases of dried flowers on the tables, posters of snowy Alpine scenes on the walls, lots of red and white checked tablecloths covering the dull plastic tables; the various bits of skiing kit that Immi had managed to blag also helped to provide some atmosphere.

'Thanks,' said Immi, draping more gingham around a window and securing it with a couple of drawing pins. 'Did you get anywhere with a snow blower?'

'Nah. I found one, but the price they wanted was howling. I said that I wanted to rent it, not buy it.' Luke shrugged. 'Still, it was worth a shot.'

'That's a shame. It would have been a good finishing touch.'

'Never mind,' said Luke. 'With what you've done here, everyone will be well impressed.'

Immi nodded at him from the top of the ladder, a satisfied smile on her face. 'Glad you like it. Dunno what I'm going to do with all this fabric when the party is over. I think I've bought the entire UK stock. If it was blue and white I could sell it to Dorothy from *The Wizard of Oz* for spare pinafores.'

Luke gave her a worried look. 'You're bonkers, do you know that?'

'Maybe.' Immi climbed down the ladder again and jumped the last couple of steps. 'God, I've been up and down today like a whore's drawers.'

'So I've heard,' he said, dryly.

'Oi, Luke, that's well out of order.'

'Sorry. Couldn't resist. Anyway, you're the one who said it.'

'Hmm.' Immi gave him a hard stare and put the fabric and the drawing pins down on the top step of the ladder. She changed the subject. 'So, who are you bringing to the party?'

'Haven't really thought about it yet.'

'You don't have a girlfriend?'

'What's it to you?'

'Just curious, Luke, just curious.' Immi fiddled with the corner of a chipped nail. 'Luke?'

'Yes?'

'Have you been to Kenya?'

'Yeah, couple of years ago. Why?'

'I volunteered for rear party but the chief clerk told me I'm going on the exercise along with everyone else.'

'Don't you want to?'

Immi shrugged. 'Not a big fan of creepy-crawlies, if I'm honest.'

Luke grinned naughtily. 'Oh, that's not good. They have millipedes out there the size of marker pens, and dung beetles

148

like tennis balls, not to mention the snakes, the flies and the bats, and that's before we get started on the things big enough to eat you alive.'

Immi's eyes were like dinner plates. 'You're kidding me,' she whispered.

'Nope,' said Luke cheerfully. 'And there's the other things you'll have to contend with, like heatstroke and insect bites. Oh, and every plant you come across has thorns on it the size of darning needles.'

'That's it,' said Immi. 'I'm going to throw a sickie. They can't make me go if I'm ill.'

'I think they probably can and almost certainly will.'

'I'll go AWOL,' said Immi with a hint of desperation.

'Honestly, Immi, you'll be fine. You're going to be back at HQ. Probably the worst you'll encounter is the RSM in a mood. No one is going to send a REMF like you into the field.'

'REMF?'

'Rear echelon mother... well, you can guess the last word,' said Luke.

Immi rolled her eyes. 'God bless the British Army – an insult and an acronym all in one hit.'

'Anyway, I was thinking...'

'Yeah?'

'Well, if you haven't got a partner for this bash we could go together. Not a date,' said Luke hastily, 'but it would stop us both looking like sad loners.'

'I am not a sad loner,' said Immi haughtily. 'I'm between boyfriends.'

Luke shrugged. 'Forget it, then.'

'No!' She realised she'd shouted. Immi lowered her voice. 'No, I didn't mean it like that. Luke I'd love to accompany you. Truly.'

'Really?'

She tried to look nonchalant. 'Yeah, if you'd like.'

And she felt as if all of her internal organs were pogoing all at once. She managed to resist punching the air and yelling 'Yesss!'

On the officers' married patch Maddy was cooking up a storm of dishes for her buffet lunch, which had seemed quite distant when she'd arranged it and now was to take place later that day. The surfaces were covered with pots and pans, wooden spoons and a couple of open recipe books, while the sink was stacked with utensils waiting to be washed up. It was fairly chaotic but Maddy was humming happily as she looked forward to the party.

She checked on the spread she'd laid out on the large dining-room table. The army thoughtfully assumed that all officers' wives – even junior ones – liked nothing better than to entertain vast numbers of people and so every quarter was issued with a table that could seat at least eight, with the chairs to match. As Maddy and Seb, when he was home, tended to eat on trays on their laps in front of the TV, their dining room was mostly a completely redundant space, but as Maddy admired the buffet she was going to be serving up to the twenty or so people they'd invited, for once she was thankful that they had the wherewithal for such entertaining. Not, she reasoned logically, that she would have been so ambitious if they hadn't.

She tweaked a napkin straight and rearranged a couple of plates of quiche, checked the cling film over the salads... There, she thought with a sigh of satisfaction. Perfect. Well, as perfect as she was capable of making it. So, just the garlic bread to heat up, the French dressing to make and Nathan to feed. Yes, everything was going according to plan. Time to gild the lily and put on something Nathan hadn't slobbered down.

Bless him, it wasn't his fault he was teething again, but it did make him dribble – a lot.

'I'm popping upstairs,' she told Seb. 'I don't suppose you could make a start on Nathan's lunch, could you? I'm rather hoping he'll go down for a nap in a while.'

'And if he doesn't?' said Seb.

'Then he can sit in his high chair or play in his playpen.'

'If you say so.'

'It'll be fine. Besides, half the people coming have kids of their own and the other half will just have to lump it. You never know, some of them might like children.'

Seb nodded. 'Maybe, although, remembering back to my time living in the mess, most bachelor officers seemed to be hard-wired to dislike kids.'

'Then they're going to have to man up. Anyway, you never know, Sam and her pal might be quite maternal. Besides, it isn't as if we're going to ask any of them to actually do anything with Nate, like change a nappy. All they have to do is tolerate his presence. It's not asking for much, now, is it?' said Maddy briskly.

By the time Maddy was back downstairs, changed, made up and scented, Seb had managed to feed Nathan, mop down the worst splodges of spat-out banana from the kitchen table and Nathan's hair and he was back playing with his toys on the floor.

Maddy glanced at her watch. 'They should be here any minute. Best I get going with the French dressing.'

As she had bustled off into the kitchen and was busy with a blender, a concoction of oil and other ingredients, the doorbell rang.

'You'll have to get that Seb,' she yelled from the kitchen, over the high-pitched whine of the MagiMix.

Seb opened the front door. And there was Michelle.

Chapter Fourteen

Sam was looking forward to meeting some of the married officers of the battalion socially and informally, and as it meant getting to know a few of the wives as an added bonus she was really looking forward to lunch at Maddy's. Michelle and she had had fun over the weekend and Michelle had enjoyed meeting Sam's mess-mates – a couple of whom had stayed over specifically to go to Maddy's lunch party – while the rest of the time had been spent experiencing the delights of shopping in Salisbury and a trip to the cinema to see a chick-flick. Topping the weekend together with lunch out on the patch, before Michelle had to drive back to Pirbright, promised to make it a pleasant ending to a very jolly couple of days. So when Sam rang Maddy's doorbell she was anticipating a fun few hours.

The door opened and there was Seb, who was, it had to be said, extraordinarily good looking: tall, tanned and very fit in every possible sense of the word. Yet, even taking that into consideration, Sam didn't think his looks merited an audible gasp from Michelle. And she knew Michelle was incredibly pretty, but the look of utterly shocked amazement on Seb's face was also odd. Sam flicked her gaze from one to the other and saw the way the pair were staring at each other – both with horrified looks on their faces. Sam's female intuition went into overdrive. There was a sub-text here and when she got Michelle to herself she was going to get the thumb screws on her.

'Come in, come in,' said Seb. He seemed to be blustering and flustered. 'I'm Seb.' He gave Michelle a look which Sam wasn't able to interpret but which she was sure was significant. The plot thickened. 'Maddy's busy in the kitchen,' continued Seb. 'Let me take your coats.'

As the two women began to undo their zips and buttons an almighty wail roared from the room behind Seb. He flung open a door to his right and said, 'Bung your stuff in there,' while he raced through another door and towards the crying.

Michelle, still looking stunned and as if she were about to cry, handed Sam her coat wordlessly. Sam was longing to ask her what the hell was going on but with Seb only yards away she didn't dare. Sam took both coats and went into the little room Seb had directed them to use as a cloakroom. It was obviously supposed to be a study but at the moment, apart from a desk and chair, it mostly seemed to be a repository for the ironing pile. Sam dumped the coats on the desk and turned to go and saw on the wall dozens of photos of rowers and their boats.

And Michelle's latest was a rower. But she'd said he was called Bas, not Seb.

Oh. Dear. God. Sebastian.

Pennies positively cascaded. Had Michelle known he was married? wondered Sam. But she instantly dismissed the thought. Of course she hadn't. Michelle might have her moments but she wasn't a marriage wrecker. Sam felt herself go hot then cold as she realised what a bloody awful mess this was. She pulled Michelle into the study. One look at Michelle's face confirmed everything in an instant. Michelle was as shocked as Sam.

'Sam, what am I going to do?' said Michelle.

'So it's Seb, isn't it? Seb is Bas. Sebastian.' Sam knew she was right, but she needed confirmation.

Michelle's eyes glittered with unshed tears and she nodded. 'I can't stay. I've got to go.'

'You can't,' hissed Sam, desperately. 'Not without endless questions. And if those start to get asked, God knows what'll happen. Michelle, you've got to fake it. Now you've turned up you can't bugger off. Stay for a while, till lunch is over, and then you can say you've got a migraine or something, anything. But you can't turn on your heel and leave.'

Michelle showed a flash of defiance. 'Why shouldn't I? I don't care what these people think of me. This mess isn't my fault.'

'And it's not Maddy's either – is it?'

Michelle shook her head. 'I don't know if I can, Sam.' Her voice wobbled. 'Bas… Seb… I think I love him, and I feel so betrayed. Sam, I feel… I feel grubby. I don't screw married men.'

'And you didn't think you had. You wait till I get Seb alone,' whispered Sam, her anger blazing out of her eyes.

'Sam, I don't think I can pull this off. I can't go out there and pretend I've never met him.'

Sam gave her friend a hug. 'Yes, you can. Just for an hour or two. You won't have met most of the others either, remember, and you barely know James or Will or the other guys from the mess. They won't be able to tell whether you're acting normally or not.' Sam made a lame attempt at some humour. 'Or as normal as you ever act.' She grinned encouragingly at Michelle, who still looked stricken. 'Please. I know you don't know Maddy but, please, do this for her. It's not her fault. Talk about innocent by-stander. However, Seb I am going to kill.'

Michelle rubbed her forehead and sniffed. 'No, I want to do that.'

'Attagirl. So, can you do this? Can you pretend you've never met Seb before? And can you pretend you are having a great time—?'

154

The doorbell went again.

'Coming,' called Seb from the sitting room.

Sam hugged Michelle again and then sashayed out of the study, patting her hair as if she'd spent the time titivating and not carrying out emergency surgery on a broken heart.

Susie and her husband, plus James and a bunch of other single officers who had arrived mob-handed, all piled into the house together while Maddy emerged from the kitchen and the lunch party got going. What should have been a jolly Sunday rapidly became, for Sam and Michelle, a nightmare, with both of them terrified they'd make a mistake and the truth about Seb and his philandering would emerge. And it wasn't just she and Michelle that Sam had to worry about; anyone with only half an eye could see that Seb was acting really strangely. He was like a cat walking on tin-tacks – all nervy and wild-eyed. He was either gazing at Michelle in utter bemusement, jumping like he'd been stung whenever she spoke or moved, or bouncing around with so much bonhomie that eventually even Maddy noticed.

'What's got into you?' she demanded to know when she got him alone in the kitchen for a second. 'You're acting like an over-excited five-year-old at his own birthday party. Calm down.'

'Sorry, Mads,' he said, contritely. 'I guess I'm not used to playing host.'

Bewildered, Maddy shook her head and handed Seb an open bottle of red and another of white. 'Keep everyone topped up with wine until I'm ready to put out the hot dishes,' she instructed him in a low voice. 'It's only going to be another five minutes. And if any of the guys want beer, there's plenty on the patio, keeping cold. Only make sure they shut the French windows after them if they go out to get some; this house is hard enough to keep warm without a screaming draught racing through it.'

'Yes, ma'am,' said Seb.

A few minutes later the garlic bread had heated to Maddy's satisfaction and she was able to call her guests through to the dining room to help themselves.

Thank God, thought Sam, that this was a buffet party, and she and Michelle could choose where they sat and with whom – and that wasn't going to be near Seb or Maddy. However, as Maddy cleared away their plates from the main course, Susie Collins, whose husband was, Sam knew, Seb's officer commanding, insisted that they all played musical chairs and moved places 'so we all get to talk to someone new'. As a result Michelle ended up on one side of the room and Sam on the other and, without Sam to ride shotgun, Michelle was firmly on her own.

Sam tried to pay attention to the conversation she was involved with but it was hard when she was also desperately ear-wigging what was going on over on Michelle's side of the room. Michelle was saying very little as far as Sam could gather, which was a total relief, and was mostly answering questions with monosyllables while listlessly picking at the apple crumble Maddy had dished up for pud. It was obvious to Sam that Michelle was finding this party the most appalling charade and the strain showed on her face. Thankfully, though, because no one else in the room had ever met her before, the others present seemed to assume that being quiet and a bit sullen was Michelle's normal persona – which was horribly unfair on Michelle in many respects but, frankly, given the situation, thought Sam, things could be a lot worse. She longed to find a way of giving her a hug – or get her away from the torment – but without being rude she couldn't think of a way out. Sam resolved to leave, dragging Michelle with her, at the first, polite, opportunity.

Thankfully, after a while, the conversation became general across the room as all the men began to talk about the upcoming brigade exercise in Kenya, which was taking place in the New Year. The fact that Michelle, stuck in a training regiment and thus not involved at all, wasn't joining in the conversation became excusable. However, neither was Maddy, and Maddy, being an excellent hostess and not wanting to see one of her guests being ignored, started to chat to Michelle.

The look on Michelle's face said it all; her misery at discovering the truth about her boyfriend was being made a million times worse by having to be nice to his wife. Sam didn't think things could be any more agonising for Michelle if someone had been dripping acid into an open wound. Sam dragged herself away from the more interesting talk about Kenya and launched herself into one about more domestic things, hoping to draw fire, as it were.

'But when's your baby due?' Sam asked Maddy. Michelle lapsed again into morose silence. If she looked sulky and antisocial, and the other guests thought she was a bit of a wet blanket, then tough shit, thought Sam a little harshly. Better that than she should suddenly burst into tears.

'Right at the beginning of March,' said Maddy.

'But won't Seb be out in Kenya?'

'No, he's on the advance party going out at the start of January so he should be first back as well. He should make it home in time – assuming that both the army and the baby keep to schedule.'

'You must be excited,' said Sam.

'Less so the second time around. You know what's in store.'

'And poor Maddy has suffered awfully from morning sickness,' interjected Susie. There had been a distinct shift in the dynamics of the room as the women left the men to talk about army stuff and the wives began to group together to talk about more domestic issues. And while Sam would have liked to have joined in with the army chat, keeping Michelle away from Seb was now her priority, so domesticity ruled. 'Poor girl, it wouldn't have been so bad if it had just been mornings but she's been a martyr to it all day.'

'Poor you,' said Michelle, but Sam could tell that she didn't really care. What was morning sickness when you were dying of a broken heart?

'It hasn't helped that Seb's been up to his eyes in some new rowing training initiative,' said Maddy. 'He's had to give up a lot of weekends recently – almost every last one.'

Sam glanced in Michelle's direction and saw her face flush.

'Not that I mind terribly,' continued Maddy. 'Sometimes it's easier when it's just me and Nathan.'

'Well, isn't that handy,' said Michelle under her breath.

Sam shot her a warning look and Michelle answered it with a hint of a shrug. Sam was thankful that, because Michelle was going to be driving back to her own unit later that day, she'd had to stay sober. What she might have said or done if she'd been the worse for drink didn't bear thinking about.

'Rowing's becoming very popular these days, isn't it?' said Susie. 'Very fashionable, like cycling. Everyone seems to be at it. Have you ever rowed, Michelle?'

Michelle looked at Seb and swallowed. Sam held her breath. 'No,' she said coolly. 'Never. And I don't think I want to, regardless of what other people say about it. Can't think of anything I'd rather do less.'

Sam breathed again.

It was getting on for four in the afternoon by the time the meal came to an end and the coffee had been served and the petits fours scoffed. How could lunch have taken so long? wondered Sam. But finally the party had staggered to an end and Sam, with complete truthfulness, citing the fact the Michelle had a long drive ahead of her, had given them the excuse to make a move. Once they did everyone else decided they ought to be going too. It was almost dark as the two girls walked back towards the mess, followed by James and Will, who were both pretty pissed. Seb might be a bastard but he was a generous one when it came to pouring drink.

'Wait for us,' called James, petulantly, but Sam refused, saying that Michelle wanted to get back to her regiment before being posted AWOL on Monday morning, and at the rate the boys were walking, that wasn't going to happen. She could see that Michelle was only just holding herself together and the sooner they found total privacy the better all round.

When they got back to her room, Sam shut the door firmly and took her friend in her arms. 'Sweetie, I am so proud of you. You were a star.'

At this point Michelle collapsed into loud sobs. 'I c-c-c-an't b-b-believe I d-d-d-didn't s-s-s-spot the signs,' she wailed. 'I sh-sh-should have guessed he was m-m-m-married.'

'How?' asked Sam. 'Men don't get "unavailable" tattooed on them once they get a wife. Although some should,' she muttered darkly as an afterthought. 'Don't you dare beat yourself up, Michelle Flowers, because he really isn't worth it. How the hell a bastard like that got a lovely wife like Maddy and a nice girl like you to fall for him, I can't imagine. Git!'

Michelle slumped onto Sam's bed, mopping her tear-streaked face. 'I really, really loved him, Sam. I was fantasising about wedding dresses and everything. When we were going out I used to imagine what it would be like to have Bas to myself; to have him coming home to me every evening, to wake up next to him every morning... I didn't know he already had a wife who was living my dream.' Another sob escaped.

Sam knelt down on the floor gave her friend another hug. 'I know, hon.' She sighed. 'But you're well out of that one. If he's

159

cheating on his wife, you could never expect him to remain faithful to you.'

'You don't know that,' snuffled Michelle, into Sam's shoulder.

'Leopards and spots,' said Sam, 'leopards and spots.'

'No,' wailed Michelle, 'it would have been different if I'd been his wife. Maddy obviously doesn't appreciate him. If she did he wouldn't have looked for love elsewhere.'

'You don't know that,' said Sam.

'Yes, I do,' said Michelle, blowing her nose. 'It's the only explanation. He can't have been happy with her. He can't have been. Not when we were always so happy together.'

'But you haven't know him long,' protested Sam, trying to get Michelle to see reason.

'Time isn't important when you were as in love as we were.'

You were in love, thought Sam. She didn't think Seb was.

'I *know* it was love this time. It was so different to when I was at uni.' Michelle blew her nose again. 'I don't know why I thought that what I felt for my tutor was love. I was just naive, I suppose. And to think I wasted all that time over that poxy bloke, thinking I loved him, when I now know what *true* love is like.' Michelle subsided into more sobs.

Oh, dear God, thought Sam, as she remembered Michelle's story about the tutor and the near-miss with a restraining order. And then she calmed down. Michelle was four years older and four years wiser, and she was posted across the other side of the country. There was no way she could stalk Seb from that distance. Besides, it wouldn't take Michelle long to realise that all Seb had been after was some extra shagging while Maddy was pregnant and, according to Susie, being as sick as a dog and probably not up for it very much. So he'd used Michelle as a stop-gap, which made him a complete bastard. As soon as Michelle realised *that*, she'd see sense, understand she'd had a lucky escape, and forget about him. Of course she would.

Seb put down the drying-up cloth. 'Is that the lot?' he asked Maddy. Yet again, while his wife was preoccupied with wringing out the dishcloth, he nervously checked his mobile.

Maddy stretched to ease her aching back. 'It's enough, isn't it?' Behind Seb, on the counter, was a stack of now-clean saucepans and glasses – the stuff that hadn't fitted in the dishwasher. 'I'm knackered,' she said.

'Not surprised. That was quite a spread you put on.' Seb took a roll of clingfilm from a drawer and covered the remains of a plate of quiche before shoving it in the fridge. 'Not much left.' He rubbed his forehead and then from upstairs came a wail from Nathan.

Maddy sagged. 'And there was me hoping for a sit-down.'

'I'll see to him,' said Seb. He glanced at the kitchen clock. 'It's a bit early for his tea. How about I take him for a nice walk around the block?'

Maddy's face lit up with a smile. 'Would you, darling? You're an angel.'

'No problem.'

Ten minutes later, Nathan and Seb, both wrapped up warmly against the December elements and Nate tucked into his buggy with the rain hood down, were strolling through the officers' married patch. There wasn't a soul around. He took his phone out of his pocket and halted under a streetlamp while he pressed the buttons for Michelle's number.

'Where are you?' he asked without preamble when she picked up.

'On the M4.'

'Then you shouldn't have answered. I don't want you causing an accident on top of everything else.'

'Hands-free, Bas. Or maybe I should call you Seb.'

Seb could hear the anger simmering in her voice, despite the background noise from her car and the less-than-perfect connection. Well, he was bloody mad too.

'What the hell did you think you were playing at?'

He heard Michelle splutter. 'Me? Maybe if you hadn't lied to me about your name and the little matter that you had a wife and kid tucked away at home, maybe I wouldn't have bothered to get involved with you in the first place. You led me on, you really did. And I fell for it, hook, line and fucking sinker. I'm not the one at fault here, Bas... Seb... whatever your name is... it's you.' Michelle severed the connection.

Seb walked on a bit further, considering her reaction. Well, of course she was cross – it'd been the shock of the encounter. God, he'd nearly cacked himself when he'd seen her standing there. For a ghastly second he'd thought she'd arrived at his house on spec – to confront him and Maddy, like some awful sort of crazed stalker. But then he'd seen Sam with her and the penny had dropped – in awful cartoon slo-mo: this was Sam's mate, the one she'd asked Maddy if it would be OK for her bring along as a plus one. And, oh, the irony, that Maddy had said yes.

He pushed the buggy on down the road and wondered how long it would take Michelle to calm down enough to talk rationally. She really did sound pretty pissed off. He thought about what she'd said and the word 'involved' leapt to the forefront of his mind. He hadn't wanted involvement. All he'd wanted was a bit of a fling. Shit, she hadn't thought their relationship was a serious one, had she? Nah, surely not.

Maybe he'd give it another five minutes, he thought. Let her calm down a bit. He pushed Nathan to the swing park at the far end of the patch and then turned to walk around the block again. On his second lap he pressed the buttons again: straight to voicemail.

He sighed. He wondered how long she was going to sulk for. Seb didn't know much about women but he'd heard stories of jilted girlfriends and what they got up to. He didn't want Michelle to start thinking of ways to pay him back. Maybe he should hold out an olive branch.

'Look, Michelle, maybe I should apologise,' he said placatingly to the answering service. Shit, the last thing he wanted was for Michelle to start looking for family pets to casserole. Not that they had any but... 'Look, I am sorry. I was shocked, that's all. And I am really sorry if you feel hurt, I'm really, really sorry. I thought it was a bit of fun. I thought you felt the same way. I never meant for things to get serious. Honestly.' That sounded a bit pathetic but what else could he say? He couldn't think of anything so he finished with 'Bye', and rang off. Would that do the trick? God, he hoped so because one thing he had to be sure of was Michelle keeping schtum. And her mate Samantha too, because he'd seen the way Sam had kept staring at Michelle and him and he was pretty certain that she'd twigged what was going on, and even if she hadn't he would bet a pound to a penny Michelle had put her in the picture as soon as they'd left the house.

Morosely Seb turned the buggy round and began to walk back home. One thing was certain, if he got out of this alive he'd never, *ever* cheat on Maddy again.

Chapter Fifteen

A few days later, Sam sat in her office and tapped a pencil on the table. Her resolve to keep right out of the awful Michelle–Seb mess was weakening, and fast. How could she pretend it was nothing to do with her when Michelle was ringing her twice, sometimes three times a day, heartbroken and sobbing and complaining that Seb was now blanking her? Sam was sympathetic, she really was, but things were beyond a joke. She knew by heart the content of that phone call Seb had made to Michelle, because Michelle had gone over and over it with her, analysing every word, every possible nuance, wondering if there was some subtext she was missing, some hidden message. Sam had tried telling her that Seb had apologised in the hope that Michelle would go away and then he could ignore what he'd done, pretend it had never happened, but Michelle was obviously deaf to such advice. And the more time that passed the more desperate Michelle seemed to be getting, and now Sam was seriously worried that her friend might do something really bonkers, like ring Maddy, or do something even more confrontational. Frankly, given how impetuous Michelle had been in the past, and that business with the threatened restraining order, Sam was getting increasingly concerned about what she might be capable of.

She grabbed her beret and made her way across the workshop floor towards the door.

'I'm going across to B Company,' she told Sergeant Armstrong as she passed him. 'I'll be about half an hour.'

'No worries, ma'am,' he called back to her.

Sam walked across the parade square towards B Company lines, wondering as she went what she was going to say to Seb.

When she reached his office, the door was open. She knocked and instantly crossed the threshold without waiting for Seb to ask her in, then shut the door behind her.

'Well?'

Seb flushed. 'Well, what?'

'You know exactly what I am talking about.'

There was a pause, then in a sullen tone, he said, 'I don't have to answer to you.'

Sam raised her eyebrows. 'No, you don't. But perhaps you ought to answer to Michelle... or Maddy.' She took a pace forward and put both her hands on his desk and leaned forward. 'Have you any idea the state Michelle is in?' She glared at Seb. 'No, of course you haven't because you haven't spoken to her since Sunday. You haven't spoken, you haven't texted her, you've just ignored her.'

'It's tricky.'

Sam's eyes widened. 'Tricky? Of course it's fucking tricky. You've been playing fast and loose with my mate's emotions, to say nothing about cheating on your wife. Your pregnant wife and the mother of your son.' She paused and watched Seb squirm, visibly. 'Why?'

'I dunno.' Then he seemed to rally. 'Anyway, I wouldn't have fallen for Michelle if she hadn't led me on.'

'Really?' hissed Sam. 'So, while Michelle was leading you on, you didn't think to mention to her that you were married? You didn't think to let her in on that little fact, so she could back away from a relationship that was bound to end in tears?'

Seb looked down at his desk.

'No, you didn't, did you?' said Sam, answering the question for him, her eyes narrowed in contempt. 'And why would you?

165

There you were, away from home, off the leash, and a lovely girl tells you she's available and you think that what happens at the rowing lake will stay at the rowing lake. Maddy will never find out, you can have a free shag and no harm done. Except it wasn't the one shag, was it? As far as I can tell, you and Michelle have been at it like rattlesnakes almost every weekend.' She stared at Seb. 'And I bet my bottom dollar that half of those rowing weekends were nothing of the sort.' She looked at the expression on Seb's face. 'No, I thought not. How could you?' she spat.

'Are you going to tell Maddy?' He looked genuinely terrified. 'Because I've already decided I won't cheat on her again. Ever.'

'Seb, it isn't up to me whether or not to tell her – not that I would anyway.' She wondered if this was the moment to tell him that while she might not, he oughtn't to bank on Michelle behaving in the same way. Maybe she'd wait and see what Seb planned to do himself. 'But you have got to sort this out, and soon. I've got Michelle crying down the phone to me every evening because she doesn't know where she stands, and you're not talking to her, which is hardly helping matters. Have you any idea how upset and hurt she is?' She raised an eyebrow at Seb. 'And what if Maddy finds out? Just because you and I aren't going to tell her it doesn't mean someone else won't.' Impossible though it seemed, Seb's face went even whiter.

'Michelle?' mouthed Seb.

Sam shrugged. 'Seb, she's hurting, really hurting. Maybe you ought to know she's not good when she's got a broken heart; she's not rational.'

Seb's jaw slackened.

'Even if she doesn't spill the beans or try and doorstep you, the army's really close-knit. It seems to me that everyone knows everyone and word may well get back to Maddy. Listen, I honestly don't know what to suggest for the best but you have got to talk to Michelle. You've got to beg her forgiveness, you've got to grovel if that's what it takes, you've got to make her see sense and then you've got to end it – gently. Very gently.'

Seb looked at his desk. 'I'll ring her,' he mumbled.

'Ring her? God, you really are a wimp. You will not ring her, you will not text her, you will not drop her a sodding line, you will talk to her. Face to face.' Sam glared at Seb till he dropped his gaze.

Seb swallowed. 'Why?'

'Because she doesn't deserve anything less and I won't be responsible for the consequences if you try and dump her by text or phone.' Sam glowered at Seb. 'You thought it was a free, no-strings shag, didn't you? Well, you were wrong and unless you want it to get completely out of hand, you'd better square things with Michelle properly, and soon.'

'You don't really think she'd do anything, do you?'

Sam shook her head. 'Seb, I'd like to say no but I can't. She's got previous. On top of that I think she's been looking for love since her mother pissed off when she was little, and it's my guess she thought she'd found it with you. This is why you've got to be really gentle with her.'

Seb shook his head. 'Just my luck,' he snapped. 'I step out of line once in my life and I pick a basket-case.'

Sam leaned forward again, her eyes narrowed again. 'No one but yourself to blame there. No one made you have an affair, no one told you to lie to both Maddy and Michelle. Did they?'

Seb shrugged. 'I suppose.'

'You suppose?' Sam's voice was half an octave higher than normal with indignation. 'For fuck's sake, Seb, you've got to take responsibility and do the right thing.'

His face was set as he nodded. 'I'll make arrangements to see her at the weekend.' He glared at Sam. 'Happy now?'

'I will be, when you've done it.' She gave Seb a salute and stamped out.

Seb sank back into his swivel chair and stared at the computer keyboard on his desk. What a shitting-awful mess. He flashed back to the moment, on Sunday, when he'd seen Michelle on his doorstep and he'd felt his world slide from beneath his feet. The dreadful feeling of nausea that he'd experienced then – that stomach lurch that he got in occasional, ghastly, falling nightmares – came right back again and he shut his eyes till it passed.

The worst of it was, Sam was right. Smug little minx. But even as that description entered his head he knew he was being unfair; she wasn't smug, she wasn't a minx and she hadn't told him anything that he didn't know, deep down, himself. The trouble was, the truths she'd told him were exactly the ones he'd been ignoring, and hearing them voiced by a third party had been heart-stoppingly shocking. His hands were shaking, he noticed, and he wondered vaguely if it was the result of having his fortune read to him by Sam or his worry about Michelle's reaction when he broke it off with her.

He pulled his mobile out of his pocket and toyed with the idea of disobeying Sam and dumping Michelle by call or text. He even began to draft a text but then he deleted it. What Sam had said about Michelle scared him shitless. And the worst of it was, she knew where he lived. He didn't think she'd do something utterly appalling, like tell Maddy, but he couldn't risk it.

Instead he lifted the receiver of the land line on his desk, dialled the number for the Aldershot garrison mess and booked a room there for the Friday night. Then he picked up his mobile and texted Michelle, asking her to meet him there.

'We need to talk,' the text finished.

He slumped back his office chair and idly swivelled it from

side to side while he considered exactly what he ought to say to Michelle. One thing was for certain, it wasn't going to be pleasant and once again the phrase 'bunny-boiler' swooshed through his mind. He closed his eyes and wished for the umpteenth time since that lunch party that he'd never, ever got involved with Michelle.

His phone pinged. A text.

Cant w8. Love you. M.

And it was M for Michelle – not Maddy.

He deleted the message and pressed the buttons to call home.

'Hiya, Mads.'

'Hi, hon.'

'Have we got any plans for the weekend?'

'Nothing much. Why?'

'Something rowing related has come up. I'm going to have to be away in Aldershot on Friday night.'

'Oh, Seb.' He heard his wife sigh. 'Well, I suppose it can't be helped.'

'Sorry, sweetie.'

'What time do you think you'll be back on Saturday?'

Seb thought quickly. The real reason for his trip meant he'd be free to leave directly after breakfast; in fact, he'd be free to leave Friday evening, as soon as he'd given Michelle the bad news, but that wouldn't stack up with the excuse for his absence. 'Erm, not sure. I should be free some time after lunch on Saturday, home by tea-time at the latest, I hope.'

'Rats.'

'What's the matter?'

'Nothing really; only an appointment to get my hair cut.'

'Again?'

'Seb, it'll be Christmas in no time and then you're off to Kenya. This is my last chance. It'll be months before I'll be able to go and get it done again without involving childminders.'

'Sorry, hon.'

He heard a sigh. 'No, don't worry. It's not your fault. I'll sort something out. Anyway, I must dash. I'll see you at lunchtime. Bye.'

'Bye,' said Seb.

He chucked his mobile on the desk and pulled his in-tray towards him. But his concentration was shot and although he stared at the work he had to do, all he could think about was the unholy mess his life was in.

Colonel Notley put his head round the door of his adjutant's office and said, 'Can I have a minute of your time, Andy?'

'Sure, Colonel.'

Andy leapt to his feet and grabbed his notepad and his desk diary and followed the CO back into his office.

The CO waved at the chair in front of his desk.

'It's about Kenya.'

'Right, Colonel.'

'I've had a phone call from the PR department at the MOD.'

'And…?'

'And they want to embed a hack from the Beeb with us.'

Andy's shoulders sagged. This was all they needed. Reporters, he knew from past experience, generally meant a whole heap of work for all concerned as they invariably needed looking after, and if anything went wrong – and on an exercise of the scale of Askari Thunder it was almost a given that something would – it was also a given that the reporter would want to ask questions, possibly awkward ones. 'Who?'

'Jack Raven,' said the CO.

Andy felt even more despondent. Not any old hack but one

of the BBC's best-known reporters who had come to the fore as a result of the Syria crisis and who now seemed to be the go-to man on all matters to do with the military, and was, apparently, the nation's favourite defence correspondent. Andy was pretty certain it was the man's film-star good looks which had got him his rating in the popularity stakes and disliked him irrationally as a result. The fact that his wife, Gilly, went all doe-eyed and gooey whenever his smarmy features appeared on the TV screen – an almost nightly occurrence – didn't help things much either. Andy's thoughts must have been reflected on his face.

'Do I gather you aren't one of his greatest fans either?' said the colonel, his eyebrow lifting a smidge in amusement.

'Not really, if I'm honest,' admitted Andy.

The CO sighed. 'Well, it doesn't matter about our opinion, we're going to be saddled with him and I really can't think who the hell I can spare to babysit him.'

Andy scratched his head. 'I'll give it some thought. Someone non-essential, personable and articulate. The trouble is that doesn't generally describe infantry soldiers.'

'Well,' said the CO, 'plenty of my officers and senior ranks are all personable and articulate but they are all essential. I refuse to waste someone of that calibre nannying Raven just to make sure he doesn't trip over his own feet. Anyway, we don't have to think about that yet but if you come up with an idea, let me know.'

'He's texted me,' said Michelle as soon as Sam answered her mobile.

Sam had no need to ask who had texted her friend.

'He wants me to meet him on Friday. He wants to talk.' Michelle sounded ridiculously excited. 'I know that means he's come to his senses and he's decided which one of us he wants. Oh, Sam, I know he's made the right decision.'

Sam's heart nose-dived into her ankles. How could she tell her best friend that this meeting with the love of her life was, almost certainly, going to be her last one?

'You think?' she asked carefully.

'Of course. He's finally realised that he doesn't love Maddy, because he wants me,' said Michelle, blithely.

'You sure?'

'Duh. You saw her, she's a mouse. I expect Seb only dated her out of pity and she probably got pregnant deliberately to snare him.'

'You don't know that.'

A sigh blew down the line. 'Whatevs, Sam. You think you're talking to someone who cares and I suppose I should feel a bit sorry for her but, honestly, I know he's got the wrong woman in his life and now he's realised it.'

He's not the only one who needs to come to terms with reality, thought Sam. 'Ring me Saturday and let me know how it goes. I'm at a party on Friday so I doubt if I'll pick up any calls. It's at the corporals' club so it'll probably be a bit raucous.'

'The corporals' club?'

'The OiC has invited me. James – remember him?'

'Sort of. I met loads of people last weekend.'

Sam rolled her eyes. No, of course her friend wouldn't remember him; at first she'd been to wrapped up in her own lovey-dovey situation to notice any of Sam's new friends, and then on Sunday she'd been too shell-shocked at discovering Seb's marital status to pay any attention to anything outside her own bubble of misery. 'Never mind,' said Sam. 'It's not important.'

'Anyway, I'll ring you Saturday,' promised Michelle.

'Good,' said Sam, already dreading the call.

*

'Jenna?'

'Hi, Maddy, what can I do for you?'

'Jenna, I'm going to have to cancel,' said Maddy as she stirred some soup made out of leftover chicken.

'Oh, that's a shame. Do you want to reschedule?'

'Jenna, I don't know if I can. It's finding someone to dump Nate on. I'd hoped Seb was going to be around this weekend but suddenly there's more rowing... I'd ask Susie but she's going to be up to her eyes next week what with the twins coming home and everything and then we're off on Christmas block leave.' She sighed. 'Never mind, it's only a trim.'

'I suppose... I suppose I could come to yours. Then Nathan has got all his toys and if he needs a nap he's got his own bed.'

Maddy felt a bit overwhelmed by the offer. Jenna had made it plain that because of her dodgy past and previous involvement with 1 Herts, she didn't want to come near the patch. 'But, you said—'

'I know what I said. But it's only the once and if neither of us draws attention to my visit...'

'As if I would.'

'Exactly. I mean, I know that the old bats on the patch are a nosy bunch but I should be able to slip through the cordon without setting off alarms.'

Maddy laughed. 'Hey, remember I'm one of the old bats.'

'No, you're not,' said Jenna. 'You were the one who was nice to me. I haven't forgotten that.'

Maddy felt a little twinge of British embarrassment at the compliment. 'OK. Then I'll see you at ten on Saturday.'

'At ten.'

There was a quiet knock on Sam's door.

'Come in,' she called. She was sitting on the chair in front of her dressing table, putting the finishing touches to her make-up before the corporals' club party. In the mirror she saw James stick his head around her door.

'You ready?' he asked.

'Just about.' Sam put down her mascara wand and swivelled round.

'The belle of the ball,' said James, appreciatively.

Sam stood up, smoothing down her short velvet frock. 'Will it do? I wasn't sure what I ought to wear. This is my first corporals' club do and I don't want to get it wrong.'

'I'm no expert,' said James, 'but you look perfect to me.'

'Aw,' said Sam. 'You are kind.'

'Hey, I'd tell you if you didn't, trust me. I've got standards, you know.'

Sam giggled. 'I do. I can imagine the last thing you want is to walk into the room and have the corporals recoil in horror at your choice of date.'

'That was *precisely* what I was afraid of. But on this occasion I think I've avoided that by the skin of my teeth.'

Sam laughed more. 'Carry on like that and I won't make the effort next time.'

'Who says there's going to *be* a next time?'

Still exchanging banter, they left her room and made their way across the barracks to the club.

Immi tried hard not to smirk as she sat with Luke and the other committee members at the central table in the corporals' club. She knew she looked a million dollars in a gold lamé dress and with her hair, freshly dyed blonde, streaming down her back. Her friends had told her she looked 'dead classy', which was exactly what she'd been going for. Luke wasn't like other soldiers and she didn't think he'd appreciate her normal, more obvious look. She still didn't understand why he had joined as a squaddie, not an officer – especially as with all those GCSEs he obviously had the brains to be an officer – but she didn't want to frighten him off by looking a bit tarty. Well, very tarty, because Immi had more than enough self-knowledge to know how she could often come across, which was perfect for pulling most soldiers, the ordinary squaddies, but not Luke, no way.

She was tapping her feet along to a Killers song and longing for Luke to ask her to dance. If her date had been with anyone but Luke she might have thrown in the towel and either told him to get his arse in the dance floor or found someone else to bop about with under the flashing disco lights. But as Luke intimidated her slightly and she was desperate to make their relationship – such as it was – a bit more permanent, she was trying hard not to rock the boat. She was even watching how much she drank; she didn't reckon Luke would approve if she got shit-faced. She was about to take her first sip of her third white wine – she'd given up on red because, try as she might, she couldn't bring herself to like it – when she saw Luke stare at the door. She followed his gaze: Captain Rosser and Luke's boss, Captain Lewis, were coming in. Immi sighed; Capitan Lewis looked fantastic in an above-the-knee, midnight-blue, velvet dress and a wonderful sparkly bolero jacket to complement it. Suddenly her own gold lamé seemed rather tawdry in comparison. Bollocks. She looked back at Luke. Bigger bollocks. Immi stared at him. The way he looked at Captain Lewis sort of confirmed what she'd suspected down at the guardroom. She felt a sharp little stab of jealousy. How unfair was that! Immi'd known all along that Luke was out of her league but she'd never expected to have to compete for him with Sam Lewis.

'Something the matter?' said Luke.

'No, why should there be?' She covered up how hurt she felt. Captain Lewis had the looks, the brains, a natty little sports car, which Immi coveted, and now she had the attention of Luke, who she wouldn't even want, not with her being an officer and everything. Bleakly, Immi wondered if she'd get Luke on the rebound.

'You don't look like nothing's the matter,' probed Luke.

'I was just wondering what that pair are doing here,' she bluffed.

'He gets an invite,' said Luke, 'because he's OiC of the club. And I suppose he asked Lewis along as a "plus one".'

'Well, that's all right, then,' said Immi, thinking it was anything but. 'As long as the officers haven't decided to gatecrash our party. And can you imagine what would happen if we did the same back to them? You'd be on a fizzer for insubordination before you could say "guilty as charged".'

Luke snorted. 'Like I'd want to gatecrash the officers' mess.'

Immi recalled his low opinion of all officers and kept quiet. She had a ridiculous ambition to one day be invited in there to be a part of a proper officers' ball or dinner night; she knew it was unlikely but, hey, a girl could dream. Although, given the way things were going with her ambition to get Luke to date her, any other dreams she might have were probably going to go the same way – down the toilet.

The newcomers came over to their table, where the chairman of the corporals' club committee leapt to his feet and found a couple of chairs so the pair could join them. Luckily, they sat down right at the far end of the table, about as far from Immi and Luke as was possible, but it didn't stop Luke from flicking disparaging looks in Rosser's direction. And Immi sat next to him, her feet tapping and head bobbing as she listened to the music and longed to be invited to dance. Then she saw the two officers stand up and make their way over to the dance floor. She sighed – shitting hell, even Lewis was getting a chance to have a bop.

She watched them stroll into the middle of the parquet floor, where they began the standard army officers' military two-step: shuffle-step-shuffle-together-shuffle-step-shuffle-together. She was vaguely thinking how nice it would be if Luke took her for a stroll around the floor too, even if it was for such a crap sort of 'dad-dance', when he grabbed her wrist and hauled her upright.

'Now listen,' he said as he propelled her forward, 'trust me, I know what I'm doing. Relax and follow me.' And with that he put her in a proper *Strictly Come Dancing* hold, thrillingly tight against his body, and then... well... frankly, fireworks, thought Immi after. She had no idea what her feet were doing, nor did she care, but she didn't seem to be kicking Luke's shins or tripping him up and yet she was being spun around, she was twirling – yes, actually twirling – and every eye in the club seemed to be on her. Luke was managing to give her signals through the position of his body and the pressure of his hand on her back, which meant instinctively she knew which direction he wanted her to move in, and as she shimmied across the floor she felt like a million dollars. Talk about being the centre of attention.

Chapter Sixteen

Sam and James headed back to the mess at around eleven o'clock, having stayed long enough to be sociable but not so long as to outstay their welcome. Besides, if they'd stayed any later there was every likelihood that one of the soldiers would have got drunk and thrown a punch or said something out of order, and it was always best if the officers had left prior to witnessing such an event – or, worse, getting caught up in it, which would only make the subsequent disciplinary action more complicated.

'So, what was all that about?' said James as they walked slowly but companionably across the barracks.

'What was all what about?'

'That dancing display put on by Blake and Cooper.'

'Dunno. Impressive, though, wasn't it? And it begs the question: just *who* was he trying to impress?'

'I don't think it was Cooper,' said James. 'I think he was showing off to you.'

Sam laughed. 'Me? Bloody hell, James, why on earth? Maybe he's planning to apply to *Strictly* and thinks a reference from me would help.'

'Maybe. But, seriously, where on earth did an oik like Blake learn those moves?'

Sam felt oddly riled by James's description of Blake. 'Blake may be an oddball but he's not an oik. Did you know he's got a Latin GCSE?'

James stopped dead in his tracks. 'Latin? Latin! You're joking.'

Sam nodded. 'Nope. He really isn't your average grunt and very far from being an oik. I did try to ask him about his past when I first arrived in the LAD, but he clammed up completely. He's a dark horse.'

'Corporal Cooper likes him, though,' said James.

Sam laughed. 'She was a bit obvious, wasn't she, the way she kept looking at him? I think she fancies him but I've got a feeling it's not reciprocated.'

'No. She's definitely punching above her weight there.'

It was her phone ringing that woke Sam the next morning. 'Yeah?' she said groggily as she picked it up, not bothering to look at the caller ID.

'Sam?'

'Oh, hello, Michelle.'

'Oh, Sam.' There was a muffled sob.

Sam swung her legs out of bed and padded across her room to where she kept the kettle and the mugs. If she was going to have to provide a shoulder for Michelle to cry on, she needed caffeine. She was only half listening as she spooned granules into a mug and boiled the kettle but it didn't matter as Michelle was on transmit rather than receive.

'And,' said Michelle, her voice almost ultra-sonic with rage, 'did I tell you that the bastard asked me what I'd been playing at? Me?'

'Bastard indeed,' said Sam as calmly as she could. Shit, not the retelling of the phone-call-after-that-lunch-party-encounter *again*? And each time Michelle retold the story her voice seemed to get shriller. Sam reckoned that at this rate she was going to be lucky to escape without hearing impairment. Honestly, she thought, it was like some awful Groundhog Day, only without the cute critter. If her English tutor at uni had been subjected to this, no wonder he'd threatened her with the law. But, thank God, Michelle was only phoning her and not anyone else… like Seb's wife.

'Well, I told him straight, didn't I? But yesterday he tried a different tack. Yesterday he said he wants us to part as friends,' she sneered. 'Like I am ever going to be friends with that git. Part as friends? My arse! He must think I'm Mother fucking Theresa because you'd need to be a saint to forgive him for what he's done. God, his poor wife is welcome to him. If you see him and can bear to talk to the slimy creep, you can tell him that I never want to have anything to do with him ever again. And he can shove rowing and his fucking boat where the sun don't shine.' Then her voice cracked and a shuddering sob reverberated down the line. Sam waited silently till her friend regained her self-control. 'Who am I kidding, Sam?' she whimpered. 'I love him. I keep wondering if I'm stuck in some awful sort of nightmare. I'd take him back in a moment.'

'No,' said Sam. 'Never. You must never do that and you mustn't tell him that's how you feel. Besides, he's not worth it. He'd only do it again.'

'But, Sam, I'm so miserable. I want him so much.'

Sam rolled her eyes. This was a worse mess than she'd thought. She'd hoped that Michelle's rage was a sign that she'd accepted what an unprincipled toe-rag Seb was and would want to keep as far away from him as possible. The last thing she'd envisaged was that Michelle would still hold a candle for him. Bugger. Somehow she didn't think this boded well. On the positive side all she had to do was keep Michelle away from Warminster and Seb until after Christmas and then Seb would be off to Kenya for weeks and weeks. Hopefully, by the time he got back it would all have blown over and Michelle would have moved on.

'Come in, come in,' said Maddy, throwing the door wide to let in Jenna and her box of products and hairdressing equipment.

Jenna stepped quickly. 'I feel like some sort of spy,' she said as she took off her headscarf, which covered up her startling platinum hair.

'A very glam one,' said Maddy, thinking Jenna looked not unlike a blonde Audrey Hepburn in her scarf and Burberry trench coat.

Jenna shook out her hair. 'Right, where are we going to do this?' She began to unbutton her mac as she looked around. 'Better quarter than the last one,' she commented.

Maddy, balancing Nathan on one hip, helped her out of her coat and put it over the banister.

'Not as lovely as your sunny little flat,' she said.

'Still, you've got it arranged nice,' said Jenna.

'Thanks,' said Maddy. 'You try and make it look as much like the last place as possible – try and keep that feeling that it's home, even when it isn't really. Now, I thought it would be easiest to wash my hair in the kitchen – and cut it there too. I can strap Nate into his high chair, give him some toys to play with and, if he really kicks off, bribe him with sweeties.'

'"Eeties,' said Nathan, waving his hands about.

'He's talking,' said Jenna as she followed Maddy down the hall.

'Up to a point.' Maddy plonked Nathan into his chair and snapped up the harness. Then she got some stacking beakers off the counter and handed them to her son. Instantly he dropped them onto the floor. Maddy bent down to retrieve them and Nathan repeated his trick.

'Nathan,' she said. 'I won't pick them up again.'

Jenna got busy opening out her big plastic box and took out the top tray, containing brightly coloured curlers, and put it on the counter by the high chair. Instantly Nathan reached for them.

'No, Nathan. Those are Jenna's.'

'Genna's,' said Nate.

'Jenna,' said Jenna.

'Genna.'

'Think that's as good as it's going to get at the mo,' said Maddy.

Nathan began to wail about not being allowed the curlers.

'I don't mind him playing with a couple,' said Jenna, 'if you don't. They're all clean.'

'He'll chew them,' warned Maddy. 'He's teething again.'

'They're only curlers.' She handed a red one and a pink one to Nathan. He grasped them eagerly and stuffed one straight in his mouth. However, silence reigned.

Maddy slipped on the gown Jenna gave her as Jenna put the shower attachment onto the kitchen taps and, while Nathan was happily diverted by the curlers, they got busy.

'So what did you say Seb was doing?' asked Jenna as she massaged shampoo into Maddy's hair and lathered it up.

'Last-minute rowing training.'

'He does a lot of rowing, doesn't he?' said Jenna.

'He does,' said Maddy. 'Every weekend.'

'Every weekend?'

'Uh huh. It used not to be that bad but suddenly… I don't know, it seems as if army rowing has taken over his life.'

'He must be bloody good.'

'He used to be. Nearly rowed in the Boat Race.' Even Jenna would have heard of that, reasoned Maddy.

'Cool.' There was a pause as Jenna began to rinse Maddy's hair. 'So what's he aiming for? The Olympics?'

'Not now. He's not in that league any more, but he coaches

for the army. He's trying to find the next generation of rowers – or something.'

'But every weekend? Can't other coaches take some of the strain? He can't be the only guy with a coaching qualification, surely. And don't the next generation of rowers want a life and a free weekend too?'

Maddy sighed. 'You'd think, wouldn't you? They must be very keen.'

'For that amount of training, they must be obsessed. What the hell are they going to do when your old man is away in Kenya?'

'Don't know. Get on with it on their own, I suppose.'

Jenna began to rinse out the suds. 'Well, if I were Seb and I had a lovely family like yours I'd be telling them to get on with it by themselves right now.'

'Don't think that's going to happen. He loves his rowing.'

'Blimey,' said Jenna. 'If my Dan was away that much I wouldn't think it was just sport he was up to; I'd think he was having an affair.'

'Seb's not like that,' said Maddy.

Jenna turned on the water so Maddy didn't hear Jenna's sceptical snort or her comment, 'He's a bloke, isn't he?'

Not long after Jenna had gone Maddy was sitting down with a cup of tea on the table and Nathan on her lap as they read a story book together when she heard a key in the door. Surely it couldn't be Seb yet? She glanced at the clock on the mantelpiece: only twelve o'clock. She wasn't expecting him back till later. What a bonus.

'Hello,' she heard his voice call from the hall.

'Seb,' she called back. 'I'm in the sitting room with Nathan.' Maddy might be content to let her husband come to them but Nathan had other ideas and, squirming like an eel, he slithered

183

off Maddy's lap so he could half toddle, half crawl to meet his father.

'Hello fella,' Maddy heard Seb say over squeals of delight from Nathan. 'Have you been a good boy?'

Seb appeared in the sitting room, cradling his son on his hip. Maddy thought her husband looked exhausted. 'How's your day been?' he said.

'Quiet. Nathan's been good, I've had my hair cut, got some ironing done.'

'Oh, yes, your hair does look nice.'

Maddy doubted Seb would have noticed if she hadn't said – he wasn't the world's best when it came to things like that.

Then he added, 'But I thought you were going to have to cancel.'

'Well, I was able to sort something out.' She decided to change the subject away from her hair. She thought it unlikely that Seb would want to know anything about the arrangements but the bigger the distance she kept between Seb and Jenna the happier she'd be. She would bet a pound to a penny that Seb would take a dim view of her associating with a woman who had caused so much trouble in the battalion only a year previously. 'You look tired. Rough training session?'

Seb nodded.

'You do too much, you know,' said Maddy. 'I mean every weekend. I know you love it and I know you're really committed but…'

Seb put his hand up. 'I agree.'

Maddy's eyes goggled. 'You agree?'

'I haven't been fair and I think my commitment might have got out of hand. So I've told the guys in charge of army rowing that they'll have to find someone else. Besides, I want to spend Christmas with my family and then I'm off to Kenya and then I'm hoping that I'll need some paternity leave so they're going to need to find someone to take over between now and Easter anyway. And if they can find someone for that long then presumably they can find someone permanently.'

'Really? Oh, Seb, that's wonderful.' And Maddy threw herself into Seb's arms.

Seb rested his chin on the top of her head as a look of utter anguish passed over his features.

Chapter Seventeen

On the Monday after the corporals' club ball Sam was at her desk, writing a whole stack of boring reports, when her phone rang. She fell on it, grateful for the displacement activity.

'Morning, OC LAD,' she said into the receiver.

'Sam, it's me.'

Michelle. Sam felt her shoulders droop. Not again. OK, she'd wanted a distraction from her mundane task but maybe not this distraction. She was so bored with the Maddy–Seb–Michelle triangle and yet she felt hideously disloyal for even thinking it.

'Hiya, 'Chelle,' she said, making a brave attempt to sound pleased. 'How are you?'

'Crap. Beyond crap. How do you think?'

Sam paused. What was she supposed to say: Oh, dear? You'll feel better soon? Move on? She sighed. 'I'm really sorry to hear that, Michelle. Truly.'

'Why do I feel as though it's my fault, Sam? I mean, it's not, is it? I didn't do anything wrong, did I?'

'No, Michelle.'

'How could he have done this to me? I thought he loved me.'

'I don't know, Michelle.' Sam gazed at the reports, which suddenly looked tempting.

'I need him to know what he's done to me. It's not fair that I'm the one whose life is ruined and he skips off back to his family.'

Sam bit back a comment that Maddy didn't deserve to have her life ruined either, which was the flip side of the scenario.

'Well, it isn't, is it?' demanded Michelle, when Sam didn't answer.

'No.'

'When am I going to see you again, so we can talk properly? I suppose you'll be spending Christmas at your grandparents, with your dad.'

Fuck. But she couldn't lie. Not to her best friend. 'Well, yes. But not with Dad. He's going skiing again, like he does, on his own.'

'That's a bit harsh,' said Michelle with indignation.

'You know what Dad is like,' said Sam. 'It's hardly out of character, is it? Anyway, I'm going to Gran's on my own and I'll get outrageously spoilt so I don't really mind.'

'Oh.' There was a pause and in it Sam could almost hear the cogs of Michelle's brain whirring. 'So your gran's other spare room is free.' Sam could detect the hope in Michelle's voice despite the miles and miles that separated them.

She suppressed a sigh. 'Unless she's suddenly decided to take in a lodger.'

'You don't suppose…'

Sam shut her eyes as if in that nanosecond of thought some perfect reason not to invite Michelle would materialise. 'Yes, I'll ring Gran. I'm sure she and Grandpa will be cool and would love to see you again.'

'Oh, that's so perfect,' squealed Michelle. 'I don't have to see Dad and the WSM and we can have a proper catch up and it'll be wonderful, you'll see.' Sam felt that Michelle wasn't even considering whether her father mightn't want his daughter to spend Christmas with him. Oh, well… 'What do you think your grandparents would like me to bring as a Christmas present? And I can bring some supplies. I'll get on the internet and order a hamper perhaps. And booze. I'll bring lashings of that...' And as Michelle rabbited on about her plans to make Christmas 'just wonderful' Sam wondered what she could plan to fill the rest of the block leave so she'd have a legitimate excuse to tell Michelle that she could only stay a few days. She loved Michelle, she did, but a little went a long way. Even if it meant living on her own in the mess for half her leave, she thought that it would be preferable to non-stop Michelle for three whole weeks. The thought of going over and over the doomed relationship with Seb for that long was more than Sam could bear. So she lied and said she'd been invited to James's for the New Year, fairly certain that, considering how obsessed Michelle had been with her own love life, she wouldn't have a clue about what was going on in Sam's – which, thought Sam, was diddly-squat, although she was happy with that. She liked being *just good friends* with the guys in the mess. It was comfortable and happy and unless there was some monumental coup-de-foudre moment between her and one of her fellow mess-mates she couldn't see the situation altering any time soon.

As Sam put the phone down the ASM appeared at her office door.

'Have you got a moment, ma'am?'

Sam nodded.

The ASM approached her desk and put the Christmas duty rota, that Sam had just published, on her desk.

Sam looked at it and then at the ASM.

'So?' she said.

'So, Sergeant Armstrong is on call over Christmas.'

Sam nodded. 'Yes.'

'He was on call last Christmas.'

'And he volunteered to do it again this Christmas.'

'It's not fair.'

'But he volunteered. He's not going away, he doesn't have kids, he's happy to do it.' She was trying not to sound exasperated but the ASM was trying her patience.

'I think you should find someone else to do it.'

'You?'

'No!'

'Then, may I suggest, Mr Williams, that until you've got another volunteer you don't muck up a perfectly serviceable duty roster.'

Mr Williams looked sullen. 'I was just trying to protect his interests,' he said truculently.

'I think, from what I know of Jenna, if she isn't happy with this arrangement, Sergeant Armstrong wouldn't have dared put his name forward.' Sam stared at the ASM and willed him to contradict her. 'Anything else?' she asked pointedly.

The ASM picked up the duty roster and left her office. Sam felt inordinately proud of having stood up to him, even though, having done so, she was left feeling wrung out.

Andy Bailey watched Immi Cooper pick up the pile of files from his out-tray and sashay out of his office. There were very few people who could look sexy in combat kit but Cooper was definitely an exception. He tore his eyes away from her rather gorgeous rear and applied himself to the citation he was writing to try and get the battalion's RSM in the honours' list before the man retired from the army. Besides, he told himself, he could hardly bitch about Gilly mooning over that bloody Raven-war-correspondent-bloke on the TV if he was ogling another woman.

He put down his pen. Of course! The perfect person to escort Raven around the exercise area would be Corporal Cooper. She was going to be a complete waste of space out in Kenya, that much was obvious, and yet there was no reason to leave her behind with the rear party, as the families officer and his team had that base perfectly adequately covered.

Andy jumped up and went to tell his boss his idea.

'Perfect,' said Colonel Notley. 'Go and tell her.'

Andy went back to his desk and pressed the intercom button.

'Come to my office for a moment, would you, Cooper?' he ordered.

Immi returned a few seconds later. 'Sir?'

'Got a job for you when we go to Kenya.'

'Oh, yes, sir. What would that be?' She sounded wary.

'There's going to be a reporter from the media covering the exercise. The CO and I would like you to escort him around, make sure he doesn't get in the way or annoy anyone, that sort of thing. You'll have a vehicle and a driver so all you'll have to do is keep this guy from sticking his nose in where we don't want it or getting himself into danger. You can do that, can't you?'

He saw Cooper swallow as she digested the task she'd been given. Then she nodded. 'OK, sir. How long is this guy going to be with us for?'

'The duration, as far as we know. The MOD will be sending us more details in due course.'

'That's fine, sir.'

'So, you're relatively happy about this?'

Cooper shrugged. 'Can't see there's anything to be unhappy about, sir. I mean, I've got no choice about going so I suppose it'll be better to be out and about with this reporter bloke than stuck in the comms tent, watchkeeping on the graveyard shift.'

'Indeed. Think of it as your very own personal safari.' But even as he said it Andy didn't think Cooper looked the intrepid traveller sort. He reckoned her idea of exotic would be a fortnight at Sharm el-Sheikh.

*

Sam was beavering away again on her dreary reports, head down, concentrating hard in order to banish some very un-Christian thoughts about her ASM, when she was interrupted by someone knocking on her door.

'Yes,' she called grumpily, not looking up.

'Sorry, you're busy. I'll come back later.'

Sam put down her pen and smiled. 'James, I'm sorry. What can I do for you?'

'Nothing really.' He shut the door. 'I was passing and thought I'd pop in a see if I could cadge a cuppa.'

'Of course.' She got up and went to the counter where the kettle lived.

'You look pissed off,' said James.

'Sorry, I am a bit. Not with you, though,' she added quickly.

'Let me guess.'

Sam gave him a rueful smile as she filled the kettle. 'Mr Williams has struck again.'

'What's he done now?'

'Something pathetically trivial, only it's got on my tits.'

'I wish you wouldn't use that phrase,' said James.

'Sorry.' Sam dropped two tea bags into two mugs.

'So, what did he do?'

Sam told James. 'And I stood up to him. He's not happy.'

'Well done, you.'

'Don't you start patronising me.'

'I wasn't, I mean it. The more you don't take any stick from him the less he'll try it on.'

'All I've got to do now is to get Blake to cheer up and stop looking like he's some sort of volcano on the brink of exploding and everything here will be fine.'

'You think Blake is about to go off on one? Have some sort of episode?' James sounded genuinely worried.

'God, no, nothing as dramatic as that.' Sam finished making

the tea and passed James his mug. 'No, he just sort of smoulders, casts a bit of a cloud around him.' Sam didn't tell James he always seemed perfectly happy in the company of others, in case it made her look either paranoid or a bit needy. After all, she was Blake's boss, not his friend, and he didn't have to look cheerful in her company.

'Then ignore him. If he wants to be a wet blanket and a miserable git as well, let him. Now then, I have another reason for my visit – other than blagging tea. Given what you've told me about your dad and knowing how you tend to stay in the mess because you don't have bolt-holes to disappear to at weekends, what are you doing about Christmas leave?'

'Ah.'

'Ah?'

'I'm going to my grandparents with Michelle for Christmas itself.'

'Michelle? The one you told me has boyfriend trouble? Doesn't sound like fun.'

Sam nodded. 'It'll be fine. She's still my best friend. We go way back.'

'And New Year?'

Sam shrugged. 'Nothing really. I'll probably come back here and watch the fireworks on the telly. Get a pizza in, a bottle of wine, live the high life.'

'Or you could come over to my folks' for a few days and on New Year's Eve we could jump on a train to London and watch them live.'

For a second Sam wondered if James had tapped her phone or was clairvoyant or something. How did he know that's what she'd told Michelle? She stared at him, bewildered.

'Sorry, you think it's a crap idea,' said James. 'And I'm not, honestly, doing a clandestine meet-the-parents-thing. It's just a suggestion. I mean, I like you but we're not dating or anything;

we're just friends. And they have a big house and several spare rooms and if I've got a mate staying I've got an excuse to go out and...' He tailed off. 'Well, the offer is there.'

'No, no it's fab. I'd love to.'

'Really?'

Sam nodded. 'Really.'

Michelle also had a pile of reports in front of her to complete. Her recruits were nearing the end of their training course and what she wrote about them could have serious implications on their first few years as serving soldiers. The reports were important – not to say urgent – but Michelle was staring at them blankly. Instead all her thoughts were directed to her meeting with Seb the previous Friday.

What had she done wrong? she wondered. Why had Seb, or Bas, or whatever his blasted name was, dumped her? Why her? Why not that dull mouse that he was married to? What the fuck had Maddy got that she didn't have? Could she have engineered the situation to get a different outcome? Could she get him back? And it was that last question that really exercised her mind. Surely there had to be a way. The trouble was, now Sam knew exactly what was going on, there was no way she was going to get an invitation to the barracks at Warminster.

Still, on the positive side, she knew where Seb and his family lived. Once again, she clicked on Google Earth and zoomed in on his quarter.

On the first morning of block leave and twelve hours after most soldiers had already charged off out of the barracks, Immi thumped her case down the stairs of her accommodation block and then dragged it down the road towards the bus stop on the other side of the security barrier. She had just passed the guardroom when a navy-blue Ford pulled up beside her.

'Want a lift?'

Immi bent down to see who was offering and when she saw, her heart gave a little skip of delight. 'Luke! I'd love one but only if I'm not taking you out of your way.'

'Where you headed?'

'Station.'

'Hop in, then.' Luke jumped out and popped the boot. 'Give me that,' he said, and with a deft heave he picked up Immi's case and stowed it away, next to his holdall.

'This is kind of you,' said Immi as she slid into the passenger seat. 'Nice motor.'

'Thanks.' Luke put the car in gear and pulled away. 'Going home?'

'Yeah. I thought about taking off yesterday straight after work but it would have been a push to get the last train... Anyway, you don't need to know about my travel arrangements. So, where are you off to? You going home too?'

'No,' said Luke shortly.

'Aren't you seeing your folks over Christmas?' probed Immi, innocently, trying to elicit any scrap of information that might help her work out what made Luke tick.

'Not if I can possibly help it.'

That's me told, thought Immi. She dropped that line of enquiry. 'So where you going?'

'Skiing.'

'That's very glamorous. Where are you doing that, then?'

'Austria.'

'Nice. I've always fancied skiing, me. Never had the bottle to learn.'

'I don't remember learning,' said Luke. 'I started when I was three.'

'So did your parents teach you?'

'My parents,' Luke spat out the word, 'dumped me in ski

194

school and ignored me. A succession of ski instructors got the job.'

'So you don't get on with them – your parents, not your ski instructors, I mean.'

'Isn't it obvious?' Luke gave her such a withering look that anyone less tough than Immi would have shrivelled.

'So what happened?'

'Shit happened,' said Luke.

And even Immi realised that she'd pushed him far enough. She changed the subject. 'You know that exercise…?'

'I'm assuming you're referring to Askari Thunder.'

'Well, yeah. There ain't any others happening this side of summer leave, are there?'

Luke rolled his eyes.

'Anyway,' said Immi, 'it looks like I'm going to be having a better time than I first thought.'

'So you're definitely going? You're not throwing a sickie?'

'Not now. There was me thinking I'd be stuck in some tent or armoured vehicle, sweating like a pig 'cos there's no air-con or nothing, and having to log-keep or act as a runner or something, but now it turns out I'm going to be the personal escort to some Fleet Street type.'

'Oh? Who?'

'I don't know.' Suddenly Immi felt a bit foolish that she hadn't asked his name. Not, though, she reasoned, that she'd know it. When was the last time she'd picked up a daily?

'You'd best hope you're not in charge of someone who wants to dig the dirt about the army; find soldiers who are racist or anti-human rights or who want to bleat about being bullied. If that's what they want in the way of a story, and you let them find it, I wouldn't want to be in your shoes.'

'There's reporters like that?' Immi was genuinely stunned. Everyone liked the army these days, didn't they? Wasn't it all 'our boys' and 'Help for Heroes' and welcome-home parades and everything?

'I think so,' said Luke. 'There's people out there dead against the army and everything it stands for. I'm not saying this reporter'll be like that but you need to be aware.'

They drove the remainder of the way to the station in silence. Immi was wrapped up in thoughts about the way things had suddenly shifted; her role had gone from being some sort of Girl Friday to a rather glamorous media type to some sleazy hack's patsy. So her view of exercise Askari Thunder was back to where it had been before: six weeks of heat, hard work, vile conditions and dodgy critters, only now she was also responsible for some guy who might be out to have a swipe at the army and who could ruin her career if he did. Well, thanks very much.

Luke pulled up in the drop-off point and got Immi's suitcase out.

'Thanks for the lift, Luke. Hope you have a blinding holiday. You'll come back from all that snow and we'll all be straight off to Africa.' And then my career might be straight down the tubes, she thought disconsolately. But she wasn't going to show Luke how rattled she was by what he'd said, so she tossed her blonde hair over her shoulder and leaned in to give Luke a kiss on the cheek before he could dodge out the way. 'See you in a few weeks,' she said as she grabbed her case and began to tow it away.

Chapter Eighteen

'I think,' said Maddy to Nathan as she surveyed the piles of clothes and presents stacked neatly in the two suitcases on the spare room bed, 'that is everything.' Nathan struggled in her arms and reached out to try and grab the bright, shiny wrapping paper on the presents. 'Sorry, hon,' said Maddy, plonking a kiss on the top of his head, 'you'll have to wait a few more days till you can open that little lot.' She glanced at her watch. 'Hurry up, Seb,' she muttered. He'd dashed into town that morning first thing and still wasn't back.

'Why?' Maddy had asked.

'Surprise,' had been the answer. Which meant she could hardly pry, although he'd promised to be back in good time for them to drive up to her parents' house for lunch. She glanced at her watch again. They'd still be in plenty of time if they set off shortly, but they had to load the car and Nate was bound to need a last-minute nappy change... Oh, where was he? Surprise or no, the clock was ticking and if he wasn't back soon they'd be late and her mother wouldn't like that.

Maddy sighed and tried to establish a feeling of calm and acceptance. She told herself that a couple of weeks ago she might have thought Seb was being deliberately selfish and thoughtless; that was a time when everything seemed to come a pretty poor second to his rowing and what he wanted. But since he'd announced he was sacking his involvement with army rowing he'd been the perfect family man, so much so that Maddy had even mentioned this transformation to Susie.

She had guffawed and said, 'Sounds like a nasty case of having a guilty conscience.'

Maddy had been horrified. 'Guilty conscience? About what?'

'About abandoning you almost every weekend for months, sweetie. Maybe someone pointed out to him that you have been a complete saint, coping with being pregnant and a toddler and the move and the house while he swanned off and enjoyed himself.'

'I think the rowing is pretty hard work,' said Maddy staunchly, but Susie had raised her eyebrows in an if-that's-what-you-want-to-believe sort of way.

Maddy carried Nathan downstairs and plopped him in his playpen along with a selection of toys, and then went back up to the bedroom and loaded the presents into a carrier bag, which she carted back down the stairs and put by the front door. She was thinking of bringing the cases down as well to reduce the time needed to load the car to a minimum when she heard Seb's key in the door.

'At last,' she muttered. 'Hi, hon,' she said as she greeted him.

Seb saw the overflowing carrier bag.

'Hey, I'd have brought that down.'

Maddy shrugged. 'I've done it now.'

'I hope you weren't considering bring down the cases?'

'Of course not.'

'Good. You're far too precious to risk pulling a stupid stunt like that. So, if you and Nathan are ready, I'll load up the car and we can go.'

'Wonderful.'

Maddy fetched Nathan and got him strapped into his car seat while Seb wrestled their luggage and all the presents into the boot, along with the travel cot and the pushchair and all of Nathan's other paraphernalia.

'Have we got everything?' asked Maddy anxiously.

'If we haven't, we'll have to cope without,' said Seb, mopping his brow and slamming shut the boot.

'You're right,' said Maddy. 'Let's go.'

She was really looking forward to this break and Christmas with her parents. And it was going to be especially nice since Seb had turned over a new leaf and was suddenly so hands-on with Nathan. He'd even been changing the occasional nappy! Over and above all the lovely things that went with Christmas Maddy was looking forward to being spoilt rotten by her mum. Even if the sickness had finally and thankfully stopped, she still suffered from heartburn, swollen ankles, backache and everything else that nature had decided to throw at her. The plan was that she would stay up in Herefordshire after the holiday was over, while Seb returned to the barracks to fly out with the advance party to Kenya. He was going to stay till New Year's Day and then go back to the quarter, collect his kit and report to Brize for his flight shortly after that.

Sam turned her car off the M5 and headed towards Exeter St Davids. Michelle had decided to come to Devon by train and Sam had promised to meet her and then drive her to her grand-parents'. She checked her ETA on the sat nav and was glad to see she was going to get in a good ten minutes ahead of Michelle. Perfect.

No, it wasn't perfect. It was going to be anything but because, at the risk of being disloyal to her best friend, what was there left to say about Seb? Five days of picking over the wreckage of the relationship. Sam wondered if she was going to be able to bite her tongue and not tell Michelle that she was being driven mad by her relentless, dreary analysis. And if she couldn't and she said the wrong thing, Sam reckoned her friendship with Michelle would come to an abrupt and messy end.

Sam pulled her car into the short-stay car park and headed for the concourse. She heard Michelle's yell over the sound of a departing train. She looked towards the shriek and there she was, still ten yards from the barrier, hurtling down the platform, her suitcase bouncing crazily on its wheels as she towed it along at breakneck speed. Except, although Michelle was obviously pleased to see her, even at this distance Sam could spot the dark shadows under her eyes and the obvious weight loss. God, and she'd only seen her a fortnight ago. Had she eaten anything during the intervening days?

'Sam! Coo-ee!'

Sam waved back and then Michelle was through the barrier and clasping her friend around the middle and trying to squeeze the life out of her.

'Hello, sweetie. Thank you for coming to meet me. So kind of you.'

Sam managed to disengage herself from the bear hug. 'And if I hadn't, how would you have got to Gran and Grandpa's?'

'I could have easily got a cab.'

Which was true, but it would have cost squillions. 'I wanted to.' Even if she wasn't looking forward to the inevitable and probably sole topic of conversation she was very fond of Michelle and it was nice to see her again. She grabbed the case. 'Let's go for a drink before we head for mine, and I inflict my grandparents on you.'

'Your grandparents are lovely, and you know it,' said Michelle as she followed Sam to her car. Sam shoved Michelle's case into the boot and then drove to a pub on the outskirts of the city and swung the car into the car park.

'You've lost weight,' she commented as she pulled on the handbrake.

Michelle turned in her seat. 'Trust me, having a broken heart is the best diet in the world.'

Sam kept schtum. She wanted to tell Michelle that Seb really wasn't worth losing sleep over, that he was a lying, cheating bastard and Michelle was well out of it, but she knew that nothing she could say would help. Michelle had to work things out for herself and that would take time. She wished she understood why Michelle still obsessed about him but, then, she reasoned, no one knew what made one person fall in love with another. It was one of life's great mysteries.

They entered the bar and she ordered a large glass of red for Michelle and a J2O for herself before they headed for an empty table. Sam took a slurp of her drink. 'Well, here's to the holidays,' she said, and raised her glass.

'I suppose,' said Michelle morosely. 'I suppose he's going to have one that's all lovey-dovey and presents under the tree, and what have I got to look forward to?'

'The same,' said Sam, briskly. 'Gran does a wonderful Christmas and you know it. It'll be lovely, you'll see.'

'But it won't, will it? The one thing I really, really want, I can't have.' She gazed at Sam over the rim of her glass, her eyes glistening suspiciously.

'Oh, hon.' Sam reached across the table and took Michelle's hand.

'And don't tell me that I'll get over it.'

But one day you will, said Sam, in her head. 'I wouldn't dream of it,' she said out loud.

'I wake up every morning and he's the first thing I think about. It's like déjà vu all over again.'

'I'm sure it is,' said Sam, knowing exactly how Michelle felt. She felt the same way every time she saw Michelle's caller ID on her mobile and guessed accurately how the ensuing call would go.

'And if he knew how much I love him, how much I'm hurting, I'm sure things would be different.'

Sam had to head Michelle off from thinking it would be a good idea to tell Seb this. The phrase *restraining order* kept popping into her head. 'Are you sure, honey? He's got an awful lot to lose.'

Michelle's eyes blazed. 'Of course I'm sure.'

Oops.

'I have to see him and tell him.'

Jesus, no! 'Are you sure this is a good idea?' And, God, how often had she said that to Michelle in the past?

'I thought you were my friend.'

'I am. And that is exactly why I am asking you to reconsider.'

Michelle took a glug of her wine and stared at Sam defiantly.

'Look,' said Sam, 'remember when we were at St Martin's and I suggested that swapping salt for sugar on the staffroom tea trolley wasn't going to go down well?'

Michelle nodded.

'And the whole year got detention as a result...?'

Michelle nodded again. 'But it was funny, though.'

'It was funny till everyone got punished. I don't think some of the girls thought it was so funny then when we missed a trip to the beach. And remember when you loosened the girth on Ella Somerfeld's pony and she broke her collar bone?'

'She should have checked it.'

Sam stared at Michelle. 'She did. You loosened it afterwards.'

Michelle shrugged. 'She had it coming, she was such a smug pain in the arse, always showing off how good a rider she was.'

Michelle did have a point... 'Yes, she was but she didn't deserve a broken collar bone for being smug or a pain or showing off.'

'Anyway, no one knew it was me… well, apart from you.'

Sam sighed. This wasn't going well. 'And when we were at Sandhurst I told you not to sew those magnets into Captain Baker's combat jacket so her compass gave the wrong reading and her map-reading lesson went to shit.'

'Now, that was funny,' said Michelle.

'It was… right up to the point when the platoon was punished with stand-to-bed at five o'clock in the morning for a whole month.'

'It was worth it.'

Sam disagreed but loyalty meant she didn't say so. 'Look,' she said, gently, 'sometimes you do things which end up causing trouble, trouble which you didn't really mean to happen.'

'I suppose,' said Michelle. 'But I can't roll over and give up.'

'Can't you?'

Michelle shook her head and eyed Sam sadly. 'No, not with Seb. I know he should belong to me. Honestly, I'll be doing Maddy a favour.'

Sam had a sinking feeling that this was going to wind up even worse than she'd imagined.

They got back to Sam's grandparents' picture-postcard thatched cottage in the heart of a picture-postcard village at around tea-time. Gran welcomed Michelle as if she were a returning prodigal daughter and swept her across the tiny hall and up the ancient, uneven polished wooden stairs to the guest room, pointing out, en route, the bathroom and Sam's room.

'But you remember this from your last visit,' she said.

'It was years ago,' said Michelle. 'It's a bit hazy, if I'm honest.'

Gran opened the door to a whitewashed bedroom, with exposed beams and a tiny window in the eaves which peeped out through the thatch, over the garden.

'Now I remember,' said Michelle as she plonked her case onto a chair by the bed. 'This is lovely. Thank you.'

'There's scones and clotted cream downstairs. Come down as soon as you're ready. And I can't believe,' continued Gran, 'how long it is since you were last here.'

'Well, after Sam and I changed schools we kind of lost touch.' Michelle saw Sam emerging from her room across the landing. 'We did, didn't we?'

'What?' said Sam, leaning against the doorjamb.

'Lost touch.'

'Mmm,' said Sam noncommittally. She knew she should have kept in contact with Michelle but she hadn't. And deep down she knew it was because of the scrapes Michelle had got her into at their prep school, and as soon as she'd been freed from Michelle's friendship, Sam had turned over a clean sheet and didn't want this new page of her life covered in horrible blots. Maybe she'd been unfair but she'd sailed through her public school without a single black mark or detention – unlike the previous years she'd spent in Michelle's company. QED, she thought.

'Well, that's all right. Now leave your unpacking and come and tell Arthur and I all about what you're up to these days. I'll get the kettle on.'

A while later the two girls clattered down the stairs to the cosy sitting room, with its chintz soft furnishings, a fat Christmas tree in one corner, laden with baubles, Grandpa reading his paper in another, the woodburner in the huge fireplace belting out the heat and a trolley in the middle of the room groaning with tea – scones, jam, cream and a lemon drizzle cake.

'And I expect you girls to tuck in.' Gran looked at Michelle. 'You especially. You look as if you haven't had a square meal in a month of Sundays.' She tutted, then bustled out into the kitchen from whence came the sound of a kettle being filled.

From his corner Sam's grandpa gazed at them over his copy of the *Western Morning News*.

'Good afternoon, Michelle,' he said. 'You've grown.'

'Hello,' said Michelle. 'You're looking well.' She went over to his corner and gave him a peck on his cheek.

'Huh,' he said, and returned to his paper. Sam winked at Michelle. Grandpa had never been garrulous.

Gran bustled in with the teapot. 'There,' she said as she put it on the trolley and then sat in her customary chair, 'isn't this nice?'

And, yes, it is, thought Sam. And while we're all here, together in this room, I'm spared talk of Seb. She wondered how long she could spin out tea for.

'Honestly,' Sam said quietly into her phone to James later that night when everyone had gone to bed, 'if I hear any more about Michelle's ex I may well hit her over the head with a blunt instrument.' She'd pulled the duvet over her head in the hope it would prevent anyone from eavesdropping, although, given the solid nature of the little cottage, she reckoned it was unlikely.

'And that would stop her?' said James.

'No, you're probably right.'

'So have you met this bloke?'

'No,' lied Sam.

'Were they engaged? Did she get jilted at the altar? She seems to be really taking this guy's departure to heart. I mean... why?'

'No they weren't engaged or anything like that. And I don't know why she's got such a thing about him.' Suddenly a memory of something Michelle had said to her about Seb popped into her brain. 'Although...' She giggled.

'Yes,' said James.

'Apparently he's incredibly... well, according to Michelle he's... you know... um... quite... um...'

'Hung like a donkey?'

Sam had to stuff her fist in her mouth to stop laughter exploding. 'Yes,' she finally squeaked through unreleased giggles. She took a deep breath and managed to get some sort of self-control. 'I was trying to be polite, and decorous and lady-like,' she said.

'You? That'd be a first.'

'Yeah, well... moving on. Anyway, I shall leave here on the thirtieth, and I should be at your parents' around tea-time. But I shall need the postcode for the sat nav.'

'That sounds perfect. I'll see you then.'

She put her phone on her bedside table and switched her light off and thanked goodness for friends like James. Nice predictable friends with no agendas or hang-ups. She sighed as she thought about the car crash that was Michelle's current love life. She wished Michelle would be more rational about Seb. Surely she had to get over him soon, she thought as she drifted off to sleep.

Michelle kicked around her room in the mess, bored out of her mind, fed up and disconsolate. Technically she oughtn't to be there as the mess was officially closed, but she'd nowhere else to go. She'd been so sure that Seb would choose her over Maddy she had made no arrangements for the holidays apart from spending a few days over Christmas with Sam. Spending New Year with her father and step-mother wasn't an option so now she had no choice but to camp in the deserted mess. With no staff around and the kitchens locked, she was reduced to making do with the toaster and the microwave in the stewards' pantry, so, when she bothered to eat, she was living off baked beans and toast. Not that she cared because her mind was preoccupied in equal parts with jealousy of Maddy and longing for Seb. Why didn't he leave the bitch? What had Maddy got that she hadn't? What was he doing? Did he miss her? How had they spent Christmas?

Her own Christmas had been, as Sam had predicted, perfectly nice. How could she not have enjoyed Sam's gran's cooking and the walks she and Sam had taken over Dartmoor? And it had been wonderful to unload her feelings onto someone who understood. Although, in retrospect, she'd felt a bit hurt a couple of times when Sam had tried to change the subject to her excitement about Kenya: really, why would anyone want to talk about some country they knew nothing about and a stupid exercise that hadn't even taken place yet?

But despite all the nice things about Christmas, ultimately it had been rubbish because the one thing she'd really, really wanted – a text from Seb – hadn't materialised. Even though she'd sent several messages to him, there had been no reply. She recalled the conversation when she'd told Sam, as they were going to bed at the end of Christmas Day.

'Of course there wasn't. And there won't be,' Sam had said. 'Listen, Michelle, it's over. You have to accept that. And you have to stop texting Seb. You're deluded if you think he's going to text you back. He's a married man with a wife and a kid – kids plural, soon – and he's not going to jeopardise all that with a fling.'

'It wasn't a fling.'

'Look, Michelle, before you fell for Seb you'd have never contemplated having an affair with a married man. You might have your faults, but you're not a marriage wrecker. And if you'd known from the start that Seb was married you wouldn't have got involved, full stop. Seb led you on, Seb is at fault, and you've got to accept that he's a fully fledged, card-carrying git.'

'Then Maddy should know. I should tell her.'

'No, leave it all alone and move on. And Maddy doesn't need you to tell her what her husband is like. Seriously, she doesn't.'

Michelle might have *pretended* to agree with Sam, but what did her friend know? What did Sam know about her and Seb and their feelings for each other? Nothing, that's what. No, she wasn't going to listen to Sam, no way.

If only she had a phone number for Maddy. But she knew where she lived, so that was something. And hadn't Sam told her that the advance party, which included Seb, was due off to Kenya right at the start of the New Year, leaving Maddy on her own.

Michelle thought she might spend the evening watching the New Year's Eve fireworks on the telly and then, the next day, head down to Warminster and create some of her own there.

Chapter Nineteen

'So this is the family estate,' said James as he greeted Sam after she pulled her car into the drive in front of a stockbroker-belt, half-timbered semi on the outskirts of Guildford. 'Please note the landscaped gardens, the work of Capability Rosser, the stunning portico and original Elizabethan beams – that's Elizabeth Windsor, not Tudor.'

Sam grinned. 'Blenheim Palace had better watch out,' she said. 'I'm surprised the National Trust hasn't made a bid for it.'

'OK, I exaggerate.' James gave her a quick kiss on the cheek. 'But it's home.'

Sam thought it looked like a happy house.

'Come on,' said James. 'We'll leave the bags. I'll drag them in for you later. Come and meet Ma and Dad.'

Sam got out of the car and followed James across the wide gravel drive. The door stood wide and framed in it was a man who Sam could only suppose was James's dad.

'You must be Sam,' he boomed. 'Welcome.'

'Sam, this is my father.'

'Lovely to meet you, Sam, and call me Duncan. Come in, come in. You don't want to be hanging about in this weather.'

No, she didn't. It was already spitting with light rain and the sky threatened worse to come.

As she stepped over the threshold a hand descended on her shoulder and gave it a friendly squeeze. 'I'm so glad you agreed to come over. James says you've got a lively sense of humour and the old fogies who live here could do with livening up. I look forward to being kept in stitches while you're here.'

Sam was a bit worried about poor Mrs Rosser being classed as an old fogie but she was more concerned about her apparent billing as the comedy turn, so she just smiled a little, nervously.

'I said nothing of the sort, Dad, and you know it,' said James. 'You'll frighten Sam off before she's even got her coat off.'

'Just living in hope, my boy, living in hope. I like a good laugh now and again.' He winked at Sam.

Sam grinned back. James's dad was obviously bonkers, but nice bonkers. She thought the next few days were probably going to be quite fun.

'It was lovely of you to invite me,' she said to Duncan.

'Nothing to do with me,' he said. 'All James's idea.'

'Even so,' she said firmly. As she spoke she took in the hallway; there seemed to be bookcases everywhere and it smelt of furniture polish with a hint of toast. In fact, it smelt like a home ought to, thought Sam. None of that fake air-freshener pong that so many houses seemed to smell of, and it was full of clutter and dust-traps and pictures and knick-knacks. Yes, it was full of all the things her father's various quarters had been completely devoid of. Yes, a happy home, a lived-in home.

'Now,' said Duncan as he glanced at his watch, 'I don't reckon it's too early to open the bar, do you? Sun's over the yardarm and all that.'

'But it's only five,' said James in protest.

'Somewhere it's gone six,' said Duncan with a twinkle. 'What's your poison, young lady?'

'I'd love a G and T,' said Sam.

'Mother's ruin! Excellent choice. I'm assuming you're on the beer, James.'

James nodded. 'We'll go and find Ma while you get the drinks, shall we?'

He pushed open a door at the end of the hall which led into a den with an Aga at one end, a couple of beaten-up armchairs, one occupied by a black Labrador with a grey muzzle and which thumped its tail when it saw James. James patted it as he went past.

'Hello, Buster, old boy. He's very ancient,' explained James. 'He doesn't do much more than totter down the garden and back these days. It's hard to think that he used to come with me on five-mile runs until only a few years ago. Now, some mornings, he has to be helped off this chair.'

Sam felt sympathy for the ancient dog's current plight, but it had obviously had a long and happy life.

'Anyway, let's find Ma.' James opened another door and there was the kitchen and the most wonderful smell of baking. Standing by the counter, with a tray of freshly baked biscuits beside her, was a woman who reminded Sam of Mrs Tiggywinkle: short, stout, with boot-button eyes and a large white apron tied firmly around where her waist ought to be. She smiled when she saw her son and her cheeks dimpled.

James bent down and kissed his mother's rosy cheek. 'Hi, Ma. Here's Sam.'

'Sam. How lovely, and welcome. I am so pleased to meet you at long last. I'm sure we're going to get on.'

'It's lovely to meet you too,' said Sam.

'Now, I hope you've got a good appetite, because it's so nice to have more than two people to cook for and I might have overdone things a bit.'

'I'm sure you haven't,' said Sam. 'And I love home cooking. The food in the mess is grand, of course it is, but nothing, nothing, beats home cooking.' She didn't mention that after being fed like a goose destined to produce foie gras by her gran she'd resolved to go on a diet. Oh well, a diet could start in the New Year.

'We,' said James's ma, firmly, 'are going to get along fine. I can tell. And I'm Betty, by the way, as James couldn't be bothered to do proper introductions.'

The kitchen door opened and in came Duncan, carrying a tray laden with drinks. He handed them round.

'Cheers,' he said.

'Cheers,' replied everyone.

Sam sipped her drink and felt her eyes goggle. Where the hell was the T in this G and T?

The two men went off to the sitting room, leaving Sam in the kitchen. Sam had a sneaking feeling that they both thought that was where she'd prefer to be, except it wasn't her natural environment at all. After a bit, her lack of domesticity became apparent to Betty and she gently suggested that maybe she'd like to sit in the den and enjoy her drink with the day's paper.

'And it'll let James and his dad do a bit of bonding, get it out of their system for the duration and then they won't talk boring old shop for the rest of your stay.'

Sam was happy to take Betty's advice, the *Telegraph* and her drink and a few seconds later she was sitting in the den with Buster.

She'd started to read the paper, and was turning to the inside pages when she heard Duncan and James's voices drifting across the hall from the sitting room.

'So... Sam,' said Duncan. 'You and she...?'

'Dad, if I've told you once I've told you a dozen times, we're just friends.'

'Oh.' Even at this distance Sam could hear the disappointment in Duncan's voice.

'Sorry, but that's how it is.'

'I don't know, son, isn't it about time you thought about

having a nice girlfriend? From what I hear, the army's much better these days about keeping families together.'

'But I don't want a family yet. Apart from this one, that is. It's early days and I really want to concentrate on my career.'

'Your mum'd love grandchildren.'

'Dad! I'm not going to rush things just for Mum.'

James doesn't sound keen, thought Sam, but then the kitchen door opened and out bustled Betty, bearing a tray of nibbles and wanting a refill and by the time the men had got back to the conversation the subject had changed to defence cuts.

As Sam went to bed, in a rather more tiddly state than she'd anticipated, she was fuzzily pleased that she and James were just good friends. She loved their uncomplicated relationship. It was, she thought, how it might have been if her twin had survived; having a man to look out for her, squire her around but wanting nothing more than companionship in return. She hoped the status quo remained. As she got undressed she realised that there was another positive to staying friends with James; she could pretend Betty was her mother. She wondered if her mother had been as good a home-maker as lovely Betty. She hoped so.

On the first day of January, Susie Collins decided she could slob for a bit with a book and a cuppa and not feel guilty, as Mike and the girls had gone out for walk. After all, she deserved it – she'd changed the beds, done the laundry and the ironing and produced a roast lunch. It was definitely time to relax. As she filled the kettle she looked out of the window.

Across the road there was a car parked. Nothing unusual in that except it was outside the Fanshaws' house and they were still away. She peered at it, through the geraniums over-wintering on the windowsill. There was someone in it. Odd. Why would someone loiter outside an empty house in the middle of winter?

Like most people connected to the armed forces, Susie was slightly wary of strangers hanging around. The days of random, drive-by shootings or terrorist bombings in the married patches were, thankfully, long gone but there were still plenty of extremists who didn't much like the military. The Woolwich murder had borne horrific witness to that fact.

She stared at the car for a few seconds with narrowed eyes as she considered the situation and then made a decision. She dried her hands on a tea-towel, headed out of the front door and crossed the street. She rapped on the driver's window. The window was wound down and Susie saw a face she recognised but couldn't instantly place. Then it clicked: it was that rather sulky friend of Sam's who had been at Maddy's lunch party and was called... Michelle? Yes, that was it, Michelle. Except she looked shocking – ill almost.

'Oh, hi,' said Michelle.

'Hi. Forgive me for being nosy, but were you expecting to see Maddy?'

'I... Yes.'

'But she's away. Seb too.'

'Away?'

'She and Seb are staying with her parents over the leave period. Maddy's going to stay on with them when Seb goes off on that exercise in Kenya with the rest of the battalion. He'll be coming home for a few days to get his kit ready before leaving with the advance party but I'm not expecting Maddy back till February, when Seb's due back from Africa.'

'Oh.' Michelle looked completely downcast.

'Looks like you've come here on a wild goose chase.' Susie felt herself soften slightly; the girl did look terrible. 'I've got the kettle on. Before you go, would you like a cup of tea – or a coffee?'

Michelle stared at the steering-wheel, seeming to consider

this offer, then finally she said, 'That's kind. Yes, wasted journey.'

Susie wondered if she was going to cry. There really was something very odd about this woman but if she was a friend of Sam's... well, the least she could do was play the good Samaritan. She waited for Michelle to get out of her car and lock it up before she led her back into her quarter.

'So, you didn't know Maddy planned to be away?' said Susie. 'Tea or coffee?'

'Oh, coffee, please.'

Susie spooned granules into a mug before flicking the switch on the kettle to bring it back to the boil.

'No... I never thought,' said Michelle. She sounded dull and utterly listless. 'Stupid of me.'

'Oh dear. You should have phoned her.'

'I don't have a number,' said Michelle.

Susie made the coffee and handed her a mug. 'Milk? Sugar?'

'Just milk, please.'

Susie gave her the jug. Not, she thought, that Michelle looked like she needed caffeine. She looked so taut and tense she could probably vibrate like a violin string. 'I've already told you I'm nosy.' She gave Michelle what she hoped was a disarming smile. 'But is something the matter?'

'No!' Michelle's voice was a little strident, a little too emphatic. 'No, nothing's the matter. I wanted to see Maddy, that's all.'

Susie felt she really couldn't pry further, although she longed to know why Michelle needed to see her neighbour. 'Can I help? Pass on a message?'

Michelle shook her head and then sipped her drink.

Susie got a tin of biscuits down from a shelf. 'Let's go into the sitting room and sit down.'

Wordlessly, Michelle followed her.

'There, this is more comfortable, isn't it?' said Susie brightly. For a second she almost wished she was back on the booze again. A stiff drink might help both of them and even if Michelle didn't want one, for the first time in an age Susie felt a real craving.

'Do you have a number for Maddy?' asked Michelle suddenly.

'I do, as it happens.' Susie got up and went to the kitchen to fetch the babysitting circle contact list. 'Here.' She handed it to Michelle. For a second she wondered about the wisdom of doing this but hell, Maddy had invited this woman into her home, they had mutual friends and she was a serving officer too, for heaven's sake. She was hardly some random off the street.

Michelle fished her phone out of a pocket and began to programme the number into it. Susie noticed her hand was shaking. Again she wanted to ask if she was all right but she couldn't keep asking the poor girl questions. It was already a bit like the Spanish Inquisition.

'Thank you,' said Michelle as she handed the sheet of names and numbers back.

'So...' said Susie, once again, 'you're not involved in the high jinks in Africa?'

'No, no, nothing like that.' Michelle took another slug of her coffee, draining her cup. An awkward silence descended. Then she dumped her mug hard on the table and stood up. 'I mustn't hold you up, I expect you're busy. Thanks for the coffee. I must be going.'

Susie thought she looked quite manic and wondered if she ought to try once again to get Michelle to open up. It was obvious that something was bothering the girl. Susie toyed for a second about offering her a shoulder to cry on, because she really looked as if she had something serious on her mind, then dismissed the thought. It wasn't her responsibility to offer counselling or advice.

'I hope you manage to get hold of Maddy. Send her my love when you do.'

'Yeah, of course.' But it was said so grumpily Susie very much doubted that the message was going to get passed on.

Curiouser and curiouser.

Michelle drove away from the married patch and headed back towards Surrey and her unit. She'd gone about ten miles or so when she spotted a lay-by at the side of the road and pulled her car into it. What a nightmare that trip had been – and a waste of time. And that bloody Susie woman prying like that. But, on the other hand, she'd got a number for Maddy so it wasn't a complete cluster-fuck. Michelle pulled her phone from her bag, stared at it, then made her mind up.

He doesnt love you he loves me.

She hit send. That'll tell her. Maddy needed to know the truth about the situation. It was only fair after all. Seb obviously wasn't going to man up and sort things out, so it was up to her.

Maddy was in her mum's kitchen, grilling a couple of fish fingers for Nate's tea, when her phone pinged. Eagerly she grabbed it. Could this be a text from Seb to say he'd made it safely back to their quarter? She looked at the display in disappointment. Pah – a mobile number, not a name. Obviously this was some spammer, not a call from Seb or even a mate. Out of vague curiosity she opened the text to see if she was being offered free laser eye surgery on her already perfect, twenty-twenty vision, or a chance to claim against some missold insurance she'd never bought, or maybe she'd got whiplash from a car accident she hadn't had. Who knew?

He doesnt love you he loves me.

For a second her blood ceased to flow though her veins and then reason kicked in. A text had been sent to a wrong number; this was two teenagers having a spat over a boy and one of them had pressed a wrong digit and the message had winged its way to her phone by accident. But even as she tapped the delete key and the message was wiped, another thought struck her... All teenagers – in fact, most people – had almost everyone they knew on their phone's system. If you wanted to send a message you didn't key in a number, you pressed the button against a name. But it was too late now to retrieve the details, she'd deleted the message and, anyway, Nate's fish fingers were ready and she really didn't have the time or the inclination to mess about with silly texts which had nothing to do with her.

Susie was getting ready for bed later that night when she saw a light on in the Fanshaws' house.

'Mike,' she said as she drew the curtains, 'I thought the Fanshaws were still away.'

Mike, cleaning his teeth in the basin in the bedroom turned around. 'No,' he said dibbling toothpaste foam down his chin, 'Seb's due back any day now.' He turned back and rinsed and spat then dabbed his chin on a towel. 'The advance party is due to fly out this week.'

'Oh, I wish I'd known.'

'Why?' Mike pulled back his side of the duvet and hopped into bed.

'He and Maddy had a visitor today. I gave the girl duff information – well, not really duff, but I didn't know Seb was going to be back today. Maybe she could have waited and seen him.'

Mike shrugged. 'Not your fault. Who was it?'

'That friend of Sam Lewis's.'

Mike shook his head, bemused. 'Who?'

'That girl who came with Sam to the Fanshaws' lunch party.'

'Oh her. Christ, she was a sour-faced piece of work.'

'She wasn't any better today. Can't see a jolly girl like Maddy wanting to be bosom buddies with the likes of her.'

Mike switched off his bed-side lamp. 'Oh, well.' He yawned. 'Night, sweetie.' He rolled over.

Susie stayed propped up against her pillow, mulling over the reasons Michelle might want to talk to Maddy. Mike might have dismissed it as being of no interest but she couldn't. Not that it was any of her business, but it was... well, odd.

Michelle checked her phone again before she switched off her light and went to sleep. Still no reply from Maddy. Huh. Maybe the silly woman didn't believe her. She'd have to tell her again – only maybe this time she'd add a bit more detail and make it a bit plainer. Obviously, despite the Oxford degree Sam had told her that Maddy had, it seemed that she wasn't so bright when it came to relationships. She'd do it tomorrow, she thought. It'd be a nice surprise for Maddy when she woke up.

Chapter Twenty

Maddy stared at her phone and noticed that the screen was juddering. Hardly surprising, given how shaky she felt. Although, despite the shakiness in her hands, her mind seemed remarkably clear as she turned over the implications of the message and tried to deduce who the sender might be.

> Seb doesnt love you anymore he told me so. If you love him let him go.

This was no teenaged spat over an unknown boy involving two anonymous rivals and a misdialled number; this was personal. This text was from someone who had designs on Seb. Or maybe it was more than that, maybe this texter was already having an affair with her husband. For a second she wondered who on earth it could be. Someone from their last posting? That new officer, Sam? But then she realised that, almost certainly, it had to be a rower. All those weekends away with those wonderful long-limbed girls who shared an interest with him. Girls who might not even know that Seb had a wife. And why would they? Maddy hadn't been involved in the rowing scene for months now. When was the last time she'd trained or gone to a regatta to cheer other rowers on? Maddy suddenly felt a wave of emotion engulf her; she was scared and worried about the implications that those few words had.

Then the initial surge of confused feelings ebbed and a chill seeped through Maddy and entered her heart, like a sliver of ice. She put her phone down and fingered the beautiful engraved gold locket that Seb had given her for Christmas – the surprise he'd had to pick up, last minute, before they'd left their quarter to travel to her parents'. When she'd opened the box on Christmas morning, she'd felt certain that he totally adored her – after all, he'd gone to so much trouble and it was such a thoughtful present, with their initials and the date of their wedding inscribed on the back. But now… now she was assailed by hideous doubts.

Had all those training weekends really been just that? She looked back over the past few months and began to add things up. Jenna had been amazed by the amount of training he'd had to commit to and Susie had thought his recent change in attitude coupled with giving up rowing was due to a guilty conscience. Well, having an affair would be enough to give anyone a guilty conscience.

Another thought struck her and with it came the reason for the vile message, accompanied with a whoosh of relief. Of course! Someone had been dropped from the squad, hadn't made the grade or had been read their fortune by Seb because they weren't putting enough effort into their training, and whoever it was resented this and now they wanted to get revenge. That had to be the answer. She almost sobbed as she clutched at this thought.

As she looked at the text the doubts reasserted themselves. She examined the last months of her marriage and knew there were plenty of reasons why Seb might be tempted elsewhere. She'd been a crap wife recently. Their sex life was all but non-existent, she'd been tired and listless and half the time she looked like shit. If he had strayed it was hardly a wonder.

Sightlessly she looked at her son, playing with some stacking cups in his travel cot beside her bed. The coldness that had gripped her now turned to a nauseating feeling of panic at what this might mean for her, Nate and her unborn child. Supposing Seb really had fallen out of love with her? Supposing he really did want this other woman instead of her? And, thought Maddy, if her rival was lively and pretty and slim and sexy, why wouldn't he? She was hardly any of those things herself, was she, these days? If Seb left her she'd be homeless. She might have derided army housing but at least a quarter provided a roof. How would she cope as a single mum with two tiny children? Shit, she'd have to move back home.

She took some deep breaths, trying to calm herself and make her brain think rationally. But whichever way she looked at the situation, however much she tried to make herself go through the evidence logically, however much she told herself the text was almost certainly a nasty, spiteful lie from someone who wanted to get at Seb, her heart kept overruling her head with the 'but what if it isn't?' argument.

She wondered what she should do. Text back? Confront Seb? Ignore it? She blinked back a tear and put her phone down on the counterpane. Thank God this text had come through while she was in the privacy of her bedroom and before her parents were up. She knew that if she was going to avoid explaining everything to her mother she'd have to find a way to put on some sort of front, but at least she had a while to get her act together.

And getting her act together was essential. Her mother had always been difficult about her only daughter's choice of husband and if she got a sniff of what was going on, Maddy knew there would be a barrage of 'I told you sos' and 'I said you should never marry a soldier', plus 'I said you were too young and you were rushing into things...' Maddy loved her mother, she did, but it had been obvious from the moment Seb had appeared on the scene that he didn't match up to her mother's expectations. From the instant Maddy had won her place at Oxford it had been transparent that her mother had expected her to Marry Well: a member of the landed gentry at the very least. An ordinary, middle-class bloke simply wasn't going to cut the mustard and even a commissioned officer was below par. Which was ridiculous, given that home was a perfectly normal four-bed detached house on the outskirts of Hereford. If she had been born with the proverbial silver spoon it might have been understandable but her mother's delusions of grandeur, when it came to her daughter, were as illogical as they were unshakable. Frankly, thought Maddy, her mother would have probably only been satisfied if she'd followed in Kate Middleton's footsteps and married into the House of Windsor. Right now, the last thing she wanted to do was give her mother any more ammunition to fire in her husband's direction, causing more trouble, before she herself had found out what the real truth was.

Suddenly Maddy wanted to be in her own home. She knew she couldn't keep up any sort of front indefinitely and once her mum had found out what was going on, it would all be finger-pointing and Seb getting blamed, and she wouldn't be allowed to even consider the possibility that Seb might be the innocent party. Quite apart from all of that, Maddy wanted someone she could talk to, a shoulder she could cry on and someone who could give her solid advice about her options if the worst did come to the worst. How long could she stay in her quarter if everything went shit-shaped? Would someone have to provide her with alternative accommodation? What would the army do to help her? And Susie would know, Susie would help and, more importantly, Susie would sit and listen and wouldn't jump to conclusions or be judgemental about Seb.

Except... how the hell was she going to tell her mother she wanted to leave early? Maddy sighed. At least this new problem

223

gave her something else to think about other than what Seb might or might not have done.

Michelle found the number for 1 Herts battalion HQ in the army directory and rang it. There was bound to be a clerk on duty even if everyone else was on block leave. The phone was answered after a couple of rings.

'Hi, it's Lieutenant Flowers here from HQUKLF,' she lied smoothly. 'I'm checking when the advance party for Askari Thunder is due to emplane from Brize.'

Unsurprisingly, the clerk didn't bat an eyelid and replied, 'They're due to fly tomorrow.'

'Thank you,' said Michelle, and put the phone down. Surely Seb would return to the quarter before he went off on exercise. And as Maddy wasn't responding to her texts and Seb was blanking her calls on his mobile it was time to try something a bit different. She had the home number, it was time to try that as a means of communication now. She took a deep breath before she dialled nine for an outside line while she brought up the Fanshaws' number on her mobile and then rang Seb's quarter. Please, please, she thought, let him be there.

Seb stared at his fellow passengers, waiting in the departure lounge of RAF Brize Norton. On the other side of the floor-to-ceiling windows a drab grey RAF passenger plane sat on the pan, as the luggage and kit for the advance party was loaded and a fuel bowser pumped avgas into the tanks. Most of the people sprawled on the seats around him were from other regiments and battalions or from the Brigade HQ and unknown to him. In fact, there were hardly any familiar faces; the exceptions were Andy Bailey, the adjutant, the blonde clerk from battalion HQ, and Sam Lewis from the

224

LAD. There were, of course, other soldiers from the battalion present, but not ones that Seb really knew, just faces he vaguely recognised.

He glanced in Sam's direction. Bloody typical, he thought. The one person he really didn't want to see and here she was. He still felt an enormous surge of guilt every time he caught sight of her because she knew what he'd done. He'd hoped that being in the advance party meant he'd get away from her and not re-encounter her till the dust had died down. Seb sighed. Just his sodding luck that it wasn't to be.

He was about to look away when she must have sensed he was looking at her because she glanced up from her Kindle and stared directly at him. Seb felt his face colour. Sam gave him a knowing look. Bitch, he thought, and returned to looking out of the window.

'You looking forward to going, sir?' said the blonde clerk. Seb glanced at the name embroidered onto the tag on her combat jacket. Cooper, of course. She'd been mates with Jenna Perkins, the woman who'd had an affair while her husband was in Afghan. Not that he could take the moral high ground about that incident now.

'It's going to get us out of the office,' he said. And get me away from Michelle. 'What about you?' Frankly, he thought Cooper would be a complete fish out of water. With her hair and make-up she looked more like she ought to be a trolley-dolly on an airliner, not a soldier about to board an RAF flight.

'Not really, sir. Not a big fan of wildlife.'

'The animals'll probably be more frightened of you than you are of them.'

'I wouldn't bank on it,' she muttered.

The tannoy bonged and an announcement told the assembled soldiers to proceed to the gate to board the flight. Instantly there was a buzz of conversation as everyone stood up, gathered their possessions and began to shuffle towards the door that led to the concrete pan and the aircraft steps.

Seb was aware that Sam was standing right behind him. He studiously tried to ignore her but she had other ideas.

'I spent Christmas with Michelle,' she said, quietly.

'Really?' He feigned indifference.

'She's very unhappy.'

'I'm sorry to hear that.' Seb turned around. 'Look,' he hissed. 'I made a mistake. A big one, but it won't happen again, so can we drop this?'

Sam nodded. 'Too right it won't happen again. If you knew the trouble you've caused...' She shook her head almost as if she didn't believe the mess herself. 'I spent the first week of my leave hearing nothing but how miserable and upset she is.'

'I've said I'm sorry,' said Seb. 'What do you want me to do – grovel?'

He got a look which told him that it was exactly what Sam expected him to do. Then she said, 'We'd better hope that with you right out of the way, she'll have the opportunity to calm down and move on.'

Seb nodded. He hoped so too.

Michelle tried for a fourth time to ring the Fanshaws' house phone and yet again there was no reply. She heard the answering machine start to kick in but she dropped the receiver before the message finished. Yes, she'd got the hint that neither Seb nor Maddy could get to the phone right now. And no, she didn't want to leave a message. What she wanted was to talk to Seb. If she could talk to him for five minutes she was convinced she could make him understand how much she loved him, make him realise he needed to leave Maddy.

She'd give it one more shot, she decided. She'd ring again in an hour and hope that maybe she'd catch him before he flew off to the back of beyond. And if she didn't get hold of him maybe she'd try ringing Maddy instead; after all, didn't she deserve to be put in the picture? It seemed to Michelle that Maddy hadn't taken her texts seriously; if she had, surely she'd have responded. So now there was nothing for it but to talk to her and tell her exactly what had been going on. It was only fair.

Maddy got out of her car and stretched. The journey had been pretty easy but having a huge bump between her and the steering-wheel hadn't made it comfortable. At least Nathan had slept for most of it, although in some ways that wasn't such a good thing because once he woke up he'd be full of beans, while she was dying to put her feet up and maybe take a nap. She hadn't slept a wink the previous night as she'd tossed and turned with worry about her marriage and Seb and her future prospects if the awful text proved to be true.

She saw Susie in her kitchen window and waved. Susie waved back and then made a 'T' sign with her hands. Good shout, thought Maddy as she answered with a thumbs-up. Much as she wanted to get into the privacy of her own home and shut the door on the world, the prospect of a cuppa before she tackled the unloading of Nathan's mountain of kit was irresistible. And maybe Nate would be able to let off a bit of steam while there were two adults and Susie's twins to chase after him, which might mean more chance of peace and quiet for her when she did get into her own house. Nate began to stir as she undid the straps of his car seat and gently lifted him out. There was a muted wail of protest as he sleepily snuggled his face against Maddy's neck, while with a free hand she grabbed her handbag and locked the car.

Susie had the door open and the kettle on by the time Maddy reached the doorstep.

'Come in, come in,' called Susie, on hearing the footsteps. She came out into the hall. 'Here, let me take Nate,' she said, lifting the half-sleeping child out of Maddy's arms. 'What are you doing home? You're not due back for weeks yet,' she added.

Maddy eased her back again. 'No, well... slight change of plan.'

Susie gave her a curious glance but said nothing. Maddy followed Susie into her tidy sitting room, where the twins were lounging on the sofa, watching *Shrek*.

'Girls,' said Susie as she laid Nate on the floor, 'keep an eye on this one for us. Maddy and I are going to be in the kitchen.'

The twins squealed with delight at being given a real live doll to play with and instantly slid off the sofa to be closer to their charge.

'And be gentle,' instructed Susie. 'You're not to pick him up or cart him around. Let him wake up in his own good time. Understand?'

The girls nodded.

'He'll be fine,' said Maddy. 'He'll squawk if he gets fed up. Nate lets people know when he's not completely happy – loudly.'

The two women went into the kitchen, where a pot of tea was steaming gently on the counter.

'So, why the change of plan?' asked Susie as she poured the tea.

'This and that,' said Maddy. Much as she wanted advice from Susie she still, even after a day thinking about her predicament, hadn't managed to formulate a way of saying 'I think my husband might be having an affair' without sounding like some sort of hysterical drama queen.

'Did being waited on hand and foot get a bit suffocating?' asked Susie as she reached for a carton of milk.

'Hmm,' replied Maddy, noncommittally.

Susie put the milk back down again and narrowed her eyes slightly. 'More than that?'

Suddenly, the weight of worry, coupled with a completely sleepless night and an argument with her mother about her sudden departure, got too much. She felt a bubble of despair well up inside. A sob escaped.

Susie gasped. 'Maddy, what on earth is the matter?' She got up from the stool and hugged her friend, which made Maddy's tears flow faster. 'It's not the baby?' she questioned as the awful thought struck her.

Maddy shook her head.

'And it isn't Seb?'

But at that Maddy's crying renewed in intensity.

'Maddy, Maddy,' soothed Susie, rubbing her back. But Maddy seemed inconsolable, so Susie rubbed steadily and made sympathetic noises until finally Maddy began to calm down. 'There, there.' She reached for the box of tissues on the top of the fridge and handed them to Maddy, who took a handful and blew her nose.

'I'm sorry,' she gulped.

Susie shook her head. 'There's nothing to be sorry for.'

Maddy forced a wet smile. 'You don't need my problems.'

'No? I think I ought to be the judge of that. Want to talk?'

Maddy blew her nose again and tried to pull herself together but juddering sobs kept escaping. She cradled her mug and stared at it.

'I suppose I owe you an explanation,' she murmured.

'Sweetie, you owe me nothing.'

Maddy blew her nose a final time and then reached for her handbag, lying at her feet. Silently she extracted the phone and after a few seconds she handed it to Susie.

There was a pause of a couple of seconds as Susie read the text and then said, 'Bloody hell,' followed by, 'Who is it from?'

Maddy shook her head and shrugged. 'No idea. I don't even know if it's true. I mean, it could be someone being spiteful, trying to wreck Seb's life because they've not made the cut with the rowing team or something.'

'It's a possibility,' said Susie, but her tone sounded doubtful.

Maddy looked at her. 'You don't think so.' Her eyes welled up with tears again.

'Maddy,' said Susie, almost desperately, 'I don't know what to think. Truly.'

'He's been away an awful lot recently.' Maddy twisted the tissue in her hand. 'So many weekends.' She gazed at Susie, willing her friend to contradict her, to say that, of course, Seb wasn't the sort to stray, but Susie nodded in agreement. 'So it could be true, couldn't it?'

'We don't know this.'

Maddy sipped her tea. 'So this is why I came back. I don't want my mum to know – not till I know the truth. Mum…' Maddy paused. 'Mum thinks…' She paused again, not wanting to sound horribly disloyal to her mother. 'Mum isn't Seb's number one fan. She thinks I could have done better than marrying a soldier.'

'An officer,' corrected Susie. 'And a fine athlete and an Oxford graduate.'

'Even so…' said Maddy. 'And I knew if I stayed with my parents I couldn't have pretended all was tickety-boo when…' She glanced at her phone. 'When it might be anything but.'

'I understand,' said Susie. She sipped her tea. 'God, this is a mess and Seb's only just flown out to Kenya. When's he due back? When will you be able to talk to him? Are there any comms out there?'

Maddy shook her head. 'No, I don't think so. Not unless I go through official channels and I can't do that – I can't expect the chief clerk or Andy to relay a message to him about something like this.'

'Maddy,' said Susie, gently. 'Look, I don't want to sound

like an old misery but have you thought about what you'll do if…?'

Maddy stared at Susie and finished the sentence for her. 'If it's true?'

Susie nodded.

Maddy sighed. 'I wouldn't be hurting like this if I didn't love him so much. And I do, Susie. I can't imagine life without him. I'd stick with him. I'd take him back in a trice. I don't want him to go… leave me. And the children…'

'Do you think it'd come to that?'

Maddy looked at Susie, desperation written clearly on her face. 'I don't know,' she whispered. 'I don't know what I'm up against. I don't know who this person is. I can only assume it's someone he met rowing.' She gave a bark of mirthless laughter. 'After all – he's got previous. It's how we met. So this is probably some young single athlete, all bronzed skin and drive and ambition, full of health and vim and vigour. Not a knackered mother whose figure has gone to pot and who has the energy of a tired sloth.'

'Don't be silly,' said Susie. 'You're lovely and you know it.'

'Hmm.'

Susie sipped her tea. 'You sure it's a rower?'

Maddy shrugged. 'No, but it seems logical.'

'It's just…'

Maddy's brow creased. 'It's just what, Susie?'

'No, it's probably nothing.' Susie took a gulp of her tea.

'Susie?'

'It's just that friend of Sam's, the one who came to your Sunday lunch party, was here, and if you remember, she was adamant she didn't row and wasn't ever likely to.'

'Who? Michelle?'

Susie nodded.

'What did she want?'

231

'To see you.'

'Me? Why?'

'She didn't really say. She was a bit odd, though.'

'No change there, then,' said Maddy. 'She was bloody odd the other time she was here. I couldn't see why a lovely girl like Sam would want her as a friend. She hardly said a word. In fact, I thought she was more than odd, I thought she was rude and moody.'

'So maybe she wanted to apologise to you.'

Maddy shook her head. 'Unlikely, especially as I had a bread-and-butter letter from her, thanking me. If she felt the need to say sorry for being such a mardy-moo she could have said so then.'

'I suppose. The thing is, when she found out you weren't here I gave her your phone number.'

Maddy stared at Susie. 'The house phone?'

'I don't know. I gave her the babysitting circle list, which has got both your numbers on it. I don't know which one she put into her mobile. It could have been the house phone, but it could have been your mobile, it could have been both. God, if I'm right, Maddy, I am so sorry.'

'But… but… it can't be her. She doesn't row, she said so, so she could never have met Seb before that lunch party. It doesn't add up.' Maddy was bewildered. 'No, it can't be her.'

But Susie wasn't so sure. She'd seen how Michelle had looked during that second visit and the words 'shifty' and 'furtive' kept popping into her mind. Along with 'deranged', not that she was going to tell Maddy. Maddy had enough to contend with already.

Chapter Twenty-One

The A330 Airbus droned southwards and Sam put her Kindle down on her tray table then closed her eyes. She was bored with reading and anyway she hadn't been concentrating properly on her book and had kept finding that she had to scroll back a few pages to pick up a lost thread in the plot.

She knew why: her mind was full of other stuff. Her thoughts kept yo-yoing between Michelle and her problems, and what she was going to find out in Kenya. The CO's briefing had been pretty unequivocal about what they might expect. He hadn't beaten about the bush when he'd opened with, 'Right, first off, almost everything you will encounter in the bush is out to kill you.'

Colonel Notley had gone on to talk about the deadly results of getting bitten. It seemed that everything from insects to lions had a taste for humans. Then there were the other dangers: the sun could burn you to a crisp in minutes; the chances of getting septicaemia from scratches or cuts were monumental; and, finally, if you were foolish enough to have sex with any of the locals you were more than likely to end up with HIV or some other STD. Frankly, thought Sam, the CO hardly sold the place as the holiday destination that civvies thought it was – although civvies got to hang out in five-star resorts.

'Of course,' the CO had said, 'I would hope that both you and your soldiers will steer well clear of the local women or, ahem, men... but I want you to drum it into every last man-jack, or woman, in your command that if we do find anyone consorting with the locals we'll take a very dim view of it.' He clicked a slide to show a map of the area. And then another slide with a larger-scale map showing the main camp in the middle – and, as far as Sam could ascertain – bugger all else. 'Featureless' and 'back of beyond' were words that sprang to mind.

He'd gone on about various other aspects of the exercise and had finished with, 'This exercise is to test the soldiers of the battalion in basic infantry skills, to test us, the officers, in our leadership skills, to test how we interact with the other units in the battle group and to test the command and control of higher formation. It will be hard, it will be hot, but, if we all follow standard operating procedures it should not be dangerous.'

But that was the thing... *should not be dangerous* kind of implied that it could be. And although Sam had known when she'd signed up that being in the army meant that her job description could include stuff like 'getting shot at' she hadn't really thought about risks like snake bites or being a lion's lunch. She wasn't sure if the butterflies that were now flapping away in her stomach were as a result of excitement at going to a foreign and rather exotic country or fear about what the country might have in store.

It didn't help matters that the colonel had also briefed them about the kit that was permanently stored out in Kenya and the state of it. The vehicles, apparently, were relatively new – well, new compared to the lot they'd replaced – but the succession of soldiers who went through the exercise area felt very little responsibility with regard to them and thrashed the engines and took them across terrain in a way they wouldn't dream of doing to their own battalion vehicles. Sam had been warned that she and her team would probably be working around the clock to keep everyone mobile.

Hot, suffering dodgy conditions and probably overworked – whoopee. Still, the other advantage of being in the back of beyond was that she wouldn't get plagued with daily calls from Michelle wanting a shoulder to cry on. Sam felt a bit mean as she thought this but, honestly, Michelle was pushing their friendship to the limit.

Michelle rang the Fanshaws' number for the fifth and, she'd promised herself, final time. It was answered on the third ring.

'Hello, Maddy here.'

Maddy! Michelle was so stunned at getting Maddy and not Seb that she slammed the receiver down. Shit, what was she doing back? Susie had said she'd be gone for ages, weeks at any rate. Michelle stared, horrified, at the phone on her desk as if she expected it to morph into a cobra or something else unpleasant.

Then she began to calm down and she thought more logically about the situation. If Maddy were home and Seb was now, presumably, in Africa – or would be imminently – maybe it was the perfect moment for the two of them to have a little chat. After all, wouldn't it be doing Maddy a kindness to put her in the picture about the sham that her marriage had turned into? Michelle looked at her diary. Good, the weekend was free. Maybe she'd take a spin down to the country.

Immi was awoken by the bing-bong of the aeroplane's tannoy and the guy sitting next to her shuffling about. She wondered how long she'd been asleep. Long enough, she thought, judging by the vile, stale taste in her mouth as she swallowed. She reached for her compact to check her appearance. Oh, God, she'd dribbled. She had dried drool down her chin. Hastily she tidied herself up and ran a comb through her hair.

'Don't worry, sweetheart,' said the squaddie next to her. 'You're still the best-looking soldier on the plane.'

'Thanks.' She preened slightly.

'Still, given what the rest of us look like, that isn't saying much.'

Immi stuck her tongue out and good-naturedly told him to piss off.

She felt the plane lurch slightly; a second bing-bong rang out.

'Ladies and gentlemen, this is the pilot speaking to inform you that we've started our decent into Nairobi's Jomo Kenyatta International Airport. We should be on the ground in about thirty minutes. I hope you have enjoyed the flight.'

Well, no, she hadn't, thought Immi, but she didn't think the RAF would be likely to listen to anything she had to say about the dozen or so suggestions she had as to how their service could be improved. Decent soap and soft loo roll in the lavs would be a start.

She amused herself for the limited remainder of the trip by thinking up all the other ways the RAF could begin to rival commercial airlines and was almost surprised when she felt a hefty thump and realised they'd touched down. She was thrown forward in her seat and bounced off the one in front as the pilot applied reverse thrust and the brakes. Another thing to add to the list – be gentler to the passengers.

As the plane slowed and began to turn Immi gazed across the aisle and out of a porthole, and thought that what she could see looked like what she'd seen on arrival at almost any other airport she'd ever landed at. A big complex of terminal buildings, a bunch of aircraft sitting on their stands and some moth-eaten grass – except this moth-eaten grass was rather browner and dustier than the stuff they'd left behind at Brize. So this was what Africa looked like.

And when she got off the aircraft she discovered what Africa felt like – nice and warm – well, nice and warm compared to the UK. And they were high here. She'd been told it was about six thousand feet so wasn't it like Ben Nevis? Which might explain why it wasn't completely baking even though they were almost smack on the equator. But it smelt of aviation fuel and warm concrete like any other airport. She pitied the lads who were on baggage detail unloading the plane; being this high it was going to be tiring. Obviously with all the guns and ammo on board there was no way the local baggage handlers could be allowed to do it so the soldiers were forming human chains and hauling everything into the eighteen-tonners that had been driven onto the pan where the huge RAF plane was parked. All being well, everything would catch up with them at their first stop – the British Army Training Unit, Kenya or BATUK as it was referred to in the endless movement orders Immi had processed only a few weeks earlier.

Immi shuffled forward with the rest of the soldiers, who were not unloading the aircraft's hold, to pass through Kenyan immigration and then into a separate holding area in the main terminal till the movement officer led them to the coaches that had pulled up outside.

Immi wasn't sure what she had imagined Nairobi would look like but, if she was honest, it was a bit of a disappointment. Actually, it was a massive disappointment. She hadn't expected to see mud huts and grass skirts but she had expected something more, well, African. For a start the roads were a joke; they seemed to be one continuous pothole. She supposed the roads might have been really dangerous if they'd managed to travel at any speed but the driver was barely managing to get out of second gear; the traffic was mad. And it was worse than mad, it was psychotically, suicidally mad, with little minibus taxis mounting the pavements to get round the jams, motorcycles going the wrong way up one-way streets, thousands of pedestrians jay-walking or stepping off pavements in front of moving vehicles, and everyone seemed to think that traffic lights and stops signs were advisory rather than mandatory. And then there was the rubbish: piles and piles of it heaped up at the side of the road, along the pavements, dumped on street corners with people in rags picking over the rotting, stinking detritus. Immi felt her skin crawl at the sight. Fancy having to do that? How desperate did you have to be to want to rummage through that sort of shit? she wondered.

The bus carried on its stop-start way around the outskirts of the city while Immi stared open-mouthed at the crazy driving and the sights of Nairobi until after an hour or so they reached their destination, the barracks where they would get their briefing about what to expect in Africa and where they would spend the night before being taken upcountry to Nanyuki, where they would start getting everything ready for the arrival of the rest of the battle group and also get acclimatised to the sun.

The convoy of buses drew to a halt and everyone got off. They were led to a hall where bottles of water were handed out before everyone took their seats for the briefing. They'd been on the go for hours, what with the journey to the RAF base, then the endless wait, then the nine-hour flight... All Immi wanted was to eat and hit the hay but now she had to listen to the training major as he droned on about standard operating procedures, casevac arrangements, the dangers of heatstroke, dehydration, insect bites, septicaemia, malaria...

And here was me thinking I might get a bit of a suntan, thought Immi. I'm not venturing outside ever, if that's what can happen to you.

'Moving on...' said the training major.

Oh Lordy, thought Immi. More? How much more was there to say? And it wasn't as if any of it would apply to her, seeing how she wasn't going to do anything but walk from her accommodation to her office and then back again at the end of the day. She wasn't going to be out in the bundu, she wasn't going to be lugging her body weight in kit around and she wasn't going to be sleeping rough surrounded by bugs and snakes. What the heck of what he was banging on about was going to apply to her? She struggled to pay attention. One of the things she'd learned about being in a huge minority, when lecturers wanted to pick on someone to answer a question, they always picked on an easy target. And being one of four women in a roomful of men meant that the odds were stacked against her if this officer decided to fire a few questions at the audience. She tried not to think about how much she wanted a hot shower, a decent meal and a sleep...

'You there, the blonde...'

Immi was jerked awake by his voice and a nudge in the ribs from the bloke next to her.

Fuck – she was right. The major was staring directly at her.

'What's one of the biggest hazards on the ranges?'

She was about to say lions as a wild guess, when her neighbour whispered, 'Civilian incursion.'

Really? OK. 'Civilian incursion,' she repeated.

The training major narrowed his eyes but Immi stared brazenly back at him.

'Thanks mate,' she whispered to her saviour, when the major moved on to cover the hazards of attacks from ivory poachers who had a particular liking for night-vision goggles – for fairly obvious reasons.

'No worries,' he whispered back. 'Besides, you don't look like someone who's going to be yomping around the bush.'

'Not if I can help it,' said Immi with feeling. And anyway, if she was out in the bush she'd be in a vehicle with the journo she was going to be looking after and she didn't think this media type would want to risk his skin either. Didn't reporters want to sit in bars, drink epic amounts of Scotch, smoke endless fags and chat up pretty girls to get the low-down on a scoop – or was that just ones in films?

Maddy was being a dreadful slob, she knew: nearly eleven o'clock on a Saturday morning and she still hadn't got either Nathan or herself dressed. But who cared? She had no plans, they weren't going anywhere, all they were going to be doing that day was playing and loafing about so what did it matter if they didn't get out of their pyjamas? Of course, if Seb knew he'd be horrified. His sense of military discipline and order would be affronted, but when the cat's away... She felt a little disloyal, even entertaining the thought, but really, life was sometimes a lot simpler without Seb around.

Nathan was happily employed stacking bricks in the sitting room so Maddy went into the kitchen to make herself a cup of tea. As she filled the kettle at the sink she looked out of the window and saw a strange car parked outside.

Her heart stilled. With ghastly certainty she knew who it was. What did she want? Though Maddy could guess, especially after those texts. She couldn't face a confrontation.

She ducked out of sight and then nipped back into the sitting room, scooped up Nathan and whipped him upstairs as the doorbell rang. She'd pretend she was out. She wouldn't answer the door.

The doorbell rang again and again and then incessantly for about thirty seconds, followed by fairly violent hammering on the door. She sat on the bed in her room, clutching Nathan to her and wondering if she ought to call the police. And then the hammering and ringing stopped. It was some time before Maddy crept back to the front and looked out.

The car had gone. She felt shaky with relief.

A couple of hours later she received another text.

Hes mine not yours and I will have him. You wont stop me.

For the rest of the morning Maddy paced about her house, unable to settle, sick with worry about her visitor and the text message. Every now and again Maddy would be distracted by Nathan or a household task that needed doing and forget to be frightened, but then she would remember the manic ringing of the doorbell and the adrenalin would kick in again, leaving her panicky and terrified. She made her mind up. If Michelle came back she'd definitely call 999. She didn't care if the cops thought she was a drama queen or a nutter with a hyper-active imagination – better that than risk anything happening to Nate.

What she really wanted was someone to talk to, someone who could reassure her, but who? Susie and Mike were taking their girls back to boarding school, and because of the extended leave period hardly any of her neighbours were back from holidays with friends and relatives. Besides, thought Maddy, she could hardly go around the patch sounding off about her marital problems to all and sundry.

It was her own fault. She should have asked Seb about the texts the instant she'd received them, she should have raced back to the house and asked him what the hell was going on. And now it was too late, now he was in the middle of sodding Africa and God only knew when she'd be able to get hold of him. What a mess.

Chapter Twenty-Two

The drive from the camp outside Nairobi to Nanyuki had been, thought Sam, a bit of a disappointment. She'd hoped for a sort of mini-safari; stunning countryside, maybe a glimpse of the odd giraffe or elephant, but instead, once they'd left the chaotic sprawl of the city they'd driven along roads lined by ramshackle villages and the only animals they'd seen had been the domestic variety – cows, sheep, goats, and dozens and dozens of donkeys all pulling carts laden with anything and everything you could think of. Where, wondered Sam, were the rolling grasslands with solitary acacia trees like you saw in wildlife films made about Africa? Where were the herds of wildebeest? Even a termite mound would be a welcome sight! Instead, it was either fields of wheat or acres of glasshouses growing flowers. Frankly, thought Sam, it seemed more like the Cotswolds than Kenya. Now and again her heart lifted when she saw a woman dressed in colourful, tribal costume with an amazing headdress of towering, sculpted fabric, or some flash of blue or green as a tropical bird zipped across the path of their coach, but mostly the journey was plain tedious.

Eventually they drove into the town of Nanyuki, the closest settlement to the Laikipia base which would be home for a while, past a sign that told them they were right on the equator; ahead Sam could see a huge looming mountain that dominated the horizon – Mount Kenya. Finally, she felt she was in Africa.

Surprisingly, despite being on the equator, when they got off the bus it wasn't the red-hot heat that Sam had been expecting. Duh, of course, they were thousands of miles high. Well, thousands of feet, at any rate. This was a pleasant turn-up for the books, she thought. Except, of course, the chances of getting really badly sunburnt were much higher; with pleasant UK summer temperatures as the norm it was going to be hard to keep remembering to slap on the factor fifty several times a day.

She looked about her. So this was going to be home sweet home for the next few weeks and it was hardly going to be luxury living. The accommodation was better than a tent, she supposed, but only marginally. Of course, like the rest of the battle group, she'd be going down, off the plateau and into the training area, but a base would be maintained back here for really serious vehicle repairs. Until the exercise proper got under way Sam had no way to judge how often she'd be required to oversee REME operations in the training area and how much she'd be needed here.

Now the buses had all arrived the senior NCOs organised work parties to unload the baggage holds on the coaches and the convoy of lorries which had followed with the rest of the kit. With surprising speed the job was done and the piles of Bergens and equipment were collected by their owners and taken to the living quarters, armouries or stores, as appropriate.

Sam, having found her luggage, approached the RQMS, the quartermaster's chief right-hand man and the person in charge of allocating bed spaces. The companies had each been allocated barn-like dorms – there were some other smaller units which had been divvied up to the officers and SNCOs, and most of Sam's LAD had opted to bunk down in the corner of the workshop. The trouble with all of these spaces was the lack of privacy. Not that Sam was a prude, but if there was any chance of separate female accommodation she'd happily go for it.

'Where am I sleeping, Q?' she asked

He sucked his teeth. 'It's a bit Hobson's choice, ma'am.'

That didn't sound hopeful. So what was the choice? Sleeping with dozens of snoring, farting soldiers or on a camp bed in the open with just a mossie net for protection.

'And?'

'There's a sort of storeroom, ma'am. I thought you and Cooper from BHQ could share it.'

Sam remembered Corporal Cooper – the pretty female clerk she'd met on her first arrival at 1 Herts and the one Blake had danced with at the corporals' club ball. That was all right. There was nothing she could object to in that.

'It's very cramped,' said the RQMS.

'That's OK,' said Sam. 'To be honest, I'd been bracing myself for much worse.'

'Wait till you see it.'

'Lead the way.'

Well, thought Sam, 'storeroom' might have been a bit generous. Cubby hole was nearer the mark but there was room for two camp beds and it had a light. Just as well really as there wasn't a window, but they could leave the door open to get some air.

The RQMS left her to settle in, which amounted to little more than plonking her Bergen on her bed. With no spare space at all, unpacking wasn't an option. Sam scratched her head. How the hell she and Cooper would both manage to get dressed in the morning in the six-inch space between the beds was a problem that would need addressing. Maybe they could take it in turns. Not that it was something to worry about right now. A shadow fell across the door. Sam turned and saw her roomie.

'Ma'am.'

'Cooper. I hope you don't mind slumming it with me.' Corporal Cooper looked bewildered. 'Joke,' said Sam.

'Oh.' Cooper gave a nervous laugh.

'A bad one,' said Sam, with what she hoped was a reassuring smile.

'Anyway, it won't be for long, ma'am. I expect I'll be off into the bush soon. Captain Bailey has detailed me to look after some reporter or other who is joining us.'

'Oh, who's that?'

Cooper shrugged. 'Haven't a clue. Anyway, whoever it is I'm lumbered with, it has to be better than log-keeping on the night shift.'

'Was that what they had planned for you?'

'Dunno, but there isn't much else I can do out here, is there?'

Sam looked at Cooper's long sleek hair, polished nails and fake tan and thought there probably wasn't. Escorting a civvy was probably a very suitable job for her.

Corporal Cooper suddenly shrieked and Sam jumped.

'What?'

'There.' Cooper was pointing, with a shaking hand, at a small lizard scuttling up the wall from behind a bed.

'Aw,' said Sam. 'Isn't it cute?'

'Cute?' squealed Cooper. 'You having a laugh? Ma'am,' she added as an afterthought.

'Well, I think so. And, if there are any bugs in here it'll probably scoff them so we needn't be worried about them either.' Sam saw the pallor on her roomie's face.

Cooper looked as if she might faint. 'Bugs?' she whispered. Maybe Cooper wasn't as interested in the local wildlife as she was.

'Well, mossies and the odd fly.' Maybe now wasn't the time to mention things like praying mantises, termites and soldier ants.

Cooper shuddered. 'Thank gawd we don't have a window,' she said with feeling. 'One less way for the little sods to get to us.'

Sam didn't think that her idea to leave the door open for ventilation was going to meet with approval.

Immi was standing at the back of the queue for supper in the huge building that had been designated as the cookhouse. No separate messes for the various ranks here, but one vast roofed space with mesh for windows instead of glass. The mesh let the air pass through but kept the bugs and creatures out, or that was the idea; climate control it wasn't. In fact, thought Immi, everything here was rubbish and as for the ablutions…! She shuddered. Honestly, she thought, she'd rather dig a hole in the ground. At least she'd know that she was the first to use it. The state of some of the lavs… She felt her flesh crawl.

'Wotcha, Immi.'

'Luke.' She was genuinely pleased to see him. 'Hey, how was the skiing?'

'Great snow, nice chalet, plenty to eat. Yeah, it was all OK. What about your leave?'

Immi shrugged. 'The usual – ate too much, drank too much, had a row with my mum…'

'I'm sorry.'

'Nah, it was blinding. Honest.'

Luke didn't look convinced. 'I'm pleased.'

The queue shuffled forward slowly and finally the pair reached the serving counter. Immi surveyed the choices, trying to decide which was the least minging option. In the end she opted for steak pie.

'Although gawd knows what animal they got this stewing steak off,' said the cook.

Immi took her meal and a large glass of water over to an empty table. Luke followed and she felt her heart quicken slightly. Being behind her in the queue hadn't been a matter of choice but luck, but now he was choosing to sit with her.

Maybe she was in with a shot. Maybe he did like her a bit. And she so wanted that to be the case because she was as smitten with him as a teenager with a crush on Harry Styles.

They sat next to each other and ate their food. Or rather, Luke ate his, wolfing it down, but Immi spent most of her time trying to find the fibres of meat in amongst gobbets of fat.

'Can I join you? Only there aren't a lot of familiar faces here.'

Immi looked up from her plate, her brow still furrowed in concentration, and saw Captain Lewis. 'Oh, yeah. Of course.' But inwardly she was sighing with annoyance. Why didn't Lewis go and sit with someone else instead of playing gooseberry with her and Luke? Bollocks.

Captain Lewis sat down and slid her plate off her tray. 'I chose the steak pie,' she announced. Then she looked at the lumps of fat arranged around the edge of Immi's plate and back at her own plate. 'Oh well,' she said, as she tucked in. 'When you've been to boarding school you can eat most things.'

Immi gazed in horror at the first forkful of meat that Captain Lewis put in her mouth. Yuck. How could anyone eat that sort of shit?

Around them the cookhouse was buzzing with conversation and the occasional burst of laughter but the three people at Immi's table munched in silence. Then Captain Lewis said, 'So, did you both have a lovely Christmas? And isn't it strange to go from winter to this glorious sunshine in a few hours.'

'Brill, thanks,' said Immi. 'How about you?'

'I spent it with friends and then New Year with more friends, so it was good. Quite jolly.'

Captain Lewis turned towards Luke. 'And how about you, Corporal Blake?'

He didn't answer. Instead, he abruptly pushed his plate away from him, despite the fact that he'd only eaten half his meal and stood up. 'Sorry, things to do,' he muttered.

Like what? wondered Immi, as he strode off.

Captain Lewis looked bewildered. 'You wouldn't think asking someone about their leave was a hanging offence, would you?'

'He's just a moody git. It's nothing personal.'

Captain Lewis looked dumbfounded for a second or two, then she said, 'I shouldn't be surprised by his behaviour; he's hardly the life and soul of the party down at the LAD. He always looks at me like... well, never mind.'

Immi was thrown. Maybe she'd read Luke wrong. Maybe he *didn't* like Captain Lewis. So much for her previous assumption. 'Well... I'm only guessing but I don't think he's got a great home life. But he can be nice, honest,' she added. 'Yesterday I caught him putting out some leftovers for those stray moggies that hang around the back of the cookhouse. He put a bowl of water down for them too.'

'Almost Saint Francis,' said Lewis. She returned to eating her lunch. 'He's not your average squaddie, is he?'

'You've noticed.'

Captain Lewis took another mouthful, chewed and swallowed. 'I *am* his boss.'

'He never talks about his background,' said Immi. 'Or he doesn't to me.' She looked hopefully at Captain Lewis.

'A totally closed book.'

Oh well, thought Immi. His mystery was one of the things that made him so attractive.

Maddy felt like a zombie. Quite apart from the fact that she was suffering from sleep deprivation due to the worry about Seb and their future keeping her awake at night, Nathan had chosen to start being difficult about almost everything, squirming and crying when she tried to do the least thing: strap him into his pushchair; dress him; change his nappy; anything.

248

Maddy simply didn't have the energy for these battles and was horribly aware that she was coming dangerously close to losing her temper with him. Maybe he was reacting to her stress, she thought. She wished she could explain to the little mite that his behaviour was hardly going to make the situation any better.

Still, she thought as she sat on the sofa, feeling sorry for herself wasn't getting anything done. She had a check-up with the midwife at the surgery and she had to get Nathan ready to go out. Maybe, once she'd got herself into town, she'd take herself for a coffee or do some window-shopping. Perhaps getting out and about, doing normal stuff, would make her feel a bit more human.

Wearily she hauled herself upright, trying to ignore the twinge in her back and the way the baby's foot seemed to have jammed itself under her ribs. Had pregnancy been this bad with Nate? She scooped Nathan up off the floor and was rewarded with a wail of protest. Maddy sighed as the wail grew louder and Nate started to bang her face with his pudgy fists, yelling, 'No, no, no.'

She grabbed his hands with her free hand to stop him hitting her. She knew she ought to try and explain to him that what he was doing wasn't nice or kind but, frankly, she couldn't be arsed. She took his all-in-one padded suit off the bottom of the banisters and sat on the stairs while she forced her now screaming son into it and did up the zip. By the time she'd finished she felt utterly drained. Sheesh, and now she had to face the next battle – that of strapping him into his car seat.

By the time she'd done that, loaded his buggy and got her own coat on, the last thing she wanted to do was drive to Warminster and spend half an hour sitting in the doctor's waiting room because the midwife's clinic always ran late. Oh the joy of not only having her own badly behaved toddler to contend with, but other people's too.

It seemed to take for ever to get weighed, measured and checked and then receive the inevitable lecture about looking after herself – 'You look very tired, Maddy, are you getting enough sleep?' – to which she'd wanted to say, 'I think my husband is having an affair, I think his mistress might be stalking me, I am out of my mind with worry, so of course I'm not.' But instead she'd nodded and forced a smile that said she was getting as much as was possible with a wriggly baby that liked nothing better than practising its gymnastic skills at three in the morning.

When she finally escaped she seriously thought about going home, but the weather was nice and Nathan was looking sleepy so she left her car in the now almost-empty surgery car park and headed into Warminster. By the time she was on the High Street her son was out for the count. So what to do now? Browse around the sales for clothes she wouldn't be able to get into for weeks and weeks, go for a coffee, window-shop…? Clothes shopping was pointless and frankly her back ached. A nice sit-down with a cuppa was what she fancied. She headed for the coffee shop.

'Coo-ee. Oi, Mads.'

Maddy stopped in her tracks and spun round. 'Jenna. Lovely to see you.'

Jenna peered at Maddy. 'You all right?'

Maddy nodded, trying to look bright and chipper. 'Yeah, of course. You know, big with child.'

'You're certainly that,' said Jenna, eyeing her bump. 'When did you say you're due?'

'March.'

'Not long now.'

'No.'

'Your old man involved with this exercise?'

Maddy nodded again. 'Yes, he went out with the advance party so, assuming it all goes according to plan, he'll be back in time for this one's appearance.' She patted the bump and was rewarded with a sharp kick that made her catch her breath.

'Something the matter?' asked Jenna with genuine concern.

'Just the baby being boisterous.'

Jenna wrinkled her nose. 'I have to say, I'm not sold on this pregnancy lark. Can't say I'm planning on trying it.'

'No? You don't know what you're missing.'

'I think I do. Anyway, you got time for a coffee?'

Maddy nodded. 'You must be a mind reader. I was on my way for one – thought I'd treat myself to a cappu and a muffin while Nate is asleep.'

'Then it's my treat – payback for last time.'

The two women strolled towards the coffee shop and while Maddy parked Nathan and settled herself, as comfortably as her bump allowed, Jenna queued.

'There we go,' she said as she put the laden tray down on the table a couple of minutes later. 'So, how's tricks?'

Maddy stared into space for a second or two and then made her mind up. 'Shit.'

'Shit?' squawked Jenna, loudly.

An old biddy with a tight blue perm shot Jenna a filthy look as the swear word reverberated around their end of the café. Jenna returned the glare but then, much more quietly, she said, 'What do you mean, shit?'

'I mean shit.' Maddy sighed. 'I don't know where to start… I think my husband might be having an affair.'

Jenna's eyes widened. 'Blimey. So what makes you think that? All those weekends away?'

Maddy nodded.

'You sure?' asked Jenna. 'Just because I said that all that time he spent away might mean he was up to something – well, I didn't mean to go and put ideas in your head. It was only a throwaway line, honest.'

'And, when you said it, I really, really thought that his rowing weekends were exactly that, rowing, right up until the moment when I started getting texts from his girlfriend.'

Jenna choked and hurriedly put her cup down. 'No! She never. What a cow!'

'Hmm,' said Maddy, nodding. 'A total cow. And I think she might have come to the house a couple of times. My neighbour saw her hanging around and then someone called when I was busy with Nate. Whoever it was, it was pretty scary – lots of banging on the door and leaning on the doorbell.'

'Oh, that's creepy. She sounds like a bit of a psycho.'

Maddy sighed. 'Thanks, Jenna. I really don't need to hear that.'

Jenna shrugged and raised her eyebrows. 'You not wanting to hear it doesn't change things, does it? Who is this woman, then?'

'I've got my suspicions.'

'Someone from the battalion?'

'No, but I think she's army. She's a mate of Sam Lewis's. Or she is if it's who I think it is.'

'You mean Captain Lewis, Dan's boss?'

Maddy nodded.

Jenna took a sip of her latte. 'Do you think Captain Lewis knows? I mean, she's nice, I really like her. She wouldn't have mates who are nutty, surely?'

'I dunno, she might. Let's face it, neither of us know her well.'

Jenna leaned forward and put her hand over Maddy's. 'Look, I know that I'm probably not the most suitable person to offer help – not if you consider what I've done in the past – but if there's anything, *anything*, I can do and if you want to talk about stuff, anything, call me. Promise.'

Maddy nodded. 'That's really kind. I appreciate it.'

Chapter Twenty-Three

Sam walked out to the vehicle park at the Laikipia base and surveyed what was parked there. Superficially all the Land Rovers and trucks looked fairly reasonable; newish, in one piece, not too many dinks and dents... However, she wasn't taken in. She'd been warned that everything had been thrashed by a succession of battle groups who had exercised here since these vehicles had replaced the old ones – the ones that simply couldn't be repaired or bodged together any more. Not that these vehicles were her worry for the moment. As long as the engines worked, the tyres were legal, the signals equipment functioned, as did the other bits and bobs of bolted-on kit, they remained the responsibility of the transport officer. However, the minute things began to go wrong then her team would have to step in and either repair or recover them. She hoped that the assessment was horribly pessimistic; she knew she wasn't in Africa to enjoy herself but getting some time off and some sleep would be nice.

She headed for a nearby Land Rover and unclipped the bonnet. She thought she'd have a quick check of the air filters and the oil level to make sure that the most superficial level of maintenance was as it should be. And it had better be, she thought, because if it wasn't... Sheesh, the amount of work just to bring this lot up to snuff didn't bear contemplating.

She was about to duck under the bonnet and get her hands dirty when she saw Luke appear from behind another vehicle, a few dozen yards away. His T-shirt was moulded to his tanned body, showing off muscles an athlete would be proud of. He had no right, she thought, to look that buff and yet be so utterly unapproachable. Covertly she studied him as he stared at the horizon with the bluest of blue eyes that contrasted with his gorgeous brown skin. Sam found herself wondering if he had any white bits. No, stop. And for once he was looking content, not brooding or dissatisfied, no scowl or frown, and for some reason Sam was glad. He often seemed troubled; maybe being in out here in this amazing country suited him. And was it the blinding sunlight that made the planes on his face so obvious? The angle of his jaw, his cheekbones... He was wiping his hands on his overalls, hands which she noticed were very long-fingered, like a musician's. Beautiful hands, which he then ran through his hair, making it slightly dishevelled. Sam had an urge to smooth it down again.

Luke turned and looked in her direction. Instantly Sam dropped her gaze, feeling guilty that she'd been caught studying him. And even more guilty about some of her inappropriate thoughts. She forced her attention away from him and back to checking the oil level. The oil was nice and clean and between the lines on the measure. OK – so that was a start. She attacked the air filter next and extracted it from its housing. It'd do, she thought. Not new but certainly in reasonable nick.

She put it back and was about to straighten up when a voice said, 'Morning ma'am,' and made her jump.

She took a breath. 'Blake,' she said as she turned.

'Sorry ma'am, I didn't mean to startle you.' He didn't sound sorry in the least. Amused more like.

'You didn't,' she lied. 'Haven't you got work to do in the workshop?'

The look he gave her insolently suggested that he thought she had too, but instead he said, 'I wanted to know how well the resident team have maintained this lot. I thought I'd spot-check a few.'

'Don't you think that's for me to worry about? After all, I'm the one in charge of work schedules.'

'Ma'am.' He stared at her and then said, 'Every little helps.'

He was right, of course, which made him even more infuriating. And worse, she wanted to know the outcome of his spot-checks but she couldn't bring herself to give him the satisfaction. 'Then maybe you should report back to the ASM with your findings.'

Luke gave her a long stare, which Sam returned, unblinking. 'As you wish, ma'am.'

Sam pushed against the hydraulic props and slammed the bonnet shut. 'I do.' She turned to move away.

'Stop!' shouted Blake.

Sam turned back. Now he'd really overstepped the mark. But he had bent down and was grovelling in the dust at her feet. He stood up again with a massive beetle in his cupped hand, his long, elegant, fingers making a cage in which he cradled it carefully.

'Rhinoceros beetle,' he said, showing her. 'You were about to squash it. Isn't it amazing?'

'Er, yes.' And it was, black and glossy with a massive 'rhino horn' protruding from the front. She'd never seen anything like it and she was glad she hadn't trodden on it. The poor bug wouldn't have deserved that.

'Here, you hold it,' he said. 'They're harmless.'

Before she could say *Not on your Nelly* he'd grabbed her hand and tipped the bug into hers.

'Thanks,' she mumbled, not looking at him, and ignoring the small shock wave his touch had caused. The beetle was surprisingly light and its scratchy little feet tickled her, but no, it *really* didn't float her boat. She wasn't scared, or even repelled, she just didn't want it crawling about on her skin, although neither did she want Blake to think she was a wuss.

She stood it for about five seconds then she tipped it back into his hand, noting that his fingers weren't just those of a pianist or violinist but that his nails were surprisingly clean for a mechanic; no ground-in engine oil around the cuticles, like all the other men she commanded.

'I think it'd be happier doing what rhinoceros beetles do, don't you?' She watched Blake looking at it with delight and fascination, examining it as it crawled over his hand. No, not your average grunt, she thought. Apart from the fact that the average grunt wouldn't have known what it was in the first place, he would also have squished it in case it could pack a punch. Kill a bug first, ask questions later. Carefully, Luke carried it over to some grass at the edge of the vehicle park.

'There you go, buddy,' she heard him say as he laid it on the ground. Then he turned back to her, saluted and walked away.

Immi sat at a desk in the shade of an awning, typing battalion orders onto a laptop. It was a slow process as every time she caught a hint of any movement she stopped and stared in that direction. Sometimes it was a bird skimming past or a dead leaf scuttering along the ground, propelled by the light breeze and, as soon as she'd reassured herself it was harmless, she returned to work. But on other occasions it would be a lizard or some massive bug and she would stare at it, watching its direction of travel, willing it not to come near her as she drew her feet up off the ground and tried not to panic.

'Those orders finished yet?' said the chief clerk, entering the 'office'.

'Nearly, sir,' said Immi.

'Well, chop-chop. I want them posted by lunchtime – today, that is.'

'Yes, sir.'

'Oh, and when you've done that, the adjutant's got a job for you.'

Immi nodded. 'I'll see him as soon as I'm done.' She returned to her task. Twenty minutes later she copied the orders to the chief's laptop for checking and took herself off to the shaded space that Captain Bailey was using as his office.

'Cooper,' he said as she approached, 'I've organised a vehicle and a driver and I want you to go to the airport and meet that journalist. He's flying in tomorrow on a scheduled flight.'

Immi nodded. 'How will I recognise him?'

Captain Bailey gave her an odd look. 'Recognise him? Don't you watch the news?'

He had to be kidding, right? 'I'm more of a Radio 1 person,' she told him. But the phrase 'watch the news' sent a little buzz of excitement through her. A TV reporter, not some Fleet Street hack. Cool.

'So you've never heard of Jack Raven.'

Immi shook her head. She knew the name Jeremy Paxman and then there was that bird who read the news who'd done *Strictly* a few years ago, but that was about it. 'Should I have done?'

'Never mind. Take a large sign with his name on it, stand right by the arrivals door and he'll find you.' Captain Bailey handed her a sheet of paper. 'All the details, flight number, ETA are on this and the vehicle will pick you up a couple of hours ahead of the landing time to take you there.'

Immi nodded. A trip to civilisation and a day away from the bugs. Result. Then she looked at the piece of paper the adjutant had handed her. She did a double take. Four o'clock. The vehicle would pick her up at four! In the morning? Captain Bailey was having a laugh. Except he wasn't.

The next morning she was standing in the airport terminal,

257

looking as smart as possible in clean combats, her hair immaculate, her beret picked clean of all fluff, her make-up perfect and trying not to yawn. The doors in front of her swished open and shut as a trickle of weary travellers hauling heavy suitcases began to emerge. The flight had touched down thirty minutes earlier and the first of the passengers had now made it through immigration, baggage reclaim and customs. Immi wondered how long it would take for her journo to appear. The plane was a Jumbo so there were hundreds of passengers to get processed. Idly she scanned the faces as they passed and suddenly her attention was caught by a fit, tanned bloke in cream shorts, a pale blue, open-neck shirt and canvas loafers. He was the sort of guy who modelled Breitling watches; that type of outdoorsy, man-of-action hero who featured in those ads for top-of-the-range luxury items. There were other men coming off the flight also wearing shorts but compared to him, they really oughtn't. If they'd known what they'd look like alongside him they would have had second thoughts. She suspected, though, that The Hunk knew exactly how good he looked in his outfit. She took another sideways glance at him as he strode towards the gap in the barriers and the main concourse. He had wavy, dirty blond hair, she noticed, eyes so blue that surely he had to be wearing coloured contacts, and a lean, rangy physique that suggested regular gym attendance.

She looked again at the fat, pasty, unfit office types, the types she assumed her whisky-swilling, cigarette-smoking journo would resemble and tried to pick out the most likely candidate. But the businessmen streamed past with a cursory glance at her piece of paper before they moved on to the other meeters-and-greeters. She looked back towards the sliding doors and nearly squeaked when she saw The Hunk standing in front of her, a tired smile on his face.

'Yes?' she said.

He pointed at her sign. 'You're here for me.'

Oh, yes! Immi swallowed. 'Am I?'

'Your sign says Jack Raven so unless there's two guys with the same name on that flight...' He smiled. 'And you are?'

'Corporal Cooper.' She gave him her best smile, the one she called her L'Oreal smile – he was worth it. 'If you'd like to follow me there's a vehicle waiting outside to take us to Laikipia. Good flight?'

'It was a flight, it was on time.'

They began to push their way through the rest of the crowd of people jostling to catch sight of the exiting passengers and made their way to a less congested part of the concourse.

'Can I take anything?' said Immi, as they headed across the polished floor to the exit. Wordlessly Jack Raven handed over his carry-on bag. Immi almost buckled under the weight, but heaved it onto her shoulder and tried not to look as if she was struggling. 'You must be tired,' she said.

'No, not really, I slept.'

'You did? But it's not proper sleep, is it? You can't get comfy, can you, when you're trapped in that little seat?'

'You can in business class.'

'Business class?' blurted Immi.

'I'm here to work. No point in the BBC sending me all this way if I can't do what I'm being paid to do from the outset.'

Immi thought about her own journey out and the way everyone had had to hit the ground running on arrival. Maybe she should suggest to the army that soldiers would function better if the RAF had lie-flat beds on their trooping flights. She suspected she knew what the answer would be.

'Been to Kenya before?' she asked as they approached the airport exit.

Jack Raven nodded. 'A couple of dozen times. The last time

259

I was here was to cover the terrorist attacks. Hopefully, this exercise will be less bloody and with a lower body count.'

Immi wanted to ask which terrorist attack but suspected if she did she'd look really stupid. And she wished she'd known who this guy was before she'd met him: she could have checked out his CV on Google and known things he'd done. If she'd had that sort of stuff up her sleeve she might have stood a chance of impressing him. But as it was... oh well. On the bright side, she was his escort for several weeks so maybe she'd manage to work some Immi-magic on him over the coming month. Although, she thought more morosely as she trudged after her charge, her magic hadn't worked on Luke. But he was odd. Maybe Mr Raven was more normal.

It was with relief that Immi handed back the hand luggage to Jack as the driver put his suitcase in the rear of the open vehicle. He jumped in the front seat and Immi sat behind. Without the windshield for protection, her hair was going to take a proper battering. She was going to arrive back at camp looking minging.

When she climbed out two and a half hours later she knew she'd been right. Jack Raven stepped out looking immaculate and she... well, she looked like a haystack after it had been hit by a particularly violent gale, she thought as she caught sight of herself in the rear-view mirror. And her make-up wasn't much better. When she'd got something in her eye at about the mid-point of the trip, she'd rubbed it and now she saw that she had a mascara smear halfway down her cheek. Shit, she'd been like for about an hour. Hurriedly she licked a clean tissue and rubbed the black smudge away. She tucked away as much stray hair as she could under her beret as Jack hauled his holdall over the side of the open Land Rover.

'Right,' she said, breezily, hating the fact she looked rank, 'I'll take you to meet the adjutant. Follow me.'

She walked off across the dusty ground towards Captain Bailey and handed over her charge, who smiled at her gratefully. Suddenly, being stuck out in Africa seemed a much better prospect now she was going to be chaperoning Jack Raven. A few weeks in the company of such a fit guy was going to go a long way to compensate for all the hardships and privations.

With Jack Raven entrusted to the care of the adjutant she was free again. She headed for the cookhouse. She was starving, having missed breakfast and she hoped the guys there would take pity on her and let her have some toast or a coffee or something.

When she got into the building Luke was at the water cooler, filling some bottles to take back to the workshop.

'Hi, Luke.'

'Where've you been?' he asked. 'You weren't at breakfast.'

Aw, he'd noticed and it made Immi feel happy.

'Nah, had to go and get that geezer from the airport.'

'What geezer?'

'That reporter bloke. You know, the one I told you I'd be looking after on the exercise.'

'Oh, right. So you know who it is now?'

Immi nodded. 'He's off the BBC. Some guy called Jack Raven.'

Luke dropped the cap he was screwing on the bottle. 'Jack Raven. Bloody hell.'

'You've heard of him?' Immi was genuinely surprised.

'Jeez, Immi, the guy's a legend. He was dodging bullets at the Westgate shopping mall attack. Did one of the best reports of the whole incident – I think he even got some sort of media award for it.'

'Westgate? That shopping centre near Shepherd's Bush?'

Luke gazed at Immi in stunned amazement. 'No, Immi, Westgate, Nairobi, not Westfield in London.' He sighed, theatrically. 'It had a massive terrorist attack. Surely even you heard about it?'

Immi was nettled by the *even you*. She gazed at Luke as he walked away. Nope, she was wrong, she wasn't getting anywhere with him. On the other hand, there was always Mr Raven. She cheered up.

Over the next few days the camp began to fill with troops and equipment; everything and everyone needed for the exercise was brought in. To an outsider it looked chaotic but there was order and everyone had a sense of purpose with a place to be and a task to fulfil: the loggies were beavering away, moving pallets of ammo, food, fuel and gallons and gallons of water; the signallers were setting up and checking comms equipment; the gunners were stripping down, cleaning and reassembling massive artillery pieces; and the infantry were being beasted through punishing PT routines to get them acclimatised to the conditions.

Jack Raven, however, was kicking his heels. He couldn't yet go to the exercise area at Archers Post, he felt he had no need to acclimatise and most of the soldiers were far too busy to have time to spare to chat to him about anything worthwhile; yes, they would tell him their thoughts on the Premiership or give him their opinions on the food but if he tried to engage them on the subject of the army's role in Afghanistan, or what was happening since the withdrawal, or the draw-down of troops from Germany or anything to do with the army's future, all he got was what the squaddies thought was the official line. It was the same when it came to their last pay rise or the quarters for the families – no one seemed to want to rock the boat. Not that he really cared because until the exercise kicked off and he would really have to start filing stories, he was on a nice BBC salary and away from the awful winter weather in the UK. He sat in the warm shade, his laptop open, stared sightlessly at the screen and tried to tell himself that he liked this feeling of semi-lethargy and that he wasn't at all bored. No, siree.

'Excuse me.'

Jack looked up and saw the pretty NCO who had met him at the airport.

'Hiya,' he said, squinting against the sun.

'I hope I'm not disturbing you—'

She was, but not in the way she meant.

'—but the QM would like you to come and get issued with some kit.'

'Like?'

'Mossie net, camp bed...' She shrugged and wrinkled her nose.

'So does this mean we're due to move out soon?'

'I think we all are.'

'Are you looking forward to it?'

'Are you kidding?' The look of total disdain on her face spoke volumes.

'But you're a soldier.'

'I'm a clerk.'

'And there's a difference? I thought everyone in the army was a soldier first and foremost and a tradesperson second.'

'If you want to believe that, go right ahead, be my guest.'

'So, that leads to the inevitable question, why did you join?'

'Good job, you get trained, decent pay, a roof...' She gave him a naughty smile. 'And I love a bloke in uniform.'

'Can't say fairer than that, then.'

'Anyway, Mr Raven, this isn't getting us to Q Stores.'

'Please, it's Jack.'

'OK, Jack, and I'm Immi.' She smiled. 'But this still isn't getting us to Q Stores.'

Jack flipped his laptop shut and shoved it in his shoulder bag. 'Lead on.'

Q Stores was a building like the cookhouse but with the addition of mesh doors that could be secured by padlocks. Inside were racks and racks of army equipment and in front of these was a line of trestle tables and a pile of forms. For signing out kit – in triplicate, no doubt, thought Jack.

He was, however, pleasantly surprised by the speed and efficiency with which he got a camp bed, a pop-up mossie net, a poncho, mess tins, KFS, water bottles, purification tablets and a Bergen to put everything in. And Immi was given the same, much to his amusement, less the Bergen.

'This ain't going to give me no privacy,' she said, poking the flimsy, see-through fabric of the mossie net.

'I won't look when you get undressed,' lied Jack. He wondered what she might look like without her dreary multicam and found the idea rather appealing – a bloody sight more appealing than the prospect of any other soldier he'd so far encountered getting their kit off.

'Too bloody right you won't,' said Immi. 'Right, I'm going to dump this lot in my accommodation and then I'm going to get some lunch.'

'Mind if I join you?'

'If you want, be my guest.' She sounded nonchalant but Jack could see the idea pleased her. Ridiculously the fact she was happy made him happy. So... if anything happened between them while they were out in the bush it would be a pleasant diversion from reporting.

Ten minutes later they were both queuing in the cookhouse for the latest offering from the army chefs.

Immi peered at the board listing the choices. 'They can't fuck up macaroni cheese too much, can they?' she asked.

'I can,' said Jack.

'Really? I had you down for one of those new men.'

Jack laughed. 'Me?' he shook his head. 'Hon, if I can ever get a woman to marry me who will run around and pick up after me, have a hot meal waiting and who will iron my clothes, and then take me to bed for a night of passion, I"ll think I've died and gone to heaven.'

Immi snorted. 'Good luck with that. You won't find one of those around here – well, apart from the sex bit.' She gave him a long, meaningful stare.

Jack grinned. He liked Immi; she didn't arse-lick, which he found rather refreshing. Being a household name – although apparently not in Immi's household – meant he, all too often, only met people who treated him like some sort of china doll; someone who had to be handled with care and kept sweet under all circumstances. And how suffocating was that?

Immi took her macaroni cheese and sat down at a table at the side of the room. Jack joined her a minute later.

He'd just loaded up a fork with the sticky, gluey pasta when Andy Bailey appeared.

'Just the people I wanted to find,' he said, rubbing his hands together.

Beside him he heard Immi say, under her breath, 'Uh-oh.' Jack suppressed a grin.

'What can I do for you, Andy?'

'There's a hearts-and-minds project kicking off upcountry. The sappers are building a bridge to replace one washed away in the last rains. It'll connect a village with the nearest school and means the kids can get to their classes without an eight-mile round trip each day to the next bridge downstream.'

Jack felt a faint tug of interest. Sure, it was a story the British army would love to get into the papers, if only to counter a couple of recent trials of soldiers 'misbehaving' with prisoners in Afghanistan, taking the gloss off the 'selfless heroes' image, which had been painstaking built up over the previous decade or so. But, from a personal point of view, it would be a chance to get away from the camp at Laikipia into the bush, and away from the brass, where the soldiers might talk more frankly. Yes, the bridge-building would provide a human-interest story of a predictable sort, but maybe the soldiers would open up about combat, separation from their loved ones, stress, conditions, camaraderie and the other facets of life in khaki, and provide an even better story. It was worth a punt.

'Sounds interesting,' said Jack.

'Good, that's what I'd hope you'd say. There's a convoy going up there with stores and equipment later today. You've got a ride if you want it.'

Jack glanced at Immi and could see the idea of being out in the bundu was filling her with horror. Her face was a study. 'Great, when do we go?'

'ETD at fourteen hundred hours from the MT section.'

Jack translated the order from army-speak to English in his head; expected time of departure at two in the afternoon from the motor transport section – wherever that was. He asked for directions.

'To the left of the vehicle park,' said Andy. 'There's a hut. Report to Robin Maynard, the MTO, he'll sort you out.'

Andy left to get his own meal and Jack turned to Immi.

'You don't look thrilled.'

She sighed. 'I'll be fine – I suppose.' She sounded highly dubious.

Immi pushed her plate aside, her appetite gone. The thought of spending days in the back of beyond didn't appeal at all – all that finding a place to have a shit in private, all those bugs, only being able to wash with a flannel and not getting a proper shower, and what about her hair? That was going to be a total train-wreck in a couple of days. She'd packed dry shampoo but it was far from an ideal solution. She excused herself from the table and headed back to her accommodation. Captain Lewis was there, getting changed to go running in her lunch hour.

'Hi, boss,' she said. She and Captain Lewis had mutually agreed that, under the circumstances, they could drop the formalities when they were on their own.

'Hello, Immi. How's tricks?'

Immi snorted. 'I'm off to God-knows-where in an hour or so.'

'Ooh, really?'

Immi goggled. Sam Lewis sounded envious.

'Hey, if you want to go instead...'

'It's got to be more interesting than being stuck here.'

'I suppose if meeting bugs, snakes, crocs, and having no running water is your idea of interesting, feel free take my place.'

Sam smiled. 'Sorry, commitments here. But time alone with Jack Raven... it's quite a pay-off.'

'He floats your boat?'

'Let's put it this way, I wouldn't object to being in a life raft with him.'

'Me neither,' said Immi. And Captain Lewis could fancy him all she wanted but Immi was going to be the one spending time with him. If anyone was going to get first dibs on Jack Raven it was going to be her. Immi pulled her Bergen out from under her bed and tipped its contents onto her bed before she began to refill it with the kit she'd need for the next few days, staring with the pile of stuff she'd been issued an hour earlier.

'How long are you going for?' asked Lewis.

'I don't know, but, however long it is, it's going to be too long.'

'You might see elephants or lions or anything, though.'

'Boss, I've seen them in the zoo.' She carried on throwing in a few pairs of clean knickers, a packet of wet-wipes, a roll of soft loo paper, mosquito repellent and some clean issue T-shirts. She sighed. 'I bet I've forgotten something.'

'And there'll be no popping to the shops where you're going.'

Immi shook her head and hefted her Bergen onto her shoulders. She staggered slightly.

'Wish me luck, then.'

'Good luck!'

Immi tottered out into the sunshine and headed for the MT office. When she arrived, a line of trucks carrying the component parts of a prefabricated bridge was waiting, along with a couple of four-tonners carrying the troops to build it. A signals Land Rover towing a large generator brought up the rear. Immi warily eyed the trucks containing the troops. The soldier nearest the tailgate was picking his nose and examining the result on the end of his finger. Immi shuddered.

A voice by her ear said, 'Imagine several hours in the company of that lot.'

Immi turned to see Jack, also looking at the four-tonners and their passengers.

'Because you're a civvy, I expect you could get a lift in the cab if you wanted it,' she said.

'If I go in the cab, you will too.'

'Really?' Immi felt her spirits lift. At least up front she'd get to see some of the countryside. She might have shown indifference to Sam Lewis about what the journey might offer by way of sightseeing but if she had a choice between travelling with a window to look out of, on a padded seat, or in the back of a badly sprung truck with no air-con and nothing to look at but dark green canvas or a nose-picking squaddie, she knew which was the better option.

Jack went to the front of the vehicle and had a word with the driver, then he returned.

'Chuck your Bergen in, we're going club class,' said Jack.

Immi squealed and then checked her enthusiasm. How uncool was that! Jack picked up her Bergen – 'Here, guys, catch' – and lobbed it into the truck, followed by his own and ignored the muttering from the soldiers about women and TV personalities and preferential treatment.

'They'll get over it,' he reassured Immi as he escorted her to the cab and gave her a bunk up to her seat. The driver held out his hand for her to grab and, inelegantly, she clambered up.

Immi settled down in front of the vast windscreen and looked with pleasure at the view it afforded. Definitely better than being sardined in the back with a load of smelly, farting soldiers.

Jack plumped down next to her and broke out a packet of smokes. He leaned across Immi. 'Want one?' he said to the driver.

'Cheers, guv.' The driver stuck it behind his ear for later. 'I'm Tyler, by the way, or Ty. Have we met?'

'I do the odd bit on the BBC news. Jack Raven.' Jack held his hand out, again, across Immi.

'And I'm Immi,' she piped up, not wanting to be left out.

'Of course,' said Tyler, taking Jack's hand and shaking it warmly. 'Bloody hell, you've been to some places.'

'Probably no worse than you,' said Jack, reasonably.

'Yeah, but I get a gun and can shoot back at the buggers. No, I really take my hat off to you. It's a privilege to meet you.'

She sat back in the high seat of the cab and looked at Jack. OK, so he was more famous than she imagined if even a bog-standard driver had heard of him. And respected him. And that made him even more attractive. She knew she was shallow, but hey, so what? It wasn't a crime, was it? Maybe being stuck for a while upcountry wasn't going to be so bad after all, not if she was going to be stuck with Jack. She moved slightly closer to him.

Chapter Twenty-Four

Maddy was at a loose end. Susie was away visiting friends, her friends who didn't have kids – or who didn't have kids of school age – were using the time while their husbands were, like Seb, in Africa to escape from the patch and quarters. Indeed, she was supposed to be at her parents' home and now, given recent events, almost wished she was. Almost... The thought of listening to her mother banging on about the unsuitability of her choice of husband was a marginally worse prospect than being stalked by some potty woman.

She was irritated with herself that she still felt intimidated by this person. It had been a fortnight since the maniacal banging and ringing on the door but the memory of it still gave her the chills. At least then she'd had a locked door between her and her caller but now she worried about encountering whoever it was outside in the open. It was ridiculous that she felt imprisoned in her own home and she really needed to get out, to go into town, to do something other than play stacking cups with Nathan. But she didn't feel comfortable going out on her own; even a quick dash to the Spar for essentials daunted her. She and Nathan had been mostly living on stuff from the freezer and store-cupboard ingredients but she really needed to do a proper supermarket shop. Was she being cowardly wanting to have a friend to accompany her? And yet who could she ask? She wondered if Jenna fancied meeting up. Maybe she'd swap an hour in the supermarket for a coffee and a bun. She got her mobile out.

An hour later she was waiting outside Jenna's flat.

She was idly listening to the radio when a tap on the window sent her heart rate into orbit. She jerked around and then felt a spasm of relief when she saw it was Jenna. Of course it was. She pressed the button to unlock the central locking.

'Sorry, didn't mean to make you jump,' said Jenna as she slid into the passenger seat.

'And I shouldn't be so nervy.'

'Any more texts?'

'Nothing,' said Maddy, as she started the engine and drew away from the kerb.

'Maybe she's given up. Or maybe she's on this exercise too.'

Maddy shook her head. 'If it is Michelle, she's stationed at a training regiment. I can't imagine she'd be sent out to Kenya.'

'No, I suppose not. Let's hope she's given up, then. Don't suppose you've heard from your old man?'

'Not a dicky-bird. You?'

Jenna shook her head. 'Wasn't really expecting to, to be honest. He said he didn't think there'd be much in the way of mobile telephone masts out there. Anyway, even if there are it'd cost a fortune. I think I'd rather he saved his money than spend it on a crackly phone call to tell me that the weather is nice and he's working hard.'

Maddy laughed. 'Very pragmatic.'

'Hey, don't use long words. I'm only a hairdresser.'

Maddy swung the car into the supermarket car park and had to hunt for a space.

'Well, you've got to expect it to be mad on a Saturday, haven't you?' said Jenna.

'Saturday?'

Jenna looked at her friend in astonishment. 'You didn't know?'

Maddy looked sheepish. 'I don't have a routine at the

moment, apart from sorting out Nathan, so the days are a bit of a blur.'

Jenna giggled. 'Blimey, when my days are a bit of a blur I know I've overdone the voddies the night before. Don't think I'm cut out to find out how they'd blur due to having a kid.'

Finally they found a vacant space and while Jenna fetched a trolley, Maddy extracted Nathan from his car seat. The supermarket, when they got inside, was as heaving as the car park.

While Maddy pushed the trolley slowly through the crush, trying not to bang it on other shoppers' shins and ankles, Jenna whizzed off, unencumbered, to fetch the next few things on Maddy's list. Finally they got to the last items and the final aisle.

'Sliced bread,' said Maddy. Jenna zoomed off, weaving her slim body through the press of people. Maddy, standing by the cakes, bunged a packet of chocolate brownies and another of millionaire's shortbread into the trolley and then followed Jenna's path. Passing the wines, she also picked up a bottle of white.

'Good shout,' said Jenna, also picking up a couple. 'After all it's the weekend.'

As they queued for the till, Nathan reached his boredom threshold and began to wail. Maddy rolled her eyes.

'Give him to me,' said Jenna.

'Really?' Maddy was stunned.

'Look, I know about kids. I'm the oldest of four. I may not be wild about having any of my own but I know about looking after the little buggers. Come here, you.' She hauled Nathan out of the trolley seat, grabbed a banana with a cheery, 'Tesco can probably afford to take the hit,' and headed for the exit. Maddy instantly felt much calmer. By the time she'd paid and was pushing her trolley out into the car park she was almost Zen-like.

Jenna was sitting on a bench outside the door, feeding Nathan with tiny bits of banana and jiggling him on her lap to make him giggle between mouthfuls.

Maddy almost wept with gratitude.

'Let's go,' she said. 'I was going to take you out for a coffee but I bought some treats. How about we go back to mine? Nathan's due his nap and he gets horribly grumpy if he doesn't get it. I think it'd be tempting providence to stay out any longer.'

'I dunno, Mads. I'm still not keen on the idea of hanging around the patches.'

'Honest, Jen, the place is almost deserted. Hardly anyone is about and all you've got to do is get out of the car and walk into the house. Go on.' She smiled winningly at Jenna.

'Oh all right. The sky didn't fall in last time I came to yours, did it?'

'Great.'

Twenty minutes later the pair were in the kitchen. Maddy was waddling around, unpacking the carrier bags, while the kettle had started to boil and Nathan was already asleep in his cot, upstairs.

Maddy scrunched up the last empty bag and slammed one cupboard door shut then opened another one to get out a couple of mugs and a jar of instant. 'Coffee?'

'It's what you promised.'

Maddy spooned the granules into the mugs, and then opened both the shortbread and the brownies and tipped them onto a plate. 'Take these through, would you. Milk and sugar?'

'Just milk,' said Jenna as she went into the sitting room with the loaded plate.

A minute or so later Maddy joined her and lowered herself into an armchair with an audible 'Oof'. 'I shall be glad when this is over,' she said.

'Not sure about that. My mum always said that kids are easier to look after when they're on the inside, and she had four,' said Jenna.

'Maybe she has a point. And I haven't got Caro to help any more.'

'No? That's a shame, you and her were good mates. What happened to her?'

'Her husband got sent to a desk job somewhere in London. I miss her.'

'That's one of the lousy things about the army – people keep moving and it's dead easy to lose touch.'

'One of the lousy things amongst a whole mountain of lousy things.'

'Tell me about it,' said Jenna. And as they munched on the cakes and sipped their coffee they compared notes about all the things that had pissed them off. Some of the time their gripes made them both laugh and once or twice it got to the jabby-finger-and-another-thing stage but they both found it hugely cathartic to get it off their chests.

The doorbell rang. 'I won't be a mo,' said Maddy, heaving herself out of the armchair and heading towards the front door.

Having someone in the house had relaxed her so when she opened it and saw who was calling, she physically reeled back.

'Michelle!'

'Surprise.'

Maddy tried to push the door shut but Michelle, taller and much stronger, pushed back and managed to squeeze through it and into Maddy's house, leaving the door open behind her.

'Get out,' hissed Maddy. She felt shaky with the shock of the encounter. Or was it fear?

'Not till we've had a chat. You've not been very co-operative, have you?'

'I've got nothing to say to you.' The adrenalin in her fired her bravado.

'That makes things easier 'cos I've got plenty to say to you. For a start, I don't care what you think about the state of your marriage, but take it from me, it's over.'

Maddy felt her anger blaze. 'No, it isn't,' she snarled back.

Michelle, unfazed, gave her an insolent stare and nodded. 'Really? If you want to think that it's fine by me but you're deluded. Seb told me himself. He said he was bored to sobs by you and he wanted out. He told me you were a waste of space in bed and that all you could do was whine and moan about how poorly you feel.'

Maddy felt as if the floor had given way under her feet. No! The anger, the shock and the initial rush of fear gave way to a tidal wave of self-pity and doubt and she battled tears. Seb wouldn't say that. Of course he wouldn't, no way. But she also knew that she hadn't been much fun in the bedroom... so... maybe... The doubt assailed her. So, had he? No, he wouldn't be so cruel, but supposing...

'No, he didn't. You're lying,' she yelled at Michelle, trying as much to convince herself as her adversary.

'Really?'

'Yes, he'd never say anything like that. He loves me, he told me so.'

Michelle guffawed. 'Just words, Maddy, just words.'

'You're wrong – he loves me. He told me so, he gave me this.' She pulled her locket out from under her blouse.

'A present to keep you from guessing the real situation. It worked, didn't it?'

Maddy felt as if she'd been punched. No! 'No. I'm not listening to you any more. You're lying. Seb wouldn't be like that. Never. Get out!'

Maddy sensed a movement at the other end of the hall.

'You heard Maddy,' said Jenna, quietly. 'You're not welcome.'

Michelle switched her gaze to this new adversary.

'This is none of your business. Butt out.'

Jenna walked down the hall. 'Maddy's my friend and she doesn't want you here. That makes it very much my business.' She leaned towards Michelle. 'So get out... or do I have to make you leave?'

Michelle laughed. 'Oh, please,' she sneered

Jenna put her hands on Michelle's shoulders and gave her a shove. She caught Michelle off guard and off balance. Michelle lurched backwards towards the still-open front door.

'Oh, so ladylike,' she said with narrowed eyes.

Jenna snorted. 'That's rich, coming from a whore like you.'

Michelle's eyes widened. 'How dare you?'

Jenna gave Michelle another shove but this time her adversary was ready and braced and she didn't budge. Michelle looked smug but the look was wiped off her face when Jenna whipped her hand up, grabbed a handful of her hair and yanked.

'Ouch,' squealed Michelle.

Jenna pulled Michelle's hair more, forcing her to bend to follow it. 'You're right, I'm not a lady and I fight dirty. Now either you get out or I start scratching.' She showed Michelle the acrylic nails on her free hand. Michelle's eyes widened.

'You wouldn't.'

Jenna flexed her hand into a claw. 'You think? I'm as hard as these nails.' She pressed her bright red talons hard against Michelle's cheek. 'Now fuck off.'

She let go of Michelle's hair and shoved. This time Michelle did reel backwards, her heel catching on the door sill, causing her to stumble in a very ungainly fashion and she half fell out of the house.

Jenna picked a dozen loose hairs off the palm of her hand and dropped them disdainfully onto the doorstep. 'And don't come back,' she shot at Michelle, before she slammed the door, hard. She turned back to an ashen Maddy. 'Good job I was here.'

Maddy sagged against the wall.

'Hey, you all right?'

Maddy could feel tears trickling down her face. She brushed them away. 'But what if you hadn't been?'

'You'd have coped. Of course you would.'

'No, I wouldn't. I can't bear to think what would have happened if...'

'If what?'

Maddy shook her head. 'Supposing...'

'Suppose, nothing. That bitch is all talk. She came here to scare you.'

'Are you sure?'

''Course. I know her type.' Jenna laughed. 'Takes one to know one.'

'You're not like that.'

Jenna shook her head. 'I wouldn't bank on it.'

Maddy's face grimaced as a sharp pain lanced into her side.

'You all right?' asked Jenna.

'The baby.' She gasped as another pain bit.

'What?' Jenna looked worried.

'It's nothing. The baby is doing somersaults. It's probably as rattled as I am.'

Jenna took Maddy's arm and led her back to the sitting room. 'Right, first off I'm going to make you a cuppa and you're going to sit down and put your feet up and then I'm going to ring the OC Rear Party and tell him what's been happening.'

'No!'

'No? Why not?'

'Let's not involve the army.'

'Maddy,' said Jenna, 'that woman is nuts. I don't think she's a real danger but she can't get away with that. She needs stopping.'

'I know, but I don't want to involve outsiders.'

'Maddy, I really, really don't want to think that she's going to go any further than she has. But you can't take that risk. And even if it stops where it is, she can't be allowed to get away with what she's done already. Someone needs to read her the riot act.'

'Yes, you're right.'

'So, you agree… someone needs to have a word with her.'

'No, I agree that she's not a danger. She's gone a bit off the rails because she's madly in love and can't have Seb so she wants to lash out. She's like a kid having a tantrum.'

Jenna snorted. 'Sorry, Mads, but you're talking bollocks. She's not a two-year-old, she's a grown-up. She knows exactly what she's doing. She's bonkers and selfish and nasty to boot and you know it.' Jenna's expression softened. 'Maddy, the authorities need to know. Look, I don't want to scare you but supposing we're wrong. Suppose she does go further. This isn't just about you. There are others you have to think about.'

Maddy sagged. 'Maybe you're right. Oh, God, who am I kidding? I just don't want to face up to any of this situation – it's just so horrible. I can't believe it's really happening.' She sighed and rubbed her face. 'I suppose I feel that if I involve other people I'm admitting that Seb really might have had an affair.' Even as she said it she felt stricken. She felt the back of her nose prickle and knew tears were imminent. She blinked rapidly and swallowed. She'd had enough drama for one day, she couldn't face ringing up Alan Milward and telling him about what had been going on. She knew she had to do it, Jenna was right, but not now. 'But let's leave it till Monday, eh?'

'I'm not sure…'

'Jenna, it'll be fine.' Maddy was trying to convince herself, as much as Jenna, that her decision was right. 'I can't face the palaver right now, not on top of everything else.'

'I don't like the thought of you being on your own on a near-deserted patch with a kid to look after and one in the oven as well. What if she comes back?'

'Tell you what, if that's what's worrying you, why don't you stay? Your old man's away, so's mine. You don't have anything to get back to, I've got nothing planned… Go on, what do you say?'

Jenna looked at her. 'Aren't there rules about officers' wives having people like me to stay in their quarters?'

Maddy laughed. 'Almost certainly! Let's live dangerously.' And then she winced again. 'Sheesh. I wish the little bugger would stop doing that. Now then, let's see what I can rustle up for lunch while you nip home and grab whatever you need for the weekend.'

'I won't be long. And, while I'm gone, don't open the door without checking who it is. Promise?'

'Promise.'

Chapter Twenty-Five

Sam was in the workshop, organising a recovery vehicle and team of mechanics to schlep out to Archers Post – the camp at the entrance to the Kenyan live-firing ranges – to sort out a couple of Land Rovers, which had already broken down. She was flicking though a sheaf of papers, trying to work out what her resources actually were and thus, what she could spare. Beside her, on the desk, the radio crackled and hissed and she kept half an ear open for her own call sign. It was unlikely that anyone would need to talk to her directly but they'd want her to answer promptly if they did.

'Am I disturbing you?'

She recognised the voice and looked up. 'James! When did you get here?' Goodness, it was so nice to see a friendly face.

James dragged a hand over his face and muffled a yawn. 'The main party landed at dawn, then we all went up to the British Army Training Unit for a briefing then back on the bus and now here.' He glanced at his watch. 'I don't think I've slept for thirty-six hours; I'm bushed.'

'Would coffee help? It's only the compo sort and condensed milk, though. Not posh Douwe Egberts and cream or anything.'

'I don't care, as long as it's hot and wet and contains caffeine. Frankly it sounds like nectar.'

Sam got up and went over to another trestle table where there was a kettle, a battered coffee container, a tin of milk and some grubby mugs. A couple of minutes later she returned and handed James his drink. 'I'm sorry, but I couldn't find the silver salver and the doilies.' She gave him a welcoming smile.

James grinned back at her. 'Numpty,' he said. He gazed at her fondly. As Sam moved around her desk to sit down again she saw Luke staring at them, the epitome of disapproval; his sapphire blue eyes blazing, his mouth compressed into a thin line and his jaw clenched. Disapproving of what? Taking a quick break? Making coffee for a colleague? Angrily, she stared back at him till he dropped his gaze.

'So, what's next?' she asked James.

'You mean after I finally get some zeds?'

'Yup.' She sipped her coffee and grimaced. Yuck, coffee and Carnation milk, horrible.

'Straight to Samburu, an overnight stop at Archers Post and then onto the ranges.'

'Aw. I was hoping to have a catch-up.' She put her mug down on her desk. 'Not that there's much time for that – everyone's flat out – but even a quick chat to an old mucker would be nice.'

'How's it going with the ASM?'

'He's still tricky, still goes his own sweet way if he thinks he can get away with it, but it's not as bad as it was. By the time I get posted out again, we might even make a team.'

James laughed. 'Keep working at it. At least it's going in the right direction.' He swigged some more of his coffee, and then yawned. 'God, I need to get to bed. Maybe drinking coffee isn't the best idea.' He took another gulp. 'On the other hand, I don't think anything will stop me from sleeping. The way I feel right now I could neck half-a-dozen Red Bulls and still crash out.'

'Given how shattered you look, I think you're right.'

James yawned again. 'Sorry.'

'Look, go and get your head down and I'll see you for supper in the cookhouse.'

'When? Five?' He handed her his half-finished drink.

'Make it half-past. It's crazy here and I never get away before that.'

He leaned forward and gave her a quick, brotherly peck on the cheek. Across the workshop a large piece of metal clanged onto the floor and the sound reverberated through the warm air. Sam spun around to see what had happened and saw Luke had dropped a drip tray and a pool of oil was spreading outwards on the ground at his feet. He stared at her defiantly before he wandered off to fetch some fuller's earth to put on the spill. Sam thought about upbraiding him for carelessness but suddenly she couldn't be bothered. Sod him.

After James had left she returned to the jobs awaiting her attention and blanked out the noise of the workshop as she concentrated on her work. Time flew by as she worked out rosters and allocated resources. Before she knew it, it was almost time for lunch.

'Ma'am?' said the ASM, approaching the trestle table.

She looked up. 'Yes?'

'We've got a problem.'

But she knew from past experience with the ASM that whatever it was it was going to be her problem, not one they were going to share. Sam felt her shoulders slump. Like she didn't have enough on her plate. 'Yes?'

'We've got real issues with a genny. The sappers building that bridge broke theirs, they've tried to fix it and from the sound of things they've made things worse.'

Sam rolled her eyes. Like they had generators to spare. 'How bad?'

'Could be terminal.'

Sam threw her pen down on the desk and sighed. 'I suppose we'd better drag another one up there, in case the team that goes to repair it can't. They can bring the dud one back here if it's in clip state and we can see what we can do in the work-shop.'

'That's what I think too. The trouble is…'

'Yes?'

'The trouble is you're the only electrical engineer we've got left who's probably got the expertise to do it.'

Sam shook her head. 'You're joking.'

'Honest, ma'am. You know how it is and all the other sparks are already deployed and run off their feet. I wouldn't ask you if there was any other option.'

For once she felt inclined to cut the ASM some slack. 'OK, fair point. How long do you reckon this is going to take?'

'Couple of days ma'am – tops. It's a fair old drive to the site and then you're going to have to see what can be done…'

Sam sighed again. 'Then you'll have to hold the fort while I'm gone.' She knew he'd love that.

'I'll cope.'

She had no doubts on that score. Besides, he'd get to do things his way, not hers. '*And* I'm going to need a driver so that'll be two of us out of the loop. There's a bit of me that says "bugger it" and that I should risk going on my own…'

'You can't. You know what standard operating procedures say. And it's in SOPs for a reason. It can be bloody dodgy out there. What with poachers and the wildlife, if you had a break-down it simply wouldn't be safe on your own.'

'I know, I know. I wasn't going to do it, really.' But even so, she felt that if there had been a sniff of a chance of getting away with it she'd have had a try. They really didn't have the manpower to spare a driver for her – a guy to be her chauffeur and to hold her hand. But, on the other hand, the Bailey bridge was being built a very long way upcountry, far too far away for it to be in any way sensible to attempt such a journey on her own. No, the ASM was right, she'd have to have a driver.

'Who can we spare?' she asked.

'Think it's going to have to be Blake.'

Sam's heart sank. Of all the guys in her LAD the one she least fancied spending a straight forty-eight hours with was Blake.

'OK, Mr Williams, you'd better tell him to get ready to move out tomorrow.'

'Ah, that's the thing.'

'What's the thing?' Sam felt her heart sink further.

'You know that BBC journo we've got embedded?'

'Yeah.'

'He's up at the bridge – doing a piece about the hearts and minds aspect of the exercise. The CO wants the genny fixed ASAP so this guy can see how efficient and wilco 1 Herts are. I don't think he wants the sappers getting all the kudos; he wants some for us as well.'

Sam nodded. 'So tell me, this means Blake and I are leaving today, right?'

The ASM nodded. 'That's about the size of it. As soon as you can if you're going to make it before nightfall.'

Great. Fucking great. 'OK.' She sighed again. 'Tell Blake that he's been spammed for this, tell him to meet me outside my room in twenty minutes.' She pulled a piece of paper towards her and scribbled a few words on it. 'And can you make sure this gets to Captain Rosser. Tell him "sorry" from me, would you, and that I'll see him at Endex.'

'Righto, ma'am.'

Sam pushed the papers on her desk into a pile and headed off to the cubby hole she called her room to grab her kit for the trip.

Jack was sitting under a thorn tree on a folding chair, tapping away at his laptop, pausing every now and again to look at the scene ahead of him. Thirty yards in front of him was a swirling brown river and on the same bank as him were twenty or so soldiers, stripped to the waist, building a bridge out of the biggest Meccano set in the universe. It was hot, heavy work but the soldiers were laughing and joshing as they laboured, making the piecing together of the complicated structure all look remarkably easy. The troop commander had told Jack that, in essence, it was a case of reading the instructions.

'A bit like flat-pack furniture. You know, you insert tab A into slot B and Bob's your uncle.'

As Jack had once been almost reduced to a gibbering wreck trying to construct an Ikea bookcase he wasn't so sure – not that he was going to admit it to this young army officer. He swatted a fly and then took off his bush hat and used it to fan himself. Shit, it was hot. He reached down beside his chair, grabbed his water bottle and took a swig. Bleuch, it was warm, but he still glugged down half of it.

A light flashed on his screen, warning him that his battery was dangerously low. Quickly he hit the save button, shoved in a memory stick and re-saved to that – belt and braces and all that – and then shut down his machine.

'Finished?' said Immi.

Jack shook his head. 'Nowhere near. But until we get a generator that works I have no way of recharging the batteries. I brought three and they're all flat now.'

'You've got to hope that one will get here today. I don't want to spend another night out here with bugger all light,' said Immi with feeling. 'God knows what was making those noises last night but it sounded big and hungry.'

'It was probably miles away. Sound carries a long way out here.'

Immi gave him a look that told Jack she thought he was talking out of his rear end.

'Truly,' he said with a grin.

'Huh.'

'Look,' he said, 'I can't write without my laptop. I thought I'd take a bunch of pictures, shoot a video. Want to help?'

'How?' said Immi warily.

'I want you to hold the camera while I do a piece to it. Think you can do that?'

Immi perked up. 'As long as it's not too complicated.'

'It's point and click. Honest. All you do is hold it steady and focus on my face.'

'OK.'

'I thought I'd go along the bank there so I can get the guys working in the background. And then I'm planning to head off to the village to talk to some of the locals about the difference this bridge will make. The hot intel is that the headman speaks good English so it should make a nice story. It's always better when the viewers hear it straight from the horse's mouth and not via an interpreter. You can come too, if you'd like. In fact, I'd really like it if you did.'

Immi didn't look too keen.

'You'd add a bit of glamour – the newsroom might like it. You'd get your face on the telly.'

That did it, but Jack could tell that Immi was trying to look casual about the prospect. 'No, you're right. It'll pass the time.'

Jack went to the vehicle where he had his kit stored and returned with a large camera bag. He got out the hand-held video camera. He showed Immi how to hold it, which buttons she had to press and stood in front of her while she had a go at filming him.

'How do you know what to say?' she said, after Jack had delivered a short but succinct piece about what the sappers were hoping to achieve.

'It's not rocket science,' said Jack. 'I say what I see. Besides…'

he gave her a grin '...being coherent in front of a camera is the day job.'

Immi shrugged and handed him back the camera. 'Here, you'd better check that I didn't screw up.'

Jack stood next to Immi so she could look at the screen too. He was very aware of her fresh clean smell. He'd had to get up close and personal with loads of soldiers in his time but Immi was a one-off. Despite the fact that she seemed the least likely person ever to have joined the army there was something refreshing about her honesty when it came to her attitude to privation and hardship. She'd shared her opinion about the latrines several times. And, in spite of himself, Jack couldn't but help respect the fact that, despite the tough conditions of the sappers' camp, she still managed to have immaculate hair and make-up. This was obviously a woman who wasn't prepared to let her standards slip because there was no running water or even decent sanitation. But he'd also noticed the way that she didn't take any shit from the soldiers. She might not be able to carry her own body weight in kit, she mightn't like wildlife, but if any of the squaddies gave her any lip at all she could issue a blistering put-down without a second thought, which always amused the other lads who were not the butt of her remarks. So, in spite of the fact that she was a girly-girl, all the guys who worked with her really seemed to like her. And Jack found that he did too.

He filmed the soldiers as they carried on building the bridge, he interviewed the troop commander and some of his men about being tasked to help the locals and got some interesting comments regarding the importance of putting something back into a country that let them have free rein to play with their kit and where, despite the less than commendable behaviour of a previous generation of soldiers, the locals were almost invariably friendly.

He began to stow his camera away.

'That you finished?' said Immi, watching him work.

'I've got what I want here. Now I'm going over to the village.'

'Is it far?'

''Bout a mile. I thought we'd walk—'

'Walk!'

'Yeah, you know, putting one foot in front of the other.'

Immi narrowed her eyes. 'Don't you get smart with me, Mr BBC Reporter.'

Jack laughed. 'I want to get a feel for what the kids have had to do to get to and from school. Only they have to walk about four times the distance, morning and night. So... you coming?'

'But what about lions and shit like that?'

Jack looked at her. 'And what do you think the kids have for protection when they walk to school?'

'But...'

Jack raised his eyebrows. 'Oh, go on. Live dangerously.'

'It's *dying* dangerously that bothers me.' Immi sighed. 'Oh, come on, then. The sooner we go, the sooner some bloody lion gets its lunch.'

She picked up her daysack, shoved several litre bottles of water into it and set off.

'Oi,' said Jack.

Immi spun around. 'Come on,' she called back.

'You're going the wrong way.'

'Fuck.' She retraced her steps and together they set off through the scrub to the village.

Maddy sat at her kitchen table, spooning mashed avocado into Nathan's mouth, while Jenna sat beside her and toyed with a glass of wine.

'I feel guilty about drinking your wine when you aren't having any,' she said.

'God, don't you dare,' said Maddy. 'You've done more than enough already and this is the least I can do to thank you.' She scraped out the bowl and shoved the last spoonful of green goo at Nathan. He banged his hands on the tray of his high chair in appreciation and smacked his lips.

'More,' he said.

'Sorry, hon. All gone.' Maddy showed him the empty bowl.

'Gone,' repeated Nathan.

Maddy handed him a breadstick to chew on and then levered herself to her feet. As she straightened up she winced.

'Ouch,' she said. She leaned against the counter and breathed slowly.

'You all right?'

'Yeah, fine. The little bugger is being really active today.' And it didn't help matters that her back seemed to be aching. Not so surprising, she thought, with all this extra weight to carry.

'Bugger,' said Nathan.

Maddy looked at him aghast as Jenna hooted with laughter.

'Ain't that typical,' said Jenna. 'You'd best hope he forgets that word again before his daddy comes home.'

'Bugger, bugger, bugger,' crowed Nathan.

'I'm going to pretend I'm not hearing this,' said Maddy. 'If I say anything I'll probably make things worse.'

She opened the oven door and the smell of warm quiche wafted into the kitchen. She looked at the tart and decided that it looked ready to serve so she hauled it out and plonked it on the table. Then she reached into the fridge and took out a bowl of salad.

'Blimey,' said Jenna. 'This is a bit healthy, isn't it?'

'Well, if it was just me I wouldn't bother much but I kind of feel responsible for junior here. I can probably survive pretty well without my five-a-day but...' She patted the bump.

They all tucked into their lunch. Maddy let Nathan use his hands to eat his quiche so she and Jenna could get on with their meal uninterrupted.

'So,' said Jenna. 'What are you going to do?'

Maddy gazed at her. 'You mean about Seb?'

Jenna nodded.

Once again Maddy's eyes filled with tears. What was the matter with her? She was so emotional. 'I don't know. I mean, I don't even know if this woman is telling the truth. Supposing she's out to cause trouble? Supposing she's lying about going with Seb.'

'Is that what you think?'

'I've got to.' Maddy gulped. 'If I'm wrong, and there really is something going on, what happens to us?' She gazed at Nathan and then her bump.

Jenna put her hand over Maddy's. 'Whatever happens, I'll be here for you. You were kind to me once. I'd like to repay the favour. But we've got to hope it doesn't come to that.'

'The thing is,' admitted Maddy, 'if it is true, can I ever trust him again? I feel sick every time I even think about it. I mean, how could he?'

'Take it from me, Mads, soldiers like shagging. Their brains are in their bollocks and they can only think with their dicks. Of course, officers might be different but that's what squaddies are like.'

Maddy gave a weak laugh. 'The trouble is what with morning sickness and now being so utterly huge Seb's not been getting much... any, really.'

'So, do you really believe that if another girl gives him the come-on...?'

Maddy sighed. 'I don't know. I don't want to believe he

would be like that. But that doubt is there now. Maybe I should pretend I've never had any contact with Michelle. Never mention Michelle, and what she said, to him or anyone. Maybe if I behave like an ostrich it'll all go away.' She shook her head. 'And if it is true, given how rubbish I've been as a wife lately, I can't really blame him, can I?

'Oh, yes, you fu...' Jenna shot a look at Nathan. 'Oh, yes, you can. Well, I would. Maybe you're a nicer person.'

'Maybe I've got more to lose. If he leaves me I become an irregular occupant and the army has the right to kick me out of this place in six months. Jen, how would I cope with being homeless with two tiny children?' Maddy's face crumpled. 'It doesn't matter if I trust him or not – I can't risk putting the kids through that. Jen, if he comes back I think I've got to pretend that nothing ever happened.'

'Then you'd better hope that Michelle plays along too. It'll be a hard act to pull off if she keeps hanging around. This is why you've got to tell the authorities and get her stopped.'

Maddy sniffed. 'You're right, and I will do it, promise. On Monday.' She gasped again. 'Hell's teeth.' She glared at her bump. 'Stop it, I know you don't like Michelle either but there's no need to lash out.'

Chapter Twenty-Six

Through the door of her tiny room Sam could see Luke sitting in the Land Rover, staring straight ahead, one hand resting on the open side of the vehicle, his fingers drumming on the metalwork. From his expression and his body language she could tell he was pissed off. Beyond pissed off.

Well, me too, buddy, thought Sam as she hefted her Bergen onto her shoulders, picked up her day sack and headed out of her cubby hole and into the bright African sun. I don't want to trek up north any more than you do, so get over it.

'Afternoon, Corporal,' she said as she rolled her pack off her back and into the rear of the Rover, where it landed with a thud next to the case of water, Luke's own Bergen, a half-dozen jerrycans of fuel and the other paraphernalia they were lugging up to the sappers' camp. She stepped over the towbar that connected the genny to the vehicle, chucked her day sack into the footwell and then settled herself in the passenger seat beside Luke.

'Ma'am,' acknowledged Luke.

'All set?' she asked.

'I was waiting for you,' he said.

'So, that's a *yes*, then, is it?' she said. She glanced across at him and wondered why she felt unnerved by his proximity. No, not unnerved but definitely unsettled. It was, she was sure, because he was such a closed book, and yet there was definitely something edgy about him. As Luke started the engine and drove towards the camp gates he looked across at her with the intensity that rattled her. She buckled up her seat belt to cover up her confusion.

On the dash was a millboard with a range map clipped to it.

'Will you need me to map read?' she asked, as she reached for it, but Luke beat her to it and snatched it away. He flipped up the map and showed her the route card he'd written out.

'I know my way,' he said.

He shoved the map back on the dash as the Rover bounced and jounced over the rutted dirt track that led through the camp. Finally they were through the barrier and then onto the black top and Luke was able to move up through the gears and get some speed on. Or he was until they hit the town of Nanyuki and the bonkers traffic of the sprawling town. Almost as soon as the houses and shops sprang up along the road the traffic increased exponentially and they were back to a crawl. Sheesh, at this rate, if they got to the sappers' base before nightfall it would be a miracle. Sam watched him carefully manoeuvre through the traffic, avoiding the other cars, the pedestrians wandering around in the warm sunshine, the stray dogs, the donkey carts and the brightly painted matatus – the local minibus-cum-taxis that were invariably overladen and whose drivers seemed to think that they were exempt from obeying the normal laws of the road. Indicating or giving way didn't seem to be conventions that applied to their drivers so Luke had to constantly hit the brakes to avoid collisions.

'Look at that,' she said, pointing at a hideous marabou stork picking over a rubbish heap.

'I'd be better off watching the road,' retorted Luke, as he swerved to avoid a wobbling, overladen bike.

'Goodness,' she said, pointing at some women in local headdress. Then, 'Watch out,' as a man stepped out in front of them.

Luke slapped his hands on the steering-wheel. 'You know, ma'am, it might be easier to drive if I didn't get the running commentary.' He shot her a look. 'Just saying.'

Sam felt momentarily crushed. 'If that's what you want,' she replied coldly.

Finally they got through the town and out onto the open highway and could really begin to motor. Once they moved past thirty miles per hour the Land Rover engine gave out the familiar high-pitched whine and Blake settled himself into his seat, his arm resting on the vehicle's side, steering with one hand. With her driver looking more relaxed Sam felt the tension leach out of her shoulders. There was still plenty to look at: farm animals wandering into the road; donkey carts ambling along; motorcycles with teetering piles of trade goods bound for the local market, or just far too many passengers; and now and again a dik-dik hurtled across the road in front of them, or a flock of bright birds flashed through the nearby trees. But best of all, dominating the right-hand horizon, was the vast majesty of Mount Kenya, with its fist of rugged rock, punching into the sky. Sam thought she could make out some snow on it.

Sometimes they drove through ramshackle villages with the houses made of breeze-block walls and tin roofs or planks and thatch but with a cat's cradle of cables hanging over the road, and beside it were rickety stalls laden with produce or market goods. Occasionally there was a mosque or a church and then a filling station, which was an exact clone of ones that you might see in the UK and so bizarrely out of place. They passed farms and smallholdings and sometimes they passed bigger farming operations, which were mind-blowing.

'Blimey!' said Sam as they drove past one of the biggest glasshouses she had ever seen. 'What on earth can they grow in a thing that size? It must cover miles and miles of land.' She stared at Blake. 'Do you know what they grow here?'

'Flowers.'

'Flowers?'

'Cut flowers, for Tesco and the like.'

'You're joking.'

'I don't joke.'

No, I bet you bloody don't. Sam lapsed back into silence and wondered why on earth a country on a continent where half the population seemed to be on the brink of starvation would want to grow something as useless as flowers. It made sense in Holland but not here.

'It's a lucrative cash crop,' said Blake.

'Thank you, Blake.'

They drove on and on, with yet more glasshouses flanking the road for miles until suddenly the glass stopped and fields of arable crops began; fields of plants that looked remarkably like wheat or barley so Sam felt she'd left the Netherlands and now she was in East Anglia. She wished it looked more like Africa. This wasn't what she'd expected at all. Mount Kenya was spectacular but she thought a lot of the rest of the country they were driving through could have been almost anywhere. Not even a hint of an elephant, she thought morosely.

And then suddenly she got her wish – or at least as far as the countryside was concerned. The road came to the edge of an escarpment and ahead was the most astounding, breath-taking view Sam had ever encountered. Stretching away to a way-distant horizon and hundreds and hundreds of feet below them was the African plain.

'Wow!' breathed Sam. For miles in front of her were the lion-coloured grasslands of Kenya, dotted with spreading acacia trees and scrubby thorns and with occasional pimples of hills popping up randomly. She followed the path of the road as it snaked down the escarpment and then shot off like an arrow across the savannah towards Archers Post. From this high vantage point she could see the signs of civilisation that fringed the road, the villages, the settlements the farms, but off to the west of the highway were miles and miles of bugger-all. Above was a cloudless blue dome of sky and the feeling of endless space was almost overwhelming. 'Wow,' said Sam again, to herself.

She was surprised when Blake pulled the Rover off the road and parked up on the scrubby, gravelly verge. He pulled on the handbrake and then got out and ambled off to a thicket of bushes. Sam guessed he'd gone off for a slash.

Sam jumped out, her phone at the ready and took a couple of shots of the scene. And then a selfie with Mount Kenya behind her and another with the plain as background. She checked the shots she'd taken.

'Want me to take one of you?'

Sam nearly dropped her phone. 'Er, yes. Thanks.' She handed over her mobile.

Blake held it up. 'Well, smile,' he said.

Sam grinned inanely. She heard the click of the shutter.

Sam looked at the image. It was quite good, she thought. At least he'd made her look human and not like a loon.

Michelle stormed into her room back in Pirbright and went straight over to her mirror. Four little crescents were still faintly visible from where that blonde cow had stuck her nails in. It was nothing a bit of slap couldn't cover up but Michelle was still angry with herself for not having fought back. It was because it had all been so unexpected. Maddy was so wet she wouldn't say boo to the proverbial, but that other woman was a piece of work. And common, thought Michelle. What on earth would Seb think if he knew the type of female Maddy kept company with? She'd looked like a hooker and sounded like a fishwife. She was the sort, she thought, snakily, who made Essex girls look positively classy.

Michelle's blood pressure rocketed when she remembered that the blonde had called her a whore. The cheek of it! The blonde was a tart if ever she saw one. She ought to have slapped the bitch there and then, but she'd missed her chance. Michelle fumed and considered her next move. Texting Maddy didn't seem to have worked and the doorstepping had been a bust. There had to be something she could do to peel that leech-like woman off Seb. She'd have to think about it.

Her phone rang. She looked at the caller ID. Her father. This was such a bad time for a call from him. She took a deep breath to try and calm down before she answered it.

'Daddy.'

'Hi, Michelle. I thought I'd ring to see what you've been up to.'

'Oh, nothing much,' she lied.

'I wondered if you're going to be around tomorrow?'

'You coming down this way, then?' They both knew that Michelle would never visit her father at home – not as long as her step-mother drew breath. Michelle knew this was a source of sadness to her father but she couldn't – wouldn't – change how she felt.

'I've got a meeting at the MOD on Monday – really early. Whichever way I look at it I'm going to have to come down on Sunday, so I've either got to book myself into a mess in London, or, I thought, I could book into yours at Pirbright.'

'I suppose,' said Michelle. She loved her father, she did, even though he'd married That Bitch, but she wasn't sure she wanted to see him at the moment. Perversely, although she wanted his attention more than anything in the world, she didn't want it right now. Now was completely the wrong time for him to want to see her. What if he got into a conversation with the other mess members and they mentioned her rowing phase which had stopped as abruptly as it had started? Her dad was bound to ask questions, dig away. And if her answers weren't satisfactory he'd keep digging some more and she knew she'd end up in shit creek. She could imagine his reaction if he found out about Seb. He'd disapprove, he'd get all sanctimonious, he'd tell her – as he'd done several times before in her life – that she was amoral, then he'd get angry with her and then they'd row... and all she wanted him to do was love her. Love her – not That Bitch. Not that smug woman who had stolen her father away from her, sent her away to boarding school and who had ruined her life.

'So can I? Stay at your mess? Tell you what, I'll take you out to dinner.'

Ah, dinner outside the mess. So maybe he wouldn't get to talk to the other mess members in the evening, and if his meeting was early he'd be off at sparrow's fart... result. 'Yeah, of course Dad, I'll book a table somewhere. I know some nice places in Bagshot.'

And maybe, when he saw her in situ, at her posting, getting saluted by the recruits, getting respect from the NCOs, he'd stop writing her off as a flake and a liability.

Maddy was starting to feel increasingly uncomfortable. The baby had obviously got itself into a really weird position and was pressing on bits of her she had never been aware of till now and it wasn't helping her back pain either. She couldn't stop herself from grimacing as she shifted the cushion behind her back to try and get comfortable. It didn't help matters that Nathan had fallen asleep on her lap and was making her legs go to sleep. She thought about putting him down in his cot but couldn't raise the energy to take him upstairs. Somehow it seemed easier to put up with the discomfort.

Jenna looked up from where she was sprawled on the sofa, watching a re-run of *Escape to the Country*, and saw her friend's expression. 'You all right, hon?'

'Yeah. You know, hot, uncomfortable, the baby's giving me gyp.'

'Erm,' said Jenna casually. 'Look, I could be wrong but there isn't something else going on, is there?'

'Like?'

'Well, you know, you've been in a lot of pain on and off today. It couldn't be, you know... labour?'

Maddy snorted. 'The baby isn't due for weeks. Ages and ages. Of course it isn't.'

'Sorry,' said Jenna. 'What do I know?'

But even so, Maddy glanced at the clock on the mantelpiece and casually logged the time. Of course it wasn't labour, it couldn't be... but she'd been feeling most odd, and the uncomfortable feelings had been all a bit... the same. And had they come at regular intervals?

'Anyway,' said Jenna. 'Of course I'm being stupid. You'd know, wouldn't you? I mean you've done it before.'

'Sort of. I had to be induced because Nathan was late. One minute I was fat and pregnant, then they stuck a drip in my arm and I was straight into contractions every ten minutes. All the stuff I'd learned at the antenatal class about the early stages of labour went straight out the window, I can tell you. So, if I'm honest I haven't got a clue about normal labour. But it can't be – not six weeks early. Not when Nate was two weeks late.'

'Of course it isn't,' said Jenna. 'I was being silly and I shouldn't have scared you. Blimey, you've had enough scares for one day without me making things worse.'

Maddy smiled. 'It's been a bit eventful, hasn't it? I'm glad you're here, though. I can't tell you how reassuring it is to have a friendly face around.'

Immi was trying to brace up, she really was, but it was hot, her boots were giving her a blister and everything, *everything*, she encountered either bit, stung or scratched. She trailed behind Jack, keeping to the centre of a well-worn path, but the branches of the thorn threes seemed to be able to reach out and snag her even though she was sure she was giving them a wide berth. And because the scratches on her arms wept very slightly, the insects seemed to be extra attracted to her. Was it like sharks and drops of blood in the water? she wondered. In fact, she thought, knowing her luck, a sodding, huge, great white shark was probably about to leap out of a watering hole and take a chunk out of her. Why not? Every other fucking critter seemed to have done. She slapped her neck again as she felt the pinprick of yet another insect bite.

'Are we nearly there yet?' she asked.

Jack turned. He was laughing. 'Are we nearly there yet?' he mimicked. 'That's the sort of thing five-year-olds say.'

'Bully for them,' muttered Immi. She took another swig from her water bottle.

'And yes, we are. Another few hundred yards. Look,' he said.

'At what?' grumped Immi. The last time he'd told her to look it had been at a rat trundling off into the bush. She shivered at the thought. What kind of weirdo wanted to look at a rat? He'd said they weren't like the rats in London. Really? Well, she for one wasn't going to get close enough to find out.

'There.' He pointed at the sky, and she saw a little trail of blue smoke drifting upwards.

'So?'

'So it's probably a cooking fire. In the village.'

Immi felt her spirits lift as she watched the smoke dissipate in the massive blue arc of sky. It really was quite close – maybe Jack was telling the truth.

A vicious pain lanced into her leg. 'Aieee,' she squealed and looked down and saw that she'd bumbled straight in to a dead branch from a thorn tree lying across the path. If only she'd looked where she'd been going. The spikes on it were all a couple of inches long. Absolutely fucking huge, so no wonder it had hurt. She pulled up the leg of her tropical combat trousers and saw blood was pouring down her shin from a series of puncture wounds. She blinked, trying to keep tears at bay. She really didn't want to cry in front of Jack. He'd probably laugh again. But, jeez, it hurt.

'That looks nasty,' he said, a genuine note of concern in his voice.

His sympathy made Immi feel even more self-pitying. 'I'm fine,' she lied, swallowing down a sob.

'Let me have a look.'

He crouched down. 'I don't think the thorns have broken off in your skin. I'm going to clean away the blood. Sit down,' he ordered, as he knelt in the dust.

Immi parked her bum in the middle of the path. Jack lifted up her leg and rested it on his thigh, then unscrewed a bottle of water and poured half the contents over her shin. He wiped away the bloody residue with a clean hanky and peered closely.

'I think you'll live,' he pronounced. 'I bet it canes, though.' He gave her a hug.

That was it. His sympathy tipped her over the brink and tears rolled down her face.

'You poor thing,' he said. 'It's all my fault.' He still kept his arm around her shoulder.

Through her damp sniffs, Immi said, 'How do you work that out, you daft bugger? I'm the one who didn't look where I was going.'

'It was my idea to drag you through the bundu.'

Immi found a tissue in her jacket pocket and blew her nose. 'I didn't have to come, though, did I?' She brushed her fingers across her cheeks to wipe away her tears. 'Bet I look dead minging now.'

Jack shook his head. 'No, you look lovely.'

Immi looked unconvinced so he took his camera out and snapped a picture then showed her the image. 'See?'

Immi peered at the little display. 'Hmm. My eyeliner's not run, that's something, I suppose.' She removed her leg from his thigh and pushed herself to her feet. She winced slightly as she put her weight on her injured leg.

'Is it sore?'

She nodded. 'A bit. Still, I don't think I'm a candidate for Help for Heroes, so best I man up.'

Jack, encumbered by his camera equipment, clambered to his feet and then held his hand out to Immi. As they moved off on their journey their fingers were linked.

'I suppose we ought to get going again,' said Sam, as she tried to imprint on her memory the view from the top of the escarpment.

Beside her, Blake nodded. 'If we're going to get that genny there by nightfall, then, yes, ma'am.'

My God, thought Sam, he's almost garrulous. She risked asking him a question. 'Is that the Rift Valley down there?' Given his GCSEs and the fact he'd been to Kenya before, she thought there was a fair chance he might know.

Blake shook his head. 'No idea, ma'am.' He paused, then he said, 'There is something down there that might interest you.'

'Yes?'

'You see where the road comes off the hill? There.' He was pointing into the middle distance.

Sam squinted and moved closer to Blake to try to look along his arm but he dropped his right arm and pointed with his left.

She had no idea what she was looking for. 'Not really.'

Blake sighed. He sounded exasperated. 'At the bottom.

There's two triangles of dust on either side of the road. See?'

Sam peered. Finally she saw what he was talking about. 'Oh yes. And?'

'There's a tunnel under the road there. It's for migrating elephants.'

'No! You're kidding!' That nugget of information made her feel bizarrely cheerful. 'How mad is that? A tunnel for elephants,' she repeated. 'Well I never.' Then, impulsively, 'Look, we're going to be stuck in each other's company for quite a while. I don't mind knocking the formality on the head if you don't.' She smiled at him. 'It's Luke, isn't it?'

Blake looked at her, his face stony, his eyes drilling into her, a muscle pulsing in his cheek. Sam had to force herself to return his gaze and feel the full heat of his anger. Then he said, 'Actually, ma'am, it's Corporal Blake. I earned my rank and I'm proud of it.'

'I see… *Corporal* Blake.'

They both climbed back into the Rover and a few seconds later they were back on the road and heading down the hill, off the high plateau and onto the plain below. With each few hundred feet they dropped so the temperature climbed. From the balmy, almost temperate climate at the top, suddenly they were heading into an oven. Sam broke out a bottle of water and cracked it open. She took a swig and without thinking offered it to Blake. He shook his head.

'If it's all the same to you, ma'am, I'd rather drink out of my own bottle.'

Silently she reached into the back of the vehicle, got another bottle out of the case and handed it to him. Deliberately she didn't crack the seal on the top. It was petty and childish, she knew, but it was no more than he deserved, she thought as she watched him struggle to open it single-handedly.

'Watch out!' she yelled. The Rover was heading off the road towards the rutted verge. Blake wrenched the wheel round and

304

the vehicle lurched as it swerved back on course.

'What the hell were you playing at?' said Sam.

'Sorry,' mumbled Blake.

They zoomed over the top of the elephant tunnel but, disappointingly, there were no elephants to see, and then on and on they drove, over the mercilessly hot and flat and, frankly, quite boring plain to Archers Post. They passed a few things of interest and Sam found she couldn't help exclaiming about some of them – the termite hills, the clumps of weaver birds' nests, a spotted guinea fowl, and a warthog that trotted across the road, its spiky tail held high at a jaunty angle.

They pulled into Archers Post as the day was cranking up to about its hottest. The actual town of Archers Post was a small community on a wide, muddy river with a road running through the middle and a few shops and bars that fronted onto it. On one side of it was the Samburu Game Reserve and on the other side was the start of the training area and miles and miles of wilderness and scrub. The camp was outside the town in a fenced compound but whether it was to protect the locals from the soldiers or vice versa wasn't clear. But this was where anyone who needed to be casevaced off the exercise would be sent initially for medical treatment. It was basically a staging post and where troops could laager up for the night and get final orders before moving off onto the ranges and start manoeuvres properly.

Blake zipped through the gates and onto the dusty track that led onto the ranges. Back off the metalled road he had to drop down the gears and slow down so they – and the Land Rover – weren't shaken to bits.

'How much further?' asked Sam, hanging onto the side of the Rover with one hand and her seat belt with the other.

'A couple of hours. We'll be there before sundown.'

'Excellent.' She reached forward and took the map off the

dash. Out of the corner of her eye she saw him flick a glance at her. Idly she traced the route across the range to the sappers' camp. Then she laid the map on her lap and went back to admiring the scenery.

Immi was glad she'd gone with Jack to the village. It was more fun and more interesting than she'd imagined. The women were wearing brightly coloured dresses and were a wonderful splash of colour in an otherwise khaki landscape. The village was mostly mud and thatch huts with a couple of houses built out of corrugated metal and nothing like any settlement Immi had ever seen before.

'Proper Africa, ain't it?' she said to Jack as they approached the compound.

'Yup, the real thing.'

They approached the houses though a gap in a high fence made from branches of thorn trees that was there to keep the domestic animals – and the inhabitants – safe from the attention of hungry predators at night. Immi had noticed that the sappers employed exactly the same system for their camp by the river. Until now, she hadn't had much faith in it, but, if the locals used it, maybe it did work after all. Maybe lions and leopards couldn't jump over it.

Following Jack closely, they'd gone across the beaten and swept earth that seemed to form a communal area for the families, and Jack had introduced himself to a tall black man wearing a bush shirt and shorts.

The chap's English was reasonable and before Immi knew it she was sitting in the shade by a hut, being offered tea by one of the women, while Jack was getting busy with his camera. The woman's English was almost non-existent so Immi communicated with the occasional smile to demonstrate that she was enjoying her tea, while Jack filmed.

In front of her a couple of women were grinding some sort of grain by pounding it with hefty lumps of wood. On the ground was a tall but narrow wooden tub, and the two women alternately raised up their bit of wood, like human pile-drivers, and smashed it down onto the contents. Immi was sweating cobs in the heat, sitting still, so how on earth did these women cope with the temperature and the physical activity? They had to be so fit.

The women saw Immi staring and beckoned her over. Not wishing to cause offence, she joined them. They were both laughing and giggling and before she knew it she had the wooden 'paddle' in her hand and was obviously expected to have a go.

Immi managed about ten 'bashes' before her arms gave out.

'You wouldn't survive here, that's for sure,' said Jack, joining her.

'Nope, I'd starve,' said Immi.

She handed the wood back to more gales of laughter.

'They think I'm crap, don't they?' she said.

Jack nodded. 'Yup, utter waste of space. Still, your attempts make for an entertaining video.'

Immi swung round. 'You didn't!'

Jack nodded.

'But I'm all hot and sweaty.'

'You're laughing and interacting with some wonderful welcoming ladies. Get over it. Honestly, it's fantastic PR for the army. Really natural and happy.'

Immi wasn't sure she agreed with Jack but what could she do? Besides, he really seemed to like her, so this little jaunt had been fun *and* she might wind up on TV. What a result – even if she did look a bit iffy.

She returned to her seat in the shade and watched as Jack and the tribal elder walked around the village, talking to the other residents and then as Jack did more formal interviews, his video camera in his hand and the local bloke doing some interpreting. Immi swigged her water and waited patiently, then dozed slightly.

'Wakey-wakey.' Immi jolted awake. 'I'm done,' said Jack.

Immi grabbed her water bottle and took a gulp of the now-warm water. Her mouth was like the bottom of a hamster cage. She swilled the water around her gums before she swallowed and wondered if her breath smelled as bad as her mouth tasted. Yuck.

'Give us some,' said Jack.

She handed the bottle over.

'All set?' said Jack. Immi nodded. 'How's the leg.'

She hadn't thought about it. She pulled up the leg of her combat trousers. Four of the half-dozen puncture wounds looked a bit angry. Bruising, probably, she thought. She pushed the fabric down again.

'Fine,' she said and stood up.

'Let's go.'

The sun might have been past its zenith but the temperature was, if anything, higher. It seemed to take much longer to get back to the river than the journey to the village had taken in the morning.

'And the kids do this and a lot more,' said Jack. 'Every day.'

'Maybe if you're born here you're used to the heat.'

'I imagine that helps,' said Jack with a grin.

'You're laughing at me,' said Immi. 'What do I know about it? I've only ever been to Spain.'

'I'm not laughing at you. I wouldn't dream of it.'

'Good.' She slapped her arm as another insect had a go at her. And her feet were hurting – the blister wasn't getting any better. And her shin was sore. 'Can we stop for a breather?' she said.

'You'd do better to keep going.'

'Yeah? How do you know? Your name Ranulph Fiennes or something?'

Jack did laugh properly this time. 'No, but it's far harder to get going when you stop than to keep going. Trust me.'

Immi sighed. 'But I've got a blister.'

'Even so.'

'Slave driver.'

'How about I give you a piggy-back?'

'Don't be daft.'

'Seriously.' Jack half crouched and held his arms wide ready to catch her.

'OK,' said Immi, 'your funeral.' She hitched her day sack up higher, grabbed his shoulders and jumped, wrapping her legs around him. Jack clasped his hands under her bum.

'A featherweight,' he said.

'I felt you stagger,' said Immi. It was nice here, she thought as she rested her cheek on his shoulder and inhaled the musky smell of his skin. She could feel his warmth through her combat jacket as he set off, his pace steady and even.

He walked for a good ten minutes before he told her he'd have to put her down.

'Not so featherweight now,' said Immi as she slid to the ground. She winced. Pain shot up her leg. Fucking blister. But then she remembered that the blister was on the foot on the other leg. Momentarily she wondered about taking a look at the manky, punctured leg but decided it would make her look a bit of a drama queen. Besides, there was nothing she could do here. It might as well wait till she got back to camp.

Chapter Twenty-Seven

The temperature was beyond a joke. Sam had been in some saunas in her time but on those occasions you could always open the door and find some respite if you got too hot. And there was generally a refreshing plunge pool on offer as well. But out here, in the equatorial African bush, the heat was relentless. All around everything shimmered with heat-haze and the sun blazed down from a cloudless sky. Even the flies seemed to have lost the energy to plague them, although the air still reverberated with the sound of other insects, rasping and chirruping with such volume they could be heard over the Land Rover engine as they belted along the road.

Sam looked back down at the map, and tried to work out where they were; how long would it be till they got to their destination and into some shade? That was the trouble with an open-topped vehicle: you might get the benefit of the breeze but there was no shelter from the sun.

She traced the route to the sappers' camp from Archers Post and looked at the contours. On the map, the long low hill that the road had been skirting was on the right of the road, but on the ground it appeared to be on the left. Maybe she was looking at the wrong hill. She tried to orientate herself using a couple of other features but still it didn't stack up. She was sure they weren't on the right road. She checked and double-checked the map and made her mind up.

'Corporal Blake?'

'Ma'am?'

'Are you sure we're heading for the right place?'

He fired a frowning glance at her. 'Absolutely.'

'So where are you planning on crossing the river.'

Blake took his eyes off the road to stare at her. 'Is this is a trick question?'

'No, it bloody isn't. Where are you crossing the river?'

Blake slowed the car down and then parked it up at the side of the track. 'What river is that, ma'am?'

Sam thrust the map under Blake's nose and pointed. 'This one.'

'So why do we have to cross it?'

Sam suddenly clicked as to what was going on. 'Where do you think the camp is?'

Blake pointed. 'Here.'

Sam sighed. 'No. The plans were changed. The sappers were ordered to camp on the same side of the river as the village so our tame hack can talk to the locals. You did check the grid reference before you left, didn't you?'

'Bollocks,' he said, quietly. He mopped sweat off his brow with the back of his hand.

'Indeed.' Sam stared at the map. 'If you ask me, we either have two choices: we either go back to here and this junction.' She pointed to a spot on the map. 'Or we cut across country to this crossing point here. You're the one who's been here before, what do you reckon?'

Blake shook his head. 'We'll be hours behind schedule with the first option.' He used the top joint of his thumb to do some rudimentary measuring on the map. 'It's four o'clock now – there's no way we'll get to the sappers tonight and sundown is at six or so. We'd have to camp out. It's too dodgy for a single vehicle to travel in darkness.' He measured the distance across country to the right track. 'If we go this way and don't hit any snags we might be there before it gets completely dark. Nip and tuck, though.'

'If we don't hit any snags. So which route?'

Blake stared at her. 'On balance, the second route. 'We'd better get on the radio and let control know what we're doing.'

'Agreed,' said Sam. 'And you're sure about the second route?'

'Cross country? Yeah.'

Sam climbed into the back of the vehicle where the radio was bolted to the chassis. She checked it was switched on, picked up the mic and depressed the pressel switch. 'Hello, Zero, this is Charlie Two Five, over.' She released the pressel and got a faint hiss of static. She tried again and got the same result. She sighed. Bollocks. 'Hello, all stations, radio check, over.' Nothing. She repeated the call. Still nothing. Her last message should have been answered by anyone on the net if they received it. Silence did not bode well. She checked the settings, the frequency – everything was apparently OK. Maybe they were in a radio dead spot.

She made a decision. 'OK, let's set off. I'll try and get through again if we get to some higher ground.'

Blake nodded and shrugged. 'Might as well. We're not achieving anything by sitting here.'

Sam got back in the front.

'Sorry, ma'am. Sorry for fucking up the route. I should have checked.'

Sam stared at Blake in amazement. 'Forget it, shit happens. Let's get across the bush and onto the right road.'

Blake engaged the gear and off they went, through the sparse bush, keeping the sun on their right shoulders so they were heading pretty much in a northerly direction. Sam tried to keep their rudimentary navigation across country on track using nearby features and the terrain to aid their dead-reckoning, but she was relying on the fact that, unless they went way off course the direction they were headed in should cause them to meet the river, then all they had to do was find the ford, turn right and they would be back on course.

That was the theory at any rate.

Sam unscrewed the cap of her water bottle and took a swig. 'Want some?' she said to Blake, waving the open bottle at him by way of acknowledging his apology and accepting it. She waited for the same rebuttal as before.

'Thanks, boss,' he said as he took it and swigged. He handed the bottle back.

'Tell me if you want any more.'

'Sure.'

The Land Rover jolted and ground its way over the rough terrain. Sometimes the scrub was thin enough and the ground flat enough that he got up to third gear, but more often than not he was zigzagging around the thorn bushes and the stumpy trees, trying to avoid fallen branches, ruts, giant termite hills, random lumps of rock or almost anything that might damage the vehicle or pop a tyre. The last thing they needed was a broken wishbone or a blow-out.

Sam hung on to the top of the door with one hand and her seat belt with the other as she was thrown around. Every now and again she couldn't help an 'Oof' escaping when there was a particularly large bounce.

'I daren't risk going slower,' said Blake. 'We're up against it as it stands.'

'I know and the sappers ought to get a working genny before nightfall. After all, delivering that is the whole purpose of the trip.' She took another swig of water and passed the bottle across again. Blake drained it and Sam threw the empty into the back and got another full one from the case lodged behind her seat. Over their shoulders the sun was considerably lower and the lengthening shadows didn't make it any easier to spot the dangers on the ground.

Sam glanced at her watch and then the map. As Blake had said, it was going to be nip and tuck to get there before dark.

Maddy and Jenna had scraped their plates clean and their trays were off their laps and on the coffee table in the middle of the room.

'I'm stuffed,' said Maddy.

'That was yummy,' said Jenna. 'You're a blinding cook. Me, I'm a dab hand with a microwave and that's about it.'

'It was only a shepherd's pie.'

'Still lovely.' Jenna took a sip of her wine. 'Right,' she said, standing up. 'Maybe I can't cook but I can stack a dishwasher. You put your feet up and take it easy while I deal with the dishes.'

'You can come again,' said Maddy in appreciation.

'Doesn't your old man take his turn in the kitchen?' said Jenna. 'My Dan does.'

'Seb isn't exactly a New Man,' Maddy admitted.

Jenna disappeared into the kitchen, leaving Maddy alone. In the quiet that followed she listened to, via the baby alarm, the faint snuffles and rustling of her sleeping son till she was distracted by another sharp twinge. She glanced at the clock. No, whatever had been going on through the day had come at such different time intervals it couldn't be labour. It was the baby mucking about, she told herself. What she'd originally thought. And given the stress and strain of the day, was it any wonder it wasn't behaving?

She lay back in the armchair and listened to Jenna clattering about in the kitchen. She wondered when she could take herself off to bed. It had been brilliant having Jenna here, and she couldn't have coped without her presence earlier, but now

314

all she wanted to do was have a nice hot bath and then a lie-down. She really needed to do something to ease her aching back. She'd have to ask Jenna if she'd mind being abandoned. There was plenty of wine in the fridge and she could watch whatever she wanted on the TV. Would she be doing anything else if she were in her own flat rather than here?

A wave of nausea swept through Maddy. She sat still till it passed. That was it, she wanted her bed. She went into the kitchen, where Jenna was all sympathy.

'Really, really good job I'm here now with you feeling poorly and all. Don't you mind me, I'm more than capable of looking after myself. I'll see you in the morning. Night-night.'

The sun had all but set and the darkness was rapidly getting more intense and Blake and Sam still hadn't reached the road. If Sam's map-reading was accurate, they still had miles to cover. Blake's estimate as to how fast they'd cover the ground had been way off. They hadn't even got to the river they had to cross and fording it in the dark would be fraught with danger. Were they going to have to stop and spend the night in the bush? Although that posed its own dangers, which were probably as significant as continuing to drive. Carry on or camp? It had to be her decision but supposing she made the wrong one and put them both in jeopardy? She could hear her father's voice in her head – don't be more stupid than you can help, girl.

At least the worst of the heat was now over, although Sam was still aware of sweat drops trickling down her spine every now and again. On the plus side she didn't need to slather on any more factor fifty. She and Blake still needed to take in plenty of water and another litre bottle was nearly empty. Maybe they ought to stop for a quick break and a really good look at the map. She was about to suggest a halt when there was the most almighty bang, which made her leap out of her skin.

'Fuck!' shouted Blake and he jammed on the brakes with such force that Sam's head almost connected with the dashboard. In frustration he banged the steering-wheel with both his palms.

'What the hell…?' asked Sam.

Blake shut his eyes and sighed deeply. 'We've blown a tyre.'

That was all they needed. They only had the one spare, so if they carried on and had another blow-out they really would be in trouble. In the poor light Blake had already failed to spot a hazard which had caused the puncture, a repeat was almost inevitable if they carried on. So, they'd change the tyre, try and make contact by radio yet again and make some sort of camp here for the night. They had plenty of water and some food – not much but enough – and they both had mossie nets. They could take it in turns to keep watch for marauding animals, they had guns and ammo, they would be safe, and at first light they'd go again. They'd be at the engineers' camp by breakfast, thought Sam. Not ideal, way behind schedule, but it'd have to do. What was the old quote… no plan survives the first contact? Well, it was something like that. You can plan in detail but when the shit kicks off you have to juggle the balls as best you can.

She tried for five minutes to get someone to respond to her insistent calls on the radio but nothing happened. That was the fourth time that day she'd tried and although she really didn't want to admit it, the radio seemed to be fucked. Maybe all that bouncing about had been too much for it. It was probably a loose wire or a faulty connection but she didn't want to start taking it to bits out here, in the dark – that really was asking for trouble.

While Blake got busy with the jack, the spare wheel and the

wheel-nut wrench Sam grabbed her daysack and tramped off to look for a suitable place for them to camp. The ground around the Rover was covered in tennis-ball-sized lumps of rock and a lot of low-growing thorns. She did a quick recce into the bush to find somewhere more suitable. About twenty yards away she found a big enough patch of flat, dusty and barren ground that would allow both of them to lie down without too much discomfort. She dropped her sack and then returned to the Rover to unload the necessary kit to make camp and start ferrying it to the spot. By her third trip Blake had managed to loosen all the wheel nuts and had got the jack in place. It was obvious that this wheel change was pretty much going as per the textbook so Sam left him to it and went back to their camp to start sorting things out.

The sound of the shot made her jump so much she actually dropped what she was carrying. Then she heard voices. Strange voices. Voices that weren't speaking English – or at least she didn't think so. Her heart was hammering so hard she could barely hear anything.

Then there was another shot and almost instantly that awful whining ping of a ricochet. And then another – and another ping.

Ignoring the sharp stones on the ground, and the spiky thorns, Sam leopard-crawled towards the Rover. At least the darkness was now a blessing rather than a hindrance. As she approached, her adrenalin kicked off again. In the faint light afforded by the last of the sun's glow on the horizon she could make out three large black men wearing tattered and dirty shorts and shirts with bandoleers of ammo slung over their shoulders and each carrying an AK47.

Blake stood in front of them, his hands in the air. Sam reached down to her belt kit and flipped open the holster that contained her Glock and pulled it out. As quietly as possible she cocked it but even as she did she knew it was an almost pointless gesture. Three AK47s against a pistol? It was laughable odds. One shot from her and this lot would start hosing out bullets in all directions. Blake would be killed in an instant and she'd better hope she followed soon after. She didn't fancy what would happen to her if they took her alive.

She lay on the ground, looking through the scrub and wishing she could understand what they were saying. One of the poachers was waving his gun around but he didn't look as though he was completely threatening. She saw Blake drop his hands and then he carried on changing the tyre. The guys around him lit up cigarettes, obviously in high spirits as they watched a white man working. But even though they looked relaxed, they held their weapons ready.

Finally Blake finished with the wheel and Sam could discern the leader of the poachers gesticulating to Blake to back off. He moved right away from the Rover. Sam brought her gun up and aimed at the leader's body – the biggest target and the place to shoot an opponent if you're not a crack shot, which Sam knew she wasn't. If the head poacher looked as if he was going to take out Blake, she'd fire.

Sam concentrated on her breathing and tried to hold her gun as steady as possible. She didn't know if it was nerves or fatigue that was making her hand shake slightly. Then the poacher laughed – she could see his white teeth – before he and the others jumped in the Rover, fired the engine and roared off. As they passed Blake one of them leaned out of the vehicle and smashed his rifle butt into Blake's head. He didn't see it coming and went down like a felled pine.

It took a few seconds for the sound of the engine to be far enough away for Sam to feel safe enough to leave her cover. Shaky with relief, she manage to scramble to her feet and run over to Blake. She knew she had tears streaming down her face but it was due to shock and the release from danger, wasn't it? She flung herself down beside Blake and checked him. There was a livid mark on his forehead where the butt of the weapon had caught his temple, but his breathing was steady. She jumped up again and raced back to the camp, tripping over rocks and getting snared in the scrub as the darkness was now absolute. She rummaged around in the makeshift camp, finding her Bergen, feeling for the things she wanted, remembering which pouches contained which items, feeling around on the ground till she found the bottles of water. With her hands full she made her way back to Blake. She slipped on a head-torch and then used a field-dressing and water to bathe his forehead. After a few minutes his eyelids fluttered and he groaned.

'Thank fuck, you're OK,' she said. There was another groan.

Blake groaned a third time and his eyes cracked open. He winced as the light from the head-torch shone right into them.

Sam whipped it off her head.

'How are you? How do you feel?'

'Shit,' Blake croaked. He raised a hand to rub his head.

Sam caught his hand. 'Don't touch it. The skin is broken, I don't want you infecting it.'

'They've gone, then?'

Sam nodded. 'They whacked you one with an AK47 as a parting gift.'

Blake gave the barest of nods. 'Oh, yeah.'

'But at least we're all right.'

Blake glared at her. 'So where were you?' he asked.

Sam pointed to a clump of scrub, nearby. 'In that, trying to get a bead on the leader.'

'Keeping your head down, then.'

Sam felt insanely hurt. 'No! I didn't think me rocking up waving a handgun about was likely to make things better.' She glared at him. 'As it was, I thought if I lay low, I might be able help if the bullets started flying. Now I can see I shouldn't have bothered.' She regretted her tone as soon as the words were out. She sounded petty.

'I'm sorry. I overreacted. I was worried about you.'

'Why? They hadn't got me.'

'No, but I didn't know that.'

'I suppose not.' She added, 'Blimey, that's twice you've said *sorry* to me in one day. You're going soft.'

'Don't push it, boss,' said Blake.

She offered Blake the water bottle. 'Like some?'

Blake, wincing, sat up and took the bottle from her. He drank a few gulps.

'How do you feel now?' she asked.

'Honestly?'

Sam nodded.

'My head throbs and I'm still shaking. But I don't think there's anything serious going on; no concussion or anything.'

'Well, that's something.'

Blake slurped some more water. 'Shit, how much of this have we got?' He stared at the half empty litre bottle.

'About four, five bottles. It's not great but at least we've got some. And I've got my Glock. Things are far from ideal but it could be worse.'

Blake sighed. ' And now Pollyanna appears.'

'There isn't any point in crying, is there? Let's face it, we're on our own. No one has got a clue where we are, we've no comms, no map and it's pitch sodding dark. We can weep and wail or we can brace up…'

'Brace up it is, then, boss.'

'Good. Because I honestly think that we ought to think about moving right now, while it's cool. We can lie up in the daytime in the shade.'

Blake frowned. 'You could have a point. If we only have

about five litres of water, we've got to make it last. What about food?'

'A twenty-four-hour ration pack.'

'Ammo?'

Sam showed him her Glock. 'A full mag.'

'Well, at least we've got some protection.'

'You don't think the poachers will come back?'

'Poachers? Shit, no.' Blake laughed. 'No, what we need is protection against every other damn thing out there that might see us as a snack.' He stood up. 'Right, we're going to ditch everything that isn't completely essential, cut down the loads we have to carry to the bare minimum. And if the army doesn't like the fact we're dumping their kit they can charge us when we get back.'

Sam liked the fact he said *when* and not *if*.

Chapter Twenty-Eight

Sam trudged on. She was tired, her boots chafed, her arms were covered in itchy bites, she had a headache and she was thirsty but she couldn't give in. She stumbled again. Not through tiredness, although she was knackered, but because, yet again, some bloody plant had done its damnedest to trip her up.

And it was still hot. Not the blistering heat of the day, but hot enough to slowly drain her energy, like a leak in a bucket will surely empty it. It wasn't only the heat that was tiring. There was also the constant battle with the scrub and knee-high dried grass that tangled itself around her ankles, tripping her up, snagging her steps and generally making the least progress a battle. Sam sighed as she trudged.

'Let's have a rest,' Blake said. 'We've been going for three hours and I for one have had enough.'

Oh, thank fuck for that. Sam stopped and eased her shoulders against the weight of the day sack before she took it off. She opened it and rationed out a boiled sweet each from their meagre food supplies and poured them each a small amount of water. She watched Blake sip his, rolling the fluid around his mouth before he swallowed it.

'How's the head?' she asked.

'Sore,' he admitted.

She put on her head-torch. 'Let me have a look… I don't think it's infected,' she said after a few seconds. 'If you feel anything, if it starts to tingle or if the headaches get worse, anything, tell me.'

'And you'll do what?'

She took off her head-torch by way of procrastination. 'Good point, well brought out...'

Blake laughed. 'Whenever an officer says that, it always means they don't have a sodding clue how to answer the question.'

No, well... The first-aid kit had been in the vehicle so if they needed more than a field dressing or a sticking plaster they were out of luck.

He looked at her and raised a questioning eyebrow. 'And the answer is?'

'Your guess is as good as mine,' she admitted.

'Then we'd better hope things stay as they are, hadn't we?'

She gazed at him steadily. 'I'm sure it'll be fine. Anyway,' she continued, 'I think we ought to stop. Get some sleep for a few hours and then start off again a few hours before dawn, when it should be at its coolest.'

'You think?'

She shrugged. 'I'm no expert but I reckon if we exhaust ourselves completely we'll make crap decisions. I think we need our wits about us if we're going to survive out here.'

She plopped down, using her day sack as a pillow as she stretched out on the ground. Blake followed suit but using the Bergen as a backrest. Sam gazed up at the stars. She laughed inwardly – some people would probably give their back teeth to see a sight like this. Ha! If only they knew that all you had to do was get bounced by poachers and nearly lose your life and you could have it for free. Still, it was good the sky was clear as it gave them a bead on the Plough. They couldn't actually see the Pole Star, it was too low on the horizon, but the Pointers were clear enough and that was all they needed to keep trekking north. They had to reach the river, find the crossing point and then head for the main road. The river ran right across their route so they were bound to come across that but the rest…? She brought her attention back to the here and now.

'How far do you think we've walked?'

'Five, six miles, maybe.'

'Is that all?'

'It's difficult to tell.'

'I suppose…' She paused and turned her head towards him. 'Look, this is daft.'

'What is?'

'Both of us pussy-footing around each other, like this. If I call you Luke I still absolutely respect your abilities as a soldier and an NCO, and if you call me Sam the world isn't going to end.'

'I dunno, boss…'

'Sam.'

'It's against all my training.'

'Supposing I told you it was an order?'

'Supposing I told you to sling your hook? With all due respect… ma'am.'

Sam snorted. 'Well, I'm going to call you Luke, anyway. What are you going to do about it? Who are you going to complain to?'

'OK… Sam.'

'You see? The sky hasn't fallen in.'

Silence fell. Or it fell for about a minute and then, in the darkness, came a rumble. They both froze and Sam felt her heart go into overdrive as a gallon of adrenalin washed through her system.

'What the hell…?' she whispered. She wished they had their night-vision goggles but they had been mounted on their helmets and, along with Luke's SA80, a hundred rounds of ammo and their vehicle itself, the two NVGs were now the property of the poachers.

'Stay still,' Luke whispered back.

The rumble came again and then there was a low animal growl.

Sam felt in her pocket and found her head-torch. She pulled it out and flicked the switch. A bright beam of light shone into the bush, which she used like a mini-searchlight. As the beam swept across the monochrome vegetation it suddenly caught a pair of bright circles – eyes caught in the light – staring back, only about thirty or so yards away. The eyes were wide apart, divided by a broad sandy-coloured nose. There was another low rumble, more threatening this time, as the eyes stared back at them, unblinking and unafraid.

'Fuck,' Luke breathed.

'Lion,' whispered Sam.

The animal kept staring steadily at the light.

Sam slipped the torch on her head, making the light dance wildly over the scrub and bushes for a couple of seconds. Momentarily the eyes disappeared and Sam was terrified she wouldn't be able to find them again, but she swept the light from side to side in front of her and there they were, unwavering, staring, scary. She opened her holster and in a fluid movement she pulled out the gun, cocked it and then shot into the air. As the reverberation of the shot died away they could hear something crashing through the undergrowth into the distance.

Sam swept her head-torch around the area to be sure the lion had gone. It was then she found she couldn't hold things together and she sank down onto her haunches and then to her knees as her trembling legs refused to hold her up any longer. She tried to put her gun back in her holster but she was shaking so badly she couldn't so she laid it on the ground in front of her instead.

Luke knelt down beside her. 'Hey, hey, it's all right. It's gone.' She felt him put a hand on her shoulder.

She turned her ashen face towards him. 'Was that the right thing to do?'

'Of course it was. The bugger high-tailed it, didn't he?'

'But supposing he comes back – you know – with reinforcements.'

Luke exploded with laughter.

Sam watched him, unamused.

Slowly Luke regained his composure. 'Sorry,' he said, wiping his eyes.

'I don't see what on earth is so funny,' she said tartly.

'Sam, it's a lion, not a member of the Taliban.'

'So? Lions hunt in packs.'

'Prides.'

'Don't you fucking correct me, Blake. I don't care what their gangs are called, it may come back with the rest of the family.'

'Sam, generally it's the female lions—'

'Lionesses,' she snapped.

'That's better.'

Sam glared at him and then shook her head, bewildered. 'What's better?'

'The fact you're fighting back is good. You're getting your mojo back.'

'Don't you psychoanalyse me.' She glared at him. Luke just grinned at her. 'You're impossible, do you know that?' she said.

He nodded. 'Anyway, as I was saying, if that male was hunting, then it was probably a lone male – one that's been thrown out of the pride because he's a threat to the alpha male's domination of his harem. He's biding his time till he can return and stage a coup and in the meantime he has to fend for himself.'

'Poor old Billy-No-Mates.'

'I wouldn't waste your sympathy on him. He wouldn't waste any on you.'

'No... maybe not.' She turned and looked at him. 'I'm glad I'm not out here on my own. I'm glad I've got you for company.'

For a second their eyes locked, before Sam busied herself by picking up her gun and putting it back in its holster.

Immi gazed at her leg. When she'd woken up, the first thing she'd been aware of as she'd come to had been the shooting pain in her shin. And now she was dressed and had had a drink of water it was still giving her gyp. It was a worrying mess. The puncture marks were bright red with a wet-looking crust on the top and around each hole, the skin was angry and tender... and raised, like mini-volcanoes. Tentatively she pressed one of the volcano-like eruptions on her skin and a fat gobbet of yellow matter trickled down her leg. No, that really wasn't right. She decided she needed to ask for advice.

She limped around the camp until she found Jack.

'Hi, Immi,' he said. He looked genuinely pleased to see her. 'How you doing?'

For some completely inexplicable reason Immi found herself very close to tears. 'That's the thing, Jack.' She pulled up her trouser leg.

'Fucking hell, Immi.' Jack knelt down in front of her. 'That's what you did yesterday, isn't it?'

She nodded.

'We need to get that seen to. Does it hurt?'

'A little bit,' she lied. It sodding caned.

'Would a sweetie make it better?'

She smiled at him. 'Think it's a bit far gone for that. You could try kissing it better.'

Jack kissed her knee, sending a shiver through Immi despite everything and then he gently touched the skin on her shin. Immi leapt. He looked at her. 'It more than hurts a bit, doesn't it? Why don't you say so, you silly moo?' He put a reassuring hand on her arm. 'I'm going to find the troop commander and if they haven't got the antibios here to sort this out, I'm going to insist you get casevaced.'

Immi nodded, blinking back tears. She might have been a bit worried about her leg before but now she was shitting it. How bad did Jack think it was?

Andy Bailey found his commanding officer in his tent at Archers Post, where most of the battalion had moved to the day before. All the troops were now preparing to move out from the staging area during the course of the day, into the bush, up to their positions on their respective start lines, ready to cross them and get going with the exercise. In about eight hours, just before sundown, it was all going to kick off and frankly Andy couldn't wait. The build-up had been intense. The admin, the orders, the logistics had seemed never-ending but it would all be worthwhile when they got down to some real soldiering. In the meantime, as always, there were a couple of last-minute hitches. And both of them, this time, were potentially serious.

'Sir, sir,' he said as he stuck his head through the flap.

The colonel looked up. 'What's up, Andy?'

'Bit of a crisis, Colonel. Well, probably not a crisis but problems that we really don't need at this stage in the game.'

The CO narrowed his eyes. 'Such as?'

'Sam Lewis and her driver haven't reported in to the sappers' camp where the bridge-building exercise is going on.'

'Why did they have to go all the way up there?'

Andy explained about the generator. 'It was a really straight-forward mission; all they had to do was drive down the main supply route through the range area, detour north over the next bridge crossing and then carry on to the sappers, drop off the new genny, kip for the night and bring the dud back. It should have been foolproof.'

'So where are they? I mean, they couldn't get lost off the MSR and then there's only one route to the sappers after the river crossing. They've got to be somewhere obvious.'

Andy shook his head. 'No, that's just it, Colonel, they aren't. It doesn't make sense. There's no report of a broken-down Land Rover, Lewis hasn't radioed in, but they've vanished.'

The colonel stared at his adjutant. 'So they've taken a detour, they've stopped off somewhere else.'

'Where?'

The commanding officer stared at his right-hand man. 'I don't know! Finding out that sort of stuff is your job, not mine.'

Andy knew it was worry making the CO so terse. 'Yes, Colonel.'

'Sam's not very experienced, though, is she? She hasn't been out here before, has she?'

'No, Colonel. But her driver is an old hand.'

'Who is it?'

'Corporal Blake.'

The CO's brow furrowed. 'I don't think I know him.'

'Bit of an oddball by all accounts but very bright and this is his third time here. He knows the ropes. Between the pair of them they should be all right. The ASM said they went off with plenty of fuel and water.' The ASM had also made some comments about his lack of faith in Captain Lewis's map-reading and his sympathy for Blake at being landed with a woman to wet-nurse. Andy had told Mr Williams he was out of order but he didn't think this was the moment to burden his CO with the knowledge that one of their warrant officers was verging on being a sexist misogynist.

'Good, so we needn't worry too much about them. They probably got delayed and decided not to risk driving at night. They've holed up somewhere. I expect they'll pitch up with the sappers any moment now.'

'Unless they've had an accident.'

329

The CO stared at Andy. His expression clearly said he didn't want to entertain such an idea. 'But if they'd come off the road on the MSR someone would have spotted something.'

'All the logistic vehicles have been informed to keep an eye out.'

'So what'll we give it? Another few hours?'

'At the most, I reckon. Then, if they're still missing, we're going to have to scramble the helicopter.'

The colonel nodded, then noted to look on Andy's face. 'There's something else.'

'Yes.'

'It's about Corporal Cooper.'

The CO sighed. He was the sort of guy who wanted solutions, not problems. 'The clerk? What's happened to her? I thought she was babysitting Raven.'

'She is. Only she's injured her leg and it looks as if septicaemia might be setting in.'

'Why are you telling me this?'

'Because she and Raven are at the sappers' camp. There is no generator because the one Sam and Blake were taking them hasn't arrived, they don't have antibiotics with them there and Raven is getting very antsy.'

'Why?'

'Why? Why no antibios or why is Raven getting in a state?'

'Both, I suppose.'

'Cock-up as regards the medical equipment. We don't know what happened but the sappers' medic wasn't issued with any, and as for Raven – gawd knows. He's very insistent she gets casevaced. Maybe he's sweet on her.'

The CO considered the idea. 'He could do worse.'

Andy decided not to tell his boss about the various fights down the NAAFI for which Cooper had been the catalyst. She might be a looker but she could also be trouble.

'So we need to get them out,' Andy said. 'Well, her out. Raven can stay put till the sappers have finished if he wants to. Or not. I don't really care what his agenda is as long as he doesn't cause trouble.'

'OK, get hold of the Army Air Corps and organise them to fly in and get Cooper. Tell them to keep an eye out for a lone Land Rover while they're en route. If they don't spot anything or if we haven't heard anything from Lewis by the time we've got Cooper back safely then we're going to have to go into full search-and-rescue mode.'

'Sir.'

Now there was a plan, Andy felt much more sanguine about both problems. He went to organise the chopper and then he would allow himself some breakfast. He had a feeling it was going to be a long day.

Chapter Twenty-Nine

Maddy woke up still not feeling right. Maybe she was going down with some sort of bug. Still half-asleep, she lay in bed, blearily trying to work out if she was really poorly or a bit... bleuch. After a little while she decided it was a case of feeling a bit under the weather rather than anything worse. She hauled herself into a sitting position and rested against the headboard while she ran through things she ought to do. The downstairs needed hoovering and the ironing pile wasn't getting any smaller – but would it be fair to do that while Jenna was around? Maybe they ought to take Nathan out, do something with the day.

Maddy glanced at the bedside clock and decided that whatever decisions she had to make it would be easier with a cup of tea. It was far too early to make one for Jenna – Maddy reckoned that her guest might well appreciate being brought a morning cuppa but not at six-thirty on a Sunday. Even Nathan was still asleep, although the baby obviously wasn't and was making its presence felt, big time. Its kicks and wriggles were probably what had woken her up. Well, that and the fact that she'd gone to bed so early she'd had much more than her eight hours' worth.

Maddy rolled onto her side, swung her feet out from under the duvet and heaved herself out of bed. She'd be glad when this pregnancy was over, she thought. Frankly, she had had enough. She wanted an end to the heartburn, the baby's somersaulting, the twinges and now this sodding awful backache. She pushed her hands into the small of her back and eased her shoulders. If anything it made it worse. Maddy sighed and plodded down the stairs and then to the kitchen.

She filled the kettle and was about to plug it in when she felt the urge to hurl, like the night before. She thumped the kettle onto the counter and then leaned over the sink while she dry-retched. After about a minute the spasm passed, although the feeling of nausea remained. She leaned against the work surface, her legs shaking, her forehead damp with sweat, while she waited for it to subside. Maybe she didn't want tea after all, maybe she needed a lie-down instead.

'You all right, hon?'

Maddy looked up. 'Hi, Jenna,' she said weakly. 'I didn't mean to wake you.'

'You didn't, not really. I was awake anyway and I heard you moving about so I thought I'd see if you were all right. And you're not, are you?'

'I'm fine,' said Maddy.

Jenna stared at Maddy and sighed. 'Don't bullshit me. You were being as sick as a dog.'

'Busted. Probably something I ate.'

'Really? So why aren't I vomming too? I ate pretty much exactly what you did yesterday.' Jenna paused. 'Can I say something... my mum says she was always sick when she went into labour.'

'But I'm not. In labour, that is. I timed those twinges yesterday and the intervals were all over the place.'

'So maybe I'm wrong, but it wouldn't hurt to ring the midwife and see what she says.'

'I don't know. They'll just tell me I'm over-anxious or some—' Maddy stopped as a bolt of pain ripped into her. Over and above that she was aware she'd wet herself. She stared at the pool of warm water around her feet, spreading slowly across the kitchen floor.

'Over-anxious my arse,' said Jenna. 'Your waters have gone.' She picked up the phone and dialled three nines. 'Ambulance,' she said.

The heat was so intense that Immi didn't know what to do with herself. That and the fact that the pain in her leg was now so severe it had left her on the brink of tears. The skin on her leg was so hot and tight she actually worried that it might split – like some revolting lava bursting open to reveal an alien parasitic species.

Marcus, the Royal Engineer troop commander, crouched down beside her as she lay on a camp bed in the shade of a poncho rigged up in a tree to act as an awning. 'They're sending a chopper to casevac you back to Archers Post,' he told her. 'You should be back in civilisation in about an hour.'

'Promise?'

Marcus nodded. 'We're going to send Jack back with you. He wants to file his story and he can't do it from out here. We'll wrap up the bridge tonight and move out at first light tomorrow. I have no idea where that generator got to – the two guys delivering it have gone AWOL, it seems.'

'AWOL?' said Immi. 'Out here? Why would anyone go AWOL in this dump?' She moved slightly and winced. Shit, her leg hurt but she'd been told she couldn't have any more pain-killers for another four hours. With any luck she'd be in a proper medical centre before then.

'I'm exaggerating. The guys have probably broken down, but whatever happened, they haven't appeared. According to the reports over the net, they're part of your battalion, apparently: Captain Lewis and Corporal Blake.'

The shock of hearing the familiar names made Immi forget the pain in her leg. 'Luke? No!'

'Friend of yours?'

'Sort of.'

'Who is?' said Jack, who had gone to fetch water for Immi.

'Luke Blake's missing, along with Captain Lewis. He's a mate… and I shared a billet with the captain.' Her eyes began to fill with tears. But even as the tears hovered on the brink, Immi knew she was worried about friends, nothing more. If it had been Jack, not Luke, who'd gone missing, she'd have been beside herself.

'They'll be found. They've probably just broken down.'

'I hope you're right. Although when we had the briefing about being out here the list of dangers was endless. Honest, Jack, they could still be in danger.'

'Don't worry about them. Save your energy for yourself.' Jack handed her a bottle of water and Immi took several greedy gulps. 'Gawd, I shove water in and it pours out again. I feel like a bleeding colander.' She got out a tissue and wiped her forehead. Jack took her hanky off her and dabbed it for her gently. She smiled at him.

'That's better,' he said.

'I'm only feeling more cheerful because I know I'm going to be out of here in a mo.' She cocked an ear. 'Listen, ain't that the best sound?'

In the distance they could hear a low thwack-thwack of an approaching helicopter.

'Taxi!' said Immi.

'Are you asleep?' whispered Sam as softly as she could.

'What do you think?' Luke answered. 'I think my brain is frying.'

The pair lay in the shade of a scrubby tree, a poncho above them strung up in the branches, which provided a postage-stamp-sized patch of deep shadow.

Sam glanced at her watch. 'Shit, it's only eleven. How hot is it going to get?'

'I dread to think.'

Silence descended and Sam put her bush hat over her face.

'It won't work,' said Luke.

'What won't?'

'Doing that. You're not a parrot.'

Sam giggled. 'And making me laugh isn't helping me get my beauty sleep either.'

'And let's face it, you need it more than most.'

'Git,' murmured Sam. Another comfortable silence fell but sleep didn't come. Sam knew that lying quietly would allow her batteries to recharge but it was also incredibly boring. After about ten minutes she spoke again. 'Luke?'

'Yes, ma'… yes, Sam.'

'Why didn't you become an officer?'

'I could tell you to mind your own business.'

'You could.'

'You really want to know?'

'No, of course I don't. I thought I'd ask to piss you off.'

'Job done, then.'

'Seriously.'

'Seriously? I didn't become an officer because – with a very few exceptions – I don't rate the officer classes at all and the last thing I wanted to do was join them.'

'Why?'

There was a silence for a while then a long sigh. 'Family reasons.'

'Did an officer do something awful to a member of your family?'

'No, an officer in my family did something awful to me.'

Sam sat up. 'What?'

Luke shook his head. 'Sorry, that's classified.'

336

'Oh. That's not fair.'

'Who said anything about being fair?'

'So, why didn't you report him... her?'

'You don't shop your dad.'

Immi couldn't walk to the Bell helicopter so Jack carried her. As Jack tramped across the grass, holding her in his arms, Immi reckoned it was almost worth being in clip state to be carried by Jack. She draped her arms around his neck as he held her against his chest and was almost sorry when they reached the air-conditioned comfort of the helicopter. What, she wondered, had she seen in Luke? Sure, he'd been handsome and clever but he wasn't in Jack's league. Probably wasn't in Jack's league when it came to pay either. Not that Jack's pay would be a deal-maker but it couldn't hurt, could it?

She strapped herself in and then Jack handed her a headset and plugged it in so they could all communicate.

'OK,' said the pilot. 'This isn't going to be a joy ride, you're going to have to earn your seat. There are two soldiers gone missing and we need to look out for them as we fly back to base.' His voice was just audible through their headphones over the whine and roar of the idling engines.

'Of course,' acknowledged Jack. 'We've already heard the news and we're as worried as everyone else is.'

More worried, actually, thought Immi. These guys were her friends.

Marcus slid the door shut and gave them a cheery wave as he dodged out from under the rotors to a safe distance and then the pilot cranked up the revs and the whole machine began to tremble and rock until with the faintest of swaying motions the skids unstuck from the ground and the machine lifted off. Immi clutched her seat as the horizon grew and grew as they soared skywards like they were in a giant lift.

Immi's stomach seemed to have been left on the ground, somewhere near where Marcus was standing.

'You all right?' said Jack, via his head-mic and her earphones.

Immi nodded and swallowed to make her ears pop. Then the aircraft stopped going upwards, tipped nose-down slightly and shot forward. She shut her eyes and forced herself not to scream. She'd been on some fairground rides in her time but this was the scariest by far.

When she opened her eyes again they were clattering over the bush and she could see giraffes. She forgot her fear and nudged Jack. 'Look!'

He nodded, 'Amazing, isn't it?'

'It's just... wow.'

'So you think Africa is better now?'

'At least there aren't any bugs up here.'

The helicopter suddenly changed course and plummeted out of the sky. Immi clutched her seat again – her eyes wide in fear.

'What the fuck!' she screeched.

'Look,' said Jack, leaning across her and pointing out of the window.

In the middle distance something was shining like a beacon. A bright shaft of reflected sunlight was sending a diamond-clear blaze of white light straight towards them. It was so blinding that it was almost like a laser cutting through the atmosphere.

The Bell thundered towards it and then hovered above and to one side at about fifty feet. Below was a military Land Rover. There was kit in the back – they could see army equipment lying higgledy-piggledy over the seats but there wasn't a sign of anyone about. It didn't look good.

'Oh, shit,' said Immi.

'We're going to put down,' said the pilot.

The helicopter slowly dropped towards the ground and then, with a barely perceptible bump, they were down. Instantly the others unbuckled and slid the doors open, ready to jump out as soon as the pilot cut the engines. Immi stayed put, craning to see out of the open door, wishing her leg wasn't in such a state that she couldn't go and have a look-see herself.

After a couple of minutes Jack returned. 'There's no blood and no bodies.'

The shock of the word 'bodies' was enough to send Immi over the edge. She began to sob.

'Shh,' said Jack, giving her a hug.

As Immi sniffled and blew her nose the two pilots began to examine the scene, trying to work out what had happened.

'There's no spare, for a start,' one noticed.

'And they've got a flat. Maybe this was the second blow-out so they decided to try and walk.'

'But why were they here? They're miles off course. It doesn't make sense. And why didn't they stay here with the water? You'd never leave your water behind out here.'

The co-pilot went back to the chopper and radioed back the news that they'd found the missing vehicle but no one was around.

'Surely they'd have stayed here if it had been a breakdown,' said Jack. 'Everyone knows that's the best course of action.' He began poking around the supplies and baggage in the rear of the vehicle.

'No rifle,' said Jack.

'Stands to reason they'd take it,' said one of the pilots.

'Well, someone did,' said Jack. He pointed to a hole in the back of the driver's seat. 'Looks like a bullet made that.'

*

'Now, are you sure you've got everything?' asked Jenna as Maddy was helped out to the ambulance. Jenna jiggled Nathan on her hip to stop him from grizzling.

Maddy nodded. 'And if I haven't I'm sure someone will be kind enough to bring it over to the hospital. Anyway, I'm not worried about that – are you going to be OK with Nathan?'

'I'll be fine. And Susie's coming back early to lend a hand too. Between us we'll be fine till your mum pitches up. Stop worrying about things this end and concentrate on yourself.'

Maddy nodded. 'I wish…'

Jenna knew exactly what Maddy was wishing. 'Yeah, but he's not. Although old Milward has promised he'll send a signal to Kenya to get Seb back as soon as possible. You never know, given how slowly things are going at the moment, he might be back before junior puts in an appearance. I know I'm no expert but I remember my mum's labour and I remember it being a bit more… well… urgent. On the plus side, your mum'll certainly be here in time to hold your hand.'

Maddy nodded. 'I suppose.'

Jenna handed the overnight bag to the ambulance driver, who stowed it by the stretcher in the back as he strapped Maddy in safely. 'Seb'll be here as soon as he can,' said Jenna. 'It's not his fault the baby has no sense of time-keeping and wants to pitch up early.'

'No,' said Maddy, 'but I can't help wondering whether the baby's decision to arrive wasn't brought on by You Know Who.'

Jenna shrugged. The thought had crossed her mind too and it was another reason to hate Michelle – as if there weren't enough already.

'All set?' said the ambulance driver.

Jenna held up a squirming Nathan to get a last kiss from his mum for a day or so, before the doors shut and she was on her way, leaving Jenna to deal with a suddenly bawling toddler.

As the ambulance drew away Jenna gave up trying to control Nathan in her arms and laid the kid down on the pavement before she dropped him. There Nathan lay on his back, drummed his heels and screamed. Jenna decided that there was little she could do to console him and it would be best for him to calm down in his own time.

'You've got some nerve,' said a voice behind her.

Jenna spun round and instantly recognised the new arrival on the scene. 'Major Milward – how nice,' she lied. Their previous encounters, back at the old posting, when she'd been having a bit of a fling behind her then-husband's back, had been more than a little tricky.

'So what are you doing here?' said Milward. 'I wouldn't have thought that even you would have the brass neck to show your face on the 1 Herts married patch.'

God, thought Jenna, he was still a pompous twat. 'Maddy asked me to look after her son.'

'Maddy did what?'

'You heard.'

'Doesn't look as if you're doing much of a job.'

'And you know all about coping with toddler tantrums, do you?'

'And you do?'

'Yes. I may not have kids of my own but I've looked after enough to know what's what.'

'So why did she ask you?'

'Because we're friends, because I'm available, because I'm good with kids.' Milward stared at her. 'So,' continued Jenna, refusing to feel intimidated by him, 'have you got hold of her old man yet?'

'I've sent the signal requesting his immediate return, yes.'

'Good. So how long's it likely to take?'

Milward shook his head. 'No idea.'

'Good job we've organised her mum to come down, then.'

'She'll take over the childcare, I trust.'

'She's going to be with Maddy to start with. Maddy needs her more than I do.' She stared at Milward. 'I do know what I'm doing, you know.'

Milward responded with a disbelieving look. 'I can't believe Captain Fanshaw would approve.'

'Like I care. I'm doing this for Maddy, not him.' Certainly not, given what she knew about Seb. She picked up the still-sobbing child. 'Look, this is none of my business...'

'So why do you think I'd be interested?'

'Because it concerns Maddy Fanshaw.'

'Then shouldn't it be her telling me... whatever this is about?'

'I know but—'

'But nothing.'

'But she's not in a position to tell you anything right now, is she?'

Milward sighed. 'So?'

'So yesterday a serving female officer came to her quarter and made all sorts of allegations regarding her husband. She was really nasty.'

'What sort of allegations?'

'That's he's having an affair with her.'

'Don't be ridiculous,' blustered Milward. 'As if an officer like Seb would behave like that. And as for a female officer behaving as you're alleging...' He turned to go.

'I was there,' snapped Jenna. 'I witnessed the whole thing.'

Milward turned back and stared at her, apparently weighing up her credibility. Jenna looked him right back in the eye. 'This woman said that Maddy's marriage to Seb was over because she's having an affair with him.'

'And is she?'

'How the fu… how am I to know? Or Maddy, for that matter. All Maddy and I know is what this woman said. She got nasty so I threw her out. It was a bit of a catfight but I won.'

Milward's eyes boggled.

'Anyway,' continued Jenna, 'I made Maddy promise to tell you this on Monday because I don't think this other woman is the full shilling and she needs to be stopped. She's obviously a nut-job and suppose she did a number with a petrol bomb or something.' Jenna saw Milward's incredulous expression. 'Well, things like that happen. I read about a case like that only the other day.' A jilted lover's revenge on her ex's family and the tragic consequences had been all over the media only a few days before and Jenna could tell from the look on Milward's face that he knew about that news story too.

He nodded. 'True. So who is she – this other woman?'

'She's called Michelle and apparently she's a friend of Sam Lewis's. Given that Captain Lewis has only just been commissioned I'd bet a pound to a penny they were at Sandhurst together. The thing is, though, neither Mads nor I know whether what this Michelle woman is saying is true or not so, whatever you do, you've got to be really discreet. Get someone to read the riot act to her about pitching up at Maddy's but don't let on about the affair, understand? The last thing Mads'll want is the whole army knowing about this.'

'This is all most irregular.'

'Irregular or not, I want you to sort this out, get it stopped. Trust me, if you don't and something happens to Maddy… well, you'll have me to answer to and it won't be pretty.'

Chapter Thirty

Seb was still having a problem believing everything that the CO had told him. That Maddy had been whisked into Salisbury Hospital, her mother had been informed and a family friend was looking after Nathan and it was all happening six weeks early.

He rammed a few more items into his Bergen, his emotions in an equally sorry state as his packing. He had been looking forward to this exercise and now he was going to miss it and, by the looks of things, the birth of his second child. He wasn't sure which was causing the greater disappointment.

Beside his tent was a Land Rover and driver, waiting to take him to Nairobi airport to wait for the next available flight. If he was lucky he might get shoved onto a scheduled flight to the UK; if not he'd have to wait for the next airtrooping one, whenever that was due in. Seb had to hope that his luck was in, otherwise he might have to wait at BATUK for ages. And how dull would that be? While everyone else was enjoying the fun of live-firing and thundering around the bush, he'd be stuck in a camp in the arse-end of Nairobi, missing the fun and the birth. Bollocks.

Andy Bailey returned to the command vehicle and his CO.

'The good news is that the RMP have confirmed that the missing Land Rover the Army Air Corps found is definitely the right one. But the bad news is there's no sign of Blake and Lewis. I can only think that poachers stole the Rover and drove it till it broke down or ran out of fuel. The question is – are Blake and Lewis with the poachers, or were they abandoned in the bush?'

'Or...' said the colonel with a significant look.

Andy nodded. He really didn't want to think about the other, awful possibility. Poachers in Kenya had a bad reputation for being ruthless but they had to hope that even they wouldn't resort to cold-blooded murder.

Colonel Notley sighed. 'We can't leave it any longer. We're going to have to start notifying the next of kin. It's coming up for twenty-four hours that this pair have been missing – their folks have a right to be put in the picture. Get the chief clerk to contact the rear party and get the wheels put in motion. We can't possibly afford to cut any corners here – especially as Raven knows exactly what's going on. Why the hell he had to be in that bloody helicopter when that vehicle was found...' The CO stopped and shook his head. 'If he puts the wrong spin on that story, my career...'

Andy bit his tongue. Wasn't the safety of Lewis and Blake a million times more important than Notley's next promotion? Instead, all he said was, 'I'll get onto it.'

'And get back to me as soon as you hear back from Milward.'

'Sir. Let's hope he's not too busy holding Maddy Fanshaw's hand to find the next of kin.'

Colonel Notley snorted. 'God, I hope not. Mind you, I should think that Milward's the last person young Maddy wants faffing around her if she's about to give birth. Any news on that front, by the way?'

'Seb's reached BATUK. They think they can get him on this evening's flight to Heathrow – apparently there's one going out with a few spare seats. As for Maddy... not a dicky-bird, I'm afraid.'

'I'll get a message through to Mrs N. to ring the hospital in the morning,' said the CO. 'I gather Maddy's mother is on her way to be with her daughter, so that's something.'

Andy nodded. 'Right, Colonel, I'll get onto the UK and get the next of kin sorted.' He left the colonel feeling stressed. Talk about never raining but pouring. As if he didn't have enough to contend with with this bloody exercise and the theoretical, tactical problems the directing staff threw at them to test the battalion, without the real-life stuff to do with missing troops and a wife in premature labour. Still, if you can't stand the heat…

He found the duty signals officer and organised a signal back to the rear party at battalion HQ. Andy had to hope that in both cases the next of kin were going to be easy to get hold of. The sooner they got the news, the sooner the MOD press office could let Raven off the leash and let him report the story he was dying to get on the airwaves and the less time he'd have thinking up some spin to put on it.

'Daddy,' said Michelle, letting her father into the officers' mess. 'Good to see you. Good journey?'

'Average,' came his brusque reply. They kissed each other on the cheek, awkwardly and stiffly. 'How's life here?'

'All right,' said Michelle.

Her father stood back and appraised her. 'You're looking peaky.'

'Really? Can't think why,' she lied, slickly. Her sleepless nights and obsession with a married man were no concern of her father's.

'Hmm.' He didn't sound convinced. 'You ought to get out more. Take up a sport. It's not healthy, hanging around the mess all the time.'

'I don't. Normally I'm very busy.' She changed the subject and looked at the holdall at her father's feet. 'Is this all your luggage?'

He nodded.

'I'll show you to your room, then.'

She led the way to the stairs. 'I'm afraid there wasn't a major's suite available for you but I guessed that as it was just for one night you'd be all right in a junior officer's room.'

'That's fine.'

'So you're just along the corridor from me.'

'Grand.'

Michelle led him to the door of his room and pushed it open. The room was bland and boring with standard issue furniture: a large wardrobe; a dressing table; a bureau and a single bed. In the corner was a cubby hole with a basin in it. From what she'd learned about the army in her short time in it, single accommodation for officers had barely changed since Wellington had stopped being the GOC. Her father would probably be right at home and have happy memories of when he himself had been a junior officer.

'This is fine, just fine.'

'Good. I'll leave you to unpack and sort out. I'll give you a knock on the door in about an hour and we can go and find some tea. Oh, and the bathrooms are down the corridor on the left and the loos are opposite.'

'I'll find them.'

Michelle turned to go back to her own room and was surprised to see the duty officer heading her way.

'Michelle,' he said.

'Yes.'

'Can I have a word?'

'Of course.'

'In private.'

Michelle felt a jab of fear. This didn't sound like one of her recruits having a problem – this sound altogether something more personal. Shit, that stupid Maddy-cow hadn't bleated about her visit? What a tart.

Michelle glanced over her shoulder and saw her father watching. She gave him a smile, brimming with confidence she didn't feel.

She ushered the duty officer into her room and shut the door. 'Yes?'

'There's been a complaint about your conduct.'

'Really?'

'Yes.'

'Who made it?'

The duty officer shrugged. 'I don't know the details. All I know is that the commandant wants to see you.'

'Today?'

'Now. And I think number two dress might be appropriate.'

Michelle suddenly felt very sick indeed. Another thought swept through her mind – what if her father found out?

Sam was beginning to feel light-headed – the combination of lack of food and water and the heat, she supposed. She wondered how long they could keep going. What was the Foreign Legion's motto? March or Die, that was it. They had a point. She concentrated on not licking her lips, not that she had anything to 'lick' with. She wondered how dehydrated she was. One thing she knew was that she hadn't had a pee for over twelve hours now; she didn't think that was good and there was a part of her that wished she knew how dodgy it was. But maybe it was as well she didn't.

She also wished she knew how far they'd walked. To distract her from the misery and the heat she tried to work it out: guessing they might have been moving at a mile and a half an hour, knocking off the hours they'd stopped to rest properly, the minutes they'd stopped for breaks... A mile and a half an hour seemed horribly slow but the reality was that picking a path through the scrub was tricky and the heat was such that even dragging one foot in front of the other was exhausting. And, as Luke had pointed out, to move faster was to risk sweating even more and they couldn't afford to do that. The pace he set was the one he reckoned was optimum – it kept them going but used the least energy and would probably result in the least amount of fluid lost through perspiration. Sam trusted him; after all, he'd been here before. Maybe the SAS could yomp it in double quick time but both she and Luke knew that if they over-exerted themselves they'd wind up with heat exhaustion. Better slow and steady than fast and dead. She totted up the hours and the miles and reckoned that the most they could have covered would have been about twenty miles – still nowhere near the river and then they had to find the crossing place. Luke reckoned they'd be able to ford it if they didn't. And if they couldn't?

She glanced at her watch and saw it was gone five: not long now till sunset and relief from the blazing sun. The shadows were stretching long and the edge had come off the temperature but it still had to be up in the high thirties or even the low forties. Moreover, at sunset they would allow themselves another break and another sip of water; the second mouthful they'd each allowed themselves since they'd given up trying to sleep and set off again, trudging through the bush, keeping the sun over their left shoulders and hoping that this meant they were heading roughly north. They didn't have the energy or resources to afford mistakes – like trekking the wrong way. As it was, they both knew that it was going to be a close-run thing to get to the main supply route before the water ran out – even if they didn't make any errors.

They hadn't discussed their precarious situation but they'd each observed the other taking smaller and smaller sips, trying to eke out their water as much as possible. Setting out before dusk wasn't part of the original plan. That had been to only move after dark when the temperature would be a shade lower but, as Luke had argued, they were sweating buckets lying in the shade, not going anywhere. With a fair amount of logic he'd pointed out that they might as well move and sweat as lie still and sweat and Sam had been too knackered and hot to argue.

So now they were trudging through the bush again, the thorns scratching them, the heat beating down on them and the bugs eating them alive.

Luke was ahead of her as they pushed their way through the bush. Now and again they were distracted by a colony of bee-eaters and their wonderfully complex nests, or on other occasions there were termite mounds to skirt and twice they crossed soldier ant trails and they stopped briefly to watch in amazement at the single-minded determination of the tiny critters, which took no prisoners as they stomped through the bush, killing and eating everything in their path.

Sam needed more than the occasional glimpse of some local fauna to take her mind off the discomfort, the worry and the heat. Besides, she was being eaten up by curiosity about Luke's background. The throw-away remark about not shopping his father had fired her imagination with loads and loads of possibilities about what he might have done to his son – and each idea seemed to be more preposterous and lurid than its predecessor. There was nothing she could do about the heat and the flies but at least she might be able to get her curiosity satisfied. Besides, there was bugger-all else to talk about.

Casually, she said, 'My dad was in the army – like yours.'

Luke gave her a sideways glance as they pushed their way through the scrub. 'Really?'

'Yeah. So we're both army brats.'

'And your point is?'

'I dunno. We probably have a lot in common.'

Luke snorted. 'Yeah, with you being an officer and me being a grunt.'

'But we both got dragged about the world, lived in quarters.' She paused. 'Did you go to a lot of schools?'

'No, I got shipped off to boarding school when I was eight.'

'Me too.' Sam slapped at a mossie biting her forearm and muttered, 'Got you, you little bastard.' Then she added, 'So what rank was your dad?' she asked.

'You mean, when I last saw him?'

'Yeah.'

'He was a colonel.'

Sam stopped dead. 'A colonel.'

'Why the surprise? If you've got a commission and stay in long enough, lots of people get to that rank.'

Which wasn't totally true, as Sam well knew, because her own father was a colonel. Lots of officers got as far as getting their majority if they made a career out of the army. To reach that rank all you pretty much had to do was keep breathing, but to get any higher… well, the competition got pretty intense. For a start it was essential to have gone to Staff College and only the very best got selected for that. Somehow, the fact that his dad had had such a successful career made it all the more bizarre that Luke hadn't tried to get a commission. Sam started walking again.

'You said when you last saw him. Don't you have anything to do with him nowadays?' she probed.

'No. And I never will if I can help it.'

'Don't you miss him?'

'No.'

'What about your mother?'

There was a beat before Luke said, 'No.' Then, 'What is this? The Spanish Inquisition?'

'Just interested. I lost my mother, she died when I was born.'

'I'm sorry.' They tramped on in silence.

It was some time and they'd covered several hundred yards before Luke said, 'So, do you miss your mother?'

'I never knew her so I can't – I *don't* – miss her, per se. But I miss *having* a mother. Dad tries, but...' she paused, not wanting to sound disloyal '... he's British and a bloke. Showing any sort of emotion doesn't come naturally to him.'

'Hmm. Mine's a cold-hearted bastard, full stop. No excuses, he just is. I hate him, I hate everything he stands for.'

Sam felt a bit taken aback. 'So did you join as an other rank to piss him off?'

Luke stopped walking and looked at her. 'I joined as an other rank because I don't want my path to cross my father's, and I thought that if being an officer turned you into the sort of human that my father seems to be, then I didn't want to be a part of it.'

'Is that what you think of me? That I'm some sort of bad person for having a commission?'

Luke stared at her before lowering his eyes. 'No, not you.'

'I'm glad,' she said, meaning it. 'Although I'm sorry about your relationship with your father.'

'Don't be.'

Sam gazed at him, willing him to confide in her, now less out of curiosity, more because she felt that if he spoke about his past it might be like lancing a boil – get all the poison and badness out of his system.

'Still, water under the bridge,' he said. He trudged on and Sam followed.

Eventually, as the sky to the east began to change colour to an opalescent blue, she glanced to her left and saw the sun was now touching the horizon. At last the heat would leach out of the day. The thought that it was about to get cooler almost made her want to cry with relief.

'It's time for a break,' she said. She took her day sack off her back and pulled out one of their remaining bottles of water. She squatted down on the ground before carefully undoing the cap and passing it to Luke. He handed it back.

'Ladies first.'

Sam was feeling too shit to argue. She took a sip and swilled the water around her mouth. It was warm but it was wet and she could almost feel her body absorbing it – like blotting paper. Just one sip, although she was desperate to glug the whole bottle. She passed it back to Luke quickly in case her willpower gave up the struggle and she necked the lot.

She stretched her legs out in front of her. Ten minutes. She dragged her day sack around in front of her and in the dying light of the sun rummaged in it to find the last bits of their twenty-four-hour ration pack. A tube of fruit concentrate, a couple of biscuits and the last of the boiled sweets. Not exactly a feast, she thought morosely. On the other hand, there was a fighting chance they might reach the river and the road by daybreak and then... rescue. She had to hold onto that thought. It was the one thing that was keeping her going. Failure to reach the road wasn't an option. She spread the fruit gloop on the biscuits and handed one to Luke. Then she divided up the boiled sweets. At least it would give them a bit of energy.

The sun dipped below the horizon and the western sky lit up like it was on fire and then, with startling rapidity, the spectacle was over. To the east the sky was already black and the stars were appearing. Sam peered to what she thought was the north and was reassured to see the Plough, roughly where she expected it to be.

She leaned back against her day sack and in the gathering gloom she munched on her biscuit. It was dry and the fruit concentrate was sticky and cloying but it was food and she forced herself to swallow it down. A sip of water would have made it easier but she'd had her ration.

'Where did you go to school?' she asked.

'Hampshire.'

'Where hurricanes hardly ever happen,' said Sam. 'It's a quote… from *My Fair Lady*.'

'Really?' He sounded supremely unimpressed.

'Did you like your school?'

'Not really.'

'Is that why you didn't stay to do A levels?'

'No.'

'So why not?'

'I got expelled.'

'I'm sorry.'

'So was I,' said Luke dryly.

'What happened?'

'I got accused of doing something I hadn't. It was a stitch-up by a gang of boys from another house, but my dad refused to believe me. He took the school's side against me.'

'So that's why you've fallen out with your father.' She reached across and put her hand over Luke's. He didn't shake her off.

'Wouldn't you? You'd think he might have listened to my side before siding with the head.'

She thought about the things her father had done in the past which had ended up with her feeling hurt or ignored and yet she still loved him, but maybe the things he'd done which had hurt her weren't in the same league as Luke's. She gave Luke's hand a squeeze. 'I don't think I'd have had the courage to burn my boats like you've done.'

'Courage wasn't involved. It was impossible to stay at home.'

'But you could have only been – what – sixteen? Seventeen?'

'Yeah, well, shit happens.' Luke pulled his hand away from hers. 'Anyway, time to move.'

He stood up and hefted the Bergen onto his shoulders. Sam followed suit, picking up her daysack off the ground. She opened a side pouch and took out the head torch.

'Here you go,' she said, offering it to Luke.

'Thanks.' He switched it on but nothing happened. He fiddled with the switch, he removed the back, took out the battery and put it back in and tried again. Nothing.

Sam sighed. 'Looks like it's dead.'

'Well, that's bleeding obvious.'

Sam felt nettled.

'Did you switch it off before you put it away?' said Luke.

'Of course I did. I'm not stupid.'

Luke stared at her. He clearly didn't believe her.

Sam slammed her day sack onto her back and stormed off into the darkness. After a few seconds she heard his boots pounding on the hard earth, coming after her. The she felt his hand grab her arm and swing her round.

His face was right in hers. 'Don't be stupider than even you can help,' he said. 'This place is dangerous and storming off like that, on your own, is asking for trouble. Although, seeing as how you are a rupert *and* a woman, maybe it isn't so surprising you're behaving like a mong.'

'Don't you dare talk to me like that, Corporal Blake.'

'Ha. I wondered how long this chummy-chummy stuff would last. So much for being equals when we're out here in the bush.'

Sam glared at him. 'You've overstepped the mark and you know it.'

'How? Trying to stop you from getting hurt – or worse? It's pitch dark. In another ten yards I wouldn't have been able to see you but there's things out here that can see in the dark very well. And you know it. And frankly, I've got enough on my plate trying to get out of here in one piece without having to fight off the wildlife on your behalf.'

'Oh, yeah? As I recall, that's not what happened the last time. I'm the one with the gun, remember. I'm the one who scared off the lion.'

They stood toe to toe, eyeballing each other, both of them simmering with rage. Under the circumstances it was beyond ridiculous and Sam suddenly began to giggle. 'I'm sorry,' she said as she pulled herself together.

'Jeez,' Luke muttered to himself, 'as if things aren't bad enough and now I'm stuck with a hysterical woman.'

'I'm not hysterical... well, not very.'

'So what the hell are you finding so funny?'

'Nothing, not really. You and me. The way we're bickering like a couple of kids.'

'I'm glad you can see the funny side.'

'Honestly, Luke, we might as well lighten up. Being as miserable as sin isn't going to help any.' She smiled. 'Want to kiss and make up?'

'Yes.'

And that was when the world seemed to shift for both of them.

Chapter Thirty-One

Michelle smoothed down the skirt of her best uniform and knocked on the door of the commandant's office. She could feel her knees shaking and hoped that they weren't making the hem of her skirt vibrate. For some reason she didn't want the commandant to know how nervous she felt.

'Come!' barked the colonel's voice.

Michelle opened the door and entered, snapping a salute when she came to attention in front of his desk. Behind her the duty officer shut the door again.

'Lieutenant Flowers, the OiC rear party for 1 Herts rang this unit earlier today and lodged a complaint against one of my officers. Looking at what he told me and various other bits of circumstantial evidence, I think the allegations might be well founded. I take a dim view of any inappropriate behaviour from any of the personnel in this training establishment and I take an especially dim view if that behaviour comes from one of the permanent staff here. I do not expect, however, to receive complaints about the behaviour of my officers. Ever.' He glared at her.

Michelle swallowed before saying, 'No, sir.'

'So when a Major Milward rings up and alleges that one of my officers visited another officer's wife and got involved in a fight I am forced to take it seriously.' The commandant steepled his fingers and looked at her across them. 'What have you got to say for yourself?'

Michelle could feel her heart hammering and she could feel the blood in her veins pounding through her body. She swallowed again but she was at a loss as to how to reply.

'You're not denying the allegation. So is it true?'

Michelle nodded. 'Sir,' she croaked.

The commandant gazed at her. 'Thank you. Your honesty spares me the trouble of getting the SIB in to investigate the case.'

Michelle felt herself sway. If the Special Investigation Branch had been involved God knows how much other shit would have hit the fan.

'Your father is a serving officer, isn't he?'

Michelle nodded.

'So you haven't just let down your own corps but you've let down me, this training regiment and your father. You are a disgrace to your uniform.'

'Yes, sir,' she mumbled, barely audibly.

'I shall have to consider what action to take. What you have done cannot go unpunished.'

'No, sir,' she whispered.

'You are, of course, confined to barracks for the foreseeable future.'

Oh, dear God. She'd have to tell her father that dinner out at a nearby restaurant was off. He'd want to know why – what the hell was she going to tell him? Her stomach was churning and she felt herself go hot and cold.

There was a pause. The commandant sighed. 'Why?' he said after a few seconds. 'Why did you do it? What on earth possessed you?'

'I... I don't know.'

'Fighting! That is the sort of behaviour I barely tolerate from the recruits but an officer! Dear God, woman.'

There was nothing she could say to that.

The commandant shook his head, seemingly appalled and disbelieving, in equal measure, at what he'd found out about her. 'Dismissed.'

Michelle saluted, about-turned and marched to the door. Once she was through it she let the tears of fear and humiliation fall as she slumped against the wall in the corridor.

Alan Milward locked the door to battalion HQ and wondered what else was going to happen. Talk about the day from hell. First young Maddy had gone into labour and he'd had to send a signal to Kenya, then there had been that allegation made by Jenna about Maddy's husband. He'd dismissed the idea that Seb had had an affair as poppycock but the story about the fight had seemed genuine enough. Why would Jenna make that up? Then, to cap it all, he'd been called out to find out who the next of kin were for Corporal Blake and Captain Lewis. He sighed. And he'd been hoping for a quiet time with the battalion away. Huh!

As he walked down the front steps of the office block the duty driver appeared with the car. Luke Blake's NOK, who lived in Andover, was close enough for Alan to break the news to personally. Sam Lewis's dad, on the other hand, was stationed in Colchester so he'd organised someone from the local brigade HQ over in that neck of the woods to visit him tell him his daughter was missing. The MOD had been put in the picture and, since there was an airtrooping flight leaving from Brize the next morning, a couple of seats had been made available on the plane if the next of kin wanted to travel out. Although what good it would do them to be there, Milward didn't know, except it would be easier to keep them informed of any developments.

He sank into the back seat of the black staff car and gave the driver the address. He hated doing things like this – being the bearer of bad news – but at least it was only 'missing' and not worse.

Yet.

He looked at the details of Luke's next of kin. A friend. Was that a euphemism for something else? He didn't think Luke looked gay but who knew these days. Anyway, even if Blake was, it was none of his business.

The driver zoomed along the main road to Andover, driving smoothly and expertly and soon they were turning off the A303 and heading into Andover itself. The driver followed the sat nav on the windscreen and pulled up outside a bike shop in a side street close to the town centre.

'Are you sure this is it?' asked Milward.

The driver looked at the address. 'It's the address you gave me, sir.' He sounded defensive.

'Fine.' Milward stepped out of the car and stared at the bike shop, then he noticed a door to the side with several doorbells. He checked the name plates and found one with the name of Blake's next of kin. He pressed it.

'Who is it?' asked a voice through the entry phone system.

'Major Milward. From 1 Herts. I've, erm… I've got some news about Luke Blake.'

The door buzzed and Milward let himself in. As he climbed the tatty, lino-covered stairs he heard a door open. He looked up to the landing and saw a young lad staring at him, looking utterly bewildered.

'You'd better come in,' said the lad.

Milward followed him into a small living room where the TV was on and there were beer cans on the table along with the remains of a take-away.

'Are you Peter North?' he asked.

The lad nodded. 'So what's happened to Luke? And more importantly, why are you telling me?'

'Because you're his next of kin.'

'What? Since when?'

'He didn't tell you?'

Peter shook his head. 'No. I mean we're mates, good mates, but we're not related or nothing. Shit, I knew he hated his mum and dad but I didn't know he hated them that much to cut them out of his life completely.'

Alan took off his beret and ran his fingers through his hair. 'OK, you obviously know a lot more about Luke than me, maybe you could fill me in.'

'Of course – as soon as you tell me why you're here.'

'Sure.'

Peter moved towards the kitchenette that led off the living room. 'Brew?'

'Please. Milk and two.' He watched Peter fill the kettle before he said, 'Luke is on exercise in Kenya and he's gone missing. He's been gone for about thirty-six hours now and the guys on the ground are getting really concerned.'

Peter switched the kettle on and turned to face Milward. He seemed to think about the news for a second or two. 'So, it sounds pretty serious.'

Milward nodded. 'It is – potentially. It might be very serious.'

'Then I think it's his dad you ought to be telling. I mean, of course I'm worried about my mate but it isn't really any of my business. It isn't that I don't care – I do – but I'm not family, am I?'

'Except you're his designated next of kin.'

'Yeah, well, his dad mightn't see it like that. And what's more his dad might make a whole heap of trouble for you if he finds out later he wasn't put in the picture.'

'Really?' Milward was perplexed. How? Why?

Peter nodded. 'You have no idea who Luke's dad is, have you?'

Milward felt faintly exasperated. Of course he didn't – otherwise he wouldn't be breaking the news to this spotty youth.

'Luke's old man is General Pemberton-Blake.' Milward felt himself reel. 'Or is it General *Sir* Pemberton-Blake now? I seem to remember he got a gong recently,' continued Peter, unaware of the effect his words had had on his visitor. 'Anyway, he's a big cheese. That's why Luke joined as a squaddie. He always wanted to be in the army but he knew if he became an officer, his path would cross his father's. They had a falling out and he told me he never wanted to see his dad again. He thought if he was in the ranks he'd be safe.'

'Bloody hell.'

The kettle boiled and clicked off.

'So are you going to visit Luke's father?'

'I think I better had.'

Andy Bailey barged into the CO's tent.

'Sorry, sir, but you've got to hear this.'

The CO looked up from a map of the ranges he was studying. 'What?'

'Blake's father.'

I thought you told me earlier he didn't have one; that his next of kin was a friend.'

'Well, that's not the case. Long story but it turns out that it's only General Sir William Pemberton-Blake.'

The CO sank into a camping chair. Then he looked up sharply at his adjutant. 'Don't be so ridiculous, Andy. Just because they share a name doesn't make them related.'

'It does, Colonel. Alan Milward's been to see him.'

'Fucking hell.'

'And he's on his way out here.'

'Jesus, that's all we need.'

'He and Sam Lewis's dad are on the airtrooping flight that gets in tomorrow.'

The CO rolled his eyes. 'I'd better go and pick them up myself. We can't send a clerk like Corporal Cooper to meet that pair. How is she, by the way?'

'On the mend. Once the medics pumped her full of antibiotics she began to rally in no time.'

'And her charge – that hack?'

'You mean Raven?'

'I do indeed.'

'Presumably, now that Blake and Sam's next of kin have been informed he's been allowed to file his story to the BBC,' said Andy.

'We could hardly stop him – anyway, MOD PR gave him the go-ahead. Does he know about Blake's father?'

'Not yet.'

The CO looked glum. 'He will, though. He's a reporter, he'll find out.'

'Would it be better if we tell him?'

The CO considered it and then nodded. 'But not tonight. We've got to hope Blake and Lewis get found before their folks get here.' He glanced at his watch. 'Actually, we've got to hope they get found before then, full stop.' His shoulders drooped. 'They can't have much water and I am getting seriously worried now. Seriously worried.'

You and me both, thought Andy.

Maddy was exhausted. The contractions were coming regularly now – every twenty minutes – but nothing else seemed to be happening. The gas and air might be taking the edge off the pain but her labour had been going on properly for well over twelve hours and so far, apart from being strapped to a monitor, there was nothing to show for it.

'Nathan wasn't this slow,' she said to her mother, who was sitting on the chair beside the bed in the delivery suite.

Her mother glanced up from her magazine. 'All babies are different, darling.'

Maddy stared at her mother. What did she know? She'd only ever had the one. She didn't have the strength to argue, besides which, if she did, she'd lose. Her mother liked to have the final word and Maddy had long since learned not to take her on.

Her mother put her magazine to one side. 'When do you think Seb is going to get here?'

'No idea.' Maddy shifted to try and ease the ache in her back. 'Look, Mum, why don't you go back to mine and take over looking after Nathan? I'm sure Jenna would like to get back home and if anything happens I promise I'll ring.'

'I don't like the idea of you being here on your own.'

'Mum, I've got a call button and half a dozen nurses who will come running if I suddenly need urgent care.'

Her mother looked at her and sighed. 'But it isn't right.'

'I'm a big girl, I can cope. Besides, there doesn't seem much point in both of us losing out on a night's sleep.'

'But Seb should be here.' Her mother tutted. 'It's not right that he's abandoned you.'

'He's got to come back from Kenya. It's not as if he's rowing or something.'

'I always knew that picking a husband who was a soldier was a bad idea.'

'Don't start, Mum.'

Her mother hurrumphed. 'You could have done so much better.'

Maddy didn't want to hear this. Her hormones were all over the place, the incident the previous day with Michelle was still playing on her mind, she was worried about imposing

Nathan on Jenna, and the last thing she needed was to have to listen to her mother's views on her husband.

'Not now, Mum.'

'You went to Oxford.'

'So did Seb,' she said wearily.

'Only because he was a rower – I don't think they'd have taken him on his academic results alone.'

'You don't know that.'

'And even then he never really made it at rowing, did he?'

Something in Maddy got pulled too hard and it snapped. 'Mum, shut up about Seb.'

Her mother stared at her. Her mouth opened and then shut. 'Really!' She said with an audible sniff.

Maddy could feel tears welling up. 'Mum, you're not helping, you know that, don't you? Now is not the moment to tell me you don't like Seb. You don't have to, you know. He's my husband, not yours.' She banged her head against the pillow in frustration. Shit, if her mother ever found out about Michelle...

Her mother picked up her magazine and then grabbed her handbag off the floor. 'I know when I'm not wanted.'

Maddy dashed the tears away with the palms of her hands. 'Mum, you are. But you'd be more use looking after Nathan rather than telling me again that you think my husband is crap. He's not, and I love him and if you can't take that on board then I'm sorry because I'm not going to leave him.' She gave her mother a defiant look as she wondered, momentarily, about the possibility of Seb leaving her for Michelle. No, she wasn't going to think about that and she certainly wasn't going to let Seb go without an almighty fight. At least she'd got that much clear in her head.

The door to the delivery suite opened and a midwife entered. 'How are we getting along?' she asked breezily, before she clocked the tense atmosphere. She looked from Maddy to her mother and back.

'You carry on,' said Mrs Peters with a sniff. 'I am leaving.' She gave her daughter a cold stare. 'Ring if you need me.' She swept out.

After the door shut there was a moment's silence. 'Oops,' said the midwife. 'I hope I didn't make things worse.'

Maddy wondered about telling her how bad things *really* were and that to make things worse she'd have to go some, but instead shook her head. 'No, nothing to do with you.'

'Do you want to talk about it?'

The kind words tipped Maddy, in her fragile state, right over the emotional edge she'd been teetering on and a sob bubbled up. Then another. The midwife sat beside her and patted her hand.

'I could tell you it's hormones, that lots of mums get weepy at this point, but my instincts tell me it's more than that. And I expect you're missing your husband.'

Maddy nodded, wetly. 'And Mum thinks he's doing this deliberately.'

'He had this all planned, did he? He knew the baby would decide to come well over a month early?' The midwife sighed in understanding.

Maddy nodded. 'Except at the rate this labour is going it's not going to get here till the due date.'

The midwife patted her hand again. 'Not on my watch. If it doesn't get a move on soon we'll crack out the dynamite and hurry things along.'

Maddy, feeling another contraction start to build, grabbed the gas and air mouthpiece and sucked on it. She puffed and panted and tried not to moan as she felt the waves of pain intensify.

'That's good,' murmured the midwife, stroking her forehead. 'You're doing so well.'

The contraction faded and Maddy began to relax again. She shut her eyes as tiredness overtook the agony. When was it all going to be over? She wasn't sure if she had the energy to see the process through.

As Michelle returned to the mess she knew that being suddenly confined to barracks would take some explaining. She also knew that if there was going to be any disciplinary action taken her father would, inevitably, hear about it. This time, she knew, she'd have to come clean. Own up to everything and not just about the fight. If, later, he found out what had precipitated it she couldn't bear to think what the consequences might be. Anyway, her situation, right now, was so dire, what on earth could make it worse?

'You did what?' Major Flowers sank onto the bed in his room and stared at his daughter. 'Why?' he said after a long pause.

Michelle shrugged. 'I… I can't explain.'

'Dear God, you've made some mistakes in your life but this one really takes the biscuit.'

Michelle hung her head. Except, even in this abject state, there was a part of her that refused to accept this was all her fault. As always, she looked about for a reason for her actions – for someone else who could share the blame. 'It's not my fault I'm such a mess. If you and Mum had stuck together, I wouldn't have ended up screwing up all the time. It's not my fault I've messed up, it's because you left Mum for Janine.'

Her father snorted. 'That's right – it's never your fault, is it? And as for what happened between your mum and me, it wasn't about Janine.'

'No?'

'No. You are making judgements on a situation you know nothing about.'

'And you aren't? You know what my relationship with Seb was like?'

'No, but I didn't go stalking third parties to try and get my own way – Janine's marriage was as dead in the water as mine. I don't care what you surmised about your mother, but it takes two to make a marriage go sour, and your mother was, and very possibly still is, neat vinegar. Let's face it, Michelle, she hasn't even had the good grace to ask to see you in nearly twenty years so don't you go blaming Janine for what happened when you were barely out of nappies.'

Michelle wasn't convinced but she'd never heard any side of the story except her father's so she didn't have much of a counter-argument.

'I wanted Seb's wife to know the truth. I felt he wasn't going to tell her what had been going on and that Maddy had a right to be put in the picture. She had to know her husband was being unfaithful. I was doing her a favour.'

Henry Flowers stared at his daughter and then shook his head. 'A favour? Dear God, I wouldn't want to be around when you decide to do someone a disservice. A favour?' he repeated. 'That's bollocks and you know it. You wanted your own way and you didn't care who got hurt as you bulldozed your way through to your objective. You've never had any regard for the feelings of other people, have you?'

Michelle felt her eyes pricking. 'Of course I have.' She blinked.

'Really? You've never given a damn about how much you've hurt Janine over the years. She's done her best to provide a home for you—'

'She got me packed off to boarding school.'

'I packed you off to boarding school to spare her from you. Besides, I thought you would get a better education if you didn't keep changing schools. Have you any idea the sacrifices

Janine and I made to find the money for the fees?' He stared at Michelle.

'But the army pays.'

'They make a contribution – and not a very big one. I really hoped boarding school would give you a brilliant start in life. But do you know what I really hoped? I really hoped that if you went away you might appreciate things when you came home, but I was so wrong.' He shook his head sadly. 'Every time you came back from school you were even more difficult, even more horrible to Janine. We used to dread the holidays. We tried not to show it, we tried to make you welcome, but whatever we did you seemed to hate and despise us all the more.'

Michelle felt the tears roll down her face. This was so unfair. She hadn't been like that in the holidays. Well, maybe a bit but that was because her father never paid her the least attention; Janine was always around, getting in the way, being the perfect bloody housewife, simpering and smiling... Gah, the thought of it made Michelle want to gag. At least when she was naughty her father noticed her.

Her father looked at her without sympathy. 'You know you can kiss goodbye to your career, don't you? I would think at the very least you'll be expected to resign your commission.'

'No,' she whispered. 'It won't come to that, surely?'

'I wouldn't be so sure. Conduct to the prejudice of good order and military discipline would be the least of the things they could charge you with. And on top of that they could add a charge of fighting. That friend of Maddy's would be well within her rights to press charges.'

'But she attacked me!'

'You're hardly in a position to take the moral high ground, are you? Barging into someone's home and then telling her you've been screwing her husband. If Maddy says her friend acted in self-defence do you think anyone is going to believe a word you say?' Her father shook her head, hardly believing the situation. 'You know, once you got to Sandhurst I thought I could stop worrying about you. I thought they'd sort you out, teach you how to be a decent citizen. How wrong I was.'

'You've never, ever worried about me. You've never given me a second thought. You've spent every living, breathing moment of the past twenty-three years trying to blot out the fact that I even exist.'

Henry Flowers stared at her – stunned. 'You really are quite stupid for someone with your intelligence and qualifications. Contrary to what you think, since you arrived on the planet I have spent every minute of every day worrying about you. There isn't day that goes by when I don't wonder what you're getting up to, what you'll tell me in your next phone call, what scrape you've got into now and wondering how I can bail you out or even *if* I can bail you out.'

'Don't lie,' said Michelle. 'You can barely bring yourself to speak to me. You've never loved me. Tolerated me would about sum up how you felt and half the time, not even that. That's why you were so glad when I joined the army. You must have thought I'd be out of your hair for ever when I did that.'

Henry looked sad and bewildered. 'No, I've always loved you. Even when you made it nigh on impossible, I loved you. Janine does too – although sometimes I wonder how she can bring herself to, considering the way you treat her.'

Michelle was crying properly now. 'No, no that's not true, you never have, either of you.'

'But of course we do.'

'Then why didn't you ever tell me?'

'I thought you knew. I'm your father – of course I love you. That's what fathers do. There are times when I don't like you very much, I'll admit that, but I loved you just the same.'

'But you didn't tell me.'

370

'I didn't think a father had to tell his daughter stuff like that.'

Michelle sniffed. 'Then we've both been mistaken. I always thought you hated me. I thought I reminded you of Mum – that's why you couldn't stand me.'

'Dear God, child, no.' Henry shook his head. 'Maybe this is something I ought to take the blame for. I'm not good at that sort of stuff – expressing myself. Boarding school and the army probably knocked it all out of me.'

Michelle gave him a wan smile. 'No hope for me, then. Second generation and all that.'

Henry shook his head again. 'Indeed.' He gave his daughter a wry grin. 'Seeing how you can't leave the barracks, how about I go and find us a take-away and a bottle or two of wine and we try and make up some lost time over supper in my room.'

Michelle sniffed and then blew her nose. 'Sounds like a plan.' As Henry walked away she knew things between her and her father were about to change for ever and for the better. Maybe things wouldn't ever be perfect but at least they'd got off the skids. She knew that allowing Janine into her life was going to take a bit longer.

Chapter Thirty-Two

Luke and Sam walked holding hands, stumbling along in the dark, exhausted, drained, hungry and thirsty.

'Time for another break,' said Luke.

'Thank the Lord,' said Sam. She swung her daysack off and extricated the water bottle. 'After this we've only got one full one left.' She gazed at the third of a litre of water that was left in it before she took a sip and then handed it over to Luke.

'We've got to be near the river,' said Luke. 'Have to be, it stands to reason.'

Sam nodded. She slumped to the ground and Luke followed her lead. 'We've got to hope. And we've got to hope we can get across it without any problem.'

'We don't need more headaches on top of being lost and running out of water.'

'No, we don't. Luke, the thing is, what if we can't get across it? I mean, what if it's too deep or there's crocs or something?'

'We can't think like that.'

'Why not? Blanking it out now isn't going to change the situation when we get there.'

'A situation that's my fault.'

'I didn't say that.'

'You didn't have to, we both know it's true. I fucked up. Monumentally.'

'It's not your fault we got ambushed.'

'If we'd been in the right place, on the right road, it wouldn't have happened.'

'You don't know that. We might have got ambushed anyway. Maybe this was our time to get ambushed.' Luke looked at her as if she'd flipped completely. 'You know – fate, karma, that sort of shit.'

'Well, even if that is true, if we'd been ambushed on the main supply route someone would have found us in no time. As it is, here we are in the Back of Bleeding Beyond, with no torch, no food, and now next to no water.'

'But at least we've found each other. That wouldn't have happened in the other scenario. You'd still hate me because I'm a rupert, and I'd try and ignore how hot and buff you are because officers can't feel that way about their men.'

'Hot and buff?' said Luke with a smile.

'Shit, yeah. That's why I made you put your shirt on that time you took me to the medical centre.'

'Ah… you were very assertive about me getting dressed.'

'You were very annoying – and verging on insolent.'

'Me?'

She nodded. 'Yes, you.'

Luke kissed Sam lightly on the lips.

'So, back to our original conversation,' she said, once her heart had quietened down. 'Any clues as to how far the river might be?'

'No. We have to keep trekking till we get there. And, if we can't cross it, we have to hope they're pulling out all the stops to find us.'

'They will be, won't they?'

'I would think so. They'll have contacted our next of kin by now.'

'Yeah.' Sam went silent for a bit as they both gazed up at

the stars and the few clouds scudding across the sky in the light breeze. 'Poor Dad. He doesn't need the grief.'

''Cos your mum died.'

'Yeah. Your dad won't know, though, will he? You've got a friend down as your next of kin.'

Sam sensed Luke nodding. 'Yeah, Pete. He's a nice guy.'

'You must hate your father a lot not to have him down as your NOK.'

'I didn't want people to know who he is.'

'Why?'

'Because… because he's Commander Land Forces. He's the big cheese.'

'He's what?'

'You heard.'

'Shit.' The penny dropped. '*Pemberton*-Blake?'

'Yup.'

'Fucking hell, Luke.' She stared at him. 'Well, that's a bomb-shell.'

'So if Pete tells the army who my real NOK actually is, the shit is really going to hit the fan.'

'Will he?'

Luke considered this. 'Possibly. Pete was never happy about the way I cut myself off from my family, so he might well.'

Sam giggled. 'I'd love to see Notley's face when he finds out.'

Luke nodded. 'Yup, that would almost make this worth it.'

'This assumes we get to see Notley's face.'

'We will.'

'But if we can't get across the river and if we can't get to the road and…'

'And we can't get rescued…'

Sam nodded. 'Luke,' she said, 'I don't want to die. Not out here.'

'I won't let you. I am not going to let that happen. We're going to get out of here. Sam, I promise you, it's going to be all right,' and he took her into his arms.

James Rosser, back at Archers Post for the CO's O Group, found Andy Bailey listening to the net in the back of his vehicle, obviously trying to get updates from all units as to the progress of the search. James had known the missing personnel were two soldiers from 1 Herts but when he'd heard the CO announce that one of the missing soldiers was Sam, he hadn't wanted to believe it. But Andy, he hoped, would have more gen, more details. Andy would put him in the picture and, possibly, fill in all the gaps that the CO had left because the information about how Sam and her corporal had come to be lost had been very sketchy.

'So, what happened?'

'We're not sure,' said Andy.

'Come on, Andy, you must have some idea.'

'We've found the vehicle, but not them. That's all we know.' Andy stared at James. 'So… your interest? Were you and she…?'

'No, no. I mean, she's a great girl. But no, not really my type.'

Andy looked a bit surprised. 'Really?'

'No.' James looked Andy steadfastly in the eye. Did he have to spell it out to him? Not that this was a particularly appropriate moment, given everything else that was happening.

The radio squawked, distracting Andy, who listened to the message being passed before returning his attention to James. 'Just be assured that we're doing everything we can to find them. The Air Corps will resume search operations in the morning, and we'll get all units to move into and search the area where their vehicle was found but we're at a loss. Their Land Rover was way off the route they should have taken and given the evidence we've found so far, we think they were ambushed.' Andy looked James in the eye. 'There were a couple of bullet holes in the chassis.'

'No!'

'We think they might have been ambushed by poachers. And, although there may have been bullet holes, there wasn't a trace of blood. We don't think either Sam or Luke could be injured. But neither do we know whether they were still in the vehicle when it was dumped or whether they were kicked out of it somewhere else. All we do know is that the bullets caused the breakdown. Something vital got hit and that's why it was abandoned, but the REME reckon it could have travelled a fair way before the engine seized.'

'So, what you're saying is they could be anywhere?'

'In a nutshell. But we are doing everything we can to find them. Trust me on this.'

'Yeah, yeah, of course you are.'

'Honestly, you have no idea. I mean, we'd pull out all the stops anyway but there's been a development that even we didn't see coming.'

James's brow creased. 'I'm not with you.'

'It's Blake.'

'What about him? What's he done?'

'Oh, it's nothing he's done, it's who he is.'

'And?'

'He's the son of the Commander Land Forces. His real name is Pemberton-Blake.'

'Bloody hell.'

'And Sam's dad, Colonel Lewis, and the general are on their way.'

'You'd better hope they've been found by the time they get here.'

'Found alive and well.'

'Show me the map,' said James. 'I know you probably have more important things to do but maybe, I dunno, maybe I—' He stopped. 'I'd like to see the lie of things for myself.'

Andy stood up and took James over to the ops tent, where the map table dominated the space. It was covered in clear plastic onto which were drawn the tactical symbols representing the various component parts of the battalion and the battle group. Out on its own, away from any of the other markers, was a small flag. Andy pointed at it.

'That was where their vehicle was found,' he said.

'And where were they headed for?'

Andy pointed at a coloured oblong out on the edge of the exercise area – the Royal Engineer's tactical sign. 'There. They were taking a new genny to the sappers building a bridge across the river.'

'So why the fuck were they there? It makes no sense at all. They're miles off course.' James studied the map.

'Look, I've got a million things to do, but if you come up with any bright ideas, let me know.'

James barely acknowledged Andy's departure as he continued to stare at the map. Why, he kept asking himself, had the vehicle ended up where it was? Even if the poachers had driven it miles before it conked out it was still too far away from the rest of the action. Where had they crossed the river? Why were they so far south? It didn't make sense. How on earth could they have got so monumentally lost?'

He traced the route to their destination with his finger, the sappers' camp on the northern bank of the river. Why, he wondered, was it on that bank? The route to get to it had to loop miles round to reach it; a huge detour off the main supply route through the exercise area. Still, who knew how the mind of a sapper worked? He went back to staring at the map and wondering where, in that vast expanse of bugger-all, Sam might be.

Colonel Tim Lewis watched General Pemberton-Blake buckle himself into his seat on the airtrooping flight and then turn to introduce himself. He knew exactly who the general was – who didn't? His picture was in every guardroom in the country, it was on the stairs of the MOD, along with the pictures of his predecessors. On the other hand, Tim knew the general would have no clue as to who he was. Even though he was a senior officer himself, he was still too junior to be on the general's radar.

'I'm Bill Pemberton-Blake.'

'I know, General. I'm Tim Lewis, Samantha Lewis's father.'

'Ah, the REME officer missing with my son. They seem to be giving 1 Herts the runaround.'

Tim Lewis was confused. Yes, he'd been up since four for this hideously early flight but he couldn't be still dreaming? Commander Land Forces' son – a squaddie in the REME? He opened his mouth and shut it again. 'But Sam is lost with her driver.'

The general nodded. 'Indeed. My son.'

Tim wondered what the correct etiquette was when it came to quizzing such a high-ranking officer about why his son had failed to get into Sandhurst. He couldn't come up with any ideas on the subject so he said, 'Oh.'

'Actually, I find he's not just a driver but he's actually a corporal in the REME. I gather your daughter is his OC LAD.'

'Oh.' God, he had to think of something more intelligent to say than that. The Commander Land Forces would think him a total moron if he carried on like this. 'I'm sorry, General, but you sound as if you didn't know your son was in the REME.'

'No.'

The RAF staff positioned themselves in the aisle and the chief loadmaster began the announcement about emergency procedures. The two officers had both heard it countless times before but knew it was incumbent on them to set a good example to the other soldiers on the flight and so they paid attention. The announcement finished and then there was a gentle jolt as the tow truck began to push back the plane from its stand on the pan.

'You were saying, General,' prompted Tim.

'Given the situation that our children are in, I suppose you ought to know why my only child is a soldier and not an officer.'

'I... I don't want to pry, General.'

The plane began to taxi towards the runway under its own steam.

'I imagine, given that the BBC's defence correspondent is out in Kenya, attached to the exercise, and given the fact that it's unlikely that Mr Raven will fail to spot my arrival due to my connection to one of the two soldiers who are in jeopardy, this is all going to be made hideously public in a matter of days – maybe less than that. The whole sorry story of my relationship with my son is bound to come out so you might as well know it sooner rather than later.'

Tim stared at the general. This was seriously uncomfortable. Generals didn't confide in other officers who were considerably junior to them, did they?

He was about to say to the general that he didn't have to when the general continued. 'My son ran away from home. Just disappeared. We had... an altercation. He was expelled from school and I was angry. Maybe in retrospect I was a bit hasty. He protested his innocence but the evidence that he'd played a part in a serious misdeed seemed overwhelming and I refused to believe him. I think I may have been wrong. Anyway,

I refused to spend more money on him and said if he wanted to get A levels he'd have to go to the local college. So he upped and left. I tracked him down to begin with. He'd got a job in a bike shop and lived with a lad in the flat over it. I wasn't thrilled but at least he had a job and a roof and I knew that to force him to return home wasn't going to heal the rift between him and me. His mother was devastated. Luke knew what he was doing to her because I sent him a letter telling him, but he refused to back down.'

And neither would you, General, thought Tim. Like father, like son.

'Anyway, shortly after his eighteenth birthday I had a message from his flatmate that Luke had found another job and had left the area. And that's the last I heard about him till the OC rear party from 1 Herts knocked on my door yesterday evening and put me in the picture.'

'I am so sorry, General.'

The general shrugged. 'He'd always wanted to join the army. I suppose he thought that if he joined as an officer he'd be recognised and I'd find out where he was. I don't think he wanted me to have any influence on his career, for good or ill, intended or not, which I think would have been inevitable.'

'Certainly it would be almost impossible for that not to happen.'

'So I suppose that's why he dropped Pemberton and joined up, pretty much anonymously.'

'Kids, eh?'

The general nodded. 'So tell me about your daughter.'

'Nothing much to tell – boarding school, uni, then Sandhurst.'

'A model child.'

'Pretty much.'

'Lucky you.'

Tim knew he was lucky with Sam. Luckier than he deserved. He'd been a rotten father, he knew that now. Well, maybe not rotten, but not the best. He'd kept her at a distance, afraid to get close to her, while poor Sam had only ever tried to please him. Everything she'd ever done had been to gain his approval, he knew that too. And yet this awful situation made him realise how distant he'd been. If... when... he saw her again he'd have to tell her how proud he was of her, how glad he was she'd done so well. How much he loved her. Maybe they could both take some time off – go on holiday together. Maybe he ought to tell her how like her mother she was. He knew her gran had told her about her mother but maybe he ought to too. He reckoned there were a lot of things he ought to tell Sam. He'd been putting it off for years, waiting for the right moment. No... he'd put it off because he didn't want to have the conversations. He was afraid that if he started to talk about her mother he'd lose control. It was cowardice that had stopped him from talking to his daughter, not tact. And now he might have missed the chance altogether.

And he couldn't bear that thought. Not Sam as well. Not as well as his wife and son.

As Tim Lewis's and General Sir William Pemberton-Blake's early-morning flight was thundering down the runway at Brize Norton, Seb's flight was touching down at Heathrow. Now all he had to do was get back to Wiltshire, but before then he wanted to speak to Maddy. He pulled his mobile out of his combat jacket pocket and pressed the buttons and prayed that not only she would be allowed to have her mobile with her in hospital but that she also had a signal.

'Hello, Seb.'

She sounded groggy.

'Hi, hon. I've landed. Am I too late? Has junior arrived yet?'

'No, although the sister promises me it's not too long now.'

'Is your mum there?'

'I sent her home to get some sleep. I think she'll be back in a while. What time is it?'

'Early. Very early. I'll get to you as soon as I can.'

'OK, hon.'

Then he heard her groan and sob and then stifle a protracted yelp of pain and then the connection went. His heart went out to her. Now he had actually heard her distress his memory of the last time came thundering back. He forgot how hacked off he felt at being hauled out of the Kenyan exercise as the realisation that she was coping with labour on her own kicked in. He remembered the last time and how much pain she'd been in and the feeling of utter helplessness as he'd watched the contractions tear her body apart. Being at this distance made matters even worse. He hurried towards the immigration hall, overtaking the sleepy passengers who were stumbling along after the knackering overnight flight. He had to hope that at this hour the queues were minimal and he could get out of the airport as soon as possible. The army had pulled the stops out and had organised a car to meet him. If everything went smoothly and the Monday morning traffic behaved, he might be with Maddy in a few hours.

Andy was heading into the ops tent, a bacon sandwich in one hand and a mug of tea in the other, when he met James.

'Just the man. I've been thinking,' said James, grabbing Andy's arm and making him slop his tea.

'What about?'

'Why were the sappers on the north bank of the river? Any tactical reason. Because it doesn't make sense. I mean, logic tells me they should have been on this side.'

Andy sighed. 'It's all down to that journalist, Raven. He wanted to be able to access the village and get a piece involving the reaction of the villagers to the new bridge going in. Of course, the MOD press office thought it was a great idea, they reckoned it would get a load of coverage on the BBC news channel. I gather the sappers kicked up a stink about having to trek round miles to reach that spot but the brass were adamant. Why do you ask?'

'Look, maybe I'm wrong, but supposing you knew that the engineers were building a bridge, and supposing you thought you knew where on the river it was all happening, wouldn't logic – unless you checked properly – mean that you headed for this position...' James stuck his finger on the map '...and not there?' He moved his finger a centimetre to the other side of the river. 'Which in turn would mean that you set out down this route...' he traced a southerly track on the map '...and not this one.' He pointed at the main supply route.

Andy stared at him, his eyes wide as he took in what James was saying. 'Which would explain why the Land Rover is on the wrong side of the river,' said Andy after a second or two, nodding.

'It would. And it means that if they're walking, my bet is that they're going to head for the river and then the main supply route as it would offer their best chance of getting found.'

'What about crossing the river?'

'I don't know. But as they haven't reached the MSR they might have been held up by it. I'll get onto the Air Corps and get them to run a low-level sortie along it. We'll mobilise some troops into the area too.'

James Rosser left the tent and started walking towards the mess tent. He would dearly have liked to join in with the search party but realistically he was too far away from the area to be involved. He might as well get some breakfast and then go back to the ops tent and see how everything progressed. He had to hope that Sam and Corporal Blake were still alive.

As he crossed the scrubby ground he saw Corporal Cooper sitting on a chair in the shade of an acacia tree, her leg, heavily bandaged, resting on a crate.

'Hello,' he said. 'You look like you've been in the wars.'

'Hello, sir. It looks worse than it is. Well, that's how it is now. It was nasty when I got casevaced here. The medics pumped me full of penicillin and now I'm pretty much better. No more light duties for me.'

'That's good.'

'Sir?'

'Yes?'

'You don't know anything about Lu... Corporal Blake and Captain Lewis, do you? Only Jack... Jack Raven... says they've notified their next of kin. That means it's serious, doesn't it?'

James nodded. 'I'm afraid it does. But I can assure you everything possible is being done. We've got to hope it all turns out for the best.' And at the moment that was all they had – hope.

Chapter Thirty-Three

Seb put his head round the door. 'Mads?' he whispered.

He saw his wife yawn and then open her eyes. 'Hi, hon,' she said sleepily. 'You missed the main event. You've got a daughter.'

She looked so beautiful, he thought. Perfect. But also exhausted. Under her eyes were huge dark shadows. She'd been through a lot in the last couple of days and she hadn't had him to help. But as always she'd got on and done it. No complaints, no retribution. She was such a star, such a great wife. How... how on earth – *why* on earth – had he ever found Michelle attractive? What had he been thinking about? As he looked at his wife, once again he was reminded that he'd made the most appalling cock-up. The conversation he'd had with Sam, back before Christmas, flashed into his head; how on earth had he ever thought he could get away with having an affair in an organisation as close-knit as the army? He'd made up his mind, back then, to do the best he could to be an ace husband, and now, seeing his beautiful wife looking so utterly wiped out, he knew he must never, ever, go back on that promise. His heart was filled with love as he bent forward and kissed her gently on the forehead. 'It's a girl?'

Maddy nodded. 'Yeah. Four pounds ten ounces and with blue eyes. And I think she's going to be a ginger.'

'Like her mum. Great.' He looked around the side ward. 'Where is she?'

'Special Care for the time being.'

Seb's eyes widened in horror.

'Just a precaution, to make sure she's feeding OK – and to allow me to get some sleep. Some of us have been up all night.'

'Yes, we have.'

They smiled at each other. Maddy reached over to her bedside locker and picked up her phone. She pressed some buttons with her thumb. 'There you are,' she said as she gave the mobile to Seb.

There on the screen was a picture of a very tiny bundle with a red, wrinkled, scrunched-up face.

'She's beautiful.'

'There speaks a doting father. I think she will be in a day or two. Right now, I think she looks like a tortoise.' Maddy heaved herself up in bed and winced.

'Sore?'

'Not too bad.'

The door to Maddy's room opened again. Maddy saw Seb's eyes pop as Jenna entered.

'Oh... hello, Captain Fanshaw,' she said. 'Hello, sweetie,' she said as she bent forward and gave Maddy a peck on the cheek. 'I've come from SCBU. Isn't she a honey?'

'Jenna!' Seb turned and stared at Maddy. 'Jenna?'

'Jenna has been a complete brick. She held the fort with Nate so Mum could be with me,' said Maddy firmly. Whatever Seb thought of her friend, she wasn't going to let him express it in front of Jenna. Not after all that Jenna had done for her.

'But... but...'

'Jenna's partner is a REME sergeant with the LAD here,' said Maddy, wondering if she ought to tell Seb to shut his mouth. He was looking spectacularly gormless.

'You didn't tell me,' said Seb accusingly.

'No. Well, I didn't think you'd be interested.' Maddy turned to Jenna. 'Is Mum all right?'

'She's fine. Susie's got Nathan so she can get her head down.'

Seb shook his head – thank goodness for the patch camara-derie; army wives were brilliant when it came to a problem like this, with everyone rocking in to help or lend a hand.

'There is one thing, though,' said Jenna. 'Nathan seems to have picked up saying "toilet" and your mum is trying to make him say "lavatory" instead.'

Maddy giggled. 'God, she's such a snob.'

'It's my fault,' said Jenna.

'Like I'm worried,' said Maddy. 'If the worst thing Nathan does in his life is say "toilet" and annoy his granny then I'll be happy.'

'Yes,' said Jenna. 'You're right. He could do much worse things. Much worse.' She turned and stared at Seb. Seb stared back and his heart crunched as a bolt of guilt skewered him. That look? Did she know something? And if so, how? But then Jenna looked back at Maddy and smiled and Seb felt as if he could breathe again.

'Anyway,' said Jenna, taking the mobile from Seb and looking at the picture of the baby, 'what you going to call her?'

'I think I need to get to know her a bit first,' said Maddy. 'Don't want to saddle her with a name that doesn't suit her. It took us a while to come up with Nathan.'

'A whole week,' said Seb. 'Your mother got quite antsy.'

'Nothing new there, then,' said Maddy.

Jenna laughed. 'I think I know where you're coming from. Anyway, I shall love you and leave you. Now you've got hubby back and your mum is around, I am definitely the pork sausage at the bar mitzvah. Bye, hon. Make sure hubby and your mum spoil you. I'm just going to take as last look at the new arrival and then I'm going home. Byeee.' She whirled out of the door again.

'Hubby?' said Seb, horrified.

'Snob. And, frankly, I couldn't give a toss how she talks or what she says, she's my friend and she has been wonderful these past few days.'

'She's trouble.'

Maddy yawned.

'Sorry, hon, you're knackered, aren't you?'

'That's what comes of giving birth first thing in the morning.'

'Tell you what, why don't I leave you to get some sleep and I'll come back when I've had a shower, a nap and something to eat. We can have a have a proper catch-up then. I'll see if I can smuggle some fizz in.'

'That's against the rules!'

'Sod it, let's see if we can't break a few.'

'Or you could wait. I think I'll be allowed to go home tomorrow. The baby may have to stay in – they're going to see how she does.'

'Can I see her?'

'Of course. Go and see the sister.' Maddy yawned again.

'I'm going to go. You need your rest. I'll go and meet junior and then I'll get off home. Bye, hon.' He kissed her tenderly again and then went to see his new daughter.

Maddy, exhausted as she was, wondered what she was going to do about her and Seb. She loved him, she knew it, but she still had to come to terms with what Michelle had told her. So, she reasoned in the relative quiet of her hospital bed, there were three possible scenarios: confront Seb and find out that Michelle was lying; confront Seb and find out it was all true; or ignore the whole sorry state of affairs. If she confronted Seb and it was true then a whole other can of worms would be opened. If, on the other hand, she decided to ignore everything she could carry on with her life and the waves that had rocked her boat would subside. Maddy looked at the picture of the little scrap she'd given birth to only a few hours previously. Maybe she was being naïve and stupid but it seemed to be the best way to her. The baby didn't need to come into a family with troubles; the third option it was, then.

She was snuggling down into the pillows when the door opened again.

'Jenna? Back again?'

'Sorry, hon, I'll only be a minute but I need to cough to something and I didn't want to tell you in front of Seb. I lurked in the corridor till I saw him go.'

'What? Why?'

'Look, I might have been bang out of order but I told Milward about the visit from Michelle.'

Maddy was wide awake. 'You did what?'

Jenna sighed. 'I couldn't bear the idea she might do something really bonkers – she needed to have the frighteners put on her. It was the only thing I could think of doing. Anyway, I don't know what Milward's done about it but I told him he ought to find out who she was and tell her boss what she was getting up to. I did say he wasn't to mention that Michelle said she'd had an affair with Seb, but I don't know if Milward would have paid any attention to that. You know what the army's like – they're not going to look kindly on an officer doing what she was doing.'

Maddy blew her cheeks out. 'And to think I'd decided to ignore it all; pretend nothing had happened.' She regarded Jenna. 'I suppose I ought to thank you but...' God, this was tricky and she was starting to feel a bit of a heel because she would have preferred it if Jenna hadn't interfered.

'But?'

'But I don't want Seb to know that I know.'

'What? Really?'

'Really. I think it's for the best. Truly.'

389

'I've fucked up,' said Jenna. She looked despondent.

'I don't know. Jenna, I'm too tired to think about it at the mo, but thanks for telling me. If you could do me a favour?'

'Yes, anything, what?'

'Get me Milward's number. Text it to me as soon as you can. The advantage of being in here is that I can think in peace and quiet with no toddler or baby making demands. The goalposts have shifted again, but, to be honest, what's done is done.'

'Sure,' said Jenna. 'And I'm sorry, but I was really worried and I thought Milward needed to know.'

'Yes, I know.' Maddy wasn't sure if she agreed or not with Jenna's assessment but she was too knackered to think about it further.

Jenna disappeared and then Maddy shut her eyes. Just when she thought she'd got a plan straight in her head...

Sam and Luke lay, side by side, still holding hands, propped up against a tree trunk in what passed for shade, both gazing at the river. All that water and they couldn't get near it. Sam empathised with the Ancient Mariner: 'Water, water, everywhere, nor any drop to drink.' And there wasn't, not any. Not a single bloody drop. None left. And the water they were looking at, apart from being filthy, and brown and muddy and probably diseased, was stiff with crocodiles, lounging on the banks, lying in it with just their nostrils and froggy eyes above the surface, lying in the cool, cool water while she and Luke sweltered in the sun, on this bank where it would be difficult for the reptiles to sneak up. Taking on one lion was one thing but there had to be about a hundred crocs right here. The odds, if they decided to attack, weren't hopeful.

'You all right, Sam?' croaked Luke.

She nodded. 'Why?' Her voice was barely above a whisper.

'Because, until very recently, you've been like the Duracell bunny on amphetamines, never bloody stopping, never shutting up, and now you've gone all quiet.'

'Oh.' There was a pause while she forced herself to swallow but her throat stayed arid and sore. 'Just tired, that's all.'

'Sam?'

'Hmm.'

'I've been a bastard to you right up till now.'

'It doesn't matter,' she whispered. And it didn't. Not now. Nothing mattered. She shut her eyes against the glare of the sun.

'It does. You need to know why.'

'I don't.'

'It's because when you walked into the LAD and I saw you, I thought you were the perfect woman, and then when I had to half carry you to the medical centre... well, it all got a bit much. I realised then I might have made a dreadful mistake in not being an officer and that I'd never have a chance with you, so to stay sane I had to keep you at arm's length. I thought if I let you get to me, if you were nice, I'd be lost. That was why I was such a git, to make sure you weren't.'

Sam smiled weakly. 'You succeeded.'

'And then I thought you were dating Rosser. I couldn't stand it, I was so jealous. It consumed me.'

'You needn't have worried. We're just mates – very platonic.' There was a pause while Sam gathered enough strength to ask Luke something that had bothered her. 'That dance,' Sam croaked, 'at the corporals' club. You wanted to show him up, didn't you?'

'Yeah. I don't know what came over me.'

'Immi enjoyed it.'

'I suppose. Anyway, now I *have* got a chance and we're together, it's all gone horribly wrong.'

Sam summoned the energy to squeeze his hand. She rolled

her head and looked at him. 'We're together,' she said. 'That's the main thing. That's enough for me.'

Luke kissed her cheek. 'You're crying.'

'No, I'm not,' she lied. 'Can't afford to waste the fluids.' She flopped back against the tree. That conversation had drained yet more energy from her. She felt exhausted, a husk and worse, she felt despair descend on her like a shroud. It was hopeless. In this temperature and with no water it was probably only hours now till it would all be over. She fingered her pistol. Should she suggest to Luke they could shorten the timeline? No, or not yet, anyway.

The heat throbbed. And the silence bore down on her oppressively. Only she realised it wasn't totally silent. She could hear the faint rasp of Luke's breathing and the whine of a mosquito and the buzzing of the ever-present flies. But there wasn't much sound. Not even a bird cry. They were abandoned. She pressed Luke's fingers again and got a stroke of his thumb on the back of her hand in response. No, they weren't abandoned – they had each other.

Even thinking was taking too much energy. Her mind drifted to nothing and she hovered halfway between consciousness and unconsciousness.

To begin with she thought the low throbbing was in her head, due to the sun beating relentlessly on it. Or was it her pulse? Some unknown insect? Or was she imagining it?

'Luke?' Her voice was a faint croak.

'What?'

'Can you hear it?'

'What?'

'Listen.'

The throbbing was louder, more insistent, more real.

Sam raised her head. Something glinted in the sunshine, something metallic in the sky.

'Oh my God, a chopper,' croaked Sam. She staggered to her feet and tottered away from the tree and into the open scrub. She began waving her hat in the air weakly. Luke joined her. They jumped, they hollered, they waved, but the chopper flew on its course, on the far side of the river, and the clatter of the rotors died away. After several minutes there wasn't a hint of aircraft noise to be heard at all.

So close...

Even in her miserable despondency, an idea came to Sam. 'Luke, have you got any cam cream?'

Luke stared at her. 'You stupid woman, we want to become more visible, not less.'

'Just answer the question.'

Sam watched Luke rummage in his combat jacket pockets. 'Here.' He proffered a small compact. Sam flipped open the lid and began to clean the mirror with her sleeve.

'You look fine,' joked Luke.

Sam shook her head. She looked like shit.

She staggered right away from the trees and then began to flash the mirror.

'You are a genius,' said Luke as he cottoned on to what she was up to.

'Don't knock us officers,' croaked Sam, 'we have our uses.'

Luke joined her. 'You've got to hope they're quartering the ground and will head back this way in a while.'

Sam nodded. She tried to smile but her lips were so cracked and dry that stretching them hurt. 'It's our last hope.'

Her wrist began to ache so she changed hands. 'Give it to me,' said Luke.

Sam handed the compact over. 'How far will this light travel?' she asked, as she watched the rays bounce off the mirror.

'We've got to hope it's far enough.'

Over the next hour they took it in turns with the mirror and between their 'shifts' they dozed. Sam was finding it harder and harder to focus, to think straight, even to keep motivated. She had to force herself to keep turning the mirror when it was her turn with the compact. She had to keep telling herself that this was *not* a waste of time, the helicopter *would* come back… She ignored the voice at the back of her head that kept saying, *What's the point?*

The sun was getting lower, and Sam's anxiety level was getting higher. She didn't think they could survive another night without water and the chopper wouldn't fly after dark. Even if it resumed the search the next day it would be too late for her and Luke, she was sure.

She nudged Luke, who was lying beside her, his eyes shut. 'Your turn.' Her voice rasped, barely sounding human.

'Uh?' Luke opened his eyes.

She handed him the mirror and he dragged himself into a sitting position.

'It's no good,' he said.

'Don't you dare give up on me, Luke Blake,' she hissed, despite the fact that she felt like she had a razor blade in her throat. 'We keep going till the sun sets. Understand.'

He nodded. 'Sorry.' He began to flick the mirror and Sam slumped, the effort of her outburst depleting her minute reserves still further. She had her arms crossed over her crooked knees and her head bowed. She shut her eyes and thought about Luke and how much she loved him.

And then she heard the pulse again, a low, thwacking beat.

'Luke?'

'Shh.'

She looked up. Luke was standing beside her, the mirror above his head, flicking it to and fro for all he was worth and this time the chopper wasn't stooging along the far side of the river, this time it was heading towards them. This time they'd been seen.

And then it was almost on top of them, the wind from the rotors beat down on them, kicking up dust and debris, forcing them to turn away and shield their eyes.

Luke and Sam still clung to each other in their relief and total joy, neither wanting to let go of the other as the chopper touched down yards away from them.

The big door in the side slid open and the winchman beckoned them over. They didn't need telling twice and with energy reserves they didn't know they had they ran across, ducking under the spinning rotors and clambered in. Instantly he passed them bottles of water.

'I take it you'd like a lift,' he said.

Sam looked at him, started to cry, and then Luke took her in his arms and held her tight.

'They've found them,' said Jack.

Immi leapt out of her chair and then instantly regretted it as her bad leg buckled.

'Hey, steady,' said Jack, catching her and stopping her from falling.

She gazed up at him. 'They're both OK, aren't they?'

'Sunburned, thirsty and the medics'll probably want to check them over but yes, as far as I know, they're pretty good for a couple who have spent that long out in the bush.'

Immi spotted James coming out of the mess tent.

'Oi, sir,' she hollered. 'It's good news.'

James Rosser charged over. 'Really?'

'Honest,' said Jack Raven. 'The adjutant heard it on the net. The Air Corps have scooped them up. They're heading back here.'

James picked up Immi and spun her round before planting

a kiss on her cheek. 'Sorry, Corporal Cooper,' he said, putting her down. 'But that news had to be celebrated.'

'Don't mind me, sir,' said Immi, pink with embarrassment and pleasure. 'I'm as chuffed as you are. Captain Lewis and I shared a room and we'd got friendly. I was so worried about her. But not as worried as you must have been, eh?' She gave James a smile and a half-wink.

'No, well...' James coughed. 'I was a bit, but really only like you were. As a friend...' He smiled back at Immi. 'Mind you, didn't I see you and Blake at the corporals' club bash together?'

'Yeah, well...'

'You and Blake?' said Raven, suddenly frowning.

'Not really, Jack. I'll admit it now, I used to have a thing for him but not any more. Let's put it this way, if we'd got it together I don't think anyone would have called it a match made in heaven. He reads books, I don't, he does ballroom—'

'Ballroom?' said Jack.

Immi nodded. 'Straight up. I bop, maybe a bit of body-popping. He drinks wine, I drink vodka and slimline or Bacardi and Coke. You get the picture.'

'So you don't know,' said James.

'Know what?' asked Immi.

'About Blake's dad.'

'About his dad?' said Immi and Jack together.

'Really?'

'Come on, sir, spit it out,' said Immi.

So James told Immi and a very interested Jack Raven who Corporal Blake's dad happened to be.

'Bugger me,' breathed Immi – almost shocked into silence, but not quite. 'Commander Land Forces.'

'The CLF,' said Jack. 'Holy cow. And I've got the scoop.'

'Nice to know that this unholy mess has brought good fortune to someone,' said James.

For a moment Jack Raven looked almost ashamed, then he laughed. 'Hey, I had nothing to do with the mess, I'm an innocent bystander.' He grabbed Immi's hand. 'Come on, kiddo, you can help me file the story. I want you to tell me what both these guys were like. I want every detail.'

As Immi followed Jack into his tent she gave James a wink.

James watched the helicopter land. Like everyone around him, he was thrilled that the two missing soldiers had been found alive and well. Even those who didn't know either Sam or Luke Blake were going about with an added bounce in their stride because the happiness caused by the good news was contagious.

James turned away as the helicopter descended onto the pad, away from the dust and dead vegetation kicking up into an almighty tornado of swirling air, aviation fuel fumes and hot exhaust. As the pilot killed the engine and the rotors began to slow and the noise from the Bell's engine lessened, James turned back and there was Sam, clambering out, looking badly sunburned, gaunt, strained and grubby but otherwise in one piece. Behind her was Luke Blake – the CLF's son, as everyone now knew. They looked ridiculously happy. Why wouldn't they? thought James. The pilot had already relayed the news back to the camp that the pair had run out of food and water and, if they hadn't been found, would probably have faced death before morning. Their rescue, in the nick of time, was enough to make anyone happy.

James watched them beginning to move away from the helicopter towards the medics who would want to check them over. They had their arms linked. No doubt they were both feeling pretty wobbly after what they'd been through – exposure to the sun for days, a lack of water and also food. Of course they'd want to support each other. And then they looked at each other and the look between them spoke volumes; of emotions, regrets, shared experiences. They stared at each other, unblinking, for the longest of moments. It was apparent to James and probably everyone else that despite the hullaba-loo going on around them they were oblivious to everything except each other. It was only when Andy Bailey walked up to them and spoke that they came back to reality.

James knew with a sixth-sense certainty that the Sam who had got off this helicopter wasn't the Sam he'd seen a few days previously in her workshop. Something had changed her and he didn't think it was the brush with danger.

As Sam walked away with Andy, still clinging onto Luke Blake, James didn't wave. He was fond enough of Sam not to want to interrupt whatever was going on between them. He knew the army wouldn't approve but he hoped for both their sakes they found a way to get around the rules and regulations about officers and other ranks fraternising. He thought it might be almost impossible. The army had unbent about many things, including being gay, but that sort of fraternising... no way.

A text from Jenna, with Milward's number, pinged into Maddy's phone. She only looked at it for a few seconds before she made up her mind and rang it.

'Hello, Alan. It's Maddy Fanshaw here. Thanks for getting Seb back when I was in labour.'

She heard him stammer a greeting. The man was such an old prude when it came to anything to do with women – like childbirth. Then he said, 'Did Seb get back in time?'

'Almost. He wasn't here for the actual arrival of the baby but he got here a few hours later.'

'Good, I'm glad. And all well with you and the little one?'

For a naughty second Maddy considered telling Alan about her stitches, but then decided that would be too cruel! 'I'm fine and the baby is too, which is great considering her early arrival. Look... Alan.'

'Yes?' He sounded wary.

'About what Jenna told you – about Michelle?'

'Yes.' He sounded even more wary.

'Can you just forget it?'

'How d'you mean?'

Maddy took a deep breath. 'I mean I don't want any action to be taken. I don't know if the girl was lying or telling the truth but Seb and I will sort things out between us. I don't want the army sticking its oar in.'

'But... but...'

'Yes?'

'But it's already gone up the chain of command. Although I only told Lieutenant Flowers' CO about the fighting, not... ahem, about the other business. Jenna was insistent that I didn't. '

Maddy breathed a sigh. Thank the Lord... the affair was still pretty much a secret. 'Even so, I don't want any action taken. I want the whole business forgotten. Everything. It's nothing to do with the army. It is an entirely personal matter.'

'But... but...'

'But nothing, Alan. Can you sort it for me, please?' She used her stern voice, the one she used on Nathan when he was being really difficult.

'Yes, yes, of course.'

Chapter Thirty-Four

Michelle was about to leave the classroom where she'd been teaching her recruits about the Geneva Convention and all its implications. The recruits were all beetling off to change for PT while she gathered up her papers, switched off the laptop and the PowerPoint projector and left the room as she would wish to find it herself. Of course, as well as tidying things up she was desperate to keep busy and occupied – anything to keep herself from thinking about when the commandant's axe might fall, anything to fill her mind with trivia rather than worry.

'Have you got a moment, Michelle?'

She glanced up. It was the admin officer for the training depot. Instantly her stomach lurched and guilt overtook her again. Shit – this was it, she had no doubt. It had been almost twenty-four hours since her last interview with the commandant so he'd had plenty of time to think about disciplinary procedures or summary punishment or both. She knew she had to expect the worst. Her father's reassuring hug before he'd left for his meeting at the MOD hadn't really helped, although he'd clearly meant it to – a show of fatherly support and love, which had touched her to the core, a demonstration which would have been unthinkable twenty-four hours earlier.

'Keep me in the loop about developments,' he'd said. 'I do care. I hope you believe that now. And whatever happens I'll be there for you.'

She'd had to blink back the tears at that. Weirdly, maybe

stalking Maddy hadn't been the disaster it outwardly appeared to be; not if it meant her relationship with her father was in a better place than it had been for almost twenty years.

She gazed steadily at the admin officer, trying to look calm, trying not to let her feeling of sick nervousness show. 'Why?'

'The commandant would like to see you.'

'I'll just finish here.'

'Leave it,' said the admin officer.

God, that last order didn't bode well. Michelle dumped her belongings back on the desk at the front of the classroom and followed the admin officer out of the teaching block and across the camp to the headquarters building. The pair didn't talk. Michelle wondered if Captain Wilkes knew the reason for the summons. And if he did, how many others were privy to the allegations? Too late for regrets now, though. What was that song that Chet had sung... *If I Could Turn Back Time*? Didn't everyone wish that occasionally? Except she seemed to find herself wishing it on a pretty regular basis. Maybe, in the future, she ought to take Sam's often-given advice and count to ten before acting.

As on the previous evening, she stood outside the commandant's door and knocked.

'Come.'

She marched in, halted in front of his desk and stood to attention as she saluted.

'Sir.'

The commandant stared at her. 'It's your lucky day, Flowers.'

Michelle swallowed. 'Sir?'

'Captain Fanshaw's wife has made a specific request that this sordid matter isn't pursued further. But, as you admitted to me that the allegations were true, there is a part of me that is inclined to ignore her request.'

Michelle's heart, which had lifted with the commandant's first sentence, came crashing back down with the second.

'Sir?'

'However, she obviously is adamant in her wishes and I imagine she wants to forget the incident so I shall respect her decision.' The commandant stared at her. 'Why she is doing this, God alone knows, although I hear she's just had a baby so maybe that explains her judgement. Or lack of it.' The disgust on the colonel's face spoke volumes. 'So... you're free to go. You are no longer confined to barracks.' Michelle felt that he'd be much happier if he'd been able to convene a summary court-martial, try her, find her guilty and order her to be shot at dawn. And frankly, that was almost what she'd expected to happen. God, the relief that it hadn't...

The colonel continued and Michelle forced herself to listen to him. 'That said, your behaviour will be reflected in the grading and my comments in your annual confidential report and I suspect the repercussions from that will affect your promotion prospects for some years to come. On the other hand, if you work very hard and don't transgress again, you may yet develop into a useful officer.'

His expression indicated that he doubted it but Michelle didn't care, she felt faint with relief.

'The ball is in your court, Flowers. Screw up again and no one will be able to save you.'

'Yes, sir,' she managed to stammer out.

'But let me make this very clear, if you so much put a single toe out of line in the remainder of your time here I will throw the book at you. Understand?'

'Yes, sir.'

'Now, get out.'

Michelle almost forgot to salute in her hurry to obey him and flee. Once she was at a safe distance with a shut door providing another layer of safety she got out her phone and texted her dad, asking him to ring her when convenient.

Her phone rang almost instantly.

'And?' said her father with no preamble.

Michelle relayed the previous five minutes. She could hear her father's sigh.

'God, you're lucky. You've been given a second chance, so make sure you don't blow it.'

'Shit, no.' And she'd been given a second chance with her father too. As soon as Sam got back from Kenya she'd have to tell her everything. She needed to ask Sam's forgiveness too, for ignoring her advice about keeping away from Maddy. Back at Christmas she'd warned her, had said it would end in tears. Well, she'd been right. Again. Maybe, thought Michelle, she really ought to accept that Sam's judgement was better than hers.

The two senior officers, weary from their flight, clambered out of the CO's Land Rover and headed into the hut that was the Archers Post medical reception station. There, side by side in the tiny ward, were their respective children, both looking red with sunburn, tired and a little drawn, and with saline drips being fed into their arms.

Sam was the first to speak. 'Hiya, Dad.'

Tim looked away and blew his nose. 'I thought I was going to lose you.' Then he let out a slow breath. 'It's been a tricky couple of days.'

'We didn't mean to get lost.' Sam glanced across to Luke's bed and saw that he and his father were also still looking at each other – neither making a move.

Then Luke cracked first. 'Hello, Dad.'

'Hello, son.' There was a pause before the general said, 'Have you any idea what a hole your rescue has just punched in the defence budget?'

'A big one, I should imagine.' Luke didn't sound the least bit contrite.

'Exactly. So in order to pay that sort of money back, I expect you to make a full recovery and return to your duties in double quick time.'

Luke stared at his father. Then he said, 'How's Mum?'

'I think she'll be better now she knows where you are and what you're doing. When you lit out…'

'I'm sorry.'

'Are you? Really?'

'I was angry with you. And Mum. Neither of you believed me. You both blamed me and you never asked to hear my side of the story.'

'I know, I was wrong.'

Sam and her father stopped shamelessly eavesdropping on the conversation taking place across the ward.

'I'm sorry, Dad,' she told him.

'What on earth for?'

'For making you worry. You don't need that sort of shit… not after…'

'Not after everything else? No, not really. I… I, erm… It made me realise that maybe I wasn't the best father.'

'You were fine,' said Sam, stoutly.

'Really?' Her father brightened.

Sam nodded. 'Yeah. Tell you what, I'm due leave when this is all over. How about you book some time off too and we go and see Gran and Grandpa together? They'd like that.'

'Why not? It's been a while since I went down that way.'

Sam knew. Years. 'They'd love to see you.'

Her dad nodded. 'Yes, it'd be good.'

After their fathers had left, Luke lay back on his pillows, staring at the ceiling. 'Bloody hell,' he said.

Sam looked across at him. 'So, you're speaking to your dad again.'

Luke nodded. 'Yeah. It's going to take a bit to really

404

straighten things out. He's mad at me for upsetting Mum.' He snorted. 'Seems I'm still not quite the favourite son. No fatted calf slaughtered yet.'

'But maybe a small steak is on offer?'

Luke laughed. 'Yeah, maybe a small steak. How about you?'

'Yeah, Dad was pleased to see her alive and well.'

'Sam,' said Luke.

'Yes?'

'I'm going to have to ask for a posting.'

Sam turned her head on her pillow. 'Posting?'

'I can't stay in the LAD with you. Not after...'

'Not after the way things have changed between us?'

Luke gazed across the space between the two beds. 'No.'

Sam stared again at the ceiling. She knew he was right. No, he couldn't stay with 1 Herts. Sooner or later the fact that they had fallen in love would get in the way of their work and the difference in their ranks would make life difficult. And apart from anything else, the fact that it was now common knowledge in the battalion that Luke was the CLF's son was going to make life awkward for almost everyone. Better, much better, that he slide off to another posting where he might enjoy some anonymity for a while, if that's what he still wanted.

'I could resign my commission,' she offered. 'I could get a job near your next posting.'

'No! If you did that I'd worry that one day you'd blame me for not achieving your potential. Maybe in a few years... maybe when you've got fed up with being mucked around by the army...' Luke paused. 'I could put *my* notice in, rather than you leave the army.'

Sam shook her head. 'The army would still disapprove if we got together. They'd know I was dating a soldier. They would do anything obvious but I'd be bound to get a succession postings to the Falklands or some training establishment from civilisation and where there wouldn't be a quarter available. Anything to keep you and me apart.'

'It just isn't going to work,' said Luke, 'is it?'

'No,' said Sam, feeling tears trickle down her temples into her hairline. 'No, it would never have worked.'

Maddy was feeling hugely rested when Seb returned later that evening.

'You are so clever,' he said, kissing her nose. 'Our daughter is the most beautiful baby. And I admit,' added Seb, somewhat sheepishly, 'I called in on her before I came to you.'

Maddy smiled. 'I was in the baby unit an hour ago, giving her a feed and a clean nappy. She's very dinky, isn't she?'

'Did *you* feed her?' Seb sounded astounded. 'But she's got a tube.'

'I had a go. We didn't get on very well so they topped her up through the tube.'

'And how about you?'

'They sent me back to the ward to get my supper and to see you. They say I can be discharged this evening.'

'Really?' Seb looked over the moon. 'That's the best news.' He glanced at the door. 'We could celebrate.' He swung a backpack onto the bed and unzipped it. Sam could see the foil top of a bottle of fizz.

'Or we could celebrate at home?'

'We could. With your mother.'

'She's not so bad,' said Maddy staunchly. 'And I'd like to see Nathan.'

'All right,' said Seb. 'So when'll you be getting out of here?'

'The doc's coming round in a minute. As soon as I've got the ⁴-clear, I can go. Why don't you go and keep junior company?
     vait to see the doc and then I'll get dressed and you can
        1e home.'

'Sounds like a plan.' Seb was about to leave when he turned. 'By the way, did you hear about Sam Lewis?'

'No, should I have done?'

'Well, if you put the TV onto the BBC news you'll probably find out.'

'It's nothing awful, is it?'

'Not now. She's had a bit of an adventure in Kenya. The BBC are full of it as they had a reporter out there in the thick of it.'

Seb left and Maddy switched on her TV. A couple of minutes after she found the BBC's rolling news channel she was transfixed. Bloody hell!

Six weeks later, the exercise was over, the RAF transports had finished ferrying 1 Herts back to the UK, and most of the chaos caused by moving a whole battalion to Africa and then back again had been sorted out. The weapons were back in the armoury, the remaining specialist kit had been returned to the Q stores, the post-exercise reports had been written and, with everything squared away, the CO cleared his troops for two weeks' post-exercise leave. During the exercise James had been on the ranges in Kenya and Sam, once she was passed fully fit, had been busy at the workshop in Laikipia, and then, having returned to England, last few days in the barracks had been madness itself. Consequently their paths hadn't crossed for weeks. But, finally, order had been restored and now, the night before block leave started, the old routines were well and truly back to normal.

James and Sam were sitting together in the anteroom after dinner. They were on their own as all the other livers-in had disappeared off to sort out their packing or make sure their washing was done and their kit was squared away, so, on their return from leave, they could hit the ground running.

While they both drank coffee James studied Sam as she faffed with the sudoku in the paper. She had definitely changed. The fun and flirty Sam had gone and in her place was a quieter, more serious clone – or maybe he was reading too much into things. Maybe she was just knackered and ready for her leave. Or maybe she was sad because Blake had been posted out of the battalion with lightning speed. Had his posting got anything to do with the body language between the two that he'd spotted back at Archers Post? Had the authorities found out too and pre-empted the awkward situation, or had Blake and Sam agreed it was for the best and arranged his posting by mutual consent? Or was it just coincidence? James longed to ask what had gone on when the pair had been lost but he had a pretty shrewd idea that even if he did, he wouldn't get a straight answer from Sam.

'You looking forward to your leave?' he said as she threw the paper back onto the table, the sudoku defeating her.

'Of course. Dad says he's going to come down to my gran and grandpa's too. I can't remember the last time we were both there together. Not for a proper holiday, anyway. He used to drop me off or pick me up. Gran's thrilled too. It's a big step for him – well, it's a big step for all of us.'

'So it's all holding together?' he asked and Sam nodded. 'I'm glad.'

'What about you? Going home to your folks?'

James nodded. 'Yup, a fortnight of Mum's baking and Dad's G and Ts should undo all the good that yomping around Kenya did for me.' He patted his stomach in anticipation. 'You'll have a nice time at your gran's,' he said. 'You spending the full two weeks there?'

'Can't think of a better place for a bit of R and R. And Michelle might come down too. Remember her?'

Of course he did. 'You'll have fun,' he said. 'No chance of

boredom setting in with her around. Well, as long as she's not still stressing about that bloke of hers.'

'No, that's all in the past.'

'I don't suppose there's any chance of you getting up to Guildford?'

'James...' She shook her head. 'You know I'd love to see you and your folks but I think I need the time with Dad more.'

'I understand.'

She stood up to go. 'I must go and pack – early start tomorrow. I'll see you when I get back. Have fun.' She leaned down and brushed his cheek with her lips.

James stared up at her. For a mad moment he wondered if she was sending him a signal about their relationship. He toyed with the idea of telling her that although he was very fond of her and liked being her friend, that was all it could ever be. But instead he said, 'You have fun too.'

'Cheers,' she said lightly, although her expression suggested an underlying sadness.

James truly hoped she'd find happiness again soon. She deserved it, but it wouldn't be with him.

Maddy could hardly believe it. It was nine in the morning and here she was, lying in bed, with breakfast on a tray and the papers. Rose was in her Moses basket beside her, and Seb had called up the stairs to tell her that he and Nate were off to the play park.

She smiled to herself. Seb had certainly changed in the fatherhood department. He couldn't be attentive enough. He even lent a hand with the cooking and the washing up, and asked, actually *asked*, if it was all right for him to go to the gym to train. And he'd been as good as his word and had stopped working for army rowing so he was home every weekend. No more endless training, no more weekend regattas, no m excuses why he couldn't help out with the house or the kids. Maddy nibbled on a piece of toast and brushed the crumbs off her nightie. Maybe Michelle had done them a favour. Not that Seb would ever know that she knew the reason for his transformation. Of course, if Seb ever transgressed again she'd batter him to death with a meat mallet, but she didn't think he would. Besides, now they had a boy and a girl they both agreed they had a perfect family so there was no need to even think about having a third child. No more morning sickness, no more being fat and bloated, and no more not fancying sex as a result.

Maddy knew it took two to make a marriage work, and also for it to go wrong, and she had to shoulder some of the blame herself for being supremely indifferent to Seb's needs when she'd been expecting little Rose. Well, all that had changed as soon as she'd been able to get back in the saddle, so to speak. She grinned at the memory of that time... and the time after and the time after that... In fact, there had been lots and lots of times since Rose's birth. She hoped that the precautions she and Seb were taking would hold up until Seb saw the doctor.

And that was another thing – he'd actually agreed to a vasectomy. She'd have put good money on him refusing to have anything to do with the notion. Could all these changes be due to a guilty conscience? Thank you, again, Michelle. No – maybe she wouldn't go that far.

She heard the front door slam as Nathan and his dad went off for their outing. She picked up her mobile from the bedside table and pressed a couple of buttons.

'Hi, Jenna,' she said when her call was answered.

'Hi, hon,' said Jenna cheerily. 'You still OK for me to come and do your hair later?'

'I am indeed.' And since Jenna had saved the day when e'd gone into labour Seb could no longer object to her ndship and neither could the other wives on the patch who knew of Jenna's rather rackety past. Frankly, Jenna couldn't have picked a better or more public way of getting rehabilitated if she'd planned it. Even Milward had had to adjust his opinion of her. 'And,' continued Maddy, 'Seb's promised to keep Nathan amused and I doubt if Rose'll be much trouble.'

'And how is the little darling?' said Jenna.

'Still little, still darling.'

Maddy heard Jenna laugh. 'That's good.' There was a bit of a silence before Jenna said, 'Um, and there's something I want to tell you. I want you to be the first to know.'

'Know what?'

'Dan and I are expecting.'

Just as well she was lying down, thought Maddy. Receiving a shock like that might have had serious consequences otherwise. 'No!'

'Honest.'

'But I thought you hated kids... well, not hated maybe, but you never seemed to be a fan.'

'I dunno, seeing little Rose, getting to hold her... Mum never let me touch my brothers and sisters when they were babies. Don't think she trusted me. She was probably right not to, back then. But holding little Rose made me think I'd like a go at motherhood myself. And Dan was up for it. Anyway, here I am, up the duff. And d'you know, I reckon I might make a half-decent mum.'

'You'll be brilliant. And huge congrats to the pair of you.'

'Thanks. Anyway, see you later.'

Maddy lay back on the pillows. What a turn up that was!

Sam couldn't believe her ears when Michelle told her what she'd got up to while she'd been in Kenya. She stared at her friend with horror, as she and Michelle strode along a track through the heather across a stretch of Dartmoor, in b sunshine but with a chill March wind nipping at any bits of exposed skin.

'You did what? You confronted his wife?'

Michelle shook her head. 'I know. I must have been mad.'

'Does Seb know?'

'I don't know. We've not been in contact – not since he saw me that last time, after that party.'

'So you went to the house and told Maddy you'd screwed her husband?'

Michelle nodded, her eyes wide with disbelief at what she'd done. 'I know. I can't think what I was at. Shit, Sam, I was so lucky I got away with it. But it taught me a lesson.'

'I should hope so,' muttered Sam. 'I mean, why? Why did you tell Maddy?'

Michelle shrugged and then shook her head. 'I honestly thought she ought to know what her old man was up to.' She held her hand up. 'And before you say anything, yes, I was wrong. Completely out of order. But, back then, I wasn't thinking straight. Sam, I'm not like you. I don't have your knack of never putting a foot wrong.'

Sam gave her a vague smile. Could she tell Michelle about Luke and just how much of a foot wrong she'd put there? No, not a foot wrong. There had been nothing wrong at all with her relationship with Luke and it would have been perfect if their career choice had been different. She had no regrets whatsoever about what had happened in Kenya but tell Michelle? She loved Michelle but entrust her with a secret…? Never.

'Oi, Sam, are you listening?'

'Busted. Sorry, I was just thinking about something.'

Not that Michelle seemed to care what her friend was thinking about because she said, 'Anyway, there's this guy…'

'Really? So you've really managed to put that whole Seb behind you?'

'Yeah, I think so, and life seems to be going really well at the moment. Even Dad and I are still seeing eye to eye.'

It was Sam's turn to shake her head in bewilderment. 'So you said. I mean, logic tells me that the Seb business should have completely put the skids under your relationship with your dad.'

'I know. I thought it was going to but…' Michelle shrugged. 'But somehow it acted like a boot up the bum. We had this huge shouting match but, for the first time, we told each other stuff – proper stuff about feelings and everything. It was weird – we'd never really talked before and even though we were yelling at each other a whole bunch of truths came out. I mean, it's still tricky between me and Janine but baby steps… And, hey, you and your father are getting on too. Although, in your case, it's so much more understandable; you've never been the huge disappointment I was and when you were lost he must have really thought…'

'He did,' said Sam quietly.

'So tell me about it? Tell me all about Kenya.'

So Sam told her almost everything – omitting the fact that she and Luke had completely fallen for each other and had mutually agreed, before they'd left Kenya, to end their relationship. They both knew it was doomed, they both knew it wouldn't work and they both knew it would ruin their careers.

'So you had no idea who this Corporal Blake's dad was before you got lost?'

'Not a Scooby-Doo. I mean, why would you make the connection?'

'I suppose. But when you were alone together… I mean, didn't you get close, confide in each other, talk?'

'I don't really want to go into it,' said Sam firmly. 'It was a really horrid experience and I want to put it behind me.' Which was a lie, but a believable one.

'Of course,' said Michelle, thinking she understood. 'And I think it's changed you.'

'Really?'

'You seem… very sad. Withdrawn.'

'I expect I'll get over it.' When I move on from Luke. Sam stopped walking and gazed into the distance, at the line of silvery-grey sea, just visible on the horizon.

Epilogue

Sam sat at her office desk, looking out of the window and watching the clouds scud across the sky. Over a year had passed since she and Luke had said farewell, here in this office, a couple of days after they'd returned from Kenya, neither touching the other, maintaining a proper corporal–captain relationship – outwardly at least. And, since then, there hadn't been a day since when she hadn't thought about him, wondered what he was doing. During his final interview, they had agreed not to contact each other again, not to follow each other's career, not to try to find out information.

'Clean break,' said Sam. She'd longed to hug him, to kiss him, to relive those moments when the terror of the bush had been at its worst and they had clung together. But the fact that her office was a far from private space meant their behaviour had to be seemly.

'Yes,' he'd agreed, although his eyes had signalled his anguish.

'Good luck in your new posting.'

'Thank you.'

'I… The team,' she corrected herself, swiftly, 'will miss you.'

She'd watched Luke's jaw tighten. 'Thank you… Sam.' His eyes, no longer angry and disapproving but utterly miserable, had rested on her face.

She remembered how he'd held her, the feel of his body, the smell of his skin. She put it behind her, she had to be resolut 'Goodbye, Luke.' She'd willed herself not to cry.

And then he'd saluted, about-turned and gone. And that was the last she'd seen of him.

And that was when she'd told herself that she had to put everything that had happened in Kenya behind her. Whatever she felt for Luke had to be forgotten. She had to get back on track, pick up the threads of her life before Askari Thunder and move forward. Outwardly she was the same old Sam – professional, clear-headed, organised... outwardly. Inside, she was a mess.

When she was alone she still found herself wondering what Luke was doing and sometimes, in the privacy of her room, she would allow herself to weaken and give in to her emotions. And when she'd blown her nose and pulled herself together she told herself that she'd done the right thing, that a relationship with an other rank would never have worked, that she needed to man up and perhaps, in a few months, she'd feel ready to think about finding another relationship, maybe one that was properly suitable.

Now she understood and empathised with Michelle about her obsession with Seb. Yeah, well, what goes around, comes around. Maybe if she'd been a bit more sympathetic to Michelle she wouldn't be in such a bad place herself right now.

Time to count your blessings, she told herself sternly. Luke may have left an aching void in her life but her father had come back into it. Surely that had to make up for everything and then some? Things could still be awkward between them but every time they met things improved a little more. And which would she rather have – Luke or her father? No, she couldn't answer that; no one should have to make that sort of choice.

She thought about the other changes that had happened around her. For a start, there were even fewer women in the battalion since Immi Cooper had decided to jack in her career the army. Her time in Kenya had finally convinced her that re were plenty of jobs she could do that didn't involve close encounters with unpleasant conditions and so she'd put her notice in and become a civvy. The last Sam had heard about her was that she was working as a PA to some smart property developer and doing very well. There was a rumour going round the battalion that she'd even got her picture in *Hello!*. Sam smiled at the thought. If it were true she was sure that Immi would be a very happy bunny. If ever there was a girl who would love to be a media star, she was it.

Another turn up for the books had been Dan Armstrong's glamorous wife falling pregnant and now she was a glamorous mum. And then there had been Michelle, who had made good her promise to sort herself out. No longer was Sam constantly worrying about what dumb ideas her mate would come up with, what pranks she would play that seemed so hilarious when she thought of them and then turned out to be such mistakes. Michelle seemed to be the model officer who never got extras and whose recruits worshipped her. Now their telephone conversations were about their work and their achievements and occasionally their social lives and Sam no longer had to listen to Michelle obsessing about Seb. Not unreasonably, though, she refused to come and see Sam in the 1 Herts mess.

'I am so ashamed of my behaviour,' she'd confided in Sam. Which had to have been a first, Sam had thought. 'Even I haven't got the brass neck to show my face around 1 Herts. Although I am so over Seb now. But it doesn't alter the past. However, there's this guy... Edward.'

'Single?'

'Totally! Only not for long if I have my way.'

'I told you it would happen, that you'd find someone else.'

All in all, life around Sam was pretty good and frankly, she told herself, if all she had to bitch about was a love affair that hadn't panned out then she should count herself lucky.

She pulled open her desk drawer and took out the file she

kept in it. She flipped open the manila cover and looked at the news cuttings. Outwardly it seemed as if she had kept the mementoes of her fifteen minutes of fame, but the reality was they represented the only pictures she had of Luke. Time to move on.

She shut the file again and went to drop it in the waste bin.

'Hi, Sam.'

Guiltily she dropped the file in the open drawer instead and slammed it shut. 'James. Lovely to see you.'

'I dropped by to scrounge a coffee.'

'Of course.' She got up and made her way over to the shelf where the tea things were kept.

'All set for the ball?' he asked as she put the kettle on.

'Yup. Looking forward to it.'

The officers' mess May Ball was, apparently, the big social event of the year. It was held to coincide with some major battle honour won by the Hertfordshire Regiment centuries earlier. The previous year the ball had been cancelled because Exercise Askari Thunder had meant the battalion hadn't got back from foreign parts in time to organise it properly. Then Sam had thought this a bit ridiculous, but since she'd been co-opted onto the ball committee she'd realised how much work went in to making it happen. This was not a slightly more grown-up version of the Sandhurst party she and Michelle had been involved in – this was a major event.

'So, how's it going?' asked James.

Sam finished making the coffees and plonked the two mugs on her desk.

'Have you any idea how difficult it is to find proper sola topis?'

James's brow creased. 'Sola topis! Why?'

'It's all the Edwardian theming. Honestly, I expect the makers of *Downton Abbey* went to less trouble to get things right than blooming Andy Bailey. Perfection doesn't come close. It's all rattan furniture and ostrich plumes and tiger-skin rugs – well, fake ones anyway – and art nouveau lamps... and... Sorry, I'm getting boring and obsessive about it and you don't need to know the details.'

'But he hasn't been like this in the past. I mean, it's always been pretty bloody good but he hasn't gone completely off on one.'

'Maybe it's because this year Pemberton-Blake is coming.'

'The CLF? But why?'

Sam shrugged. 'Search me. I reckon it's because old Notley got a bit chummy with him when he had to come out to Kenya and now he wants to capitalise on it. We all know what Notley's like when it comes to the main chance for advancement.'

James laughed. 'Good shout. You're probably right. I wonder what happened to his son.'

Was it Sam's imagination or was he staring at her, as if he expected her to know something? She stared back as steadily. 'Not a clue. He got posted out and that's the last I heard, so your guess is as good as mine.' And not a word of a lie there. But then she couldn't help herself. 'Why do you ask?'

'Oh, I don't know, except that you two went through a lot together so I thought you'd take an interest.'

'Nah. Not really.' She took a sip of her coffee.

'Hey, talking of guests,' said James, 'I hear Jack Raven is coming to the ball too.'

Sam felt a small ripple of relief at the change of subject. 'Yes, I heard that. Another one old Notley wants to keep in with.' Sam laughed. 'Jeez, he's a bit obvious, isn't he, when it comes to who he associates with – CLF, the BBC defence correspondent... Makes you wonder who else will be turning up.'

'Never mind. It won't stop everyone having a good time, will it?'

'No, I can't wait. It'll be a great evening.'

Sam looked about the mess with a degree of satisfaction. It was, she thought, very *Downton Abbey*, with antimacassars on the chairs, loads of potted palms, faux stained glass made from cellophane decorating some of the windows, a wind-up gramophone in the corner and jazz playing over the mess's proper music system, plus all the other props she'd managed to beg, borrow or hire to give it that authentic Edwardian feel. 'Great job,' said James, standing beside her in his mess kit and looking extraordinarily handsome.

'You think?'

James nodded. 'I think you've really captured the period. Well done.' He stared at her. 'Although I was rather hoping to see you wearing that natty little number you wore to the corporals' mess that time.'

'Not appropriate, Captain Rosser, not appropriate. The dress code for officers is mess kit.'

'I think there ought to be an exception made in your case.'

'Ha. So much for equality. I can hear Mrs Pankhurst spinning from here!'

The mess began to fill up with couples and although the wives and girlfriends had done their best to outshine their male partners they still looked like peahens next to the men dressed in their peacock, mess kit finery. Many of the wives had entered into the spirit of the evening and had found dresses that gave a nod to Edwardian fashions with ostrich plumes, beaded embroidery, long ropes of pearls or fur tippets. The consensus of opinion was that the whole eve-of-World-War-One theme was perfect.

At last, as the party really began to get under way, Sam felt she could relax, and when the band struck up with some ragtime numbers (which were possibly not of the era, but who cared?) Sam and James put down their glasses of Buck's Fizz and joined the others thronging to the marquee on the lawn and crowding on to the dance floor.

By the time they'd had a third dance they were both hot and thirsty and they made their way back into the main mess building in search of a cold drink. Sam stood at the periphery of the even-more-crowded bar as she watched James fight his way through to the counter. Over the heads of the others around her she saw the CO and Mrs N. He must have arrived with his house party.

'Hello, boss.'

Sam spun round. She recognised that voice.

'Immi!' Immi Cooper? What the hell...? And there was Corporal Cooper in a show-stopper of a turquoise blue ball-gown with a fish-tail train that made her look like a mermaid.

'Immi... what the heck? I mean, it's wonderful to see you but what a surprise!'

Immi looked as bit abashed and she smiled shyly at Sam. 'I'm here as a plus one,' she said as an explanation. 'I always dreamed of getting an invite to a swanky ball like this in the officers' mess and I can hardly believe I'm really here.'

'But that's great,' said Sam, meaning it. 'Wonderful, and you look amazing. How's the leg?'

Immi raised the hem of her skirt a few inches and showed Sam her scars – a line of four purple splodges on her shin. 'They're fading but I still don't like showing my legs off. Still,' she said cheerfully, 'long frocks cover a multitude of sins, eh?'

'And your dress is gorgeous,' said Sam, meaning it.

'That's the advantage of being a civvy – I get to wear what I like. Not,' she added swiftly, 'that you don't look lovely in your outfit.'

Sam looked down at her taffeta dress with the bumfreezer jacket that went over it. 'But it's uniform, isn't it?'

'You ought to have worn the dress you wore to the corporals' club that time. That was dead classy. And Lu—' But before Immi could continue she gave a squeak and jumped. 'Jack! I wish you wouldn't do that.' She turned to Sam. 'My fiancé,' she explained. 'His idea of a greeting is to pinch my bum. You remember Jack, don't you?' She flashed her left hand at Sam and showed her the stonking diamond on her third finger.

Sam goggled at the ring before turning to Jack. 'Of course I remember you, Jack. Good to see you again. And in rather nicer surroundings. And congratulations.'

Jack Raven kissed her on both cheeks. 'You're looking well. Certainly better than when I last saw you.'

'Thanks. I think that's a compliment.'

'It is,' said Jack. 'I think this look suits you better than the Wild Woman of the Jungle.'

Sam laughed. 'I was a bit unwashed that time, wasn't I?'

'Hello,' said James, returning with the drinks. 'Is this a private conversation or can anyone join in?'

Sam smiled at him and took her drink gratefully. 'James, you remember Immi Cooper, don't you? And Jack Raven?'

James did a double take when he realised who Immi was. 'Crikey,' he said. 'You look a bit different out of uniform.'

'I should hope so,' said Immi, giggling and swishing the fabric of her gown.

'So, I want to hear all of your news,' said Sam. She took Immi's arm and towed her to the edge of the room, where there was more space and slightly less noise to contend with. 'And the boys can talk shop and war stories. So... spill. What have you been up to in the past year, apart from getting engaged?'

Immi stared at Sam, her eyes shining. 'Ma'a... Boss...'

'Sam,' said Sam firmly. 'It's Sam now.'

'Sam, I can't keep the secret any longer. Jack doesn't want ʹou to find out just yet, but I disagree. You need to know *now*.'

'What secret? What do I need to know now?' Sam was intrigued.

'You've got to come with me,' said Immi.

'Where?'

'Just… please?'

Sam shook her head, feeling bewildered as Immi led her around the edge of the room.

'There,' said Immi, triumphantly.

Sam stared. There was the CO and Mrs N., both schmoozing the CLF, General Sir William Pemberton-Blake, and a small woman who Sam assumed to be Lady Pemberton-Blake, and with them was a REME officer with his back to her.

'And?' said Sam.

Immi rolled her eyes. 'Look!'

And then the REME officer turned and Sam didn't notice the hand holding her drink go limp and the champagne pour out of the glass onto the floor, nor did she notice the triumphant look on Immi's face, or the chatter of the people around her. Everything faded away, as if it was some amazing special effect in a movie, leaving her and Luke Pemberton-Blake, Lieutenant Luke Pemberton-Blake, in a bubble. Beside her Immi was babbling about the look on the CO's face when not one but two of his ex-soldiers turned up on his doorstep for a house party, but Sam was oblivious to it. All she could see was Luke, in his mess kit, an officer… like her.

'Hello, boss,' he said, coming towards her.

'Luke? Why? When?'

'I went for a commission.'

Sam nodded. 'I can see. But you hate officers.'

'Not all officers,' he corrected her.

'No…' She lowered her eyes, confused by the surge of emotions. She'd spent over a year – a whole year – trying to put her feelings and her memories of him behind her, to move on with her life because a relationship between them was impossible, and all the time it had been for nothing. 'Why didn't you tell me? Have you any idea…?'

'I was afraid I might fail.'

'Fail? But you're the CLF's son.'

'So? They expect more, not less. You're expected to excel if you have my sort of background, and to do well isn't enough. Sam, I couldn't tell you. I couldn't bear to raise your hopes and then let you down.'

James came towards them.

'I see congratulations are in order, Luke. Well done on the commission.'

'Thank you, sir… James. Sorry, it's tough to break habits. I called you sir for so long.'

James took Sam's arm and drew her to one side. 'I am so pleased for you, Sam.'

'Sorry, James, I haven't a clue what you are talking about.'

'Yes, you do. Don't fib to me, Sam, I've known all along about you and Luke. When you got off that helicopter back at Archers Post, I thought I spotted something. I was pretty certain something significant had happened between you and him.'

Sam stared at him, the crease of a frown between her eyebrows. 'But how?'

'Because you looked at Luke in a way that should have made me insanely jealous. Of course it didn't… you're not, ahem, my type.'

Sam gave James an understanding smile. 'Oh, James, you are so lovely. And far too good for me, even if I had been "your type".'

'You guessed?'

'Put it this way, I had a suspicion, only because I felt so completely safe in your company.' Sam gave him a peck on the cheek.

'And now Luke can take over the job of keeping you safe.'

'He may not want it.'

'After he went and got a commission? Come off it, Sam.'

Sam shrugged. 'Well, maybe. And thank you. Thank you for being a friend. You made me feel welcome here from the start and when I felt lonely, after Luke left, you were always there. You couldn't have done more.'

'It's been a pleasure,' said James. 'Only now you've got Luke back in your life I hope you won't forget me.'

'Never,' said Sam with feeling.

'So go and say hello to Luke properly,' said James, sternly.

Sam turned back to Luke and let him fold her into his arms. Ignoring the scandalised look from Mrs Notley and Lady Pemberton-Blake, she then let Luke kiss her long and deeply.

Acknowledgements

There is a danger, when you start to acknowledge the assistance people gave you when you were writing a book, that the 'and-thanks-to' list can get dangerously out of hand and lengthy ... and thanks to my mother for giving birth to me, the stationers for supplying me with paper – that sort of thing. But, seriously, there are some people who were endlessly patient when I pestered them with questions, or helpful, or just plain supportive and it would be unfair of me not to recognise their contribution. My son deserves a medal for the advice he gave me about Askari Thunder, as do Jo Thoenes of BFBS Brize Norton and her friends Patricia and Jonathan, who have all lived in Kenya and made sure I got the details right. The team at Head of Zeus have been amazing but especially my editor, Rosie de Courcy, who has been such a lovely and encouraging person to work with, and I must thank my agent, Laura Longrigg, who makes sure my early drafts are fit to be seen *before* I send them off to my publisher. I am also blessed with some great friends who cheer me up, keep me going and generally make sure I stay focussed – none more so than the Chez Castillon crew; Janie and Mickey Wilson who own Chez Castillon and who provide the most wonderful writing space (and the most delicious meals!) and Katie Fforde, Judy Astley, Jo Thomas, Clare Mackintosh, Jane Wenham-Jones, Jan Sprenger and Betty Orme-Smith who are the best writing companions an author could hope to find.

Freedom's Banner

Born in Essex, Teresa Crane still lives
north of the county. Her first novel, *Sp*
Web, was published in 1980 and was foll
by *Molly*, *A Fragile Peace*, *The Rose St*
Sweet Songbird, *The Hawthorne Herit*
Tomorrow, *Jerusalem*, *Green and Pleas*
Land and *Strange are the Ways*.

'This fine effort . . . sweeps readers along w
a blend of drama and social history.'

Publishers Wee

TERESA CRANE

FREEDOM'S BANNER

HarperCollins*Publishers*

HarperCollins*Publishers*
77–85 Fulham Palace Road,
Hammersmith, London W6 8JB

This paperback edition 1995
1 3 5 7 9 8 6 4 2

First published in Great Britain by
HarperCollins*Publishers* 1994

Copyright © Teresa Crane 1994

The Author asserts the moral right to
be identified as the author of this work

ISBN 0 00 649018 2

Set in Trump Mediaeval

Printed in Great Britain by
HarperCollinsManufacturing Glasgow

'Yet, Freedom! yet thy banner, torn but flying,
Streams like the thunderstorm *against* the wind . . .'

BYRON, *Childe Harold*

PART ONE

Bath, England
1860

CHAPTER ONE

It was a certain fact, an exasperated Constance Barlowe reflected, that Mattie Henderson was one of those unfortunate people who could drive a saint to distraction without the batting of an eyelid or the lifting of a finger. Surreptitiously she adjusted her shawl to cover the stain on her green silk where baby Nicholas had dribbled that morning, tucked a few strands of mousy hair back up inside her neat-fitting bonnet, and attempted to conduct amiable conversation whilst fixing aggrieved eyes upon her cousin, willing her to smile, to chatter, to laugh, as those about her were politely smiling, chattering and laughing.

Mattie, sitting with a group of younger folk in the pleasant, dappled shade of a small birch grove a few yards away, did not notice the look. Mattie indeed did not appear to be noticing anything. Constance breathed a small, long-suffering sigh. What in the name of heaven did the girl think she was about?

Around them the summer air twittered with the light, untroubled sound of voices. Sitting poised and straight-backed upon the wrought-iron garden seat next to Mattie, Sally Brittan fluttered her fan becomingly and chattered like a jay at a tall, thin-faced young man who stood beside her, his head with its large, sun-reddened ears bent dutifully to her. Every now and again he fingered his stiff collar as if it were choking him and a prominent Adam's apple bobbed disconcertingly as he attempted to edge the odd word into the one-sided conversation. On the grass at Mattie's feet that little hussy Alice Thompson, her pink skirt spread like the petals of a full-blown peony, her face bright with laughter, was openly – one might even say brazenly – teasing the young Hopley lad. Now there was a match that would be made by the end of the month, or Constance Barlowe was a Dutchman. Even the very plain Miss

3

Esme Spencer was sitting austerely to attention upon a canvas chair, thin hands folded about a drooping daisy chain in her muslin lap, talking with decorously lowered eyes and with a clear trace of heightened colour in her wan cheeks to a middle-aged man whom Constance recognized instantly as Mr Ashby-Jones, a widower of Eastbourne, who was in Bath – according to the omniscient Mrs Johnstone – to take the waters and to find a wife.

And Mattie? Mattie was sitting, calmly composed, staring into the middle distance with a tranquil and distracted concentration which cut her off from her companions as effectively as a firmly closed door. She might as well, Constance thought, with a spurt of enraged indignation, hang a sign about her neck and have done with it: 'Strictly private. Keep out!' The problem with Mattie – Constance pursed her lips and reframed that thought – one of the problems with Mattie was that she had absolutely no idea how to behave in smart company. She would sit so for hours, quietly, taking no part in the gossip about her, exuding what could only be described as a polite disinterest, enough to dampen the kindest of interest or effort. It was her father's fault of course – a vexed frown marred the pale smoothness of Constance's forehead for a moment – oh, yes, entirely Cousin Henry's fault. The Lord only knew what he had thought he was about, bringing up a child – a female child! – in such a ridiculous and contrary manner! Constance winced, remembering her own dear Herbert's understandable embarrassment the evening before upon being drawn into an unsuitable discussion about the outrageous theories of that dreadful Mr Darwin. But then, in charity, one could only give Mattie the benefit of Christian sympathy; whatever could be expected from such a very odd background? In fact it really had to be said that it was a positive blessing that Henry had died when he had; or this awkward orphaned daughter of his might well have been altogether beyond saving, completely unmarriageable, and thus a burden to herself as well as to others. Constance smoothed her crocheted gloves over plump fingers and graciously acknowledged the greeting of a newcomer. Of course even that would not have been such a very bad thing if her own

4

original plan had worked out a little more satisfactorily. But, alas, it was not to be. The idea of her lonely, bereaved second cousin as friend and helpmeet to herself, and nurse and tutor to the children, properly grateful for a roof over her head and the kindly companionship of a happy family, had been seductive. But at the time of its promising conception Mattie and Constance had not met in ten years, since Constance's marriage, when Mattie had been no more than twelve years old. To be sure, she'd been an odd little thing then, but it had not occurred to Constance that her cousin's daughter could have retained such eccentricity into adulthood. Henry's fault, all Henry's fault! What young woman could possibly have grown up in any normal fashion in that great uncomfortable barn of a house with no company but her father and those peculiar – why, one would simply have to say in some cases downright disreputable – friends of his? Constance smiled sweetly again and nodded, acknowledging a distant, lifted hand as a small party of ladies and gentlemen strolled by at the far end of the garden, taking the fresher air of the terraces that overlooked the city. The smile faded rapidly as she noticed amongst them the portly Mr Andrews, a London banker, escorting much too attentively the well-rounded but nicely proportioned figure of Miss Faith Edwards. Too late, then; there was yet another chance that Mattie had let slip. Really, one could almost imagine the trying girl didn't want to make a match!

Constance turned her head a little, her attention caught by a sudden murmur of interest that had lifted like the buzz of bees about a flower bed from the lawns behind her. Mrs Johnstone's voice called in shrill greeting. 'Why, Mr Sherwood! How delightful to see you! How very kind, to grace our little gathering – Anna, my dear, make a place for Mr Sherwood.'

Constance watched, as enthralled as anyone. A tall, gracefully built young man, deeply tanned, was making his way from the open windows of the house across the paved terrace to the garden. His broadcloth cutaway coat was dark green, the waistcoat and trousers beneath it a soft fawn and obviously, like the coat, of expensive cut and material. His soft-collared shirt was

5

a spotless white and the dark green silk neckcloth faultlessly tied and fastened with a gold scarf-pin. In one hand he carried hat and gloves, in the other a small book. His thick and shining black hair, parted in the middle, fell forward like a boy's onto his forehead. His eyes gleamed dark as the jet beads that bedecked his hostess's ample bosom, and his expression was apologetic. 'Mrs Johnstone – Ma'am – I do hope I'm not unforgivably late? I had a meetin' in Bristol yesterday with our mutual acquaintance Mr Salisbury, who, by the way, sends his best regards to you –' he bowed his dark head a little, impeccably courteous '– a meetin', as I said, concernin' some final details of the shippin' arrangements for next season's Pleasant Hill cotton. I have only just returned.' The voice was pleasant, the slow drawl magnetically attractive set as it was against the clipped English accents. Heads turned. Eyelashes fluttered. Fans were lifted and a small sibilance of whispers scurried around the garden like a summer breeze.

'My dear boy, of course not! Come – join us for tea. It's a warm day for travelling.'

'It is indeed, Ma'am.' With the exquisite manners of which every Mama in Bath had taken approving note, the young man subsided with good grace and a charming smile onto a narrow bench beside Mrs Johnstone's daughter Anna.

Mrs Johnstone leaned forward, handing him tea in a dainty flowered cup. 'So very delighted to see you, Mr Sherwood. We were quite cast down when we thought you wouldn't come. Anna was saying just this morning how fascinating she found your stories of your home in the romantic South – and how much she hoped you might be here this afternoon and willing to tell us more.'

On cue, Anna blushed, becomingly.

Constance sniffed. So that was the way of things, was it? Trust Emma Johnstone to have her predatory eye firmly on the most eligible of the young men in evidence this year for her own pert offspring. That explained Mrs Johnstone's ill-humour the other night when this same young Mr Sherwood had so inexplicably sat out of the dancing and had spent almost the whole of the evening with – of all people! – Mattie Henderson, earnestly discussing, so Mattie had mildly insisted, the ideas and poetry of Mr Shelley and Lord Byron. Constance had not believed a word of it then, and still did not. Mattie could be a sly one sometimes, there was no mistake about that. She glanced again at her cousin. Mattie's hands were idle in her lap. Her eyes were fixed upon the distant, shining ribbon of the river that wound through the city beneath them. Her wide, pale mouth drooped a little. It was perfectly obvious that she had not noticed the newcomer, nor was she making the slightest effort to join in the talk and laughter around her.

For just one moment Constance had the almost overwhelming desire, hastily suppressed, to slap her.

Constance was right. Mattie Henderson's thoughts were very far from this garden, from this gathering – far, indeed, from Bath itself. Watching the play of sunshine upon the distant river and the golden spires of the Cathedral Church she was indulging in what she was perfectly well aware was an absolutely disgraceful bout of self-pity. As the silly, inconsequential talk and laughter fluttered unnoticed about her ears she was at that moment back at Coombe House, much-loved home of a childhood she knew she should long have outgrown, but that had only truly come to an end on that day five months before when her father had died, in his sixty-eighth year and her twenty-second. The rigidly formal manicured garden where she now sat, high on the hillside above a city that, for all its airs and its still-fine classical buildings, was showing unmistakably the first signs of a genteel decay, was a far cry from that other garden her heart knew so well. That garden – empty now, she thought desolately, an unkempt graveyard surrounding an equally betrayed and abandoned house – was lush and beautiful; flower-filled, half-wild, secret; hidden in a tree-filled valley in the quiet Kentish countryside, its western boundary a fast-moving, singing stream. That garden, as she so often remembered it, had been full of birdsong, and windsong, and her father's voice. With a painful twist of her heart she could hear that voice now, far clearer than these others; deep and well-modulated, edged more

7

often than not with laughter, or with passion, engaged in one of those usually amiable and always subversive wrangles in which he so loved to indulge. 'My dear old chap, of *course* we can keep the ungrateful natives pacified in the short term; it will be a long time before they – or we! – forget the lessons of the Mutiny. Why, they have an Empress now, of their very own, the lucky fellows! But the long term, my boy – look at the long term! The greatest of empires tumbles at last – see for yourself, for otherwise you and I would be sitting here draped in sheets, crowned with laurel and conversing in Latin! Mattie, my dear, come share this excellent wine and support your old father – Albert here seems to believe that God has given the vast and treasure-filled continent of India to the British for India's own good and on an entirely permanent basis!'

Mattie took a very slow and rather careful breath. This was simple, perverse self-indulgence. It could serve no possible purpose. Think of something else.

'You'll grieve, my dear – of course you will,' her father had said at the end. 'But it will pass. I promise you. The time will come when you will remember me simply with affection, and I hope with laughter. I've been a wickedly selfish old curmudgeon, to keep you here beside me for so long. You're young. You have a life to live. Live it knowing that my love and my blessings are with you always. And remember – the pain will not, cannot, last for ever.' And he had been right, of course, as he almost always had been. The devastating, the agonizing pain of loss had eased. If it had not she might well have eschewed good taste altogether and lost her reason. The problem was that what now stood in its place was, if anything, worse; the emptiness, the numbing ache in heart and soul, the certain knowledge that nothing would ever again be as it had been, that she would never again see that dear face with its wise, bright eyes, hear that special note in his voice that was for her alone . . .

'Miss Henderson?'

A darker shadow stood in the dappled light. Disconcerted, she lifted her head, blinking up at the tall figure beside her, aware even in her surprise that an interested silence had fallen about her, that bright, inquisitive and astute eyes were watching. A dark-skinned, well-shaped hand was extended towards her. In it was a small and very scuffed leather-covered volume. 'I promised I wouldn't keep it too long, Ma'am,' Johnny Sherwood said, in his soft, intriguing drawl, 'though it's with great reluctance that I return it.'

Mattie rose, smiling, and took the book, refusing to betray the slightest hint that beneath the calm there might be any unsettling sensation of excitement, of quickening blood. 'You enjoyed it, then?' Her voice was satisfyingly composed, coolly friendly.

His reply was a moment in coming. He did not smile. 'Enjoy is too insignificant a word, Miss Henderson, when you talk of genius.' Formally he extended his expensively clad crooked arm. 'Please – might I ask you to walk with me awhile? I'd very much like to talk with you.'

Mortifyingly Mattie found herself to be blushing; an occasion so rare as to be all but unique. In wary silence she placed her gloved hand upon the proffered wrist. Beneath the strong smooth weave of the broadcloth she was unnervingly aware of the warmth of him, of the horseman's strength in the steady arm; as they stepped together into the sunshine she caught Constance's astonished eyes upon her, unblinking. The pale gaze was so disbelieving, so truly thunderstruck, that it almost brought open laughter, the constraint of which at least helped to overcome those mystifying sensations that had for a moment surprised her into awkwardness. She ducked her head, hiding her amusement beneath the wide brim of her flower-trimmed straw hat and, wide skirts swaying, accompanied her escort along the paved path that led through rose-hung pergolas to the terraces.

They walked for some moments in silence, returned the polite salutes of a couple who passed them on the way back to the house, the two young women manoeuvring the silk-swathed cages of their crinolines like bright flowers nodding greetings to each other in a summer's breeze. 'Confound the thing,' Mattie said, conversationally. 'And confound its inventor. Did you ever see a more ridiculous and constricting fashion?'

Johnny turned upon her a quick smile that lit his darkly

9

handsome face like a gleam of sunlight. With warmth in her cheeks that once again could not be entirely attributed to the balmy day, Mattie looked away, apparently absorbed in the view of the city that unfolded beneath them. Unconventional she might be, and to Constance's permanent chagrin not brought up in the fine and mannered fashion of declining Bath, but even she knew how very rude it was to stare. 'I find them very becoming,' Johnny said.

'That well might be because you don't have to wear them.' It was a small triumph to discover that she could return his smile in her most unflustered fashion, to take the bite from the words. She lifted the book. 'So – do I gather that you approved of my Mr Shelley?'

'Miss Henderson, I think you know that approve is not – cannot be – the word.' All levity was suddenly gone from the boyish face. 'The man, as I said, possesses pure genius. I had read a little –' he spread his thin, strong hands '– a very little I fear; small excuse, I know, but there seems little time for such leisurely pursuits at home. So of his lyrical dramas I knew nothing. I cannot thank you enough for introducing me to them.'

Mattie was holding the small book to her breast, her hands folded around it almost protectively. She glanced down at it. 'I'm glad you liked them so much. I truly wish I could have given you the book. But – it's very precious. I couldn't bring myself to part with it.'

They had reached a small terrace, bounded and perfumed by tumbling roses, at the far end of which was set a shaded stone bench. Beside the seat, in a little fountain-splashed pool a mermaid gazed with stony concentration into a large shell. With one accord they stepped from the path and strolled towards it.

'I couldn't help but notice that the book is signed to your father from Mr Shelley himself.' Johnny helped her to arrange her skirt so as to make the business of sitting at least possible if not entirely comfortable. 'May I ask – did they know each other?'

'Yes, they did.' Mattie laid the book upon the pale lemon silk of her skirt. Earlier she had found herself wondering what had prompted her to the extravagant caprice of wearing this, just about her only flattering and fashionable day dress and certainly her most expensive, to accompany Constance upon her visit to the abominable Mrs Johnstone this afternoon. Now, in honesty and not altogether comfortably, she knew, and the knowledge was disconcerting. She was not used to deceiving herself. 'They were at University College together, at Oxford. In eighteen hundred and ten, or thereabouts – '

He cocked his head. 'Fifty years ago? Your father – he wasn't a young man when he died, then?'

She shook her head. 'No.' Her low voice had taken on that note of warmth and animation that it always held when she spoke of her father. 'He just seemed it. As for Mr Shelley, he came often, I believe, to Coombe House – where we lived. I never knew him, of course. His tragic death occurred some years before I was born. Father always spoke of him with great respect and affection, and wouldn't hear a word against him, though there were always plenty to try.' Beneath the calm she had the most absurd and disorientating feeling that she was talking utter nonsense, that there was no connection whatsoever between what was going on in her mind – in her heart? – and the words she spoke so crisply. Firmly she tried to focus her thoughts. 'I was brought up on his poems.'

Her companion slanted a dark, questioning look at her face. 'The dramas too? Strange fare for a small child, Miss Henderson.'

'Yes. It was. As many, of course, were ready to point out. But then I suppose I was an odd child.' Mattie could not prevent a small, caustic smile. 'Just ask poor Cousin Constance.'

She thought she caught an answering flicker of amusement in his eyes but when he answered his tone was sober.

'Didn't such reading matter produce nightmares?' he asked, and then with the smallest of smiles, 'even for a child as odd as I grant you might have been?'

She would not rise to his bait. 'Only occasionally.' She turned from him, folded her hands about the book and let them rest peaceably in her lap. The scent of roses flooded the warm air about them, a perfume to drug and to drown the senses.

Determinedly she looked not at her companion but at the distant, diamond glitter of the river. Face and voice were obstinately schooled. Fluttering fans and palpitating hearts were for the likes of such as Sally Brittan. He must take her – or, her practical heart told her, more likely leave her – as she was. 'My father was always there, you see. He knew so much – could explain so much – there seemed nothing that he could not explain –'

Johnny was watching her with frank interest. 'You talk a lot about your father. You must have been very close?'

'Yes.'

'And – you had no other family? No brothers, or sisters?'

Mattie shook her head. 'No. No mother either – she died when I was two and I don't remember her at all. There was just Papa and me –' she half smiled '– and a positive colony of cats and dogs. And many friends, who came and went as they pleased.' She looked out for a moment, distracted, across the sunlit city to the green hills beyond. Then she took a small, brisk breath. 'And you, Mr Sherwood? You have a family?'

He had half turned to face her. Disconcertingly, she found herself looking full into the lean, brown face; a situation she had been doing her level best to avoid. Even more disturbingly she found her hands, still clasped about the book, taken impetuously in his. Felt the strength, the callused skin of hands well-kept but most certainly used to wielding more than a silken handkerchief or a snuff box. 'Yes, Miss Henderson.' He emphasized the polite formality of the name with half-humorously lifted brows. 'I have a family. I have a father and three brothers. And a sister-in-law, sent from the devil to plague us, who is a perfect Louisiana Belle, as was my mother, who was a Creole, and a beauty – of course – and who also, sadly, has been dead these many years. We too have dogs, and horses – Pleasant Hill's Arabian strain is famous.' The hands holding hers were firm, very steady, and confusingly were, like the clear dark eyes, somehow saying more than the voice.

She swallowed, with some difficulty. Struggled on. 'Louisiana, Mr Sherwood? Is that where your home is?'

'No, Miss Henderson. My home is in Georgia, as I'm sure I told you the other night. The most beautiful place in the world, about which I will tell you absolutely anythin' you wish to know but —' pausing at last for breath he lifted a finger '— not before we have finished our conversation about Mr Shelley.'

She eyed him cautiously. 'We haven't finished it?'

'We most certainly have not, Miss Henderson. When a backwoods Sherwood is so struck by a piece of poetry that he takes it into his head to spend an uncomfortable journey from Bath to Bristol and back again in memorizin' it, why that is such an unusual occurrence that it seems to me that the very least that a kindly person might do is to give him a chance to recite it!' He was openly laughing now, the dark eyes as mischievous and challenging as a boy's.

Suddenly light-hearted, she capitulated. 'And I am that kindly person, Mr Sherwood?' God forgive me, she found herself thinking, I have after all listened to Sally, and to Alice, and to all their sisters in flirtation, once too often!

The teasing gleam brightened. 'Why, most certainly you are. I can think of no other to whom I would rather dedicate my new-found devotion to Mr Shelley. You'll listen, Miss Henderson?'

'I'll listen, Mr Sherwood.' Mattie knew, in that split second, the mistake she had made, the trap into which she had stepped like any empty-headed child, like any green girl who did not know her Shelley from a shopping list at Jolly's. She could have recited the poem with him; it was one of her favourites. She did not. She sat fighting the colour that lifted relentlessly in her face at his effrontery.

> 'The fountains mingle with the river,
> And the rivers with the ocean,
> The winds of heaven mix for ever,
> With a sweet emotion —'

He paused for a moment, watching her.

Colour high, she schooled her face and said nothing.

> 'Nothin' in the world is single,
> All things by a law divine,

In one another's bein' mingle,
Why not I with thine?'

'Mr Sherwood,' she said with an attempt at severity that fell far short of its aim, 'I really don't think –'

'See the mountains kiss high heaven,
And the waves clasp one another,
No sister flower would be forgiven
If it disdained its brother;
And the sunlight clasps the earth
And the moonbeams kiss the sea –'

He hesitated again. His eyes searched her face. His voice was very quiet.

'What are all these kissin's worth,
If thou kiss not me?'

'I think,' Mattie said, in the lamentable absence of any other inspiration, 'that we should walk a little further.'

Wordless he stood, and extended a polite hand. She took it, stood, straightened her wide skirts.

'I've offended you?' he asked.

She lifted her face to look at him levelly. Shook her head. 'No. I don't think so. Not offended.'

'What, then?' He was watching her intently.

She hesitated. Then, 'Confused,' she said, with the honesty that was her bane and her pride. 'You confuse me, Mr Sherwood.'

He fell into step beside her. 'I can't imagine why. It surely can't be the only time, Miss Henderson, that a man has wanted to –' he hesitated, sent her a look sly as a cat's '– recite a poem to you?'

She had to laugh aloud. 'Are you always so devious, Mr Sherwood?'

The sun was dipping westwards, rose-tinted now, and fiery. The light slanted, etching his dark profile against the brightness of the sky above her. Mattie was not small, yet she came only to his shoulder. He moved with ease, his hair, a little too long for fashion, curled thickly about his face and neck. He was, indisputably, a very handsome young man.

And what was such a young man doing reciting love poetry to too-tall, too-thin, and above all too-opinionated Mattie Henderson? Mattie had few illusions about herself; indeed what few she might have had had been well dispelled by Cousin Constance and her cronies over the past months. 'My dear, what a shame it is that your shoulders are so very thin – ah, well, perhaps a shawl –' and 'Oh, Mattie, whatever are we to do with this hair? So long and so heavy and so very straight. I declare it gives me a headache simply to look at it! The irons won't even crimp it unless you consent to have it cut!' And 'Cousin, really, you must learn to be a little more –' fluttered fingers, butterfly sighs '– appealing in company –' What then was this contrary and unalluring creature doing leaning upon an ivy-clad stone wall beside this attentive and attractive young American that every girl in Bath – and every girl's Mama – had set her cap at, gazing out over a city that was lit with the glory of a summer's evening and that suddenly, and alarmingly, held some perilous enchantment far beyond its usual comfortable charm?

She turned. 'Mr Sherwood –'

'Johnny,' he said, quietly. 'My name is Johnny. And yours is Mattie, I know. May I call you Mattie, Miss Henderson?'

She was utterly taken aback. 'I – why, yes, Mr Sherwood – Johnny – I see no reason why not –'

'And would it bore you if I told you of Georgia, and of Pleasant Hill?'

A little more positively she shook her head, smiling. 'Of course not. Far from it.' Had he offered to recite the alphabet for her she would at that moment have accepted with pleasure, she realized. And indeed she listened almost without hearing as he talked in that slow and pleasant drawl, before the glamorous spell woven by the sheer sound of his voice wore off and it dawned upon her with a shock what he was actually saying. He spoke of the green splendour of Georgia's countryside – the

15

mountains to the north, the vast and verdant forests, the wide rivers and the rich, lush plantation lands, most of them cleared and planted within the last generation – of the growing, gracious towns and the houses with their oak-planted parklands, of the people with their fierce pride, their high temper, their ready laughter, their open-handed hospitality. He spoke of his childhood and his home, of his three older brothers, William, Robert and Russell, and of the plantation upon which they lived, Pleasant Hill, with its wide-porched house, its cotton fields and its people.

It was then that it hit her.

She turned to face him. 'You – your family – you're slave holders?' She could not, for her life, keep the sudden horror from her voice.

He stiffened. Every line of his face hardened. When after a moment he spoke the warmth had gone, his address was formal. 'Pleasant Hill is a working plantation like any other, Miss Henderson. We have to run it. We have a livin' to make. How else would you expect us to do it?'

'But – slavery! It's – it's an abomination!'

He looked at her in silence for what seemed a very long time; long enough for her to realize how great had been her lapse of manners, and to blush for it; long enough to realize that the fragile enchantment of the evening was gone. Long enough for the shadow of a wish to form: that she had, just once, kept a curb on her intemperate tongue. In defiance she dismissed the thought.

'What do you know about it?' he asked, at last, pleasantly enough.

The frankness of the question caught Mattie unawares. 'I know – I know what any reasonable person surely knows, that it is utterly wrong to own a man or a woman as if he or she were a beast –'

'Ah. An' it's as simple as that, is it?' He leaned against the low wall, watching her. 'It must be mighty reassurin', Miss Henderson, to be so very certain of one's ground. But then, of course, like any good little Abolitionist you will have read Mrs Beecher Stowe's much admired book?'

'Yes.'

'And will have condemned – as any reasonable person surely must –' the mimicry was harsh and deliberate '– the cruelty depicted therein; the tortures and the floggin's, the tearin' of babies from their mothers' breasts?' His quiet voice remained relentlessly pleasant.

Temper stirred. 'Yes, of course. And you can make me sound as much of a sanctimonious fool as you wish – it does not change facts –'

'But what are the facts, Miss Henderson? Do you know? Can you be so sure?' The depth of his anger, the strength of his effort to control it were obvious in his still, clenched hands, his fierce eyes. His face was dark with it. 'I can give you some facts, if you are ready to listen. The first is this: if the Union is dissolved and bloodshed should come to my homeland, which God forbid, though there seems no guarantee that He will – Mrs Beecher Stowe will bear a very great responsibility for it; I only hope she can square that with her fine, self-righteous Northern conscience! And the second: on Pleasant Hill we do not sell our people down the river. We do not flog them to death, nor rape and torture their women. We do not sell children from their mothers nor husbands from their wives unless some circumstance absolutely demands it. We do not abuse the loyalty of our "Uncle Toms".' The last two words were invested with a singular scorn. 'Our folk live good, modest, Christian lives. They marry and beget children, for the most part in safety, in comfort and in peace – which is more than can be said for many in this world. Tell me, Miss Henderson –' Mattie had opened her mouth to speak but he pressed remorselessly on '– would you say that there is no slavery in England?'

'Most certainly I would!'

'Then you'd be wrong. Have you seen your factory workers, enslaved to their industrial masters, your mineworkers in thrall to the coal barons, the little children worked to death in mills and up chimneys? The babies that die of want and disease in your slums, the girls forced to sell themselves to keep breath in their abused bodies? No child on Pleasant Hill is worked till he drops, Miss Henderson; no child is expected to work at all

17

until he is old enough and strong enough to do so. Don't talk to me of slavery, Miss Henderson. Not until you have seen how the great majority of your own people live!'

How many times had her enlightened father said much the same thing? And how many times, stubbornly, had she answered? 'Two wrongs can never make a right, Mr Sherwood.'

'And which, then, would you count the greater wrong?' he challenged, quietly.

'The institution of slavery can never be anything but abhorrent. I'm sorry, Mr Sherwood, but it seems to me that the owning of one soul by another can be nothing but degrading to both. I accept that what you say is true – that not every slave holder is wicked, or licentious, or weak – but the institution itself is constantly open to abuse. Surely you can't deny that? These people have no rights, no law protects them. They are treated like animals –'

'As are the men and women who pull trucks like beasts in your coal and tin mines!' It had become a full-blooded, passionate quarrel, and there was nothing either could do to stop.

'It is a different thing, Mr Sherwood!'

'And still I beg to differ, Miss Henderson! Tell me of these people's freedom, tell me what choices – what real choices – they have, these so-called free men? Are they able to choose where and when to work, or for whom? No. Can they choose, even, where to live? No – except in such choice as exists between one squalid slum and another. Might they be able to choose that their women and children should not work from dawn until beyond dusk? That their young be educated? That they should breathe clean and healthy air? No! Can they choose to be doctored for their ills, to be paid a livin' wage for their labour, to refuse to be exploited by those set above them, to be certain of a safe and comfortable old age? No again, Miss Henderson! So I ask, where are these freedoms of which you are so certain and so proud?'

In the pause he took for breath, and before Mattie could speak, the melodic sound of the dinner gong reached them from the house.

They stood in hostile silence for a long moment. Then, 'We

should go back, I think,' Mattie said, very coldly and very quietly, 'for Mrs Johnstone is extremely particular about the timing of her meals.' With the blood still high in her cheeks, she turned and lifted her skirts a little, to walk back up the steps and the sloping paved paths to the lawn above. In equally chill silence he fell into step beside her, escorting her politely, opening gates, drawing away stray rose branches from the silk of her skirt.

Upon the lawn they found the company awaiting them.

'Mr Sherwood, Mattie, my dear –' Mrs Johnstone trilled, her eyes sharp as blades upon Mattie, '– we wondered where ever you might have disappeared to! Anna, there, you see? I said Mr Sherwood would be back in time to take you in to dinner. Come, my dears, lead the way – I really don't think we need to bother with too much formality, do you?'

'I'm sorry, Ma'am.' Johnny took his hostess's hand and bowed above it. His back, to Mattie – all she could see of him – looked straight as a steel rod, and about as ungiving. 'I fear I can't stay. Family business, you see – as you know I have little time left – I sail for home in just a few weeks' time, an' there's much to be done.' His voice was still harsh with anger and he made little attempt to make the excuse believable.

'How very vexing for us all,' Mrs Johnstone said, casting a stony glance at Mattie's calm face. 'But, my dear, you will oblige us for our musical afternoon on Thursday, will you not? We spoke of it last week, if you remember – we are all so looking forward to hearing you sing again.'

Johnny agreed rather more gracefully that yes, indeed, he remembered and would be there. With reluctance Mrs Johnstone relinquished his hand. He nodded to the company, still unsmiling, murmured farewells, studiously avoiding Mattie's eyes.

Mattie watched the tall, broad-shouldered figure cross the lawn and enter the house, aware of speculative glances, all interested, a few relatively friendly, others decidedly less so. She lifted her head, taking battle to the enemy. 'I'm sorry,' she said, quietly, to Mrs Johnstone, painfully aware of the avid silence that cradled her words, 'I fear I have offended Mr Sherwood.'

As she turned she caught a glimpse of Cousin Constance's face, a picture that might under other circumstances have afforded her amusement, before allowing her arm to be taken by a portly gentleman in black broadcloth and a canary yellow waistcoat. 'Cheer up, my dear,' he said, the words kindly meant. 'It's dinner time – and dear Mrs Johnstone does keep a wonderful board.'

Dear Mrs Johnstone did indeed. As soup was succeeded by three kinds of fish, a joint of mutton and a joint of beef, a choice of duck, quail or chicken and a mountain of sweet things that must, Mattie thought, have stripped some far island of its year's crop of sugar, she sat smiling emptily and nodding, toying with her food and speaking inanities whilst attempting not to remember the awful things she had said to Johnny Sherwood; and for the first time in her life she found herself close to some accord with Cousin Constance. 'Do try not to *think* quite so much, Mattie. And never – never! – answer back. It doesn't go down well with the gentlemen, you know.' Well now, she supposed, she did know. The worst of the matter was that, again for the first time in her life, she cared. And there was nothing she could do about it. No amount of wishing could take back the words she had spoken, the offence she had obviously given. She accepted yet another titbit from her portly escort, smiled politely and gave herself up to a sudden and overwhelming misery. A misery, however, that held within it an intransigent core of resistance. She had been right, surely she had? She had been, perhaps, too vehement, too provoking. But for all Johnny Sherwood's well-argued rebuttals, that did not make her wrong. She just wished she could forget the whole stupid, miserable episode. But she could not. Because, beneath the acutely embarrassing memory of the quarrel lay another memory; of intent dark eyes, and a soft voice: 'What are all these kissin's worth, If thou kiss not me?'

Cousin Constance would not – could not, Mattie thought, tiredly – let the incident drop. All the way back to their lodgings in Great Pulteney Street, where the Barlowe children had been left in the charge of Kate, the young nursery maid, she scolded and chattered like a bad-tempered sparrow.

'– Truly, Mattie, if you will not think of yourself, then you might at least have the grace to think of others! Why, I thought I might die of embarrassment! How could you? First to monopolize Mr Sherwood for so long – quite *noticeably* long I might add! – and then so to have offended him that he left the gathering, and with such a black face! Lord knows what you might have said to him to create such temper!'

'Connie, it was neither my fault nor my doing that Mr Sherwood chose to spend time with me. I'm sure he regrets it now, and won't make the same mistake again, so you can rest easily on that score at least. As to the other –' Mattie stopped.

Constance glanced up at her, waiting, blatant curiosity in her pale eyes.

'As to the other, it really is no-one's business but ours. We had a disagreement. I spoke perhaps a little too forcibly.' She ignored Constance's sharply clicking tongue. 'The thing is done. There's no use going over it.'

'Well, I must say I wish you realized how very awkward it has made things for me –'

'I can't see why.' Mattie's temper was getting shorter and shorter.

'With dear Mrs Johnstone, of course! Oh, Mattie, you are so very thoughtless! We go to the Pump Room with her and with Anna tomorrow. And then there's Thursday's soiree – Mattie, for goodness' sake, do slow down a little – you know I can't keep up with you when you stride away so! I declare you walk like an Amazon! It really is most unladylike!'

'I don't think I shall go to the soiree on Thursday.'

'Nonsense. Of course you must go. Mrs Johnstone told me she was quite relying upon you to play the piano.'

'Anna can play the piano.'

'Not as well as you can, dear. And anyway –' Constance stopped.

And anyway, Anna must be left free to circulate, to hand around the cordial, to simper and to pretend to be the empty-headed fool that Mattie knew perfectly well she was not. Anna must not be tied to the piano stool all afternoon. 'I'm sorry, Constance, but no. I'll not be going on Thursday. I'll take the children on the river. I've been promising them for weeks.' It had been at one of Mrs Johnstone's musical afternoons that Mattie had first met Johnny Sherwood. He had sung, very pleasantly, a duet with Anna, and had, with his impeccable courtesy, congratulated Mattie on her playing.

Infuriatingly Constance chose that very moment to produce one of the few perceptive remarks Mattie had ever heard her make. 'Well,' she said, lifting her vast, swaying skirts as she negotiated a broken paving slab, 'I have thought you many things, Mattie Henderson, and have made no bones of it, as you know – but I must say that I never thought you a coward.'

They finished the walk to the house in a somewhat dangerous silence. Once there, and having rescued poor Kate from a screaming Nicholas, a bad-tempered Elizabeth and an eight-year-old Edward who indignantly denied being the cause of both, Mattie set about organizing bath and bedtime, Constance as usual having produced a sudden and convenient 'head'.

'– and Master Edward threw Miss Elizabeth's best doll from top to bottom of the stairs – and she stamped and screamed so I really thought she'd have a fit, and fret herself into a fever, that I did – and that's what woke the baby, you see, and you know what the mite is like once he's started –'

Mattie did indeed. 'It's all right, Kate. Come, give Nicholas to me – you go down for the children's milk.'

'Master Edward says he won't go to bed. He says his Mama told him he could stay up as late as he wished, and Miss Elizabeth says if he's staying up then so's she. I tell you, Miss Mattie, I couldn't do a thing with them –'

'Leave them to me, Kate.' Mattie's tone was grim. 'I'll have them in bed in the shake of a lamb's tail.'

The girl left, trailing down the stairs, muttering aggrievedly. Mattie sent up a small, heartfelt prayer that she would not give in her notice with the milk. She was the third nursemaid in as many months and Mattie had no inclination to get used to a new one.

It was later, after she had retired thankfully to her own small room at the back of the house, that she realized that she had, in the confusion of the afternoon, left her father's Shelley at Mrs Johnstone's house. She shook out the hair that so offended Constance – thick, straight as black rain, almost to her waist – and picked up her brush. Stopped, watching herself in the mirror. Her thin face was sharp and pale, the too-long mouth set. 'Drat the thing,' she muttered, and then, a little louder, 'and drat Johnny Sherwood with it!' And felt, after such childishness, a little better. The book was safe enough. She'd pick it up next time she was at the house.

Constance's words came back, clear and sharp. 'I have thought you many things, Mattie Henderson, and have made no bones of it, as you know – but I must say that I never thought you a coward.'

Mattie outfaced her own reflection for a moment, scowling. Very well. If childishness was to be the order of the day, she'd well and truly give in to it. And she'd pick up the wretched book on Thursday afternoon, when she went to play the piano at the ghastly Mrs Johnstone's ghastly party.

CHAPTER TWO

'Mattie Henderson, for goodness' own sake! Whatever is that you're wearing?' Constance, standing in the hall resplendent in turquoise silk and a muslin cap with peacock ribbons that could not quite bring themselves to match the dress, eyed her cousin in scandalized disbelief. 'Why, it's surely the dress you wore for the spring cleaning? And in the garden when you helped Taylor clear out the pond? You cannot – you cannot – seriously mean to wear it to Emma Johnstone's this afternoon? Please, dear, go and change, quickly. We're quite late enough as it is.'

Mattie firmly reached for her own bonnet and jammed it on her head. 'I'm going to play the piano, Constance, not to an audience with the Queen. I don't need to get dressed up for that.'

'But – you look like a – a governess! Or a shop girl! And with your hair scragged back like that! Mattie – please! I have to insist!' From the nursery upstairs came an ill-tempered roar and a childish screech of rage. Constance cast uneasy eyes upwards. 'Hurry, Mattie, do.'

'Constance, I am quite happy with my appearance, thank you. As happy as anyone afflicted with my shortcomings can be, that is, of course.'

Irony was not one of Constance's strong points. With one ear still nervously upon the growing pandemonium upstairs she tapped her parasol sharply upon the polished floor. 'But, Mattie!'

'I come as I am or I stay behind.' Mattie's mouth was stubborn. 'A crinoline makes it quite impossible to sit comfortably at the piano. This will do. It's decent and it's clean. What else should one require of one's clothes?' She knew she was being childish, but there seemed to be nothing she could do about it. She had spent the past few days trying to erase from her memory the disastrous and ill-tempered exchange with Johnny Sherwood. Finding that impossible, she had attempted instead to rationalize it; they were two strangers who held differing opinions on a thorny issue. What did it matter what he thought of her, her opinions, or the way she expressed them? But there was the rub. It did matter. However much she tried to deny it, she did care what he thought. And upon that rock her sensible ship foundered and she resorted to miserable anger; anger at herself, and at Johnny Sherwood; anger at the world that trivialized great issues and magnified small ones until one doubted one's own judgement of which was which; at a world that had, above all, so arbitrarily taken her father from her – her stay and prop in time of trouble. He would have known what to do, how to handle this absurd situation; a little frighteningly, she had found some of her fury levelled even at him. What business had he to leave her to face alone a world for which he had never prepared her? Every ounce of obdurate recalcitrance that she possessed – and that, even her indulgent father had been heard to admit, was a considerable amount – had asserted itself. She did not need Johnny Sherwood's approval, nor Constance's, nor Emma Johnstone's, nor the world's. And to prove it, absurdly, she had donned her dullest and most out-of-fashion dress – a poor washed-out thing of greys and blues and tired thread – thus, she well knew, with spectacular success cutting off her nose to spite her own face. She would have died, however, before she would have changed it for the lemon silk, or indeed for anything half-way becoming. She planted herself foursquare in front of Constance and defied her to try to make her.

Constance had all but lost interest. Upstairs full-scale war had broken out. Kate could be heard, clearly in tears, calling on Jesus, Mary and Joseph to restore order to the battlefield. If they did not leave now they never would. Constance could see her gossip, her cordial and cakes, her comfortable niche in the detestable Emma Johnstone's coterie of chosen intimates being snatched away by elves of misfortune anxious to substitute an afternoon of motherly responsibility for three fractious and uncontrollable children. Mattie's appearance rapidly lost any trace of importance. She turned and scurried through the door, leaving Mattie to follow and close it behind them.

The first thing that Mattie realized as they made their way, late, through the chattering crowd in Emma Johnstone's over-warm and over-furnished parlour, was that all her fine and silly defiance had been for nothing. Johnny Sherwood was not there.

'So here you are, you naughty pair!' Mrs Johnstone bore down on them like a galleon under full sail. She eyed Mattie's less than impressive toilette with a bemused but by no means affronted glance. 'My dear, how very neat you look. Anna – see – here's Mattie to play the piano. Fetch your music, my love. And dear Mr Allen – would you consent to sing for us first?'

It was a very long afternoon. Mr Allen rendered one insipid romantic ballad after another; Anna contributed a little more life with her spirited rendering of 'A Soldier's Dream'. The com-pany, some more in tune than others, afterwards joined in a variety of choruses. Mattie was at last left to herself for a while, and lost herself, as best as she could, in a sonata, newly dis-covered, by the young Johannes Brahms before being called to order by half a dozen young people who were demanding the newest Strauss waltz. It was then she saw Johnny, dancing with Anna Johnstone, smiling down into her laughing face as she instructed him in the dipping, graceful ways of the dance. There could be no doubt about it; they made the most handsome and well-matched pair imaginable. Stiff-fingered Mattie increased the rhythmic, mesmerizing pace of the music. Laughing, the couples twirled, cannoning into one another and into the furni-ture, clasping each other in an embrace that would under any other circumstances have been totally unacceptable. Indeed, many a matron looked on with disapproving eyes; so much so that when the dance finally ended, despite the eager clamour for more, Emma Johnstone shook her head and firmly drew Johnny forward, patting his hand in a maternally proprietorial way that for some reason grated on Mattie's nerves like sharp chalk on a slate.

'Mr Sherwood has consented to entertain us again with some of his fellow-countryman Mr Foster's songs. Mattie, you have the music?' Mattie sat like a statue as Johnny leaned above her, arranging the sheet music upon the holder. 'Ladies and gentlemen, Mr Johnny Sherwood with "Old Folks at Home".'

He had an extremely pleasing voice, a light tenor with a clear, precise tone, and his timing was better than most. He went on to 'My Old Kentucky Home', and had the most disapproving chaperones beating time and singing along with 'Oh Susannah'. But it was with a rousing song called 'Dixie', which none of them had heard before, that he raised the roof. Mattie, struggling a little with the unaccustomed, martial accompaniment, glanced at Johnny's face above her and sharply wished she had not; the clear and fierce pride that lit it would fuel still further, she knew, those dreams against which she had set her mind and was struggling to set her heart. She sat, hands perfectly still on her lap, as the applause filled the room. Sensed his movements beside her as he spoke.

'Thank you,' he said warmly, the excitement and emotion of the song still upon him. 'Thank you for your kind applause. Thank you for the support and friendship which I know you and your countrymen bear us and upon which in the future we in the South may well come to depend.'

'Sing us something else, Mr Sherwood. Please do.'

'A duet,' Mrs Johnstone said, positively. 'Come, Anna – a duet with Mr Sherwood.'

Anna came forward. Once again Johnny Sherwood leaned across Mattie, murmuring an unsmiling and impersonal apology as he did so. Mattie was aware of small, knowing glances. There was no-one in the room who would not be remembering the scene in the garden; no-one who would not be noting her fall from grace. Colour mounted in her cheeks. She stiffened her backbone and rested her hands upon the keys. 'Oh, no,' she heard Anna say, easily, 'I can't manage that one, I'm afraid. Mattie can, though. I've heard her. Mattie – come – sing with Mr Sherwood.' There was mischief in the bright eyes, innocence in the voice. For a fierce and frightening moment Mattie could have struck her dead where she stood.

'Miss Henderson? Would you mind?' Johnny Sherwood's voice was cool and quiet above her. She looked not at him but blindly at the music he had placed in front of her, and laid her fingers once more to the keys.

Small ripples of music filled the suddenly quiet room. 'Oh, for the wings, for the wings of a dove...' The gentle song had always been one of her favourites. 'Far away, far away would I rove.'

Beside her he had picked up the tune and was humming, his voice harmonizing with hers.

'In the wilderness build me a nest...' How many times had she sung this for her father, and watched him smile? 'And remain there forever at rest...' She lost herself in the song, aware of Johnny's voice in perfect accord with her own, a sweet partnership that left an empty, aching void as it died with the last notes of the piano. Through the patter of applause she could not look at him; by the time she lifted her head to do so he was gone, with polite and quiet thanks, moving through the smiling audience to where Anna Johnstone awaited him with an eager look, a glass of cordial and a plate of cakes.

Mattie went back to Brahms.

She found her father's copy of Shelley's poems waiting for her on the hall table as she left. Her thanks to Mrs Johnstone were dismissed. 'If you left it in the garden, it must have been the gardener who found it, or one of the staff. Anna probably recognized it – oh, goodbye, dear Mrs Brittan – Sally – thank you so much for coming.'

There were a couple of rose petals caught in the leaves of the book. Mattie opened it to the page that they marked. Her eyes automatically scanned the words she knew so well, registering them before she snapped the little volume sharply shut.

'My soul is an enchanted boat,
Which like a sleeping song doth float,
Upon the silver waves of thy sweet singing . . .'

She let the petals flutter down upon Mrs Johnstone's fresh-brushed carpet, pushed the book into her pocket and followed Cousin Constance out into the summer evening.

Perhaps it was Johnny Sherwood who had found the book,

28

she found herself thinking acidly. Perhaps he was memorizing yet another poem. For the delectation and entertainment, no doubt, of Anna Johnstone.

'Mattie,' Cousin Constance said crossly, 'I keep telling you – I simply can't keep up with you when you walk at such a pace –'

Mattie, try as she might, could not bring herself to enjoy – as Constance so determinedly enjoyed – those mornings so essential to the social round of the summer visitors to the city spent gossiping and taking the waters in the Pump Room. Always the place was too hot and too crowded. Always the small, down-at-heel orchestra struggled with admirable if misplaced optimism to be heard above the carelessly raised voices, the chink of china and glass and the clatter of cutlery. Mattie, sipping her spa water with a grimace of distaste, felt truly sorry for them; most especially for the harassed-looking second violin, a portly, middle-aged man who appeared to be wearing someone else's suit. Perhaps he was also playing someone else's instrument; he certainly wasn't playing it very well – 'I'm sorry?' she murmured, unable to hide her abstraction.

'Mattie Henderson! You aren't listening to a single word I say, are you?' Anna Johnstone did her best to sound offended, but could not prevent her laughter. 'Whatever are you thinking of?'

'I was thinking,' Mattie said, honestly, 'how demoralizing it must be to be a second-class musician playing second-class music to –' she hesitated, and good sense for once asserted itself '– to people who don't want to listen.'

Anna dismissed the irrelevance with an impatient gesture. 'Oh, for goodness' sake! Mama is right – you do say the most peculiar things, you know. Ugh! I refuse to take another mouthful of this foul stuff! It tastes like warm metal polish!' Turning, she tipped her glass of water into the nearest potted palm and curled her fingers about her steaming cup of chocolate. Across the table Mrs Johnstone and Constance were talking earnestly, entirely engrossed – for all the world, Mattie thought drily, as if they actually liked each other – their voices pitched against the babble of the Pump Room. Kate sat, baby Nicholas asleep on her lap, glumly watching Elizabeth demolish her eighth cinnamon biscuit; this after having eaten her own Bath bun as well as Kate's. The child gobbled the biscuit with a self-absorbed intensity that would have well become a starving waif rather than the plump and rather too well-fed child that she was. Edward, quite deliberately, braced his feet against his sister's chair and pushed with sudden violence. The chair rocked. Not surprisingly Elizabeth choked. Equally unsurprisingly no-one took the slightest notice, with the exception of Kate, who pushed a small glass of the warm spa water towards her. The child grabbed it, took a mouthful and, with an outraged yell and to Edward's huge enjoyment, promptly spat it out.

Mattie raised her eyes to the pillars and the plaster ceiling of the elegant room. The Pump Room's Georgian glories, though faded, were still evident. She liked to imagine what it might have been like sixty years before, when Beau Nash and his cronies had made of Bath the most fashionable and glittering of the English spa resorts.

'Mattie!' The sharp exasperation drew attention from the other side of the table. Anna smiled agreeably at her mother and Constance and added in a quieter and conversational tone to Mattie, 'If you don't pay attention and talk to me I shall pinch you. Hard.'

'I'm sorry.' Mattie turned to face the other girl. 'I'm listening. I promise.'

'I don't want you to listen! I want you to talk!' Anna hissed, moving her chair a little closer and speaking in a rapid undertone. 'Now do come on – I'm dying – truly dying! – to hear about your passionate argument with the delightful Mr Sherwood – oh, don't you think he's the most divine-looking man you've ever seen? I do hope by the way that you didn't mind my making you sing with him? I thought it might help.' Her tone was just a shade too ingenuous. 'It didn't seem to, though. A pity, I thought.'

There was a very short and, Mattie hoped, appropriately repressive silence. 'Of course I didn't mind. And of course it didn't help, as you put it, since there was nothing at all to help,' she said. 'I didn't have a "passionate argument" with Mr Sherwood. We had a difference of opinion. I'm afraid I was a little too frank. Mr Sherwood, as you saw, took objection. I suppose he is not to be blamed for that.'

Anna waited.

Mattie said no more.

'Well?' prompted Anna, impatiently.

'Well, nothing,' Mattie said, shortly. 'Apart from the musical afternoon – and nothing happened then that you did not observe for yourself – I have neither seen nor spoken to Mr Sherwood, and I greatly doubt if I ever will again.' She folded her hands and her lips and fell to determined silence.

Anna shook her head in disbelief. 'Really, Mattie, you're no fun at all, you know! Why, everyone could see that the man was pursuing you –'

'Pursuing me?' Mattie was genuinely startled. 'Oh, no, Anna – you have that entirely wrong. We spoke of poetry – of Mr Shelley and Lord Byron. There was no "pursuit", I assure you.' 'And the sunlight clasps the earth, And the moonbeams kiss the sea...' She pushed the sudden memory of those words, of that voice into the deepest recesses of her mind, looking for a door to slam and lock upon them. Stubbornly they echoed, as they had so often in these last days. 'What are all these kissings worth, If thou kiss not me?'

Anna smiled mischievously. She was, Mattie thought, not without the smallest twinge of envy, a very pretty girl. 'Well, if I'd aroused that amount of interest in the man, I'd have converted it into pursuit in very short order, I tell you that!'

Mattie sipped her chocolate. It was thick, hot and very sweet. She set the cup steadily upon the table. 'Well, the field is clear,' she said, very lightly. 'It was, to be sure, never anything else. So –' she looked at the other girl with sudden interest '– will you set your cap at Mr Sherwood? Are you truly so eager to marry?'

Anna's bright eyes gleamed subversively above the rim of her own cup. 'You've asked two entirely different questions there, dear Mattie.' She glanced at her mother to make certain that her ears were entirely occupied with Constance's shrill inanities. 'If

31

I were honest I'd admit that I don't want to marry Mr Sherwood. I don't want to marry anyone. I want to run off to Paris and live a life of sin. Or go on the stage and capture a Duke as my admirer. Or live in a garret in Rome with a poet who beats me and adores me by turns. But I'm not honest, of course, so I shall deny it all and say: yes, I shall most certainly set my cap at American Johnny. It will please Mama.' She pulled a small and very droll face, the merest twitch of the muscles. 'And it will please me too in that it will set what I believe is a rather large ocean between me and her. Hopefully for ever. Is it true that you never knew your mother?'

'Yes.'

'How very sensible and clever of you. But then, you are a very sensible and clever person, aren't you? Oh look – I do believe Elizabeth is going to be sick.'

Fifteen minutes later Mattie sent a damp and subdued Elizabeth escorted by a Kate still queasy at the smell of vomit back into the Pump Room to Constance. Mattie's own spirit, faced with the heat, the packed roomful of perspiring humanity and the sweet smell of chocolate, failed her entirely. 'Convey my apologies, please, Kate. Tell Mrs Barlowe that I'll see you all back at the house later. I have silks to buy, and the pink ribbon for Miss Elizabeth's hat. And Elizabeth – don't for Heaven's sake eat anything else! Kate, do try not to let her devour absolutely everything in sight – '

'I do, Miss, I do! But she do put on such a turn if she's thwarted!'

Mattie tapped the child briskly on the shoulder. Sulkily Elizabeth lifted her head. 'Did you enjoy being sick?' Mattie asked, brightly.

The fair head with its tortured, corkscrew curls shook.

'Well, if you eat anything else – anything at all – between now and supper, I can virtually guarantee that it will happen again. And since I'm leaving you to go off shopping, and since Kate seemed more inclined to join you at the bowl than to help, that leaves only your Mama to care for you. Or Edward perhaps.' She waited for a moment for that message to sink in. 'Now, off you go. Don't forget to apologize to Mrs Johnstone. And to your

Mama, of course. And Elizabeth, please, do try not to glower so – it's not in the least becoming.'

Alone at last and breathing the fresher air – the day was bright and breezy and cool for the time of year – Mattie stood for a moment in the busy square outside the Pump Room, relishing freedom. Constance would not be pleased; there would be pained recriminations and charges of wanton thoughtlessness, selfishness and caprice. There always were if Mattie contrived an escape, for however short a time. There was, however, absolutely no doubt in her mind; just to be alone, just to be left to think and be still for a moment was treasure, and worth the price. She turned her footsteps towards the magnificent west door of the Abbey Church, her favourite refuge.

The interior of the great church – known for its light and beauty as the Lantern of the West – was still and quiet; a deceptive peace, she knew, for great plans were afoot to change and modernize the place and already building materials cluttered corners and doorways, and a ladder was propped against the huge screen with its magnificent organ and ancient carved wooden figures. The screen was to be demolished, and the organ repositioned to open up the nave to expose the great east window and the altar beneath it, a worthy aim, she supposed, and one thoroughly approved by many who had far more right and say in the affairs of the building than she had; but she could not help wishing that the lovely old place could be left to its simple, graceful self. She had seen many pictures of this lofty nave in its fashionable heyday some hundred years or so ago; she liked in her imagination to people it with the men and women of that elegant era who, with their wigs and their patches, had paraded and promenaded beneath this same ancient plasterwork ceiling – that, she feared, would also fall victim to 'improvement' – at a time when the church had been as much a part of the social scene as the salons, the Pump Room and the gardens of Bath.

Mattie walked slowly, the sound of her heels echoing in the quiet, the hubbub of the square outside cut off by the towering walls and the massive doors. Wind buffeted the tall, leaded windows that were set high above her. Beyond the screen she

33

manoeuvred her wide skirt into one of the old choir stalls, sat, quite still, her eyes upon the altar, and let her mind drift gently in the benevolent quiet. She was not a particularly religious person – no daughter of her father could have been – yet she never failed to appreciate the blessing bestowed by a quiet church; often she thought that God, if He were in attendance, would understand and accept these quiet moments as a kind of prayer, since she found it impossible to indulge in the more conventional kind. Indeed she sometimes comforted herself with the thought that perhaps He might prefer it; at least she never disturbed His peace or tried His patience by begging favours.

She found herself thinking, with a touch of laughter, of Anna's desire for a life of sin in Paris; found herself then comparing, with much less amusement, the shrewd and intelligent Anna she knew to exist with the one that she so often saw at Mrs Johnstone's soirees, simpering and affected, sometimes downright silly. Was this truly what most men wanted of a woman? If so, then Constance was certainly right in one thing; Mattie's own father had clearly ruined her chances of ever finding a husband, since Coombe House and the small income that went with it would never be enough as dowry to counter the independent mind he had so cavalierly fostered. And though she would determinedly show nothing but unconcern about that to the world at large, to herself she could admit a certain despondency at the thought. She had spent most of her life in an atmosphere of love, mental stimulation and warm companionship. It had not, for a long time, occurred to her that there was any other way to live. The difference between that world and the one in which she now so uncomfortably found herself was that there she had belonged, and had been accepted as a thinking and comprehending person – hampered sometimes, admittedly, by a too-quick tongue and a too-quick temper, but never made to feel inferior simply because she was a woman. No-one, including her father, had made any allowances; if she joined a discussion she was expected to hold her own and to take the same punishment as others. An ill-thought-out theory or an illogical argument would receive short shrift in that circle, whoever espoused it. On the other hand, no one view was considered superior to another simply because of the sex, or the age, of the person who held it. In short, she had been brought up to believe that she should think for herself; and this, it seemed, perplexingly, was a thing most fiercely frowned upon. She knew herself too well to believe that she could now produce some obnoxious and despised alter ego, as Anna had done, to simper and trill prettily to entrap some poor man into marrying her. Yet – she could not deny it to herself – the thought of being alone for the rest of her life, never to share a thought or a feeling, never to know that wayward, romantic love about which she had heard and read so much, but of which she knew nothing, daunted and dismayed her. She sat up a little straighter and lifted her chin in deliberate defiance of the thought, that seemed somehow disloyal. Things could be much, much worse; she could find herself married to someone like dull, upright, respectable – thick-witted – Herbert; and *that* would teach her to mope, and no mistake! The thought brought a small, graceless smile to her face. She felt her father's precious, delighted approval as if he had been sitting by her side. An approval, she told herself stubbornly, that was worth all the handsome, bright-eyed young men in the world.

Or was it?

The unguarded thought had opened that dangerous door again. 'What are all these kissings worth, if thou kiss not me?' Cruelly lovely words. And accompanying them a jeering treacherous imp, that mocked her self-deception. And if you had known? it seemed to ask, if you had seen what Anna apparently saw, what you have subsequently come perhaps half to recognize yourself? Where would your fine principles have led you then? Why did he leave? Why? If he had not cared for your opinion, why would it have mattered so much to him? A young man whose good manners are the talk of Bath – to stalk off like that, with so little excuse – think about it, Mattie, think what you might have said, might have done if you had understood – if you had not been caught so much off guard. And you dare to condemn Anna, who is, in her way, more honest than you are?

Meticulously Mattie cleared the nonsense from her brain,

packing the words, and the imp, back into their dark cupboard, locking and barring the door. Briskly sweeping all trace of them away with common sense. The whole thing was a silly, futile fantasy; she was altogether too old and too sensible to allow rein to such self-indulgence. His attitude to her on Thursday afternoon at Mrs Johnstone's should surely have dampened any absurd hopes she might ever have harboured. She stood and slid carefully out of the choir stall, automatically protecting the fine stuff of her skirt from the splintered wood, her eyes still upon the altar and its dull-gleaming crucifix. Drawn from herself for a moment, she wondered again, as she had wondered so often, at that terrible – and truly heartbreaking – icon.

And then she turned to discover that the tall figure of Johnny Sherwood stood within the shadows of the doomed screen, watching her.

He spoke first, which considering the paralysed state of Mattie's own vocal chords, was just as well. 'Miss Henderson, I can do nothing but apologize – I saw you outside – followed you – an unforgivable thing to do, I know, but I so wanted to speak with you –'

She stood as immobile as the ancient wooden figures above the screen, and as wordless.

'I trust I'm not interruptin'?' His voice was quiet, his eyes flickered towards the altar.

She shook her head, unable to deny or explain.

He came to her swiftly then, with that loping, long-legged stride; made as if impulsively to take her hands and then withdrew a little, standing awkwardly for so graceful a man, a couple of feet from her. When he spoke the words came rapidly, as if he feared she might stop him. 'I realized when we met the other afternoon that you hadn't forgiven me; Miss Henderson, I can't tell you how much it means to me that you should. I thought to write – but then could not find the words. I'm no Mr Shelley, I'm afraid.'

'Mr Sherwood, I –'

'Please. I must say it. I feel so very badly about the way I behaved the other day – to leave so – and to make it so clear that we had had – that we had had words. It was unpardonable.

But Miss Henderson, I promise – I would do anything before I would offend you.' His dark face was intense; there could be no doubting his sincerity. 'I have thought about it – dare I say about you? – day and night since. I wanted so much to speak of it at the musical afternoon – indeed, to be truthful, that was the purpose of my attending – but alas, understandably you made it very clear that you did not wish my company –' She blinked at that, shook her head slightly. He talked on rapidly. 'When I saw you in the square it seemed like a sign. I followed you in here because I simply had to speak to you alone. To beg your forgiveness. Please may I hope that you will accept my sincere apologies?'

Mattie found her voice properly at last. 'Mr Sherwood, no. Absolutely, no! It was I who gave offence. I who should apologize. It was unforgivable of me to speak as I did.' Somewhere far away the imp cackled with laughter and was quickly silenced. 'I too –' she faltered a little '– I too have found myself greatly regretting our quarrel.' The word had an oddly intimate sound. She felt colour rise in her face.

Footsteps sounded in the nave, and a woman's voice murmured, answered by another.

'I feared you would never speak to me again,' Johnny said, dropping his voice a little. In his relief he smiled. Mattie thought, a little bemusedly, that someone must have lit a candle upon the dark altar. She thought she had never seen anything as beautiful.

'And I was certain I would never hear another word from you.'

'I asked you to sing with me.'

'Ah no, Mr Sherwood.' Ridiculous happiness was rising, just to listen to his voice – to stand so, openly, and look at him. 'That was Miss Johnstone. It was with Miss Johnstone, too that you danced.'

'I left the rose petals in your book.'

'I feared that too might have been for Miss Johnstone.' Her clear eyes were steady and bright on his.

Another small smile lit his intent face. 'For – for Miss Johnstone?'

'You do her a disservice,' Mattie said. 'There is more to her than she allows you to see.'

'I don't want to see *Miss Johnstone*,' he said calmly. 'I want to see you.'

She looked at him for a long, openly astonished moment.

Johnny waited to see if she would speak. When she did not, he stepped to one side, offering his arm as he did so. 'Miss Henderson – Mattie – dare I ask, would you care for a stroll to the river? It's a little windy, I fear.'

Quite surprisingly, she felt, her composure survived even that. She moved to him with a commendably sober step. 'As a matter of fact I rather like the wind, Mr Sherwood,' she said. 'And I love the river. So yes, thank you, a short walk in the fresh air would be most welcome.'

Johnny Sherwood's swift courtship of Mattie Henderson was the talk of Bath. Mattie Henderson's astonishing luck in capturing such a prize as Johnny Sherwood kept tongues wagging even faster. Mattie cared neither for the gossip nor for the unflattering and oft-expressed amazement that accompanied it. She lived in a world suddenly grown warm again with love. Even Constance could not discompose her.

'Well, I declare, Mattie Henderson, you really are the darkest horse I ever knew! And keeping it all to yourself, Miss Slyboots –' Constance would not have it, no matter how often she was told, that Mattie had had no more idea of Johnny's feelings than had anyone else '– and now here you are being squired hither and yon by quite the handsomest young man in town. I must say Emma Johnstone was quite puce with envy when I mentioned it to her the other day – indeed she became quite unpleasant – said she could not understand in the least what he sees in you!'

Mattie, quietly and quite without artifice, had asked much the same thing, as she strolled with Johnny by the waters of the Avon, watching the placid, graceful progress of a pair of swans upstream. He had taken a moment to reply. Then, 'Because I love you,' he had replied, simply. 'And because you are the right woman for me. I knew it the first time we met.'

'But – why? Johnny – why? If you wanted an English wife, why, you must know that you could have carried off any girl in Bath! Girls far more beautiful than I!'

He had lifted her face to his. 'Beautiful? Who says there is anyone more beautiful than you? Have I said it? You have a beauty all your own, Mattie; what better kind is there? What do you take me for – do you think I would look for a bright and shallow beauty that could be had by anyone for the asking?' It would have taken someone of far more experience than Mattie to recognize the bitterness behind the words. He had looked away then, watching the lovely birds that moved serenely, hardly rippling the water. His face had been in shadow. 'There are plenty of those to be had at home, believe me, without looking further afield for them. It's you I need, Mattie. You!' The hand holding hers had tightened, paining her.

His vehemence had surprised and disturbed her a little; but it had excited her too. And his words she had treasured like a miser, bringing them out for her own pleasure in quiet, private moments, hoarding them. She looked into her mirror, studying the face that had apparently inspired this love, noting a little nervously that in her own doubtful opinion it had not changed a bit; the hazel eyes were clear enough – her father had often likened their colour to spring water – but unremarkable as ever, the face thin, the mouth wide, the black hair still obdurately lacking in curl.

They spent hour upon long hour talking. They talked of poetry and of music. They talked of Charles Darwin's exciting yet strangely disquieting new theories. They marvelled at the African adventures of those brave souls determined to open up that arcane continent to the avid and often greedy gaze of the rest of the world. They spoke of the cable that had been laid across the Atlantic which miraculously made possible instant communication between two continents. Mattie told Johnny of Coombe House and of her life with her father; and in speaking of it for the first time, the grief eased at last, as her father had predicted it would. She could, as he had promised, think of him now with gratitude and affection but without pain and regret.

39

The vacuum was filled. Of one thing, however, they did not talk, except in the lightest and most passing of fashions. When, just five weeks after their meeting in the Abbey Church, Johnny Sherwood had proposed marriage and Mattie, eagerly and with love, had accepted, she knew no more about his home or his family than she had on the day of the quarrel in Mrs Johnstone's garden.

There was plenty of time. A lifetime.

Quite wilfully she set her mind against any misgiving. She loved Johnny. He loved her. No differences in their background could come between them. There were no difficulties they could not overcome. Mattie had never been in love before; she knew no better.

And Johnny, who had, did not try to find the courage in his craven young heart to enlighten or warn her.

PART TWO

Georgia, USA
1860–1865

CHAPTER THREE

The sun shone from a sky of tropic blue on the late September day in 1860 that the SS *Pride of Liverpool* ended her four-week journey across the Atlantic and steamed past the salt marshes of Tybee Island and beneath the guns of the sturdy brick-built fort of Pulaski, which stood in defence of the wide mouth of the Savannah River.

The long voyage had been by no means as trying as some of the passengers had feared; ocean and weather had been comparatively kind. Indeed the worst buffeting they had received – apart from a memorable three-day storm one week out of Liverpool – had been the day before this landfall, as the ship had approached the American coast through the warm waters of the Gulf Stream; a small tropical storm, as the captain had nonchalantly informed them, that had fortunately decided not to turn into a hurricane. 'Remind me,' Mattie Sherwood had said in heartfelt sincerity, her hand snug in Johnny's, 'never to be at sea in a large tropical storm that decides otherwise.'

They stood together now at the flaking, salt-crusted rail, narrowing their eyes against the shimmering glare of sea and sunlit sky, the marshy flatlands of the Savannah stretching into blue, green and golden distance on either side of them, watching for the first signs of the city that proudly bore the same name as the river that served her. Here on the water, for all the heat of the sun, the breeze was fresh and cool. Sea and river birds wheeled above them, calling welcome. The mere sight and smell of land, after the last featureless weeks of ocean seascape, was exciting. What Mattie saw and scented was the land of America – if she looked to the left she looked across the State of Georgia, to the right across South Carolina, until now simply names spoken in Johnny's softly drawling fashion, holding no

43

substance, no thread of recognition, making this arrival, so much anticipated, quite exasperatingly unreal; dreamlike. This was her new home. This was the start of a new life. A new life with Johnny. 'Would it be dangerous to pinch myself?' she asked, lifting her head. 'Would this all disappear in a puff of smoke?'

He bent his head to hers, eyes still watching the wide brown waters of the river ahead. 'If there's any pinchin' to be done, honey,' he said softly, voice mingling with the breeze, 'I'll do it. Tonight.'

Her sudden laughter was so spontaneous that several people, watching with them, turned smiling to the source of it. She coloured furiously. Johnny's hand curled about hers. She turned to look up at him. Mouth crooked in a smile he looked ahead, knowing her eyes were on him. It was just six weeks since the day that she had, to the astonishment of Bath Society, walked up the aisle in the Abbey Church, past the very spot where they had talked that memorable day, to become Mrs Johnny Sherwood. And those precious weeks had been as happy as any she had known.

'There,' he said suddenly, lifting a hand, 'there – see? Savannah, bless her pretty heart!'

A small buzz of excitement lifted around them.

The sea was far behind them now. The river had curved to reveal, upon the distant left bank, a cluster of buildings, long, low and businesslike. Mattie was for a moment taken aback; used to ancient Bath, booming Bristol, and more recently the black giant of Liverpool, she had, to be honest, expected something a little more impressive. But beside her she sensed Johnny's excitement, felt with him the emotions of home-coming.

Surprising herself, she found herself speaking in the silence of her mind to the God in whom she only half believed: please let me share this with him. Let me give him this; let me love his country as he does.

There was a band on the quayside to welcome them, and much activity. The wharves swarmed. Cotton bales from a bumper crop were stacked and piled in mountains, waiting to

44

be carried to the mills of Lancashire and the ports of France. Wisps of cotton wafted in the air, tickling the nostrils and bringing sneezes. Mattie already knew that the ballast the *Pride* carried was cobblestones, to be used to pave and extend the streets and byways of Savannah, free to anyone who wanted or could use them. The activity as at last they tied up beside the wharf was frantic. And, suddenly, the air was so humid that she could barely breathe.

'There's Young Peter.' They were still on deck, watching as the ship docked. Johnny pointed. 'Aunt Bess must have sent him.' Beyond the bustle a shining two-horse open carriage stood, and at the horses' heads was a figure in dark green livery. 'Come. Let's get the formalities over and done. They'll be waiting for us.'

The city of Savannah stood on a bluff overlooking the river, a little over twenty navigable miles from the sea, the small defensible lift of ground on which it stood the very reason for its existence; for in troubled times any high position in these lowlands, especially any that oversaw the highway of the great river, was invaluable. In the past peaceful, industrious and prosperous years, however, the warehouses and offices had moved down more conveniently onto the waterfront and idiosyncratic iron walkways had been constructed to connect the upper storeys of the wharfside buildings with the bluff above, to give the cotton factors and rice exporters easy access to their offices. Steep cobblestoned ramps led behind the warehouses and beneath these 'bridges' up to the residential city above the waterfront. Still bemused with the excitement of landfall, none too steady on her feet after four weeks at sea and finding it all but impossible to breathe, let alone move, in the heavy, humid atmosphere of the city, Mattie found herself bustled through the formalities of arrival and whisked to where the Negro Johnny had called Young Peter waited with the carriage. The sun was westering in a sky smokily red. Never in her twenty-two years had Mattie experienced such heat or humidity. She was greeted by Young Peter – a man of middle age and a

45

dignified mien well in keeping with his neat and understated uniform – as 'Miss Mattie' and helped into the carriage. Thankfully she settled into the well-polished and well-sprung leather upholstered seat and raised her parasol. She had felt in the touch of Johnny's hand as he led her to the carriage the tension of his excitement. He sat forward now, hands clasped between his knees as the horses laboured up the steep cobbled incline towards the city. 'You'll love Savannah, Mattie, I know you will – wait till you see the trees – I'll lay money you've never seen a prettier place. Every other block of the city is laid out as a garden – look, see the big tree there? The oak? Do you see the Spanish moss hanging from it? I always think it's real pretty, the Spanish moss, like a girl's hair. Peter, how is everyone? What's been happening?'

'Tol'able well, Mast' Johnny, tol'able well.' Straight-backed and impassive, the driver concentrated for a moment upon manoeuvring the carriage around the sharp bend at the top of the ramp and into the treelined streets of the city. 'Bin some excitement 'round here 'bout them No'therners an' their speechin' – whoa, there, Sassy, car'ful now – Mast' Henry and Mast' Edward they sho' gets mad now an' again when they read them No'thern newspapers.'

Johnny nodded. 'I'll bet they do. I'll just bet they do.'

They had left the waterfront district now and were into the residential area of the city. Mattie was looking around her in delight. Johnny was right; Savannah was as beautiful a place as she had ever seen. Elegant houses, of brick, of stucco, of white-painted clapboard, graced every gardened square. Wide porches, tall windows, sweeping steps, classical, fluted columns; the effect was of space, of beauty and of opulent wellbeing. And everywhere was the lush green of shade-trees and shrubs; the great spreading canopies of the live oaks decked, as Johnny had pointed out, with the delicate hanging tracery of the curious silver-grey Spanish moss. Sharp-leaved palms and bright, late-blooming bougainvillaea were exotic in the late afternoon sunshine. The streets, though busy, somehow held none of the mindless bustle of other cities Mattie knew; here the pace was leisurely – in the heat, indeed, it could be nothing

46

else – and in the shaded squares frilled parasols and wide, swaying skirts vied with the shrubs and flowers to please the eye. But to Mattie, who had never until now left her native land, the most astonishing thing was the variety of skin colour in the faces about her. Every shade of black, white and brown seemed to be represented in this Southern city.

'We're nearly there – see – the house on the corner, with the iron railings – that's it –'

The house Johnny had pointed out stood foursquare and well-proportioned, taking up half a block. It faced onto a park where groves and avenues of young oaks shaded lawns and walks and, in the distance, a graceful white fountain. The house was three full storeys high, a wide sweep of marble steps leading to the main entrance on the shaded porch of the first floor. The windows and the double doors were tall, the pillared porch was screened by ornate wrought iron. As the carriage turned in the street to come alongside the gate, a small black child who had been perched upon the top step ran into the house shrieking like a steam whistle. 'They's here! They's here! Mast' Johnny done come!'

Johnny swung from his seat and came around the carriage to assist Mattie to alight. Above them the door flew open again and a babble of excited cries and exclamations burst about them; Mattie received the swift impression of ringlets, ruffled skirts, lace-edged petticoats and small slippered feet. Johnny grinned widely. 'Hold onto your hat, honey,' he said. 'Here come Aunt Bess and the girls.'

It was three days before Mattie extricated herself from aunts, uncles, cousins and assorted friends and well-wishers for long enough to write her duty letter to Constance; three days in which, as she wrote, only half in jest:

'I swear, Connie, my two feet have not stayed upon the floor for more than a moment at a time! It apparently slipped Johnny's mind entirely to tell me that he's related to half of Savannah – and that the half that he isn't

actually related to is "cousin-by-marriage" to the half he
is! The whole city has streamed to the door, I swear it!
There are Mornings, Afternoons, Luncheons, and Teas –
even breakfasts have their share of guests! Johnny's
Aunt Bess, "our" Aunt Bess I should say, for she is most
insistent upon it, and I have promised, is – in the way, I'm
coming to believe, of most of these Southern people – the
warmest-hearted person imaginable. She won't hear of
our starting out for Pleasant Hill until I have, as she puts
it, "quite rested my precious self" (!) One would think we
had come from China rather than simply across the
Atlantic! And, truly, how one could possibly describe
as "rest" life in a household that is in the throes of
perpetual comings and goings, eternal eating and drinking
and absolutely constant chatter is quite beyond me! The
ocean gales were positively restful compared to the
Packard household! (I should explain here that Aunt Bess
is sister to Johnny's mother, who died when Johnny was
born. She is married to Mr Henry Packard, a merchant
and cotton broker, who, though a little daunting upon first
meeting, is in fact as kindly and warm-hearted as his
wife; their hospitality has been – there is no other word
– overwhelming.) The four young people, cousins Edward,
Dorcas, Clarrie and Maybelle, are equally (I almost said
alarmingly) welcoming; the girls exclaim constantly over
me (my speech – my hair – the "English delicacy" of my
skin!) and are quite determined to make a romantic story
of our precipitate courtship. It seems that we will not be
able to extricate ourselves for some time yet. (I read what
I have written there and am ashamed, for all is done
with such love and enthusiasm that I know it to be
churlish to think in such terms – it is simply, I think, that
I am now a little nervous of my meeting with the family
at Pleasant Hill and would, given my own choice, get it
over and done with as speedily as possible.) For his part
Johnny seems quite happy to stay for a while in
Savannah; I'm not surprised, since Aunt Bess and the girls
coddle and pamper him so! He is also much taken up, as

is everyone else, with the political trouble that seems to be brewing here; all over the city one hears nothing but talk of states' rights and Northern interference. The view here seems to be that South Carolina will certainly leave the Union if Mr Lincoln is elected President in November, and that if that should happen many sister states, including Georgia, would feel called upon to do the same. For myself, I am an outsider and find it hard to share the passions that the matter obviously arouses; yet it is difficult to conclude anything but that, despite the rhetoric and the fire of patriotic indignation, the central issue is the institution of slavery, though few here in the South can be brought to admit it. And even with regard to that great debate, I now find myself torn; here in the Packard house the servants are black and, yes, they are slaves – but I have seen no whips, heard no cries, observed nothing, in fact, but a benign, even affectionate regime that many a free servant in England would be delighted – lucky! – to be a part of. I admit to confusion and – Cousin, I think you will not believe this –'

Mattie paused for a moment, half smiling, wryly. She had allowed her pen to run away with her; Cousin Constance would neither believe nor disbelieve. This last part of her letter would almost certainly be passed over with a dismissive click of the tongue and an impatient hunt for far more interesting and important information. Herbert on the other hand might well have a fit at her diversion into politics. The thought brought faint satisfaction. She shrugged a little, dipped her pen into the ornate inkwell that stood upon the desk in the huge, comfortable room she shared with Johnny.

'– I am learning to watch, and to listen, and to keep a still tongue. There are many things to learn, many certainties to be tested –'

She stopped writing again, lifted her head for a moment, looking sightlessly out of the screened window to the little shaded garden beyond. It was very hot and so humid that each movement brought perspiration. A small, pale flash of colour caught her eye. In the garden Maybelle sat upon a swing seat under a live oak tree, a book resting upon her lap, the light muslin of her dress drifting in the breeze created by the moving swing. At the foot of the tree a young black boy pulled with sleepy rhythm at the rope ingeniously rigged to the seat's chains, back and forth, back and forth; from where she sat Mattie could hear the faint squeak of the chains. The picture was perfect. The girl's bowed, ringleted head, her young, intent face, were the very incarnation of innocence and beauty. Pale muslin drifted in the moving air. The tree itself, enclosing the scene, draped with the magical drifts of moss, was something from a fairy tale.

But the child – the black child, sleepy, well-fed, untroubled – was a slave, owned body and soul by his Packard master.

Mattie sat for a very long time, watching, the letter forgotten, a troubled furrow in her brow.

' 'Belle? 'Belle, do come.' Dorcas's voice, her slow drawl so pronounced that she made two syllables of her sister's diminutive. 'The Perry Street Smiths have arrived – they're askin' for you, sugar – '

Maybelle threw aside the book and slid from the swing, straightening and fluffing her billowing skirts, putting a hand to her hair. Mattie smiled a little as she watched the girl drop her shoulders and lift her chin prettily before stepping with carefully graceful steps towards the house. Maybelle was thirteen years old, her sister Dorcas fifteen and already a woman engaged to be married; the younger Packard daughter, Clarrie, had just passed her twelfth birthday and was already wearing her hair up and her skirts long. In this society – and this climate – girls did not remain children for long.

Mattie picked up her pen again; if she did not finish this letter now she never would.

The boy beneath the tree had come to his feet, and started towards the house behind his young mistress. 'Belle stopped for a moment, pointing, speaking sharply. The child scampered back, collected cushions, books and a small handkerchief from the seat. Both disappeared from sight into the house. The swing moved, settled, was still.

'– I must tell you something of the house.'

As Mattie wrote she could almost see Constance's pale eyes settle upon such an important issue with an interest entirely unaroused by what had gone before. She sighed a little. It really was very hot.

'Because of the extreme heat experienced in this part of the world, the ceiling of each room is very lofty, and the windows and doors *very* tall, to allow the flow of air. Most rooms have fans depending from the ceilings that are worked by a clever contraption of rope, a little like those I have seen pictured in houses in India. The room in which I sit – a bedroom, but prettily furnished as a sitting room too – has ceilings at least fifteen feet high, and doors and windows of perhaps twelve feet. The bed was made at a local plantation and is huge – one must climb three steps to reach it! – and the rest of the furniture is in complete and very attractive perspective. Consequently, tall as I am, I feel a little like Tom Thumb.'

Mattie pushed the pages from her abruptly, dropped the pen, lifted her hands to her damp, heavy hair, longing to take out the pins that held it wound about her head, weighty as a Saracen's helmet, longing to divest herself of the constricting corset, the frilled layers of her dress. Lord, it was so very hot! She grabbed the pen again, splashing ink in her haste to have her task done.

'Fashions here, like everything else, seem a little exaggerated – the hoops are wider, the hats larger, the feathers more feathery and the fans a sight to see. And waists are definitely smaller. Elizabeth would not like it at all, since it is considered the very worst of manners for a girl to eat healthily in public; Dorcas, 'Belle and

Clarrie all stuff themselves silly before going to a party, to prevent hunger pains from shaming them. I of course am a matron, and am allowed to eat what I wish.'

She was aware that her writing was deteriorating in direct relation to her patience.

A tap on the door brought her head up. 'Yes?'

A black maid, in neat dark green uniform and spotlessly white turban and apron entered the room, a wide smile on her pleasant face. 'Miss Mattie, Miss Dorcas and Miss 'Belle sent to find you. There's visitors to see you.'

'Thank you, Rosie. I'll be there directly.'

As Mattie turned back to her letter, the maid did not move but stood in silent if still smiling reproval, watching her. 'You want that I should do your hair for you, Miss Mattie?' the girl asked at last.

'No, thank you, Rosie.' Mattie scribbled a last few words then, with a sense of enormous relief, signed and sanded the letter.

Rosie stood, still watching. Still reproving.

'That will be all, thank you, Rosie. Please tell Miss Dorcas I'll be down in a minute.'

'You want one of your pretty dresses out, Miss Mattie? The yellow one, perhaps? I'll just –' The girl moved a little tentatively towards the huge wardrobe that stood in the corner of the room.

'I really don't think so. This one is quite –'

'But Miss Mattie, the yellow sure does suit you – an' with company and all?'

Mattie sighed, and acquiesced. As she was beginning to learn one almost always did. 'Very well, Rosie. The yellow.'

'And them pretty green earbobs?' It was barely a question as the girl bustled to the wardrobe.

'And the green earbobs.'

The double parlour of the Packard house was on the main floor, across the hall from the curving staircase that swept gracefully from the first floor to the second. It was a lovely room, the polished wooden floor and white-painted panelled walls giving an impression of space and coolness on the hottest of days. It was, in effect, two rooms with no dividing wall, each a faithful reflection of the other. At either end an identical, elaborate fireplace stood, the grates filled now with flowers; there were, too, identical chandeliers hanging in the centre of each ceiling, their beauty reflected in the mirrors that hung above the fireplaces. The furniture was very fine, much of it brought from Europe some fifteen years before, where Bess and Henry Packard had travelled on their wedding trip, the house itself having been the young couple's wedding present from Henry's parents. Today the tall windows at one end of the room had been closed and shuttered against the sun. At the opposite end they were open, though screened, to allow the circulation of air. The scent of flowers was everywhere.

The far end of the room was full of people. All the Packards were there, and Johnny. Standing talking to Johnny and his uncle was a tall, distinguished-looking man with a luxuriant moustache.

'Why of course the British and the French would support us,' he was saying as Mattie quietly opened the great, easy-moving door. 'Where else are they goin' to get the cotton they need? I tell you, their own good sense will lead them to recognize us, never mind the natural goodwill they undoubtedly harbour towards us! Where would the European economics be without King Cotton? An' they can't get cotton from the Yankees, that's for sure!'

'There's something in what you say, Samson, no doubt about it. It's a pity this year's crop has been so good, though – seems there'll be a lot of cotton around for a while –'

'Not enough. Never enough!'

'Does it matter if they support us or not?' A tall, fair, handsome lad who had been talking to 'Belle turned to join the conversation. 'We don't need their support, Pa. We don't need anyone's support! If the damned Yankees – pardon me, ladies – want a fight then we'll give it to them! And we'll whip 'em. What do you say, Edward?'

'We sure enough will.' Edward, small, slight and dark, with his mother's Creole looks, flashed white teeth in an excited grin. 'Any Southerner can whip any two Northerners with one hand tied behind his back, and that's a given truth! Why, most of 'em can't even ride, let alone shoot straight! I tell you – you could almost feel sorry for 'em.'

'I couldn't!' 'Belle exclaimed, her eyes, dark as her brother's, fixed upon the tall youth beside her. 'That I couldn't! I couldn't feel sorry for them at all! If they won't stop interfering with us they deserve everything they get!'

Mattie stood listening at the door, waiting for someone to notice her.

'Belle's remark received general approval from the other young people; only another tall young man, so like the object of 'Belle's attention that they surely must be brothers, shook his head a little, unsmiling.

'What's the matter, Arthur?' Edward's grin showed a glint of good-natured malice. 'Don't you fancy your chances against them puny Yankee factory boys?'

The lad shrugged. 'That's just it. It ain't the Yankees we've got to beat – it's their factories. You can't fight iron with cotton. You can't sink ships with pea-shooters.'

There was a small, dangerous silence. 'You sayin' that the South couldn't whip the No'th in a week an' be home in time for Sunday dinner?' Edward enquired, his voice deceptively gentle, his drawl slower than ever.

'I'm sayin' it isn't that simple, is all –' The lad broke off as, lifting his head, he caught sight of Mattie standing at the other end of the room. She thought she caught a glimpse of relief in his eyes at her timely entrance.

At the same moment Aunt Bess had seen her and hurried to her now, soft, plump white hands extended. 'Mattie, darlin' – here you are! Come meet our good friends the Smiths – they live on Perry Street – the pink house I pointed out the other day, you remember, honey? Everyone, here's Johnny's English bride – isn't she just precious?'

*   *   *

54

Later that night, alone at last with Johnny in their room, Mattie returned to the subject that had cropped up time and again during the day. Over Rosie's scandalized protests she had insisted that she was perfectly capable of making her own preparations for bed – the first time she had actually managed to win that particular battle – and was sitting at the vast dressing table, at which she was certain a family of six could comfortably have eaten dinner, wearing a blessedly loose dark silk robe, brushing her hair. Beyond the window the crickets called noisily, a sound still so foreign to her that she found it distracting. Candlelight flickered about the pale walls and high ceiling; the mosquito net that hung from the tester had been drawn about the great bed, making a cavern of shadows in the centre of the room. A candle stood beside the mirror. Mattie drew the brush through her straight, heavy hair with long strokes, her face abstracted. 'Johnny?'

'Mm?' Johnny, in shirt and breeches, his coat and waistcoat tossed over a nearby chair, had been standing by the screened window that overlooked the garden. At the sound of her voice he turned.

'All this talk of war. It isn't really going to happen, is it?' She had stopped her movement, the brush poised above the dark hair that was spread upon her shoulders. The face the mirror reflected was pale and serious. She watched him in the glass, half expecting laughter, easy reassurance.

She got neither. For a long moment Johnny stood, a shadow in shadows, silent. Then, 'I don't know,' he said, honestly. 'I hope to God not. But things have certainly been stirred up these past months. And if Lincoln wins the election –' He shrugged. 'I don't think he'll let the slaveholdin' states leave the Union. And I sure as hell don't think the slaveholdin' states will stay with him as President. So – who knows?'

'But – war? A civil war between North and South? It's horrible!'

'Of course it is.' Johnny's voice sharpened a little. 'But remember this, Mattie – whatever happens, none of this is of the South's choosing. We aren't the ones trying to change things. All we ask is to be left alone. *We* aren't trying to force *them* out of business, to tamper with their lives, their rights, their own way of doing things! Like I say, we just want to be left alone, that's all. We won't attack them, be very sure of that. Why should we? But if they attack us – if they won't leave us be to live our own lives in our own way – what would you have us do? Roll over on our backs an' invite them to walk all over us?'

'No. No, of course not. But –'

'You've a lot to learn about the South, Mattie – but here's a pretty simple lesson to take to heart; you back a Southerner into a corner and he'll fight. To the last breath he'll fight, and the last drop of blood. No matter what the odds.'

'And what are the odds?' she asked, very quietly.

He did not reply.

'The young Smith lad was right, wasn't he? The North has the factories – the armaments – the ships – the men. Their resources vastly outweigh yours –' Too late she realized what she had said. 'Ours,' she corrected herself after a small, difficult silence.

Johnny had come to stand behind her, looming tall in the shadows. His skin was dark against the fine white material of his shirt, which lay open at the neck. Mattie suddenly wished with all her heart that she had not brought up this awful subject.

'England won't recognize a breakaway Confederacy,' she said. 'You know it. The Abolitionist sympathies are too great, the Abolitionists themselves too influential. No government could withstand them. And without England, France won't act. The South will be alone. Johnny, you know it – you must have spoken to people in England – whatever their private sympathies they won't risk confrontation with the North.' She tilted her head to look at him. She could feel the warmth of him, wanted so much for him to touch her that it was like a physical pain.

'England must do as she wishes,' he said. 'And France, too. It's our fight, not theirs. We don't want to leave the Union, Mattie, though by God we'll defend our right to do so if we have to. For God's sake, it's as much ours as anyone's; some would say, with justice, more so! Some of the slaveholdin' states are the oldest in the Union! That should give us more rights, not less! You can surely see that we cannot – will not! – have the North dictate to us – force us to our knees – destroy us and our way of life – without fightin' for our cause and our country.' The last words were spoken very quietly, yet so forcibly that they might have been shouted aloud; a cry of pride.

Despair filled her; despair, and love, and a sudden surge of fierce and unexpected admiration. 'You'd fight?' she asked into the quiet. 'If it comes to it, to war – you'll go?' She was surprised to see the bright sheen of tears in the eyes of her reflection. For a treacherous instant the image of Coombe House rose before her, infinitely dear, infinitely safe.

'Yes,' he said. His long, brown hand reached and took the forgotten hairbrush from her still hand. 'Yes, I'll go. What else would you have me do?' He began, very gently, to brush her hair, pulling it back over her shoulders, lifting it, heavy, in his hands. She closed her eyes, feeling still the tears behind the lids, and tilted her head back against him.

She had had very little idea of what to expect from the physical side of the marriage union; there had been no-one either to warn or to encourage her. In this even her father had failed her. Cousin Constance had paled and threatened to faint when she had tried to touch upon the subject, and even Anna Johnstone had proved to be disappointingly ignorant, for all her hints and knowing looks. So Mattie had approached this particular unknown with some understandable qualms. But to her delight and astonishment, after the initial, undeniable shock, the intimate pleasures of the marriage bed had enthralled her; not simply the love-making, though that seemed to her to be an almost wickedly beguiling activity, but the lovely, lulling sense of warmth that simply lying beside him brought, listening to his quiet breath in the night, knowing that if she were to reach a hand he would turn, arms open, to her. She had not understood before her marriage the physical thrall of love; now she did. Unladylike she knew it must be, but there could be no denying that the touch of her husband's hand, the sight of his lean, handsome face, the tall, easy-moving body quickened her blood in the most embarrassing way and at the most inappropriate of moments. That this both surprised and amused Johnny she had known from the start; how much it pleased him she was only just coming to understand.

Outside the window, in the warm and heavy-scented darkness, the crickets kept up their cacophony of sound. Beyond and above it, a night bird called.

Johnny drew her from the stool, tossing the hairbrush aside. She laid her face against his chest, eyes still closed; felt the lean, hard hands that slid down her back, catching upon the silk of her robe, cupping her buttocks and pulling her close to him. Somewhere in the dark house a door closed, footsteps sounded, and it was quiet again.

'Will it happen?' she asked.

'I don't know. No-one knows. Shall I ring for Thomas?'

She sniffed. Lifted her head. 'Useless Southerner! Can't you undress yourself?' Her hands were already busy at his shirt buttons. The tears were drying saltily on her cheeks.

'For God's own sake, woman – you aren't suggestin' I should take off my own boots?' The drawl was lazily exaggerated.

'No,' she said, sinking to her knees, smiling now, as he had intended, shaking off the thoughts of slaughter. 'No, I'm not.'

Much later they lay beneath the mosquito net, which hung pale and ghostly as cobweb above them, naked, drawing apart for coolness, on the edge of sleep.

Mattie waited for a long time, trying not to ask, trying not to bring up yet another subject that had in some obscure way that she did not understand become awkward between them. Then, 'Johnny?' she said, quietly.

He grunted.

'My dear – don't you think – isn't it time we moved on to Pleasant Hill? Won't your father be expecting us?'

He shifted a little.

'Johnny?'

'Soon,' he said. 'We'll go soon.'

CHAPTER FOUR

Given how quickly Mattie was adapting to this new life, she should not, she supposed, have been in any way surprised that 'soon' could stretch with so little apparent effort on anyone's part to a month or more. Despite the fairly frequent exchange of messages from Pleasant Hill to Savannah and back – the content of which she suspected had become more demanding as the weeks passed, since Johnny had stopped reporting them word for word and simply conveyed his family's vague best wishes – they stayed in the city for the whole of the golden month of October, being wined, dined and congratulated on their marriage.

'Why, my poor, precious dears,' Aunt Bess was wont to say at intervals, if the subject of leaving was raised, 'who in the world knows what's to happen next? A weddin' trip's a weddin' trip, whatever the circumstances – why, Mr Packard and I were away in Europe for a full two years! We brought our darlin' Edward back with us! No, no, let that naughty old Pa of yours wait! He'll have you for long enough! Mattie, honey, I have the *best* surprise for you! Remember the Greens – the charmin' people we met at Aunt Sophie's the other day? They want to hold a party for you and Johnny in a week or two. Now really, my dear, that's a *chance* you can't think of passin' up.'

Mattie's own reaction to the delay was ambivalent; she was, as she had admitted to Constance, more than a little nervous at the thought of her first encounter with her new family, and her instinct was to get the meeting over and done as soon as possible. However, she was also well aware of the truth behind Aunt Bess's words; once in the country – Macon was over one hundred and seventy miles inland from Savannah, and the plantation some ten or fifteen miles on from there on the strangely named Ocmulgee River – there could be no knowing when they might come back to this green, beautiful city again, and to the friends they had made here. It would have taken a greater kill-joy than she to reject such warm-hearted and generous hospitality. Yet one part of her longed to be away from here, and alone with Johnny, to start their new life.

But here, too, lay a small disquiet.

'Where shall we live?' she had asked, many weeks ago, in the exhausting whirl of activity that had preceded the wedding.

'We'll build a house, on the plantation, a mile or so from Pleasant Hill. I know just the spot – a clearing beside the river – shaded with trees so old that people say the Indians thought the Spirit of the Land lived in them.'

But the house in the clearing was as far in the future now as it had been then. Until it was built it was clear from the way Johnny spoke that she must first expect to live with a father-in-law, three new brothers and a sister-in-law in the house called Pleasant Hill. Johnny would not be hers alone for yet awhile. So – why cut short so happy an interlude as this? Despite the fiery and excitable talk of secession from the Union, despite the growing excitement and self-righteous anger she sensed about her, despite the drilling in the streets and squares of the city of small and picturesque bands of young men, watched and admired from beneath silken parasols by ringleted girls in wide skirts and lace gloves, whose light and pretty voices expressed notions if anything even more bloodthirsty than those of their beaux, it was hard to believe that war could really come to this lovely, indolently graceful land.

And so they stayed on in Savannah, and Mattie, for those few magical weeks, allowed herself to be lulled for the one and only time in her life into that sense of unthinking, uncritical, secure and self-centred happiness that, a part of her well knew, her father would unhesitatingly have described as living in a fool's paradise; a paradise that lasted only until the day in early November when a gangling, slow-spoken railsplitter born in the Kentucky wilderness and raised on the tough Western frontiers of this still-expanding young nation was elected President of the United States, and suddenly the deadly talk of war was, even by the most optimistic of observers, no longer to be taken lightly. Mattie, along with most others, read with growing concern the firebrand reports in the Southern newspapers. Abraham Lincoln had taken the Presidency without achieving a single electoral vote in the South; indeed, in five of the Southern states he received not a single vote of any kind. Here was a man who just three years before had publicly condemned the institution of slavery as a 'moral, a social and a political wrong', and who had declared himself in favour of a policy that would treat it as such. His views and those of his party were anathema to the slaveholding states. Unless the North accepted the right of those states to secede from a Union of which they no longer felt a part, his election must surely be the match laid to the long, slow fuse leading to conflict.

It was in subdued mood that Mattie supervised the packing for the journey to Pleasant Hill. Around her the house, like the city, buzzed with excitement and outrage. Johnny, she knew, was closeted with his uncle and cousin discussing the development, predicting – indeed hoping – that this would mean the final break from the detested Yankees and their interference. The girls, too, had been vociferous in their contempt and anger. 'I declare,' young Dorcas had exclaimed at breakfast that morning, the colour high in her cheeks, dark eyes glittering, 'I'll just die if Dalton doesn't join Colonel Lawton's Volunteers straight away – why, if he doesn't an' the Yankees come they'll be whipped and it'll all be over before he gets into uniform!'

'Lance Smith said Colonel Lawton told him that the first thing the Volunteers would do would be to garrison Fort Pulaski.' 'Belle cast a sly, sidelong look at her older sister. 'Lance has been in the Volunteers since July. He and the Colonel are real good friends.'

Mattie had watched them, wondering at their unnerving certainties. Nothing she had known or experienced before coming to America, and most certainly nothing she had heard since or learned from the Southern newspapers indicated that an armed struggle, if it came, would be so easily won. Quite the contrary. Her eyes had gone to Johnny, his dark head turned as he talked animatedly to Edward. God forbid that she should ever see him in uniform; and even as the thought had taken form she had heard him say to his cousin, 'Pa said in his last letter that there are volunteer units forming at Macon. Seems if it comes to it my best chance would be there –'

She glanced now about the untidy bedroom. Trunks and bags lay open on the floor. Rosie, whilst managing, Mattie had noted wryly, to do as little as possible herself, was supervising three other girls as they folded and packed. 'Primmy, you no-count niggah! What in the world do you reckon yo're about with that?' Rosie snatched a shirt from one of the other girls, shook it out, spread it on the bed to refold it. 'You-all want them folks at Pleasant Hill to think a Packard niggah cain't decently fold a shirt?' It was a strange convention, Mattie had discovered, that no well-mannered and self-respecting white person would call one of his or her slaves a 'nigger' as a term of abuse, though she had heard Henry Packard address a favoured servant so almost as an endearment; yet frequently the word was so used between themselves. She watched the busy black hands, the closed black faces. What did they think of the fuss that was going on about them? They were neither deaf nor stupid; Aunt Bess had openly admitted that the house slaves of the city knew a great deal more of what went on than did most of their masters. Did they know or understand how influenced their lives might be by the result of this election? Did they care? And if war were to come – what would they do?

War. Suddenly the very word sounded barbarous; horrifying. 'Rosie!' she found herself snapping irritably. 'For goodness' own sake! If you're going to insist on refolding everything all the time we'll never be ready in time for the train!'

Rosie said nothing, withdrawing into a dignified and offended silence, the shirt receiving, Mattie noted, even slower and more meticulous attention. The other girls sniggered, glancing at each other and at Mattie from beneath lowered lids. Mattie turned her back on them all, looking out of the window.

The freshness had gone from the garden. The long hot summer and autumn were all but past, the short winter would set in fairly soon.

And then what?

Suddenly a future that had seemed serene and safe was uncertain. Suddenly she knew that she did not after all stand on as steady ground as she had over these past weeks convinced herself. She did not want Johnny to go to war; above all she did not want him to go to war for a cause that she knew deep in her heart to be wrong. She had listened to the passionate arguments, had even to some extent been swayed by them. She had seen how fiercely held were these peoples' views and convictions, and had understood their anger; yet, for all her attempts to pretend otherwise, to herself and to others, she knew that she believed them to be mistaken.

'My ancient faith teaches me,' Abraham Lincoln had said, 'that all men are created equal, and that there can be no moral right in connection with one man's making a slave of another.'

What treachery to stand here, in this house, in this place, amongst these kindly and hospitable people, and to know that she agreed with him.

She stared sightlessly into the empty, dusty garden.

What a betrayal of the man she loved to be in sympathy with his enemies, to condemn something for which he, his brothers, his friends were ready to fight and to die.

'Mattie, honey, are the cases nearly done? You've only a couple of hours before the train leaves –'

Mattie jumped. Aunt Bess had bustled into the room behind her, accompanied as always by the rustle of satin and a drift of flowery scent upon the air.

She turned. 'Yes. Nearly done.'

'Oh, sugar,' in warm and genuine distress the older woman held out both arms to her, 'don't look so very sad, my precious girl! Lord knows we don't want you to leave – oh, if only that *dreadful* man hadn't won! If only the Yankees would mind their own business and leave us alone!' Her normally light and pretty voice was almost venomous. 'Oh, I tell you, Mattie darlin', I could bring myself to hate those wicked people for what they're doin' to us – an' here you are, havin' to leave –'

Wryly and affectionately Mattie found herself almost smiling at that, wondering how concerned Mr Lincoln would be to know that the ire of at least one Southern lady was directed at him because Mattie Sherwood had to leave Savannah. 'We were going to have to go anyway, Aunt Bess. I believe Johnny's father is becoming impatient – one can't blame him – he's been expecting us for the past month.'

Aunt Bess sniffed briskly, enfolding Mattie in her arms. 'Now, don't you let that ol' Logan Sherwood bully you, darlin'. He likes his own way, there's no denyin' that – an' those boys of his, big as they are, 'most always give it to him – well, I don't count Robert in that of course – that boy's got more of his mother in him than I have, an' she was my blood sister! – Primmy, for land's sakes! What are you *doin'* with that pretty dress? It'll be ruined before it gets half-way to Macon, packed like that!' Aunt Bess released Mattie and pounced on the unfortunate Primmy, pushing the girl, snatching the dress from her and shaking it out. Rosie cast a small, smugly hurt look at Mattie, which Mattie sensibly ignored.

'I'd better go and find Johnny,' she said, knowing Aunt Bess to be far more capable of overlooking the packing than she. 'I'm sure he's forgotten the time. He always does.'

She lifted her skirts and ran swiftly down the curving staircase. Apart from the bustle upstairs the house was quiet. Mattie stood for a moment, her hand still resting upon the carved newel post, listening. The murmur of male voices came from the parlour. She walked to the door and pushed it open.

'Mark my words,' Henry Packard rumbled in his low, slow, heavy voice. 'South Car'lina will leave the Union. She's sworn to. Nothin'll stop her. Then what can we do in Georgia but join her?'

'Nothin', Pa. It's natural. An' Virginia, an' Mississippi, an' all the others. They cain't stop us!' Edward's voice, young and excited.

'There's no choice left to the South.' Johnny was quieter, more thoughtful. 'But then what? Will the Yankees accept it? Will they let us go?'

Mattie stepped into the room. 'No,' she said. 'No, they won't. You know it.' She was aware of three astonished pairs of eyes turned upon hers; levelly she returned their gaze. 'They think they're right. They know they're right. As you think –

know – you are. There's no compromise to be reached. No reconciliation.'

There was a small glint of disapproval in Uncle Henry's eyes as he courteously acknowledged her presence and her interruption. 'Mattie, my dear.'

Mattie's eyes were on Johnny now. It was to him she spoke the words, the passionate convictions, that she had battled to contain for the past weeks. Knowing as she did it that this was neither the time nor the place; helpless to stop herself. 'To argue secession to offer to die for it! – is sheer madness. No amount of courage, no amount of fortitude, can overcome the odds! Why can't you see it? Johnny, in the end it simply can't happen! The North won't accept it, and no-one in Europe will support you; whether you wish it or not a war of secession will be seen as a war to preserve the institution of slavery. No European government can be seen to support that, least of all the British.' She stopped, watching her husband, suddenly seeing that there was more than disapproval in Johnny's eyes – there was real anger.

'England and France need our cotton, child,' Henry Packard said, sharply.

'Not as much as they need trade with the North. Not as much as they need Abolitionist support for their own governments. Not as much as they need to assuage their own guilt in the whole slavery issue –' She had gone too far and she knew it. Face suddenly suffused with colour, she stopped.

'Guilt?' Johnny enquired, after an oppressive moment, very gently.

Mattie clasped her hands and said nothing. She had never found it harder in her life to keep her eyes steady upon another's.

There was a small, unpleasant silence.

'You no doubt came,' Henry said after a moment, courteous as ever, 'to remind Johnny that it is almost time to leave?'

'I – yes.' Helpless, Mattie saw the cold anger in her husband's face, and could do nothing about it. 'We haven't said goodbye to the girls, and we need to leave in an hour or so.'

'I'll fetch them, of course. Like all of us, they aren't happy to see you go.' Uncle Henry nodded pleasantly enough and left them. Edward after a slightly awkward moment followed him, his bright eyes curious upon Mattie, as if, she thought with a quick spurt of something close to temper, she had unexpectedly become some freak in a sideshow.

'I'm sorry. That was unforgivable of me,' she said quietly, when it became obvious that Johnny was not going to break the difficult silence; but somewhere anger of her own was stirring. Why was she apologizing? She had believed – did believe – everything she had said. Certainly – surely? – she had the right to voice her opinion on something that affected her as closely as it affected anyone else?

'Yes. It was.' He strode past her and out of the room before she could open her mouth or do anything to stop him. She stood alone, face set against the sudden, miserable tears that would betray her and leave her helpless in a way that anger would not.

After a moment she stalked after him, up the stairs and into the still chaotic bedroom. Aunt Bess was gone. 'Oh, for goodness' sake! Aren't you finished yet? I swear I could do better on my own with both hands on my head! Rosie – stop fiddling with that and get that case shut! And you –' she levelled a finger at a small girl who had jumped as if she had seen a bogeyman when Mattie had burst into the room '– take that stupid look off your face and help her! Primmy! I've had quite enough of your nonsense! Go tell Jeremiah to come up and take the trunks! Now!'

The journey to Macon was not a happy one. They each treated the other with an acrimonious politeness that was worse than anger. As the train chugged steadily into a fertile countryside of forests, fields and startlingly red earth, Mattie kept her head turned to the window, apparently absorbed in the vast tracts of land that reeled past it. Here and there a cabin, or the glimpse of a white plantation house with its sprawling village of attendant buildings clustered about it, caught the eye, or a rust-coloured, rutted road, or the gleam of water; but for the most part the red land stretched to the horizon cloaked in the green of its trees, its pastures and its crops. The cotton had been picked clean; the great fields rested in the cool autumn air. They clanked through villages where children waved and horsemen doffed their wide-brimmed hats.

Johnny said nothing.

She stood it for as long as she could before giving in and making her peace. She had for long enough seen her arrival at the Sherwood plantation as an ordeal; to endure it with Johnny withdrawn into a frigid and unfriendly silence was more than she could contemplate.

'Please, Johnny – I'm sorry I interrupted your talk this morning. Sorry I upset you. It was very bad-mannered of me; I can't think what got into me. It's just – all this talk of war –' She let the words fade into silence. Then, 'Don't let's start off at Pleasant Hill bad friends?' She despised her own bowed head, the small voice that was all that she could manage if she were not going to shriek at him.

He held out for perhaps half an hour before tentatively taking her hand in his. She let it rest there. A short while later he pointed through the window. 'See the roof over there? With the big chimneys, just there through the trees? That's the Baineses' place, on Turkey Creek. Old Mr Baines was a real good friend of Pa's. Got himself killed a year or so ago – thrown from a horse – broke his neck. His son Jeff's got the place now, and making a damned fine job of it. We were at school together. Mighty nice lad, is Jeff.'

Mattie accepted the olive branch with grace. 'Why yes, I see it. What a delightful-looking house! It looks quite like a wedding cake with all those verandas and windows.'

He smiled at last, laced his fingers lightly through hers. 'I'll take you to visit there if you'd like. Last I heard Jeff was courtin' a real nice girl from Augusta.' The smile widened, irresistibly, and suddenly the tension was gone. 'I'd sure like him to meet the real nice girl I courted for myself in England!'

They steamed into the depot at Macon late in the afternoon. The air was cool, though far from cold, and the sky had clouded over. As the train pulled clanking into the town Mattie saw a pretty, prosperous-looking settlement grown up about a wide river, much smaller than Savannah but not unlike that city in the style of its houses, the white spires of its churches and in the green of its gardens and treelined streets. They were the only passengers to alight; barely had their feet touched the dusty ground before, with a whoop of greeting, three tall young men surrounded them, grinning, slapping Johnny on the back, pumping his hand.

'Son of a gun! Took you long enough to get here, John-boy!' The tallest of the three, a huge young man with shoulders that strained the seams of his strong broadcloth coat, gave Johnny a friendly shove that all but sent him sprawling. 'We'd nigh given up on you!'

'Or sure enough thought you had on us!' Another, as like to Johnny as a pea to its neighbour in the pod, made a fist and punched him on the arm, white teeth gleaming in a grin to split his handsome face.

'Johnny! Johnny – it's real good to see you.' The third, a smaller, slighter version of the others, turned, smiling, to Mattie. The hubbub died to an expectant silence.

Johnny, the recent disagreement forgotten in the excitement of homecoming, took Mattie's hand and drew her forward. 'Mattie, I want you to meet my brothers. The big one's Will. The noisy one's Russ. And the little one's Robert.' They all grinned wider at this obviously well-worn joke; Robert, certainly the smallest of the four, nevertheless topped six foot. 'Boys – meet Mattie.' He hesitated for only the space of a heartbeat. 'My wife.'

Their hats were off now, black hair gleamed in the fading light. 'Real nice to meet you, Mattie.' Her hand was engulfed three times over in strong, leather-hardened palms, three pairs of dark eyes smiled at her. She sensed and understood their curiosity; wondered what they saw as they looked at her, these young men who were to be her brothers – if she was as they had imagined her. She smiled, murmured greetings. There was a small, tongue-tied silence broken by Will.

'Well, y'all – let's get organized here. That your stuff down there, Johnny?' He pointed to where their luggage was being stacked by two Negroes. 'Damn' good job – beg pardon, Mattie – we brought the cart as well as the carriage! Pa said you'd need it and by gosh he was right! Hey, Saul! Get yourself on over here and get this stuff to the cart for Mister Johnny an' Miss Mattie.'

A beaming young Negro standing not far away doffed his cap. 'Yes, sir, Mister Will. Welcome home, Mister Johnny – it's sho' nice to see you.'

'Thanks, Saul. It's good to be here. Is that Shake I see over there?'

'Sho'ly is, Mr Johnny – wouldn't be nohow left behind when he knowed we was comin' to meet you.'

'Mattie – we can call you Mattie, can't we?' It was Robert, beside her, offering his arm. The train, in billowing clouds of steam, was beginning to move. The engine shrieked its farewell.

Mattie laid her hand on the proffered arm. 'Of course.' She walked beside him to where a small and shining, well-sprung open carriage waited, together with four saddled horses, magnificent animals whose meticulously groomed coats shone like new-peeled chestnuts, their reins held by a young black lad astride a sturdy mule. Beside the carriage an elderly Negro, dressed in neat black suit with a spotless white shirt and a dark cravat, waited.

'This is Dandy, our coachman,' Robert said. 'Dandy, this is Miss Mattie, Mister Johnny's new wife.'

'Sure pleased to meet you, Miss Mattie. Here now – you be real careful climbin' up here.' Between them, he and Robert handed her into the carriage, and tucked a warm rug about her knees. Behind them she could hear the others, shouting and scuffling good-naturedly, howling with laughter like small boys let out of the schoolroom.

As she settled herself, Johnny came to the side of the carriage, laughing, his arm thrown across Will's broad shoulders. ''Lo there, Dandy. You comfortable, Mattie? We'll be – ' He stopped as his eyes moved beyond her to the horses, his face lit as if by a lamp. 'Arrow! By God, you brought Arrow!' As he ran to the horses one of the animals, a handsome beast with a white blaze on its face, lifted its head to watch him, nickering softly. Johnny put his face to the animal's strong, smooth neck, rubbing its ears, talking quietly. His brothers watched, beaming. The lad on the mule tossed the reins to Johnny. 'I took care of her good for you, Mister Johnny. Real good. Though she sartin' has missed you.'

Leading the mare, Johnny came back to where the others stood watching, thrust a hand out to Will, who shook it, grinning. 'Thanks, Will. Thanks, boys. Now I really feel I'm home.' He turned and swung into the saddle with an easy, effortless movement. Russell let out a high, yodelling yell and ran for his own horse, followed closely by the others. Red dust lifted as the animals, catching the boisterous high spirits of their riders, danced and circled like circus horses.

Dandy clambered onto the high seat of the carriage and picked up the reins, clicking his tongue gently. The tall wheels turned. Behind them the mule-drawn cart carrying their luggage and two or three young Negroes, who sat on the tailgate swinging their legs, moved forward also and the small cavalcade swung out into the rutted road, the young men, still chafing each other, leading the way, holding back their powerful mounts to the gentler speed of the rocking carriage.

Mattie sat, hands folded in her lap, a fixed smile upon her lips, watching her husband. Watching a stranger. She had never seen him on horseback before; it should not have been a surprise that he rode as gracefully, as easily, as his brothers. But – was this her Johnny? Was this the young man who had walked with her in the gardens of Bath, talked of Byron, and Shelley? 'What are all these kissings worth, If thou kiss not me?'

A sudden and demoralizing panic all but overwhelmed her. She wanted him here with her, beside her, as they travelled towards Pleasant Hill and the life that awaited them there. She wanted to talk to him, to have him reassure her. Yet he rode ahead with his brothers, straight-backed and laughing, and she found herself battling helplessly against a feeling of loss. Pleasant Hill had claimed him, as she somehow had known it would; as the small procession moved along the blood-red dusty roads of Georgia she found herself wondering if she would ever wholly get him back.

Mattie's first glimpse of Pleasant Hill was of distant, welcoming lights twinkling through the trees as they wound their way in darkness up the mile-long dirt drive that led from the road. It had been a long journey; she was tired, stiff and uncomfortable. Robert had dropped back and was riding beside her; the other three walked their horses in front of the carriage, talking more soberly now, their voices quiet against the background of hoof-fall and creaking saddles in the darkness. 'Pa says there'll be war for sure now. Reckons there's no way the South will stand for that Yankee nigger-lover Lincoln as President.'

'Colonel Bransom over at Silver Oaks is raising a troop. Thought we might ride over there tomorrow an' talk to him.'

'Cousin Edward's already signed on for the First Volunteers. Savannah's sure fired up over this whole business. They talk as if the navy's goin' to sail up the river any minute.'

'P'raps they're right. Pa says the first thing the North'll do is blockade the ports.'

'We're nearly there.' Robert leaned over in the saddle to speak to Mattie, pointing. 'See the lights ahead? That's Pleasant Hill. Looks like the whole household has turned out to welcome you.'

Certainly as they drew closer to the house that loomed pale against the dark sky, its windows brightly lit and its wide front door open, it could be seen that the great porch and the steps leading up to it were crowded with people. Nervously Mattie smoothed her gloves, adjusted her bonnet. Johnny wheeled his horse and rode back, taking up his position on the other side of the carriage from Robert. Will and Russell spurred forward, dismounting and tossing the reins to the waiting hands of two small Negro boys. With a sense of the dramatic that would have done justice to a parade master, Dandy too touched the tired carriage horse with the whip and brought him to a canter so that the carriage, flanked by the two young men on horseback, broke with some style into the lighted clearing before the house, to pull to a halt before the crowded steps.

A spontaneous cheer went up. Every eye was turned upon Johnny as he swung from Arrow's back. 'Welcome home, Mist' Johnny,' a woman's deep voice called, and the cry was picked up with gusto. A little shakily Mattie stood up. Johnny strode to her, lifted his arms and picked her from the carriage as if she had been a child. She wished she had not been so suddenly and clearly aware that he had never done such a thing before. There was a buzz of laughter, a smattering of applause. Then the eager crowd shuffled backwards, clearing a way up the steps to where a man stood, and a trim-waisted girl in the widest-hooped skirt Mattie had yet seen. One look at Logan Sherwood was enough to see where his sons had got their build and strength. His shock of silver-white hair fell almost to his collar; there was about his face a high-boned cast that reminded Mattie in that first, brief moment of pictures she had seen of the Red Indians who had roamed these lands a generation before. Her hand on Johnny's arm, she climbed the steps on legs that trembled after the long, cramped ride. For a moment, at the top, Johnny stepped away from her for a brief embrace with his father. 'Pa.'

'Welcome home, son.' Logan released him, turned his eyes to Mattie; light, clear eyes so unlike Johnny's and his brothers' that it was a shock to meet them.

Johnny drew her forward. 'Pa – Cissy – I want you to meet Mattie. My wife.'

The older man smiled and took a step to her, bending to brush a kiss upon her cheek. His mane of hair was soft as silk as it brushed her face. 'Welcome, Mattie. Since we heard Johnny's news we've looked forward to this day. Cissy, come say hello to your new sister.'

The slight, fair-haired girl, who had been standing in shadow, stepped forward. As she returned the softly drawled greetings and a light, cool kiss, three things struck Mattie forcibly; the first was that William Sherwood's wife was a child, no more than fifteen or sixteen years old at the most, the second that she was one of the prettiest girls Mattie had ever seen. And the third that in the bright blue eyes was a look of frank and daunting dislike that her sister-in-law was making not the slightest attempt to disguise.

'Come – you must be tired, and hungry.' Logan Sherwood offered his arm, turned to lead her indoors.

Johnny was looking about him, a small frown on his face. 'Hey, Pa, where's Joshua?'

'Over at the Brightwells' place. Miss' Brightwell has a parcel of Eastern cousins stayin' there. She begged the loan of Joshua for a couple of days to help organize.'

'An' Josh sure left like a bullet from a gun,' Russell grinned. 'Even when he knew you were comin'. Somethin' tells me that Ellie, Sally Brightwell's girl, had more than a little to do with that!'

Johnny's face lit with laughter. 'Joshua's *courtin'*?'

'Sure seems like it.' They clattered indoors, the house servants streaming, chattering behind them.

Mattie caught Johnny's sleeve as, still laughing, he came to her side. 'Johnny,' she asked, 'who's Joshua?' Surely, she wondered, half despairing, not some other far-flung Sherwood relation she had yet to meet? 'You've never mentioned anyone called Joshua.'

He patted her hand soothingly, called smiling greetings to the excited crowd on the steps. 'Best damn' butler in the county, sweetheart, that's what Joshua is. Born an' bred here – best Pleasant Hill stock there is – half the county'd jump at the chance to buy old Josh if Pa would let him go, which he wouldn't.'

They passed through wide double doors and into the house. Logan Sherwood turned, hands held high. 'Shoo off, now, all of you,' he said, 'Miss Mattie'll meet you all tomorrow. We won't burden her with introductions now. Lucy, take Miss Mattie to her room and help her freshen up. Supper will be ready in an hour, Mattie, so rest awhile. Lucy will bring you tea if you'd like. Johnny – a word with you, lad, in the library. Sol, bring a bottle, will you? Oh, and Will, there's trouble with the gin machinery again – go see to it, would you?' All this was spoken against a background of excited noise in quiet and conversational tones; yet within seconds, as if by magic, the spacious

73

hallway in which they stood was cleared, Johnny and his father had disappeared through a door through which Mattie glimpsed a comfortable, masculine-looking room with a battered leather desk and several deep armchairs, and Will and Russell were striding back out of the door, the heels of their boots loud upon the polished wooden floor. Only Cissy stood, small white hands clasped in front of her, pale blue skirt belling around her, unsmiling, watching Mattie.

'This way, Miss Mattie.' The girl called Lucy, tall and slim with lustrous black eyes in a light-skinned face, bobbed a small curtsey.

'Thank you.' Uncertain, Mattie hesitated, her eyes still on Cissy. The girl's fair, heart-shaped face was closed against her. Alone in the wide expanse of the hallway she looked more of a child than ever. Impulsively Mattie said, 'Cissy – I have some lace, brought from England. A present. Would you like to come and see it?'

Cissy did not for a moment answer, nor did her face change. Then she shook her head. 'I don't believe so, honey,' she said, slowly. 'Will likes me to rest before supper. He don't like me gettin' overtired.' And with no apology and no farewell, she walked past the silent Mattie to a door at the far end of the hall, the sound of her small feet clipping lightly upon the floor ringing loudly in the quiet.

Mattie stood, caught between astonishment and dismay.

Beside her Lucy expelled a small, sharp breath and said quietly, 'Lord bless us all, iffen that ain't the spoiltest chile Ah ever did meet! This way, Miss Mattie. Doan' pay Miss Cissy no mind. Joshua's had your rooms done up real nice for you.'

In silence Mattie followed her to the same door through which Cissy had disappeared, surprised to discover that when opened it led to another, narrower open veranda at the back of the house, from which two flights of stairs ascended to similar balconies above. Beyond it, in the yard and fifty or so feet from the house, loomed a two-storey square building, a little like a cottage. Through the open door she caught busy movement, the glimmer of fire- and lamp-light and the smell of cooking, and guessed, having seen similar arrangements in Savannah, that this must be the kitchen, built independently from the main building to keep the Big House cooler and to minimize the risk of fire.

Lucy led her along the veranda to the wooden staircase that climbed to the second floor. At the top of the stairs she took Mattie along the open, railed balcony to a door at the far end of the white clapboard wall of the house. 'Mister Logan said you an' Mister Johnny should have these rooms, same as Miss Cissy an' Mister Will have the ones at the other end. They're real pretty, Miss Mattie. Ah sure hopes you like them.'

'I'm sure we will.'

The two rooms, connected by a door, were indeed pleasant, though a little small after the lofty proportions of the Packard house. One had been furnished plainly but comfortably and with some pretty touches as a sitting room, the other as a bedroom, the centrepiece of which was a large, carved bed not unlike the one in which they had slept in Savannah. On the open walkway outside the door their trunks and cases were stacked.

'We packed away the stuff you sent on, Miss Mattie. Mister Logan said t'would be best for us to do the rest while you-all are at supper,' Lucy explained. 'But iffen there's anything you need, Ah'll search it out for you now?'

Mattie shook her head. 'No, thank you, Lucy. If you could just bring in the small leather bag – that's the one – everything I need for the moment is here.'

'You should rest, Miss Mattie, like Mister Logan said. Here, let me help you with them buttons – Ah'll send for warm water for you – an' iffen you give me that –' Mattie had taken a clean but crumpled blouse from the bag that Lucy had deposited on the bed, to have it whisked determinedly from her hands as she held it up '– Ah'll get it pressed and freshened for you to wear to supper. You need anything while Ah'm gone, you jest pull that there cord.' She pointed to where a bell rope dangled beside the door. 'An' someone'll be with you direc'ly.'

'Thank you, Lucy.' In the quiet after the girl had gone Mattie looked around. The plain, comfortable room was lit by candles upon the table and in wall sconces. The bed looked altogether too inviting; aware that if she allowed herself to climb upon it and lay down it was extremely unlikely that she would be able to drag herself up again, she ignored it and wandered into the sitting room. This too was candlelit, and was obviously on the back corner of the house since there were two tall shuttered windows on the far wall. She walked to one of them and folded the shutter back.

Lights showed from a line of cabins some distance from the house. An open fire flickered, blood-red flames lighting the figures that moved about it. Beneath the window at which she stood, a Negro boy carrying a lamp led one of the horses across the packed dirt towards a stable building some hundred yards away. She could make out the dark bulk of trees, and something not too far off that could have been the glint of moving water. Two slave women, figures foreshortened, dark dresses merging into the shadows, white aprons and turbans ghostly bright in the darkness, walked slowly together towards the cabins, from where came the sound of a man's voice, singing. Mattie closed her eyes for a moment, listening. The sound was indescribably haunting; it took no great flight of fancy to hear in it an echo of black Africa, a lament for lost freedom.

This was her new home.

The door opened behind her. 'Miss Mattie?' Lucy's gentle voice. 'Here's Samson with warm water for you. Now, why ain't you-all lyin' down like Ah said?' The words were reproachful. 'After all that journeyin', a lady should rest! Why, Ah've never been further than the old Sloan place, just across the river, where mah Mammy lives an' Ah swears it wears me out just gettin' there an' back once in a whiles! Come on, now – let's loosen them bones an' brush that pretty hair. There's still time for you to close them eyes for a few minutes –'

Mattie pulled the shutter to and turned, drawing breath, to face the relentless cosseting to which a Southern lady was obviously expected to submit before she could possibly eat supper.

76

CHAPTER FIVE

It was while Lucy was helping her to dress for breakfast the next morning that Mattie learned that there was to be yet another celebration of her marriage; more, that the arrangements were already well under way.

'Why, whatever is you expectin', Miss Mattie? The county ain't about to miss out on such a chance fo' a party! It'd nigh be a hangin' offence around here to have a weddin' without a party!'

Mattie laughed. 'I suppose it's just that the wedding does seem rather a long time ago now.'

'Maybe to you, but not to no-one here.' There was a sudden unguarded note, rueful and heartfelt, only half-humorous, in the girl's voice. Mattie glanced at her, sharply. Lucy ducked her head and turned away, diligently searching in a small box that was set upon the dressing table. 'Now, where is them pins? I declare your hair's so heavy, Miss Mattie, you need twice as many as Miss Cissy.'

There was a long moment of thoughtful silence. Lucy found the pins, came round behind Mattie and began to brush her hair. Mattie watched her in the mirror. Lucy avoided her eyes.

'Lucy?' Mattie asked at last.

'Yes, Ma'am?' Lucy made great play of ferocious concentration; her voice was innocent.

Mattie waited. Lucy, still managing to avoid the steady, questioning gaze, folded her full lips into a stubborn line.

With an effort Mattie lightened her voice. 'It must have been a shock? Hearing that Mister Johnny had married in England?'

'Oh, no, Miss Mattie.' The words came much too quickly. The lustrous eyes flickered to Mattie and away. 'Folks was real pleased. Real happy. We all knowed Mister Johnny wouldn't do

77

anythin' – ' the girl fumbled for a minute, dropped a hairpin '– too hasty. Course, iffen it'd been Mister Russ – he's the hell-raiser all right, no knowin' what he'd *ever* do!' She rolled her eyes in what even Mattie perceived to be a parody of exasperation. But the girl's face was not happy. She glanced again, obliquely, at Mattie, a clear plea in the look.

Mattie said no more.

Breakfast at Pleasant Hill was taken in the dining room, a well-proportioned square room at the front of the house with double doors opening onto the wide porch. Behind it, opening onto the narrower veranda and the staircases at the back was the room, of similar size and proportions, known as the library. On the other side of the wide hall was the parlour, which ran the length of the side of the house. The hall itself, having no staircase, was in fact a large room in its own right, containing several big, comfortable chairs and settles, a table and a piano (which Mattie had already discovered was woefully out of tune), and stretched through the centre of the house from front to back. As Mattie followed Lucy down the outside staircase and into the hall, Logan Sherwood, dressed in riding breeches, boots and thick woollen shirt, came out of the library. He made a striking figure, tall and broad-shouldered still, his shock of white hair and pale eyes emphasizing the sun-darkened skin of his high-boned face. In his gloved hand he carried a wide-brimmed hat; at his heels were two smooth-haired black dogs.

'Mattie, my dear,' he said, courteously, 'you slept well?'

'Like a log, thank you, Mr Sherwood.' Mattie found herself warily studying the quality of his smile. Was there a reserve? A trace of disapproval? 'I'm afraid I've overslept quite disgracefully. Johnny's been up and out for hours.'

'No matter, no matter. You've had a very long journey. It will take time to get over it. I thought it best to give orders that you were not to be disturbed. Tell me, do you ride?'

It was the question, in this equestrian household, she had dreaded being asked. 'Not well, I'm afraid.'

He shrugged a little. 'We can find somethin' for you, I'm sure. Johnny shall take you for a look over the place later on. I gather he has his eye on a patch of land down by the river?'

The directness of the man took a little getting used to. 'I – yes, so I believe,' Mattie said.

'We'll see, we'll see.' They had reached the door of the dining room. Her father-in-law turned to leave; the dogs lifted their heads expectantly.

'Mr Sherwood?'

He waited.

'Lucy – said something about a party? A celebration of some sort?'

'Ah yes. Next month, I believe. A little before Christmas. Joshua has the handlin' of the arrangements. He'll give you the details. Discuss them, that is, if that's what you'd like?' He settled the hat upon his mane of hair very firmly. 'Now – if you'll excuse me?'

'Of course.'

She watched him stride away, dogs obedient at his heels, to where the ever-attentive Sol waited by the door. Together they clattered out into the softly damp November day.

Mattie breakfasted alone, for which she could be nothing but grateful. It was, she was discovering, a strain to be permanently in company, permanently on guard. The thought caught her by surprise. Against what, against whom, was she guarding? She smiled her thanks to the girl who served her a daunting plateful of honeyed ham, scrambled eggs and pancakes sweet with syrup and a cup of strong, fragrant coffee; with, she considered, no small show of courage she waved away the bowl of grits the girl offered. Her dislike of the strange, rough-textured stuff had caused Johnny much amusement. She would not, he had told her, ever become a true Southerner if she did not learn to appreciate grits. She tinkered with the food upon her plate, sipped her coffee, crumbled a soft muffin between her fingers. The girl who had stayed to serve her watched her, curiously.

'Sum'p'n else you's wantin', Ma'am?'

Brought from her reverie Mattie shook her head. 'No. No, thank you. I'm – just not terribly hungry this morning, that's all. I'd like more coffee though.'

The girl collected her cup, refilled it. 'Beggin' your pardon, Ma'am,' she said, shyly.

'Yes?'

'Ah sure does like the way you talk.'

The odd, unsettled mood that had been with Mattie since her conversation with Lucy lifted in laughter, as if by magic. 'Thank you. I do wonder sometimes if people can actually understand me.'

The girl regarded her seriously. 'Oh, t'ain't easy, Ma'am. Takes some gettin' used to, I's tellin' you that. But it sounds real pretty, even so.'

Mattie was still smiling when she opened the door that led out onto the porch and stepped into the soft, damp air. It had rained overnight. The leaves of the evergreen live oaks that sheltered the house shone with moisture, and the red earth was dark with it. For the moment the wide, swept dirt clearing in front of the house was empty. Smoke rose from the slave cabins and she could hear the sound of children playing. From somewhere in the direction of the river an engine throbbed rhythmically. In the house a voice was raised, scolding, and another was lifted in laughter. She leaned upon the porch rail, taking in the view.

The house stood upon a small rise, in a copse of trees. Beyond it she could see the curve of the river and the vast stretches of Pleasant Hill land, some of the arable fields ploughed and ready for planting, the bright earth turned to red mud by the rain. In one of the great barns over to the right a cow bellowed. She moved to the top of the steps and then stopped, listening. There were voices coming from the side of the house, and footsteps. As she watched, Robert and Johnny came around the corner, deep in conversation, Johnny with his head turned from her, bent towards his brother. She smiled to hear their easy laughter.

'Johnny! Robert!' Heart lifting at the familiar sight of him, Mattie picked up her skirts and ran down the steps. 'Johnny – wait –'

The two men stopped, and turned towards her.

Mattie's steps slowed; the man with Robert was not Johnny, though even as she came closer to him it was easy to see why she had mistakenly assumed that it was. Now, however, she could see that his build was rather slighter, his shining hair thick and smooth and without the trace of curl that made Johnny's so unruly, and his skin, where Johnny's was always burned brown by the sun, was of a smooth, attractive olive, almost Mediterranean tone. She slowed her pace further, confused, finding herself running swiftly through in her head Johnny's talk of his family. Will. Russ. Robert. Surely she had met them all? There had been no mention of another brother, yet here, undoubtedly, was a Sherwood – a cousin, perhaps?

Then she saw the men's expressions and for a moment was more confused than ever. The stranger had turned to her and stood, suddenly immobile and no longer smiling. The dark eyes were utterly expressionless. Robert stepped forward quickly, a hand stretched to her, swift understanding and then some small flash of anger, quickly subdued, and not she felt directed at her, on his face.

'Mattie,' he said, rapidly, 'this is Joshua. We spoke of him last night, remember? He's been over at the Brightwell plantation, across the river, came back just this morning.'

Mattie felt as if the ground had dropped from beneath her feet. She stood, struck to silence. Joshua. This was *Joshua*? If Robert had hit her she could not have been more taken aback.

'Joshua, this is Miss Mattie. Mister Johnny's new wife.'

The tall man nodded, still unsmiling. 'How do you do, Miss Mattie. Welcome to Pleasant Hill.' His voice was very deep, his accent, unlike that of the other house servants, no more pronounced than Robert's own.

She cleared her throat. 'Thank you.'

'You were looking for Johnny?' Robert asked, gently.

'I – yes – Mr Sherwood suggested – that we might ride around the plantation this morning –' Try as she might, she could not keep her eyes from Joshua's face. The resemblance to Johnny, and indeed to Russ, who like Johnny had inherited his father's high, slanted cheekbones and lean good looks, was positively startling. The planes of the face, the line of the jaw, the set of the handsome head was the same, and, indefinably, something about the expression. There could be no doubting the startling likeness.

81

'Johnny was down by the dock a little while ago,' Robert said. 'Joshua, perhaps you'd go fetch him for Miss Mattie?'

'Yes, Mister Robert.' Joshua nodded, turned, strode off. Mattie and Robert stood and watched him go in a silence that held, on Mattie's side at least, acute embarrassment.

They turned and walked slowly towards the house.

Robert made no attempt to deny the obvious. 'Johnny didn't tell you?' he asked after a moment, quietly. 'About Joshua?'

'No. No, he didn't.' A slow anger was beginning to burn beneath her confusion, and a terrible mortification that churned her stomach like sickness. Why hadn't he? Why hadn't he told her? Why hadn't he foreseen her shock, the possibility of embarrassment? 'Robert,' she said, 'I don't understand – I thought – I thought Joshua was a slave?'

'He is.' The words were quiet.

She stopped walking. Turned to look at him. 'But – surely?' She could not go on.

'These things, I'm afraid, tend to happen in the best-regulated of families,' Robert said, after a moment, his voice dry, all but expressionless.

'Joshua is –' Mattie struggled for a moment both with the enormity of the idea and with the problem of expressing it '– is your father's son?'

'Yes.'

She had stopped and was staring at him, horror in her eyes. 'He's – your *brother*? – Johnny's brother?'

'Yes.' He was watching her calmly.

'And – and a slave?'

'Yes. As his mother was a slave. He also, as it happens, is the best friend I've ever had, though I can see you'd find that hard to believe.'

'I find the whole thing hard to believe.'

'Yes. I expect you do.' They walked on, up the steps and onto the porch. 'Johnny should have told you.'

'Yes, he should.' Embarrassment and anger seethed still. The thought occurred to her: what else? What else had he not told her?

'Mattie, listen. This is the South. There are attitudes here that you'll never change. Deeply held convictions that nothing will ever shake, no matter how wrong – evil, even – they might be.' Robert caught her sudden, startled look and grinned wryly. 'Oh, yes, something else Johnny obviously hasn't told you. He has an Abolitionist brother. But an Abolitionist who at least knows and sympathizes with both sides of the argument, which is more than any Yankee outsider can possibly do. You think Pa should have freed Joshua.' He shook his head 'Pa won't – can't – do that. He can't do it because it would go against everything he believes in, would undermine a way of life he has fought for, and loves. If you look at one Negro and see a man, then you're lost; for if he is a man then so are his brothers. If you free him, you must free them also.'

'Even if that man is your son?'

'Even then. Pa's done what he believes is right by Joshua. He has his own quarters, he has a position of trust and responsibility – in fact he more or less runs the household; I guess you could say he has more of a say in what happens at Pleasant Hill than the rest of us put together. And if this girl he's taken a shine to over at the Brightwell place turns out to be the one he wants, Pa'll buy her for him. But he's still a slave, because his mother was a slave, and whilst there's a breath in Pa's body he always will be. Mattie, if you're going to live here you have to understand; there are many good people who are convinced that the institution of slavery is God-given and right. Who truly believe that the Negro is an inferior being, no better than an animal, incapable of thinking or caring for himself. They can't – daren't – believe anything else.'

'And what does Joshua think of that for an idea?' Mattie could not keep the acid from her voice.

Robert turned to face her, held her eyes. 'That isn't for me to answer, is it? Ask Joshua.'

She nodded, biting her lip. 'I'm sorry. That was unforgivable.'

He turned back to the rail, leaned his elbows upon it, looking to where two tall figures, deep in conversation, were walking across the clearing. Johnny and Joshua were exactly of a height; even their gait was similar. 'No, Mattie. There are a few things that are unforgivable. Anger at injustice isn't one of them.'

83

They watched the oncoming figures for a moment in silence. As the implications of what Robert had just said took on a sudden clear meaning, the brutal dilemma in which he surely must stand became clear. Mattie felt a swift surge of sympathy for the quiet young man, so unlike the other Sherwood boys, who stood beside her. 'Robert?'

He glanced at her enquiringly.

'What will you do if there is a war?'

His face closed as surely and as sharply as a slammed door. He pushed himself from the rail, standing to his full height. Johnny saw them, lifted a hand in greeting. 'There isn't going to be a war,' Robert said, flatly. 'It's all talk. We're a nation; a civilized nation. No-one could be that stupid.'

Johnny and Joshua had reached the bottom of the steps. They stood in a moment's further conversation then Johnny raised a friendly hand to Joshua's shoulder before the Negro turned and walked towards the stables. Johnny took the steps two at a time and dropped an easy kiss on Mattie's cheek, apparently completely unaware of any tension. 'Good morning, Mrs Lie-abed Sherwood.' He looked young, healthy and full of vigour. 'Joshua tells me you want to survey the kingdom. He's gone to tell 'Ziah to saddle the horses – all right, don't worry – there's a little old pony over there who'd carry a newborn babe without dropping him! Coming, Robert?'

Robert shook his head. 'I'm going into town; Pa's not happy with the new cotton factor and wanted someone to go talk to him.'

'You'll be back this afternoon, though?'

Robert shook his head. 'No. No, I won't. Thought I might go visit the Morrisons while I was about it. Well, enjoy your ride, Mattie. Don't let this young scoundrel get you jumping fences just yet.' He put a hand upon Mattie's arm, very lightly. There was, she saw, clear warning in his level gaze, one that she had no difficulty understanding. She swallowed her anger. Robert was right; this was neither the time nor the place to take Johnny to task. She turned to her husband, who, a small, straight furrow between his dark brows, was looking after Robert, who had disappeared into the house.

Mattie, still struggling with her own precarious temper, had the sudden, certain feeling that she had missed something. 'Johnny? What's happening this afternoon?'

'The boys and I are riding over to Silver Oaks, to see the Colonel.'

'Which Colonel?'

He turned to her, smiling again. 'Colonel Bransom, honey. He's raising a troop of local boys. We reckon to be in it.'

Mattie glanced towards the door through which Robert had gone. 'All of you?'

'Reckon so. We've always done things together. Can't see goin' to war should be any different.' His voice was flippant.

'Johnny!' She stared at him in horror.

He laughed aloud, his arm about her shoulder. 'I'm jokin', honey. Just jokin'! Of course it won't come to that. But if there's fun to be had, we'll have it, you can count on that. Hey, look, here comes 'Ziah with the horses. Now just don't you worry, Patsy'll do you fine. She's the most docile creature I ever did come across. Run up and change. We'll ride upriver to the place I told you about.'

For the first little while Mattie was too uncertain of her control over the horse, quiet and well-mannered though the animal certainly was, to indulge in too much by way of conversation, though questions seethed in her mind. They rode single file southward along the narrow towpath, the mare Patsy following behind Arrow with a plodding concentration that at least enabled Mattie to focus all her efforts simply upon staying in the saddle and did not require her to guide the beast. In perhaps ten minutes they reached a pretty little clearing by the river and Johnny lifted her from her perch to set her upon the ground beside him. 'There. We'll make a horsewoman of you yet, you'll see.'

She shook her head, smiling.

He spread wide his hands, indicating the glade in which they stood. 'Well? How do you like it?'

'It's lovely.' The words were absolutely sincere. Even on this dull day there was a beauty, a quality of peace about the place. The red-brown waters of the river swirled between wide, over-grown banks. The huge trees spread their canopies as if to shelter the ground beneath.

Johnny reached for her, pulled her to him. 'Wait till you see it when the magnolias are out. It's the most beautiful sight in the world. This is where we'll build our house, Mattie, and this is where we'll raise our children.'

Mattie said nothing.

Johnny did not notice. 'The land over yonder's Brightwell land. Old Mr Brightwell's talked often enough to Pa of selling. Added to Pleasant Hill, it'll make us the biggest place in the county – it's what Pa's always wanted, what he's worked all his life for, us boys here, together with him – working Pleasant Hill land.'

'You wouldn't think – of buying somewhere of our own?'

'Why, heck, Mattie, it would be our own!' In his own enthusiasm it did not occur to him, despite the quiet question, to doubt hers. 'We'll build the best house in the county, see if we don't!' His arms were about her, his laughing mouth on hers. He was irresistible. Her arms went about his neck and her body moulded itself to his, her face laid against his chest. A house here, in this lovely place, would be wonderful. Of course it would. A house in which to bear Johnny's child. His children. A whole tribe of them! A house with a wide, shaded porch, like Pleasant Hill's. A house filled with music, and laughter, and books. A house where the children read Byron, and Shelley, and had no nightmares because their father could banish fear. Could explain injustice, pain and suffering –

'Why didn't you tell me about Joshua?' she asked.

Johnny's arms did not release their hold. His cheek was resting against the top of her head; she could not look at him. Only the sudden, subtle stillness of him spoke.

'I'm afraid I made the most terrible mistake.' Her voice was almost nervelessly normal. 'I think I must have upset him badly. I thought he was you. I called him – called him Johnny. He was walking with Robert, you see, and I didn't know – wasn't expecting –' Remembering the disciplined rage in

Joshua's dark eyes as he had turned to her, she flinched, and was silent. Then, 'You should have told me, Johnny,' she said, suddenly fierce. 'You should have told me!'

She felt Johnny take a long, slow breath, filling his lungs, loosening shoulders that had become tense. 'I'm sorry, hon,' he said, 'honestly sorry. You're right. I should have explained, warned you. It didn't occur to me that you'd meet like that – and somehow it seems we've lived with the likeness for so long that we forget how strong it is.'

'Forget? Oh, Johnny, how could you say such a thing? Forget?' He is your brother. Perhaps fortunately she could not bring herself actually to speak the words.

He put her from him, holding her by the shoulders. 'Joshua's mother was a slave, Mattie. Joshua was born into slavery, as was every other darky on the place –'

'Darky?' Mattie shook her head disbelievingly. 'Johnny, how can you say that? Joshua's *white*! His skin is lighter than yours!'

'That's as may be.' There was a small, dangerous edge to the words. 'But his mother was an octoroon. One eighth black blood. She was a lovely woman – Pa has a picture of her somewhere.'

'A picture?' Mattie spread helpless hands. 'I don't understand this. I don't understand anything about it.'

'Of course you don't! I've told you before. You're an outsider.' His hands tightened, almost he shook her. 'Mattie – Mattie, honey – you can't change these things – you have to learn to live with them! You married me. You have come to live in Georgia. And Georgia is the heartland of the South.' He was now openly struggling to keep his patience. 'By law the son of a slave woman is a slave. By law, Mattie. That Joshua's mother was seven eighths white means not a thing. He's black. He knows it and so do we. And he's a Pleasant Hill slave. But I ask you, as I have asked you before, do you see an unhappy worker on Pleasant Hill? Have you seen drivers with whips? Drunken overseers to abuse our people? Do you talk of the children that crawl up the chimneys of London? Of the sweated labour, the coal mines, the cotton mills? I've seen those mills – you haven't! You can't judge, Mattie. You mustn't! You must learn to live with it.'

He was right, she thought suddenly, and her heart was leaden. It was she who was wrong; she who had knowingly married a man whose life and background was so at odds with her own. She who had deliberately blinded herself. 'I'm sorry,' she said; for it was all that she could say.

He misunderstood entirely, as she supposed she had known he would. Relieved, he took her hand, turned to walk with her towards the bank of the river. 'It's all strange to you, Mattie darlin', I know that. It'll be all right, I promise you. Everything will be all right.'

She walked in silence beside him.

'Pa treats Joshua real well.' There was a defensive note in his voice.

'Yes. That's what Robert said.' And had he believed it? She could not be sure; that Johnny did she was certain. She turned her head to look at him. 'Are Joshua and Robert particular friends? He said some such thing?'

'They used to be thick as thieves. They were born within a couple of days of each other. Grew up together, I suppose. We all did; but Joshua always used to follow Robert around like a puppy.' There was the faintest edge of impatience in Johnny's voice. Perfectly obviously he wanted the uncomfortable subject dropped.

'I see.' She wanted all at once to ask: what did your mother think? How did she live with it? And are there others, less obvious in their paternity? And you, Johnny? Would you expect me to accept it too? She picked a twig from a tree, tossed it into the slow-moving waters. They both stood in silence and watched as it drifted, spinning, out into the current. 'Is the river very deep?'

'Pretty deep, yes. It's navigable for shallow draught. We take the cotton down on barges.'

'To Macon?'

'Yes. Then it's shipped on to Savannah by rail.'

They fell again to silence. Then, 'It's a very pretty place to build a house,' she said, quietly.

He smiled.

88

Mattie tossed another twig, watched it with apparent absorption as it drifted and eddied in the quiet waters by the bank. 'Johnny?' The twig had been caught by the current now and drifted, spinning, downriver. 'What does your father – the family – think of us? Of our marriage?'

The silence this time lasted for so long that she had to turn, had to look at him. He took her hands. 'Does it matter?'

'Yes,' she said, steadily. 'It does. Of course it does.'

He hesitated for a moment longer, then shrugged. 'He fears that perhaps I – we – married in haste.'

Haste. That word again. She remembered, clearly, Lucy's embarrassed confusion that morning. 'That's the word that Lucy used,' she said. 'Hasty.'

He smiled, a shade too beguilingly. 'What a word to use of a courtship that lasted all of five weeks.'

She smiled a little, but her heart was not in it. 'Johnny?' she asked after a moment, quietly. 'There is something, isn't there?'

He looked down at their linked hands for a long moment, avoiding her eyes. Then lifted his head. 'I suppose – yes. There is something I should have told you.'

'Something else?' The words were sharp.

He shrugged. 'Yes. I suppose so. Something else. But, Mattie, I swear it means nothing. Nothing! I only feel I should tell you at all because – well, because if I don't then someone else certainly will, and you could – misunderstand. I can see why Pa and the others might think that I made a hasty decision. But, Mattie, I want you to know – to believe – that I love you and only you.'

She spoke steadily through the discomfiting hammering of her heart. 'Why wouldn't I believe it?'

'Because sooner or later somebody –' he cocked a wry eyebrow '– and very probably a somebody called Cissy Sherwood – is going to tell you that a year ago I was engaged to marry someone else.'

In silence she absorbed it. In silence she watched him.

'Her name is – was – Charlotte Barclay. She is now Mrs Bram Taylor.' No effort could keep the sudden bitterness from his voice.

'What happened?' she asked.

'She ran away with him. Just under three weeks before she was supposed to marry me. Lottie is a creature of impulse.' The attempt at humour did not come off. His eyes were savage. 'I was too – gentlemanly – for her. No excitement. She found Bram irresistible. For a while anyway. I hear it's worn off. But then, with Lottie, it always would.'

'You loved her?'

'Yes, I loved her. No point in denyin' that. I'd loved her since we were children.' The words were perilously simple; the anguish behind them painfully clear.

'And – after she ran away – you went to England?'

'Yes. Pa thought it would be good for me to get away –'

She drove relentlessly through the words. '– went to England, and met me.'

'Yes.'

'And made this – hasty – marriage.'

Silence.

'No wonder your father has – reservations.' She would not show her shock, her hurt. The words were tart. 'Tell me, you don't feel – didn't feel – that perhaps you should have told me?'

'Yes! Oh, of course I should! But, Mattie, I was afraid! Afraid you'd think that –' He stopped.

'– That I might think that, as they say, "many a heart is caught on the rebound"?' In that moment she could not herself have said which was strongest, pain, humiliation or sheer rage. Joshua, for the moment at least, was entirely forgotten. This was a very personal hurt.

'That isn't true, Mattie, I swear it!'

'*Then why didn't you tell me?* Why let me face everyone without knowing? The Savannah cousins? Aunt Bess? They knew?'

'Yes.'

'Of course! Of course they did! And you say you love me? Johnny Sherwood, I could *kill* you!'

'Mattie, Mattie!' He caught her to him, fiercely. 'Stop it, now! I never dreamed you'd take it so badly –'

She stood, shaking, against him. 'In the name of God how did you think I'd take it? Do you still love her?'

'No.'

She struggled free of him, to look him in the eye.

'No,' he said again.

'You mean you didn't marry me to – to spite this Charlotte? To show you didn't care?'

'No!'

Mattie turned from him and walked to the water's edge. A log was jammed against the bank, the red, muddied waters eddying about it. Numbly, she watched the patterns, the dull sheen of light on the water, her arms crossed tightly over her breast, her shoulders hunched against him, against his betrayal. Of all things, she had not expected this.

She felt him come up behind her. Very gently he turned her to him, rocking her in his arms as she stood.

'The fountains mingle with the river,
And the rivers with the ocean –'

He spoke the words clearly and strongly, against the rippling of the river. Fiercely she resisted him. Shaking still she tried to pull away from him, but he would not let her go.

'Nothin' in the world is single,
All things by a law divine,
In one another's being mingle –'

'Stop it!' she snapped, through tears and gritted teeth. 'Just stop it, Johnny Sherwood! Or I *will* kill you! I swear it!'

His arms simply tightened. Once again, fiercely and in genuine fury, she struggled; he held her as easily as he might have held a child. 'What are all these kissin's worth, If thou kiss not me?' He bent his head to hers. Forced her mouth to his. Kissed her very hard, and then again more gently, brushing his mouth against hers, over her wet eyes, the damp hair at her forehead. She stopped struggling. To her dismay it took every ounce of willpower she possessed not to kiss him back. She stood straight and still in his arms. 'Believe me,' he said, 'what went before has nothing – nothing! – to do with us. But I'm sorry, truly sorry. I should have told you.'

She took a breath. 'Yes. You should.'

'Forgive me?'

She chewed her lip.

'Mattie – sugar – forgive me?'

'No!'

He waited.

'Well – not completely. You can't expect that.'

She saw him catch his lip between his teeth to prevent the laughter that, in love, can so quickly follow upon fury. She scowled at him, ferociously, trying to preserve her anger, trying not to see how very beautiful he looked with his dark hair awry across his brown forehead, his eyes bright with relief and with the laughter he was trying to suppress.

'But you do forgive me a little?'

'I suppose so.'

Johnny made a fist and grazed it gently along her tense jaw. 'Then why don't you climb aboard that apology for a horse and come and see the rest of the plantation?'

Knowing herself lost, she managed at least to make him wait. 'Is it worth seeing?' she asked, at last.

He had produced a huge, snowy handkerchief, was shaking it free, laughing openly now. 'Bits of it, I guess.'

'Then I suppose I might as well.' Mattie let him mop her face, submitted with charity to another kiss. His body was warm and strong against hers. He was her husband. She loved him. She did not want to quarrel – to spoil things. Above all she did not want to spoil things. She stood for a quiet moment, her head resting against him. Then they walked together to where the horses, reins trailing, were cropping grass companionably. As she stood, her hands on his shoulders, waiting for him to lift her to the saddle, she said, suspiciously, 'I do hope I'm never going to be expected to meet this Charlotte Whatever-her-name-is, who has such a lamentable taste in men?'

He had the grace to look faintly abashed. 'Um. Well – as it happens – I'm afraid so. They're – well, neighbours. Up you go.'

Propelled by his – she suspected – deliberately overenthusiastic strength she scrambled with no grace at all for the saddle, hooked her leg awkwardly over the horn. Patsy moved a little. Mattie clutched at Johnny's hand. 'Oh, for goodness' sake! Can't you make the beastly animal stand still? What do you mean, you're afraid so? When? When is this – this neighbourly confrontation to be?'

'At the party.' Johnny swung effortlessly into the saddle. Arrow danced with pleasure. Patsy tossed her head.

'Johnny!'

'Just hold her. Let her know who's boss.' He leaned over, took the reins, shortened them, handed them back.

'That's the problem. She does know. What party?'

Johnny, urging Arrow on, did not reply.

'Not – not our party? Not this wedding party that Joshua has so competently been arranging, and that the county can't live without? Oh, Johnny – no! You can't mean it!' In her exasperation she drummed her heel into Patsy's side, trying to catch up with her husband. Patsy, with a plaintive sideways look across her dappled shoulder, stopped dead. 'Johnny!'

One handed, and laughing again, he wheeled Arrow to bring her back.

'You great junkhead! Stop laughing and do something!'

He reached over and slapped Patsy's firm haunch sharply. Like the outraged matron that she was, the mare snorted and set off at a dignified, swaying and very determined pace down the trail. And Mattie, as she knew Johnny had intended, had once more to abandon both elegance and conversation in favour of the serious business of keeping her precarious, jolting seat.

Cissy found them about half an hour later as they emerged from a stand of trees on the ridge of land above the house. Together they watched the small, flying figure perched upon a horse every inch the size of Arrow as it approached them across a wide swathe of hedged meadowland. Will's young wife rode with the verve and confidence of a fearless child, putting her mount flat out across the grass, soaring apparently effortlessly over a hedge that even Mattie could see would have given pause to most grown men, to pull up beside them, bright-faced and laughing, eyes teasingly upon Johnny. 'I'll bet cash money that poor old Arrow's forgotten how to do that while you've been away.' Like Mattie, she rode side-saddle, but there, Mattie was well aware, any similarity between them stopped. Cissy sat straight and graceful, the velvet sweep of her riding skirt rich and dark against the bright chestnut of her mount. The only disarray caused by the wild ride across the meadow – strands of fine, fair hair curled about her cheeks and against the tiny feathered brim of her hat – actually enhanced the prettiness of the picture that she made, as Mattie was sure she well knew.

'Arrow has better manners,' Johnny grinned, 'than to show off so in front of poor Patsy.'

The girl's laughter pealed; her horse danced close to Patsy. Mattie, with no small effort, resisted the temptation to drop the reins and make a grab for the saddlebow.

Johnny made the quiet, chucking sound that urged Arrow on. Cissy, with nothing beyond a small, barbed smile as greeting for Mattie, kneed the chestnut in beside him. Patsy – knowing her place, Mattie thought wryly – fell in behind the other two animals, bringing up the rear as they skirted the hedge and walked at steady but unadventurous pace downhill towards the distant house.

'When are y'all going to Silver Oaks?'

'This afternoon.'

The light voice took on a note of excitement. 'I wish I was a man! I wish I could come too!'

Johnny laughed in affection and amusement. 'You?'

The small, fair head came round, pale eyes blazing. 'An' why not? I can ride as well as any of you – an' shoot too, you know it!'

'An' you'd sure enough look pretty as a picture in uniform!' Johnny conceded, grinning.

Cissy pulled a face, not unflattered. 'I don't see why y'all should get all the fun! I'd show them Yankees a thing or two!'

'I'm sure you would.' Johnny turned a little in the saddle to look back at Mattie. 'You all right, Mattie?'

With every plodding step Mattie felt as if her back were being torn apart. Her hands were sore and her leg painfully cramped. 'I'm fine.'

'Your Pa says the Yanks won't last two weeks against our boys. He says most of them don't know one end of a gun from the other. He says that's easy proved by lookin' at the generals in the US Army. All the best come from the South – Lee's a Virginian, Beauregard comes from New Orleans. If the South secedes, the North won't have a general worth his salt to fight for them.'

Mattie, wondering if she could summon the courage to suggest that she walk the rest of the way on her own two feet, tried to close her ears to this interminable talk of secession and war. The clouds had lifted a little, the air was remarkably warm. The red and fertile land lay tranquil about them. From the ridge upon which they rode she could look down not only upon the roofs and chimneys of Pleasant Hill, but across the river to the Brightwell plantation, partly hidden amongst a grove of trees. In distant fields she could see small figures moving; much of the cotton in the fields furthest from the house had not yet been picked. Along the red line of the road that led down to the river tall-sided carts piled high with the precious crop were moving slowly, the mules' feet plodding patiently along the rutted way. Smoke rose from the kitchen chimney and she could see the white dots that were the ducks and geese grazing the grass and weeds of the orchard at the back of the house. In the paddock behind the barns two young horses trotted, tossing their heads in high-spirited play. It was an idyllic picture. Could it possibly be that war could come to this peaceful land? Would these hotheaded Southerners truly put all this at risk in order to wrench themselves from a Union of which they no longer felt a part? She found herself thinking of Robert's words to her that morning: 'We're a nation; a civilized nation. No-one could be that stupid.'

' – The best men and the best horseflesh in the world,' Johnny was saying to Cissy, 'that's what'll tell. Them Yankees'll run like rabbits at the first sign of trouble, you'll see.'

A flock of birds rose, cawing and screeching, from the trees. In the distance a dog barked.

Cissy was laughing, that unstable thread of excitement back in her voice. 'Rabbits is just about all that fat ol' Arrow could chase at the moment, I reckon,' she challenged, dancing her own bright mount forward, glancing back at Johnny in clear, goading invitation.

Johnny grinned, accepting; they were off then with no word, no thought and no caution, thundering shoulder to shoulder across the field towards a wide, five-bar gate. Mattie drew rein and sat watching them, her heart in her mouth whilst, as reckless as a pair of daring children, they set the horses at the barrier. Cissy reached it first, lifting her mount clean and clear above it, the great animal appearing for a moment to defy gravity. Seconds behind her, Arrow too gathered for the jump. Mattie, despite herself, shut her eyes. When next she looked, hearing Johnny's shout, she saw that the mare had landed awkwardly, stumbling a little and losing her stride. She watched as her husband with expert grace retained his seat, regained control of the animal and, leaning across her neck, urged her on after the fleet figure of his young sister-in-law. They thundered with no diminution of speed straight into the shadows of the woods, ducking beneath low branches that could, given a moment's inattention or a misjudged movement, have swept them from their saddles; and Mattie was left, alone in the silence, sitting with aching back on the quiet horse and knowing in certainty and something close to despair the answer to the question she had just asked herself. Yes, these people would fight. With the same thoughtlessness, the same pride, the same reckless, feckless dash with which they lived. They believed themselves God's children; invincible. Their arrogance, like their dauntless courage, was bred into them; they believed themselves right and they believed themselves betrayed. Suddenly, in the serenity of this most peaceful of moments, Mattie looked ahead and was shaken to the soul by what she saw.

It was long minutes later before, grateful at least that Cissy's derisive, and Johnny's amused, eyes were not upon her, she slid very much less than gracefully and showing more leg than could ever be called ladylike to the ground and, taking Patsy's reins in her hand set off – to the relief she felt of both of them – on limping foot for the house.

CHAPTER SIX

Joshua, Mattie very quickly came to understand, did indeed occupy a place of trust and privilege in the Sherwood household – a position exemplified by the fact that he had his own private quarters in the half-basement beneath the house beside the pantry and the well-stocked cellar, to which only he and Logan held a key. The relationship between these two baffled her. Logan rarely used with Joshua the easy, paternalistic tone that he employed with the other slaves – a sometimes deceptive gentleness upon which they trespassed, she noticed very quickly, at their dire peril. Neither was Joshua's attitude to the man who was both owner and father to him in any way akin to the other slaves', although he was never anything but flawlessly and courteously attentive to Logan and to the rest of the family. There was a distance between Joshua and the rest of the world, with the single obvious exception of his affection for Robert, that took no great effort to understand; yet there was more than simple obedience in the excellence of his service, and more than simple patronage in Logan's dependence upon him to run the house in a pleasant and civilized manner. Joshua neither fawned nor fussed. He ran his domain with the same singlemindedness and pride as Logan Sherwood ran his; Mattie understood readily, but with misgiving, that no-one would be allowed to usurp that position, not even young Mister Johnny's new wife. Perhaps, given the unfortunate circumstances of that first meeting, *especially* young Mister Johnny's new wife – faced with Joshua's unfailing and austere civility, she could not be sure. The only certainty was that Joshua knew a great deal more about running the complicated household of Pleasant Hill, or indeed anywhere else, than she did; and most assuredly he needed no assistance when it came to planning a party. The matter of the wedding celebration was clearly well in hand, and her tentative interest in the arrangements was discouraged with intransigent politeness. Perfectly obviously the young mistress was expected to keep her meddling fingers occupied elsewhere. The date was already set – the twenty-second of December, since by then the cotton harvest would be finished and Christmas almost upon them, giving everyone more reasons than one to celebrate – the guest list had been drawn up, approved, and the invitations sent – and with regard to food, drink, hospitality and entertainment, the well-oiled wheels of household management were already turning. The whole county knew, and Mattie was speedily assured, that a party organized by the Sherwoods' Joshua would be an event to remember; to attempt to interfere would be as unnecessary as it would be graceless. She was therefore in that first month left with little or nothing to do but to accompany her difficult young sister-in-law on the occasional call, attempt – in vain, as they both privately accepted – to improve her relationship with Patsy, and to practise upon the piano that Joshua, solicitously, had had brought up to scratch if nowhere near perfection by a piano tuner from Macon. The piano, Mattie noted with a certain degree of dry satisfaction, was the one thing in the house for which she was in no competition; no-one else could play it. The instrument, which had been Johnny's mother's, was hers alone.

The situation in which she found herself was an odd one by any standards. She very soon came to realize that at Pleasant Hill, which had been without the hand of a free woman since Johnny's mother had died twenty-five years before, little had survived of the traditional role of mistress that had not been taken over first by Joshua's grandmother – a formidable old slave woman called Bella, who had died the winter before at the venerable age of ninety, and about whom many of the plantation slaves still talked in awe-stricken tones – and later, with the active approval of Logan Sherwood, by Joshua. Will's marriage to Cissy the previous year had created not the slightest ripple upon the smooth surface of the house's waters; Cissy was no more interested in running Pleasant Hill than she was in hoeing the fields or picking the cotton, and that suited everyone. This was the precedent that Mattie was clearly expected to follow. The house ran like clockwork, as it always had. The furniture and floors gleamed with polish, the food was well-cooked and varied, and the house servants were well-mannered and less careless than most. Preserves and pickles lined the shelves of the pantry, candles and soap were made and stored on a regular and efficient basis, the linen well-sewn and kept crisply laundered. Joshua himself overlooked the kitchen gardens and the orchards, as he did the household accounts and the small infirmary that saw to the needs of the slaves. Prudence, the cook, reigned supreme in the kitchen, the only two people of whom she took the slightest account being Logan Sherwood and Joshua himself. Mattie's presence, or absence, made no impact whatsoever upon the routines of the house. As the cooler weather set in, the hogs were slaughtered, the hams salted and smoked, the sausages made. And in the same competent way the party to celebrate the youngest Sherwood son's interesting and hasty marriage was planned.

Cissy, as Johnny had predicted, took the first opportunity to mention that Mr and Mrs Bram Taylor were back from a prolonged wedding trip to Paris and would be at the party. The two young women were in the open carriage on the way to visit the Brightwells across the river. Forewarned, Mattie was able to express unruffled and quite genuine curiosity, not about Mrs Taylor but about her husband, who must surely be a most extraordinary young man for anyone to prefer him to Johnny? Her sting thus pulled, Cissy subsided into a sulky silence for the rest of the journey; a circumstance, Mattie thought just a little wearily, that could only be welcomed. She was finding the younger girl's unnecessary and unrelenting hostility tiresome, but could think of nothing to do about it. As she got to know Cissy better, she had come to understand a little of her attitude – much akin, she often thought, to that of a spoiled only child's antagonism towards a new and unwelcome sibling – but the understanding got her nowhere. Cissy was treated by the Sherwood men, including her husband, as a pretty child to be petted, fussed and indulged; it was, Mattie thought, therefore hardly Cissy's fault if she reacted as just such a child would.

Such charity, however, did not preclude the occasional unnerving desire to scream, or better still to box Cissy's pretty ears when she was behaving particularly pettily. It was a relief at least, since neither of them particularly enjoyed the other's company, that Cissy did not often choose to seek her out. Mattie did not in the least mind that this meant, with much of Johnny's time taken up either with the plantation or by playing soldiers with the troop over at Silver Oaks, she spent many hours of each day alone. Or at least as alone as she could ever hope to be in a house full of people whose only duty was to serve her and where her wishes, it seemed, were anticipated with the most infuriating prescience, almost as soon as they were formed. She had her books and her piano. She wrung from Joshua the indulgence of embroidering sheets, pillowslips and tablecloths. She walked, or occasionally nervously braved Patsy's broad but still unaccommodating back, to explore the plantation. And above all, she spent hour upon hour in attempting to train Johnny's homecoming present to her: an ungainly, golden, four-legged fiend with paws the size of a grown man's hand and a compulsion to gnaw anything that did not move, a dog called Jacob.

These hours, at any rate, were wasted, she was convinced. Told to sit, Jake would stand, watching her eagerly, pink tongue lolling, huge flagged tail waving like a banner. Ordered to stay, he would take off after one of Joshua's geese, barking in demented delight until the thing turned on him, upon which he would skid to a startled halt and scamper back to the shelter of Mattie's skirts. Tied up as a punishment for too boisterous behaviour – an all too common occurrence – he would lie reproachfully motionless, nose on paws, aggrieved and mournful eyes turned towards wherever he expected her to appear; and her every appearance was greeted with a bouncing, wet-tongued ardour that was entirely unacceptable in a well-trained dog, and as entirely endearing. Within a very few days and against all good sense, Mattie discovered that she loved the silly, perverse animal to a quite alarming degree, a situation made considerably less uncomfortable by the fact that, despite firm effort and much good-natured derision, almost everyone else did too.

Banned from the house after a regrettable incident with a prized silk cushion, he would lie on the back porch awaiting Mattie's coming, being petted and fed by every hand, black or white, that came near him. Logan Sherwood's two aristocratic and disciplined hounds treated him with flawless disdain, despite his every friendly advance; with the other dogs on the place he quickly became firm and excitable friends. If Jacob had been her only wedding gift Mattie would have been both well occupied and well content.

Unfortunately he was not. Logan – with, she suspected, perhaps oversensitively, clear malicious intent – gave her Lucy.

Mattie was appalled, Johnny furious at her reaction, Logan apparently unperturbed and Lucy, demoralizingly, openly hurt. 'Lord, Miss Mattie – doan' you want for me to be your own girl? I'se tried real hard –'

'Oh, Lucy, now stop it! I know you have! And I don't want anyone but you looking after me! But –' Mattie spread her hands in despair. 'I can't! I can't!'

'What cain' you do, Miss Mattie?' The girl's soft, questioning eyes held hers too steadily for comfort.

Mattie folded her hands in her lap, turned her gaze sightlessly to the gloves and riding crop that Johnny had thrown down in anger before storming from the room. 'I can't – Lucy, I can't own you.'

'But, Ma'am – I cain' understand why?'

Mattie, battling a predicament she had foreseen, dreaded, and for some time cravenly managed to persuade herself she would not be called on to face, did her best to lose her temper. 'I simply can't! I don't have to explain myself to you.'

'No, Ma'am. That you doan'.' Calmly Lucy picked up the gloves and crop, laid them upon the table, busied herself with a dress that lay upon the bed. The silence lengthened.

'I'm sorry,' Mattie said, at last. 'Lucy – I'm sorry.'

'No call for that, Miss Mattie.'

'Please try to understand. I'm not – not used to – to the way things are here –' She stumbled into silence.

The girl finished her business with the dress, hung it tidily in the wardrobe. Straightened up the bottles and jars on the dressing table. Adjusted the mirror to the exact best angle. Turned. 'Iffen you is talkin' 'bout the bondage of slavery, Ma'am – an' I jus' reckon you mus' be – then you sure not makin' much sense.' She hesitated, lifted her head. 'An' I knows you could have the hide off me for sayin' such a thing.'

Mute, Mattie shook her head, sharply.

'Seems ter me that iffen I serves you, in this house, I serves you as a slave. Same as Joshua, Prudence, Sol, Dandy –'

Mattie looked down at her own long, pale hands, clasped upon her lap.

'You goin' ter stop eatin', Miss Mattie? You goin' ter live out there in the yard, under them there trees? You goin' ter pick your own cotton, weave your own cloth, make your own pretty frocks?'

'Lucy!'

The soft voice continued, emotionless and inexorable, putting into simple words the dilemma with which Mattie had been struggling for weeks. 'What diff'rence it make who owns me, Miss Mattie? I'se your girl. I serves you. An' I serves you as a slave.'

Mattie lifted her head at last, to meet the girl's eyes. And was silenced utterly by the clear plea in them.

'Miss Mattie, iffen you won't take me for your own self, take me for my sake!'

'But – why, Mattie? Why must I? Mr Sherwood – the others – they aren't unkind to you?'

The black head shook. 'No.'

There was a long, quiet moment. 'You think I'll free you?' Mattie asked at last.

Lucy made a small shrugging movement. 'I doan' know, Miss Mattie. I doan' know. But one thing's fer certain; Mr Sherwood sure 'nough never will!'

Logan Sherwood was in the library, sitting at the massive desk, pen in hand poised above a huge ledger that lay open before him. Sol stood by the window, the two hounds at his feet, all three watching their master, and waiting.

Mattie summoned every ounce of courage she possessed – at that moment it seemed to her to be a cloak that covered her trepidation all too thinly – and knocked upon the open door.

'Come in.' Logan lifted his massive head. 'Ah. Mattie, my dear.' His handsome, clear-boned face was politely enquiring, for all the world as if every soul in the house did not know what had passed between them just a couple of hours before. Courteously he stood as she walked into the room.

'Mr Sherwood – if I might have a word with you?' She heard herself how her effort to control her nervousness produced a crisp, English clarity in the words that could easily have been mistaken for arrogance. Well, there was nothing she could do about that. She lifted her chin, jaw set, and waited.

'Why, of course.' Her father-in-law waved her to a chair, himself sat down again behind the desk, fingers steepled before him. His pale eyes were impenetrable.

She glanced towards Sol. She simply could not accustom herself to having her every word overheard. 'Might I – speak to you alone?'

A look of genuine puzzlement flitted across his face before, with a glint of what looked uncomfortably like caustic amusement, he nodded. 'Of course. Sol? Take the dogs outside, please. I'll be along in a minute.'

'Yes, Suh, Mr Sherwood.'

As the big door closed behind the man, silence settled.

Logan Sherwood watched her with affable expectancy. For one short, savage moment Mattie almost hated him. Hated him, and most certainly feared him. At Pleasant Hill this man's authority was greater than the law's. The land was his; he had fought for it and with it and put his mark upon it. His power, his ruthlessness, which he disguised so well beneath the polished veneer of his courtesy and his slow, drawling speech, was absolute. He had been given nothing; what he possessed he had taken, and would hold. He would not be defied. Suddenly, and with clarity, she understood why Johnny had tarried with his new and impulsively wed wife for so long in Savannah, rather than face his father. Yet even as she thought it, she knew that this was but half the story. Logan Sherwood loved his sons with the same fierce and single-minded intensity that he loved his land. And in return any one of them, and even some of his slaves, would have died for him, and he for them. For they were not outsiders, as she was. Such intemperance did not disturb them. They were Georgians, and these extravagances had been bred into them. 'I came to apologize,' she said, and heard again, surprised, the coolness of her own voice.

'There's no need.' He leaned back in his chair, watching her still.

'Of course there is. To refuse a gift can never be anything but discourteous.'

He said nothing. He was, disconcertingly, smiling.

'I came to apologize, and to ask –' The words stuck in her throat.

He leaned forward again. 'If you might change your mind?' he suggested, mildly.

She blinked. 'Yes.'

'Why?'

She met his gaze steadily. 'I've thought it over. I realize that I was being not only unforgivably impolite, but stupid. Self-deception is not my favoured vice, Mr Sherwood.'

His smile broadened. 'No, Mattie. I never suspected for one moment that it might be.'

'I'm married to Johnny. I'm a Sherwood –'

'– a Sherwood of Pleasant Hill.' His voice was gentle.

'Yes.' She hesitated for a moment.

'And when in Rome?' he supplied, helpfully.

Mattie took a quick, defiantly angry breath. 'I'm doing my best to be honest, Mr Sherwood. With you and with myself. If slavery is wrong, then it surely must be as wrong to take advantage of the slaves of another as it is to own them yourself.'

'And – you believe it to be wrong?'

'Yes. Yes, I do.' God in heaven, what was she saying? 'But Lucy serves me; and Lucy is a slave. It is absurd to pretend that the fact that she serves as your property rather than my own absolves me from the responsibility that involves. To refuse your gift was cowardice.'

'Yes. I rather think it was.' His voice still showed no sign of rancour. He was watching her with interest.

She could do nothing but hold her temper and her tongue, which had already run too far.

Logan Sherwood closed the ledger upon which he had been working, aligning it precisely upon the desk. 'I think,' he said into the silence, 'that maybe you've been talkin' to Lucy?'

The warm colour that flooded her face was admission enough.

He came to his feet with an easy movement that belied his age and walked to the window that looked over the back yard and the neat, two-storey kitchen, standing with his back to her. After a moment he turned. 'So, daughter-in-law – daughter, if you'll allow me?' He did not wait for a reply. 'We are bein' honest with each other?'

'Yes.' The word was short.

He nodded, thoughtfully. 'Very well.' He came to lean upon the desk, the shock of his shining white hair gleaming above her in the December light 'First, yes, you may change your mind, an' yes, I will give Lucy to you. But I will not allow you to free her.' The words were spoken perfectly pleasantly, almost kindly.

She clung to the shreds of her defiance. 'Can you – can you stop me?'

'What do you think?' He allowed her a moment to answer. When she did not he continued, evenly, 'Second, in answer to the question you have not asked – yes, I was, and am, extremely displeased – justifiably as it turns out, I think you'll agree? – that Johnny chose so precipitately to marry someone from outside his own circle, someone who, whilst possessin' grace, intelligence and I suspect a fair share of courage –' despite the fact that these were the most flattering words he had ever spoken to her it took all of Mattie's strength not to shrink physically away from the sudden fierceness of tone and eye '– nevertheless is so far removed from the realities of his life that I can see nothin' but eventual misery in the union for either of you.'

The brutality of it took her breath away. She sat like a statue, watching him, unblinking.

'However, the matter is out of my hands an' there is nothin' to be done. But I'll have you understand one thing, young woman; in this house, at this time, you'll kindly keep your sanctimonious Abolitionist nonsense to yourself. There's a war comin', sure as eggs. If my boys are goin' off to fight in it they'll know that they leave behind them nothin' but loyalty, nothin' but support. You understand?'

'Yes. I understand.' One question would have destroyed him, she realized. One tempting, cruel question.

'The South is fightin' for her life.' He struck the desk sharply with the heel of his hand and straightened, turned back to the window. 'Blood red is the colour of our earth,' he said, quietly. 'And with blood it will run before we bow to that renegade redneck of a crooked lawyer, Lincoln!'

And what of Robert? How would he answer that question, this proud and unbending man who was so sure of his power over those around him? What of the son who has obdurately refused to join the troop, whose voice is never raised in the frequent vehement condemnation of the North and its anti-slavery stance? Why did she not ask? Was it the reserved good manners acquired over the years despite the efforts of her dear, subversive father, in a society that preached respect and deference to age and to the male sex? Or was it, more likely, sheer cowardice? Moments later she wished with all her angry heart that she had.

Her father-in-law turned from the window, relaxed now, smiling a little. 'So, Lucy is yours, Mattie my dear. An' I know well that she's in safe hands.'

Mattie stood. 'Thank you.' She was at the door before she realized that he was still speaking.

'– Somethin' to occupy you an' to give you purpose – get yourself with child, daughter. You'll see, that'll keep you out of mischief –'

She managed, just, not to slam the door. By the time she reached the rooms where Lucy sat placidly by the window sewing the pretty pale green dress that Mattie was to wear to the party, she was in a towering rage. The girl looked up, startled, as Mattie burst into the room, clutched at the fine material, crushing it in long, strong fingers. 'Laws, Miss Mattie! Whatever is the matter?' Her eyes widened in misery, swimming with quick tears. 'Mister Sherwood – he won't let you have me now? 'Cause you done once said no?'

Mattie shook her head impatiently. 'No, no. He gave you to me all right. Along with a piece of good and considered advice.'

Lucy sniffed mightily, rubbed her hand across her eyes. Lifted her head, smiling like a Madonna. 'What that, Miss Mattie?'

Mattie ground the answer out through teeth still gritted together in helpless fury. 'He suggested that I might be best kept occupied if I – if I became – if I –' she summoned into her head all her most livid and detested images of Constance and her puling prudishness and forced the words across her tongue '– if I produced a baby!'

Lucy began to pack away her sewing. 'Well, Miss Mattie, iffen you ask me, doan' seem like all that bad an idea?'

Mattie's monthly flow had started that morning, frustrating once more her dearest and most fervent hopes.

Upon the bed lay a small box of pins. Suddenly overwhelmed by frustration, misery and sheer temper Mattie picked them up and flung them at the wall. The box broke. Glittering and sparkling, the pins flew in all directions. There was a moment of uncertain silence. 'God preserve us,' Mattie said, evenly, 'I'm getting more like Cissy every day.'

'No, Ma'am. That you ain't.' Unruffled, Lucy moved to pick up the pins.

'Leave them.' Mattie hated the treacherous tears that were sliding down her face; hated the fact that anyone else was there to see them. 'I'll do it.'

'But, Miss Mattie!' For the first time Lucy was truly shocked.

'Leave them, I say!' Mattie dropped to her knees, leaned blindly forward to pick up the tiny, shining things. 'Or I'll have your hide, you hear me?' There was a small, almost hysterical note of self-deriding laughter behind the horrible words.

Lucy did not move.

'Please, Lucy, go and do whatever it is that you do when you aren't with me. Go!'

'Yes, Ma'am.' The door closed quietly behind the girl.

'What is the point –' Mattie demanded of the shining waxed floor, through the veil of unrestrainable tears ' – in having a slave, if you can't order her about? And why –' she sat back on her heels, brushing the back of her hand fiercely across her eyes ' – oh, why aren't I carrying Johnny's child? In God's name, we're trying hard enough!'

Five days later, with the house in a crisply organized uproar preparing for the wedding party the following day, and with personal conflicts more or less submerged in the roaring torrent of excitement and activity, the news that was spreading through Georgia like wildfire reached Pleasant Hill. The state of South Carolina had seceded from the Union, and the eager dogs of war were howling anew, and straining at their leashes.

The first carriage emerged from under the sheltering trees of the long red drive late in the morning. By lunchtime the house was packed, with more riders, more carriages turning up each moment. Children ran shrieking around the porch and up and down the staircase getting under everyone's feet and provoking Jake to a manic excitement that, as Mattie had feared would happen, necessitated his early banishment to the confines of his kennel in the barn. Upon the great table laid out in the hall the pile of presents grew, as she and Johnny received family after family at the door. She shook so many hands, kissed so many cheeks, acknowledged so many greetings and congratulations that not one name in three registered and she was reduced to a helpless, smiling bemusement. The house hummed as neighbours, both near and far-flung – some having travelled since before dawn – came together over Prudence's excellent food and chilled tea or Joshua's faultless choice of wines from Pleasant Hill's cellars to exchange news, gossip, and the high-tempered talk of secession. With a lull in the flood of arrivals, Mattie found herself seated beside Johnny at the head of the long table that had been laid in the parlour, picking at her food, smiling at anyone who caught her eye, and listening to the talk around her.

'– An' her a married woman an' all! My, Mrs Talbot, can you imagine? I tell you, I was that scandalized!'

'– Kentucky an' Tennessee? They'll join us for certain. Their future's with the South, an' they know it –'

'I ain't so sure about that, Seth. Seems to me t'ain't as clear-cut as that fer them border states –'

'Clear-cut? We'll make it clear-cut for 'em, they jump the wrong way!'

'Georgia's next, by damn! Got to be! Georgia – Alabama – Mississippi – Louisiana – the Confederate States of America! An' we've got Europe in our pocket. They need our cotton, they won't see us blockaded –'

'– The little one's ailing again, did you hear? Not strong, that family, three in the graveyard and only two in the cot –'

'– Seems we'll be comin' out of the Union for sure now.' Johnny half turned from Mattie to talk to his neighbour, a long-faced man with lank black hair. 'Pa says that ever since –' He stopped abruptly. Up and down the table eyes shifted to the door. There was an odd, expectant lull in the conversation.

In the attentive quiet the girl who stood framed in the doorway smiled, a little defiantly it seemed to Mattie. 'Well.' The husky voice, all Georgian, divided the word into two clear syllables. 'We'd quite given up on ever arrivin' at all. Seems like the whole state's buzzin' like a bechive.' Behind her a tall, fair young man waited, his eyes wary.

Johnny stood up. 'Lottie. Bram.' He smiled, woodenly. 'Welcome.'

Mattie came to her feet beside him. Together Charlotte and her husband entered the room. Conversation resumed around the table, though less boisterously. A few greetings were called to the newcomers. Bright, curious eyes watched as Johnny bent to brush Lottie's cheek with his lips, stiffly extended a hand to her husband. Perfunctorily Bram took it; dropped it again too quickly. And Mattie was sure that she was not the only one who sensed the current of fierce antagonism that flashed between the two young men like a bolt of lightning. Johnny drew her forward. She acknowledged their greetings, found herself briefly embracing the girl her husband had once loved. Once? How could that be so? Was it possible that any man who had loved this girl would not be bound by her for the rest of his life? Even standing as she did now – defensively poised, obviously uncertain despite the bright and defiant smile – she glowed with restless and vivid life. By no means did she possess the classic beauty that Mattie had somehow expected, nor even the conventional prettiness of which Cissy was so proud. But the nut-brown curls shone and danced as she moved, the remarkable green eyes were lit as if by sunlight and the creamy skin glowed with health and vitality. Her nose was small and tilted like a child's, her mouth wide and made for laughter. There was about her a bright and magnetic quality that Mattie sensed could draw even the most reluctant to her if she chose to exercise it.

'You had a good journey?' Mattie asked, politely. And tried desperately to ignore the unnecessarily fierce grip of her husband's hand upon her own, the look in those brilliant green eyes as they flickered to Johnny's face, and hastily away.

'Thank you, yes. Why, look – there's Russ, an' Robert, too. I declare I do believe they're both bigger than ever – don't you ole Sherwoods ever stop growin'?' The girl extricated them all from the difficult situation with grace, almost dancing to where Robert and Russell sat, planting playful kisses on each proffered cheek, bringing laughter from both as she whispered something into Robert's ear.

The moment had passed. Conversation swelled again. There were more arrivals at the door.

Mattie rose with an enthusiasm born of relief to greet them.

The party had been organized with a meticulous eye to everyone's comfort and enjoyment, from the youngest to the oldest visitor. In the cool, crisp afternoon there were children's games beneath the trees, the boys running races, the girls skipping, and dragging reluctant brothers into clapping and ring games. In the house the older ladies were ensconced in the parlour with tea, biscuits and cakes, whilst their young charges reluctantly rested in the bedrooms upstairs in excited anticipation of dancing in the evening. In the library, Logan Sherwood and his contemporaries enjoyed an excellent Madeira, smoked their cigars and discussed secession. In fact, Mattie thought, mildly exasperated, as she paused for a moment to watch the house servants transform the long hall into a ballroom for the evening's revels, one could be forgiven for thinking there was nothing else in the world to talk about. Even those young married women who had chosen to take advantage of their independent status and eschew the detested afternoon nap talked over their tea and cordial of little else; whilst their husbands, brothers and cousins gathered in small, noisy knots on the porches and in the dining room cursing the damn' Yankees with picturesque enthusiasm and raising their glasses – some of them already none too steadily – to the great and glorious Confederacy, to which South Carolina had so decisively shown the way. She tried not to watch Johnny; tried not to check every minute of the afternoon where he was, to whom he was talking. It was, she well knew, mean-spirited and unworthy to suspect that every minute he was not under her eye he was searching out the company of Lottie Taylor.

'Mattie, my dear.' Mrs Brightwell, a plump and beaming vision in velvet and feathers, caught her arm with small, soft hands. 'Do come and have a word with my good friend Mrs Hampton Deverell – she was in England just last year, and my dear she simply adored it.'

Supper was served in the dining room and in the parlour, every table and chair of any size or shape in the house having been pressed into service – some of the older guests indeed, knowing the problems of such a gathering, having brought their own chairs with them. The unmarried girls had fluttered down the stairs and back into the house like so many brilliant butterflies, decked now in silk and lace for the evening's festivities, fans, programmes and tiny pencils dangling from gloved wrists, hair piled and ringleted, shoulders smooth and bare in the candle-light. 'Laws! Miss Mattie,' Lucy had exclaimed earlier on, as she had helped her mistress change into the pretty pale green silk gown she was to wear for the evening, 'the way some of the young ladies do take on! To say nothin' of their uppity nigger gals – airs an' graces is the most of it! Nuthin' ain't good enough fo' them!'

In the ballroom a small dais had been erected, upon which was seated the orchestra. Every plantation musician from miles around had been ruthlessly poached by Joshua and the result was a very passable collection: a pianist, two violins, a cello and a trumpet. Mattie knew that they could play well together, for they had done nothing but practice in the back yard for the past forty-eight hours; she knew by heart every note of every piece they were to play during the evening.

'Miss Mattie?' She turned to find Joshua at her elbow. 'If you and Mister Johnny are ready? We can start the dancing when-ever you care to.'

Mattie glanced around a little nervously, alarmed to discover herself unprepared for the small responsibility of taking such a decision. What in God's name was the hothouse atmosphere of Pleasant Hill doing to her? 'Do you think it's time?'

The level of sound was deafening. Some people still sat at the table, others stood in groups, talking, arguing, laughing. The children had long since been taken home or packed off to bed in the small building known as the garconnier, a guest-house with three bedrooms upstairs and two down, which stood a hundred yards or so from the house, well away from the noise. Two busy house servants, neat and smart in white jackets and black trousers, were replenishing glasses. As Mattie stood un-decided, a group of young men came in from the front porch, where no doubt they had been savouring Logan Sherwood's excellent cigars, and his even more excellent whisky. The tall, fair figure of Bram Taylor was one of them. 'Damnation to the Yanks, I say!' His voice was far too loud, the words a little slurred. He ignored the half-hearted attempts his companions made to quieten him. 'One Southerner's worth any ten of them factory-broke hirelings! We'll make 'em eat their own –' The end of the sentence was cut off abruptly as a large red-headed young man with admirable presence of mind clapped a hand across his companion's mouth.

'It's time, Ma'am.' Joshua's deep voice held a thread of amusement, and as Mattie glanced at him she caught in that intelligent, normally impassive face a sudden and unguarded gleam of laughter. And again there was that uncanny and unnerving likeness to Johnny. For the first time since the disaster of their first meeting, she smiled at him openly and without embarrassment, sharing his amusement; and was surprised at her pleasure when, as openly, he returned her smile.

'Thank you, Joshua. I think you're right. If you'll find Mister Johnny for me?'

Mattie and Johnny opened the dancing, waltzing together as the onlookers clapped. As young men around the room claimed their partners and stepped onto the floor, she looked up into her husband's face. He smiled down at her. 'You're enjoying our party?'

'Yes. Very much.'

He grinned. 'It isn't Bath, I'm afraid.'

She laughed aloud, aware of his arms about her, aware of the perilous depths of her feelings for him. Trying not to remember Lottie Taylor's lovely, vivid face. Trying not to care that there was not, yet, a baby. 'So far as I'm concerned that's something to be thankful for!'

She danced with Russell, who made her laugh so much that she fell over her own feet, and with good-natured Will, who tried hard to concentrate but spent a greater part of the time gazing over her head to where Cissy danced with the large red-headed young man who had silenced Bram Taylor's intemperate tongue. She sat out with Robert, who declared himself so bad a dancer that anything was better than braving the floor with him. His conversation was light and quite scurrilously funny as he gave her potted histories of the families in the room. 'I don't believe a word of it!' Mattie said, glad that he could be so light-hearted, wondering if – hoping that – he had perhaps come to terms with his own personal demon now that the choice was apparently to be forced upon him.

'Which just goes to show,' he said, bending over her hand with an entertaining show of gallantry, 'what exceptionally good taste in women my young brother has. Though what on earth a clever girl like you ever saw in him is way beyond me.'

She had drunk just a little too much wine, she knew it, though the feeling was far from unpleasant. As the evening wore on and the evidently quite genuine goodwill towards her of most of these people – Johnny's friends, neighbours and relatives, most of whom had known him all his life – was borne upon her she felt herself relaxing. Despite the talk of war, her heart and her spirits were lifted. This, after all, was her wedding party; and of all the celebrations that had gone before, this was, she realized, the one that mattered. This was her family, these now were her neighbours and her friends. She moved from group to group, joining in the talk and the laughter, accompanying an elderly gentleman in the shabby splendour of a long-tailed, velvet-collared coat that must have come out from England at least fifty years before, onto the dance floor for a remarkably spritely reel. Restoring him to his obviously astounded wife, she slipped into the empty dining room. It was cool and quiet. The tall windows had been opened to allow the flow of air. She walked to them, stood for a moment breathing deeply, savouring the freshness upon her hot face. She felt just a little dizzy, and quite alarmingly happy. Soft in her velvet slippers, she stepped out onto the porch.

The two figures at the opposite end of the wide, shadowed veranda did not notice her. Lit by the flaring torches that had been set about the house, they stood in a world of their own, neither touching nor speaking, simply looking at one another, the girl's brown, shining head thrown back, ribbons streaming from her curls across her shoulders and down her back, the man, tall, broad-shouldered, dark, looking down into her face as if no other sight in the world would ever satisfy his eyes.

Mattie stood as if struck to stone; and stone, suddenly, was her heart, heavy and cold.

Johnny lifted a hand very slowly, his eyes still not leaving

Lottie's face. Mattie could see the tears now, gleaming in torch-light. In a gesture more tender, more terrible, than she had ever seen, her husband touched the girl's cheek gently with the back of his curled fingers. For the briefest of seconds her small hand came up to cover his then, wide skirt swaying at the abrupt movement, she stepped back a little, away from him, pressing herself against the balcony railings as far from him as she could get, shaking her head despairingly, her eyes still clinging to his. Johnny dropped his hand and threw his head back in a sharp and savage movement of pain, his throat and jaw clenched against sound.

'Johnny – oh, Johnny, please!' The girl pushed herself away from the rail and stepped into his arms, her hands reaching to pull his mouth down to hers.

Mattie stepped back through the film of the curtains into the dining room. She felt as if every last drop of blood had drained from her heart and from her body. She was trembling, ice cold; her stomach had curdled to nausea.

'Miss Mattie?'

She looked blindly towards the sound of the voice.

Joshua took two swift strides, caught her shoulders, held her upright. 'Miss Mattie! What is it? What ails you?' As he spoke the curtain billowed. He looked towards it, then back at Mattie. Mattie stood as if deaf, dumb and sightless. Satisfied that she could stand alone, his hands dropped from her shoulders. Watching her still, he moved lightly to the window.

Within a moment he was back, his hands firm on her arms, his voice soft, fierce and steady. 'Go back to the party, Miss Mattie. Go find Mister Robert. Dance with him.'

'I – can't.'

'You can. You must. Miss Mattie, listen – look at me.'

With an effort she tried to focus her eyes upon his face. He spoke rapidly and urgently, his face intent as he willed her to understand. 'No-one must know they're out there! You hear me? No-one! It'd mean blood – blood and death – Miss Mattie! Listen!'

'I'm – listening.' Listening but not understanding.

'There's bad blood already between Mister Johnny and the

Taylor boy – they've both been drinking. Given half a chance they'll be at one another's throats. Miss Mattie, *think*!'

She blinked, her eyes focusing at last. 'You mean, Bram Taylor would try to – to kill Johnny if he thought –'

'Nothing's more certain. There'd be murder done, one way or another. Miss Charlotte never could keep control, of herself or of others.' His low voice was savage, then again urgent; she felt his hands tighten, as if he would shake her. 'Miss Mattie, think what could happen – think of the scandal – think of the family –'

Think of the family. Think of my marriage. What marriage? Think of the child, of the child that I want so much, and that never comes. Is it my fault? Think of Johnny, dead, the red blood of his treacherous, lying heart seeping into the red earth of this cursed land –

Joshua was still talking; but his face was softer now, his quiet voice compassionate, persuasive. 'Miss Mattie, please! It doesn't mean anything! It doesn't! Give him a chance to explain. Go back to the party. I'll get Mister Johnny in, before anyone else sees them. Apart from anything else, if his father finds out he'll have his hide in strips.'

'You think that should bother me?' Mattie was shocked at the venom in the words, in her low, shaking voice.

'No. But the trouble that could come from this should. You've not had an easy ride, Miss Mattie. I know it. But believe me, if you throw a fit now and create a public scandal it'll do nothing but make things worse. For you and for everyone. It's in your hands, Miss Mattie. I'm asking you to go back to the party. Go to Mister Robert. Tell him if you have to, though better not – but no-one else! Please, Miss Mattie?'

The shock was wearing off. The chill was ebbing, to be replaced by a pain and rage worse than she had ever felt, even at the death of her father. 'Very well,' she heard herself saying, suddenly composed, aching to hurt someone. 'I'll go. And I won't tell anyone, certainly not Robert. What do you think I am? The silly child you people seem intent on making me? Don't worry, Joshua. I'll safeguard your precious, unflawed – contemptible – family honour.' She held his eyes for a moment, letting her own ask, as openly as words, You? You speak of their honour? and was bitterly rewarded by a subtle but unmistakable answering flare of anger, quickly veiled, in his. Somewhere a new Mattie noted that Joshua was not, perhaps, quite what Joshua purported to be. 'I'll protect my husband's worthless hide. Just don't tell him, you hear? Don't let him know that I saw them.' She lifted angry, defiant eyes to that face so like, yet so unlike, Johnny's in which now she saw suddenly an unexpected and wholly unwelcome sympathy. 'Leave me that pleasure at least.' She wrenched herself away from his supporting hands, put her hands to her hair, turning from him, composing herself. Then with no backward glance she walked out through the door and back to her wedding party.

The trials of the night were not quite over. At midnight those revellers, young and not so young, who were still on their feet insisted upon escorting the happy couple out onto the back porch and up the stairs to their rooms amidst showers of rice and dried flower petals, and much ribald advice. It had been easy enough to avoid Johnny until then; not easy at all to prevent herself from snatching her hand from his when he took it, from slapping his face with all her strength when he asked, solicitously, above the racket if she were tired. As they left the hall, running the gauntlet of arched and lifted arms, she caught Joshua's eyes upon her, impassive once again.

Their rooms were quiet; a small fire burned in the grate of the sitting room, the bed was turned down. Every other room in the house had been turned virtually into a dormitory for overnight guests but, given the nature of the celebration, it had been agreed, to Cissy's disgust since she and Will were sharing their rooms with a family with three small children, that the newlyweds' rooms should be left to them. Both Lucy and Johnny's man, Shake, had been given the night off from their private duties to help the overburdened house servants. Johnny, still a little breathless, loosened his cravat. 'Some party!'

'Yes.'

He glanced at her. 'You tired, honey?'

'Yes.'

'That ain't surprisin'.' His laughter, Mattie thought, was strained. She turned her back on him. She was tired. Bone tired. Tired, she thought, almost to death. She did not want to look at him, to talk with him, to touch him. She had gone beyond fury to a hurt and a misery so deep that she felt nothing would assuage it.

'You want me to help with that?' She had reached behind her to the tiny buttons that fastened the back of her dress.

'No,' she said, too swiftly, then realizing that in fact she could not manage on her own, nodded. 'Well, yes, please. If you would. Just these top ones. I can manage the rest.'

He undid the buttons neatly and, without touching her, retreated to the fire. Suddenly she understood. Tonight he no more wanted her than she did him. The thought brought nothing but relief.

'Hon?' His voice was tentative.

'Yes?'

'There's – well, there's a game goin' on over in the big barn – I wondered – you bein' so exhausted, an' all?'

'A game?'

'A card school. Poker –' He watched her, warily.

She shrugged. She knew it to be true. She also knew that Bram and Lottie Taylor had left for Macon with a family everyone called the 'Macon Joneses' with whom they were staying, an hour or so before. 'Go on over. I don't mind.'

Johnny was gone with an alacrity that might, under other circumstances, have been wounding. As it was, she endured his peck on the cheek, nodded at his injunction to sleep well.

After he had left Mattie undressed, slipped a warm woollen gown, loose and belted, over her nightdress, and lay for a long time on the bed, eyes wide and staring into the lamplit shadows. Then, with the sound of revelry in the house below at last beginning to die down, she sat up abruptly, rummaged in the wardrobe, slipped her feet into a pair of stout shoes and opened the outer door. The yard was deserted, the kitchen quiet at last, the fires still glowing through the open door. Swiftly she slipped down the stairs and out across the packed dirt yard.

Jake heard her coming from fifty yards off. 'Sssh!' she whispered, fiercely, as he bounded about her, tangling her in his chain, making it impossible to free him. 'Be still, you great stupid animal!'

The dog quietened a little, more because his long, rasping tongue had found an interesting taste of salt upon his mistress's face than for any reason of discipline. With diligent, loving enthusiasm he worked to clean it off. 'Jake, stop it! And quiet! That's right. Good dog. Here.' She tied a length of rope around his neck. 'Now, do behave, or you'll choke yourself – or someone will hear us – there – that's better.'

Mattie never discovered if Johnny ever knew that she spent that night curled upon their bed with her arms about the huge dog, safe in his uncomplicated devotion, her face buried in his warm and comforting fur. Her groom, in company with a fair few of his friends, drank himself into a stupor over a cut-throat game in the barn and slept it off in the straw until daylight.

CHAPTER SEVEN

Any attempt to celebrate Christmas in a normal or whole-heartedly festive fashion that year was out of the question. In common with most of the rest of the state, indeed with most of the rest of the country, the talk around the Sherwood table was of nothing but the timing of the inevitable secession and the now apparently equally inevitable coming war. In such circumstances the celebration of birth, the promise of peace and the hope of salvation came a very poor second. At Pleasant Hill, too, there was an added uncomfortable dimension, as there must have been in many homes up and down the land as a course of events was set in train that could so easily set brother against brother. As the others, with blithe and perilous eagerness, made plans for the troop to enlist as a body the moment that war became certain, Robert remained inflexibly silent. Against the ever more edgy banter of his brothers and through a couple of blistering interviews with his father, he stubbornly held out; he would not fight. He believed in the Union and he believed in democracy; it was not his opinion that secession and war could serve either cause. No-one, including Robert himself, mentioned his views on the institution of slavery.

Cissy it was who, with typical lack of discretion, voiced most flatly the inevitable consequences of such a stand. On the fourth day of the new year the family sat at table discussing the seizing by state troops of the arsenals in the Southern towns of Charleston and Mobile, and the fact that young Edward Packard, to his Sherwood cousins' envy, had likely been with the Volunteer Militia who the day before had marched into the massive brick fortress of Pulaski at the mouth of the Savannah river, taking it for the South without firing a shot. Cissy regarded Robert's closed, attentive face with bright and challenging eyes. 'You can stay silent or you can talk till you're blue, Robert,' she said, suddenly, 'you must know there's not a soul round here but'll think you're showin' the white feather iffen y'all don't go off with the others.' She cast a defiant glance at the faces about her. 'Who'd blame them? After all, just about *everyone's* talkin' about goin'.'

In the silence that followed, Logan Sherwood folded his napkin very neatly, laid it by his plate. Looked up. 'Well,' he said, easily and quietly, 'we all know how to deal with anyone who ventures such an opinion, do we not?'

'Sure do, Pa.' Will came as close to a disapproving scowl as ever seemed possible with him as he looked at his young wife. 'We sure do.'

'I'm only sayin' what people'll *think*.'

'People,' Logan said, mildly, 'may of course think whatever they wish. But should anyone choose to voice any such thought about any one o' my sons I for one would take it very – personally.' His disconcerting, light gaze moved again round the table. Johnny and Russ, mouths full, nodded vehemently.

Robert had flushed deeply. 'Pa –'

Logan ignored the interruption. 'And since I'm sure that most of our friends and neighbours would understand that, I somehow doubt that the situation will arise. Now, I've two suggestions to make. First that you boys should make your choice of a servant each to go with you; could be that it'd be a good idea to start to take the darkies with you when you go over to Silver Oaks – teach 'em the ropes – and since it's beginning to look as if the running of the plantation well may have to be put on an emergency footing before too long, I suggest that you make a list of your responsibilities about the place that require supervision by Robert or myself, for discussion within the next few days.' He turned with a faint and caustic smile to Cissy. 'For I too, my dear, will not be takin' up arms. It seems from enquiries I have been makin' that there's no place in the army for an old wolf like me. Fightin's for the cubs, they say. Appears they think I'm better occupied here on the land, with the women an' the children –'

'Pa!' Johnny stared at him. 'You? You'd have enlisted?'

'If they'd had the sense to let me, of course.' The huge white head came up. His fierce, pale eyes were focused upon Robert's face. 'My homeland and my way of life is threatened; in the cause of honour, in the cause of truth and in the cause of justice, what else would you have had me do but try?'

There was a long, awkward moment of silence before Robert pushed his chair away from the table, nodding in courtesy to Mattie and to Cissy, addressing his father. 'You'll excuse me, Pa? I've got some of the hands out by the swamp mendin' that fencin' that came down in the winds. I'd best go give an eye to them.'

'Perhaps,' Mattie ventured a little later that evening to Johnny, 'perhaps it's just as well that Robert feels as he does? Your father might find it hard to run Pleasant Hill single-handed?' They were in their small sitting room. The short Southern winter had set in; rain drove in gusts against the shuttered windows.

'Pa could run Georgia single-handed. Shake, you no-good nigger, what d'you think you're playing at? You want me to take some other boy to war with me?'

'No, Sir, Mister Johnny.' Shake allowed himself a wide grin; they both knew the likelihood that Johnny would take anyone else away with him was slight. 'Sorry, Mister Johnny.' He set himself to draw the skin-tight boot from Johnny's foot with slightly less exuberant force.

'No, when Robert goes, Pa'll take care of everythin' real well, you'll see.'

Mattie laid her embroidery upon her lap, turned her head to look at him. 'When Robert goes? When he goes where?'

Johnny stretched his long legs and wriggled his toes before the fire. 'When he enlists, of course.' He turned a genuinely amused face to her. 'You don't take all this talk seriously, do you? Lord, Mattie, this is *Robert*. He's never been any different; when I was five years old I remember he couldn't go fishin' without callin' a committee meetin' about it!'

'And – you think this is the same?'

''Course it is! Just wait till it happens; wait till we go. Wait till the first time we take on the Yankees an' make 'em run!

He'll be out there to join us like a bullet from a gun, I'd lay my life on it! Robert's as much a Sherwood as any of us. It just isn't always as obvious. That'll do, Shake. Off you go.'

'Yes, Mister Johnny. Goodnight, Mister Johnny. Miss Mattie.'

'Goodnight, Shake.'

Johnny had stood up, huge in his stockinged feet, and stretched, his eyes on Mattie. She felt the sudden familiar, treacherous stirrings of warmth, in her body and in her face, under his gaze. He smiled. 'Dove's in the dovecote, turkey's in the barn. Time you an' me was in bed.'

She stood up. 'You'll never rival Mr Shelley, I'm afraid.'

'Don't aim to.' He came to her, reached to the pins in her hair, his big hands deft. 'Don't send for Lucy. No need.'

She let him undress her, let him, as he liked to do, carry her into the bedroom and lay her upon the bed. She let him veil them both in her hair, let him touch and stroke her, with hand and with mouth; more, she did for him those things that he had taught her brought him pleasure. And, painfully, they brought her pleasure too – painfully, because through it all a small, clear voice in that hatefully detached part of her soul that not even Johnny had ever touched asked: how could he? And how could I? How could he, who loved another woman, speak the words he spoke, caress her body with such ardour, penetrate her with such tender and restrained force that they both cried out in the delight of it? And how could she, who had seen him lift a hand to another face, who had seen his tears, heard his unspoken cry, how could she allow this? Worse, how could she allow it without telling him that she knew? Without confessing that she distrusted him for every single minute that he was out of her sight? That her imagination supplied him with more illicit opportunity to meet his other love – his real love – than practicality could ever possibly allow, given the distance between them? In the first twenty-four hours after that awful night – the hours of anguish in which she was determined to wreck them both in the cause of justice and her own brutal hurt – they had hardly passed a moment in each other's company, and the opportunity simply had not presented itself. Even in her misery and rage Mattie could not bring herself to the humiliation of a public quarrel. And by the time the house had settled and the last guests had left it was Christmas Eve, rumours of troop movements were rife, serious talk of secession and war had taken over, and she had found herself forced to face the fact that at any moment Johnny might be taken from her by more than the lucent green eyes and gallant smile of another woman. To bring it into the open would have been to force a crisis; a crisis that might have driven him from her for ever, and at such a time. What then? Was that what she wanted? It was a cruel situation, made worse because she had no-one to whom could she turn, no friend in whom she could confide. Christmas was upon them; Johnny's greetings were apparently loving, his gifts thoughtful; how could she not accept them? His lips were warm on hers; how could she not respond? It seemed more and more certain with each passing day that he would be going to war. And, faithless or not, perfidious or simply fallible, he was her husband and she wanted desperately to bear his child. So, despising herself, she did not tell him of what she had seen on the night of the party. She buried the searing memory as deeply as she could, although never deep enough, and tried to pretend that nothing had happened. She lectured herself, stretching charity to the limit. Johnny and Charlotte had been childhood sweethearts – there would always be special affection between them, and rightly so. Bram Taylor, on short acquaintance, did not strike Mattie as being a man she would wish her worst enemy tied to; of course Johnny would feel badly about what had happened. Too much wine, and too bright an eye; if even the most respectable of novels were counted to reflect life, then many a less susceptible soul had been carried away by such circumstances. The scene she had witnessed meant nothing – nothing! – in balance of the fact that it was she, Mattie, that Johnny had married, it was she, Mattie, with whom he laughed, discussed his day and to whom he turned each night. It was she, Mattie, who would some day bear his son.

Only on these nights when he lay beside her, breathing quietly, his arm flung across her breast, his dark head heavy and still upon the pillow did she lie and ask herself: how could he? How could I? And, cruellest thought of all: as we loved, did he think of her?

Within the month, state after state followed South Carolina's lead and left the Union. Mississippi, Florida, Alabama – and, on the nineteenth day of January, Georgia, to be followed a week later by Louisiana. The four Sherwood brothers went to Milledgeville, the state's capital, on that day to hear the proclamation; when they returned the tension between Robert and the others was palpable. Questioned by Mattie, Johnny was curt and unforthcoming; that there had been argument was obvious. Acceptance of secession was by no means entirely universal. Some there had been in Milledgeville to unfurl the old Union flag in defiance, and to preach peace and reconciliation, but there had been few to listen.

'Laws! Miss Mattie, I surely wish I knowed what was goin' ter happen now.' Lucy's quick fingers rested for a moment upon the petticoat she was mending, her large, soft eyes lifting to Mattie's. 'Them Yankees – they goin' ter come here? I's real scared, Miss Mattie. Ol' Mose says them Yankees'll hang any nigger they can git their han's on.'

'Oh, Lucy, for goodness' sake! Things are bad enough without such talk! No, the Yankees aren't going to come here. And, anyway, they don't have horns and a tail, you know.' Mattie pulled herself up and raised rueful brows. 'Though you'd better not say that I said so. It isn't a fashionable view around here.' She laid aside the book she had been reading and walked to the window. 'Heavens, this rain! It's as bad as home!' She stopped, surprised at the sudden wrench of pain that the memory and the unthinking word engendered. For a moment the green fields and lush woodlands of Kent superimposed themselves upon the alien landscape of red mud and moss-hung trees beyond the window. She saw the ancient, comfortable, wood-panelled rooms of Coombe House, the low, rambling passages, the stone-flagged kitchen – she blinked, and cleared her throat a little.

'It must be real strange, Miss Mattie, to come way cross the ocean – an' be set among strangers?' Lucy's voice was soft with sympathy.

'Yes. It is.' Mattie kept her back resolutely turned. Not for the first time the irony struck her; if she had to name the one person in this house that she counted as a friend, that person would be Lucy. In the past days and weeks the girl had served her devotedly; more, had supported and encouraged her in a way that no-one else had. Sometimes Mattie wondered how much Lucy knew, how much she divined, of the strains in the relationship between her mistress and the young Mister Johnny. Mattie had been in Georgia for long enough now to believe, as Aunt Bess had maintained over and again in Savannah, that there was little of any note that a personal slave did not know or perceive of his or her owner's affairs.

Before the fire Jake stretched and yawned, lifting his great golden head to lay it upon the fallen book.

'Why, you big ol' devil, look what you doin' to Miss Mattie's book!' A touch over-indignant in her effort to lighten the moment, Lucy jumped up, scolding, to rescue the little volume. 'Git off there, you slobberin' houn'! You done creased it up!'

She brought the book to Mattie, wiping the page with her sleeve. 'Don' know what that great ol' nuisance is doin' bein' allowed in here!' she grumbled, smiling.

'Yes, you do. You know very well.' Mattie took the book, smoothing the pages. 'Why, look, Lucy – here's your name!' She pointed to the word. 'You see? L.U.C.Y. Lucy.' She held the book for the girl to see.

Lucy leaned forward, her face suddenly intent. Her dark finger with its pale pink nail rested for a moment on the book, tracing the letters. 'That say Lucy? That say my name?'

'Yes.'

'An' this? What it say 'bout me?' She ran her finger along the line that followed the word.

Mattie laughed. '"Lucy for her part had not a care in the world",' she read, '"but that the birds should sing, and the sun shine. She was young, and it was summer. Tomorrow's troubles could wait their turn."'

'It done says that?'

'That's what it says.'

Lucy's serene smile lit her face. 'Sounds good 'nuff to me.'
She turned again to the book. 'Miss Mattie? Where it say "sun"?'

'Here – see? S.U.N. Sun.'

'Ess? Why you says ess? An' why me?' The girl's mystified
interest was edged with the slightest degree of frustration.

'Because that's what the letter's called. Ess. And I didn't say
"You", I said "U".' Mattie stopped, shaking her head. 'Oh dear.
Perhaps I'd better start again.'

A long time later, Lucy broke into their absorbed and self-
appointed task to straighten and ask abruptly, 'This ain't like
teachin' me to read, is it, Miss Mattie? Mister Logan – he sends
me to the barn for sure, iffen he knows you's teachin' me to
read. Laws! When Poge came out an' just *asked* to learn the
mass'er done wore him out in that barn an' then sent him out
to the fiel's – never let that nigger back in the house ag'in. I
would'n' wan' that, Miss Mattie! Sure wouldn't!'

Mattie stiffened, her finger still upon a word. 'I suppose – I
suppose, yes, these are the first steps to learning to read.' She
turned her head to look into intelligent eyes that had become
huge with fright. 'But, Lucy, there's no question of your being
sent to the barn, nor to the fields for that matter.' Floggings
were not frequent events on Pleasant Hill; when accounted
necessary, a whipping would be administered in the big barn
and sometimes, for the purposes of discipline, in front of the
assembled hands. The shackles upon the barn door were a grim
and permanent testament to the building's use on these
occasions; the mere threat of being 'sent to the barn' was usually enough to curtail any misbehaviour. 'Mister Sherwood gave
you to me. I should never allow such a thing to happen. However, if it worries you, then of course I shouldn't dream of continuing.' She snapped the book shut.

Lucy made a small protesting movement with her hand, then
stilled.

Mattie eyed her coolly, knowing her own irritation to be not
only unjust and unkind, but levelled at the wrong person. That
Logan Sherwood's relentless hand should show itself here, in

127

her own small domain, was certainly intolerable; it was hardly poor Lucy's fault. 'Well?'

'I – don' know, Miss Mattie.'

'Please yourself, Lucy. Just let me know when you've decided.'

'Yes, Miss Mattie.'

Mattie lifted the book with a sudden quick smile. 'It would of course be an entirely private arrangement. Just between you and me. No-one need know.'

Again that lovely smile lit the creamy-dark features. 'Yes, Miss Mattie. Jus' us two? That'd be diff'rent for sure, wouldn't it?'

The troop at Silver Oaks had become the pride of the countryside; there was hardly a plantation in the area that did not have its representative in 'The Colonel's Boys'. That most of them had known each other from birth, wrestled each other, swum in the same rivers, climbed the same trees, ridden the same horses, courted the same girls, made for a camaraderie, a true *esprit de corps*, that many a more professional outfit might have envied. There was, however, another side to this coin; they were a reckless bunch, and their blood was high – it was only to be expected that old rivalries, and in some cases old antagonisms, would also be perpetuated. So on the day that Bram Taylor rode up to Silver Oaks on as spirited a piece of horseflesh as any in the troop could boast, his rifle at his saddle, his boy Zach at his heels, his wide-brimmed hat on his saddle horn and his fair hair a defiant pennant in the cool winter breeze, the odds were on for a fight.

It was not long in coming.

By the middle of February the young nation of the Confederate States of America had been born and was growing and thriving. She had her own Constitution and her own unanimously elected president in Jefferson Davis – a man born, in space and in time, uncannily close to that other President, whose seat was Washington and whose person was the most unequivocally detested in the South. By an ironic quirk of fortune, the two presidents had been born barely a year apart, and within one hundred miles of each other in the state of Kentucky. It was one of those unlucky border states between North and South whose divided loyalties had and would cause heartache and bloodshed for its people. Spirits in the South were high. It was only a matter of time before Virginia, Tennessee, North Carolina and probably others joined the fight to protect old freedoms. Europe would back the Cotton States, and would not see her ports blockaded for long, for reasons that the pragmatic recognized to be as much to do with trade as with sympathy. And if it did come to conflict – what could the industrialized, money-grubbing, immigrant-ridden North produce to match the gallant, dedicated young of the South? Such loyalty and honour could not be bought, such sense of fierce pride instilled overnight into a nation of accountants and factory hands. If an attack should come, it would come from the North; the South did nothing but defend her own soil. A soil sacred, or so the legend ran, to every Southerner who drew breath.

Bram Taylor, who had married – in circumstances of which no man in the troop could fail to be aware – the only child of an old Georgian family, actually hailed from Arkansas, a state that had not yet declared her allegiance to the star of the Confederacy. Johnny Sherwood, backed by his brothers, was ready and willing to make all that could be made from that, and did. If everyone knew, or at least suspected, that the actual causes of the enmity between them ran deeper than that, it was of no consequence; the result in the end was bound to be the same.

Mattie was throwing sticks into the river for Jake when she heard the drum of hooves on the dirt track that could only signal the return of the three young men from Silver Oaks. She called the dog, stepped back laughing as he shook himself dry, and turned to go back to the house. It was a day in early March that showed every sign of spring, though the ground was still sodden from torrential rain the day before. She picked her way onto the track, waved as her husband and his brothers came into sight. Jake bounded amongst them, barking. Shake, riding behind the three brothers with the other two servants, slipped from his saddle and collared the big dog, dragging him away from the skittering horses.

'Good day, young Miz' Sherwood.' With ceremony Russ swept the stylish, wide-brimmed, plumed hat that was part of the troop's new uniform from his head and bowed courteously in the saddle, grinning. 'Y'all got room for three hungry soldier boys at your table today, Ma'am?'

Mattie regarded him with tranquil eyes, joining the game, emphasizing her clipped English accent. 'By all means, Captain, providing you-all take your muddy boots off first. The last troop I had in simply ruined the Aubusson. To say nothing of – Johnny!' She stopped, startled into normality. 'Johnny – what have you done?' Turning to her husband she had seen his face, which had until now been shaded by the brim of his hat. A large, picturesque bruise, purple and green, swelled upon his cheekbone, half closing his right eye.

Russ laughed, urging his horse forward. 'Don't worry about him, Mattie – you should see the other fella!' He grinned widely, and his horse, restless and full of energy as its rider, danced around her. Easily, one-handed he controlled it, swinging away from her, his bright face full of mischief.

As his brothers moved off, laughing, Johnny swung from the saddle to walk beside her, his arm about her waist, Arrow stepping daintily behind them. 'Now don't fuss, Mattie.'

'What did he mean? What other fellow?'

'Don't be silly – Russ was joking. I took a tumble, is all. We aren't playing ring o'roses, you know. These things happen.' He grinned down at her. There was an air of high-strung excitement about him, his eyes were fierce with laughter.

She laid her head against his arm for the briefest of moments. 'Oh, Johnny, I do wish you'd be more careful! You really do all look on this as a game, don't you?'

'A game?' As she looked up at him he shook his head. 'No, Mattie – not a game. An adventure. A crusade!' He swung her to face him, planted a kiss on her mouth. 'You'll be proud of us all, Mattie, see if you won't!'

* * *

130

They were at supper when Joshua came swiftly into the room to bend to Logan Sherwood's ear. The talk about the table died down in surprise, but before Logan could react to Joshua's urgency they all heard it; a man's voice from beyond the door that led to the front porch, lifted in bitter, drawling challenge. 'You there, Johnny Sherwood? You ready to take me on man to man, 'thout your big brothers steppin' in to look after you?' The words were very slightly slurred.

Johnny stood up abruptly, his chair rocking dangerously.

'Johnny! Sit down!' Logan Sherwood lifted a sharp finger.

'But, Pa!'

'Sit down, I say! Joshua, I'm sure we can leave this to you? Kindly inform the young man that we are at supper, and that we have ladies present. If he wishes to speak with me or with any of my sons in a civilized manner later, we will be at his disposal. Offer him refreshment, if you will – something other than alcohol, I think.'

'Johnny Sherwood! You hear me? You think I'm gonna let you get away with it? Sniffin' 'round a man's wife like a –?'

Johnny was out of his chair and at the door before anyone could stop him. With a roar he flung himself out onto the porch. 'You hold your filthy tongue, Taylor, or by God I'll cut it out, you damn' drunken Yankee! What I started this afternoon I can finish, here an' now –'

Joshua had moved almost as fast as Johnny, and was behind him as Johnny braced himself, hands on the balcony rail, to glare at the figure who stood below him, feet braced, defiant but by no means entirely steady. Just out of the circle of light cast by the lamps in front of the house, feet shuffled in the mud, and shining eyes in faces dark as the surrounding shadows watched, bright with interest.

'Well, I just bet you think you can.' The words were spoken aggressively slowly and with precise, drunken venom. 'An' ain't that just why I'm here? To show you diff'rent. I don't care for – unfinished business – of whatever kind.'

'What in the devil's name is this all about?' Logan snapped at Will.

Will shrugged huge shoulders, glancing at Russ. 'There was

a bit of trouble over at Silver Oaks this afternoon, Pa. Johnny and Bram – well, they had a bit of a scrap – we had to pull 'em off each other. The Colonel was real mad – sounds like Bram's bin off somewheres an' got himself a skinful.'

Mattie had frozen in her seat, her face set.

'You wan' to come down here an' face me, Sherwood? I done showed you once, last year, who was the better man – you wan' me to pound it into you? You wan' me ter make you tell me what you been doin' sneakin' 'round my wife when my back was turned, or you goin' ter do it your own self?'

Johnny launched himself too quickly for Joshua to prevent it. His feet were on the rail, and his big body, agile as a cat's, was propelled through the air to fell the other man in one move-ment. They rolled in the sticky red mud in a savage, grunting tangle of arms and legs.

Cissy uttered an excited shriek, jumped from her chair, lifted her skirts and ran out onto the porch. White-faced with anger, Logan Sherwood strode after her. The other three boys sat for a moment, looking from one to the other, obviously at a loss. Mattie flinched as there clearly came the crack of fist against bone and one of the combatants rasped in pain.

'Johnny!' Logan Sherwood roared. 'You get back up here this minute, you hear me, boy?'

The answer was another grim smacking of bone and flesh.

With one accord Will and Russ moved fast from their chairs to join their father on the porch. Mattie was left facing Robert. She sat quite still, trying not to listen to the savage sounds beyond the open doors. Robert reached a hand in silence. After a moment she took it, accepted its quick, warm grip of sympathy, then stood composedly and went out onto the porch with the others.

At first glance, in the darkness and after that initial ferocious, muddy scramble, it was difficult to tell one man from the other. Both were plastered from head to toe in red mud, blood smeared both faces. But Johnny had the height, the weight and the reach, and Bram was slighter, and drunk. Even Mattie, appalled, could see that it was no contest.

'Enough!' Logan's voice cracked like a whip. 'Johnny! Enough!'

Again Johnny's fist connected with his opponent's face. Again the other man rocked, and refused to fall.

'*Johnny! Enough, I say!*'

Grimly, open-handed this time, and unloosing every savage ounce of power in shoulder and arm, Johnny struck again, knocking Bram Taylor completely off his feet. The man sprawled in the mud.

Johnny bent and with blind and terrible strength lifted him by his shirtfront. Again open-handed, he slapped the other man's face, back and forth, his own teeth bared like an animal's.

'Johnny! Stop it! For God's sake! Stop it!' Mattie was at the rail, her hands gripping it as if it were the only solid thing in the world.

'Joshua,' Logan Sherwood said.

'Dog!' Johnny lashed out again. Bram staggered, blinded. 'Yankee bastard!' Another precise blow. The fair, handsome face was wrecked, swollen and bleeding. Obstinately the drunken man struggled upright once more, fists flailing.

Mattie put her hands to her face.

'Joshua, you have my permission to stop this.'

'Yes, Sir, Mister Logan.'

With an economy of movement that blurred the eye, Joshua stepped forward, slid a long arm about Bram Taylor's narrow waist and lifted him, swinging him bodily away from the next blow, depositing him with neither apology nor ceremony on all fours in the mud before turning to face Johnny's poised fist. Every watcher held his breath. For one moment it looked as if Johnny would not be able to control himself and that massive fist would explode into Joshua's dark, shadowed face. For the moment of a long breath they stood so, Joshua still and impassive in the torchlight. Then Johnny's arm fell to his side. He shook his head, as if waking.

'Johnny. Get back up here.' Logan Sherwood's voice was quiet, contained, and brought every eye to his expressionless face. 'Joshua, have Mister Taylor cared for, please, and escorted home.' His cold eye cast beyond the torchlit circle. With no sound the watchers began to melt into darkness. Mattie turned and walked back into the dining room where the meal sat congealing on the table, and two wide-eyed house servants stood, waiting, only their eyes moving from face to face as the family came, silent, into the room. Johnny, muddy from head to foot, blood running from his nose and his knuckles raw, stepped last through the door, to face every gaze.

There was a very long moment of quiet.

'I'm sorry, Pa,' Johnny said at last, brushing the back of his hand across his marked face, and avoiding his father's eyes.

'So you should be, son. A more unseemly show I've not seen in a lifetime.' Logan let a significant silence develop. 'But seems to me there's someone else deserves your apology more?'

Mattie, as all eyes turned to her, would have given every last drop of her blood to be elsewhere. For a moment she looked obdurately at the carpet. Then, gritting her teeth, she lifted her head to face her husband.

'I'm sorry, Mattie,' he said. But she could see the anger and resentment in him, sensed her own rising to confront it. Despair gripped her.

'You'd best get yourself cleaned up.' Logan's voice was impersonal.

'Yes, Pa.' With no look to left or right, Johnny left the room. Beyond the door they heard his barking voice: 'Shake? 'Ziah? Fetch some water, an' quick about it. Joshua – you got some salve?'

Mattie stood for a moment longer. She was alarmed to discover that every smallest part of her was trembling, imperceptibly, like an aspen leaf in the breath of a summer breeze; she was surprised to find that her limbs and her voice obeyed her with every appearance of composure. 'If you'll excuse me?' Head up, she followed the sound of her husband's defensively angry voice out of the room and up the stairs to their rooms.

She watched in silence as his hurts were bathed and doctored. In a silence no less painful, Johnny withstood the ministrations. With the slaves dismissed the room was quiet, deceptively peaceful; the fire flickered in the hearth and the candles in their sconces cast a gentle light.

'I saw you,' Mattie said, with no preamble. 'On the night of the party. You and –' she swallowed, hating the feel of the name on her tongue '– you and Lottie Taylor. On the porch.'

It was obviously the last thing he had expected. She saw the shock in his eyes and was fiercely glad.

'Now this.' She lifted her head to look at him. 'Is it true? You've been seeing her?'

'No!' The word was violent. He came to his feet, lifting his big, bandaged hands. 'No. Mattie – not – seeing her –'

'What, then?'

'Once,' he said. 'Just once. I had to go.'

'Why?'

'Mattie, I've known her since we both were children – I had to know – if she was happy –'

'You already knew she was not.' She was astounded – horrified – at the biting calm of the words.

He set his jaw in stubborn, defensive anger.

'Johnny?' She forced his eyes to hers. 'Why did you marry me?'

The ensuing silence was too long ever to forgive. She turned from him, fingered blindly the lace of a tablecloth. 'Tell me – do you ever tell me the truth about anything?' she asked, quietly bitter.

'Do you? Are you so damned sure of your own self?' The sharp words were followed by the sound of a drawer slamming open.

She turned, puzzled.

Johnny threw a small slate and a piece of chalk, which broke as it fell, onto the table. 'You do know,' he asked, quiet in the silence, 'that it's against the law of this land to teach a slave to read and write?'

Mattie looked at him in horror. 'You've been spying on me?'

He shook his head impatiently. 'In God's name, when will you learn? There's no need to spy in a house like Pleasant Hill. I grew up with most of these niggers. What they know I know.' He leaned to her, black eyes bright with anger. 'You know what could happen to Lucy, iffen I told Pa?'

She stared at him for a long, quiet moment. 'You're despicable,' she said, still precariously calm.

His flushed face reddened further.

'You hear me?' She had never in her life been so angry. That he had lied to and betrayed her was one thing; that he could think to counterattack with threats to Lucy was unforgivable. 'You think you're so brave, so gallant, so – honourable –' She invested the last word with such disgust that she saw him flinch, and was furiously glad. 'But you know what you really are? You're a child! A spoiled child, playing games. You married me to spite Charlotte, and wouldn't admit it, not even to yourself. You and your poetry, your declarations of love! Playacting! That's what it was. Like this damned silly playing at toy soldiers at Silver Oaks! In God's name, has it occurred to any of you what war will really be like? Do you ever think of the blood, and the death, and the mutilation?'

'Shut up, Mattie!' He towered above her, glowering, his damaged face dark with rage, and, had she but seen it, with the shadow of fear. 'Just shut up!'

Tears spilled onto her face. Angrily, she rubbed them away with the back of her hand. 'Do you remember what you said this afternoon, Johnny? You said I'd be proud of you! *Proud* of you? Tell me what there is to be proud of ? Brutality? Deception? What of honour, Johnny, that you all talk about so much? Integrity? Decency? Where are they in all of this? Where's the decency in marrying me when you loved her still? Where's the integrity in lying to me, in seeing her behind her husband's back? And this – this *honour* you're all so proud of, so certain of – what honour is there in a society that treats half its population like animals, that could strip a girl like Lucy naked and flog her because she wants to learn to read? No wonder you think you can do as you like! No wonder you can lie to yourself as well as to me, and not even understand that you're doing it!' Her unstable voice had risen.

Johnny's control snapped; he reached for her, caught her by the shoulders and shook her like a doll. For an instant, seeing the lacerating fury in his bloodied face she was truly frightened. Then he let her go, so that she stumbled, and almost fell as he stepped back from her, a hand in front of his eyes. 'Mattie – I'm sorry –'

'What for?' she asked, bleakly and very cold, turning from him, knowing the risk she ran, unable to prevent herself. 'For marrying me? For taking me from everything I knew and bringing me here? For being a liar and a cheat? For fighting in the mud like an animal over another man's wife?' She was so hurt, her love for him so violated, that she wanted in that moment only to inflict pain. 'I hope there is a war, Johnny Sherwood. At least it means you'll go away, far away! At least it means I won't have to watch you thinking of her when you look at me, when you touch me –' She stopped, appalled, knowing it was a barbarous thing to have said.

Behind her the door slammed. Johnny's footsteps clattered along the narrow balcony and down the steep stairs, away from her.

Slowly Mattie bowed her wet face into her hands; a still figure in a silent room that still rang with the vehement echoes of anger.

The quarrel did not mend easily. As events picked up a momentum of their own, and early one April morning at Fort Sumter, in Charleston, the first shots were fired that were to signal the start of conflict, Mattie and Johnny lived in a cool and open estrangement cloaked only in the necessary civilities of daily life in a household full of people. They slept each night with backs obstinately turned, barely spoke at all on those odd occasions when they could not avoid being left alone.

True to their plans, Will, Russell and Johnny made preparations to leave. The troop was riding together, north to Athens, to join Colonel Thomas R. Cobb's Georgia Legion. In the middle of April another wave of secessions began as Virginia joined the Confederacy, soon to be followed by North Carolina, Arkansas and Tennessee. The South's ports were blockaded. In North and South tempers and hearts were high and young men answered the impassioned appeals of their chosen governments and flocked to the recruiting stations.

It was not until the very night before the troop was due to leave that the awful restraint between Mattie and Johnny broke.

Heartsore though she still was, and grievously hurt, Mattie could not see him go with such unnatural animosity lying still between them. It was hard to perpetuate a quarrel now that war and parting were actually upon them. As she helped Lucy to lay out his grey and blue uniform, with its shining buttons and its jaunty, plumed hat, it was almost as if for the first time she understood that he was truly leaving, truly riding to war, to an experience in which she could have no part and from which it was possible he might never return. In bed that night with no words she turned to him, and as wordless he came to her, ardent and loving as he had ever been. Later, much later, he slept, his head pillowed upon her breast, while the unstoppable tears slid all but unnoticed down her cheeks and into the tangle of her hair.

The next morning, in their last moments alone, Mattie gave him the small leather-bound volume of poetry that had been her father's and had seemed to be, to her at least, the first token of their love. 'Take it,' she said, over his protests, 'I want you to have it. It may help pass a few empty hours. At the very least it will remind you of your quarrelsome wife.'

Johnny bent to her and hugged her for a long, fierce moment, almost lifting her from her feet, crushing her to him as if he would never let her go. With strange detachment then she followed him downstairs and into the house where his brothers, sabres and pistols at their sides, unfeigned excitement in their faces, awaited him and, as calm as if he had been setting out for the market at Macon, watched and waved from the porch with the rest of the household as the brave little cavalcade wheeled smartly and with a rhythmic jingling of harness away from the house and into the dappled sunlight beneath the moss-draped trees of the long, red driveway. Just before they disappeared Johnny turned, lifting his plumed hat in a sweeping wave of farewell. Smiling, she lifted her hand. And then they were gone, and all seemed very quiet.

'God be with them,' Logan Sherwood said.

'Amen to that,' Joshua added firmly and quietly; and, turning, Mattie saw to her astonishment that there were tears in his eyes too.

CHAPTER EIGHT

Those first months of war were, as had been the months that had preceded them, as much a matter of tub-thumping and posturing as of fighting. There were a few skirmishes, none of them serious or telling except to those who fell in them. In one, at a place called Big Bethel, Federal forces lost seventy-six men to the Confederates' eight; clear proof, if any soul in the South had needed it, of the simple truth that one Southern fighting man was worth any ten Yankees. Speeches were made, patriotic feeling stirred to combustion point. Roads and railways, north and south, were clogged with the movement of volunteers, their horses, their supplies, their arms. No-one, it seemed to Mattie, listening to the fiery talk in Milledgeville and Macon, or reading the equally inflammatory newspapers, asked any more what this fight was actually about; quite simply the battle lines had been drawn — you chose your side, the side of the angels, and you abhorred the other, the side of the devil. That the two forces, which were growing and strengthening every day, had in fact much in common with each other — that many of the professional backbone of both armies had been at military college together, had served together in the US Army in Mexico and in the West — meant nothing; a die had been cast, and a demon's game was in progress. Nothing now it seemed could stop it.

As the weather warmed and spring moved towards summer, they heard often at Pleasant Hill from one or other of the three brothers who were kicking their heels at a training camp in Virginia. Occasionally one of them made it home for a few days, full of talk of constant drill and occasional manoeuvres, of the boredom of camp life and the hair-raising escapades they devised to relieve it, and of the certainty of swift victory. It would all be over by Christmas at the latest, everyone knew it. All that was needed was to bring the damned Yankees to a confrontation, whip them soundly, and they'd give up and not stop running till they reached Canada.

In May the capital of the Confederate States was moved from Montgomery, Alabama to Richmond, Virginia; and the ironic quirk of fate that had placed the places and times of birth of the two opposing Presidents in such oddly close proximity was replicated in their seats of power. The two cities stood a bare hundred miles from each other, and in those first weeks it was the Northern capital that was least advantageously situated; the tiny District of Columbia was surrounded on three sides by a by no means undividedly loyal Maryland, whilst across the great river of the Potomac upon which Washington stood was the openly hostile state of Virginia. For the whole of the month of April, the Northern capital had been ill-garrisoned, its supply routes virtually cut off. Only by the end of that month were the railways to the north secured and ten thousand men bivouacked in and about the capital for its defence. On the Northern side as well as in the South there was a strong conviction that one good battle could win this war; the Federal warcry was 'On to Richmond!', whilst in the young Confederacy the view held that in righteously defending home, hearth and land, the South could not fail. As the warm and tranquil days of an early Southern summer followed one upon another in a Georgia that considered herself to be the very heartland of the Confederacy, heads nodded sagely over juleps on the porch; there was no doubt about it, the boys would be home before the cotton harvest was under way. Didn't the South have the pick of the generals, the best of the cavalry, the sharpest and steadiest of marksmen and, above all, right on her side? One engagement would send Lincoln's Yankee hirelings home with their tails between their legs and the new nation would be saved.

In the middle of June, Cissy came down with a fever, caught, she insisted, because Mattie had, with cheerful determination and to her own surprise, persuaded her to take her turn at the plantation infirmary. Mattie, guiltily aware that in all probability she was right, nursed the sick girl herself, sponging the fair, flushed face, spooning the mixture that everyone in the house still called 'Bella's herb tea' into her mouth, sitting with her through the long, restless nights. On the third afternoon, when Cissy's temperature soared yet again and with the girl's condition quite obviously deteriorating by the hour, she searched out Robert in the stables. 'She's getting worse. Someone's going to have to go to Macon for the doctor.'

With no question Robert put aside the harness he was inspecting. In this unhealthy clime and at this time of the year, no-one underestimated the potential danger of these infections. 'I thought she was improving?'

'She was. Or seemed to be. But –' Mattie shook her head worriedly, pushed a strand of hair from her eyes.

'I'll go. Doc Morrison is still in town.'

'Please be quick.'

'I will.'

Mattie went back into the sickroom. Liddie, Cissy's personal servant, whom Mattie had left on watch when she had gone to look for Robert, sat huddled on a stool beside the bed, her hands over her face, keening as if for the dead. The room was like a hothouse and smelled abominable.

'Liddie! What is it? She isn't –?' Her heart in her mouth, Mattie flew to the bedside, scrambling up the wooden step to bend over her patient. Cissy thrashed feverishly, muttering. Liddie shrieked on.

'Liddie!' Exasperated, Mattie jumped down to the floor again, catching her toe in her voluminous skirt, hearing the material rip as she wrenched it free. Whilst in the sickroom she had abandoned her hoops. 'Stop that! Will you stop it? Liddie!'

'She dyin', Miss Mattie, oh my little Missis is dyin'! I knows it! I seed it before!'

'Liddie, just hold your tongue! Make yourself useful – go fetch some cold water and –'

'T'ain't no use, Miss Mattie! T'ain't no use! She dyin', I tells you! Oh my poor little Miss –'

Fury lent Mattie a strength she did not usually possess. Bending, she took the girl by the shoulders and hauled her to her feet, shaking her. 'Will you be still! Or I swear I'll tell Mr Sherwood to send you to the barn!'

The girl sobbed mournfully on, but at least the threat had reduced the volume of her cries. 'No good you tryin', Miss Mattie. She dyin'. You cain' do nothin' 'bout that.'

'Mr Robert's gone to Macon for the doctor. Now go and get some more cold water and some flannels. And send Lucy up. And, Liddie, stop that screeching or I swear I'll slap you myself – hard!'

The next few hours were terrifying. More than once Mattie wondered if the hysterical Liddie were not, after all, right about Cissy's chances of survival. As day waned into evening and they awaited the arrival of Doctor Morrison, there was little they could do but helplessly watch the fever mount. Delirious, Cissy struggled against their every ministration, clamping her teeth against the bitter herbs, crying out against the sting of the cold flannels on her dry and burning skin. In the past days she had lost flesh, the bones of her pretty face stood sharp and fragile, her eyes and cheeks hollow as death. Informed of the crisis, Logan Sherwood came in from the fields, sustained the heat and stench of the room for as long as any hale man who was as ill-acquainted and ill at ease with sickness as he was might be expected to – about four minutes, Mattie guessed wryly – and then repaired gruffly to the library and the plantation accounts, requiring to be called if circumstances changed. Quiet black feet shuffled about the shadowed room. Black hands administered to the frail, restless figure in the huge four-poster bed. And Mattie sat on, watching grimly and with failing confidence her young sister-in-law's fight against death. It was closing dusk when the sudden sound of horses' hooves and the spinning wheels of a light carriage heralded at last the arrival of Robert with the doctor. As the man, a brisk and rotund figure a full head shorter than Mattie, bustled into the room, she was ashamed to discover that her first feeling was of huge relief; not for Cissy, but for herself. Here was someone far better qualified to shoulder the responsibility of the sick girl's fight for life. She suddenly felt very tired indeed.

'Mrs Sherwood?' Shrewd eyes held hers. 'Might I suggest you

take yourself off for a half-hour's rest and a cup of tea? It will do no-one any good to have a second invalid to deal with. And I have a feeling that it is going to be a very long night.'

It was. At first it seemed that the doctor's medicines were to have no more effect upon the fever than the herbs and roots with which Cissy had already been dosed. Later, Mattie found herself wondering which in the end had truly been more effective. Certain it was that when the crisis came, in the early hours of the morning, Doctor Morrison could do no more than Mattie had already done. 'She's young,' he said quietly, his voice tired, 'and strong. All that can be done has been done. Now it's up to her.'

With the dawn the fever broke. The restless, painful tossing ceased. Sweat drenched the tangled fair hair, soaked into the thick cotton of Cissy's nightgown. She looked like a child, Mattie thought, still and pale and sleeping the sleep of exhaustion. Or like the young princess whose finger had been pricked by a needle, evilly enchanted.

'The next few hours will be crucial.' Doctor Morrison was collecting his things, packing them methodically into his bag. 'She needs constant attention. But not from you, young woman.' He lifted his balding head sharply, darting a quick look at her. 'Leave her to the darkies now. They know what to do. And you go to bed. For a day. Two if you can manage it. Or I'll be gettin' another call, and Pleasant Hill is a danged inconvenient way from Macon.' His tired eyes were twinkling.

Mattie smiled in return. 'I will. And thank you. Can I get you something? A cup of tea, perhaps?'

'You most certainly may. But tea? Beelzebub's curse on the awful stuff. You can tell Joshua to break open one of Logan's best bottles of Madeira, and if the old man isn't around to help me I'll drink it alone.'

She smiled again. 'He's in the library, I think. Sol said he had refused to go to bed.' She walked with him to the door. All at once she was so weary she could barely put one foot in front of the other. The skirts that dragged about her ankles felt like lead weights. 'I'll take you to him.'

The pearly dawn had brought at least a little coolness to the air; it revived her as she stepped with him out onto the outside veranda. 'Your sons – they're safe? You've heard from them lately?'

Doctor Morrison stood back for her to precede him down the stairs. 'Sure have. Howard's with the troop in Virginia with Will, Russell and Johnny of course. But Jerry's out in Missouri. The lad's already seen some action and patched up some heads from all accounts. At Camp Jackson, back at the beginning of May –' He stopped short.

The door below them had opened, and Robert had stepped out onto the back porch, head lifted to their voices. 'Mattie? Is that you?'

'Yes.' Mattie descended the last few steps to him.

'How is she?'

'The fever's broken. She's still bad, but she is better.'

'Thank God for that.'

'God and Doctor Morrison,' Mattie said, lightly, and only then sensed the fierce and unmistakable hostility that emanated from the still, sturdy figure on the stairs behind her. The portly little doctor had stopped abruptly, stood rigid a little above them, scowling down at Robert. Gracefully and with a small, self-effacing gesture Robert stepped back, leaving the way clear to the door. Doctor Morrison, with what undoubtedly would in most circumstances be considered a gross lack of manners, stumped down the last stairs, past Mattie and, without so much as a glance at Robert, on into the house. Mattie stared after him. Looked at Robert, who shrugged a little, though not easily. His face was shadowed.

'For goodness' sake!' Mattie said, quietly. 'What in the world –?' The old doctor was, she knew, a family friend. His boys had grown up with the Sherwood brothers. There had even been, according to Lucy, talk of some attachment between one of the lively, pretty Morrison daughters and Robert. At last her tired brain caught up with itself. 'Ah,' she said.

Robert smiled his small quirk of a smile, but without a trace of humour.

'Joshua? Joshua!' the doctor's voice roared out from within the house. They heard the door that led into the semi-basement,

Joshua's domain, screech open. 'Where are you, you son of Satan? Better still, where are the cellar keys?'

Mattie put out a hand. 'Robert –'

He shook his head sharply. 'It's all right. I understand. I know how he feels. I understand how they all feel.'

She stood quiet in the strengthening light of dawn, looking at him. His face was calm, his head high, but he could not in that vulnerable moment hide the weary strain in his eyes.

The week before, she had been in Macon with him on a shopping trip. He had left her to Dandy's protection whilst in the town, and a few minutes' observation as he had walked away from her down the main street had told her why. She had seen the quiet snubs, the smiles not returned, the drawing aside of skirts, the old friends who had openly crossed to the other side of the street rather than speak to him. Logan Sherwood may have been right in one way; no-one would dare to come out and accuse a Sherwood boy to his or to his father's face of treachery or of cowardice – but there were more ways than one to make a point, and patriotic feelings ran high in Georgia. Robert was right; he understood them. The problem was that they did not understand him. She wondered, sometimes, if he understood himself.

They walked together in silence into the spacious hall. Doctor Morrison was still at Joshua's door, calling down the steps. 'Joshua! You hear me, boy?'

'I hear you, Doctor.' Unruffled, Joshua appeared, ascending the steep steps, improbably immaculate as always, a bottle in one hand and two glasses in the other. 'They probably hear you in Macon.' It was said gently, and with no obvious trace of humour.

The little doctor rubbed the heels of his hands into tired eyes and grinned like a boy. 'You were mine I'd have you sent to the whippin' shed, you uppity nigger,' he said, amiably.

'Yes, Sir, Doctor, ah knows you would.' Joshua bestowed a tranquil look upon the other man, the slyly accented words apparently innocent. 'Mr Sherwood's in the library, Sir, awaitin' you. I hear Miss Cissy's going to be all right?'

As always Mattie found herself registering astonishment at the efficiency of the jungle telegraph that kept the servants informed of everything in the house almost before it had actually happened.

'Hopefully, Joshua, hopefully. Though these things can never be taken for granted, as we all know.'

'Yes, Sir.' Joshua had glanced past the doctor and seen Mattie and Robert. He nodded. 'Morning, Miss Mattie. May I get you something?'

Mattie shook her head, smiling tiredly. 'No, thank you, Joshua. Sleep is what I need.'

'I'll send for Lucy.'

'No. No, don't bother her at this hour. I'm perfectly capable of seeing to things myself. Just ask her to see that I'm not disturbed, would you? Oh, and Jake could do with some exercise. I've neglected him horribly these past few days.'

'I'll see to it, Miss Mattie.' Joshua's dark eyes moved to Robert, standing still and silent beside Mattie. 'And you, Mister Robert? Shall I bring another glass?'

The little doctor's head turned sharply, wiry brows drawn to a pugnacious point above suddenly ferocious eyes. He looked, Mattie thought tiredly, a little like a terrier challenging a wolfhound.

Robert shook his head. 'No, Joshua, thank you. I think I'd best go write to Will. I hope the doctor will be kind enough to take a letter to the post in Macon?' It was not lost on anyone that he did not speak to the other man directly. For the first time Mattie wondered what had taken place between the two men on the long ride from Macon.

'A letter to young Will? Why, most certainly I will. I'd ride to Virginia with it my own self if I had to.' The words were as openly belligerent as the look that accompanied them. 'Believe me, there's nothin' I wouldn't do for one of our lads who's fightin' for his country like a man.'

The heavy emphasis tried even Robert's seemingly limitless patience. His mouth tightened, and he levelled a long, quelling look at the smaller man. Never, Mattie thought, had his likeness to his more hot-tempered brothers been so clear.

Doctor Morrison, to his credit, was not to be intimidated. He set a bellicose, if small, jaw, and stared right back. He looked exhausted.

Robert turned without a word and left them, shutting the door very quietly behind him.

Mattie shook her head. 'Doctor Morrison, you're being unfair to Robert –'

He spun on her. 'Unfair? *Unfair!* Young woman, with respect, I'd advise you to hold your tongue and go to bed. You've done a grand job and you can be proud of yourself. That fly-by-night sister-in-law of yours probably owes her life to you. Don't spoil it now by meddlin' in affairs about which you know nothin'. I've no doubt but that, like most of your sex, when it comes to the world's affairs you can do nothin' but talk out of your pretty hat. What do you know of honour, an' pride, an' the perils of war that our young men are facin'? Unfair? Why, if I had my way, the likes of young Robert would be horsewhipped through the streets of every town in the South. He knows it and so does his Pa. If truth be told, I'm dang' certain Logan would agree with me. Unfair indeed!' His face had coloured quite alarmingly. In his anger and tiredness he could barely keep control of his tongue, and the words came in a spray of spittle. He jabbed a finger. 'My boys are out there, ready to die if needs be for our great country. Your own husband – the husband of the girl that lies sick upstairs – that young scoundrel's own brothers! – have taken up arms to defend you, to defend this house!' He threw his short arms up in an all-embracing gesture. 'To defend this land! Your Yankee-lovin' brother-in-law is ready enough to accept their protection, to allow them to fight – to die! – for him, and you say that I'm bein' unfair?'

'But it isn't as simple as that –'

'What do you know of it? Get back to your embroidery, girl, and leave the world to those that know what's goin' on, and know what needs to be done about it.'

Mattie was tired, too; and as outraged as he. 'The men, you mean?' she asked, remarkably calmly.

His already perilously empurpled face darkened further. 'Who else, child?' Even in her anger Mattie could not resist a certain helpless amusement that in the past few moments she had regressed from a young woman to a girl and now back into childhood. 'What would you have? A world run by petticoats and poke bonnets? Tell me this, girl –' his hand shot out again, a finger pointing to where the pearl of dawn showed through the window '– can you till that land? Can you handle those field hands? Could you take up rifle and sword to defend your rights? To defend your life and the lives of your children? Pah! Of course not!'

'That doesn't mean I can't think,' she said, not unreasonably.

'Think? *Think?* Satan's whiskers! There isn't a woman I know who doesn't think with her – with her –' he caught himself, shaking his head '– with her heart. Charmin' I'm sure, an' God bless the ladies for it. But it's no good in this hard world, young Mrs Sherwood. No good at all. You just get yourself a batch of children and spend your time bringin' 'em up. That'll keep you occupied.-'

'And in my place,' she supplied, smoothly.

'And in your place,' he agreed, placid now, and sure of himself. 'The place where you belong; the place where you'll be happy. What more can God give you?'

She opened her mouth. Closed it again.

'Nothin' to say?'

'Oh, yes. I've something to say.'

He contemplated her with repressive gaze. Only the faint twitch of his mouth indicated, infuriatingly, that tired anger had demonstrably slid into equally tired mirth. 'I had a feelin' you might have. Go on, then, Mrs Sherwood. Fire away. Don't let an old man's sensibilities stop you.'

Mattie gritted her teeth.

He laughed outright then, by no means unkindly. 'Go to bed, my dear. You're exhausted. Joshua –' he jerked his head towards the door of the library '– old Logan must have nodded off. Go wake him up and open that danged bottle.'

'Yes, Sir.' Impassively Joshua moved towards the study door.

Doctor Morrison bowed courteously to Mattie, eyes still twinkling with laughter. 'Goodnight, Mrs Sherwood. Sleep well.'

She watched him almost to the door before she found her breath and her tongue. 'Doctor Morrison?'

He turned, waiting. Joshua, his hand on the doorknob, waited too, watching her with suddenly disconcertingly interested eyes.

'It seems to me a very great pity,' Mattie said, with stubborn calm and clarity, 'that a man of such sensitivity and intelligence should hold such barbarous views. And I say again, you're wrong to treat Robert so.'

There was a moment's fragile silence. The little man stood, tired, dishevelled and thoughtful, watching her. 'There is the remote possibility, Mrs Sherwood, that you could be right on both points,' he said at last. 'But don't take heart from that, my dear. As soon try to teach that scruffy hound of yours to be a scented lapdog as try to change the ways of a stubborn old fox like me. To say nothin' of takin' on the world. We like things the way they are.'

'That doesn't mean that things won't change.'

'No. It doesn't. But we're sure ready to fight like hell to make certain they don't.' He nodded affably. Joshua pushed open the door. Beyond them Logan Sherwood was seated in an armchair, nodding. As the door opened, he woke like a big, raw-boned cat, lithe on his feet. He held out a hand, his greeting lost as the door closed behind them.

Mattie stood alone in the big hall, fighting exhaustion and contemplating the firmly shut door. 'I'd noticed,' she told it, drily. 'I had noticed.' And turned to meet Joshua's eyes, in which for a fleeting moment she thought she detected something close to a gleam of subversive laughter.

Cissy's convalescence was long, slow, and trying for all concerned. The first week or so was the easiest time; she was too weak, too sleepy, to be any trouble at all. At the lift of a finger she was calmed, cosseted, soothed to quiet. Later, things became more difficult.

'You-all tryin' to poison me?' Pettishly she pushed Prudence's lovingly made, nourishing broth from her, slopping it over the bedclothes. 'Tastes like the water the dishes were washed in! Mattie, for goodness' sake! Can't you do better than this?'

'It's what Doctor Morrison recommended –'

'Oh, for cat's sake! Doc Morrison? What does he know? Mattie – Mattie! – get me somethin' nice? – somethin' I could fancy?'

'What do you fancy, Cissy? What can we get you?'

The thin face, surmounted by its cloud of silver-blonde hair, had taken on the haunting beauty of a fairy child's. 'I don't know. How do I know? I'm too ill to think of such things. Liddie, let me have some of the medicine that stupid man left. Yes, that one. No, you silly fool – the blue bottle. That's it. Oh, Mattie – Mattie! – when will Will come? He's comin', isn't he? Robert said he'd come.' She pulled restlessly at the stained bedcover.

Mattie took the thin hand, stopping its feverish movement. 'No, my dear. Robert said he'd written to tell him what had happened. Robert said he'd come if he could. And he will, of course he will. But, Cissy, no-one knows when he'll be able to come. There are – things happening – Will isn't a free agent.' She shied from telling the sick child that all the signs were that the battle of which everyone had spoken with such certainty, towards which everyone had looked with such determinedly convinced optimism, was about to take place. Even less could she tell her that the news that had begun to filter through from Virginia was less than reassuring. The Federal army was on the move towards Richmond. A number of relatively small but strategically important engagements had taken place, and in most of them the honours had gone to the North. The situation was, by any measure, a strange one. Two inexperienced armies were mustering against each other; in one, the lowest bugle boy obstinately expected his democratic rights to be observed, and reserved his right to be regarded as an equal to any leather-booted colonel when it came to the giving and the taking of orders. In the other, an able officer would find it difficult to impose discipline upon young men who had little time for, or experience of, such restraint and who, in that other life, so soon to be resumed, held higher social station than his own. The crucible of battle had not yet done its work; Northern columns broke to pick berries and to swim in a calm pool, Southerners at a reckless whim would put their horses to the highest fences, drop out from line with no thought to visit cousins and the cousins of cousins. But the feeling was abroad that an accounting was imminent. 'He'll come when he can, Cissy,' Mattie reassured the fretful girl. 'He'll come when he can.'

He came with a bare twelve hours to spare with them. 'The Colonel said he'd have my hide if I was longer. Cissy – Cissy darlin', just look at you – you're skin and bone!'

'She's looking much better,' Mattie said, cheerfully. 'If she would just eat a little more –'

'Cissy, sweetheart, I can't stay. Truly I can't. But I'll be back. I promise I will. Soon, and for a proper stay.' Will left his weeping child-wife with tears in his own eyes. 'Mattie – God, but she looks so poorly!'

'She'll be all right, Will. Leave her to us. You look after yourself and the others. We'll take care of Cissy for you.' Mattie hesitated. 'Is it true? Is there a battle coming?'

'Sure looks that way.' Will swung into the saddle. His horse, well rested and fed, danced in a tight, excited circle, anxious to be gone. Mattie could not help but feel that the animal was doing nothing but reflecting her rider's own impatience to be away, despite Will's genuine concern for his young wife. There was a high-strung and expectant edge to the man; his thoughts as he saluted her were patently already elsewhere. 'Will, give my love to Johnny,' she called as he left, but was far from sure he had heard her.

Five days later, by a stream called Bull Run near the town of Manassass, the Creole General Beauregard's green Southerners opposed an equally inexperienced Federal army led by Beauregard's old West Point classmate General Irvin McDowell in an attempt to prevent a Federal march south and an attack on Richmond. The site was less than thirty miles from Washington, and the politicians and socialites of that city rode gaily to the heights about the battlefield on horseback or in buggies and gigs, their picnics stowed safely beneath the seats, the ladies' fair skins well protected beneath parasols or fringed canopies, to watch the fun. This, after all, would be their only chance to see the arrogant Rebels taught the lesson they so richly deserved.

The gods of war, however, decreed otherwise.

In a battle notable more for confusion and chaos than for strategy and discipline, for singular and independent displays of courage than ordered tactical successes, it was, in the end, the Confederacy that took the day; though not before coming heart-stoppingly close to losing it. It was a day upon which reputations were made, and lost, and a famous nickname bestowed; it was the Georgian General Bee, leading his men on his own authority into the fiercest and most perilous of the fighting, who observed the staunch defence being put up by General T.J. Jackson and his Virginians. 'There's Jackson, boys, standing like a stone wall! Let us determine to die here, and we'll conquer!' And die, indeed, he did, whilst the name he had unwittingly bestowed lived on.

It was, too, on that day, at the turning point of battle, when a Federal army that had so nearly broken through the grey lines of the South was itself broken and scattered in panic that the savage, keening sound that became known as the Rebel Yell was first heard. 'Yell like furies!' Jackson had told his men and, like hounds baying at the heels of the quarry, they did; a sound to haunt the nightmares of those that fled the bloody field in disorder and defeat, overrunning the civilian gigs and carriages as they went. And as a drizzling darkness closed upon that field and the inevitable grim accounting was taken, the scales of pride and of victory were weighted for the South. The numbers of dead were relatively light; three hundred and eighty-seven Confederates had given their lives against four hundred and eighty-one Federal troops. Despite the Southern victory, her wounded outnumbered the enemy's, fifteen hundred to eleven hundred. It was, however, in the number of prisoners taken that the greatest triumph lay. No less than fifteen hundred Yankees had thrown down their arms and surrendered; the number of missing Confederates was eight, and no-one believed for an instant that a single one of them had been taken anything but fighting. In Richmond that night, and in the South itself in the next few days as the news spread, there was joy and relief; independence was assured. The war was won.

News of Bull Run came to Pleasant Hill on the day following the battle, and it was Doctor Morrison, paying one of his regular visits to check upon his patient, who brought it. Mattie read the news to Cissy from the paper that the doctor had given her. Still frail and fractious, Cissy could see the news in nothing but a personal light.

'Does it mean that Will and the others will come home? Does it mean we can stop all this silly war talk and doing without things and go back to normal?'

Mattie had noticed months before that all Cissy's bold enthusiasm for the war had evaporated speedily once Will and the others had left and boredom and loneliness had set in. Now it seemed that the girl had lost her taste for it altogether. 'Perhaps.' She did not think it helpful to share her own worry, that the casualty lists had not yet come through to Macon, and that this victory, great and welcome though it was, would bring sorrow and bereavement to some. Try as she might, she could not rid herself of the thought of Johnny dead or dying upon the field at Manassass. Knowing him, knowing them all, she could not but believe they would have been in the thick of the fighting.

The first lists came through the following day. Logan Sherwood himself, accompanied by Joshua, made the trip into town, and came back sombre but openly relieved. 'Young Morrison's gone. An' both Dickson boys are hurt bad. But our lads seem to be safe.'

'Well, of co'se they're safe!' Cissy, much encouraged at the thought of the menfolk of the house coming home, had made considerable improvement over the past twenty-four hours and sat tucked into a rocking chair on the front porch. She looked fragile as glass and very beautiful in a day dress of pale silk. The air was hot and almost unbearably humid. Beside Cissy, upon a low stool sat Liddie, stoically patient, fanning her mistress with a large palmetto fan. 'What would you expect?' Her eyes, unnaturally large and bright, shone with excitement. 'My, what times they must have had! I'll just bet they were the bravest!'

'Morrison?' Mattie asked. 'Howard Morrison? The doctor's son?'

'Yes.' Logan Sherwood sat heavily upon a sturdy chair. 'Whisky, Sol.'

'Yes, Sir, Mister Logan.'

'But – that's awful –'

'Yes.' The big man leaned back, the shock of his long white hair bright against dark cushions. He rubbed the back of a brown hand thoughtfully against a tanned cheek.

Mattie watched him. In the trees beyond the clearing the crickets chirped in monotonous harmony.

'When do you think they'll be home?' Cissy smoothed the flimsy silk of her skirt, little hands restless as ever. 'Will it take them long, do you think? If the war's over, there's nothin' to stop them –'

'The war isn't over, Cissy.' Logan Sherwood stood and walked to the balcony rail. The summer screening had been put in place. The world beyond it was drawn in soft focus, smudged and shadowed. 'At least the Yankees don't think it is.'

'You mean – ?' Cissy's mouth set in a familiar line. 'You mean they won't be coming home? You mean this – this stupid business is goin' to go on?'

''Fraid so.' Logan took the glass that Sol had proffered on a tray and took a long, slow mouthful, his back to the two young women.

'How very vexin'.' Cissy's voice was small; miserable.

Mattie felt an unbidden surge of sympathy. She reached to take the other girl's hand. 'Don't worry, Cissy. It won't be for long.'

Cissy suffered her hand to be held for the very briefest of moments before extricating it. 'Any time's too long. Liddie, what are you about? Isn't it time for my medicine?'

'Not yet, Miss Cissy. Not till bedtime.'

'Don't be such a fool, girl. Four times a day, Doctor Morrison said. Can't you count? Go get it, at once.'

'Yes, Miss Cissy.'

Logan Sherwood turned. 'My hat, Sol. There's work to do.

I've time to check on that field down by the brakes. Tell them to bring Dancer round.' Most of the Sherwood horses, together with some of the mules, had been, with no small heart-wrenching, surrendered to the Confederate army. Only Dancer, Logan Sherwood's own big black stallion, was still safe in the stables, kept company by one old mule, a couple of workhorses and one ageing carriage horse.

'Yes, Sir, Mister Logan.'

Mattie searched her father-in-law's face. 'Mr Sherwood? There – there isn't anything else?'

He hesitated for a telling moment; realizing it, he nodded. 'Bram Taylor's missing,' he said, flatly. 'It seems pretty sure he's dead.'

Mattie said nothing at all.

'Liddic!' Cissy called, her voice strengthened by petulant exasperation. 'Where's my medicine?'

It was a couple of weeks later, six or seven days into the enervating heat of August, that Shake appeared, mounted upon a Sherwood horse, skirling up the drive in an ostentatious and unnecessary display of red dust, well aware of and well pleased with the drama of the occasion. He brought with him letters, messages and news. The Sherwood brothers were indeed safe. Will and Johnny had both been offered commissions in other regiments, which they had turned down in favour of staying together, and Russ had been threatened with a court martial for seducing a brigadier's daughter. Questioned about the battle, Shake averted his eyes and became a little less loquacious. The young masters would want to tell their own stories. It had all been very noisy, very confusing.

'Will thinks he'll be able to come home for a while,' Cissy announced, perusing her letter. 'At the end of August. For a whole month, he says.'

'Good.' Logan Sherwood was crisp. 'That's just when I could do with an extra pair of hands.'

*　　*　　*

Will arrived unexpectedly, well and in good spirits, just a couple of weeks later, his furlough having been brought forward for compassionate reasons. He looked leaner, somehow tougher, than when they had last seen him, and his skin was tanned to the colour of mahogany. The uniform that had been so smart and elegant when he had left Pleasant Hill showed some signs of wear. He took the steps of the porch two at a time, made straight for the little figure of his wife, picking her from her feet and spinning her dizzily around, her skirts flying free in the air. Logan watched, smiling. The hands gathered, talking excitedly.

'Will! Will!' Cissy was beside herself with excitement. 'What are you doing here? We weren't expecting you for at least another two weeks!'

'Couldn't wait to see my sweetheart.' Will kissed her soundly, as the onlookers cheered, and then set her upon her feet, to turn to his father and brother, big hand outstretched. 'Pa. Robert. How're things?'

They trooped indoors, Will sweeping off his battered plumed hat and using it to beat the red dust of his journey from his clothes. 'Joshua! Good to see you!' Grinning, he clouted the tall, smiling Negro on the shoulder. 'You still growin', boy? I swear you get bigger every time I see you! You still courtin' that little gal over to Brightwell's place?' Joshua smiled a little and shook his head, but Will was looking around, smiling still, enquiring, 'Where's Johnny? That son of a gun still in bed or what? He sure swore he was goin' to sleep for a week.'

There was a small, surprised silence.

'Johnny?' Logan Sherwood asked, puzzled, half laughing. 'Why, Will, how would we know where Johnny is? We thought you'd be tellin' us.'

Will turned, his open, good-natured face guilelessly confused. 'Well, he left three days since – his furlough came through first. If he isn't here –' He stopped. Cleared his throat. Beneath the sun-darkness of his skin a deep flush was spreading. His suddenly wary eyes slid to Mattie and hastily away again.

'Well, now.' Logan filled the awkward moment, throwing an arm about his son's shoulder, another about Cissy's small waist, ushering them both towards the parlour, followed by Robert and the chattering servants. 'Come in, son, come in. It's grand to see you.' At the door he propelled them forward, turned back to where Mattie stood alone, still and pale with shock and growing anger.

'Wait, Mattie,' he said very quietly. 'Don't jump to conclusions. There's an explanation –'

'Oh, yes,' she said, with bitter clarity, 'there's an explanation.'

'Anything could have happened. His horse could have gone lame.'

'Pigs might fly, Mr Sherwood. But it's unlikely.'

'Mattie – give him a chance. You don't know – you can't know –'

'I think I know where Johnny is, Mr Sherwood. And I think you know too. For all I know the whole wretched county knows.' She marched past him into the drawing room, trembling with anger and humiliation. Will caught her eye and ducked his head, miserably, as if it were he who had been caught in mischief. She walked straight to him, slipped her arm into his, smiling. 'Goodness me – it looks as if Cissy isn't the only one who needs fattening up! What are they feeding you in that army of yours?'

Johnny rode home into the storm two days later. By then Mattie knew at least the bare bones of the story; Johnny's furlough had come through first, and he had left, telling his brothers that he was riding straight to Pleasant Hill. Within three days of his leaving Will too was unexpectedly on his way home, his own furlough having come through two weeks early. Johnny could have had no idea that his older brother would arrive home so soon, expecting to find him there. They all knew that had bad accident or mishap overtaken him upon the road, they would have heard by now; though still they pretended to believe that some small misfortune may have befallen – a thrown shoe, perhaps, or some muddle with officialdom. In truth, no-one at Pleasant Hill believed that Johnny Sherwood was anywhere but somewhere he had planned to be. Not even Cissy, by no means the most sensitive of souls when it came to other people's feelings, spoke too often of the absentee in Mattie's presence.

In the forty-eight hours that followed Will's arrival, Mattie obstinately refused to show her hurt. With an almost savage calm she continued her usual round, head high, manner unruffled, heart almost paralysed with pain. When news came to the house that Johnny had been sighted on the road, she went upstairs to change for all the world as if the news were welcome.

'The lemon silk, I think, Lucy. It's cooler than the blue.'

'Yes, Miss Mattie.' Lucy was subdued. Like all the household she knew what had happened; it was an indication of the depth of Mattie's unhappiness that she had not been able to bring herself to talk about Johnny's behaviour even to her. 'An' that pretty scarf with the rosebuds?'

'Yes.'

Lucy turned, the gown draped across her arms, her eyes upon her mistress' face. 'Miss Mattie –'

'Yes?'

'Miss Mattie, I doesn't want to speak out o' turn –'

'Then don't.' Mattie turned her back. 'Undo these buttons for me, please. And I think perhaps the amber earbobs, don't you?'

She was waiting, with the others, on the porch, apparently perfectly composed, when Johnny rode out from under the moss-draped trees. Only the faint puffiness about her eyes, the pale and shadowed texture of her skin, betrayed her. Not unexpectedly, Will was beside his brother, having ridden out to meet and to warn him. Mattie was neither surprised nor particularly offended at that; she had been at Pleasant Hill for long enough to know that no Sherwood boy would let another step into such a tricky predicament unguarded and unprepared, no matter where the fault lay. With detached calm she watched as Johnny smiled welcome to the hands who gathered about him, taking his horse, his sword, the bedroll from his saddle. She studied him; like Will he had lost weight, and his skin was darkened by sun and wind. He looked fit and handsome, his uniform, again like Will's, a little faded, a little worn, emphasizing the height and grace of him. With an odd, dispassionate detachment, she wondered how he would face this embarrassing homecoming.

His eyes found hers. The noise around them died. For a moment they might have been alone in the world. She did not smile.

He shouldered his way through the crowd, ran swiftly up the steps onto the porch. Came to her, took her hands. 'Mattie, I'm sorry. Arrow lamed, just outside Augusta –'

Mattie turned her gaze to where the horse, perfectly hale and stepping as always in lovely and faultless rhythm, was being led away to the stables 'That's a pity.' She presented a cool cheek to his kiss. Stepped back. Let her eyes speak clearly. Liar, they said. And as clearly she saw the defensive tightening of jaw and of mouth.

Greetings, a little subdued, were exchanged. Logan Sherwood it was who paved the way to the confrontation that everyone knew was unavoidable. 'You'll want to clean up, son. You go right ahead. There'll be time to talk later.'

Upstairs Johnny dismissed Lucy brusquely. 'And take that damn' animal with you.' Lucy looked to Mattie, uncertain. Mattie nodded, her eyes upon her husband. When the door closed quietly behind the girl and the reluctant dog, she continued to stand, still as a statue, hands clasped loosely in front of her, watching him. 'Five days,' she said, at last, quietly. 'Where have you been for five days, Johnny?'

He took a quick breath to reply.

She made a small, warning gesture with her hand. 'Don't lie to me. Don't do that. If there's anything left between us at all, then I want the truth. That isn't too much to ask, is it?'

He stood tongue-tied. She saw, suddenly, that he looked very tired. His hair had grown; it curled about his ears and neck like a girl's. One brown, strong hand still held his hat, crushing the brim, the knuckles showing tense and white.

Mattie turned and walked to the window. Outside, red dust smothered everything; the buildings, the trees, the scrubby grass. It was so hot that the slightest movement brought perspiration. 'We heard that Bram Taylor was missing, presumed killed. You, I assume, have later information?'

'Yes. Bram's dead. It was confirmed before I left camp.'

'And you, in your capacity as old family friend —' she could not believe the unsparing chill in her own voice '— took it upon yourself to console the grieving widow.' There was no question in the words.

The silence behind her was damning in itself.

She turned. 'I'll never forgive you for this, Johnny,' she said, her tone still intransigently conversational. 'Never.'

The tension that held him broke. Cursing, he flung his hat upon the bed, stepped towards her, stopped as she pulled back from him, her hands warding him off. 'Don't touch me. Please don't touch me.' Again the words were spoken almost nervelessly calmly. Just a few hours before she had spent the worst and most miserable night of her life in this very bed. The memory was too fresh; her tears were spent. 'Just tell me — tell me the truth. Grant me that dignity at least.'

Johnny stood tense for a moment, then turned from her. She found herself studying the broad shoulders, the set of the handsome head, and wondering that the sight of him could move her so little. It was as if something within her had broken; something that, at this moment, she felt would never mend.

'All right. I did go to see Lottie,' he said.

She waited.

'For God's sake, Bram might not have been much, but he was her husband!'

Still she did not speak.

'I thought — I thought that I should check that she was all right. That she didn't need any help.' His voice that had started a little uncertainly was stronger, as if the sound of his own reasonable words were convincing him that he was right and she wrong. 'We're old friends. I've known her all my life. What else would you expect me to do? Mattie, in God's name, will you please say something?'

'I don't think I've anything to say. Not anything that you'd want to hear.'

'Like what?'

'Like what took you five full days? Like why didn't you tell the others you were going to see Lottie? Why tell them you were coming straight to Pleasant Hill? Why not come home first and then pay your – your duty visit? Did this – Christian urge – to comfort the bereaved afflict you quite suddenly, perhaps, between Virginia and Georgia?' She could not believe how calmly she was speaking, how cool was her voice.

He shook his head, helplessly.

'You've never stopped loving her, have you? Oh, I don't blame you for that. How could I? But I'll tell you what I do blame you for, Johnny. I blame you for marrying me. For marrying me when you didn't love me –'

'No!' Johnny swung around and caught her, roughly, by the arm. 'That isn't true! Mattie – believe me –'

She said nothing, but stood quite still in his grasp, head lifted to look him levelly in the eyes. He it was who broke away first, letting go of her, dropping onto the bed, bowing his face into his spread hands. 'I thought I loved you.' His voice was desperate, and so low, so muffled by his hands that she could barely hear it. 'Mattie, I swear I thought I loved you. I did love you. I needed you. Until – until –'

'Until you saw her again.' Abruptly she turned from him, arms folded tightly across her breast, to gaze again, sightlessly through sudden tears, into the hot and dusty afternoon beyond the window.

'What are we going to do!' he asked at last. And this time her silence was forced upon her; she could no more have spoken than grown wings and flown.

Johnny came up behind her. Stubbornly she turned her face from him. Very gently he put an arm about her shoulders, drawing her to him with no passion, holding her quietly. 'Mattie, I'm sorry,' he said, reaching for her hand, bringing it to his own wet cheek. 'I am so very sorry.'

They struggled through the week that was left to them before he had to return to Virginia. In the end it was a positive relief to see him go, to end the nightmare of pretence, of knowing that as he walked and talked with her his thoughts, his hopes, his heart were elsewhere. Convention ruling to the last, Mattie stood with the others to wave him off, her hand upon Jake's soft, shaggy head. The dog followed her eagerly upstairs, falling over his own feet in his enthusiasm to stay beside her on the narrow steps. The shutters had been closed against the heat; the rooms were shadowed and very still. Empty.

Placed in painfully careful symmetry upon the table in the sitting room lay a small book. She stood looking at it, her lip caught between her teeth. Here was a more final farewell than any words they had spoken.

She picked up the cruelly familiar little thing, carried it to the window, opened the shutter to let in a shaft of hot afternoon light. The battered leather cover of the Shelley had a new stain upon it, a smear of mud that had also marked a few of the pages. She did not open it – she dared not – but held it tightly in both hands as the helpless tears, of which there had been so many in these past days, rose again. Jake, sitting beside her, leaning his weight against her legs, lifted his head, watching her with mute and loving eyes.

Mattie's shoulders dropped, her knees buckled, and like a child she knelt beside the dog, her arms about his warm, heavy shoulders, her face buried in his fur, weeping as she had not wept since the day her father had died.

CHAPTER NINE

The river swirled, red-brown, between the almost tropical lushness of its banks. The little clearing was still in the heavy air of the afternoon, the riotous growth of the woodland jungle-like about it, and the cries of birds still unfamiliar to Mattie echoed through the spreading canopy of branches. Midges buzzed about her. High above the clearing a huge bird of prey hovered, hanging all but motionless in the quiet air before gliding out of sight. Jake snapped with happy and entirely pointless enthusiasm at a bright butterfly that danced above his head, then trotted back to Mattie, worrying at the stick that she held, forgotten, in her hand. Absently she threw it, watched as the dog bounded after it, pawing it out from under a fallen log before chasing back and eagerly dropping it at her feet.

Why in God's name had she come here, of all places?

Jake barked, a short, excitable yelp, and pranced about her, waiting for her to throw the stick again.

It was over a month since Johnny had left, and in that time she had heard not a word from him. Neither had she written to him. Formal and general greetings were conveyed to everyone in his brothers' letters, and that was all. It was, she thought, like being stranded in limbo, neither wife nor free, and unable because of the circumstances to take any action or come to any final conclusion. Like that of this agonized and divided nation, her future held little but the certainty of more trouble, more pain. With the Northern blockade tight about the ports of the South she could not, even had she decided to, go home. She had no idea what Johnny wanted; all she knew with certainty was that he did not want her. So why had she come here?

Jake barked again, a different, excitable sound, and bounced noisily into the dense undergrowth. Absorbed in bitter thought,

Mattie did not notice. She was taken completely by surprise when a moment later Logan Sherwood rode quietly into the clearing, his hounds at his horse's heels, Jake gambolling and yelping about them like an overgrown puppy spoiling for fun.

'Darned animal.' Her father-in-law doffed his hat to her, swung from the saddle, looped the reins over a branch. His voice was easy, and his smile took any sting from the words. 'Iffen the tyke was a field hand I'd have him hogtied and sold at market.'

Jake had come to Mattie's call, and now sat beside her, head lifted to her hand. Mattie had long since learned to take no notice of such disparaging comments about her pet; there was no-one in the house, she suspected, Logan Sherwood included, but that would defend the silly animal with his own life if necessary.

Logan's own two dogs settled beside Dancer, eyes attentive upon their master.

He came to the point, as was his way, with no preamble. 'We must talk, daughter.'

It was all she could do not to flinch at the word.

He looked around the little clearing; the clearing where she had believed that Johnny had planned to build a house, to build a life, to build a family.

'Why did you come here?' There was clear curiosity in his voice.

'I was just wondering the same thing myself.'

Logan Sherwood walked to the fallen log, sat down, his head lifted to her, his pale gaze direct. It was not lost upon her that he could have remained standing, towering above her, master upon his land. She held his eyes, but neither smiled nor moved.

'You have to give him time, Mattie.'

'Time for what?'

'Time to come to his senses.'

'I fear, Mr Sherwood, that that's what he thinks he's done.' Her voice was austere; she yielded not an inch to the sympathy in his eyes. To have done so would have flawed the shield she had built with such painful obstinacy, and that she had determined not to do.

'Mattie, my dear, the circumstances —'

'The circumstances, Mr Sherwood, have absolutely nothing to do with the case — if, as I take it, you mean the circumstances of war — of Bram Taylor's death?'

'Yes. That is what I meant.' He was studying her intently; it was impossible to fathom the thoughts behind the look.

'Johnny loves Charlotte Taylor. He does not love me. Oh, he thought he did — that I believe at least — but he was wrong. Which means, of course, that you were right.' Mattie let the words challenge him for a moment, but he did not speak. 'Those are the facts, and neither war nor death nor the destruction of Paradise can change them. The — circumstances, as you call them, may well have changed the actual course of events. For that I should be nothing but grateful, don't you think?' For her life she could not keep the sudden bitterness from her voice. 'At the very least we've all been forced to honesty.'

He shook his head. 'Mattie, listen to me; you're young, you're proud, and you're terribly hurt. I understand that.'

She gritted her teeth against caustic comment; the man, she could only suppose, meant well. She just wished, with all her heart, that he would leave her alone; and knew as she thought it, wearily, that he would not.

'Johnny is your husband. For better or for worse —'

'To love and to cherish —' She flashed the quote at him in quick anger, and then stopped.

He nodded. 'Till death do you part,' he supplied quietly. 'Isn't that what you promised?'

'What we both promised, Mr Sherwood. It's your son who has betrayed his word and my trust. Your son who didn't think our promises to each other, our life together, were worth fighting for! From the moment he saw Lottie Taylor again he was lost, and you all know it. And if Bram hadn't been killed — don't think it would have made a ha'p'orth of difference!' She was truly angry now, and with a surge of relief she let the anger fly, assuaging at least some of the hurt she had hugged so closely to herself in these past weeks. 'If war had not broken out, if Bram had not been killed, Charlotte Taylor and your precious, honourable son would still have become lovers!'

There was a small silence. 'You believe that?' Logan Sherwood asked.

'Yes. I do.' In the oppressive heat she felt the sweat that sheened her face trickle uncomfortably between her breasts and down her back.

He was quiet for a long time. Around them the crickets took up their monotonous song again. Then, 'And what do you intend to do about it?'

The straightforward question, which she had asked herself so often and so fruitlessly, took her aback. 'I – don't know.'

'That, at least, seems to be a good sign?'

'Don't take it as such.' She shook her head grimly. 'It simply means that I don't know what I can do at the moment. The blockade precludes, for the time being at least, any possibility of my returning to England.' She saw the swift shock in his eyes at that, and coolly ignored it. 'It had occurred to me to suggest a visit to Aunt Bess in Savannah –'

He lifted his head sharply, frowning. 'I wouldn't hear of it. The city's bound to be a target if the Yankees decide to attack from the sea. I won't have you exposing yourself to that kind of danger.'

'With respect,' Mattie snapped back, very coldly, 'is my welfare, or my marriage, any of your business?' and knew, with an odd mixture of misgiving and sudden, astonished mirth, that possibly no-one had ever spoken to Logan Sherwood in such a manner in his whole, privileged life.

The thought must also have occurred to him. He stood, unfolding his spare frame, his brows a straight, repressive line above pale eyes that glinted anger. Straight-backed and belligerent, she faced him, chin up. For a moment it seemed he might explode into wrath; then, completely unexpectedly, he flashed a frank, swift smile so like Johnny's that it was as if a knife had been turned in her heart. Thoughtfully he rubbed the back of his hand against his cheek in characteristic gesture. 'Darned if that son of mine isn't a greater fool than I took him for,' he said.

Jake had found his stick again and was playing with it, tossing it into the air and then pouncing on it.

Mattie, disconcerted, ducked her head, watching the dog.

Johnny's father came to her then, put a big hand lightly on her shoulder. His voice when he spoke was less certain, less assertive, than she had ever heard it. 'Mattie, please – I want you to promise me something?'

She turned her head to look at him.

'Don't do anything hasty. Don't take any decisions. Not yet. Wait. Be patient. And above all, don't leave Pleasant Hill. We've grown very fond of you, girl. We need you. You're part of the family – yes!' Mattie had been unable to prevent the fierce and bitter shake of her head. His grip on her shoulder tightened, preventing her from pulling away from him. 'Yes, I say! In God's name, girl, what do I have to say? I'm askin' you to stay. I'm askin' you – and I know what I'm askin' – not to do anythin' until things return to normal, until Johnny's had time to come to his senses. Mattie, I know what the boy's done to you. I know he deserves nothin' from you! But, whatever you think, however he's hurt you, this is no time to come to hasty decisions. He's at war, Mattie! He's riskin' his life –'

That was too much. She wrenched herself from his grip, turned on him in outrage. 'You think I don't know that? You think I don't know that every minute of every day and every night? You think I don't know that with every miserable breath I take? Who do you think you are to tell me what I should think, how I should feel, what I should do? Go away! Will you please go away!'

He shook his head. 'Not until you answer me. Not until you agree to stay. At least to give that idiot boy of mine another chance.'

She shook her head, tiredly. 'He doesn't want one.'

'Perhaps he doesn't know he wants one.'

She studied him. 'You can't manipulate everyone, you know.'

He smiled again, that quick, unexpected smile that each one of his sons had inherited. 'You're sure teachin' me that, Mattie,' he agreed, in graceful and devious capitulation. And in that moment they both knew he had won.

They walked back to the house together, Logan leading Dancer, the dogs at their heels. They talked of the uncertain progress of the war – for every Confederate advance news came, it seemed, of a setback and the hoped-for recognition from Britain and France still had not materialized, though hearts were still high and conviction of eventual victory unshakeable. The three Sherwood boys had not seen battle since Bull Run and were champing at the bit. Rumours grew, every day, of the possibility – at one time regarded as totally unacceptable – of conscription in the South. 'What will Robert do?' Mattie asked, glancing up at her father-in-law. 'If conscription comes, I mean?'

A small nerve throbbed at the base of the man's jaw, but his voice was equable. 'Why, Mattie, he'll join his brothers, of course. What else would he do?' Ahead of them the elegant bulk of Pleasant Hill rose, white against its setting of dark, moss-hung trees. From the direction of the slave cabins came the sound of children playing. Woodsmoke drifted in the heavy air. 'Look at that, Mattie.' Logan Sherwood came to a sudden halt, put his arm about her shoulders, drawing her to him. 'Look at it! Isn't that worth fighting for?' He relinquished Dancer's reins to Sol, who had come from the house at first sight of them.

'Anything's worth fighting for, Mr Sherwood,' she found herself saying, 'if you love it enough.' And wished immediately that she'd kept a still tongue.

'That's the girl!' He squeezed her shoulder delightedly. 'That's the girl!'

Cissy sat, rocking herself a little, upon a chair on the porch, Liddie beside her with the inevitable palmetto fan, watching them as they climbed the steps together. Since her illness, her moods had become more unpredictable than ever. Today her colour was high and her eyes held a waspish brightness. 'My!' she said, lightly, 'y'all looked real friendly walkin' across there!'

'An' why shouldn't we, Cissy my dear?' Logan Sherwood bent to drop a fatherly kiss on her cheek. 'We're all one big family here, aren't we?'

Cissy's bright, hostile gaze rested squarely upon Mattie's face. 'Really?' she asked, innocently enough, and laughed.

Mattie, deciding that murder was no way out of her predicament, reached down to Jake's collar. 'I'd best take him round the back.'

As she left the sound of the charming, childish voice followed her; 'I heard from Mama an' Papa today, Mr Sherwood. They both send their best wishes. Mama is findin' the war just so tryin'! She's wearin' last season's bonnets made over! Not that she minds that of course – it's for the Cause, after all – but she says she truly dreads the comin' of winter, with no trip to Europe to look forward to. They're talkin' of leavin' N' Orleans an' movin' down to Florida for the duration of the war. Mama says she's just sure there won't be any fightin' down there – she says if the Yankees come we must be sure to go join them. Liddie, go get my medicine, will you? Why, Florida always sounds just such a charmin' place to me, don't you think, Mr Sherwood?'

Logan Sherwood's reply was lost as Mattie turned the corner of the house. She slowed her steps a little. From the steep-roofed kitchen the delicious smell of the stew called gumbo drifted. Prudence's voice could be heard, scolding, and another answered. A wagon creaked towards the stables, one of the field hands, straw hat flopping, sprawled upon the driving bench, two others on the tailboard, legs swinging, half asleep in the autumn sun. The scene looked absurdly idyllic. To all intents and purposes nothing had changed; she had noticed no open difference in the attitudes of the slaves to their masters, no sign that these people knew or understood what was going on around them. But could it possibly be so? In the months since the war began, two field hands had absconded, a rare event at Pleasant Hill, and the runaways had not been recaptured. Mattie knew many of the local planters had tightened security and taken on extra overseers. If, as everyone so confidently predicted, the South held her own and successfully defended her independence, then the likelihood of real trouble from the slave population would presumably be slight, though a few incidents had been reported. But if not? The very thought, she knew, would be counted treachery, not to say heresy, by most. She snapped her fingers at Jake, calling him away from Joshua's geese. What a strange and fearful muddle it all was.

Over by the stable buildings two men stood deep in conversation. As always she was struck by the resemblance each bore to the other. Joshua stood, erect and graceful, the sun gleaming blue-black in his hair. As always she wondered: what does he really feel? What stirs in him when he looks at his brothers and sees them free? Where, now, does his allegiance lie? Yet, watching them now, of one thing she was certain: the link of kinship between these two transcended even that most brutal of gulfs. Whatever else was certain, Logan Sherwood could not live for ever. Mattie had been long convinced that Joshua's eventual freedom, if Robert had any hand in it at all, must be assured. She would, she realized, probably never know. Before any such thing could happen she planned, Logan Sherwood's pleas notwithstanding, to be far from here; back, safe and quiet, in Coombe House.

As the months dragged on and the war showed no obvious signs of coming to an end, the tensions between Robert and his father became more obvious and open. When in November the towns of Beaufort and Port Royal, barely fifty miles from Charleston, fell to Union attacks from the sea and the plantations of family friends were seized by the Union, the bitter row between the two over Robert's continuing adamant refusal to join his brothers in Virginia could be heard all over the house, and the atmosphere was frigid for days. When the news came through a couple of days later of the Confederate victory at Belmont, Missouri, tempers were lost again. And when Russell, to his father's open and unusually demonstrative delight, fought his way home for a few days through roads that had dissolved into liquid mud in the rains of December, it was noticeable that even he had become cooler towards his brother. Through it all Robert remained obdurately and quietly determined; he would not fight. Upon the persistent and growing rumours that by the spring the Confederacy would have its conscription laws and he might be forced into service he would not comment; time enough to make a decision when it happened.

Mattie, meanwhile, one chill wet winter's day, was faced with an unexpected problem of her own.

She had in the past months taken a great interest in the

Infirmary; at least she felt here was a place where she could be of active help. It was late one afternoon when she realized that she had left the notebook, in which she had been making notes about the effectiveness or otherwise of the various medicines and treatments administered to the sick, in the drawer of the little desk that she had taken as her own in the cubbyhole of an office at the back of the Infirmary. While she was retrieving it she heard a noise in the room beyond, where the medicines and herbs were kept and in which no-one, at this time of day, had any business to be. Upon opening the door she was surprised to see Liddic, wide-eyed and obviously frightened, one hand tucked swiftly behind her back.

'Liddie? What are you doing here? What's that you've got?'

The girl stood, mute and terrified.

'Liddie, I asked you a question.' Mattie stepped forward, hand outstretched. 'Give it to me, please.'

Liddie shook her head and stepped back.

Irritated, Mattie sharpened her voice. 'Liddie, I insist!' She held her hand out again. 'Give it to me!'

'Oh, Miss Mattie – no! – I cain't – 'tisn't my fault, Miss Mattie, I swears it!'

'What isn't! What are you talking about? Liddie – will you give me whatever it is you have there, or do I have to call Mister Sherwood to deal with you?'

The girl burst into tears.

Mattie leaned forward, took her hand and prised the fingers open, taking the small bottle that had been hidden in her palm. She looked at it for a long time as Liddie sobbed noisily beside her, her apron to her face. ''Tisn't my fault, Miss Mattie, oh, 'tisn't my fault! Miss Cissy said I had to! She said I done dropped the other bottle an' broke it – but I didn't, Miss Mattie, I swears I didn't. Don't let them whup me, Miss Mattie, I didn't mean no harm –'

'Do be quiet, Liddie. Of course I wouldn't have you whipped.' Mattie held up the bottle. 'You say that Miss Cissy sent you for this? Why didn't she ask me for it?'

The wailing, which had subsided, began again. 'She done said no-one was to know. She done said she'd have me whupped for breakin' the other one – but I didn't, Miss Mattie! I didn't! – an' oh, Miss Mattie, doan' tell Miss Cissy you done seen me, please! She'll whup me her own self if you do.'

'Nonsense.' Mattie pocketed the phial. 'I think perhaps I should see Miss Cissy myself about this. She's in her rooms?'

'Yes, Miss Mattie. But, oh, she'll have my hide off me for this!'

'No, she won't.' Mattie's voice was flat. 'I'll see to that at least.'

Cissy was seated in a comfortable chair before the fire in her little sitting room. Her small hands rested upon an open book in her lap, but her eyes were fixed in distant reverie upon the flames. She did not look round when the door opened. 'Liddie? You have it? Bring it here, girl, for goodness' sake, don't –' She looked round then, and stopped. 'Mattie? What do you want?'

Mattie advanced into the room. Held out her hand. The small green bottle lay in her palm.

There was a very long silence.

Cissy lifted pale, raging eyes. 'Spyin'? You're spyin' on me now? Don't y'all have anythin' better to do with your time, Mattie Sherwood?'.

'No, Cissy, I'm not spying on you. But when it comes to sending Liddie to the Infirmary to steal laudanum for you –'

'Steal? You accusin' me of *stealin'*? How dare you?'

'What else would you call it? Why didn't you ask for it in the normal way?'

'Because I didn't want to get that stupid cat into trouble, that's why! She dropped the bottle –'

'She says she didn't.'

'Well she would, wouldn't she? You takin' her word against mine?' Blazing, the girl came to her feet, snatched at the bottle, but Mattie was too quick for her. She put her hand behind her back, out of reach. For one astonishing moment she thought her furious sister-in-law might physically attack her. After a moment Cissy turned from her, wide skirts swirling angrily. Mattie waited for a moment, but the other girl did not speak.

'Cissy? Why are you taking laudanum still? It's been months since you were sick.' Her voice was quiet, almost gentle.

'It's for my nerves. Doc Morrison said I needed it for my nerves.'

'He said nothing to me.'

Cissy turned on her. 'Why should he? What business is it of yours?'

'You've been taking it – ever since the summer? Ever since you were ill?'

The moment's hesitation was damning. 'No. Of co'se not. It's just – sometimes I need it. For my nerves. I told you.'

'And the other bottle? The one you said that Liddie broke?'

'She did! She did I tell you!'

'Where did that come from? I'd have noticed if it had gone from the Infirmary.'

'So you admit I didn't –' Cissy cast her a withering look '– steal that?'

'From Macon?' Mattie asked, steadily. 'You've been getting it from Macon?'

'It's none of your business.'

'But, Cissy, it is!' Mattie stepped forward, taking the other girl's arm. 'Cissy, don't you see? Laudanum is addictive! It's dangerous!' On the slow walk from the Infirmary to the house, many things had become clear: Cissy's extreme swings of mood, the later and later mornings, the missed meals, the disappearances, sometimes for hours at a time, to 'rest'. 'Dangerous,' she said again, 'if it's misused.'

'An' you're accusin' me of misusin' it?' Cissy's eyes glittered dangerously. She threw Mattie's hand from her arm with a contemptuous gesture.

'No. No, of course not. I'm just not sure that you understand –'

'Oh, I understand, all right. I understand that you can't keep your pryin' nose out of my affairs!' She was shaking. 'Now – get out! An' stay out! Of my rooms an' of my business! Liddie! *Liddie!*' Her voice rose to an ungovernable shriek.

Mattie had to recognize defeat. The bottle still firmly in her hand, she turned. At the door she hesitated. 'One thing, Cissy. I don't want to hear of Liddie being punished for this. It wasn't her fault.'

'Liddie's none o' your business either. I'll do as I like with her.'

'No. No, you won't. Not this time.'

'Oh? You figgerin' on stoppin' me?'

'Yes. I am. You lay a finger on that girl and I take this bottle straight to Mr Sherwood. You can explain to him what happened to the other bottle – I assume you have the pieces since you are so certain that it was broken and not used up? And you can explain to him why you sent Liddie over there to take it instead of asking for it. I mean it, Cissy. I promised the girl she wouldn't be punished, and I'm going to make damn' sure she isn't.'

The look Cissy sent her verged on hatred. Had it been a dagger, Mattie had no doubt whatsoever that it would have struck straight for the heart.

She took to locking the medicines into the Infirmary cupboard after that, though she had no doubt at all that Cissy had another source of laudanum, probably in Macon. She thought of approaching Doctor Morrison, but with every other medical practitioner in the town now away with the army the man was so overwhelmed with work that she hesitated to bother him. Nor could she bring herself to approach Logan Sherwood with such a delicate problem. And as for Robert – he had troubles enough of his own. The person who really should be told was Will; but not by letter. She would wait, wait until Will came home again – it surely couldn't be too long? – and then she would tell him. Meanwhile her relationship with her sister-in-law, never close or particularly friendly, had now deteriorated into enmity. Another reason to get away from Pleasant Hill. To go home.

If only this wretched war would end.

In the spring of 1862 the whole of the South was cockahoop with the news of Stonewall Jackson's exploits in the Shenandoah Valley. At least it took the mind off the rising prices, the facts that the bottom had fallen out of the slave market, gold was selling in the Confederacy at a premium of fifty per cent and there was still no sign that Britain and France were desperate, as had been so confidently predicted, for the cotton that was piled up on wharves and in warehouses all over the blockaded South. Good old Stonewall, running rings round three Union armies, cocking a snook at the best the North could throw at him; with the world's toughest fighting men at his back he was showing Lincoln a thing or two! The news also went a considerable way to wiping out the memory of the surrender of Forts Henry and Donelson, on the Tennessee and Cumberland Rivers, which had lost western Tennessee and the state of Kentucky for the South. From those engagements another nickname had come; Brigadier-General Ulysses S. Grant's message to the defenders of Donelson – 'no terms but an immediate and unconditional surrender can be accepted' – tied in too well with his initials to be ignored, and 'Unconditional Surrender' Grant he had become to a celebrating North. Most of the nicknames his enemies bestowed upon him did not bear repeating.

It was towards the end of that March, with growing signs that the Federal armies were, after this first year of war, being moulded by their leaders into a daunting fighting force that, at last, things came to a head between Robert and his father.

During the winter another two field hands had fled north. Of even more concern to Logan Sherwood was that a favoured house slave, a young man called Mose, had also attempted escape. Dragged back by the patrollers and their hounds, the boy had been strapped to the barn door and savagely flogged before the assembled hands and then, despite the pleas of his mother, sold off for little more than pennies to a sharecropper in Alabama, stern warning to any that might think of following his example. The awful business set yet more barriers between father and son; quite clearly Logan was convinced that Robert's stance was putting subversive ideas into his people's heads, encouraging them to believe that the war would free them. The contest between these two, as too often between those who love deeply but who find themselves divided, was becoming more bitter every day.

On the last day of March, with signs of spring bright and beautiful in the fields and woods of Pleasant Hill, another absconding slave was hauled back in chains to the plantation by a patrol that had caught him an ineffectual ten miles upriver, heading, he had defiantly told them, for the place where Mister Lincoln lived; for Mister Lincoln was the slave's friend.

'Friend, boy?' The brutally casual blow accompanying the words had knocked him from his feet. 'You ain't got no friend. Who in the world told you such a story?' In his hand the patroller, held a rope, fashioned into a noose. As he spoke he swung it, thoughtfully. The men around him grinned, and the dogs, which had already tasted blood, lunged, snarling, at the fallen man, to be pulled off at the last minute by their handlers. There was no fun to be had turning the dogs loose; it was all over too quickly.

Terrified, the captive cowered from them. 'Done heard Mister Robert talkin' to Joshua,' he wailed. 'Done *heard* him!'

'Well, you – done – heard – wrong, – boy.' Each word was accompanied by a precisely placed, vicious kick from a booted foot.

'Mister Robert?' one of the men asked of his companions.

'Sherwood,' said another, menacingly quiet. 'Of Pleasant Hill.'

They arrived with their captive and their story in the early afternoon. Logan and Robert, called in from the fields, sat upon their horses in a closed-faced silence and listened. Mattie and Cissy watched from the porch. Mattie was aware of Joshua, standing behind her, still as a carved image. The recaptured slave had not been treated gently. Blood had dried dark upon his dark skin, and glistened still, bright and horrifying, in the woollen thatch of his hair. Bones had been broken, and he could barely stand. He was in a state of terror that took him almost beyond speech. Only the sight of Robert had galvanized him. 'Mister Robert – Mister Robert, please – doan' let dem string me up – doan' let dem hang me –'

Rage glittered in Logan Sherwood's pale eyes. 'Thank you, gentlemen,' he said, courteously, to the slave's captors who sat their own mounts, hard-eyed and watchful. 'You may with confidence leave this with me.'

The leader shifted a little in the saddle, his hand moving to the noose that was slung across it. 'Seems to me, Mister Sherwood – with respect, you understand? – there's an example to be made here.'

'Right. And Robert will make it.' Logan turned his head, looked at his son for the space of half a dozen heartbeats before turning back to the scene before him. The slave – Benj, Mattie remembered he was called – was on his knees, bloodied and terrified, on the hard-packed red earth, hands chained behind him, the rope by which he had been led here still about his neck. About him, carelessly, danced the hooves of his captors' horses. The hounds snarled, watching him as if he were prey. Her stomach roiled suddenly and she turned away.

'Squeamish, darlin'?' Cissy asked, spitefully pleasantly.

Despising herself for allowing herself to be goaded, Mattie gritted her teeth, and turned back.

'– take him to the barn. Put him up on the door,' Logan Sherwood was saying, crisply. 'Sol, sound the bell – get the hands in from the fields. The house servants too. Everyone. In front of the barn, in an hour.' He reached for the big whip that hung always at his saddle, turned, straight-backed, in the saddle, to hold out the coiled, wicked-looking thing to his son.

Robert sat like stone.

'You flog him,' Logan Sherwood said, very clearly, 'or I hand him back to our friends here.'

'No, Mister Robert, no!' It was a scream of pure terror. 'Doan' let dem take me! They'll string me up for sure – they'll let them houn's have me!'

Robert flinched. Mattie looked away. Cissy smiled.

'A whippin'?' The leader of the patrol shook his head. 'Now I ain't real sure that –'

'A whippin', Sir, yes.' Logan had turned back to him, his face grim. 'This is Pleasant Hill business on Pleasant Hill land. As a general rule it is not my policy to string my people up on the nearest tree, whatever the offence.' His voice was edged with acid. Mattie saw the other man's lips tighten. 'However –' Logan looked at the upturned faces around him, well aware of the impact of his words '– if my son refuses to do his duty then you may take that – ' his eyes flicked in cold contempt to the sobbing man on the ground '– and do as you will with it. I think, however, that you may rest assured that a flogging will be administered that no-one on this plantation, slave or otherwise, will ever forget. Robert?' Still he held the coiled whip, steady in his extended hand.

For a moment it seemed that Robert would refuse.

'Please, Mister Robert –' Benj was sobbing uncontrollably '– you whup me – please! Doan' give me back to them.'

Robert took the whip.

Soft-footed, Joshua spun on his heels and went back into the house, the door closing behind him with a sharp click.

'Well,' Cissy said, much diverted, 'there's a thing.'

'If you don't mind, Mr Sherwood –' for all her effort, Mattie could not keep her voice as precise as she would have liked '– I'd rather not witness the –' she swallowed '– the punishment.'

Logan Sherwood appended his signature unhurriedly to the paper he was studying, looked up. They were in the library. Outside the plantation bell tolled, calling in the hands from the fields.

'But I'm afraid I do mind, my dear.' His expression, like his voice, was unruffled. 'In fact I find myself havin' to insist. Everyone, I said. And everyone I meant.'

'But –'

'No buts, Mattie. Believe me, I would not subject your delicate sensibilities to such a test if I did not feel it to be necessary.'

The anger that had been boiling in her ever since the brutal scene of half an hour ago was making her tremble. Within the fullness of her skirts she clenched her fists, willing herself to calm. 'You aren't punishing Benj,' she said, 'you're punishing Robert.'

He had picked up his pen. He looked at it for a moment before, with the slightest of patient breaths, setting it down again and looking at her. 'How very perceptive of you, my dear.'

Mattie flushed to the roots of her hair.

He shook his head. 'I'm sorry. Sarcasm is not my favourite form of wit. I apologize.'

She shook the apology off with a fierce movement of her head. 'Mr Sherwood – please! – don't make Robert flog Benj. From the look of him the boy's crippled for life already. Isn't that enough? To flog him could kill him.'

He lifted his eyes. For a second so brief she wondered if she had misjudged it, she was taken aback by the naked, savage pain she glimpsed there. Then, 'Possibly,' Logan Sherwood said. The word was cold.

'But how can you force your own son –'

He interrupted her, very sharply, hand lifted. 'Robert will do his duty. In this if in nothin' else. It's a matter of principle –'

'No principle that I recognize, Mr Sherwood!' Mattie's voice was unsteady with anger. The man stood, leaned his hands upon the desk, looking at her levelly, his own face schooled now and all but emotionless. 'I'm sorry, Mattie,' he said at last, his voice very cool and very quiet, 'I hadn't realized just how much I had overestimated your backbone. Strange, how wrong one can be about people. Very well, perhaps you're right. If you haven't the stomach, then by all means you're excused.'

She glared at him for a long, precarious moment. Then 'Go to hell, Mr Sherwood,' she heard herself say, surprisingly quietly but very clearly indeed, before she turned and strode, skirts belling awkwardly about her, to the door.

Behind her the silence was perilous.

She shut the door upon it, furiously, outfacing the panic that she knew might overwhelm her if she actually considered what she had just done.

The house was still, tensely so. No voice lifted, no slave hurried soft-footed about the rooms. Apart from the austere tolling of the bell, there was no sound. Almost without thought, Mattie let her momentum carry her on to the door that led to the only person in the house she could think of who might find some solution to this barbarous situation.

She pulled at the bell rope. Below her she heard the bell ring. Nothing happened. She opened the door. 'Joshua? Are you there?'

She had never before ventured into Joshua's realm; she peered into the shadows. Wide stone steps led down to a brick-paved hallway from which opened several doors. Daylight filtered from a tiny window close to the ceiling. 'Joshua?'

Still nothing. Gingerly she lifted her skirts and stepped carefully down the worn stairs. 'Joshua!'

The first two doors she tried were locked; the third opened onto a room neat and spare as a monk's cell, containing bed, cupboard, chair and table and a small shelf full of books. The floor here was brick, too, and the low ceiling was the unpainted wooden boards of the floor above. The curtainless window was set high, and level with the ground outside.

Joshua sat at the table, barefoot and in shirtsleeves and the wide cotton trousers of a field hand, his big hands wrapped around a glass. Beside him stood a half-full bottle of whisky. He did not move as she pushed open the door.

'Joshua, I'm sorry – I don't mean to disturb you. I couldn't think of anyone else –' The words trailed into the silence. The man had lifted his head and was watching her, waiting. Every taut line of his face was a line drawn in relentless pain and an agony of anger.

Mattie had come too far to back out now. She stepped forward, her hands held urgently towards him. 'Please, Joshua! No-one's *doing* anything – no-one's even trying to stop this. There surely must be something we can do?'

He turned away from her. Very steadily he poured more whisky into his glass, and without looking at her lifted it to his lips.

'Joshua! For God's sake! Don't you care?'

His sudden movement, arrested as swiftly as it had begun, made her jump. She flinched at what for one unguarded moment she saw in his face. 'Oh, I'm sorry – I'm sorry! Of course you do – I just can't bear just to stand by and see this happen – not to try to do something –' She was close to tears.

He spoke at last. 'Do somethin', Miss Mattie?' he asked. 'Now what in the world does you suggests this poor foolish nigger ups an' does?' The drawl was exaggerated to parody. 'Go beg the mass'er to be kind, an' please not to whup poor ole Benj?

Ast him ter send away them nasty ole pattyrollers an' their houn's?'

'Stop that! Stop it!'

'Yes, Ma'am.' His mouth clamped to a straight and bitter line.

'Joshua, I'm trying to help – I thought you might think of something –'

'No, Ma'am.'

'It'll kill Robert to flog that boy.'

The dark eyes lifted again, intelligent, pain-filled and distant. Mattie got the feeling that he hardly even saw her. 'Likely it'll kill Benj too,' Joshua said, very softly.

The bell had ceased its ringing. Joshua poured himself another drink.

Mattie watched him helplessly. 'I just told Logan Sherwood to go to hell,' she said, not knowing for the life of her why she said it.

For a moment it looked as if he would not even answer. Then, his expression unchanged, ''Bout time someone did,' he said, quietly, and then with the briefest glimmer of a grim smile added, 'You tell anyone I said that and I'll be the next one on the barn door.'

'I won't tell anyone.'

He looked back down at the bottle, the smile gone. 'I never thought you would, Miss Mattie. I never for a minute thought you would.'

She stood watching him, wordless. 'I'm sorry,' she said at last, bleakly. 'I shouldn't have come. If I'm honest I don't know why I did. I can't think what I imagined you could do when the rest of us are helpless.' She turned from him, walked to the door.

'Wait. Miss Mattie – wait!' Joshua's voice stopped her as she reached the threshold. She did not turn. All she wanted now was to leave. She could not bear the thought of this man seeing her break down and weep like a child. She heard the chairlegs scrape as he pushed the chair back from the table. 'Wait,' he said again. His voice suddenly was its normal self, deep, husky and quiet. 'It isn't for you to apologize. It's for me to be thankin' you – for comin' down here. For believin', even for a moment, that I could do somethin' to help. I appreciate that, Miss Mattie. You're wrong, but that ain't your fault. You did it for the best.'

'For the best and for nothing,' she said, her back to him still, unable to keep the sound of bitter tears from her voice.

Joshua had moved behind her, silently on bare feet, standing very close. She could feel his warmth, smell the faint smell of whisky on his breath. She bowed her head, buried her face briefly in her spread hands, furiously fighting off the desire to give way to a helpless and useless storm of tears.

'There, now, Miss Mattie. There, now. No need to take on so. Brave lady like you?' The touch of his hand was light upon her shoulder. She felt his other hand on her hair, smoothing and stroking with easy, comforting rhythm. 'One thing in this life to learn, Miss Mattie. Ain't no use takin' on about somethin' you can't do a damn' thing about.' The musical voice was soothing, gentle. Oddly and disturbingly tender. She stood, still tense and trembling a little. Then for a single, shocking moment, she let herself lean against him, let herself be lulled by that deep, lovely voice, gentled by the stroking hands. She dropped her own hands from her face, lifted her head, turning it into his shoulder, eyes still closed. His hand brushed her cheek, the thumb resting on her lips.

Each pulled away from the other at the same moment. She backed away from him slowly and carefully, her eyes locked on his. Light gaze and dark held for a moment, as if hypnotized, lucid and fearful. Joshua's gleaming eyes narrowed. He shook his head, sharply.

Mattie, heart pounding, turned and fled for the stone stairs.

The punishment did not kill Benj, though it came close. Nor, from any expression he permitted to show, did the savage business openly cause Robert any distress. Mattie, goaded as Logan Sherwood had known she would be, had steeled herself to be part of the silent throng who gathered to watch the whipping. She thought she had never seen anything so demeaningly brutal, and was certain that the sound of Benj's screams as the lash lifted and fell with intolerable regularity upon his bleeding back would stay with her for ever; though the silence at the end, when the screaming was done and the blows fell dully upon a sagging and all but lifeless body, was worse. Sweat sheened Robert's face, dripped from his hair, stained the back of his shirt. Benj's mother and sister keened quietly, their aprons over their heads. It was not until Mattie herself was close to screaming that Logan Sherwood at last lifted a finger to stop the merciless beating. Robert lowered his tired arm. The man lashed to the barn door did not move. Flies buzzed about his raw, striped back.

'Well, Sir?' Logan faced the patroller, who sat his horse to the side of the crowd, watching. 'Are you satisfied?'

The man nodded, grinning. ''Bin quicker to hang him. An' cost a mite less energy,' he said, and, touching his hat, kneed his horse round and walked him off down the drive.

'Joshua. The brine.'

Joshua, stripped to the same shirt and trousers he had been wearing when last Mattie had seen him, stepped forward and dowsed the still figure upon the door with two buckets of salted water. She averted her eyes.

Benj made a sound like an injured animal.

'Take him down. To the Infirmary. Careful, there! You – 'Lilah – go with them. Robert –' He stopped.

Robert had turned, the bloodied whip coiled in his hand, staining it. Silently he came to his father. The two stood for a long moment, eye to eye some yards from each other, before, with no word, and with a gesture that verged on the contemptuous, Robert tossed the whip at Logan's feet, and turned to stride back towards the house, the crowd parting for him in utter silence as he went.

Logan watched his son's retreating back with narrowed eyes.

'I declare,' Cissy said, a bright excitement still in her eyes, 'how very strangely Robert does behave sometimes.'

The next morning the last Sherwood son was gone from Pleasant Hill.

Robert set his horse upon the road before dawn, leaving behind no message, and a household utterly divided.

As he rode north, his brothers, unknown to him, were also jubilantly on the move at last; on the move, and fast, with a Confederate army, towards a place on the Tennessee River – a place that took its name from a small log-built church upon a tranquil hillside; a church whose name had been translated by those who knew about such things as 'the place of peace'.

As Robert, anguished and solitary, rode slowly to his enemies, his brothers rode, singing, with their comrades, towards a place called Shiloh.

CHAPTER TEN

The Battle of Shiloh, claimed as a victory by the North, never
accepted as a defeat by the South, was in real and human terms
a disaster for both sides, the first intimation of just how bitter
and how costly this struggle between sister states was to
become.

The Confederate army, commanded by generals Johnston and
Beauregard, with which the Sherwood brothers rode, pushed
fast and hard for Tennessee. Initially winning the race upon
which they had embarked, they took Grant's Federal troops by
surprise, and at a savage cost in casualties on both sides, overran
the Yankee positions and their camps, forcing them back to the
river. It was a Sunday in early April; the weather was atrocious
and the Rebels, after their forced march, were tired and hungry.
As they swept through the captured encampments many
stopped, whooping derisively at the fleeing bluecoats, to breakfast by the Yankee campfires on the ham, eggs and soft white
bread that Grant's green troops had abandoned in panic. But
the day was by no means easily won. Dug in to a sunken road
that became known by the Southerners who tried to take it as
'the Hornets' Nest', courageous Federal soldiers held out for
several obstinate and bloody hours, obstructing the advance,
their casualties and those of their attackers rising into thousands
before they were finally forced to an exhausted and honourable
surrender. In brutal confusion, field by field, wood by wood, and
through the blossoms of a ten-acre peach orchard, the Southerners fought on towards the river, in some places knee-deep in the
dead and dying of both sides. Nor was it only the common soldier
who died; at the height and in the midst of the battle, the able
and popular General Johnston was killed, a shattering loss for his
men and for the Confederacy. But, defying even the death of such

a leader, the Rebel blood was up and the day was going their way; weary before they started, hungry and footsore, still the promise of victory bore them up. That the bluebellies made a last stubborn stand at the river as the sun sank, and fought their wildly screaming attackers to a standstill, mattered nothing; the day was the Confederacy's. Word was, confidently, that the Yanks would surrender at sun-up.

Before turning in within the comfort of an enemy tent, General Beauregard sent a wire to his President in the Southern capital of Richmond, reporting that the Confederate states' army had won a convincing victory, and that the enemy was driven from every position.

In the sodden fields and woods men in grey and in blue dropped where they stood, heads pillowed on their packs, despite the drumming rain that swept over the stiffening dead and the slumped, exhausted living alike. It was a nightmare of a night, riven by thunder and by lightning, by the shrieks from the surgeons' tents and by the sound of the indiscriminately fired shells that sang a song of death from the Federal gunboats that still patrolled the Tennessee River; nevertheless, in exhaustion, they slept.

It was from the river that the Union reinforcements came; over twenty thousand of them, fresh, hardened and ready for action. When the sun rose on the second day over the bloody fields and mangled orchards of Shiloh, General U.S. Grant and his second-in-command – a thin, hard-faced, red-headed Ohian named Tecumseh Sherman – had more men at their command than they had marshalled on the first, notwithstanding the desperate losses of yesterday; the Confederates, on the other hand, scattered, exhausted and badly mauled despite their successes, had no reserves on which to call. Instead of attacking, the weary Rebels found themselves attacked. Instead of sealing a hard-won victory, they found themselves fighting for their lives against aggressively fresh troops. To their credit, pushed relentlessly back across the ground they had won at such cost, they held the line and did not break; but the heart had gone from them, and the slaughter this time was too much. By early afternoon the retreat had begun, the long, dispirited column struggling through sleet and rain and a quagmire of mud, harried by Sherman's cavalry; they left behind them on that field over seventeen hundred dead and nearly a thousand missing men. Over eight thousand wounded travelled with the retreating column, or were abandoned to the untender mercies of a Northern prison. And despite their claimed victory, the Federal casualties almost exactly matched the defeated Confederates'. One hundred thousand men had come to the riverbank at Shiloh Chapel; of them, almost one in four had been wounded, captured, or had died – losses comparable with the equally savagely fought Battle of Waterloo, forty-seven years before.

The difference was that the battle that had seen the final downfall of Napoleon had decided the outcome of a war; cruelly, this one had decided nothing.

Beauregard's confident and premature claim to victory slowed and confused the news of disaster and loss in the South. Days after the battle, reports were still contradictory. It was on the Thursday of that week in April that Logan Sherwood decided to ride into Macon with Joshua on the dual errand of a visit to the cotton factor and an attempt to gather any positive news.

No-one had dared to speak Robert's name since he had left.

Mattie divided that day between the Infirmary, where she was reorganizing the medicines cupboard, and the supervising of half a dozen female slaves who were making lye soap; no-one mentioned that up to a few months ago such supervision would have been unnecessary. It was an accepted fact now; even the female slaves had to be watched – and since Cissy was, as usual, conspicuously absent, the task fell, as it now almost always did, to Mattie.

She was in the Infirmary when Logan Sherwood and Joshua returned from town. Hearing the familiar, even sound of the horses' hooves upon the red earth she came blinking from the shadows into a clear spring afternoon, wiping her hands on her apron, tucking a stray strand of hair behind her ear. As her eyes adjusted to the light and she saw the riders more clearly, she stopped in midstride, every instinct telling her that something was badly wrong.

The two rode slowly, at walking pace, and as always in single file, Joshua a yard or two behind his master.

Mattie narrowed her eyes, watching them. It was something about the set of the old man's head, about his carriage, rigid and ungivingly erect, so unlike his usual easy and graceful stance, that had alerted and alarmed her. Joshua too rode with none of his usual ease. The afternoon, which was full of birdsong and the scent of magnolia, seemed to hang dark about them. As she started forward again towards the oncoming riders, her eyes upon Logan's stony face, shadowed beneath his wide-brimmed hat, Mattie was suddenly aware of her own heartbeat, slow and heavy, all but choking her.

Logan Sherwood, at all times and even at his most arrogant the very soul of courtesy, rode past her as if she had not existed, his gaze fixed like a blind man's directly ahead.

Nothing had ever frightened her so much.

Joshua's eyes, black as pitch in the grim, carved mask of his face, flickered to hers; and, in anguish, the beat of her heart almost stopped altogether.

For a moment she could not move. She stood as if rooted and watched as the horses came to a well-behaved stop at the foot of the steps. The usual fleet-footed boys had appeared at the sound, waiting to take the reins. Mattie saw in their shocked, upturned faces the same expression she knew must be upon her own as they looked at their master. There was a strange silence about the scene; a terrible silence.

Mattie broke it. 'Mr Sherwood? Mr Sherwood, what is it? What's happened?' She picked up her skirts and ran across the packed red earth to where the two men stood.

Logan Sherwood had dismounted stiffly, and already started up the steps, slowly and heavily, his gait that of an old, infirm man.

The sight struck her to horrified silence.

At the top of the steps he paused for a moment, his hand on the rail, his back still to Mattie. 'You tell them, Joshua,' he said, very quietly. 'For, by Christ's own suffering, I can't, and that's the truth.' As he spoke he turned his head a little; and for the first time she saw the tears.

She was sick with panic now, and with dread. As always, the strange and wordless communication of the slaves was at work; the area in front of the house was filling with men and women on quiet, naked feet. Others were coming from the house, their eyes in awe upon their master as he walked unseeing through them. A girl threw her apron over her turbaned head and began to wail. Lucy, beside her, calmly pulled the apron clear and slapped her, hard.

In the sudden hush Mattie asked, as steadily as she could, 'Joshua? What's happened? It's –' she swallowed ' – it's bad news?'

He stood, tall, broad, the bruised and shadowed image of his brothers. 'Yes, Miss Mattie. It's real bad news.' His deep and musical voice was very quiet.

She waited, watching him, still trying to control the awful, muffled thump of her heartbeat.

'Mister Will. Mister Russ.' He hesitated for a fraction of a second. 'Mister Johnny. They're gone, Miss Mattie.'

She looked at him, stupidly. 'Gone?' Her own voice had risen. With an effort she mastered it. 'What do you mean – gone? Gone where? Not – not deserted, surely? No, of course not – how stupid – you mean captured? Taken prisoner?'

The shadowed face was still and expressionless as granite. 'They're dead, Miss Mattie. Killed at Shiloh, all three.'

'Dead?' She spoke the word as if she had never heard it before, as if it had no meaning to her. She felt as if someone had hit her, very hard, in the solar plexus. She could not breathe. Nearby a woman was keening, wailing wordlessly into the clear spring sky. 'Dead?' she repeated, faintly.

'Yes, Miss Mattie. Their names were on the list at the telegraph office.'

She shook her head sharply. 'Don't be ridiculous. They can't be. Not – not all of them. Joshua – there's a mistake. Of course there is. There must be.'

Joshua was silent.

The sound of tears, of noisy grief, was suddenly all about

them. Mattie turned, furiously. 'Shut up, you stupid things! You hear me? Be still – or I'll have the skin off you, I swear it!' She spun urgently back to Joshua. 'Joshua, there must be some mistake! They can't all be – be dead! It's unthinkable. These lists – they aren't always right – they're made up in the confusion of battle – they're often wrong –'

He was shaking his head. 'It was in the paper too, Miss Mattie – and a story about what happened – see – Mr Sherwood threw it away – but I picked it up.' He pulled a torn, crumpled newspaper from the pouch at his belt and handed it to her.

Mattie could not for a moment focus upon the small, black print. Utter silence fell about her. With an effort she forced her eyes and her brain to obey her. The words danced queasily. She gritted her teeth. In the Yankee counterattack on the second day of the Battle of Shiloh, newly promoted Lieutenant Russell Sherwood had made a defiant and courageous stand with a handful of men to protect a road down which the shattered Confederate army was retreating. His brothers, hearing of the action, had, against orders and against common sense, turned back to help him; too late. Outnumbered and outgunned, Russell and his companions had already gone down. Will and Johnny had run directly into the butchery of the Yankee advance; they had sold their lives dearly. The State of Georgia had lost three true and gallant sons, sacrificed to the cause. Heartfelt sympathy was extended to the Sherwood family, well known in the state . . .

Mattie stopped reading; she could not, in any case, see through the tears. She stood, head bowed, fighting a wave of mind-numbing grief. She no longer doubted; the story rang too bitterly true. Obdurately rejecting the pictures that were trying to force themselves into her mind, of three tall, laughing young men cut to bloody shreds by the Yankee bullets they had always so despised, she did not hear the silken rustle of skirts above her, the shuffle of feet about her as the gathered Negroes stepped back from the sparkling smile of the newcomer who stood on the porch, fair and young as the spring sunshine, looking down in surprise at the gathering below. It was one of Cissy's good days; she had had a letter from Will the day before promising that on his next furlough they would go to visit her parents in Florida. 'Why, gracious me,' she said, the small beginnings of a questioning frown marring her high, pale forehead. 'What in the world is goin' on here?'

Between Logan's grief and Cissy's, Mattie hardly had time for her own; except in the dark, exhausted nights, when unhappiness and guilt and a helpless sadness mercilessly combined to drive out sleep and annihilate peace of mind. For a week her father-in-law locked himself in the library and would not come out, nor speak to anyone, not even Sol, who moped beside the door in company with the dogs, also banned from their master's sight. It was in desperation that Mattie turned to Joshua. Since that strange and disturbing moment in his room on the day of the flogging they had, in an unspoken and delicate mutual agreement, avoided each other's company as far as was possible. In this crisis, however, Mattie could think of no-one else who might be able to bring Logan from the dark seclusion of his grief.

'Please, Joshua, would you try? It's wrong for him to shut himself away so. Speak to him – try to persuade him –' She stopped, shrugged helplessly.

Joshua shook his head. 'Best to leave him, Miss Mattie. You don't know him as I do. Best to leave him to himself.'

'To himself and a case of whisky? Joshua, he'll kill himself if we don't stop it! Please!'

He was quiet for a moment, watching her. She was on the edge of nerve-strung tears. 'All right, Miss Mattie. If you say so. I'll try. But I still think it's a mistake.'

He was right. It was a mistake.

Flinching, she heard – everyone heard – Logan's raised voice from beyond the door: 'Get out of here you no-good Goddamn' nigger! When I want you I'll call for you, you hear? Get away – get out of my sight, or I'll have you in the fields pickin' cotton.' As the door opened she saw Logan's face, ashen with rage; saw too the empty bottle upon the desk, and the untouched tray of food that Prudence had taken to him some time before.

Joshua strode past her, stone-faced.

'An' stay out, you hear me? Uppity Goddamn' nigger! Stay away from me!'

Mattie, gathering her courage, went to the door. 'Mr Sherwood –'

'You, too, Mattie.' His voice was level, and hardened against emotion, his hair was dishevelled and his eyes red-rimmed; but the habit of command was still with him. 'An' keep him away from me, you hear? Just keep him away!' Behind him on the wall, portraits hung; Russ and Will, captured upon canvas together in healthy and glorious youth, Johnny, the youngest, alone, his arm about a favourite hound, the quirk of that reckless smile upon his lips. A blank, light square where once Robert's image had been. And in each of those faces, the shadow of Joshua.

Cursing herself for the fool she knew she had been, Mattie shut the door, very quickly.

Joshua was gone.

Cissy, too, refused to leave her room; refused, in fact, to leave her bed. She swung between paroxysms of hysterical weeping and periods of total, miserable silence. The only thing that gave her comfort or any measure of peace in the days that followed the news was the laudanum that Mattie could no longer deny her.

It was a week before the letter arrived from their commanding officer confirming the deaths of the Sherwood boys, commending their courage and gallantry, sympathizing deeply with the family, assuring them that the brothers had not died in vain; victory for the cause was assured whilst the South had such men to defend her. Mattie hoped that the words did not ring as emptily for Logan and Cissy as they did for her.

Two days after the letter arrived, another field hand escaped, and was not recaptured. A week later, Shake came home.

He hobbled up the drive, barefoot and clad in nothing but a pair of ragged trousers and a dark blue uniform jacket, torn and bloodstained, too short in the sleeves and too tight at the shoulder. As always it was the slaves who saw him first; by the time Mattie came out onto the porch he was already surrounded. Seeing her, he pulled himself erect and attempted a salute. He was thin, and grey-faced with exhaustion.

For one moment Mattie allowed herself to hope; then, looking into his face, the faint, absurd glimmer was extinguished.

'Got ter see the Massa, Miss Mattie,' he said. 'Got ter tell him – tell him what done happened to the young masters.'

'You were there?'

'Yes, Ma'am.' The man was almost at the end of his tether. A filthy bandage showed beneath the torn cuff of his trouser leg.

Mattie stood back. 'Come. Mr Sherwood's in the library. Afterwards, come to the Infirmary. And I'll get Prudence to get you some supper.'

'Thanks, Miss Mattie. Sure could do with that.' Painfully he hauled himself up the steps to the porch, brushing down his stolen tattered jacket. 'Hopes Mr Sherwood'll not take it bad that I's not clean.'

Mattie shook her head. 'He won't take it badly, Shake,' she said, gently, then, as she lifted a hand to knock on the library door she hesitated for a moment. 'Shake?'

'Yes, Ma'am?'

'They – they are dead? There's no mistake?'

He shook his head tiredly, his face set in lines of grief and exhaustion. 'No mistake, Miss Mattie. I was there. I done seen it. When Mister Will an' Mister Johnny saw Mister Russ go down they waded into them bluebellies like they'd done lost their minds. They didn't stan' no chance, Miss Mattie.'

She could see it as clearly as if she had been there. 'No,' she said, 'I'm sure they didn't,' and knocked sharply upon the door.

Shake's return, his eyewitness account of the disaster at Shiloh, at least had the effect of giving the tragedy substance. Until then Mattie had not realized how much hope she – and she presumed the others – had still secretly nursed, how unreal the whole business had seemed. Shake's first-hand account of the Sherwoods' deaths – and, incidentally, of the speedy desertion of Will's and Russell's servants, who had apparently taken the opportunity to flee north – laid all of that to rest; it made grief real, and very painful, but it also focused the mind. Will, Russ and Johnny were gone. In the fraught days that followed the confirmation, Mattie found she had no choice but to force her own grief for those lost young men, her own agonies about the unfinished, now unresolvable, relationship with her husband, to take second place to the struggle not to be dangerously overwhelmed by the very real crisis their loss had produced. Even her longing to be home, away from this torn and alien land, was utterly swamped by the everyday exigencies of keeping the grief-stricken household running, by the need to see order restored to Pleasant Hill. For order, certainly, had fled, and she sensed too well that peril might well stalk close on the heels of any unusual relaxing of discipline, whatever its cause.

After Shake's homecoming, Logan came out of his self-imposed isolation; but the fire and the heart had gone from him, and the youthful vigour that had so characterized him. For the first time Mattie realized, with a shock, that he was an old man. He spent most of the time sitting in a rocking chair upon the porch, whisky glass in hand, rocking slowly back and forth, his eyes, still pale and bright, looking with abstracted concentration towards the place where the long, winding drive emerged from its tunnel of oaks. Mattie wondered often if he watched, despite everything, to see one of his boys come riding up to the house. He ate little, and drank too much, though she never saw him anything but completely clear-headed. His great frame seemed to have shrunk. He would not, or perhaps could not, look at or speak to Joshua; his orders, such as they were, were relayed through Mattie. He received the sympathetic visits of friends and neighbours with a tart and touchy resignation; he made no-one welcome, and they did not stay for long. Through these outside contacts Mattie learned of the fall of Fort Pulaski to the Federal navy, and of the taking of New Orleans by the Yankees. Baton Rouge and Natchez followed; only Vicksburg now flew the Confederate flag over the waters of the Mississippi. If Vicksburg fell, the South would be split in two. A disastrous spring for the Confederacy was turning into an even more disastrous summer. Logan, apparently, did not care, any more than he cared that weeds grew in the cotton fields, that a fire, possibly deliberate, half destroyed one of the barns and reduced the garconnier to ashes, that even the house slaves were getting lazy. Only once did the old Logan reassert himself, and that was when Mattie unwisely mentioned Robert's name. Knowing the dangers, she had so carefully planned what she might say that inevitably she did it clumsily. Logan, after all, still had a son; should they not try to find him – to tell him of his brothers' deaths?

The great head came up, pale eyes in a gaunt face blazing. 'Mattie, don't mention that name to me. Ever. You hear me? Not ever! My sons are dead. All of them. I have no sons.'

'But –'

'And if the coward you just mentioned ever dares to set foot on Pleasant Hill land again, by Christ I'll kill him myself.' The words were flat.

'Mr Sherwood – surely – you can't –'

He leaned forward, the old intemperate wrath at being challenged flaming in his face. 'Don't tell me what I can or can't do, girl.' He lifted a long, thin, but still strong hand, palm out, as if taking an oath. 'I swear this to you, on everythin' I've ever held holy – on my dead boys' heads – if that craven runaway ever shows his face in this state of Georgia, never mind on my land, I'll kill him, sure as eggs. I mean it. Hangin's too good for his kind. I'm shamed to have sired him.'

And Joshua? Are you ashamed of Joshua too? Mattie did not have the courage to voice the question; she believed in any case that she knew the answer. Logan Sherwood was too entrenched in his ways and beliefs to feel any shame at having bedded a slave girl, or kept his own son in bondage. His present antipathy to Joshua was purely and simply rooted in the fact that this other Sherwood son looked so like those young men who had ridden away in such high spirits, whole and healthy, such a very short while before. Sometimes she feared quite desperately that the old man might sell Joshua, or give him away, to spare himself the sight of him – and was certain, though he never said anything, that the same thought had occurred to Joshua himself. With no word, the two of them, Mattie and the slave, embarked upon a conspiracy to keep him from his master's eyes. Mattie knew, if Logan did not, that without Joshua Pleasant Hill would fall apart, and for that reason – and for that reason alone, she told herself firmly – there could be no question of allowing Logan, in the irrational state of mind caused by his grief, to send him away.

And so it was that throughout the hot and difficult days of that summer and on into the humid weeks of autumn, it was Joshua who ran the plantation, Joshua who supervised the work in the fields as yet another unsaleable crop of cotton came into bloom, Joshua who ordered ditches dug and fences mended, nursed the few cattle and hogs left to them through the summer heat, walked the fields of corn, potatoes and peas that would hopefully see the household through the winter; Joshua who knocked down a slave whose insolence was simply a symptom of the general disintegration of discipline on Pleasant Hill. Mattie it was who consulted with Logan, who conveyed to the rest of the household his occasional orders and suggestions, though in truth the man did not seem to know or care that his land was, despite Joshua's efforts, suffering neglect and his people showing the first dangerous stirrings of discontent. For Mattie too that summer was a hard one. The strong hand that had held the plantation together was gone; and with it had gone the efficiency and obedience she now realized she had taken so much for granted. She could spend the whole day supervising a task that should have taken a couple of hours, to find it still not done, and yet never be able to put her finger on the reason why. She gave orders that were forgotten, or ignored. Dust accumulated in corners and the store of candles and of flour ran out, far quicker than they should have done. She suspected thieving. And, each night, there was the lonely room to face; the guilt, the grief, the endless, unanswerable questions. The small, much-thumbed book of Shelley's poems, as much a torment as a comfort.

And then, there was Cissy.

Cissy's grief, though undoubtedly genuine, was entirely self-centred. She saw and understood nothing of the crippling blow that had been dealt Logan, and was openly scornful of any tears Mattie might shed. What had Mattie to cry about? Why, she and Johnny hadn't even written to each other in months, everyone knew that – whilst she, Cissy, and Will – such a train of thought invariably led to hysterical outbursts, which took ever larger doses of laudanum to calm. And even as time and youth worked their alchemy and the sharpest edge of her grief was blunted, her whole concern continued to be for her own plight. What was she to do? A widow, for goodness' sake, before her eighteenth birthday – and with this dreadful war going on – how was she ever to find another beau? Who would care for her, who would protect her now?

'Oh, Cissy, do stop!' Mattie cried one hot and trying September day, thoroughly losing her temper at last, dropping the sheet she was darning and putting her hands to her ears, as the whole litany was repeated again. 'Anyone would think you were the only one to suffer so! Don't you know what's going on out there? Thousands of men have died! Thousands! And still are dying! God only knows how long this awful business is going to go on! And all you can think of – all you can talk about – oh, I don't know how you can be so selfish!'

She was stopped by a screech of indignation. 'I, selfish? I! Why, may you drop dead where you sit, Mattie Sherwood! Everyone knows how *miserable* you made poor Johnny! An' the way you try to order everyone about – oh, I declare, you are the most detestable creature!' Cissy's voice lifted, edged with hysteria, and she hauled the inevitable handkerchief from her sleeve. 'Just because you don't care what you look like – just because you don't mind seein' no-one, talkin' to no-one from one week's end to the next, doesn't mean I have to be the same! Stuck here with you an' that damn' dog an' a mad old man for company –'

'Cissy!'

'Why can't we go live in Macon? At least there's some life there! Why must we stay out here, in the middle of nowhere?' She was crying in earnest now. Mattie noted in some exasperation and not for the first time that Cissy even managed to do that to the prettiest effect. 'Nothin' will ever happen here.

Nothin'! My life's over, Mattie!' Her voice rose to a wail again. 'Oh, it isn't fair! It isn't *fair*! Liddie – go fetch me my medicine –'

Mattie never knew whether the overdose was deliberate or not. Thinking about it later, she gave the child the benefit of the doubt and decided not; at the time it hardly mattered. All she knew was that her young sister-in-law lay as still and pale as death upon her bed, the hysterical Liddie shrieking and crying beside her.

'Shut up, Liddie! Take her other arm – no, I can manage – the child weighs nothing. Go and find Lucy quickly, you hear? And Joshua –'

'I doan' know where he is, Miss Mattie –'

'Just find him! Fast!'

'But he might be out there in the fiel's – I doan' like goin' into the fiel's – them hands are downright –' Liddie backed away smartly as Mattie turned on her. 'All right, all right, Miss Mattie – I's goin' –'

Mattie hauled Cissy to her feet. 'Cissy, wake up! Cissy!'

The girl moaned, her head rolling.

Awkwardly, Mattie slapped her. 'Cissy!'

Cissy coughed and mumbled incoherently.

Mattie swung her around, caught her by the shoulders, shaking her. 'Wake up! Cissy, wake up!'

'Miss Mattie?' It was Lucy at the door. 'What is it?'

'Get over to the Infirmary, quickly. Castor oil. Lots of it. Cissy!'

They brought her through it in a squalid and panic-ridden mess of vomit and tears. Later, filthy and exhausted, Mattie stood on the balcony outside, breathing the stifling autumn air and trying to control her shaking legs; trying too not to think of what might have happened if Liddie had not found the girl when she had.

'You all right, Miss Mattie?'

She turned her head. Joshua stood beside her.

'Yes. Yes, I'm fine, thank you. Thank God Liddie found her when she did.'

He nodded.

In the room behind them Lucy's quiet voice spoke, Liddie's light one replied, sharp and quarrelsome.

Joshua stirred in the darkness.

'You should get some rest, Miss Mattie. You've been up all night.'

She slanted a quick and weary smile over her shoulder, then turned, unwarily, to face him. 'So have you.'

He shrugged a little.

From the compound beneath them came the sound of singing, soft and melancholy. The sudden and telling quiet that had fallen between them as she had lifted her eyes to his stretched on. Too tired to resist it, she leaned against the wooden rail, watching him, trying to fathom the look in that intent, high-boned face. 'Rest, Joshua,' she said at last, softly. 'You've been working too hard. We all have.'

He neither moved nor spoke. For a single, outrageous moment she was tempted to the impossible: to take that small step forward, into arms she was certain would open to her, would hold and protect her. He moved, very slightly, and she caught her breath.

'– good-for-nothin' little cat that you are!' Cissy's door flew open. Lucy stalked out onto the balcony breathing righteous anger. 'Miss Mattie – you done told me to help nurse Miss Cissy or you didn't? You done tell this no-good Liddie that!'

Mattie took a long breath. Turned from Joshua. 'Oh, for goodness' sake! Can't the two of you get on for two full minutes at a time?' Behind her she could still sense the man's quiet, powerful presence. It was with some relief that she heard his light foot-falls as he slipped away down the stairs and into the house. 'Liddie, I'd have thought you'd have been pleased to have some help!'

Cissy stayed in bed for three days. On the fourth she was busy in her room – evidently, from the amount of coming and going she was engendering, recovered. On the fifth she appeared on the porch, still a little pale but dressed fetchingly for travel, albeit in the grey and lilac trimmed with black that had been her concession to mourning, and with a tall young male slave and a nervous-looking Liddie behind her, the one carrying a small trunk and the other a large bag. Mattie, who had been reading to Logan a week-old newspaper – which contained, at last, a little good news – looked up in surprise. 'Cissy? Where are you going?'

'Home,' Cissy said serenely, though there was a wary defiance about her. ''Lijah, put the trunk down there, will you please? And go ask Dandy to bring round the carriage. Tell him we're goin' to the train station in Macon.' She turned back to Mattie, ignoring Logan completely. 'I'll send for the rest of my things later.'

'Home?' Mattie repeated, faintly.

'To Mama and Papa.' Cissy's voice was light but her chin was set stubbornly. 'Home,' she repeated.

'But – but Cissy – you can't go running around the country on your own!'

'I shan't be on my own. 'Lijah and Liddie are coming with me. They're both mine. I brought them from N'Orleans with me.' She cast a small glance of mixed fright and defiance at Logan Sherwood.

He had picked up the newspaper and appeared to be taking no interest in the proceedings at all. 'Indeed they are,' he said, calmly, from behind the spread pages. 'And indeed you did.'

Mattie stood up. 'But, Cissy –'

'Let her go.' Logan Sherwood neither looked up nor raised his voice; but the words cut across Mattie's like a blade.

Cissy threw him a look of sheer, unadulterated dislike.

Mattie was struck to silence; the two girls stood so, with Liddie fidgeting behind them, for what seemed an age before the small two-wheeled carriage drawn by an elderly, slow-moving horse who until the war had been honourably pensioned off to grass, came around the corner and drew to a halt in front of the steps.

'Well,' Cissy said, very brightly, 'I'll be goin', then.' She sounded, Mattie thought bemusedly, as if she were going into Macon for a few yards of ribbon. She proffered her cheek to Cissy's soft lips, watched as Logan, with no show of emotion whatsoever, did the same. 'My Papa will be in touch with you, I expect,' Cissy said.

He tipped his head to look at her, forbiddingly, at last. 'Oh?'

'About –' she hesitated, delicately, cleared her throat '– about anything that – that may be coming to me – through Will, you understand?'

Mattie held her breath.

'Get out, Miss,' Logan Sherwood said.

The last Mattie saw of her young sister-in-law was a straight back and the curling grey plume of her bonnet that waved in the breeze of the carriage's movement.

'Good riddance,' Logan said, quietly, beside her. 'I never could abide that silly child, for all poor Will was so fond.' The carriage turned the corner of the drive and was lost to sight. Woodsmoke drifted on the air above the slave quarters. He tilted his head for a moment, as if listening. 'Are they really gone, Mattie? My boys? Will, and Russ, and Johnny?'

She reached a hand to cover his.

He allowed it to rest there for the space of a breath. Shook it off. 'Sol? You there, boy? Another tot, if you please.'

CHAPTER ELEVEN

Shiloh was, of course, by no means the last nor even the bloodiest of the engagements that were fought with increasing bitterness and ferocity in this fraternal struggle. Indeed, less than six months after Shiloh, on an embattled ridge at Sharpsburg, what was to prove the bloodiest day of the war claimed over twenty thousand casualties, five thousand of them killed; and again the result was indecisive, again no end to the slaughter was in sight. For a while, in December of that same year, after the great Southern victory at Fredricksburg that saved the Southern capital of Richmond and sent Grant's armies running for their lives, the outlook for the Confederacy seemed optimistic; but as battle after battle was fought and more and more young men died or were disablingly wounded, it became ever more difficult to ignore the obvious. If the war could not be brought to a swift and successful end the South, like so many of her young men, would simply bleed to death. No amount of personal valour, no amount of fierce and patriotic dedication, no amount of sacrifice could produce men, military equipment or the basic necessities of life from nothing. For every man who fell in the Federal armies, there was another, grumbling but whole, to take his place. For every captured gun or spent shell there were factories working overtime to produce more. In the South it was a different story. The resources, both human and material, were finite, and it could only be a matter of time before they ran out. Grant well understood that when he brought to an abrupt halt the until-now civilized exchange of prisoners; his own lost men he could manage without, and if his action left them imprisoned in a South that was finding it harder and harder to feed its own people, let alone enemy prisoners, so be it. For the South every captured man unreturned was a loss as crippling as a death.

Around the coasts the blockade tightened. Shortages began to be felt by civilian and serving man alike. Many in the rebel armies marched barefoot, even in the worst of the winter weather; many of those that did not were shod, and in a lot of cases clothed, from the corpses of the fallen. A dead man, whether friend or foe, needed no boots. In May 1863 the South suffered a terrible blow in the loss of Stonewall Jackson, a national hero, at Chancellorsville – ironically one of the Confederacy's great victories – and then, in July of the same year, came Gettysburg, a brutal defeat for the Rebels, a disaster compounded by the equally calamitous loss of Vicksburg on the same day. Yet even with the Mississippi lost and the Confederacy to all intents and purposes cut in half by the Federal gunboats that patrolled its waters, the optimists doggedly refused to accept any thought of defeat. The mistake, they argued, had been to try to defend too great a territory. Now the Southern forces could be concentrated at the perimeter of the Southern heartland; and let the Yankees do their worst, not another foot of ground would be conceded.

Deep in that heartland, the household at Pleasant Hill, like most of their neighbours, survived first one and then another difficult, unpleasant winter. They survived too the rapid devaluation of their currency, the even more frightening runaway inflation, and the requisitioning of many of their stores and of their remaining horses and mules – with the exception of the old carriage horse, Star, for whom the Confederate army could find no use but in a stew, and, as the army quartermaster quite seriously told Mattie as he rounded up the last but two of her cows, things hadn't got to that state yet. As they struggled through that second winter of cold and mud and driving rain, they began to hoard what little gold they had left – the Confederate paper money was all but useless, even in the Confederacy – and bartered with neighbours, or with the townsfolk of Macon. For the past two seasons Joshua had overseen the planting of long rows of okra on the borders of the cotton fields – matured okra seeds tasting much more like true coffee than any of the other inventive cereal substitutes – and this above everything else became their currency. They patched their clothes and they turned the sheets and they got used to living with shortages of absolutely everything. There were times when Mattie thought that if she ever saw, let alone tasted, another unseasoned grain of rice, hunted for another recipe to make the slices of dry, rubbery apple that was one of their staples edible she would scream and run mad. But yet they survived – even becoming used to the hardships. What was harder to come to terms with, no matter how much time passed, was the change in Logan Sherwood. It was as if, with the loss of his sons, the purpose of his life had fled, and with it any great interest in what went on around him. He was healthy enough; he simply rocked on the porch, or sat for hours closeted in the library, living it seemed in some inner world of his own, as if the real world about him, with its trials, challenges and difficulties, did not exist. All of the everyday decisions fell to Mattie, and to Joshua, without whom, she was certain, Pleasant Hill would have disintegrated completely. Not that Logan ever gave any sign of acknowledging that. Though he no longer banned Joshua from his sight, to Mattie's knowledge neither did he ever show the slightest gratitude for the feat of organization that kept the household fed at least adequately, and, more importantly, that held firm the fragile thread of discipline that prevented unrest and a mass escape – as had happened on a plantation upriver – or worse. What kept Joshua loyal, what made the man work his fingers to the bone, break his back and maybe his heart, for a master who showed no interest in and no gratitude for what he did was beyond Mattie. She could not ask him, for through these dark and difficult months it seemed to her that Joshua had put up a barrier between them that she could not breach. He was courteous as ever, quick to help or to counsel, but – deliberately, she was certain – he never approached her when she was alone, nor attempted to speak of anything beyond the everyday running of Pleasant Hill. Almost she began to wonder if she had imagined those fleeting, strangely intimate moments of contact between them. Meanwhile there were other things to occupy her hands and her mind; but, busy as she was, nothing could fill the void of loneliness in which she lived. There were times when she longed, from the bottom of her heart, simply for someone to talk to. But times had changed and allegiances were inevitably shifting with them; it came as a shock to discover that even Lucy, whom she had considered her friend, was no longer entirely to be trusted. It was lucky for the girl that it was Mattie who found her, one afternoon, behind the street of slave cabins, reading aloud a pamphlet about Lincoln's Emancipation Proclamation, which declared free any slave held by a master in rebellion against the government of the United States – whilst declining to do the same for any belonging to a master in a loyal state – to an intently listening crowd of slaves. Mattie had been surprised at the sense of betrayal that had filled her.

That night, silently, Lucy came as usual to her room to attend to her. 'Why, Lucy?' Mattie asked. 'You know the trouble the Proclamation is causing! What are you trying to do?' She had not been able to bring herself to report what she had seen and heard to Logan or to Joshua – even to mention the detested Proclamation was virtually a hanging offence on any plantation – but neither could she ignore her own hurt, or the immense danger of Lucy's subversion.

Lucy stood quietly.

'Lucy? Will you answer me, please? Don't you understand the danger of the Proclamation? Do you really know what it means?'

'I know what it means, Miss Mattie.' The girl's eyes had met and held hers. 'It means we're free.'

'It means Mr Lincoln says you're free,' Mattie said, sharply, 'which means precisely nothing. Mr Lincoln is the president of a foreign country. His word means no more here than – than the King of Timbuktu's might. You know that.'

'Yes, Miss Mattie.'

'Then – why?'

'They're my people, Miss Mattie. They have a right to know.' There was pride in the lift of the girl's head. 'You taught me to read your own self, Miss Mattie. For what? On'y to read the things you want me to see?' The girl shook her head. 'Don't work that way, Miss Mattie. You know it.'

Mattie knew it indeed; and, despite her own loss, was nothing but relieved when, a few days later, Lucy absconded in company with a young field hand called Peter, part of a steady trickle of runaways who were taking advantage of the growing disorder in the countryside to run north.

It was early summer again, the summer of 1864. War notwithstanding – whilst in Richmond the guns of battle could be heard, the peace of Pleasant Hill remained unbroken – the sun shone, the birds sang, the flowers gave their heavy perfume to the warm and fragrant air. For days now, sometimes weeks at a time, Pleasant Hill was as good as cut off from the world. Their single ancient horse was too precious an animal to use unless the trip was absolutely essential, and the days were gone when a slave could be trusted to walk the long miles to Macon and back without supervision, so news came to them from passing travellers, of which there were few, or from the occasional newspaper that Joshua brought back with him when he did risk old Star in the shafts of a light carriage and make the trip into town to barter precious fruits, vegetables or eggs for staples they did not produce themselves such as sugar, tea or the inevitable rice.

It was from such a newspaper, already two days old, that they learned of fighting in the north of Georgia, a bare hundred and fifty miles from them. The Union commander was that same Tecumseh Sherman who had fought at Shiloh. Mattie remembered, uneasily, other things she had read about him in the past couple of years; how in Mississippi he had openly encouraged his men to live off the land they took, regardless of the needs of its people, how the wholesale looting and destruction of plantation houses had left those landmarks that had come to be called 'Sherman's Tombstones' – the fire-scarred chimneys that were all that was left after the red-headed Ohian and his men had passed through. She scanned the page – there seemed no doubt that the Confederate General Johnstone would hold against the attack; surely, he must? For if he did not, the great Southern storehouse and railhead of Atlanta lay vulnerable, less than a hundred miles south, and only forty or so miles as the crow might fly north-west of Pleasant Hill itself. It was unthinkable that the Yankees should strike so far and so deep into the very heart of the Confederacy.

Yet that was what they intended, and that, as those anxious summer weeks wore on, was exactly what they did. Whilst in Virginia General Beauregard stubbornly held out at St Petersburg, thus preventing Grant from besieging the Southern capital, in Georgia Johnstone, outgunned and outmanoeuvred in a coolly planned and increasingly vicious campaign by Sherman, was pressed back day by day and week by week until, after eleven weeks of savage fighting, the exhausted Rebels fell back for the last time and the enemy, like a wolf, was at the gates of one of the most strategically important cities of the South.

Atlanta panicked. The trains that were still running south from the great terminal through unoccupied Georgia were packed with wounded men and with military supplies being salvaged from the storehouses; there was scant room available for frightened civilians. Those unlucky souls who could not find a space on the requisitioned trains left the doomed city in any way they could; in carts and in carriages, or if necessary on foot. Many chose not to follow the main route through Macon, for fear of being overtaken by the ogre Sherman, and took instead the smaller roads that wound through the countryside bordering the Ocmulgee. The first intimation the inhabitants of Pleasant Hill had of the exodus was when an exhausted family in a mulecart piled high with possessions stopped to ask for food and water; Mattie noted that the wife, a small, worn woman with a tight mouth and thin, greying hair, eyed the Negroes who served her with a dislike and distaste that put Mattie's teeth on edge despite her pity.

'Y'all best be gone soon as you can,' the man said, spooning grits into his mouth, and speaking through them as he chewed. 'That devil – once he takes Atlanta, an' he will sooner or later, you'll see – he's gon' fire ever'thin' he can lay torch to. Done it in Mississipp' – he'll do it here all right, no reason ter think he won't.'

His wife nodded. Looked around with eyes that burned with envy and a scarcely veiled satisfaction. 'Place like this – be the first he makes for, most like.' She slapped at a whining child. 'Be still, Sam! An' keep your hands from that brute. That's a slave-hound. He'll have your hand off iffen you ain't careful.'

Mattie bit back temper. 'Here, Jake.' The dog looked from the small, sticky, inviting fingers he had been licking to his mistress, decided for once on obedience. Mattie turned back to the man. 'But – why would the Yankees come here? If Sherman takes Atlanta he'll have the railhead, won't he? That's what he wants, isn't it? Won't they stop there?' she asked, uncertainly. 'There's nothing for them here – the railroad runs a long way south –'

The man lifted his grizzled head. 'That's as may be, lady,' he said, softly. 'But I had a cousin up in Mississipp'. An' he reckoned Ol' Sherman surely hates the South for rebellin', an' that's the truth. No tellin' where he'll stop, lady. He's goin' ter wipe out Atlanta, that's for sure; but whether he'll stop there –' he turned and spat over the porch rail, '– our lads're startin' ter run like rabbits – there's no-one to stand against him for long, I'm tellin' yer that. Won't be a lot left iffen he does take it into that cursed red head of his to come through here, you mark my words.'

'If you want to get to Macon by dark, Sir,' Joshua said quietly from behind Mattie, 'then you'd best be on your way as quickly as possible. I've had the kitchen pack a few supplies for you.'

The man grunted. Mattie threw Joshua a swift glance of thanks. No-one else thanked him.

They stood together and watched the rickety cart off down the drive. 'Joshua? Do – do you think there's anything in what he said? If Atlanta should fall, is Sherman really likely to come this way?'

Joshua shook his head. 'There's no telling, Miss Mattie. There's no reason that I can see that he should. And anyhow, the way it seems to me, we're not going to do any better running off down the road like chickens with our heads cut off than staying here. At least till we know what's happening.'

She nodded, swallowing the sour taste of fear. 'You're right, of course.' She glanced towards the library door.

Joshua nodded. 'Someone has to tell him.'

A thought – a conviction – struck Mattie at that moment. 'We can tell him till we're blue,' she said with resigned certainty. 'We won't get him to leave. Not if Lucifer and all his avenging angels were coming.'

Joshua allowed himself a rare, if bleak, smile. 'My thoughts exactly, Miss Mattie.' He turned away.

'Oh – Joshua?'

'Yes, Miss Mattie?'

'Where's Peg?' Peg was the girl who had taken the missing Lucy's place. 'I haven't seen her since last night. Is she ill? Does she need anything?'

His reply did not come quickly. 'She's gone, Miss Mattie.'

'Gone? You mean – run away?'

He nodded. 'Last night. With Tige, Betsy, Jo-jo, –' he spread his hands ' – an' maybe a dozen or so field hands. There's no way you'll stop them now, Miss Mattie. Not with the Yankees so close.'

'No. No, I suppose not.' She stood for a long time after he had gone, still and thoughtful, her hand resting upon Jake's soft, warm head, her eyes distant. With the departure of the mulecart and its unpleasant occupants there was a strange quiet about the place, a hush, as if the world held its breath.

And then, rolling menacingly beyond the horizon like distant thunder, she heard the sound of guns.

Mattie was right. When told of the situation – though even he had already understood the meaning of the far-off, continual sound of the Federal bombardment – Logan listened calmly and politely, shrugged a little and said simply, 'They come or they don't. If they do – then let 'em. They won't take Pleasant Hill easily.'

Mattie shook her head, exasperated. 'Mr Sherwood, if worst comes to worst, you can't take on the whole of the Yankee army on your own!'

He fixed her with a level eye. Suddenly he looked like the old Logan, firm and authoritative. 'Are you suggestin' that I run away, my dear?'

She shook her head, helplessly. 'It isn't running away. It's — it's being sensible —'

'An eminently praiseworthy thing to be under normal circumstances. However —' he shook his head, gently '— not these circumstances. If they do come then you, of course, must go.'

Crossly Mattie picked up a cushion, banged it back into shape and dropped it back onto the chair. 'Don't be ridiculous.' She straightened and held wide exasperated hands. 'You see? This wretched place has infected me at last. Even I've stopped being sensible —' and was rewarded by the glimmer of a smile.

Throughout that month of August they got used to the sound of the bombardment, and the sight of the distant flickering glow in the sky at night. It was obvious now that Sherman's intention was to reduce Atlanta to rubble. Yet still the routes to the south were open and still a small but steady stream of refugees called at Pleasant Hill. Had they been feeding as many mouths as before, their supplies would have been strained to the limit; but with the Yankees so close, as Joshua had predicted, those slaves that were left now deserted en masse. Only Joshua himself remained, and Sol and Dandy, and Prudence the cook with her daughter Sapphire, and Shake, who was sweet on her. Between them, they did their best for the unhappy, half-starved travellers who trailed up the drive; and on almost every occasion the advice they were given was the same: leave. Leave while you can. Don't stay within Sherman's reach. They spoke as if he were the devil himself. On one occasion a group of ragged, grey-clad soldiers came to the porch; deserters, Mattie was almost certain. They were hungry as hyenas, and less well-mannered. They each carried a long, well-honed knife, and each looked more than ready to use it. To Mattie's huge relief, when they arrived Logan had taken himself off to walk Pleasant Hill's neglected acres, a pastime he indulged in more and more often lately. Where his chancy temper would have led them with these particular visitors she dreaded to think. When they left, discretion having been by far the better part of valour, the Rebel deserters went clad in Sherwood coats and boots — albeit too big for three out of four of them – and each carrying a bottle of Logan's dwindling and precious whisky supply, to say nothing, she was fairly sure, of a few trinkets tucked into their pockets. Only the firearms they had demanded had not been handed over. When they had casually splintered the stout gun cupboard it had been to find it empty apart from an ancient carbine and a damaged hunting rifle.

'What did you do?' Mattie asked Joshua in amazement, in no doubt that no-one but he could have worked such a trick.

In answer he walked to a corner of the hall, bent to lift the edge of a floorboard, artfully notched. There in the cavity beneath lay the handguns and rifles that would normally be kept in the cupboard. 'Never thought I'd have to hide them from white folks,' Joshua said, with one of his surprising and caustic flashes of humour.

In the relief of the moment Mattie could not help a small explosion of laughter. 'Well,' she said, 'that's one miracle. Now you're going to have to work another.'

'Oh?'

'You're going to have to explain to Mr Sherwood where four of his precious bottles of whisky disappeared to!'

Atlanta fell at the beginning of September. Mattie, on a trip to Macon with Joshua, watched with helpless pity the straggling, scarecrow columns of shuffling men in ragged grey or homespun uniform that marched in exhausted retreat from the fallen city, saw too the long and terrible lines of trucks full of dead and dying men that clanked perpetually over the rails in defence of which so many had died. Many of the fighting men, like the civilians that Sherman turned mercilessly from their homes in the captured city, were clearly sick and looked half-starved. The streets of Macon were full of distressed and displaced people, many of them having lost everything in the bombardment and ensuing fighting. Mattie stayed for three days with the Morrisons, helping in the overcrowded hospital and in the small canteen Mrs Morrison had organized to help feed the refugees. To her surprise and embarrassment, however, Joshua refused utterly her order to return to Pleasant Hill without her. 'The master'd have my hide, Miss Mattie,' he said, in calm dismissal, when she tried to insist.

'But, Joshua, we can't leave Mr Sherwood out at the plantation alone. And Star – you know what danger the poor old thing is in here – those that don't want to steal him for transport are after him for the pot!'

'That's right, Miss Mattie. But if you stay, I stay, and Star stays with both of us.'

In the end it was Mrs Morrison herself who persuaded Mattie back to Pleasant Hill. 'My dear, of course you've been the most tremendous help, but the pressure's easing now, and we've plenty of hands, I promise you. The doctor does think you should go tend to Logan – there's no knowing what the silly man will do, left to himself.'

Mattie was all too conscious of that worry herself. Moreover, at three that morning, a boy of eighteen she had nursed for three days had died in her arms, screaming; she was in no fit state to argue. To her tired embarrassment she cried almost the whole of the way back to Pleasant Hill, snuffling apologies to Joshua, who suggested, oddly and gently, that her tears were probably good for both of them.

Week followed week, strung with uncertainty. The stream of people fleeing the city died to a trickle, then stopped altogether. It was strange, almost unnerving, no longer to hear the constant rumble of the bombardment. Towards the end of the month rumours began to circulate that Sherman had openly declared his next objective to be Savannah; if it were true then Pleasant Hill might indeed be in danger. But on 28 September the President of the Confederacy, Jefferson Davis himself, visited Macon to lend his support to a benefit for impoverished refugees from Atlanta. The event – as it was supposed to – boosted morale and spirits enormously. Surely there could be no danger if Davis himself could show his face so near the fallen city? The arguments that Mattie heard that day were optimistic and convincing; Sherman had stretched himself too far. He could not defend his lines of communication for much longer against the daring and successful raids of the Confederate cavalry led by the legendary Nathan Bedford Forrest. Sherman, sooner rather than later, would have to leave the city and retreat or he himself would be cut off and besieged.

Heartened, Mattie returned to Pleasant Hill to labour with Prudence and Sapphire over the autumn's curing, pickling and preserving. Nothing that could be stored and used was wasted. There was a long winter ahead.

It was on a chill night in the middle of November that something woke Mattie.

Curled on the floor beside her bed Jake was growling, a low and somehow dangerously uncertain sound that raised the hairs on the nape of her neck. She swung her legs from the bed, reaching for her woollen robe. As she pulled it on, the soft material snagged harshly on a sore patch on her roughened hands and she caught her breath.

One of her shutters was broken, and rather than struggle with it she had left it open. Beyond it the sky to the north-west was filled with the merest suggestion of light; a slight, rosy glow that might, in the east and on a summer's morning, have been taken for the first herald of dawn. Drawing the robe around her, she ran to the window and swung open the other shutter. There could be no doubt; the horizon was warm with a faint, unnatural, smudgy light.

In the darkness Jake had left her, and she heard his big paw scratch at the door, the growl turned to an expectant whine.

'Be quiet, Jake.' Her eyes were still on that glowing sky.

Again the dog made that small, excited growling sound, and again his blunt claws raked the door.

Then she heard it, soft but unmistakable. The faint whinny of a horse.

Her heart all but stopped.

Jake growled again.

Somewhere in the house she thought she heard a door close, very quietly.

Mattie forced her suddenly paralysed brain to something approximating rational thought. She could shout an alarm; but who would hear her? Certainly not Joshua in his quarters underground. And Logan, who had taken to sleeping on the couch in the library, had grown in these past years more than a little hard of hearing; would he hear her? She doubted it.

The dog whined, snuffled at the door. She steadied a little; he was protection if anything was. All she had to do was to get to Logan – he slept, she knew, with a handgun by his side.

Leaving her robe buttoned but loose, she pulled the belt from around her waist and slipped it about Jake's shaggy neck before opening the door.

Out on the balcony the glow in the sky was more pronounced than ever. Fire. A huge fire, and in the direction of Atlanta. She fancied she could smell it, borne on the breeze.

Jake towed her down the stairs to the door that led into the main hall. Before opening it she yanked him fiercely to her, hissing at him. Trembling with excitement he sat, his weight fully on the hem of her robe, dragging it down. She wrenched it free, gently turned the door handle.

A small lamp was burning, very low, upon the long side table. In the moment she had before the dog leaped forward tearing the makeshift leash from her sore fingers, Mattie saw a figure standing, half-lit; saw the gleaming gold insignia upon the neat, dark Yankee uniform, the long, glinting sword and the pistol in the polished leather holster. As she filled her lungs to scream he turned fully to the light, Jake tore himself free to leap upon the intruder and she froze as if struck to stone.

The uniformed man – the Yankee soldier – dropped to one knee and threw his arms about the dog. 'Jake, Jake! Hello, old boy!'

Very, very slowly Mattie closed the door behind her, leaned on it for support. Her legs were trembling.

Robert straightened, the dog still worrying happily at his leather-gloved hand. 'Mattie,' he said, quietly.

'Robert? Wh-what in the world?' How she reached him she did not know, but she was in his arms, clinging to him in a sudden flood of tears, the dog dancing in mad circles about them.

'Mattie – Mattie, there now, no need to cry –'

The sound of his voice brought her to herself with a jolt. 'Ssh!' She laid fierce fingers across his mouth, took his hand in hers, pulling him towards the doors that led into the sitting room, picking up the lamp as she went and carrying it with her. 'Be quiet! If he should hear you!' She pushed open the doors and drew him into the room, closing the doors behind them, opening them again a second later as Jake indignantly scratched at the wood. 'Oh, you damned nuisance of a dog!' Her voice was still far from steady, her face wet with tears, but the shock had passed and she was thinking clearly. She turned to Robert. 'Your father mustn't find you here. He's sworn to kill you. Sworn it. Robert – he means it. He won't have your name spoken – he won't – he can't – forgive you.' She hesitated for one moment and then blurted, 'The others – your brothers – they're dead –' and could have cut out her own tongue at the clumsiness of it as she saw his face drain of expression and colour in the shadowed light of the lamp. She took his hand, holding it tight. 'I'm sorry. It's a terrible way to tell you. But it's a terrible thing, and there's no time – no time for gentleness.'

'When?' he asked. 'Where?'

'Shiloh.' She had lived with it for so long now, wept so many tears, that she could speak of it almost dispassionately. She spoke very rapidly. 'Just after you left. Russ was defending a road, during the retreat. The others heard of it and went to help him. They were all caught in the Yankee advance –' For the briefest of moments she allowed her eyes to flick over his sober uniform, could not curb the sudden and even to her unexpected edge of bitterness in her voice.

Robert made no attempt to disguise the pain in his eyes. And this time she was ashamed. 'I'm sorry,' she said.

Jake, whining, scratched at the French doors that led out onto the front porch.

'Jake! Quiet!'

But Jake was well awake now, and wanted to be out amongst the rabbits. The whining grew louder. He looked at her expectantly and gathered his breath to bark.

'Oh, for goodness' sake! You'll wake the whole house!' Mattie flew to the doors, unlocked them, shooed the dog out. Then stood, looking at the reflected glow in the sky. 'What is that?'

Robert came to stand behind her. For a moment she closed her eyes. The height, the breadth – the very smell of him – reminded her so –

'It's why I'm here.' His hands on her shoulders, he turned her to face him. 'Mattie, you have to take Pa and get clear away from here. Now. Tonight. Sherman's coming. He's vowed to march to the sea through Georgia, and he's promised to make the state howl as he does it.' He saw her eyes turn to the glow in the sky again. 'Atlanta's burning,' he said, quietly. 'Destroyed. And that's what he'll do to anything in his path – he's a man who keeps his promises.'

'Burning? But – why? The city surrendered! Surrendered a month ago! Why burn it?'

'Because it's his way. Mattie, I had to come, to warn you – get Pa away from here – and Joshua –' he paused for a second, a flicker of doubt in his eyes '– Joshua – he hasn't gone? He's still here?'

'Oh, of course he is. What would you expect?'

'And – the others?'

'Most are gone. Run north, or to the Yankees.'

He nodded, drawing her back into the room. 'Listen. Tell Joshua –' He stopped.

The inner door had opened.

Mattie was pulling on Robert's arm. 'Robert – go! Please go!'

Robert resisted her. Stood straight and still as his father walked into the room; kept his eyes unflinching on the older man's face, ignoring the small gun that was levelled steadily at his breast.

'How dare you, Sir?' Logan Sherwood said, very quietly. 'How dare you defile this house with your filthy presence?'

'Mr Sherwood, please – he came to warn us –' As she stepped towards Logan Sherwood, Mattie found herself caught from behind and swung ungently clear. She stumbled away, catching at a chair to prevent herself from falling.

'Stay out of this, Mattie.' Robert had stepped not away from but towards his father.

The gun came up, perfectly steadily.

'Pa, will you please listen?'

The flame of fury that flared through Logan Sherwood at the unthinking, affectionate diminutive was almost tangible. He stepped forward and with his free hand struck his son a brutal, backhanded blow across the face. Robert staggered, regained his balance. A bright bead of blood broke and threaded down his cheek. He stood, hands loosely by his side, making no move to avoid the next blow as his father raised his hand and hit him again, with all his considerable strength, open-handed. Despite being prepared for it, Robert's head rocked with the force, and another smear of blood appeared upon his broken lip.

'Stop it!' Mattie shouted. '*Stop it!*'

'Get away, Mattie!' Robert held up his hand, still watching his father. 'Sir, all I ask is that you listen to me – please!'

The gun had come up again. 'I swore I'd kill you,' Logan Sherwood said, 'And by Christ I'll do it –'

'Please!' said Mattie, desperately, 'you can't!'

'At least your brothers died in honour. You, Sir, deserve only to die in shame.'

Robert's face was bone white. He took a quick breath to reply, and in that fatal instant his attention was distracted.

'Drop the gun, Mr Sherwood,' Joshua said softly from the door.

Logan Sherwood's head lifted sharply. Mattie never afterwards could have said which gun fired first. Robert went down as if poleaxed. Logan Sherwood staggered, dropped his gun, grabbed at the back of a chair, bringing it crashing down with him.

Joshua stood, arm hanging by his side, the gun a sudden dead weight in his hand.

Mattie suffered a moment of shocked paralysis. Robert lay spread-eagled, knocked almost through the open doors and onto the porch by the force of the bullet that had taken him full in the chest. One look at his face was enough to recognize death. Logan Sherwood lay curled upon the floor moaning, blood-covered but alive. She ran to him. On the edge of her vision she saw Joshua cross to where Robert lay, kneel by the blue-clad body and take it in his strong arms, holding the dead man to his chest like a baby, rocking back and forth, fierce and sound-less, as if he would will life back into the body.

'Leave him, Joshua,' Mattie said. 'He's dead. Please, help me here –' She dropped to her knees beside Logan.

Joshua ignored her. Suddenly, shockingly, still clutching the body, he threw back his head and howled like an agonized animal. It was the most savage, most harrowing sound Mattie had ever heard. She hunched her shoulders for a moment, trying to close her ears and her mind to the awful cry. Then, shaking, she reached for Logan. Blood was pumping messily from his shoulder. His eyes were open. 'If I help you, can you walk?' she asked.

Teeth clamped against pain, he nodded his head. She slid an arm under his good one, gave him a wad of material to hold against the wound.

Joshua ignored them, sitting silent now, and rocking still, his face sheened and shining with tears. Robert's arm hung stiffly, lifeless, like a doll's. Mattie determinedly averted her eyes. With huge effort she hauled the semi-conscious old man upright, dragged him towards the door. In the hall the door had burst open to admit Shake and Prudence, both wide-eyed and frightened.

'Shake, give me a hand here – carefully now! Take him into the library – put him on the couch – gently for goodness' sake. Where the devil is Sol? Prudence, we need bandages – and – and perhaps a knife – I don't know if the bullet's still in there.'

It wasn't. In the only fortunate circumstance of that dreadful night, the bullet had driven through Logan, from back to front, leaving a dreadful, gaping hole where it had exited. Having poured half a bottle of whisky into the old man and the other half over the broken flesh, with shaking hands Mattie did her best to clean and close the wound, tying the bandages that Sapphire brought as tightly as she could about it to stop the gruesome pumping of the blood. 'Prudence, where's Sol – he surely can't have slept through this?'

Prudence avoided her eyes. 'Doan' know, Miss Mattie. Doan' know where he be.'

'We have to go to Macon.' Working as swiftly as she could,

218

Mattie was thinking out loud. If Pleasant Hill indeed lay in the path of Sherman's advancing army then circumstances were bad enough; the consequences of facing the Yankees with a dead Federal officer in the house did not bear thinking of. That the dead officer was Robert was something she was firmly putting from her mind; hysterics would mend nothing. 'Someone get Dandy and tell him to bring the biggest cart Star can haul to the front of the house. Prudence, when we've finished here, go to the kitchen and collect what supplies you can. Shake, when the cart comes round, you and Sol – if you can find him! – make a bed in it for Mr Sherwood – I'm sure that we shouldn't move him, but I don't see –' She stopped. Even in her abstracted state she could not but notice the silence that had fallen about her.

'Dandy ain't here, Miss Mattie,' Shake said, gently. 'Nor Sol. They gone.'

Her hands stilled, Mattie lifted her head sharply, her face incredulous. 'Sol? *Sol*'s run?'

'Sure has, Miss Mattie.' Shake held out his hand to huge Prudence, who had with difficulty dropped to her knees beside the couch with Mattie. Prudence took it and with strange and somehow reluctant dignity came to her feet. 'We's goin' too, Miss Mattie.' Shake's voice still held a quiet, almost tender note of regret. 'I's sorry, but there it is. This –' he indicated with a wave of his hand the bloodstained cloths, the man who lay still as death on the couch '– this ain't nothin' to do with us. We don't have to stay no longer. The Yankees is here – we's free – Lucy told us that –'

'Well, Lucy told you wrong,' Mattie said, very calmly. 'Come now, Shake, don't be silly. Go and get the cart.'

Shake's ebony face was sober. 'No, Miss Mattie. We's goin'.'

'Where?' Mattie came to her feet, faced them obdurately, defying the panic that given the slightest chance would, she knew, overwhelm her and set her screaming. 'Where will you go? Have you thought of that?'

'To the Yankees, Miss Mattie. That's where we's goin'.' Prudence found her voice.

'Just like that?' Mattie shook her head. On the couch Logan

Sherwood stirred and groaned. 'The Yankees don't want you. Don't you know that?' She knew, looking at their closed, determined faces, that she could not win. There was a long moment's silence. Then, 'Go, then,' she said, coolly. 'Find out for yourselves. But don't come crawling back here when Sherman's devils drive you off. Go starve somewhere else.'

For one moment she thought she saw doubt upon Prudence's bewildered face. But Shake was not to be sidetracked. He reached for Prudence's plump arm and drew her after him to the door. In the silence of despair, Mattie let them go.

It took half an hour for her to pour enough whisky down Logan Sherwood's throat to send him into an uneasy sleep, the only thing she could at the moment think of to keep him still. Once she was sure he was all but unconscious, in dread she crossed the hall to the sitting room.

It was empty and clean, and perfectly tidy.

She stood tiredly, frowning at the straightened furniture, the closed doors, the clean, polished floor. No sign of violence remained; and Robert's body was gone.

'Joshua?' she asked, then called louder, into the still house, 'Joshua?'

Outside the closed doors Jake barked excitedly.

She opened the front door. The winter darkness was still lit by the menacing glow over burning Atlanta. 'Joshua! Joshua!' She thought she might tear the skin from her throat.

Jake bounded to her, panting.

'Jake? Where is he? Where's Joshua? Find him!'

The dog wagged his great friendly tail and grinned his doggy grin, nudging her hand for a stick.

'Find Joshua!'

He had no idea what she was talking about, but he was ready for anything. He sat down, watching her expectantly.

Mattie ran down the steps, her robe billowing about her, and into the centre of the wide, packed-earth clearing in front of the house. 'Joshua! Joshua – please!'

Jake, at last catching scent of her distress, whined a little.

She turned and stumbled back towards the house, the sobs she had until now restrained choking in her throat. At the foot of the steps she could go no further. She sank down, buried her face in her hands, weakly letting the tiredness and the terror overwhelm her. Like a child she sobbed and, like a child, between the sobs, she begged for help; and it was Joshua's name she called, over and over, Joshua with whom she pleaded.

But Joshua too, it seemed, was gone.

CHAPTER TWELVE

In a smoky winter dawn, Mattie woke on the floor beside the couch upon which a grey-faced Logan Sherwood lay breathing slowly and heavily, blood dark upon the bandages about his shoulder. She felt half dead herself. Eyes and head were heavy with tears and exhaustion, her neck was stiff and her right arm was painfully cramped where she had pillowed her aching head upon it.

The house was very quiet about her; the quietest she had ever known it. It was cold, and, worse, a frightening and unnatural air of emptiness, of desertion hung about it. She struggled to her feet, shivering, wincing at every movement.

Logan moved slightly, and groaned, uneasy in sleep. Mattie stood looking down at him. A moment at a time, she told herself, grimly, that's the only way I'm going to get through this. A moment at a time. So; dress first. Then tend the old man. Then find some breakfast. Afterwards, we'll see.

She attended to the tasks, dressed in an old woollen riding skirt and jacket as being the toughest and warmest clothes her wardrobe could provide, changed the stained and sticky bandage, packing the wound with clean lint and tying it tightly in place with torn sheets. Logan Sherwood was awake, pale eyes watching her calmly as she handled the wound with inexpert hands.

'So,' he said, as she stood at last, her hands full of soiled bandages. 'Where is everyone?'

'Gone,' Mattie said, briefly. Her head was thumping like a steam engine.

'What about that murderous nigger? He gone too?'

'Joshua? Yes, it seems so.' She bent to pick up a fallen bandage. Turned unfriendly eyes upon him. 'And talking about murder –'

'The boy's dead?'

'Yes.'

He grunted. 'Good.' His eyes did not flinch from hers.

She stuffed the bandages into the linen bag she carried. 'You're a vile old man. It's a pity Joshua didn't shoot straighter.' She turned to the door.

His voice rasped, painfully. 'You may well be right, girl. Where you goin' now?'

'To get breakfast. And to get you another blanket. Though why I don't let you freeze to death is beyond me.'

In the kitchen she found the remnants of yesterday's none-too-lavish meal, and some stale but eatable bread. Stirred up the fire and boiled water for tea. At least it was warm in the kitchen. She tried not to think of Robert; tried even harder not to think of his warnings, of a troop of dark-coated soldiers riding up the long avenue of live oaks.

In the stall that Joshua had built beside the kitchen for the household's last precious cow, the animal was bellowing mournfully. 'Oh, God,' she said conversationally to the kettle, 'I can't.'

By mid-morning she had to; the cow's udders were bursting with milk, and the animal was restive with the pain of it. The operation ended, of course, in exasperation and tears and with little satisfaction for either party. Most of what little milk she did extract was wasted when an irritable hoof caught the bucket and flung it against the wall. Doggedly she tried again, and was surprised when, for a moment at least, she acquired something of a knack and achieved several juicy squirts that relieved her almost as much as it did the cow.

With what little he ate at the midday meal, Mattie produced a very large glass of whisky for Logan. 'It'll take more than that to put me to sleep,' he said nastily.

'We've got more,' she said. 'And if that fails I'll hit you with the bottle,' and pondered in some surprise upon this habit she seemed to have acquired of speaking in sentences of few words and less generosity.

In the afternoon, with Logan Sherwood uneasily asleep, needing to think she walked with Jake a little way into the woods that stretched towards the river. Somewhere here, she thought, Robert must be buried – for surely, that must be what Joshua had done before he had left? The thought brought back the ache she had been trying to deny; the ache for companionship, for order, for strength. The ache, she suddenly realized, for Joshua. She stopped, listening. 'Joshua?' she called, hoping, she knew, against all reasonable hope. 'Joshua!'

The air was acrid still with the smell of burning. Ash had settled, a grey dust of mourning. Mattie climbed a small rise and looked westward. In the distance, against the grey cloudlike pall of smoke that hung above the burned city, and undeniably closer, a single smudged column rose into the still air.

That night she dragged a mattress into the library to lie beside Logan Sherwood. Drugged by alcohol, he slept. The wound, thank God, seemed so far clean and clear of infection. She lay, staring wide-eyed into the darkness, trying to organize her thoughts.

In a day, perhaps two, with luck, the old man would be well enough to move without too much danger. They should leave Pleasant Hill and go into Macon, to the Morrisons, where someone else could take care of the wounded man, and where, if Sherman's men did come, they would have at least some protection – the thought was such a relief that she realized for the first time, uneasily, just how frightened she was. It had, she knew, been an act of charity on Shake's part not to take old Star with him when he went.

Mattie could not get used to the unsettling stillness of the house, the silence outside. Even Jake, brought in to the room together with Logan's own dogs for companionship and protection, had insisted on lying close against her, his length almost the same as hers as he stretched, twitching, in sleep.

She shut her eyes, and saw etched against her lids every vivid detail of Robert's dead face, staring.

She opened them again.

Logan snored on.

Somewhere, far in the distance, there was a sound that might have been gunfire.

It was not an easy night.

Mattie spent most of next day caring for the old man and preparing in absurdly meticulous detail for the journey to Macon. She tried to ignore Logan's increasing restlessness, the bright colour in his cheeks, the slight puffiness of the wound. Just twenty-four hours, she prayed as she went about the house, just give me twenty-four hours. Then we'll be safe. She gathered and packed carefully the most precious of their depleted stores – one could not in these days simply wish oneself upon a household without some payment in kind – and she planned to take the cow, tied behind the wagon. Mrs Morrison at least would be pleased to see *her*. The chickens would have to be left; perhaps someone could come out to pick them up later. She collected some of her own small treasures and tried to elicit, unsuccessfully, from Logan what was most precious to him in the house.

'We're not leavin', girl, an' that's flat. So it's immaterial.'

She was too fraught for good manners. 'We're going. One way or another. You can leave things or you can take them, it's up to you.'

'You'll carry me out feet first!'

Mattie bent over him. 'Yes. And if necessary I will! And it's time you came to realize that there isn't a single thing you can do about it!', and left, consoling herself with the furious thought that if she were a bad nurse Logan Sherwood was a far worse patient.

She did not, that day, call for Joshua. What was the point? she asked herself, desolately. If he had any sense he'd be at least thirty miles away by now, and probably safely with the Yankee army.

She did watch in a trepidation she could neither quell nor deny the drifting spirals of smoke that, slowly but surely, seemed to be encircling them. Ash drifted on the breeze like a shadowy and menacing snowfall.

That night, surprisingly, the mattress upon the floor was as welcome and as comfortable as a feather bed when she threw herself, fully clothed and exhausted, upon it. Her last thought before she drifted into a sleep as deep as death was that tomorrow, before they left, she would find some hiding place in the woods for the valuables in the house – just in case.

The thought came too late, much too late. For, very early the next morning, the Yankees came.

The dogs heard them first, and set up a clamour that would have wakened the dead. Mattie started, heart pounding to choke her.

'What is it?' Logan asked from the couch.

Groggily she scrambled from her makeshift bed, ran her hand through her straggling hair. 'I don't know.' She was pulling on her jacket with shaking hands.

Growling like one of his own dogs, Logan tried to push himself into a sitting position.

'For God's sake!' How many times, she wondered, had she taken the Lord's name in vain in the past few days? 'Lie down! Do you want to kill yourself?'

'Damn' nigger's done that for me.' Still he struggled.

She pushed him back. 'I'll do it for both of us if you don't behave yourself.' The words were furious. She was utterly terrified. She ran to the door, ran back, pulled her boots on. 'Stay there,' she said. 'Don't dare move.'

When Mattie opened the door the dogs shot out as fast as their four legs could carry them, barking like the hounds of hell.

She closed the door behind her, stood for a moment in the dark hall, trying to control her shivering limbs and uncertain stomach. She could hear it now: the jingle of harness, the trample of hooves, the sharp and musical calling of orders.

And then, above it all, the clear sound of two shots.

She flew onto the porch. Stopped, clinging to the rail, aghast, looking at the scene below her.

Dark uniforms, dust-covered from the red Georgian roads. Sleek and well-groomed horses.

An officer, middle-aged, dark and tired-faced, sitting his mount with ease and not a little arrogance, one hand resting lightly on the hilt of his sword.

Logan's two dogs lying dead in their own blood upon the ground, and the smoking muzzle of the gun that had killed them lifted towards the maniacally barking, totally harmless Jake.

'No!' Mattie almost tore her throat out with the scream.

Very precisely the trooper took aim at the dancing dog and fired. Horribly, after the bullet took him the animal leapt once more, twisting, into the air before the body landed, paws still scrabbling at the red earth.

Silence fell.

Mattie walked steadily down the steps and over to the dying dog, her eyes only upon Jake, utterly ignoring the circle of faces above her.

'Slave-hound,' somebody muttered. 'Sure as hell. Seen its teeth?'

Mattie dropped to her knees beside the dog. Felt the life drain from him as she laid a hand upon the bloody golden fur and, seeing the dreadful wound, was thankful. The towering, venomous rage that filled her drove out any fear – outweighed, for the moment, even her grief. She stayed for a second or two sitting back upon her heels, head bowed, hand gentle upon Jake's still body, controlling her anger, hoarding it in place of calm strength. When she stood, though her face was wet with tears, her voice was collected and ice-cold. 'So,' she said, chin lifted, making no attempt to disguise the blistering anger in her eyes as she looked at the mounted officer, 'having bravely murdered three harmless pets, what next? Will you murder me? There are, what –' she flicked a scornful glance around. One or two of the men avoided her eyes '– a dozen of you? The odds are about right, I'd say, wouldn't you?'

He was not abashed. 'Who's in the house?'

'One old, sick man. Oh, and a couple of cats. Shall I bring them out for you so that you can use them for target practice too?'

His eyes still on her, the man turned his head a little. 'Bartlett.

227

Prescott. Brown. And you, Spender, search the outhouses. You know what to do.'

'Yes, Sir.' The men swung from their horses.

'Martin, Burroughs and Stevens, take a look around the back – and you two –' he pointed '– get down to the wharf and fire that cotton.'

Mattie stood, her dead dog at her feet. The officer's eyes flickered down to the body and back to her face. 'We have orders to exterminate any hound that's been used to hunt down slaves.'

'And you automatically assume that anything on four legs that barks has been used for such a purpose?' Still the bitter, liberating rage burned, clear and steady in her brain. 'Is your cruelty and blind stupidity wilful, Sir, or does it come naturally?'

'Abuse will get you nowhere.'

'And an appeal to your better nature would?' The words were bleakly mocking. Her voice shook.

'Ma'am, please.' A young man swung from his horse and stepped towards her, snatching his hat from his head as he did so. 'We were not to know –'

'You didn't wait to find out.' She turned and strode, straight-backed, towards the house.

He walked beside her. When he spoke his voice was low. 'Please. It would be best if you co-operated.' He hesitated as she flicked him with a withering glance, then added with obstinate perseverance, 'Is there really an invalid in the house?'

'Yes.'

'And no-one else?'

'No.'

'The menfolk –' he paused again '– they're with the Rebel army?'

They had reached the bottom of the steps. Mattie stopped and turned to face him. He was small and slight, her face was almost on a level with his. 'The menfolk, Sir, are dead. At Shiloh. All of them. Except –' suddenly the smallest flicker of something kindled in her mind '– except for the one who is fighting in the Union army,' she said levelly. 'I'm sure he'll be interested to hear about this.'

'You have someone fighting for the Union? Your husband?'

'My brother-in-law. Sherwood. Robert Sherwood. He's with your army, I believe. It's his father who's sick in the house.'

'Lieutenant Rivers? Over here, please.' It was the other officer. His voice was impatient.

'Coming, Captain.' The young man lowered his voice again, speaking very rapidly. 'Ma'am, listen – we're under orders to burn Rebel homes, destroy crops and stores – but you just might be able to save the house, if you really do have an invalid in there and you can prove that one of the sons really is in the Union army.'

From the direction of the barn came the sound of shouting, laughter, and the frantic squawking of chickens. Two troopers appeared, carrying in each hand a couple of hens, held by their legs. The birds flapped and screeched indignantly. Casually they were tossed to a couple of mounted men, and as casually those men wrung their necks and tied the birds to their saddles.

Desperately now Mattie needed time to think. 'May I go and see to the old man? He should be told what's going on.'

'Yes. Of course.'

She ran up the steps and into the house.

Logan had manoeuvred himself half-off the couch, his feet on the floor. His grey face ran with sweat. 'What's happening?'

'The Yankees are here. They've killed the dogs. They're stealing everything they can lay a hand on – be still!' Logan, with a surge of furious energy, had all but pulled himself to his feet. 'Listen for once! There's one, just one, who seems half-way decent. Logan, is there any way – any way at all – that we can prove that Robert served – is still serving – in the Union army?'

The old man's mouth clamped to an iron line.

Mattie banged the palms of her hands together in frustration. 'I can't think of anything! Not anything!'

'Why should you want to?'

'The young lieutenant seemed to think it might help – might even prevent them from firing the house.' The energy of anger that had propelled her through the last ten awful minutes suddenly drained from her. To her horror she felt the rise of helpless, frightened tears. Logan watched as she turned from him, battling them, hunching her shoulders against him, fighting for control of herself. 'They killed Jake,' she said, 'Oh, Logan, they killed my poor, silly Jake!'

'There's a letter,' Logan said, roughly. 'In the bureau.'

'What?'

'In the bureau. A letter.'

Mattie turned to look at him, startled from her tears. He gestured impatiently. Galvanized, she flew to the bureau. 'The key – Logan, where's the key?'

'Over there. On the shelf.'

She ran to fetch it, fumbled with the lock, threw open the bureau. 'What am I looking for?'

'A letter. In the damn' pigeonhole at the top.'

She found it, opened it with unsteady fingers. There was a brief moment of silence. 'You never told anyone,' she said.

'No business of anyone else's.' His face was stubborn. 'I wrote back an' I told him, by damn – show your face here, I said, and by Christ I'll kill you.'

She threw him a single, furious look before she ran from the room, the letter in her hand.

The grim-faced captain sat on his tall horse and looked at the paper for a long time, before passing it, expressionless, to his young second-in-command.

'It – looks genuine enough?' the lieutenant ventured.

'It would be a little difficult, wouldn't it,' Mattie asked, crisply, 'for a Southerner to steal paper with the crest of one of Sherman's own regiments on? And prescient to the point of clairvoyance, I should have thought, to mail it from Mississippi upwards of two years ago?'

'Please understand,' Robert had written, 'it is because you have brought me up in honour and in truth that I can do nothing but fight for what I truly believe to be right.'

Mattie pushed the words away from her, together with the memory of that staring, dead face.

'The house will go to Robert now, when his father dies,' she said, forcing her voice to some small measure of conciliation.

'The other boys are all dead, lost at Shiloh. Mr Sherwood is a very sickly old man. The loss of his sons, you understand – and the shortages – it's been very hard.'

The man on the black horse frowned a little, thoughtfully. Billows of smoke rolled by them from the barns, which had already been fired. Old Star and the cow were tethered together behind one of the Union horses. Mattie could hear the yelps and shouts of the soldiers who were busy systematically destroying what was left of the vegetable garden.

Lieutenant Rivers glanced towards the bloodstained carcasses of the dogs. 'Is there need to fire the house, Sir,' he asked, quietly, 'in the circumstances?'

'There does seem to be some –' The captain stopped, his blue eyes lifted, looking beyond Mattie.

She heard him behind her, closed her eyes for the space of a heartbeat to battle a frightened fury in which she knew that if she turned and found him within reaching distance, she would kill him in cold blood.

'An' might I ask, Sir, just what you an' this rabble think you're doin' on my property?' Logan was leaning upon a long old rifle that had hung above the fireplace in the library, using it as a crutch. His great head with its shock of white hair was up, the pale eyes burning in a paler, all but translucent face. His southern drawl had never been so strong, yet the words were clear and precise, defying his pain. The scarlet patch of seeping blood upon his shoulder, exposed by the rags of the shirt that Mattie had torn from his body to get at the wound, was bright and garish in the cold morning light as the fresh mark of sin upon a snow-white soul.

Mattie took a long, long breath, and wished him, and his pride, and his stubborn, disastrous courage, stone dead.

Very slowly the captain kneed the big, well-schooled horse forward. His eyes were narrowed. 'This,' he asked, dangerously mildly, 'is your invalid?'

Mattie stood wordless. She saw the young lieutenant's eyes flicker to her and away.

'That ain't no sick man,' a trooper said, laconically thoughtful, leaning an arm upon the high pommel of his saddle, and turning to spit into the dust, 'that's a man with a gunshot wound, or I'm a Dutchman's aunt.'

'Well, old man?' The captain straightened in the saddle, his voice still quiet.

'An' what business might it be of yours, Sir?' Logan Sherwood might have been at ease in his own drawing room correcting an ill-mannered child. Even whilst she raged at the stupidity of it, Mattie could not suppress something that was beyond good sense, beyond even the urgent need for self-preservation; something close to pride.

'I'll tell you what business it is of mine, old man.' The captain kneed the animal closer to the porch, so that his eyes were on a level with Logan's own. 'You ever hear tell of Reb vigilantes around here? You ever hear tell of the bunch of murderers who ambushed a troop of our men up by Jonesboro? Or of the Rebel scum who tried to blow the bridge at Covington?'

'No!' Mattie had found her tongue. 'No, Captain, you're wrong. Mr Sherwood has nothing to do with any such group. He was shot a couple of days ago by an escaping slave —'

The man did not even look at her. His eyes, bright and hard, were still fixed upon Logan's face. 'We got orders to hang any outlaw Reb we find,' he said, his voice hard. 'You want to tell me now how you got shot, old man?'

Logan Sherwood drew himself up and stood silent.

'I told you. It was a runaway slave,' Mattie said. 'For goodness' sake, look at him. Does he look capable of riding around the country fighting Yankees?'

'Yes,' the man said, flatly and with impervious hostility, 'he does. Him and his kind — they're the ones started this business.' At last he looked at her, and his eyes were malevolent. 'You got ten minutes, lady.'

'Ten minutes for what?'

'To save what you can of personal belongings. Nothing of any value, you understand. All such property is forfeit.' He pulled a gleaming watch from his pocket. 'Ten minutes. Then my men go in, and then we fire the place.' He leaned forward, watching Logan again. 'And one move, old man — just one move to stop us, and I'll string you from the highest tree we can find. You understand?'

'You burn Pleasant Hill,' Logan said, 'and you burn me with it.'

The man nodded brusquely. 'It's your choice, old man.'

Logan turned to go back inside the house.

Mattie sprang to him. 'No! Logan, please! They'll do it!'

'I daresay. Out of my way, Mattie.'

She shook her head.

'Out of my way, I say!'

'Logan, please – don't be so stupid!' The words were despairing; even so in some strange recess of her mind she registered the disrespect in front of strangers, half expected a rebuke. 'Get away from the house. Let me save what I can.'

He shook his head obstinately. Behind him she saw that the young lieutenant had dismounted and was coming up the steps towards them. 'Hold him!' she snapped, and pushed Logan hard, with both hands. Taken entirely off guard, the old man teetered for a moment, then lost his balance and keeled over backwards. The young Yankee threw himself forward, and he and Logan finished in an awkward heap at the foot of the steps. 'Keep him out!' Mattie did not wait for a reply; did not pause to ascertain that no permanent damage had been done. Heart hammering in panic, she turned and ran back into the house.

They allowed her to bring out the personal mementos she had gathered together to take to Macon, the photographs of the boys that Logan had had in the library, some clothes for both of them. 'There are some books,' she said, holding up the small, mud-stained Shelley for him to see. 'Just a couple. May we keep them?'

The captain shrugged, impatiently. 'I suppose so.'

Logan sat under guard upon a chair beneath a moss-hung live oak, watching the activity, stone-faced, as his home – his life – was raped by the strangers who might have been the men who had killed his sons. Upright and bloodstained, his white hair wild about his great head, he looked like a fearsome and vengeful prophet from the Old Testament; it was a wonder, Mattie thought wearily, as she joined him with the pathetic bundles she had been allowed to save, that the whole troop were not destroyed by a thunderbolt, or swallowed up by the earth. But they were not. Systematically they looted Pleasant Hill, and then as systematically they fired it. The lovely old house, wooden-clad and tinder dry, went up like a funeral pyre – which indeed it was, since, at the last moment, a trooper had dragged the carcasses of the dead dogs up the steps of the porch and flung them inside, though the bloodstains remained, red on the red earth.

Mattie stood, hands clenched about the back of Logan's chair, watching through resolutely silent tears as the flames danced and licked from the windows, which had been flung open to increase the draught. Glass shattered and tinkled. Sparks towered into the air with the column of smoke marking this barbaric act of intolerance and unforgiveness that would breed, for a hundred years, more and more of such. Men had to shout to be heard above the vengeful roar of the conflagration. When the roof collapsed, the blast of heat that swept the clearing might have been the breath of hell itself.

The soldiers left not long afterwards, when it was clear that the house could not be saved, trotting down the drive in orderly column, leaving Logan still in his chair, his smoke-reddened eyes upon the burning ruins of his home, Mattie kneeling beside him, her hand, numbed from the pressure, clamped tightly into his. Before they rode away the young lieutenant, one eye upon his commanding officer, hovered apologetically, trying to catch her eye. She ignored him stonily. There were a couple of troopers too, she noticed, who did not apparently relish this work of destruction quite as some of their comrades did. It made no difference; she hated them none the less. As the sounds of their departure died, and only the hungry crackling of flame, the occasional sound of structural collapse from within the inferno filled the clearing, she hated them all, from the very depths of her heart and soul. And with hatred came despair. She was alone, with an injured old man and nothing but destruction about her. Gently she freed her hand. She did not look at his face, which she knew was riven by tears that she understood would shame him, no matter how needlessly. Instead she rummaged in the bundle she had dropped beside her. Produced a slightly battered-looking, leather-bound volume.

'Well,' she said, with a sturdy attempt at bravado that did not quite come off, 'it's a good job that God-forsaken Yankee didn't want to know why a respectable woman like me would have wanted to save this.'

Logan turned his head a little, blindly.

'The Scarlet Letter,' she read from the spine, 'by Nathaniel Hawthorne.'

He nodded.

'Joshua told me,' she said, hoping – praying – for some reaction, some anger, even; anything.

He turned his face back to the still-burning ruins of the house.

Mattie fiddled with the small metal lock upon the book, opened it to reveal a cavity cut into the pages, the glint and clink of gold. She looked at it bleakly. You couldn't eat gold.

'My boys will never forgive me,' Logan said, 'for allowing this to happen.' And then, 'I would give my soul,' he added with a deadly rancour that seemed to take the last of his energy, 'to see those bastards dead in their own blood.'

The slave cabins had been left standing, having been considered too poor in pickings to be looted. They stood, cold and empty, in their street not far from the smouldering pyre. Mattie found the soundest and most comfortable, brought primitive furnishings from the others and moved herself and the old man in. Logan Sherwood was feverish and exhausted; otherwise, she felt, he might well have insisted upon sleeping in the open before he occupied one of his own slave cabins. The ruins of Pleasant Hill still smoked, the embers were red hot; at least she had no difficulty in kindling a fire in the small fireplace in the single room of the cabin. With the old man sleeping restlessly at last she wandered the devastated and trampled gardens, gathering what she could, though it was precious little – a few potatoes, some carrots and some old, wrinkled apples on the hacked-down apple tree. A couple of chickens wandered discon-solately from the woods, and flittered back, refusing to be caught.

Logan's fever mounted.

The Infirmary was in ashes; nothing had survived. Mattie brought water from the well and bathed his face and his body. The wound was unhealthily discoloured and looked appallingly inflamed and painful. His temperature was obviously perilously high.

The day wore on; she was so tired she could hardly put one foot in front of the other. Her sore eyes ran and her throat was raw from the smoke. She moved like an automaton, empty, utterly exhausted. She wanted to lie down, to sleep for ever. She wanted to scream. She wanted this not to have happened; could not understand why it had.

Quietly and with care Mattie tended to Logan, doing every-thing within her power to ease the pain, to make him comfort-able, though no amount of stoic courage on the old man's part could conceal from her the obvious truth that it was not enough.

Determinedly she banished thought, and feeling. One moment at a time. That was the only way to survive nightmare.

The interminable day ended at last; dusk turned to darkness and, cold and hungry, having shared a boiled potato with the feverish Logan, she wrapped herself in a blanket and lay upon the hard wooden pallet she had set beside his.

Outside in the darkness the charred ruins of Pleasant Hill glowed in drifting smoke, whilst the two strong, fire-marked brick chimneys reached still, like accusing fingers, towards the clouded sky; Sherman's Tombstones. But in those last exhaus-ted and unguarded moments when Mattie at last could no longer prevent herself from giving way to miserable tears, it was not for the wanton and terrible destruction of the graceful old house that she cried, nor was it in sadness for the way of life that had irrevocably gone with it. It was — absurdly she supposed, even through her distress — for Jake; for the poor, harmless, trusting animal whose uncomplicated affection had seen her through so many trials and whom she had been unable to save from slaughter. She lay, chill, lonely and frightened, and ached for his silly, boisterous, undemanding companionship, the soft reassurance of his fur beneath her hand, the roughness of his tongue upon her skin; could see nothing as the hot tears slid down her face but his body, stiff, bloodstained, ugly in death as he never could have been in life, sprawled, a sacrifice to unthinking hatred, upon the red earth.

When at last she dozed off her fitful sleep was full of menace; each time she slipped from consciousness the flames roared, Jake twisted, screaming in the air, and manic images filled her head. Unknown voices babbled and shouted.

And then she woke in a cold, clear panic and knew that what she had heard was no figment of her imagination; there was someone – something – moving outside the hut.

The door had neither bar nor lock. As she watched, by the light of the small oil-wick lamp she had left burning near the sick man, the wooden latch was slowly and carefully lifted.

Almost without thought Mattie flung herself off the narrow pallet and grabbed for the ancient rifle that Logan had used to support himself. 'Stay where you are,' she called, shakily, backed against the mud-plastered log wall. 'I have a gun.'

The door swung open. Had the weapon she held been operative she would have pulled the trigger upon the empty, smoky square of night it revealed.

'Who's there?'

'Miss Mattie? It's me. Don't shoot. I'm coming in.'

The wave of relief that engulfed her was so great she almost collapsed where she stood. 'Joshua? Joshua – is it you?'

A shadow in the darkness, his big frame blocked the doorway for a moment, then he slipped inside, bare feet silent on the packed earth floor, and closed the door behind him.

'Joshua,' she said, faintly. 'Oh – Joshua!'

'I'm sorry, Miss Mattie,' he said, in the deep, musical voice she would have recognized anywhere, 'I didn't mean to frighten you.'

Mattie had dropped the useless gun and, unthinking, stepped forward and across the tiny room to him before he had stopped speaking. 'Joshua? It's really you? Oh, thank God.' She reached to grasp his warm, strong hands in hers. 'The soldiers came – they burned the house – and killed –' she was crying uncontrollably '– the dogs – and took everything. Oh Joshua, I've been so frightened, and I am so very, very pleased to see you!'

'I saw from the bluff. Thought I'd better make sure they were really gone before I came down.'

'You've – you've been here all the time?'

He nodded.

She bit her tongue, but could not control her face.

His grip upon her hands tightened a little. 'I'd have done you no good at all dancing from a tree, Miss Mattie. The Yankees'd string me up as quick as any Reb would for shooting a white man.' He turned his head to look down at Logan. 'And he'd have told them all right. We both know that.' He bent forward, listening to the other man's difficult breathing. 'He's alive, then?' His voice was dispassionate.

'Yes. But bad. I was going to take him into Macon, but the Yankees came – they took Star, burned the wagon. And I've nothing to help him – the Yankees burned the Infirmary – Joshua, we've nothing to eat –'

'Wait till morning, Miss Mattie. There are places the Yankees didn't know where to look.' He smiled a very little. 'Places you wouldn't know where to look. Get back to sleep. I'll watch the old man.' Gently he released her hands, put her from him. 'I'll wake you if he needs you, I promise. Get some sleep, Miss Mattie. That's what you need most, I reckon.'

She stood for a moment, her face tense, the catalogue of disasters still singing in her tired brain. Joshua pulled her pallet over by the fire, replaced it by Logan's bed with a battered wooden chair. 'You get some sleep, Miss Mattie,' he repeated, coaxing. 'I'll wake you if it's needed, I promise.'

The thought of a secure, guarded rest was almost overwhelming. She settled herself down on the pallet; the fire warmed her back like a benison. 'Joshua?' she began.

Joshua was bent over Logan, his face intent, one hand resting gently upon the sick man's forehead. Something about the sight faintly worried her.

Joshua straightened the blanket about the old man, laid a

quiet hand upon his forehead, turned his head to look at Mattie. 'Yes, Miss Mattie?'

Mattie, sound asleep, did not hear him.

She woke knowing what had worried her. She was scrambling to her feet almost before thought.

Logan lay very still, one hand thrown wide. There was no sign of Joshua.

She laid a not quite steady hand to the old man's cheek. It was warm; too warm. As she touched him, he moved a little, muttering.

Her pulse and her heart slowed, and panic died.

'He's still alive, Miss Mattie.' The voice from the door was quiet. 'What else did you expect? I promised I'd wake you if needed.'

'Yes. Yes, I know – it was just – you weren't here – I –' She stopped in confusion.

His steady dark eyes looked past her disjointed words and to her uneasy thoughts. 'It's just that you went to sleep and left a sick man in charge of the renegade nigger that shot him,' he said.

'No, I –'

He did not let her finish. 'I went to fetch these. They might help.' He lifted his hand. In it he held fresh herbs, and a small pot of salve. On the table by the window Mattie now noticed several pieces of primitive cooking equipment that had not been there the day before, and a small stack of bags and tins. 'I found some food, too – no banquet I'm afraid, but better than nothing.'

'Where?' Mattie had moved to the table. There was flour and corn, ham and butter and biscuits and honey, and fresh eggs. 'Where did you find this?'

'Where de Mass'er don't look,' he said.

'Well de Mass'er's damn' well looking now.' Logan's voice was thin, and was interrupted by a bout of painful coughing. 'Damned murdering nigger I'll see you hanged, see if I don't –'

Mattie ran to him, pressed him back against the stained straw-filled pillows. 'Lie still! You'll kill yourself!'

Pale, malevolent eyes were fixed upon Joshua. 'Get it right, girl. If I die he's the one who'll swing for it –'

'Logan, calm down and stop it! We need Joshua.'

'Need him? By God I *will* die, an' happy to do it, before I'll depend on this Judas nigger for my life.'

'Life,' Joshua said gently, 'consists of many things,' and pulled from his pocket an almost full bottle of whisky, which he placed with great care upon the small, rickety table next to Logan's bed.

Logan turned his head away, but not before they had both seen the flash of pure longing in his face. 'Poisoned, is it?'

'Hold still, and stop talking nonsense,' Mattie said, very briskly, cringing before she ever got near the task, 'I'm going to get rid of this old dressing. Joshua, do you have a knife? Or scissors? I think it's probably better to cut it away.' She accepted the small, sharp knife that he handed her, and set herself to the task, trying to ignore the feverishly venomous glow in Logan's eyes as he watched Joshua over her shoulder. 'Joshua, could you stir up the fire a little and boil some water? We're going to need –' She stopped abruptly as the dressing came away. Appalled, she saw the fiery threads of infection spreading like strong and ghastly roots up the sinewy shoulder and down the arm, smelled the sweet, foul beginnings of corruption in the wound.

Logan's eyes, which had closed upon his pain as she had pulled the dressing off, opened and met hers, in them a sudden and surprising clarity. Mattie looked away. His good hand found hers. 'Don't fuss, girl,' he said. 'What is there now for me but this? Where others have gone in pride before their time, d'you think I'm afraid to follow?'

She made a great business of collecting together the pieces of bandage. 'You?' she asked, caustically. 'You're too much of a plague, Logan Sherwood, to die of a scratch like this. You won't let us all off so easily, I know.'

He took two long, painful days and nights to die. In the end he accepted Joshua's whisky gratefully, which until then he had stubbornly refused, cradled in his son's strong arms, drifting in and out of consciousness, fevered and in agony. They took it in turns to watch over him, to ease his pain as best as they could. Towards the end of the first day he rallied, and it looked for a couple of hours as if his indomitable will would triumph over even this. 'I'll survive to see you swing,' he told the impassive Joshua. 'Treacherous hound. I'll have your hide. See if I don't.' But by nightfall he was delirious again, back in the world where his tall, strong, handsome boys rode with him and he was sovereign in this kingdom of his, fortunate beyond all men, benign and all-powerful. Perhaps, Mattie thought sadly as she watched through the desperate final hours of the second night, when the light of life glowed so low that it could barely be detected, and the face that had been so dauntlessly authoritative fell lax into the defeated lines of approaching death, it was just as well. Logan's time was gone. His life could only have ended in bitterness and hatred. To live on in a defeated world could only have diminished him.

He died in the grey dawn three days after Pleasant Hill had burned.

In drifting rain Joshua dug a grave square in the middle of the red earth clearing in front of the cold, charred remains of the house, with its blackened, foul-smelling ashes and its strong, accusing chimneys. They raised a rough but true cross as tall as a man, so no-one could miss it, with his name upon it and the date of his death. Mattie, thinner than ever, bedraggled, still wearing the clothes she had thrown on that first morning of disaster four days since, said over the grave what words of the funeral service she could remember. A chill breeze blew, and the cold drizzle drifted like the mist of death through the trees and over the quiet, sodden ruins.

Even the most distant sounds of battle had long since receded. The stillness was bizarre, a parody of peace.

She stood at last, straight and silent, remembering. Here she had been driven as a new bride in the Pleasant Hill carriage, escorted by those high-tempered, laughing outriders. Here Bram Taylor had screamed his outrage and his challenge to Johnny. From here those three had ridden, plumed and feathered, laughing still, to glory. To death. Here she had said to Logan, 'Anything's worth fighting for, Mr Sherwood, if you love it enough.'

'Come away. You're getting drenched.' Joshua was beside her, his own jacket offered to cover her shoulders. In these past, fraught forty-eight hours she suddenly realized he had not called her by name once. And knew why.

Mattie turned to him, under the jacket he held and so, inevitably, within the curve of his arms. He settled the garment over her shoulders, his shirt drenched already and clinging to his body. 'Come away,' he said again. And did not take his supporting arm from about her shoulders as they walked back to the hut.

They built up the fire. Their clothes steamed. It was odd – almost disorientating – not to have Logan to tend to. Half the whisky was left. He ignored her automatic refusal.

The first mouthful was, she thought, the most abominable thing she had ever tasted. By an enormous effort of will she managed not to choke, though her eyes ran. Politely she applied the mug to her closed lips, pretending to sip, unwilling to reject his obviously well-meant gesture. Joshua put a plate of thick-cut ham and biscuits in front of her. 'Eat,' he said, gently, and she felt the soft touch of his fingers upon her hair.

Mattie nibbled the ham. It was sweet and succulent. And a warmth was spreading through and from her belly that was far from unpleasant. She sniffed at the tin mug she held cupped in both hands. The warm pungency of it cleared her head a little. When she sipped again, the fumes still in her nose and her throat, she was able to savour the smooth liquor as the fire spread again from tongue to throat and then down into her stomach.

Unselfconsciously he stripped the wet shirt from his back, rubbed his thick, soaked hair.

She watched him for a moment, then turned her eyes back to the fire. Sipped the whisky. They had hardly exchanged a word since the old man had died.

Shirtless, Joshua pulled on a jacket, reached for his own mug, drained it. Took the bottle to the light of the fire. Splashed more into her mug. The afternoon was dark.

What seemed a very long, quiet time later she said, 'I'm tired, Joshua. So very tired.'

'Sleep,' he said.

He drew the pallet with its corn husk mattress close to the fire, piled blankets upon it. Mattie lay down, drowsily, watching the flames and his still strong silhouette against the glow.

She woke slowly, blinking, aware only of comfort and of warmth. Nothing had changed. The freshly made-up fire threw dancing shadows upon ceiling and walls, limned in light the head and shoulders of the man who sat, staring into the flames. 'Joshua?' she asked.

He moved his head, looking towards her. She could not see his face. He watched intently. Then quietly he came to her and, with that grace of movement so characteristic of him, sank to his knees beside her. Firelight gleamed upon his face. She put a hand to his cheek, touching it with one uncertain, questioning finger, tracing the line of it to his mouth. 'Joshua.'

Very, very slowly he leaned and kissed her, gently and long. It was a cherishing kiss, a kiss to calm, to expel and expunge the horrors of the past days; she savoured every blessed moment of it. Then she it was who pulled him to her, fiercely, her fingers buried in his hair, she who slid the jacket from his shoulders and spread her hands upon the smooth skin of his back, warm and vibrantly alive to her touch. He was whole. He was life. He loved her with strength and with tenderness, and as if she were the first and only receptacle of his love; and willingly she yielded to him, safe for this fleeting hour from the squalor and terror that stalked the shadows beyond the firelit cabin.

They slept together on the narrow pallet, limbs entangled, until the new day broke. Then in the silvery light of dawn they coupled again, in joy and even in laughter, outfacing a harsh and alien world, savouring the discovery of love.

CHAPTER THIRTEEN

The weeks that followed were undoubtedly the strangest, yet in a disorientating and dreamlike way perhaps some of the happiest, that Mattie had ever experienced. It was as if, after the horrors that had come upon them so swiftly, they had been granted a respite, a time of peace and discovery. They lived in total isolation and with the minimum of comfort though, with the few surviving chickens, the small hoard of the slaves' stolen food that Joshua had unearthed, what they managed to salvage from the ruined land and what game Joshua managed to trap in the woods, they ate quite adequately and there was plenty to burn. And in any case a hardship shared, and shared with strong if fledgling love, was a hardship halved, or simply ignored altogether. They furnished their small home with anything serviceable from the other cabins, finding blankets and more cooking utensils. Joshua whitewashed the cabin walls and Mattie, hating the dark eye of the empty window, contrived a pair of curtains out of a pretty patchwork bedspread. They spent long hours wandering Pleasant Hill's neglected acres, and came back to the warmth of the small cabin to lie together upon the corn-husk mattress of the wide bed Joshua had constructed, to talk and to make love. Joshua showed her where, in the darkness of that night of violence, he had buried Robert, deep in the quiet woods near the river, and they fashioned for him a cross as they had for his father, with his name and the dates of his birth and death upon it. Joshua knelt, head down, beside the grave and shed silent, difficult and bitter tears.

'It was for him, wasn't it?' Mattie asked quietly. 'It was for Robert that you stayed all these years, when Logan treated you so ill, for him you held Pleasant Hill together, didn't run with the others, when of all of them you would have made the best future free, and away from this place?'

'Yes. It was for him. My friend and my brother. He swore he would come back. When we were free.'

'Both of you.'

He glanced up at her, eyes bright with tears, and with awareness of her understanding. 'Yes. Both of us.'

'What will you – what will we do now?' It was the first time she had dared to think the question, let alone ask it.

Joshua shook his head and reached up for her hand. 'Don't think of it, Mattie. Not yet. We have today, and that is all we have. We'll plan when we know there's a tomorrow to plan for.'

They were not left entirely undisturbed; Joshua was fishing in the river, with Mattie sitting beside him basking in a spell of soft winter sunshine when, a couple of weeks after the destruction of Pleasant Hill, they heard the slow sound of approaching hooves.

'Down!' Joshua hissed.

They crouched in the undergrowth, peered through the trees. Along the winding avenue of evergreen oaks a mule plodded, head down, its rider's legs swinging. 'It's – it's old Mr Brightwell,' Mattie hissed into Joshua's ear. 'From across the river. The Yankees burned them out, too – I saw the smoke – he must have come to see –'

'Ssh!'

They moved quietly closer. The old man had reined in and come to a halt in front of the burned-out house. He sat for a very long time, shoulders slumped, looking at it. Then, stiffly, he swung from the mule's back and walked slowly to Logan's grave, taking off his battered, wide-brimmed hat and resting a gnarled hand for a moment upon the cross before bowing his head and covering his eyes with his hand. Mattie felt tears prick her own eyes; she remembered the man well, a gentle, quiet soul, happily henpecked by his lively wife and daughters, in that other life that seemed so very long ago.

He stayed at the grave for perhaps five minutes before, with a last glance towards the grim ruins, he clambered awkwardly back upon the mule and turned its head down the avenue of oaks towards the road. When the last sounds of his passage had died, Joshua and Mattie emerged into the clearing and walked to the grave. 'It's hard for them, Joshua,' Mattie said at last. 'However wrong they were, however wronged your people are, it's hard for them.'

'I know it,' he said.

They talked for hours, as neither of them had ever talked to anyone before. 'After you came,' he said, 'I knew – thought I knew – that I would never take a woman of my own.'

She frowned. 'But – why?'

He shrugged.

'But – Joshua – you were so distant! You hardly ever even looked at me!'

'What else was there for me?' He smiled a little, and still the bleak edge of bitterness was there. 'To see you so unhappy – to sense, as I sensed, that you were drawn to me –' He shook his head and looked into the firelight. 'Such things happen. Everyone knows it. The white mistress and the slave. What pride is there in that, Mattie? Would you expect it of me?'

She was silent; reached a hand to him. Rain drove into the roof and dripped from the eves.

One day of wind and rain, lying together in front of the fire, he pressed her to tell him every detail she could remember of her life from her very earliest memory to the day their paths had finally crossed. Remembering that day Mattie still blushed. 'And I thought you were Johnny.'

Joshua turned to her, leaning above her, kissed her. 'I know.' He kissed her again. 'And now? Do you still think I'm Johnny?'

'No. Oh, no.' She pushed him back, settled her head against his shoulder. 'Now. It's your turn.'

'What for?'

'Life histories. Your turn.'

'No,' he said, gently and adamantly. 'For I have no history, until now. A slave's past is not history.'

Mattie turned her head to look at him. 'You aren't a slave, Joshua. You're a man.'

'Yes,' he said. 'Now I am.'

She read to him from the Shelley, and found to her relief that no ghosts rose to haunt her. She began, crazily, to form an idea in her mind, an idea that she took out and looked at every so often, like a small treasure, hoarded and kept from the eyes of others. One day, tentatively, she mentioned it. 'Joshua? Would you – would you come to England with me if we could somehow manage it? This awful war can't go on for ever – for all we know it might be over already! – and surely there must be some way?' She waited. He said nothing. 'I told you – I have a house there,' she said softly, remembering, unaware of the longing in her voice. 'We could live there – we could marry –' and laughed, suddenly, bright and uneasy at his silence. 'There! My cousin Constance always knew I was a forward hussy! And here I am, proposing to a man!'

But he did not join in her laughter. 'Wait, Mattie. We must wait. To plan too early would simply be to court disappointment.'

She turned on him, suddenly and fiercely. 'You don't believe we're going to be able to stay together at all, do you? You think the world will catch up with us – and part us –'

'It's a possibility,' he said, drily.

'No! No, it isn't! Not if we don't let it be a possibility!'

He took her shoulders, turned her tearful face to his. 'You still don't understand, do you? You still think this war is going to change something. Don't you know what would happen to me if any white man – Northerner or Southerner – caught me with you? Don't you know what would happen to you?'

'Oh, for goodness' sake! What do you take me for? I'm not thinking of parading down Macon Main Street with my arm tucked in yours, dearly as I'd love to! Of course it isn't that simple! But, Joshua, no-one but us knows what happened here! We can say what we like – make something up to suit ourselves! And people will believe me, if they wouldn't believe you – oh, my love, don't look like that! If we have to play their game for a little while, what does it matter? In England, no-one would know.' She knew him well enough by now not to say what was in her mind; that Joshua looked as white as any of his brothers,

247

and so deception would be easy. She had learned so much, at least.

'Not yet,' he said, the words brooking no argument and no further discussion. 'It's still too dangerous. Mattie, Mattie, I keep telling you we can't – we mustn't – think about tomorrow. Not yet –'

It was the closest they came to disagreement during those strangely idyllic days.

They had no way of knowing of the disasters that those same quiet weeks were dealing to the South. When Mattie, to her amazement, worked out upon the calendar she had designed at the back of one of the salvaged books that Christmas must have arrived, she could not know that the city of Savannah had capitulated in terror the day before, with no shot fired, to the victorious Sherman and his fearsome raiders, who had left in the wake of their march to that lovely city a trail of devastation, death and hatred. Nor could she know that now, his mission accomplished to rend, raze and terrorize the rich and arrogant heartland of Georgia, the red-headed Ohian had turned his narrowed gaze to that cradle of rebellion, South Carolina. If Georgia had suffered, and had deserved to suffer, the Carolinas must be wracked and burned to ashes for their treachery. Grant, still staunchly held at bay by Lee and his starving scarecrow army, was nevertheless throwing a ring of iron about Richmond. Sherman's march with fire and sword northwards through the Carolinas would bring the two Federal armies together, ensure a final, bloody defeat for the Confederacy, and bring the Secessionist States to their knees, once and for all.

At Pleasant Hill the new year of 1865 slipped in strangely peacefully, and within a very few weeks the buds of new growth were veiling the devastated countryside with the first gentle promises of spring. The weather warmed and Joshua and Mattie worked side by side in the garden, or each occupied with their own tasks in this most simple of lives, but never too far from one another. When Joshua went down to the river to fish, or into the woods to trap, Mattie watched every moment for his return, and for his part he rarely let her out of his sight for any length of time. Neither spoke of the perils they knew threatened them beyond this strange, small world of theirs; both went more in fear for the other than for themselves. Indeed, as week succeeded week, Mattie found herself becoming more rather than less apprehensive, more rather than less desperate to know what was happening beyond the borders of Pleasant Hill; for she had come to understand, as Joshua had understood from the start, that anything that happened outside this retreat could only in the end be a threat. They could not stay hidden here for ever. She tried to live each day, with its surprising and beguiling gift of love, moment by moment and hour by hour; but it was difficult. It was as if they dwelt within a magic circle lit by the fragile light of a single candle flame. Beyond was darkness and uncertainty, and they could not know how long the flame would last, nor what might happen when it was extinguished. If either or both of them went to Macon to buy supplies and to discover what was happening – obviously the safest and most sensible option – it would be the end of their happiness together. There could be no question of their association continuing beneath the spiteful scrutiny of the outside world and, if either of them showed their face in the town, there would be too many well-meaning questions to be answered, too many unwanted offers of help to be ignored; they would never be left in peace again. Their present isolation was owed simply to the fact that no-one knew they were there. No other neighbours came to discover what had happened at Pleasant Hill – presumably Mr Brightwell had drawn his own conclusions and spread the word amongst whatever acquaintances might be left in the area, and people had more pressing things to do than to come to gawp at yet another deserted ruin. As spring advanced and the weather warmed and the rutted roads dried, they were more at risk from the increasing numbers of ragged soldiers that straggled along the road past the gate; deserters, Mattie assumed, or Rebels wounded or cut off from their units during Sherman's devastating drive through the state.

'I think it must be more than that,' Joshua said thoughtfully, after a band of half-starved, desperate-looking men, filthy, barefoot and unshaven, and in a patchwork of uniform that defied any recognition, had fortunately decided not to explore the

Pleasant Hill drive, seeing at its end the forlorn, firemarked chimneys and the blackened remnants of the house.

'Nothin' there,' one had said, wearily. 'Bastard Sherman got here first, God rot his balls. Won't be enough left to fill the belly of a cockroach.'

'Must 'a bin a real purty house,' said another.

'Sure must.' A big, raw-boned man in tattered grey shot a stream of brown tobacco juice expertly into the ditch. 'An' tell you what, Ezekiah Johnson, you'd 'a got no more a welcome there before it burned than it'd give you now, an' that's a certain fact. Your great dirty feet wouldn't 'a crossed that porch, you can be sure o' that. Round the back with the niggers, that's where you an' me would have bin sent – an' the lady o' the house drawin' her skirts aside so's not to be polluted by the likes of us. Quick enough to make us fight for 'em though, eh?'

There was a mutter of assent.

Mattie and Joshua, hidden in the trees, watched them go. 'More?' Mattie asked.

'These can't be men left behind after Atlanta. It's too long ago now, and they've the look of having travelled.'

'You mean – deserters? From – another battle? Another defeat?'

Joshua shrugged. 'They look in a poor way.'

Mattie folded her arms across her breast, absently rubbing her rough fingers upon the threadbare material of her jacket. 'If only we knew. If only we knew what was happening.'

He shook his head, his black eyes fathomless. 'Leave it. Don't think of it. We'll find out soon enough.'

A week later, another such group descended upon Pleasant Hill and Mattie and Joshua only escaped detection by sheer luck. The weather was warm and they had not lit the fire in their cabin. Encouraged into the pale sunshine, Mattie had packed a frugal meal and they had followed the path upriver to a favourite fishing spot. The fat, waxy buds of the magnolias were bursting into fragrant life and the air was noisy with birdsong and the spring gossip of the crickets. Mattie felt the benevolent warmth of the sun creep into bone and nerve, and relaxed, shutting her eyes against the brightness of the sunshine, breathing deeply of the fresh, balmy air.

The shots shredded the quiet of the afternoon like claws ripping rotted fabric. She leaped to her feet, taking a breath to cry out. With a movement swift as a cat's, Joshua was beside her, hand over her mouth, shaking his head as he held her. 'Ssh!'

They stood in silence, listening. There came another volley of shots, and the sound of laughter, from the direction of the house.

'Wait here,' Joshua said.

Mattie grabbed his arm. 'No! I'm coming with you.'

He hesitated for a moment, shrugged and took her hand. They slipped back along the path then struck into the now-overgrown woodland beside the live oak avenue.

In the clearing in front of the burned house a group of men were building a fire, dragging fuel from the ruins of house and barns. Several dead rabbits lay upon the ground. A man staggered around the corner of the house with a bucket in each hand. 'There's a well back there — the water's good —'

'Keep the water.' A tall, thin, unshaven man unsteadily lifted a bottle to his lips. 'This'll do me.'

'Hey, Stevens, whadja think you — you're doin'?' Another man snatched the bottle from him. 'Greedy son of a bitch — 's ours too, y'know.'

'They're drunk!' Mattie whispered.

Joshua nodded, his hand tightening on hers in warning.

The man called Stevens swung a wild fist at the other, and missed, fell to his knees, swearing. Like most of the others, his filthy feet were bare; like all of them, he was weather-beaten from a winter spent in the open, gaunt to the point of emaciation and dressed in butternut rags not fit for a scarecrow. Another man placed a bare foot upon his buttocks and pushed, gently. He subsided flat on his face on the red earth and lay there, spread-eagled and snoring.

'Leave him.' The apparent leader of the group aimed a kick at the prone man as he passed. 'An' Jake, lay off that for a while, will yer?' He snatched the bottle from the other man. 'There's only three left. Leave 'em till later. Get these things skinned, Willy.' He tossed the rabbit to a weary-looking youngster who grabbed for them and missed. 'An' you, Robbie, get over there behind the barn – there's a bit of a garden there – fetch some vegetables.' He straightened to his considerable height, grinning crookedly.

Mattie gritted her teeth, thinking of the tender growth of their fresh vegetables. Joshua pulled gently at her hand, indicated with a jerk of his head that they should leave. A safe distance from the house he said, 'We'll have to stay away until they go. Go back to where we were fishing – at least we've some food there.'

'Where are you going?' She would not release his hand.

'Back to the cabin. If we're going have to stay out all night, perhaps two, we need some supplies.'

This time Mattie had to let him go. She made her way back to the river and waited, rigid with fear, for his return. She could hear shouts and laughter; waited for the yell that would tell of Joshua's discovery.

It did not come. He emerged from the trees like a shadow, carrying blankets and extra food. 'We'll go upriver, then cut up into the woodlands on the ridge,' he said. 'Then we can keep watch and see when they leave.'

'Supposing – supposing they don't?' she asked, a little shakily.

He took her hand in silence, hitching the blankets over his shoulder.

The renegades stayed for two nights. From the quiet darkness of their ridge, Mattie and Joshua could see the leaping light of the fire, hear the drunken singing and brawling.

'I don't understand,' Mattie said. 'Where did they get the drink? They don't seem to have anything else.'

Joshua shrugged in the darkness. 'Stole it, I suppose.' He could not bring himself to tell her of the drunken bragging he had overheard when he went back to the cabin; he remembered, as Mattie did, the Brightwell family from other, better times. The thought of the old man and his wife, having returned against all good sense to the wreckage of their home, slaughtered in cold blood for the sake of what had been salvaged from the plantation cellar, sickened him. He saw no reason to burden Mattie with it; but he was fierce to the point of anger when she wanted to stretch her legs away from their hiding place. 'You stay right here, you hear me? You don't move a muscle you don't have to! Keep down and keep out of their sight! For God's sake, Mattie, these men are animals, and drunken animals at that!'

On the morning of the second day he slipped down to the makeshift camp to watch as the leader of the deserters kicked his men awake, groaning and bleary-eyed. 'Get up, you skunks! On yer feet!' He bent to wrench an empty bottle from an all but unconscious man's arms and tossed it over his shoulder to shatter in the embers of the fire, the last drops of spirit flaring. The man on the ground, who had been cuddling the bottle as if it had been a woman, muttered obscenely in protest and got the toe of the other man's boot for an answer. 'Up, you stupid, sodden sons of bitches! Up. Time to move on.'

Joshua watched as they straggled down the drive towards the road.

'Hey, Willy.' A man, staggering, threw a companionable arm about the boy's thin shoulders, as much to support himself as anything else. 'What you goin' ter do now this bastard war's nearly over?'

'I'm goin' home, Seth.' The boy had stumbled and nearly collapsed under the other man's weight. 'Just goin' home, to Ma an' Pa an' the farm. That's all I want. Tell you straight, never wanted nothin' else in the first place.' The reedy voice was almost tearful. 'Ain't never gon' leave again, Seth. No, Sir, not never.'

Joshua did not hear the other man's reply. When all sound had died he walked over to the fire, and the filth and the wreckage the men had left around it. Stood for a long moment stirring the still-smoking embers with his foot, thoughtfully. To stay? Or to go? Which was the more dangerous? And if they decided to leave, where, and how, would they go? Was the war nearly over? And if it were, how did it affect them? How safe was it to move? And then again – round and round like a rat on a treadmill – how safe to stay?

They were still debating the question five days later, when their precarious peace was brutally shattered and all chance to take a decision was lost.

If it had not been for a capricious, chill turn in the weather they might once again have escaped. But the men came at night this time, and followed the smell of smoke directly to the cabin door. The first either Joshua or Mattie knew of the invasion was when the door was shouldered open, breaking the bar and slamming it back on its hinges, and two men stepped into the glowing firelight, rifles levelled almost casually. Mattie was in bed, Joshua sitting at the small table mending a broken fishing rod by the light of a single candle. He leaped to his feet, the chair flying backwards. Mattie gave one small cry, then sat frozen, the bedclothes clutched about her.

'Evenin', folks.' The words were flat, lacking in the smallest amount of human warmth. The man who spoke them was much like every other they had seen in these past weeks; thin, dirty, hard-faced, tired. He wore faded and threadbare grey trousers and a Union jacket that hung open over a filthy home-spun shirt. Hair and beard were ragged. He chewed as he spoke; his teeth were stained from the tobacco. Grinning, he doffed a crushed and shapeless hat to Mattie. 'Pardon me, Ma'am.' He emphasized the pronoun with affected deference, and his companion sniggered.

Mattie looked at Joshua, suddenly aware of his acute disadvantage in such a situation, willing him to shake off the instincts and reflexes of a lifetime of slavery and take the initiative, as a free man would. In the dim light his skin shone pale – paler, if anything, than that of the intruders, who had spent these last long, tough months in the open. That these were Southern deserters could not be in doubt; the situation was fearful enough without their guessing who and what Joshua was.

Joshua was there before her. 'What the hell do you think

254

you're doin', Sir?' His deep, cultured voice was quiet, polite, hard as steel; he had not lived that same lifetime with his father and his half-brothers without learning the inflections of command and inbred superiority. 'How dare you intrude in this way?'

The man chewed ruminatively, watching him. Spat into the fire, which hissed and crackled. 'You the folks from the house?'

'Who else would we be?'

He shrugged. 'Could be Adam an' Eve for all I know.' He chuckled at his own wit, glancing at his partner who sniggered again, obediently. His eyes had barely wavered from Mattie, her hair about her shoulders, the bedclothes pulled up to her neck.

She clutched them tighter.

Joshua settled his feet firmly upon the floor, standing tall and easily. 'If it's shelter you're lookin' for, why then we can certainly supply it – you're welcome to use one of the huts. As you see, our hospitality has been gravely limited by a visit from other, more demandin' guests.' He allowed himself the shadow of a bleak smile. 'We have too some few supplies you're welcome to share. Anythin' more valuable – ' he spread his hands, shrugging a little, and for an unsettling moment Mattie could not believe that she was not watching Johnny, three years dead '– if you can find it you're welcome to it, though I have to tell you our Northern visitors did a pretty good job, an' if there's even a Confederate dollar bill left we haven't been able to find it.'

The other man grinned appreciatively. 'Wouldn't do you much good if you could.'

'Quite. My opinion entirely, Sir.'

'Things ain't worth nothin' but to wipe shit with – beggin' your pardon, Ma'am.' The apology was perfunctory in the extreme, but the bravado was obvious; the man had certainly been disconcerted and, Mattie suspected, put just a little in awe. Just so had first his masters and then his officers spoken. He had lowered the rifle. With something of a swagger he toured the room, inspecting it, lifting up a pot from the mantelpiece, a dish from the table.

His companion's unblinking gaze was still upon Mattie.

'So,' Joshua's voice was perfectly firm and calm, 'if you wouldn't mind?' He made a courteous gesture towards the door. 'There's plenty of fuel should you feel the need for a fire, and the water in the well is fresh and untainted. We can talk, if you wish, in the mornin'?'

Almost it worked. The man could not disguise the hesitancy in his eyes, the reflex of obedience. He scratched his unkempt chin. 'Well –'

'In the mornin', Sir.' Joshua's voice brooked no argument. 'Until then I'll thank you to leave me an' my wife to our privacy, inglorious as it may be.'

The door opened.

With some relief the man turned. 'Jeb. What kept you?'

'I bin lookin' round.' The newcomer spoke from the shadows beyond the door. 'Bin enjoyin' the fuckin' view an' thinkin' of old times. Bin' thinkin' that this ole war's not bin all bad iffen it means the bastard Sherwoods got their comeuppance.' The newcomer stepped into the light. 'Well, well. An' what do we have here?'

The silence was absolute, and terrifying. Mattie stared at him, trying to place him.

'So one of you bastards survived, did you?' The man carried a rifle. He hefted it in his hand, laid it carefully in the crook of his arm. He was watching Joshua, a faint and dangerously puzzled frown creasing his weather-beaten forehead.

Joshua said nothing.

'Remember me? Jeb Sangster? Remember my Pa, share-croppin', strugglin' to hold body an' soul together down south of the river by Silver Springs? Remember your Pa an' his fancy fuckin' friends houndin' us out? Killed my Ma, between you; always swore I'd see you in hell for it –' He stopped. That faint, suspicious frown was still there, and his light eyes had narrowed.

'Mr Sangster,' Mattie said, in desperation; anything to draw that shrewd, suspicious gaze from Joshua's immobile face. 'Please, can't we discuss this tomorrow? I'm sure if there's anything we can do to help you –'

The appraising eyes were on her now. She could almost see

the brain behind them working. 'You're the piece Johnny Sherwood brought back from England after that happy bitch Lottie Barclay floored him,' he said. 'But this –' He shook his head slowly, eyes steady once more upon Joshua, and then flicking about the room, taking it in, absorbing the intimacy, the sense of home.

'What, Jeb? What's up?' The man who had been watching Mattie so intently was the last to catch on that something was afoot. Sensing the odd tension in the air, he looked perplexedly from one to another.

'This – ain't – Johnny Sherwood,' Sangster said, very slowly. 'An' what's more, it ain't –' He stopped. Then he smiled, a huge, savagely malicious smile. 'It's a mother-fuckin' niggrah,' he said softly. 'By Christ, it's a niggrah *and* a Sherwood!' He took two steps and had Joshua by his shirtfront, his face thrust close. 'It's the uppity – Sherwoods' – uppity – niggrah – ain't it?' he asked, screwing the shirt tighter about his fist at every word. 'It's Joshua.' He breathed the word softly, filled it with venom and hate. 'Ain't it?'

Mattie, barefoot and clad in nothing but one of Logan Sherwood's oversized nightshirts, scrambled without thought from the bed and flew at Sangster like a harpy. 'Get away from him! Get away!' She threw herself upon him, shrieking, blind with terror and with fury, and for a moment, taken off balance, he let go of Joshua and staggered back before her onslaught. The door was open. *'Joshua! Run!'*

There was one moment when he could have fled, when the three men, bemused by the fury of Mattie's attack and the pitch of her furious screaming, were, as she had hoped, watching her, not him. He did not take advantage of it. As Jeb Sangster drew back his hand to slap Mattie away, Joshua launched himself upon him. Within seconds he was pinioned, arms twisted behind his back, a savage hand buried in his thick hair.

He fought like a fury for a moment or so and then, knowing himself overwhelmed, he subsided, standing quiet, head forced back, in their ungentle hands.

'Joshua,' Mattie said. She too was held. The man who had been staring at her had caught her and twisted her around, her back to him, his rough hands hard across her breasts. She could feel his body against her, moving, disgusting her. 'Joshua!'

'We hang uppity niggrahs,' Jeb Sangster said, conversationally, twisting Joshua's arm harder, hearing it crack. 'Don't we, boys?'

'Sure do.'

'Dark for it.' The man who held Mattie grinned. 'Quicker to shoot him.'

'Quicker, yes,' Jeb Sangster said softly. 'All the more reason to hang him. I remember this bastard. Thought himself better than us white trash. Didn't you, niggrah?' He gave a last vicious turn to Joshua's arm, which brought a grunt of pain. 'Hold him, Gus.' He let go and stepped back, grabbing his rifle and lifting it to threaten both Joshua and Mattie. 'OK, boys. Let them go. Gus — the fishing line. Tie them up. Then we'll have us some fun.'

'Yes, Sir, Jeb.' The man let go of Joshua and reached for the line coiled neatly upon the table.

'No,' Mattie said, and then again, 'No!' Once bound, Joshua would have no chance at all — they would drag him out and string him, choking, to the nearest tree. 'No!' For that moment she did not care if she lived or died. Ignoring the rifle, she launched herself towards the man who reached for the fishing line. In the same second Joshua swung clumsily, one arm hanging uselessly at his side, at the man closest to him.

The rifle spoke, thunderous in the enclosed space. Mattie screamed. Joshua grunted and dropped where he stood. Jeb Sangster, feeding an old hatred, took aim very precisely and fired again. 'Pity,' he said, as blood and brain splattered the dirt floor. 'A hangin' would 'a bin better. Slower, like.'

Mattie's assailant had her pinned to the floor, leaning above her, his face bearing down onto hers. The other man stood watching, grinning. 'Need any help, Amos?'

'You want niggrah leavin's?' Jeb Sangster asked, true disgust in his voice. 'Take 'em. I'll see you outside.'

As he left he aimed a kick at the struggling Mattie's side that took her breath and allowed her attacker time to grab both her hands and mount her. He was speaking, low and intense, obscenities repeated over and over again.

'Go it, Amos.' The other man was laughing, down on his haunches watching. 'Go on, boy. Get in there. Christ, Amos – never knew you had it in you –'

She lay for hours after they had left, shocked into a state of near insensibility, curled upon the bed, her eyes fixed upon the bloodstained sheet that she had flung over Joshua's body. It was full daylight before she dragged herself to her feet and set about the only task her numbed mind could encompass. She sprinkled the precious oil they had been so carefully conserving for the lamps over the sheet, and the furniture, stood for a moment, a glowing brand in her hand, looking down at all that was left of Joshua Sherwood. She did not pull the sheet away – she knew too well what lay beneath it; it would haunt her for ever. She made her goodbyes, quiet and tearless, then tossed the torch upon the oilsoaked cloth, staggering back, her arm flung up before her face, as it exploded into flame. She had not intended to leave the cabin; she had intended to burn there with him upon his funeral pyre. Yet somehow she found herself in the open, watching as the cleansing flames licked and crackled from window and door, towered into the air. It was then at last that the tears came, and, filthy and bloodstained, the nightgown all but ripped from her body, Mattie crumpled to the ground, sobbing, and willing herself to die.

Almost she succeeded. She never afterwards knew how long she lay there, or at what point she dragged herself into the darkness of another slave hut and lay upon the board bed, her face turned to the wall. She drifted in and out of consciousness, in and out of nightmare. She ate nothing and drank little. She spoke to Joshua. She spoke to her father. She pleaded with God to let her die. Light-headed, she relived again and again the terrible moment of Joshua's death; saw the man Sangster's livid, hate-filled face as he pulled the trigger. Cried until there were no more tears, no more feeling. Until the moment that she opened her eyes, sensing a presence beside her and saw to her horror another of the scarecrow men that had haunted her, one-armed, filthy, the rags he wore bloodstained; and this was no spectre, but a solid, foul-smelling reality. Weak as she was, Mattie surged up, screaming, fingers clawed.

Even one-armed, he held her with ease, and the terrible spurt of energy soon died.

'Mattie,' he said. 'Oh, God, Mattie – what's happened here – what?' He was crying, tears sliding down the filthy cheeks and into the wild black beard.

She lifted her head, narrowing her sore, reddened eyes against the light that streamed through the door, and found herself looking into the changed face, haggard and marked by pain, privation and grief, of Russell Sherwood.

She kept her secret, and Joshua's. There was enough to tell without that. Russell nursed her devotedly in the days that followed, and she used the time well. When at last he deemed it the time to ask, gently, what had happened, she had concocted a tale that was near enough to the truth to withstand scrutiny, but which neither incriminated Joshua in the death of Logan nor told of her own involvement with him. She also spared Russell any suspicion that Logan had killed his own son. It was easy to blame the death and destruction around them first on Sherman's men and then on the gangs of deserters that Russell knew all too well were infesting the countryside. Robert, she said, had come to warn them of danger but had been unable to get away in time and had died defending the house and his father. Logan had been shot, and had later died of his wounds. Joshua and a couple of the other slaves had stayed loyally with her, until the arrival of the deserters, when Joshua had been killed and the others had fled. It was all very plausible.

'But you, Russell? How are you here? We were told you were all dead. Shake said he saw it. The others?' She lifted her eyes to his.

Russell shook his head. 'No, Mattie. No hope of that. They're dead. I saw them die. And Shake would have believed me dead, too. I nearly was.' He lifted his hand to his hairline, parting the dark hair to show a deeply grooved scar on his forehead. 'I woke up in a Northern prison camp, so sick I hardly knew who I was, let alone where I was. Later I sent a message – it obviously didn't arrive.' He shrugged a little, as if shaking off the intolerable memories. She reached a thin hand and he took it in his, laid it against his unshaven cheek. 'Mattie, poor Mattie. God knows, you did nothing to deserve any of this. I'll make it up to you, Mattie. I promise. Anything – anything I can do – '

She waited a long, quiet moment. Then, 'I want to go home, Russell,' she said. 'I just want to go home.'

It took three months to arrange passage to England; the war was over, and the blockade lifted, but trade with the shattered South had not yet resumed, and there were few ships as yet sailing from Liverpool. Mattie spent the last anxious month in Savannah – the city, unbelievably, as graceful and lovely as it had ever been, apparently untouched by war – haunting the shipping offices, standing hour by watchful hour upon the bluff, looking downriver towards the sea. She stayed in a small hotel not far from the waterfront, having begged Russell not to let anyone know she was there. He had misunderstood entirely the reason for her anxiety, as she had intended, and had willingly and gently agreed. With an unexpected delicacy he had never questioned her about her own experience at the hands of the deserters who had murdered Joshua; but certainly he guessed what had happened, and believed that he understood her reluctance to face people and their well-intentioned, prying questions. Having escorted her to Savannah, he was concerned at the thought of leaving her there alone, but Mattie insisted. The war might be over, but a new battle awaited him at Pleasant Hill; plantations were being confiscated, broken up, sold off. If he stayed away too long he could well find he had nothing to go back to, and after all that had been sacrificed such a thought was unbearable for both of them. Mattie knew one thing. While there was breath in Russell's body, one-armed or not, he would fight to protect Sherwood land.

And so she waited, alone and with hard-held patience. When

at last the ship that was to take her to England drew away from the quayside – that same quayside at which she and Johnny had disembarked in such expectation five long years before – she watched as Savannah dropped rapidly astern with nothing but an overwhelming sense of relief.

She was safe, and the secret she guarded was safe with her.

As they passed beneath the ruined bulk of Fort Pulaski, lying wrecked and deserted in the summer sun, and surged through the running tide towards the open sea, the child within Mattie quickened and stirred for the first time.

PART THREE: INTERLUDE

Coombe House, Kent
1883

IT HAD BEEN A LONG and lovely summer. The Kentish countryside basked still beneath an autumn sun, the slightest breeze drifting from a balmy westerly direction, bearing with it the smells of hops and of harvest.

The soft bricks and mossed tiles of Coombe House gave back the warmth of the sun; bees hummed in late honeysuckle and perfumed scarlet petals dropped from September roses. The river, beside which two distant figures strolled, curled lazily beyond the green lawns and lost itself, glittering, beneath the drooping green canopy of the woodland trees. A single swan sailed placidly upon its waters. The voices and laughter of the two young people who walked beside it drifted back to the open windows of the house.

'I must say, Mattie, the garden is looking truly splendid. I said as much to Mr Wheeler just the other day.' Angelina Wheeler turned from the window, looked affectionately at the tall, lean-built woman who was pouring tea. 'You really do have the greenest of green fingers!'

Mattie Sherwood smiled. 'Thank you, Lina. You're very kind.' She carried the cups to her friend's side, stood with her looking out over the peaceful scene. 'It is, as you know, one of my passions.' As she moved, a big old dog, shaggy and golden, ambled beside her, and sat leaning heavily against her legs. She laughed. 'Jake, for goodness' sake! You'll push me right over!'

'He's getting fat,' the other woman said, laughing with her.

Mattie bent to fondle the big, soft head. 'He's getting old.'

'Aren't we all?' There was a harmless coquettishness in the question that made Mattie smile. Angelina, ten years Mattie's junior, was almost as pretty as her daughter Carolyn, with whom Harry walked by the river, and she well knew it. Her satin afternoon gown, a becoming shade of rose, flounced, beribboned and bustled, showed off her softly rounded figure to perfection. Her fair hair was tucked beneath a feathered bonnet.

Mattie, who, on her guests' unexpected arrival, had been caught on her knees in the very garden of which Angelina was so admiring, and was herself wearing her favourite and most serviceable – and therefore most shabby – skirt and blouse, laughed again. 'What nonsense! Look at you! Dressed to the nines and as pretty as a picture! You look no different to when we first met – what? – seventeen years ago?'

Angelina blushed, pleased. 'Seventeen years! Is it really so long? I suppose it must be! Such happy years – they've flown so quickly!' and then, with the slightly anxious generosity that was so much a part of her character and which Mattie had always found tiresome and endearing in about equal parts, added quickly, 'But, Mattie, no matter how I tried I could never look as you do, you know.'

'I?' Mattie had turned to the window, watching as the two youngsters moved from the water towards the house. 'Good heavens, whatever can you mean?'

'Distinguished,' Angelina said, sturdily. 'Handsome. That's the very word dear Mr Wheeler used about you only the other day.'

'Handsome?' Mattie turned astonished eyes to the other woman. 'Oh, lord, Lina, what a thing to say about a grey-haired old biddy of forty-five who spends most of her time with dirty hands and fingernails you could plant a good crop of potatoes in!'

'Oh, don't be silly! Your hair isn't grey, it's softest silver, and it suits you well.' Angelina raised a small, mockingly warning finger. 'If you aren't careful I shall tell you what else George said.'

Mattie cocked her head to one side, adopted a low, masculine tone with a touch of a Yorkshire accent. 'I can't think why our Mattie hasn't remarried in all this time. T'isn't natural, that's what – handsome woman like that. T'isn't as if she hasn't had her chances -'

Angelina squealed in delight. 'Oh, Mattie, that's it! That's it exactly! You have dear George to a "T"!'

'Hardly surprising after seventeen years of being told the same thing,' Mattie said, gently dry.

Her friend joined her at the window, slipped an arm through hers. 'You know it's only because we care for you – because we're concerned for you.'

Mattie laid a garden-roughened hand on hers for a moment. 'Yes, I do know that. Of course I do.' She smiled again. 'As with quite relentless determination do, quite independently, my Cousin Constance and my Sherwood brother-in-law – both of whom heartily agree with you and urge me in every letter to find myself a sensible and well-set-up husband who will deliver me from my self-imposed and unsociable state and make of me, they hope, a normal, respectable woman.' Mischief glinted in her eyes. 'What you all fail, I fear, to understand, is that I have remained unmarried by design rather than by accident. Lina, my dear, I actually like living alone – except, of course, that I don't. I have Jake. I have the house. I have the garden.' Her eyes rested for a long moment on the two figures who, together, approached across the soft green grass. 'And I have Harry. Why should I need more?'

The smaller woman opened her mouth, and then with unusual self-restraint shut it again. There was a moment's silence. Then, 'Would you never think of marriage?' Angelina asked, clear curiosity in her voice.

Mattie considered. 'Yes. But only to a man who understands me. Who doesn't only love me, but likes me.' She laughed, with a clear ripple of true amusement. 'And since, I suspect, no such paragon exists, then I shall do very well as I am.'

'You don't think that Harry has missed having a father?'

'He had a father, Lina,' Mattie said, evenly.

'Well, yes – of course – I didn't mean –'

'We've spoken of it, of course we have. There have been offers, as you know.' Mattie's eye were still soft, upon her son, who laughed and lifted a hand in greeting as he saw her standing in the window. 'If Harry had wanted it I would have married. For him. But always he said no. Always he said – we're happy as

267

we are. And always we have been.' She turned abruptly, moved towards the fireplace. 'I'll ring for more tea. This has gone cold, and I expect the children would like a cup.'

Angelina laughed, watching the young couple who strolled towards them. 'Children! You always call them children!'

'Well, of course! That's what they are.' Mattie tugged at the bell pull.

'Hardly.' Angelina sat in a straight-backed chair, arranged her skirt about her, glanced archly up. 'Our Carolyn is just seventeen, and young Harry will be eighteen next week, will he not? Caro is in a great fuss over what to buy him. Mr Wheeler and I were only saying the other day what a very handsome pair they make.' She put her head on one side, hopefully, watching Mattie.

There was a small but marked silence. Then, 'Handsome seems a word much bandied in the Wheeler household?' Mattie said, lightly, but with the faintest edge to her voice.

Angelina leaned forward a little. 'Mattie, my dear – they are very fond of each other –'

'Well, of course they are. They were practically brought up together.' The words this time were brusque. 'They're like brother and sister. Of course they're fond of each other.'

Apparently unaware of any agitation her words might be causing, Angelina trilled laughter again. 'Mattie! Brother and sister? Why, my dear, where ever are your eyes? That may have been true in the past – but now? Oh, no, I think not, you know. Brother and sister indeed! Why, Caro is already six months older than I was when I married dear George.'

'Angelina, Harry is far, far too young to consider marriage. It's absurd!' The tiniest flicker of panic made Mattie pause to take a deep and audible breath.

'Well, of course – we realize they would have to wait – but we're perfectly happy about that, my dear. You know how dear Mr Wheeler is about his little girl – what Carolyn wants she must have –'

'Lina!'

'He even suggested the other day that we might talk about a position in the company for young Harry. We have no son of our own, as you know, and we are so very fond of him –'

'Lina!'

Angelina stopped, astonished.

'I'm – I'm sorry. I didn't mean to be so sharp. It's just –' the panic had increased, was building, had almost paralysed Mattie's tongue. Angelina was right; these past, contented years had raced by far too quickly. She wasn't ready – dear God, she wasn't ready! When he's a man, she had told herself, when he's a man – then I'll tell him, then I'll explain, then he'll understand. They had been so close. She had told him, by inference, so many, many lies – she could not face telling him the truth. Not yet. Not just yet. '– it's just that Harry's so young yet. I really don't feel I should be pushing him into something before he knows what he wants.'

Angelina stood, smiling, hands extended. 'But, dearest Mattie, it's as plain as the nose on your face! He wants Caro!'

'No,' Mattie said. 'No, you're wrong.'

The other woman's pleasant smile faded. 'Mattie? Mattie, surely I haven't upset you, talking of it? We do understand – Harry being all you have, and being so very close to you, closer than most, I know – but, dearest, you must know it can't last for ever? Children grow up. We have to let them go sometime.'

'It isn't that. And no, of course you haven't upset me –' Mattie stopped as the French doors opened to admit the two young people, faces sunflushed, hands linked.

'Mother, any tea? My throat feels like the Sahara. Aunt Lina, Caro wants one of Sedge's puppies – may she have one?'

'Oh, please, Mama. They are the very sweetest things.' Carolyn Wheeler's forget-me-not eyes turned upon her mother, her pretty lips curved into a coaxing smile. Mattie saw with a suddenly leaden heart the expression in her son's dark eyes as he watched her, the pink-and-white Dresden beauty of her small face, the little, graceful hands, the tiny waist; oh yes, Lina was right, a handsome pair they made indeed. In God's name, how had she not seen it? Had her self-induced blindness been deliberate? How had she reached this moment unprepared? As she poured tea and passed biscuits, carried on light and teasing conversation, admired Carolyn's new dress and hunted out a book of recipes for Angelina, Mattie tried to ignore the rise of panic. How often, in these past eighteen years, had she thought of having to face this moment? How often had she swung from one decision to the other; to tell him, or to take the chance that his father's blood – Joshua's blood – would not taint the coming generations? Taint. The brutal word made her feel sick.

'Mother? Are you all right?' Harry, ever sensitive, was watching her, a faint frown upon his clear, boyish brow. She never could look at him without seeing his father, whom he so much resembled, without remembering those short, fierce days of their love; yet it was a secret she had kept from everyone. So far as the world knew – so far as Harry himself knew – he was the son of Johnny Sherwood, a hero dead in the American war, fighting to defend his brothers and his cause. A cause now enshrined romantically in a past that must seem as distant to the boy as the moon.

'Yes. Yes, I'm fine, darling. It's a little warm in here, that's all. Perhaps you'd like to open the other window? The breeze is very pleasant.' Mattie watched him move, lithe and graceful, to the window. His ivory skin took the sun each summer and tanned to gold. His black hair fell in tangled curls that Carolyn often teasingly asserted were wasted on a boy, and his eyes were Joshua's eyes, dark, long-lashed and lustrous. He was bright, carefree, volatile and hopelessly impulsive in all things. And she loved him more than life itself.

But she had kept from him all these years the secret of his true parentage; a secret that clearly was no longer hers to keep.

Later, Harry and Mattie sat together, as they often did in the evening. Mattie gave Harry the letter that had arrived from America that morning, and watched him as he read it. She had always felt grateful to Russ for his delicacy in never questioning Harry's paternity. He no doubt assumed the boy to be the product of rape, as was more than one child in the aftermath of that terrible war.

Harry folded the letter and handed it back to her. 'It's good that Pleasant Hill is still doing so well, despite the difficulties. I should like to meet Cousin Johnny. And little Will. We will visit one day, won't we?'

'Of course,' she said, stopping the conversation there. Russ had married a local girl, and their two sons had been named after his dead brothers. Fortuitously the third child had been a girl, named Dorcas, after her mother.

Harry leaned to the fire, holding his hands to the warmth. 'Mother? You've been quiet today. Is anything wrong?'

So well did they know each other. Mattie smiled a little, shook her head. Her hand moved softly upon Jake's shaggy head. 'I'm a little tired, that's all.'

He turned, smiling. 'Caro's taking two of the puppies.'

'What will she call them?' She watched his quick, restless movements; he was never still.

'Byron and Shelley.' He caught her swift glance and coloured a little beneath his tan. 'We were reading that little book you gave me – that Father took to the war –'

'Were you indeed?' What are all these kissings worth, If thou kiss not me?

Harry ducked his head, shaking his hair out of his eyes, scooped a piece of well-chewed wood from the floor and spun it in the air, catching it deftly as it fell. 'Honestly, that dog – you let him get away with more than I can! Supposing I hauled a bit of chewed old wood onto your favourite carpet, what would you do?'

'Shoot you, probably. Or send you to your kennel.'

He grinned.

'Harry? You're – very fond of Carolyn – aren't you?' She tried to keep her voice quietly neutral.

He glanced at her in surprise, and a little shyly. 'Well, of course I am. As a matter of fact –' He stopped, and again that tell-tale colour lifted in his dark cheeks. He spun the piece of splintered wood again. Memories of the kiss he had stolen under the willow by the water – by no means the first and he fervently hoped not the last – filled him with an odd and delightful confusion of feelings; and when he allowed himself to dwell on the feel of the creamy-smooth skin of her shoulders beneath his hands, the bright eagerness of her blue eyes – he tossed the wood again, and missed it.

Mattie took a long, sighing breath. 'Harry –'

'She's a marvellous girl, isn't she? Don't you think? I mean, she isn't just pretty like most other girls. Caro's – well, she's different. She's fun. And – nice. Don't you think? Ma?' he added, softly, when she did not reply. 'Don't you think?'

'Oh, Harry,' she said, 'you are so very young.'

He dropped to his knees beside her chair. Jake nudged him companionably. Harry ignored him. The dog, resigned, spread himself upon the floor like an untidy rug.

Harry was watching his mother intently. 'Not that young, Ma. Not any more. I'm eighteen next Thursday –'

'You must know it can't last for ever? Children grow up. We have to let them go some time.' The words had echoed in her head ever since Lina had so innocently spoken them.

Mattie took his hand. 'Harry – darling – I'm sorry. There's something I must tell you – something I think – I know – I should have explained to you a long time ago –'

When he left her, the terrible storm of disbelief and recrimination had not blown itself out. Mattie sat, shaking, as darkness closed in on the room, seeing before her Harry's young face, tear-marked, incredulous; blazing with hurt and accusation.

'Why did you have to tell me?' he had shouted at last, still not understanding. 'You've lied to me for this long – why tell me now?'

'Because,' she had said, steadily, 'don't you see? Any child you may have –' and had stopped, stricken to silence by the horror in his eyes.

'Oh God! Oh, dear God!' It was then he had fled, sobbing, leaving her here alone, in silence, with her helpless regrets, her bitter self-reproach.

'Mrs Sherwood?' A small, frightened face had appeared around the door. Betsy, the parlour maid, was not the staunchest of beings at the best of times; raised voices were enough to terrify her. 'Shall I light the lamps, Ma'am?'

'No, Betsy, thank you.'

The door closed softly. She sat on in the twilight, living Harry's distress with him, knowing she deserved his anger, his contempt. She should have told him long, long ago. She should not have lied to him, and to herself; in refusing to face the problem she had in the end made it worse for him. Her prevarication had done nothing but harm to them both.

And now, she knew, she had lost him.

The old dog, sensing her unhappiness, came to her, resting his nose on her knee.

Somewhere in the house a door slammed, very loudly.

He spoke of it only once more. The following evening, after avoiding her all day, he came to where she was pruning the roses in the garden. She felt his presence, clipped on with steady hands, not looking round until, without preamble, he spoke. 'You said that – the men who came – who killed him – you said they –' He stopped.

'Raped me,' she said calmly, watching him. 'Yes.'

His young face, marked still by the aftermath of tears, was defiant. 'Then how do you know – how can you know –?'

'That you are his child? Because you are his living image.' Mattie waited. Harry said nothing. 'Were you hoping,' she asked, 'that you were the product of rape?'

The bitter confusion in his face answered her.

'Oh Harry,' she said, quietly, 'I am so very sorry.'

Three miserable days later, on the eve of his eighteenth birthday, Harry Sherwood left home, leaving no word as to where he was going. A month after that he donned his first uniform.

PART FOUR

Egypt
1898–1899

CHAPTER FOURTEEN

'Sir?' Captain – lately and lamentably briefly Major – Harry Sherwood stood meticulously to attention and addressed, as was expected of him, the smoothly polished panelling just to the right of his commanding officer's ear. He put a cautious question into the word.

The colonel waited, not without a certain – and, Harry felt, faintly alarming – patience.

Beyond the windows of his office the teeming, stinking, often squalid but always colourful world of Cairo went about its devious and noisy business.

Harry, mindful of recent indiscretions, chose his words with care. 'Sir, I am of course most flattered that you would consider placing your niece in my care.' He saw the flicker of grim amusement in Colonel Standish's eyes, and wished he had phrased it a little differently. The thought of the briskly capable Hannah Standish in anyone's care did not exactly ring true. His heart sank further. 'But – I wonder – would it not be better to use someone with a little more knowledge of the river and its – ' he hesitated ' – its archaeological attractions? With respect, Sir, I'm a soldier, not an Egyptologist. In fact I have to admit that the more arcane pleasures of the country have rather passed me by. Lieutenant Windsor, on the other hand, is a positive expert on these Pharaoh chappies and their ruins – he's never happier than when he's poking round in the sand and picking up bits and pieces. Knows what he's looking for too, so they tell me. Doesn't seem to me – Sir? – that I'm really the best man for the job.' He ended the sentence on a note of qualified hope.

The colonel tapped his desk top with a pencil, the sound small and sharp in the quiet room. 'My niece,' he said, pensively, 'said much the same thing. She too mentioned young Windsor.

Appears they've been on a couple of sand-scraping expeditions together already.'

Harry cheered up a little. 'Well, then, Sir?'

'No, Harry.'

'No, Sir?'

The colonel shook his head. 'No.' He waited for a moment, added blandly and without the least attempt to disguise the implied threat, 'As a matter of fact young Windsor's being assigned to the railway project in the south. Of course, I suppose once the leg's better, arrangements could be made –?' He left the sentence hanging in the air.

'Er – no, Sir. Thank you, Sir.' Of all the postings in this God-forsaken waste of a country, the protection of the builders of the railway that was cutting deep into the southern desert to carry troops and arms into the Sudan was, with reason, the least popular. Thirteen years before, the Sudan had been abandoned to the Mahdi and his fanatical followers after the fall of Khartoum and the killing of General Gordon; now, however, the territory was of renewed interest to the European powers, who were battling for their own interests in Africa. With the Mahdi himself dead, but his followers led equally ably by their new leader, known as the Khalifa, Britain, using the power and influence she already wielded in Egypt, had decided to reconquer the barren desert state, thus avenging the murder of Gordon – of whom the British public had made an unlikely national hero and martyr – salvaging British pride and, most important of all, securing the crossroads of Nubia against the African ambitions of the old enemies France, Belgium and Italy. It was an open secret that nothing would suit those countries better than that the Anglo-Egyptian army sent against the Khalifa should be bloodily annihilated, as the one sent against the Mahdi had been.

Silence had settled upon the room for a moment. The colonel stood up and walked to the window, unshuttered in the relative cool of the early morning, stood with his back to Harry, looking down onto the wide, dusty parade ground, where a small squad of native troops marched in less than perfect time to the exasperated bawling of their British non-commissioned officer.

Years of discipline kept Harry standing like a well-turned-out statue, eyes and stance perfectly steady despite the thumping of his head and the furred thickness of his tongue. The still-uncomfortable twinges from his healing thigh he hardly noticed. The summons from his commanding officer had taken him by surprise: the suggestion that had just been made – or to put it more bluntly the orders he had just been given – had surprised, and dismayed, him further. Like the rest of the relatively small garrison, he had heard of Hannah Standish's intention to travel up the Nile to visit the various sites and antiquities in the steps of her heroine and one-time mentor Florence Nightingale – it had, after all, been her declared aim in coming to visit her uncle a few weeks before – and had assumed that some hapless officer or other would be detailed to accompany her. But the possibility that the unfortunate might be himself had, for many cogent reasons, never so much as crossed his mind. It was by no means a duty for which he would have volunteered; the thought of a month, possibly two, prowling around every bloody ruin between here and Nubia at the beck and call of the formidable Miss Standish was not the most appealing he had ever entertained. Its one and only recommendation was that it would get him away from Cairo for a while; away from Cairo and from Fenella and her incessant and increasing demands. He winced a little at the thought, and his head thumped harder.

Colonel Standish returned from his survey of the world outside and stood leaning against his desk, arms folded, shrewd blue eyes upon the subordinate officer. Harry Sherwood was one of those soldiers, not uncommon in the colonel's experience, who were at once the blood and bone of the British army and the bane of their commanders' lives. In a tight corner, or given a whiff of the smoke of battle, the man was a wonder; a born fighter, a fierce, intelligent and brave officer whose men would follow him anywhere, and whose loyalty was unquestioned and unquestioning, all of which had been proven beyond doubt in the south just a couple of months earlier. However, convalescent and bored, kicking his heels in camp or barracks, it was an exasperatingly different story. A quiet life did not suit

Harry Sherwood, and if there were no ready-made excitements to keep him happy, then with cheerful disregard for his own or other's comfort or safety he would make his own in as entertaining a manner as he could devise. Old enough to know better, he could be the most subversive of bad influences on some of the more impressionable young officers, his reputation alone enough to ensure their eager attention and – worse – desire to emulate. His effect on the apparently equally impressionable garrison wives could be even more marked. A professional soldier to his fingertips and to the elegant, shining toes of his boots, yet the very qualities that made him such a good man in a fight – as the Dervishes had so recently encountered to everyone's cost, not least Harry's – tended to make him a disruptive influence in the well-ordered administration of a posting such as this. Promotion on the field had proved, not for the first time, an experiment ending in failure. Now the colonel had a new idea. And even if nothing concrete came of it, it possessed two clear benefits: it ensured that Hannah and her relentless organizational abilities were set afloat on the Nile and thus, to her affectionate uncle's relief, as far away as possible from him, and it removed Harry Sherwood from the vicinity of Major Hampshire's wife, Fenella, before real mayhem could ensue, as most certainly it would if Harry remained in Cairo.

'The leg – it's mending, Harry?'

'Yes, Sir. Mended, I'd say. Good as new.' Harry looked hopeful. 'Ready to get back to the fight any minute, Sir?' Again he imbued the statement with a hopeful question.

The Colonel shook his head. 'Not what the Doc says, I'm afraid.'

'But, Sir!'

'You speak French, I understand, Harry?'

The conversational interruption took the other man by surprise. His eyes flickered to the colonel. 'Er – yes, Sir. Of a kind.'

Heavy brows lifted. 'Might I ask what kind?'

Harry grinned a little. 'The gutter kind, Sir.'

The Colonel nodded; he had expected as much. Among the most believable of the regimental rumours that had gathered about Harry Sherwood over the years was the notion that he had started his military career at an early age in that toughest of schools, the French Foreign Legion. Given his known exploits since, to say nothing of unsubstantiated rumours of the wilder sort, Colonel Standish did not find that too hard to credit. The Legion was a crucible that toughened or destroyed the men who passed through it; it also fostered a certain reckless, intransigent defiance of the world and its conventions, and upon that evidence alone the colonel was inclined to believe the story. He studied for a moment the proper, disciplined stance of the man before him, which somehow was at odds with the unconscious arrogance of the lifted chin, the spare, defiant line of cheek and jaw. No doubt about it, the man was an enigma; a role he himself, the colonel was aware, appeared quite happy to perpetuate. At a time when a man's family connections were of paramount importance in the army, as in society at large, Harry Sherwood apparently had no family. Rumour, again, had obligingly furnished him with many backgrounds, each more exotic than the one before. He was the illegitimate sprig of an ancient aristocratic family. He was a disgraced younger son driven into the army to escape prison and a vengeful husband. He was the offspring of a forbidden liaison between a great lady and her gypsy lover; this last fantasy well born out by his dark good looks, his flamboyant skill on a horse and the excessive grace of his carriage, all of which so endeared him to the ladies. Whatever the truth, Harry Sherwood had proved convincingly and more than once that he was not a man to challenge on the matter of his privacy; he kept his own counsel and his own secrets.

At least most of the time.

The colonel was not in a position to know that just the night before, faced with a woman more determined than most and with a head for liquor stronger than any man's he had ever met, as Harry's own head this morning bore graphic witness, more of the truth of his background had come out than he was happy to remember – indeed, than he actually could remember. He pushed away the unease. God, he felt like hell!

'– mischief brewing in the south. We suspect the supplying of arms, and we suspect the French –'

'I'm sorry, Sir?' This time Harry did turn his head, looking directly at the other man, his bright, dark eyes suddenly sharp. By God, the colonel thought wryly with a startled touch of envy, with looks like those no wonder the man's learned to defend himself so well; he's probably needed to, in many a Mess and for more than one reason.

'At ease, Harry.'

Harry moved his feet, relaxed a little, but warily. 'I'm sorry, Sir, you were saying?'

Colonel Standish took his time. He reached into the box on his desk for a cigar, cut and lit it, sucked on it for a moment. 'The French, Harry. The bastard French again. It's the old story. As you know, they have their own designs on the Sudan, their own reasons for seeing General Kitchener and our lads stopped in their tracks by the Dervishes. They want us held up before we can push further south: and to do it we suspect – we're almost certain – they're illegally running arms to the Khalifa and his followers. It's more than likely that they're coming overland – from Ethiopia, perhaps. The Emperor had a fine array of French guns to use against the Italians at Adowa, remember? And he's the wiliest bugger on this benighted continent, he'll have his fingers in anything he can. But there are other rumours. Rumours that some of the arms may be going upriver under our very noses. It's unlikely. But it isn't impossible.' The blue eyes had narrowed, peering through the pale haze of the smoke. 'I thought, if you should keep your eyes and ears open, on this trip upriver – well, who knows? You may hear something, see something, significant. This country's the very devil for intrigue and gossip, as you know. Where there's one faction doing one thing there's usually another that's ready to sell them for a couple of piastres, or betray a friend for a half inch of advantage. Didn't I hear some story about your passing yourself off as a fellah for a bet?' He paused, waiting.

Harry winced a little. There were no flies on the Old Man, that was for sure. He hoped his information did not include the purpose of the deception; the pleasures of the Cairo bazaars did not begin and end with the joys of shopping. 'Er – yes, Sir.'

'Quite. Well. You see what I mean, then.' The older man drew again on his cigar. 'Not that I'm advocating any daft cloak and dagger stuff, you understand. And nothing – absolutely nothing! – that would in any way endanger Miss Standish's comfort or security. I just thought you might keep an ear to the ground.'

Harry had visibly brightened. Here was something a good deal more interesting than playing nursemaid to the colonel's strong-minded niece. 'Do we have any solid information, Sir?'

The colonel shook his head. 'Unfortunately not.' He toyed with the idea of telling the other man about the two bodies, scarcely recognizable, found floating in the Nile that very morning, and decided against it. There was little evidence to connect the torture and murder of two native scouts with this business. In his honest opinion, the likelihood that Harry might pick up any information on this trip was almost nil, but anything was worth a try, and Abdo had been insistent that Harry, French-speaking and after a few months of Egyptian sun as dark as many a native, was the man for the job. 'Look, your main job will be to look after Miss Standish, smooth the way, handle the natives, get her where she wants to go, make sure she doesn't get herself into any difficulties –' Ye gods, what an assignment! French gun runners would be a tea party beside it! '– that sort of thing. I'm simply suggesting you stay alert. If the arms are going up the river then someone knows who's involved. You'll meet people on your way. Talk, gossip, just see if you can ferret anything out. My man Abdo will be with you –' the colonel raised pained, bushy eyebrows, '– seems his father was on the expedition with Miss Nightingale more than forty years ago, would you believe it? Once Hannah discovered that, you may be sure that no-one else would do!' He breathed a gusty sigh. He had had to balance the loss of Abdo and the consequent lapse of comfort and efficiency in his small household against the stress of standing in Hannah's way once she had made up her mind, and the peace and quiet that must ensue once she left. He had capitulated with a quite shameful lack of argument. 'You can trust him absolutely, of course. As a matter of fact he's rather astute for a native. You may find him helpful – use him as a runner if needs be. The river – you know what the river is to this country – you may pick something up, however small. You'll be in mufti, of course – better that way.'

'Yes, Sir.'

'You'll leave within the week. The weather is warming nicely, and the winds are steadying. We'll talk again in a day or so, before you leave. Oh, and Harry – '

'Yes, Sir?'

'Mum's the word, eh? You're just escorting Miss Standish upriver, understood?'

'Yes, Sir.'

Smartly Harry about turned and left.

Colonel Standish looked after him with something close to sympathy. In truth the bait of the arms being run to the Khalifa was a little less than fair; there were other eyes and ears seeking the source of the guns that were undoubtedly trickling through to the Dervishes, and despite Abdo's usually sound instincts the colonel felt that the chances of Harry Sherwood finding anything on his trip with Hannah Standish up the river were minimal. But at least it had salved the man's pride and perhaps made up for his being appointed to what he no doubt saw as the post of nursemaid to Hannah; at the same time the embarrassing, even dangerous, possibility of Harry's affair with the Major's wife becoming even more noticeable than it already was had been headed off. Colonel Standish was well aware that some eyebrows might be raised at the idea of his sending a well-known womanizer, however good a soldier and despite being officially convalescent, to escort his niece, unmarried though long betrothed, on a several-hundred-mile journey up the Nile; but only, he thought, relighting his cigar, eyebrows belonging to those who had no acquaintance with that niece. No, on the whole he was rather pleased with himself. This was as good a solution to a couple of thorny problems as he could possibly have devised. If he could not yet be sent back on active service, Harry Sherwood was at least put under Hannah's eye, where assuredly he could do little harm, and cause less scandal, and Hannah could set off on her tiresome Odyssey. And, it had to be said, in as much affection as he held her, the sooner the better. Her firm and well-intentioned attentions were driving him, a middle-aged and determined bachelor, to distraction. It was self-evidently true that Harry Sherwood was not inexperienced when it came to the ladies. That meant, presumably, that he knew how to deal with a lady, even such a one as Hannah.

The colonel settled behind his desk with his cigar, reached once more for the matches and, quite sincerely, wished his captain luck.

Harry stepped with relief from the blinding sunshine into the cool shadows of the building which housed the quarters he shared with Archie Douglas. His head now was thumping so hard that it almost defeated thought altogether.

Archie, booted and spurred and dressed for riding, his feet resting, ankles crossed, upon a small table, was reading a letter. 'Mail's in.' He glanced up, grinned. 'Lord, you look like God's gift to a mortician! Where the hell were you last night?'

Harry shook his head, the effort of speech too much for him. He reached for the single letter that rested on the table near his friend's shining boots, glanced at it and tucked it into his pocket. Archie watched, curiosity in his eyes, but said nothing. No amount of probing had ever elicited from Harry who it was that wrote to him with much regularity each month; the only certainty, from the delicacy of the envelope and the femininity of the decorative writing, was that the faithful correspondence came from a woman. Archie sometimes wondered if Harry did not, after all, have a wife and family tucked safely away somewhere in England. Experience, however, had taught him that speculation was as far as he would ever get in the matter. 'What did the Old Man want?'

Harry dropped onto his narrow bed, right leg propped straight before him, sank his head into his hands for a moment, long fingers buried in his thick black hair.

Archie, sensing fun, swung his long legs from the table and sat forward, forearms resting upon his knees, watching the other man with interest. 'Well?'

Harry flung himself backwards on the bed, one arm shielding his eyes. 'I'm off on a trip, Archie. Off on a trip.'

'What sort of trip?'

There was a short silence, then, resignedly: 'A trip that traces the footsteps of Miss Florence Nightingale over forty blasted years ago up the River Nile in company with a student of that same Miss Nightingale – '

'Hannah Standish!'

Harry sat up, face sober. 'Laugh,' he said, 'and I'll flatten you.'

The other man was already all but choking. 'You?' he managed. 'The Old Man's landed you with it? Serves you right, Harry! Serves you bloody right!' He flung back his fair head and let out a roar of mirth. 'Oh, serves you bloody right!'

Harry glowered. 'What's so funny?'

Archie did not feel the need to reply.

Later, when the other man, still chuckling, had left to ride to the pyramids of Ghiza with the latest impressionable and starry-eyed young female tourist to arrive via Mr Thomas Cook's good offices, Harry read his letter. The weather was cold in England, Mattie reported, but unseasonably dry. The latest Jake was a roamer; the countryside was being populated with shaggy golden puppies, to the outrage of the neighbours. The roof had been all but blown off in a gale in September, but had been secured in time for the winter. She hoped that he was enjoying this posting better than the last; the glories of Egypt must be amongst the most exotic sights in the world. She signed, as always, restrainedly, 'your loving mother'.

Harry folded the letter haphazardly, shoved it into a small box crammed full of similar notes that had found him, in the past fifteen years or so, in almost every outpost of an Empire that had established itself firmly in every continent of the world. He answered, briefly and impersonally, perhaps once or twice a year; the only thing he had done meticulously since his flight from the Legion into the more respectable arms of the British army was to let his mother know where he was from posting to posting, and thus ensured that the cheerful and undemanding letters kept coming. He had never brought himself openly to admit the reason; it had, he always told himself, simply become a habit. He moved to the window, looking out into the bright and dusty world beyond. For one moment, his mother's words in his mind, he could see her. He could see

286

Coombe House, smell the crisp, sharp smell of a chill December morning, see a shaggy golden dog bounding towards him, coat burr-covered and wet from the frosted grass –

'Sir?' A huge man, sweating in his scarlet uniform, had appeared at the door.

Pained, Harry turned his head.

The man grinned unsympathetically. 'They're ready for you, Sir. As ready, that is, as they ever are for anythin'.' Sergeant Thomas never attempted to disguise his contempt for the native troops he tried day in and day out to lick into something approximating British Army shape.

Harry took a breath, steadied his brain and his stomach against his hangover. 'Very well, Sergeant. I'm coming.'

'You did *what*?' Colonel Standish bellowed, glaring at his niece in the manner that was, after years of practice, guaranteed to reduce the bravest of men to doubt and confusion.

Hannah was unimpressed. 'I invited her to join me. Really, Uncle, you should be careful, you know. It's terribly bad for you to get into a state about every little thing.'

The colonel gritted his teeth. 'I am not, as you choose to put it, getting into a state. I simply want to know how it is that every time I make arrangements – any arrangements – you effortlessly and without thought manage to –' he fought against the words he would have used to a male subordinate, and ground out, finally '– change them.'

Hannah shrugged briskly. 'For goodness' sake, I haven't changed them – I've simply added to them. It's hardly the end of the world, is it? Laila wants to go upriver to join her father in the Winter House. She's bored with Cairo and would like to come with me. What on earth is wrong with that? I think it's a perfectly splendid idea. I like the child, and it seems she likes me. The company will be pleasant for both of us, and her father seems quite happy about it. Really, Uncle, I can't see why you should make such a fuss.'

The colonel reached for his cigars. 'Hannah, you really do have a lot to learn about this country.'

Hannah, tall, lean as a whippet, as always immaculately clad in neat pale grey trimmed with white that seemed to defy the heat, the startling, wiry hair that was so much at odds with the austerity of her features confined beneath a severe scarf and an untrimmed straw hat, frowned a little, questioningly.

Her uncle breathed an overtly patient sigh. 'You, at the last minute, invite Ayman el Akad's only daughter to accompany you on this trip –'

'She invited herself, actually.'

'That makes it worse, if anything. For it indicates she may have known something you didn't –'

'Which is?' Hannah was wary.

'Your escort on this benighted trip is to be Captain Harry Sherwood.'

There was a very long moment's silence. Then, 'Ah,' said Hannah.

'Ah, indeed.' The colonel took his usual stance by the window, chewing furiously on his cigar.

'Can she have known?' Hannah asked.

Her uncle shrugged. 'I don't see how. But that doesn't mean she didn't. In this place it seems to me that you can't –' the colonel battled again against his natural choice of words. God in heaven, he simply wasn't used to addressing females! '– can't breathe without someone hearing you and passing comment to his neighbour! She may have done.'

'To Captain Sherwood's credit, he seems not to have encouraged the girl's attentions. As I understand it, he rode with her a couple of times, simply as a member of a party – to the Pyramids, and to the Sphinx – but I believe he declined gracefully any further contact when it was pointed out to him that the child was becoming – interested. I'm sure the captain is quite capable of fending off such attentions. Quite apart from anything else he may be, the captain is no cradle-snatcher. His tastes, I understand, actually run to something a little more –' she raised well-defined eyebrows with something disconcertingly close to dry amusement '– shall we say a little more mature? And certainly very much more attached.'

Her outspokenness, as always, left him floundering.

Hannah smiled coolly. 'Really, Uncle, I don't think you need to worry. We have Mary for protection.' The glint of humour was back; it could not be denied that Hannah had spent a good deal more time protecting her timid maid than Mary had spent safeguarding her mistress, and the girl's nervous terror at the prospect of setting sail upon the swirling, crocodile-infested waters of the Nile with nothing but a bunch of wild Dervishes for company would have been funny had it not been so exasperating. 'And Laila has Abdo's and my protection against any dastardly designs the convalescent Captain Sherwood might have.' Her grey eyes twinkled with laughter.

The colonel detested being teased, was aware that his dislike of it always made him pompous, and consequently, in Hannah's case, tempted her to further lengths. 'Hannah, you don't understand. Ayman el Akad is one of the richest, most powerful and certainly most influential men in Egypt. He's no run-of-the-mill merchant! He's connected by birth to every important family on the Nile, and there isn't an influential man in the country – up to the very top! – who doesn't owe him money, or a favour, or both! He's the piper who calls the tune, however far behind the scenes he stays. It's essential that we keep his goodwill. The slightest breath of scandal concerning his daughter –'

'Oh, Uncle, there won't be the slightest breath of scandal! Use your common sense! Are you honestly suggesting that Harry Sherwood doesn't know all that? He'd have to be insane to encourage the girl's interest – and she is, after all, little more than a child!'

'They grow up very young out here,' the colonel said morosely.

'She's half Irish!'

'That,' he said, 'makes it worse.'

Hannah laughed outright at that, the clear, unfettered laughter that so characterized her forceful and uncomplicated personality. Her uncle's reaction to it fairly represented his reaction to her; it exasperated and embarrassed him in almost exact proportion to the admiration and real affection it inspired. Lord, life would be so much simpler once she was gone!

'So, it's settled then.' Hannah was brisk. 'We leave after

luncheon next Tuesday. You will join us for a meal aboard before we sail, won't you?. I'll be so very disappointed if you don't. Abdo has helped me find a very comfortable dahabeeyah, which we have named the *Horus* – don't you find it rather charming, this habit of renaming a boat for every trip? – with what seem a reliable captain and crew. The boat is smallish, we are after all a small party, but I must say the accommodation is quite acceptable. Abdo as always was splendid, the price is quite a bargain –'

Colonel Standish admitted defeat. 'I can't think why you can't travel upriver on a steamer, as any normal and sensible person does,' he grumbled.

She was neither impressed nor discomfited by the inference. 'You know very well why. Miss Nightingale travelled under sail; so shall I. Her tales of the Nile were the most enthralling stories I have ever heard. I formed the intention long ago to follow, so far as is possible, her itinerary exactly, and I can only do that under sail. And in any case, there can be no comparison between a noisy, smelly, crowded steamer full of those dreadful sightseers from Shepheard's and one's very own dahabeeyah silently gliding upon the face of the most fascinating waters in the world.'

'Gliding against adverse winds and flash floods. At least the steamer gets there.'

'We'll get there, Uncle, you see if we don't.' Hannah stood composedly, awaiting his peck upon her cheek. 'I really must go. As I'm sure you may appreciate, there are an awful lot of things to be seen to before we leave – the indispensable Abdo has of course obtained a first-class dragoman for us, but I don't want to give him an entirely free hand. Some purchases I wish to supervise myself.'

The colonel delivered the kiss, a dry, awkward thing, as she had expected, and saw her from the room, remembering too late that he had once more forgotten to ask about her long-suffering betrothed. Hannah had been, as he remembered, a perfectly ordinary and acceptable child, a girl of whom his dead brother could have been justifiably proud. Now look at her. In the straightforward and, he was ready to admit, old-fashioned colonel's books, the odious Miss Florence Nightingale had many things for which to answer; and in his firmly held opinion the subversion of such well-bred and normally sensible young women as Hannah Standish, came very high on the list.

The two-masted *Horus* was neatly moored against the eastern bank of the Nile, one of several vessels awaiting their passengers and leaving within the week. Three boats were to sail today, two carrying related families of French travellers and the smaller *Horus* with her British contingent. Harry went aboard at ten in the morning. The sun was already high, and hot. The tasselled awning that shaded the passenger deck was more than welcome. In the days since he had been given this assignment he had become, on reflection, rather more enthusiastic at the idea of the trip. If he couldn't yet get himself sent back to where the real excitement was, what better break from the hot, humdrum life of the barracks than to sail up the Nile in a native boat, however tourist-orientated both river and boat might be? And if Miss Standish were not the most perfect companion, at least she would make few demands. And as for his other unexpected charge, the little Egyptian girl, he had no doubt whatsoever that Miss Standish would have her own ideas about the proprieties where she was concerned, which suited Harry admirably. After Fenella, though he did not like to admit it, he felt the need of a rest.

And then there was the matter of the guns.

He was smiling as he stepped from the narrow gangplank onto the shallow, flat-bottomed boat to be greeted by Hassan, the Reis, master of the vessel. 'Effendi, welcome! Come, I show you to your cabin – very nice cabin, Effendi, very comfortable.'

It was indeed, Harry noted with approval, though small, both nice and comfortable, as was the rest of the boat. Miss Standish, Hassan informed him with a wide, stained smile, and a man-to-man gesture with his long-fingered, dirty hands, had been aboard since the day before. Did not the Effendi admire the way she had arranged things? In honesty, the Effendi did. There were flowers in his sleeping-cabin as well as neatly stacked fresh sheets and towels, and there was, luxury of luxuries, a bar of European soap upon the washstand. The mosquito net was fresh, clean and reassuringly whole. There were flowers too in the saloon and on the open, awning-shaded upper deck with its comfortable chairs, small tables and scattering of rugs, as well as books, magazines and guides to the antiquities of Egypt, sketching and painting materials and a series of small pictures upon the walls of the saloon. Bright shawls had been thrown over some of the couches and chairs, and comfortable tasselled cushions added. Bowls of fruit had been set upon the tables. 'Well –' Harry looked around in approval, grinning at the incongruous sight of a small piano tucked into the corner of the saloon '– quite home from home!'

'Yes, Effendi. Of course, Effendi. The Miss Standish, Effendi – she has gone to fetch her companion. She said to tell you she would be back in time for luncheon. The Colonel Effendi is coming – we have very nice food, Effendi, very nice. The cook – he is good, you'll see. The *Horus* – she's the best dahabeeyah on the river, Effendi, the very best.'

'I'm sure. Thank you, Hassan.' Refusing politely the offer of a servant, Harry packed his sparse possessions into the cupboards of the cabin himself and then, moving with determinedly even strides, went up onto the awning-shaded passenger deck. Within a moment a silent, barefoot servant was by his side – would the Effendi care for tea? Well satisfied, Harry settled comfortably into a deep armchair, enjoying the cool breath of wind from the water and watching the bright, colourful life that flowed like a river itself along the bank.

Hannah Standish arrived, brisk and energetic despite the heat, an hour later. With her were the little Egyptian girl, a large woman attendant swathed to the eyes in musty black and Abdo, the colonel's body servant. Abdo was a Nubian from the southern deserts and, like others of his people, the bones of his face were strong, the skin black as pitch and of the texture of velvet, light-absorbing and without sheen. He was a giant of a man, though lightly built, graceful and easy-moving, a striking and remarkably dignified figure even barefoot and in his khaki shirt and shorts. Harry had once seen him in the city, on an errand of his own, walking through the shaded, carpet-hung bazaar dressed in the simple robes of his people, and had been startled into a moment's unexpected admiration both for the grace and for the oddly powerful presence of the man. That night he had watched as the Nubian, with quiet efficiency, had served the colonel at dinner, and wondered at the contrast. Certain it was that the colonel was known to trust the man, literally, with his life. Looking at him somehow it was not hard to see the reason. For all his grumbling it was a measure of the colonel's affection for his niece that he was ready to put up with the faithful Abdo's absence for a month or more.

Beside him on the quay, her small, proud head only a little higher than his elbow, stood Laila, daughter of the merchant Ayman el Akad. She was dressed today in Egyptian style, the folds of her robe in no way disguising the slender, softly rounded figure beneath. Her skin was golden, her hair beneath its filmy veil shone black as the wing of a raven; but her eyes were the eyes of the exiled Irish girl who had been her mother, blue as sapphires. Harry surveyed her with a mixture of feelings. The child was a beauty, there was no doubt about that, and there was a liveliness and generosity in her nature that was extremely attractive. Unfortunately she was also indulged, capricious, swift-tempered and dangerously self-willed. In a few years she would be a fascinating woman; with her father's power to protect her she would always be a dangerous one.

Hannah had seen him and given a cheery wave. Harry could hear her rapid-fire instructions above the hubbub of the quay. The unexpected, wiry cloud of red hair glinted like fire beneath the sturdy straw hat. 'Careful with that crate, Achmet – we want the chickens alive, not dead! Well, not yet, anyway! Abdo, you will make sure they put the grains and the rice in the earthenware jars? And you'll instruct someone in the use of the rat trap?'

Amused, Harry pushed himself away from the rail and returned to his chair. The *Horus* was obviously in capable hands.

Hannah joined him on the deck a few minutes later. 'Captain

Sherwood.' She extended her hand. 'I hope you're looking forward to the trip?'

'Very much, Miss Standish.'

She nodded. 'Good. Heavens, I could do with a cup of tea, but I suppose it's too near luncheon. Poor Uncle will have a fit if I don't tidy and change. Letting the side down and all that. Your cabin is comfortable?'

'Perfectly.'

'Splendid. Laila and I are on the other side of the boat. Mary was to have had the cabin next to yours –'

'Was to have had?'

She nodded composedly. 'Mary isn't coming. She threw one too many fits. I really couldn't stand it any longer, the girl's a dear but quite unsuited to travel in what she calls "foreign parts". The poor thing has become a liability; I spend more time coping with her vapours than I do concerned with my own affairs.' She had turned away, moving towards the stairs. 'Anyway I've allocated her cabin to Laila's nurse – the old thing is utterly devoted and threatened to follow us upriver in a rowboat if she wasn't allowed to come!' Her clear laughter sounded for a moment.

'But – your uncle – does he know you're leaving your maid behind?'

At the stairs Hannah turned, looked at him steadily. 'My uncle won't learn of the change of plan until it's far too late for him to cause a fuss,' she said, calmly. 'I don't need a lady's maid, Captain. I need peace and quiet to study and to paint. I've coped with Mary and her nerve storms for convention's sake for quite long enough. Life will be much easier, for both of us, if she stays in Cairo. Luncheon is in an hour, Captain, and we sail at three.' She smiled, suddenly, her wide, pale mouth curving, the glint of delighted excitement in her face unguarded. 'The fulfilment of a dream, Captain. Not something that happens every day.'

Hassan's cook, surprisingly, was excellent. For two months the year before he had been in the employ of a Frenchman, whose gastronomic demands were higher than most. Lunch was delicious, and was washed down with a more than drinkable date wine. The colonel was in expansive mood, Hannah quietly amusing and Laila, under the eyes of her nurse, who squatted on her haunches beside the girl's chair, quiet and demure, the brilliant blue of her eyes veiled by lashes as dark and silky as her hair. Harry felt himself relax. A month or so of this would be a very welcome break from the tedium of barracks life. At the end of the meal Abdo produced a more than passable brandy, and Hannah Standish played for them on the piano. At ten minutes to three the colonel took his leave and retired to the quay to watch the last-minute preparations for departure. Exactly on the hour the great sail was hauled up, the muskets fired in salute and farewell, and the *Horus*, trailed by the small felucca tied to her stern and waved off with friendly cheer by the crews and passengers of the other boats, slid gracefully away from the bank and into the stream, sail belling in the wind. Hannah joined Harry on deck, watching in silence as the roofs and domes and minarets of the city, glinting in the sun, dropped away behind them. The great, mysterious pyramids of Ghiza dwindled as they watched, though they remained in sight for a long time, appearing to float, shimmering in the dusty heat haze. When at last the *Horus* rode the wide waters below the city, heading south between banks dressed in the lush green of gardens and palm forests, and edged beyond with the golden distances of the desert, Hannah drew breath and lifted her face to the vast, bright sky. 'The Nile,' she said, softly. 'At last!'

CHAPTER FIFTEEN

Hannah Standish knew – and was not discomfited by the knowledge – that she was not entirely the person she allowed the world to think her. Some facts, of course, were indisputable. Certainly she was thirty years old and as certainly – to the bewildered exasperation of her family and despite a friendly and long-standing arrangement with a kindly man of whom she was extremely fond – she was in no hurry to change her marital status from that of independent spinster to dependent wife. There were times when she herself wondered if it were not some perverse flaw in her nature that had prevented her, at the time when her contemporaries had been determinedly – in some cases desperately – set upon marriage, from pursuing the path considered the only suitable one for her sex. Again she knew, and did not particularly care, that this was the general belief. No-one but she ever seemed to consider the possibility that quite simply the man for whom she would, or could, sacrifice her freedom had never yet crossed her path; she had long ago accustomed herself to the thought that he probably never would. As a girl she had been too tall, too thin – her mother had said too plain – and too outspoken to be much in demand with the young men who had courted her sisters, her cousins and her friends. There had been no white knight to stride into her mother's overpoweringly velvet-draped and stuffy drawing room and lay before her a different world, a different notion of love than that which she observed about her. The best she had managed was an irreproachably proper and extremely dull young solicitor's clerk called Hubert. She smiled still, wryly, when she recalled her mother's astonishment when he had offered for her, her outrage when she had refused him. Later, after her grandmother's bequest had added modest independence of means to independence of mind and she had achieved her dearest ambition in going to London to meet and study under Miss Nightingale, she had met Leo, dear Leo, bookish and wise, who had in friendship and with humour suggested the mutual benefit of marriage. She supposed that the world assumed she would one day come to her senses and marry him; she herself sometimes thought that she would. But something, always something, held her back. She had long grown used both to the occasional loneliness and to the satisfaction of her eccentric independence. She well knew the persona that she showed to the world, and indeed the Hannah who was so crisply displayed was no fake. Her sharp, sometimes impatient intelligence, her capable good sense, her caustic dislike of the pettiness and triviality of unnecessary convention, were absolutely honest and as intrinsically a part of her character as were the slightly wayward sense of humour and the occasional unnerving and mule-like obstinacy with which she managed sometimes even to exasperate herself. It was that other Hannah, who had once so absurdly and impenitently dreamed of chivalry and the enchanted gardens of the soul, who was of necessity most severely kept in her place. Standing now beneath the fringed awning of the passenger deck of the *Horus*, her elbows upon the rails, watching the stately flow of this wide, brown river that had for so long exercised her imagination, and the passing of its green, flood-fed banks that lay fertile and rich between the shimmering mystery of the desert and the life-giving, death-dealing waters of the Nile, she knew, and was pleased to know, that in her unruffled grey-and-white striped cotton and her no-nonsense scarf and hat she looked as if she might be considering how to curb the enthusiastic extravagances of their dragoman or counting the hours lost by yesterday's adverse winds rather than, as was the truth, dreaming of the splendour of desert cities and of god-kings, of power and the chanting of priests, of the infinite enigma of a lost civilization.

'Miss Standish? I'm sorry – I'm not interrupting?'

She turned. Tall as she was, Abdo towered above her. She liked his voice; it was deep and gentle, and lacked entirely the note of whining servility adopted by some of his countrymen. She liked too the calmness and dignity of his demeanour, the straightforwardness of his dealings, with her and with others. She liked his black, handsome face, more Arab than African, and his easy, erect carriage; in short, she liked Abdo, and became more delighted each day at having secured his services as general factotum on the *Horus*. She was still surprised that her uncle had let him go. 'Abdo, of course not. What can I do for you?'

He smiled. 'Reis Hassan wished me to tell you that we will be in Benisuef by sunset. But he says the wind is dropping again. The afternoon's journey will be slow.'

Hannah lifted her face to the breeze. 'The wind still seems strong.'

'The Reis is certain it will drop.'

'Then I expect he's right. He certainly seems to know his business. I suppose – ' she glanced towards the lower deck where barefoot, robed crewmen sat in circles about their cooking pots ' – I suppose that means we must track again?'

'It does.'

She made a small grimace. 'Oh dear. Well, if we must we must, I suppose.' On the second day out of Cairo, with that city still hovering on the horizon like an enchanted mirage, the wind had deserted them and the crew had had to resort to the practice of tracking; nine or ten men harnessed like oxen pulling the great, sluggish *Horus* against the current from the towpath. Hannah had found it an uncomfortable experience to stand at leisure at the rail whilst human beings slaved so. 'Benisuef – it's a fair-sized town, I believe?'

'Indeed it is. The Reis would like to stop there for a day or so to add to our provisions.'

'Most certainly. I should like the chance to see a little of the city myself. Miss Nightingale found it a poor place – a place of sordid mud and clay is how she described it.'

'A harsh judgement, I think,' said the quiet voice beside her. 'And from a stranger who knew little of the land.'

Hannah glanced at him sharply. Although the same thought had occurred to her, it startled her to hear it so bluntly put by

298

a man who was, after all, little more than a servant. And yet, of course, he was right. In the three days since they had left Cairo she had been constantly impressed by the man; under his hand the routine of the boat ran like clockwork, all the small details that Hannah had devised for their comfort had been attended to meticulously. He was intelligent, diplomatic and hard-working; he was also, she told herself severely, entirely entitled to his opinion, even on Miss Nightingale's caustic judgements, and was surprised at herself that such self-censure should be necessary. She stored the thought away for future examination. 'You're probably right. Is the captain back yet?' Harry had taken the little felucca and gone ashore on an errand of his own some time earlier.

'No. He's expected at any moment, I believe.'

A veiled woman had come to the bank and beneath a canopy of palms was filling an earthenware pot with water. Beside her a donkey stood, patient and docile. Beyond her, a huddle of mud huts all but disappeared into the line between desert and flood-fed fields. She lifted her head, raised a shy hand as the dahabeeyah passed. Hannah smiled and waved back. 'I must say that Captain Sherwood does seem to have acquired a quite remarkable habit of disappearing. Where does he go on these little expeditions, do you know?' The question was idle, and half-humorous, but the small silence that followed it drew her attention.

Abdo's face was expressionless. 'No, I'm afraid I don't. Miss Standish, if you'll excuse me? I have duties still to attend to. If the wind is going to drop then the cook will be called in for other duties than in the kitchen. I'd like to make sure that the arrangements for dinner are made.'

'Yes. Of course.' She watched him walk away, barefoot and graceful. As he disappeared down the narrow flight of steps that led to the lower deck, she surveyed her small kingdom. The awninged deck with its rugs, its divans, its books and its flowers looked a very haven of peace and tranquillity. Laila and her nurse were still below decks; the post-luncheon rest for guardian and charge was sacrosanct. A blessedly solitary, leisurely hour stretched before her, her favoured companion Amelia

Edwards's extraordinarily evocative and informative book *A Thousand Miles up the Nile*, written just twenty years earlier, and as thumbed and earmarked as Hannah's signed edition of the Florence Nightingale letters. At the thought of those, she remembered Abdo's gentle remonstrance and found herself vaguely discomfited. To observe a place was one thing; to pass judgement was something else again. She should not have needed Abdo to tell her that. She glanced towards the east bank. The small felucca, skimming the water like a bird, its tall, triangular sail bending to the slightest breath of breeze, raced on a tack that would bring it alongside the *Horus*. She saw Harry at the tiller. He lifted a hand. She waved back. The breeze blustered, and died. Above her the great rust-coloured sail, which had been taut with the steady, driving energy of the wind, flapped, faltered, and fell slack. Hannah felt the dahabeeyah lose way, was suddenly aware of the surge of the current against them. A streaming flight of birds, white, glistening like a silver shoal in the sunshine, wheeled and dipped across the soft, relentlessly flowing waters. The *Horus* slowed, and slewed towards the bank.

Harry came back aboard as they pulled into the bank, just as Abdo with his usual miraculous timing appeared with a tray of tea. Harry and Hannah drank it on deck as they watched the preparations for tracking the boat the rest of the way to Benisuef.

'It's no good.' Hannah shook her head. 'I know they don't seem to mind, but I do hate to see the men harnessed like animals. It doesn't seem right.'

Harry shrugged a little. He had lost interest in the activity and had picked up a magazine. 'As you say, they don't seem to mind. I daresay they wouldn't do it if they did.'

'But of course they would! They have to earn a living.'

Harry smiled, blunting the edge of her indignation. 'Don't we all?'

'Don't laugh, Captain Sherwood.' She leaned forward, putting her elbows on the table, linking her hands, resting her chin in earnest thought upon them. 'Don't you see the importance of understanding such things? To me, to see men chained like donkeys or mules is degrading – but I'm seeing it, aren't I, with

European eyes? Here it is the norm, here it is accepted. So do I have the right to judge? Abdo said something of the sort this afternoon.'

Harry tossed the magazine aside, still smiling. A genuine, and, to Harry at least, surprising friendship was well on the way to growing between these two. Against all his expectations in the days since they had left Cairo, he had found himself slipping easily into the pleasant routine of life aboard the *Horus*; a routine that had been largely, with unfussy good humour, thought out and instigated by Hannah. He found it remarkably refreshing to be with a woman who neither fawned upon nor attempted to challenge him. Hannah did not coquet, nor did she treat him with the provocative disdain he had long grown to recognize as just another ploy in the perilous give and take of sexual attraction. He could relax with her; and if on occasion, as now, she showed an alarming tendency to lecture, he found himself at least equally as often drawn into a spirited discussion or argument that was as entertaining as any flirtation, and far less dangerous.

'And yet, surely, there are some things that are basically right, basically wrong? Murder, for instance, can surely never be justified. Or gratuitous cruelty. And slavery. That slavery is normal practice in a community, as it was in Ancient Egypt, cannot be an excuse to justify it, can it? Captain Sherwood? Is something wrong?'

Harry had moved abruptly, standing up, turning from her, leaning upon the rail apparently freshly absorbed in the activity upon the bank. 'No. Nothing.'

'Did you know —' she joined him at the rail '— that according to Abdo there is still an established illegal trade in slaves here in Egypt? If it's true it's absolutely scandalous. Slavery has been outlawed in the Empire for sixty years! Yet Abdo says that many of his own people are taken by the Arab traders. I have to say I find it hard to believe, for surely that must mean some kind of official condonement of the wretched business? But Abdo said —'

'Abdo seems to have been talking rather a lot today.' The attempt at lightness did not work. His voice was sharp, hard-edged.

She looked at him curiously. 'Captain, there is something wrong. What is it?'

Harry shook his head, forced mild apology into his smile. 'I'm sorry. Too much sun, perhaps. I walked a little way into the desert this morning. It really was most impressive. Perhaps while we're at Benisuef you'd like me to arrange a trip for you? There are camels or ponies for hire.'

'Yes. Thank you. That would be nice.' The words were absently spoken; the attempt to change the subject was so transparent that, characteristically, she simply ignored it. 'Captain – would you mind if I asked you something? Something you might regard as a little personal?'

'No. Of course not,' he said stiffly.

'Is there some reason why you don't like Abdo?'

The question shocked him. 'Of course not. Why should there be? He's an admirable and reliable servant. Why should you think such a thing?'

Hannah shook her head. 'I don't know. I'm sorry. There just seem times when –' she considered for a moment '– when you aren't at ease with him.'

'As I said, the man is a servant, Miss Standish and –' he hesitated '– and a native. Are you suggesting I should treat him as a personal friend?' This time he made no attempt to disguise the sharpness in his voice.

'No. No, of course not. And now I have made you angry. Forgive me, Captain, I had no right to ask such a question. Ah – see – we're under way at last. And Laila, my dear, how absolutely enchanting you look! – you rested well? I'm afraid the captain and I have quite finished the tea! I'll ring for some more.'

The Egyptian girl, who had come onto the deck as they were speaking, smiled vividly from one to the other. 'That would be nice. Thank you.' Her English was almost perfect, with only the trace of an accent. She was dressed today in European style, in fine, pale cotton sprigged with flowers that matched the wonderful sapphire of her eyes. A wide straw hat, also flower-decked and tied beneath her chin with an embroidered ribbon, framed her small, pretty face. Her nurse and shadow padded to the edge of the deck and squatted, black-shrouded, watching. Harry turned to the newcomer with something like relief. 'Miss Akad. I trust you're well?'

'Very well, thank you, Captain.' The words were demure, the shy set of the head was demure; the spark in those remarkable eyes was not.

On much easier and more familiar ground, Harry moved a chair a little, out of the sun, making a small bow in the direction of the smiling girl. 'There. I think you'll find that cooler.'

She glanced at him again from beneath lustrous dark lashes. 'Thank you, Captain.'

'Laila, have you seen this? I thought it might interest you. You can have it if you'd like, I've entirely finished with it.' Hannah had picked up a small book.

Harry moved away from them, aware that the little Egyptian girl's eyes followed him, but for once not ready to play the pretty game of flirtation they both usually so enjoyed. Hannah was right – her impertinent question had angered him; but its perception had disturbed him too. In that unwary moment he had been surprised into a flash of clear-sighted honesty. He well knew that, as Hannah had so bluntly pointed out, his relationship with Abdo was not as easy as it might have been. There was an awkwardness, always, a reserve, that Harry knew emanated entirely from him. What he had seen in that instant was that, had Hannah Standish but known it, it was partly her own easily friendly relationship with the Nubian that for Harry touched some obscure sore spot; a sore spot he did not care to probe. To have Hannah, or anyone else, even suspect its existence would be utterly intolerable.

He stood for a moment longer looking down onto the activity upon the lower deck. As if conjured by his thoughts, Abdo stood, a giant amongst the smaller Egyptians, talking to Reis Hassan. As if sensing Harry's presence he looked up, and their eyes met. Unsmiling, Harry made a small movement of his hand in greeting. After the slightest hesitation Abdo nodded.

Too quickly, Harry turned away.

* * *

They spent a night and a day and then another night in Benisuef. At Hannah's request, Abdo and Harry escorted the ladies through the shaded, teeming, carpet-hung bazaars, with their silver- and goldsmiths, their stalls of brass and copper platters, bowls and cups, their silks, their spices and their quarrelsome dogs. A dust haze hung within the crowded, mud-built alleys, pierced by the shafts of sunlight that struck shining blades through the patched matting strung high across the narrow streets. Every shade of complexion moved through those busy, shadowed alleys, from the velvet black of Nubia through elegant degrees of brown to a scattering of pale or red-faced Europeans beneath palm-leaf hats. There were turbans and tarbushes, ragged fellaheen and graceful Bedouin, stately in their desert robes. The party from the *Horus* shouldered their way through the crowds, stepped aside for docile, heavily laden donkeys and for disdainful camels strung with brass bells and multicoloured swinging tassels, heavy wooden saddles swaying to their rhythmic gait like the battle decks of a fleet of fighting galleons. They strolled through the slipper bazaar, delighted at the bright, beaded footwear, made to every size and every pattern – toes turned up, toes made round, toes made flat, any style that took the fancy. Hannah loved the rugs and prayer mats that abounded; the boy from the *Horus* who accompanied them could soon barely be seen for the pile he was carrying to enhance their temporary home. With Abdo's help and encouragement they bartered with the merchants who sat smoking their coiled pipes in the midst of their glittering Aladdin's cave of wares. They bought brightly painted plates and bowls, a set of copper saucepans that fitted one into the other and a bukray – a Turkish coffee pot in brass and silver – in which Hannah fancied flowers might look very well. They bought sweetmeats and cakes, dates and fruit, fragrant tobacco for Harry and as a present for the Reis. Laila spent little, but might easily have acquired more than any of them had she wished; just the mention of her name was enough in most cases to bring an obsequious smile and the offer of the best merchandise, often brought from the small dark shops behind the stalls. She bought a pretty gold tissue scarf for Hannah, a bright leather pouch for Harry, and a string of intricately fashioned beads in her favourite sapphire blue for herself. They watched in fascination as a charmer enticed a gleaming and perilous-looking snake from its basket, and refused the temptation of a fortune-teller. Harry found time for a swift but unsatisfactory conversation with a vendor of singing birds whose name had been mentioned in Sakhara, and then found himself invited to smoke a pipe with a camel driver from Minieh, who seemed eager to talk about a Frenchman, whose name had cropped up more than once before. Abdo obligingly guided the ladies towards a small kiosk of glittering stones and gleaming metal whilst Harry, with grace, accepted the invitation and noted the information. It was a tired but satisfied party that finally boarded the *Horus* that evening and ate their meal upon the awninged deck by the light of the candles Abdo had acquired in the bazaar, washing it down with a very passable date wine produced by Christian monks in the fastness east of the city.

The next morning, in the improbably glorious light of a desert dawn and to the eerie call of the muezzin from a nearby minaret, the *Horus* raised her sail once more and surged into the tide of the great river, heading south.

The next few days, sailing towards Osyut, were uneventful but for a routine visit to some ancient tombs and an expedition into the desert organized by their dragoman from a village in which a suspicious number of people knew his name and his face. The man who owned most of the camels was his cousin; the man who owned the rest was enough like him to be his brother. Laila, to whom neither desert nor camels were a novelty to be enjoyed, but rather a curse to be avoided, declined to join the party. Hannah, once the awkward and perilous business of boarding the animal was accomplished and she had come to terms with the distance that stretched between her and the ground, was amazed at the comfort, the positive pleasure, of the ride. She had no difficulty in adapting herself to the even, rolling gait, was fascinated as she watched the great splayed feet plant themselves in the shifting, hot sand, safe, steady and reliable as a dog's paws upon turf. By the end of the day she had privately determined that the camel was a singular beast and was entirely entitled to his scornful and grouchy independence.

The air shimmered with heat, the sky was a brazen bowl above them. They rode to the ruins of a monastery whose origins were long lost and whose only significance was as a point of reference in those vast golden spaces. They picnicked in a ruined courtyard encircled by the forlorn remains of a masonry wall. The men who had accompanied them took wary station as the visitors ate.

'They fear the Bedouin,' Abdo said simply, in answer to Hannah's question.

'Is there much trouble still with the desert tribes?' Harry asked.

Abdo shrugged. 'Enough. It troubles a man if death, or slavery, can be the result of an unwary moment.'

Death or slavery. The words repeated themselves in Hannah's mind as she sat her swaying mount as they made their way back across the apparently trackless hills and valleys towards the river. Death or slavery – which would be the least evil, she wondered, suddenly sober; and found herself shivering at the thought of either.

She voiced the question later that evening as they ate dates and English cheese after the main meal, with the *Horus* tied close to the western bank and the river rippling peacefully about them. The last colours of a glorious sunset still touched the sky, dying quickly as the swift desert night claimed them.

'Death,' Harry said without an instant's hesitation or thought.

Laila glanced at him from beneath the shadow of her lashes. 'Really, Captain? You surprise me. There are some forms of slavery, surely, that are less arduous than others?'

Harry smiled, acknowledging her meaning yet still a shade grimly, shaking his head, saying nothing.

'You're very positive,' Hannah said.

He looked at her in some surprise. 'Aren't you? Would you, could you, allow yourself to be enslaved?'

'But is it that simple? Would one have such a choice? If one were born to the condition of slavery?' She trailed off for a moment, thinking. 'Or even if one were captured and enslaved – to die would be to end all hope of freedom.'

'To live,' Harry said, 'would be to end all hope of honour.'

She frowned, considering that. 'That's a very harsh judgement, is it not? And possibly based upon our own fortuitous certainty that such a choice would never be forced upon us?'

'No, Miss Standish.' The words were very cool. 'I can assure you that isn't so. There is always a choice. It is simply my opinion that any man who allowed himself to be enslaved – by anyone –' he lightened the moment by turning to Laila and bowing a little, lips curved in a smile, though the gleam in his eyes was hard '– is nothing but a worthless coward. There is no question but that it would be better to die.'

Hannah picked a date from the dish, contemplated it. 'Men!' she said, conversationally. 'What a very simple world they do inhabit, date!'

Harry, happy to lighten the moment, leaned forward, addressing the fruit as seriously as she. 'Women, date!' he said. 'How they do like to impress we poor, simple men with the subtle depths of their reasoning.'

Hannah popped the date in her mouth. 'Touché,' she said, affably, and laughed her clear, sudden laugh.

'Captain Sherwood,' Abdo said from the shadows behind them, 'would you care for coffee? Or for brandy?' He stepped into the light, his face impassive as always; and as always Harry found it infuriatingly difficult to meet the steady gaze. He stood up, stretching his stiff leg. 'Neither, thank you, Abdo. If the ladies will forgive me I intend to get an early night.' He bowed his goodnights and left the deck.

Behind him he heard Hannah say, 'Abdo, these men you say still trade in slaves – who are they?'

One thing could be said about Hannah Standish, Harry thought ruefully as he let himself into the small, stuffy cabin. Once she got her teeth into something she rarely let go until she had torn it to shreds.

* * *

They continued peacefully on their way. Most of the ancient sites that Hannah was so anxious to visit were further upstream, around and beyond Luxor, and much of this part of the voyage was spent simply enjoying the warm and lazy days upon the shaded deck, watching the passing, ever-fascinating life of the great river as the *Horus* forged steadily south. There was always something to see: small mud villages huddled beneath shadowed groves of palms, their miniature minarets and domes shimmering in the bright, hot air; water buffalo laboured in the fields beside the river, strings of camels plodded in sober line, tassels swinging, great loads moving in rhythm with their steps, and donkeys, heavy-laden or carrying riders whose bare feet almost touched the ground, picked their surprisingly dainty way along the stony desert tracks. Veiled and robed women came to the water to do the family's washing and to gossip, and their barefoot children waved and shouted as the dahabeeyah sailed by. The occasional crocodile, the menace of the Nile, sunned itself, deceptively innocent, upon the mud. And always there were the birds, singly and in flocks: egrets, swallows, long-legged herons and great pied crows. Hannah spent hours with her easel set up in the prow of the *Horus*, sketching and painting, eager to capture every picture, every impression of the great river. The waters were alive with the tall triangular sails of the little feluccas used by the villagers for fishing or commerce; the Nile was a highway, not least for the great steamers that ploughed past them, cheerfully waving tourists lining their rails, the wash setting the *Horus* bobbing like a cork.

Hannah laughed as one of the steamers sounded a last salute before disappearing around a bend in the river. 'We really shouldn't allow ourselves to feel so dreadfully superior, you know!' she said. 'I'm quite certain they must be extremely comfortable in their own way. But oh, so *unromantic* compared to dear old *Horus*!'

There were other dahabeeyahs on the river, most bigger than the *Horus*, and often one or more would moor together, and the occasion would become a social one, with visits back and forth and meals shared in saloons or on decks. The days drifted by in an altogether pleasant way. Sometimes they landed and rode into the desert to visit rock tombs or the sand-sifted ruins of temples. On other occasions Laila and Harry, accompanied sometimes by Abdo and always by three or four members of the crew, would hire horses and ride upstream for the pure pleasure of it, meeting the dahabeeyah when she moored in the evening. Hannah, who was no rider, always cheerfully declined any invitation to these expeditions; she was happy alone with her books and her paints, and knew the other two enjoyed each other's company. Sometimes she wondered if Laila were not perhaps just a little too taken with Harry, and if Harry, beguiled by the easy-going regime of their days, was not being a little incautious in his attentions to the Egyptian girl, but such faint worries were always short-lived; except on their desert rides, Laila's nurse was always with her, and when they rode they were always surrounded by people. There could be no question of any impropriety, and Harry himself was always the soul of discretion. Soon enough, no doubt, Laila would be compelled to marry a man of her father's choosing; there could surely be no harm for her in this mild and innocent flirtation?

For Harry, the trip he had undertaken with such misgiving was proving unexpectedly pleasant. His duties were far from onerous and his leg improved with every passing day. There was only one fly in the ointment. Though he still haunted the souks and squares of the villages and towns they passed through, no scrap of information had he managed to pick up since his talk with the camel driver in Benisuef.

The trail, such as it had been, had apparently run cold.

Osyut, the capital of Middle Egypt, was a small but busy city of sun-dried mud houses and minareted mosques set a little way from the river and backed by mountains in which were many ancient tombs. The *Horus* sailed into her mooring on a cool, clear afternoon, in company with another dahabeeyah, the *Ra*, with whom they had made contact several times in the past few days. The passengers on the *Ra* were an elderly English couple called Rainsford and a Scots family of four – mother, father and two grown-up sons – the MacDonalds. Hannah had in particular been pleased to meet the Rainsfords, since it seemed they were on their way to visit an eccentric relative of theirs, a reclusive but respected Egyptologist who lived in the mountains beyond the city and to whom, to Hannah's delight, they had offered to introduce her. The *Horus*, of necessity, would be staying in Osyut for at least two days, since, as was usual, Hannah's agreement with Reis Hassan had included permission for the crew to spend a day baking a batch of the bread that was their staple diet in one of the public ovens of the city. There was little hardship in that, however – as well as the mountain of tombs, known as the City of the Dead, Osyut was reputed to have the best and most varied bazaars in the whole length of the river. There was street after street of booths and stalls devoted simply to the sale of the red-and-black pottery for which the area was famous, besides other souks in which virtually anything could be purchased, from a button to a fine-tooled saddle, a singing bird to a docile wife. Hannah, surfeited with riverbank scenes and picturesque feluccas, planned to do some sketching in the bazaars.

They dined that night with the Rainsfords and the Mac-Donalds, and plans were made for the party from the *Horus* to accompany the Rainsfords to lunch with their Egyptologist the day after next. The following morning Hannah watched the preparations for the bread-making for a while before, accompanied by a burly and well-natured crewman known simply as Ali, she packed her sketchpad and pencils and set out for the main bazaar. She spent an industrious and happy morning sketching and drawing; a turbaned head here, an excited, hand-waving group about a stall there, an old man with a wispy grey beard that reached to his skinny abdomen, crouched over a hookah pipe. A blind beggar, lifting his face to the passers-by. A high, almost windowless wall from which projected a single narrow balcony, entirely protected from the world by a beautifully wrought metal screen; what secrets were hidden there? A fountain set in an ancient curve of wall, its very sound seeming to cool the hot and dusty air, worn brass drinking cups resting upon the glimmering, beautiful tiles that edged the water. A veiled woman riding upon a brightly caparisoned donkey, earrings and bangles and anklets chiming as she rode, bright eyes enticing above the flimsy protection of her veil. Utterly absorbed, Hannah tried to capture the spirit of the noisy, exotic, dirty streets. Smoke from a hundred cooking fires wreathed the narrow lanes, and the savoury smell of meat was on the air. Her attention was caught by a group of Bedouin, their cream-and-chocolate striped woollen robes immaculately elegant, seated easily, cross-legged on the ground, drinking coffee in a small courtyard off one of the streets. As her pencil flew she was half aware of two newcomers, tall, hooded and robed, one of whom moved with an excessive grace. For a moment she could not think why the figure appeared familiar. Then she realized – the man, whose dark face was obscured by his soft, folded hood, must be a Nubian. The grace of his carriage was exactly that of Abdo. For a moment, pencil still busy, she pondered as she often had before the illogical puzzle of national characteristics. People were people, as Leo was very fond of saying – there were bad and good, tall and short, fat and thin in all races. It was absurd to try to classify men by the arbitrary rule of blood. He was of course, most certainly right. The illogic of assuming that the man who moved as Abdo moved was Nubian was well illustrated by the fact that the man who followed him, dressed in the same desert robes as the Bedouin she had been sketching, might, by his height and his bearing, be taken for that most English of officers, Harry Sherwood. Smiling at the thought, she finished her sketch, packed up her things and let Ali lead her back to the *Horus* and a cool and welcome drink.

Sheldon Rainsford lived on a hillside above the city in a simple, airy house set about a vine-wreathed courtyard garden in which a fountain played. He was a stockily built, sandy-haired man with an abrupt manner and the bushiest eyebrows Hannah had ever seen. His main emotion upon greeting his relatives, with Hannah, Laila and Harry in tow, appeared to be irritation, but it soon became apparent that this was the norm; habitually he snapped his words as a dog might snap at a passing stranger.

The monosyllabic gruffness with which they were received, however, eased a little as the afternoon wore on. Hannah got the distinct impression that Sheldon Rainsford simply regarded the social graces as a waste of precious time, and was in fact making courteous and considerable effort – as he would with the customs of some primitive people – to pander to his visitors' tribal expectations.

Luncheon was simple in the extreme and was served by a silent, barefoot servant in a sparsely furnished, cool room upon a trestle table, hastily erected. The conversation, at first, was stilted and to the guests from the *Horus* almost incomprehensible, since it consisted almost entirely of messages and news from relatives of their host. Hannah had to suppress her amusement at the fact that he seemed no more acquainted with the senders of the messages, nor of the import of their content, than was she. As the afternoon wore on, however, and the date wine, cool and rich, flowed with the same steady cheer as did the water in the fountain beyond the open colonnade, the talk at last turned to Egypt, her Pharaohs and her gods.

The man, Harry conceded, certainly knew his stuff. Unusually amongst European Egyptologists he was not in favour of removing the priceless artefacts, which were day by day being unearthed, from what so many perceived as the feckless hands of the Egyptians, whose past and history they so vividly illustrated. 'Take an obelisk, a mummy, half the side of a temple, the simplest drinking vessel, to the British Museum, and what do you have? A nothing. Or rather – a thing. A dead thing. A thing out of context, out of its living environment. A thing we have no right to possess. A thing that bears no relationship to its surroundings – '

Harry, pleasantly impressed by the quality and quantity of the wine, listened to Hannah's earnest arguments and, later, to her graceful capitulation with equal pleasure. Rainsford, self-evidently happier now that the subject of the conversation was more to his taste, at a diffident question from his cousin, explained why, whilst temples and statues and magnificent tombs abounded there was nothing in Egypt of palaces or great houses.

'My dear Sibyl, have you understood nothing of what you've seen here? The ancient Egyptians believed in an afterlife as certainly as we believe that the sun will rise tomorrow! Their earthly homes they built of sunbaked mud; why build a fragile paradise on this earth, when the certainty is of a life beyond the trials we suffer here? Would we could all have such faith!'

The atmosphere was not, however, so easy when the conversation moved to the pantheon of the Egyptian gods; tiny Mrs Rainsford, rebuked over her perfectly innocent question, and who had not partaken of the wine, became a little pink about the ears as Hannah and Sheldon Rainsford discussed, more or less earnestly, the symbolic significance of that part of Osiris's anatomy that his wife and sister Isis had been unable to recover after his murder and dismemberment by his brother Set. The consequent comparison of the birth of Horus and the virgin birth of Christ clearly distressed the lady to the point that Harry, who had in their few meetings conceived something of a true affection for the dauntless little woman, offered a smile and a supporting arm and led her into the courtyard.

Laila, who had waited more than patiently through a boring afternoon, watched them go with a veiled, steely eye.

Harry was surprised, a little later, to be joined by their host, Sibyl Rainsford having long ago scurried back to the safety of her husband's side. Harry stood, thoughtful, beside an aperture in the courtyard wall that gave onto the mountainside and the gold and ochre desert that stretched to Osyut. The sun was setting, the sky glorious with colour, the mountains and the desert reflecting rose, gold and shadowed blues; almost as he watched the light shimmered and changed as the sun dipped further towards the horizon. Below the house a small village huddled in palm trees, its mud construction making it all but disappear into its surroundings. Only the minaret of its tiny mosque threw a stark shadow in the desert sunset.

'You know,' Sheldon Rainsford said from behind him, 'that the origin of the minaret is Christian?'

Harry started, and turned. 'No. I didn't.'

'There has always been conflict – conquest. When the Christian knights took infidel territory, the first thing they did was to build churches, and bell towers; when the infidel took back his own as always he used what he found. The bell towers made a perfect platform from which to call the faithful to prayer. They simply became taller and thinner. And in my opinion more beautiful.' The stocky figure turned, moved closer to the water. Harry followed.

'Captain Sherwood,' Rainsford said, reflectively, 'of Her Britannic Majesty's army.'

'Yes, Sir.'

'The British should not be in Egypt, did you know that?'

Harry contemplated a variety of answers, opted for tact. 'No, Sir.'

'Not just Egypt. And not just Britain.' Rainsford hunched huge shoulders, staring into the water. 'A mistake, my boy. An historic and self-evident mistake, this scrambling to divide a continent.'

Harry was truly intrigued. 'A mistake, Sir? That isn't the way it's seen in London, I think?'

Rainsford smiled a huge, stained, almost beatific smile. 'Ah. London,' he said. 'That's where the idiots live who think the criminally stupid Gordon should be avenged, is it not?'

There was a breath of silence. 'I think, Sir,' Harry said, hearing the stiffness in his own tone, 'that I should perhaps rejoin my party – it may be that Miss Standish is ready to return.'

'Don't be stupid, man.' The words were remarkably mild. Sheldon Rainsford returned his gaze to the splashing waters. 'Did you know,' he asked, conversationally, 'that in the Topkapi Palace in Istanbul there is a bedroom in the centre of the harem – a very beautiful bedroom I believe – within which a fountain plays constantly?'

Harry was ready to go. He shifted his foot, glanced towards where voices and laughter rang. 'No, Sir. I didn't know that.'

The sandy, leonine head lifted. 'The sound of water is remarkably diffusive, did you know? It's difficult – no, I think impossible – to overhear a conversation held beside running water.'

Harry turned, and waited.

'I hear that you've been making certain enquiries, Captain Sherwood,' the other man said.

Harry hesitated for the space of a breath. 'Yes.'

'Regarding – certain shipments to the south?'

'Yes.'

Rainsford's hesitation was longer than Harry's had been. 'I may – only may – be able to help you.'

In the silence the fountain sang.

'Arms are being run to the south.' There was an open reluctance in his voice. 'And as to that I have to admit to very mixed feelings, Captain Sherwood. Why should the Dervishes not acquire arms? What disaster might befall the tribesmen if they come to face the might of the British army with bows, and spears and knives?'

'Bows, spears and knives were enough to finish off General Gordon and his companions fairly comprehensively, Sir,' Harry suggested grimly.

'That was entirely the general's own fault, Captain, the British public's view notwithstanding. The man was a fool and invited his fate.' The words were tart. 'If indeed he did actually die as reported, which appears to be by no means certain. However, with regard to your recent enquiries –'

Harry, who had believed those same enquiries had been conducted with a maximum of discretion, winced a little. 'Yes, Sir?'

'You've heard that a gang of slavers is working the river?'

Harry hesitated. 'I've heard – some such story, yes.'

'It's no story, Captain. I'll tell you this; find the slavers and you've found your gun runners. They are one and the same. I have many friends amongst the native population. I hear many things. I have a name for you. A Frenchman –'

Harry experienced the only glint of pleasure he had felt in the whole of this difficult interview. 'Would that be a Monsieur LeFeuvre?'

The other man smiled drily. 'One of his names, certainly. Try also LaFitte, or Montand. If the man changes his shirts as often as he changes his name, his seamstress must be a rich lady indeed. I have an address. A warehouse in Luxor –'

'Captain Sherwood?' It was Laila, moving gracefully through the vine-draped colonnade. 'We're ready to leave.'

Behind her Rainsford's silent servant appeared, awaiting his orders.

Even Rainsford was not immune to the girl's gazelle-like beauty. He smiled. 'A moment, my dear.'

The short-lived sunset was over. The sky in the east was dark, whilst the colours in the west were fading rapidly from vivid reds and golds to a vast wash of pearly pink. The very land seemed to have changed colour, darkening mysteriously. The river glittered like a winding silver ribbon in the distance. Several huge birds of prey wheeled and hovered high in the still air. Rainsford spoke rapidly.

'Sheldon? We really must go.' Sibyl Rainsford appeared along the colonnade.

'Why?' Harry asked, quietly, as they followed the others to where the saddled ponies waited. 'Why, if you feel so strongly about the British position in Egypt, are you willing to help?'

The older man stopped. 'If there's one thing I hate more than the arrogance of the European powers in believing they can carve up Africa to suit their own plans and pockets,' he said, 'it's the cruelty of brother enslaving brother. Had it simply been a case of the guns for the Dervishes I would not have told you what I know. The British army is perfectly capable of looking after itself. The Sudanese who are being enslaved and sold cannot; anything I can do to help them I will.'

Harry nodded, held out his hand. 'Thank you anyway, Sir. I'm grateful.'

'Be careful.'

'I will.'

They rode through the warm evening beneath a sky that still showed the last drifts of colour painted by the glorious sunset. The town ahead of them looked magical in the dying light, its minarets and domes drawn dark against the pale sky, mysterious and enticing, a scene from *The Thousand and One Nights*. Hannah, suddenly oddly restless, kneed her pony forward to ride beside Harry. 'You're very quiet, Captain?'

He shook his head, smiling, but did not speak. Hannah, not, she was aware, for the first time, found herself watching him; the sharp, clear-cut profile, the set of his shoulders. Her own lips twitched to a self-deprecating smile and she looked away, into the wide distances of the desert. That would never do. Most certainly not. Laila looked at Harry so, when she thought no-one was watching. Practical Hannah Standish had much more sense. She must beware these wonderful Egyptian evenings – their effect obviously might be felt by the most unromantic of souls.

'Why, look,' Mr Rainsford pointed, 'there's a steamer arrived. Moored a little further upriver, see it?'

The steamer was lit festively, lanterns swinging from awnings and strung about the decks. An hour later the party rode past it towards the dahabeeyahs moored snugly in the shadows downstream. Music drifted across the water and there was much talk and laughter. A group of people standing by the rail with glasses in their hands waved energetically. 'Cooee!'

Mrs Rainsford, dutifully waving back, said in heartfelt tones, 'Goodness. How very noisy. I am so glad we decided to travel under sail.'

They approached the dahabeeyahs, the *Ra* moored before the *Horus*. They handed the ponies back to their patiently waiting owners, stopped for goodnights, decided against the offer of a nightcap aboard the *Ra*. A good steady wind was blowing; the boats with any luck could sail at dawn.

The *Horus* was moored in shadow. On the lower deck a small group of cross-legged men talked and smoked their pipes. A single lantern gleamed beneath the awning of the passenger deck. A couple of the crew hurried to help them aboard. One of them said something which Hannah did not catch, pointing to the passenger deck. Abdo was nowhere to be seen. The sounds from the steamer, softened by distance, echoed in the darkness.

'So there you are at last.' The soft voice came from above. All three looked up. Leaning against the railing of the passenger deck was a smiling, lush-figured vision in ivory satin. Fair hair and pale skin gleamed in the light of the lantern. The earrings she wore swung, striking fire, beside the creamy smoothness of her neck; the cunning cut of her evening gown revealed a provocative shadow between full breasts.

'Harry, my dear,' Fenella Hampshire smiled, brilliantly and beguilingly, delighted with the small drama she had so effectively created. 'Cairo was just too, too boring without you. I couldn't stand it a moment longer!' She let her large eyes drift with calculatingly insulting indifference to Hannah and then, for a longer and much more malicious moment, looked down into Laila's pretty, bewildered face. 'See what a mischief I am!' She extended a hand glittering with rings towards Harry. 'I've come to join your harem!'

CHAPTER SIXTEEN

'Mischief's the word!' Hannah said, straightfaced, a bruising half-hour later, after their uninvited guest, escorted by an openly terrified crewman, had stormed back to the steamer that had brought her to Osyut. 'Mrs Hampshire is, I fear, a very angry lady.' She cocked a warily amused eye in Harry's direction. 'She's a very – forceful person, isn't she?'

Harry winced and hunched further into his cushioned wicker chair, hands cupped firmly about his second extremely large glass of brandy.

'I hope,' Hannah continued after a moment, mildly, 'that I was not too –' she considered for a moment '– forthright? Mrs Hampshire is, after all an old friend of yours.'

Harry dismissed any thought that the gleam in her eyes could be laughter. 'Good heavens, no You were quite splendid. There aren't many who can stand up to Fenella like that.'

'Perhaps she won't,' Hannah said.

'Won't what?'

'Be waiting in Luxor.' Too innocently Hannah echoed their departing guest's sweetly venomous parting shot.

This time he glanced at her more than sharply. 'Hannah! This really isn't funny, you know!'

Hannah made grave but wholly ineffective effort to discipline both her uncharitable amusement and the unexpected flicker of pleasure that his unthinking use of her Christian name had brought. 'No. Of course not. Or at least it certainly wouldn't have been had she succeeded in her aim of joining us! Mrs Hampshire doesn't strike me as being the most peaceful of travelling companions, and the poor little *Horus* would have been quite overwhelmed by her presence, I think.'

Harry groaned.

She laughed outright. 'It's all right. She's gone; I don't suppose she'll come back.'

'But she'll be waiting in Luxor.'

The gloom in his voice brought another small peal of laughter. 'I do wish you'd stop laughing!'

'I can't help it! Oh, Harry – you don't mind if I call you Harry, do you? You just called me Hannah perfectly naturally and all this Captain Sherwood and Miss Standish business, at least in private, is really very silly, don't you think? – Harry, just think about it. Of course it's funny!'

He resisted a moment longer, then, half-hidden in the darkness, she caught the sudden flash of his smile, though he quickly sobered. 'It won't be funny if her husband takes it into his head to question what suddenly prompted a woman who has as much interest in Ancient Egypt as she does in training elephants to steam up the Nile on one of Mr Cook's steamers!'

Hannah stood up, shaking out her skirt. 'If the man were going to question his wife's activities at all,' she said, tranquilly, eyes steady and still caustically amused beneath raised brows, 'I should have thought he would have done it before?'

Harry had the grace to flush, very slightly.

'Now –' Hannah decided she had extracted as much fun out of his discomfiture as was kind '– why don't you finish your drink and read your letter? I'm off to bed.'

Harry lifted his head. His smile was warm. Floored as he had been by Fenella's sudden alarming appearance, he had to admit that without Hannah's resolute and courteous calm under fire the situation might well have resolved itself differently, and the *Horus* might have been carrying another, and unwelcome, passenger. 'Goodnight, Hannah,' he said. 'And thank you. You ought to be recommended for a medal. In fact you ought to be recommended for several!'

She watched him, smiling, for a long moment, surprised at the words that hovered upon the tip of her tongue, before, 'Goodnight,' she responded, and left him.

Harry turned the letter – the delivery of which had been Fenella Hampshire's flimsy excuse for tracking him down –

over in his hands. It was lucky that Fenella had actually given it to him before she had realized that, astoundingly, she was not going to get her own way; it was certainly not beyond her to have destroyed it in a fit of temper. He frowned a little, oddly reluctant to open it. It was unusual for Mattie to have written twice in a month. A faint disquiet stirred; with a sudden movement he slipped a long finger beneath the flap of the envelope and tore it open.

Below decks Hannah followed her well-organized bedtime routine as usual; the water that had been put out for her had cooled, but the evening was warm and she did not bother to call for more. She slipped into a loose and comfortable silken robe she had bought in one of the bazaars at Benisuef – it was the most glorious shade of green, and in a rare moment of self-awareness she had known how well it became her bright hair and pale skin – and perched upon the stool in front of a mirror, brush in hand, lifting her eyes to those of her reflection.

Her movements stilled.

For a surprisingly long time she sat so, her gaze thoughtful, a small furrow between her brows. Then with a small, impatient, almost angry movement, she shook her head, lifted the brush to attack the wiry shock of her red hair with an energy that made it crackle.

A little later, as always, before she crept beneath the mosquito netting that tented the narrow bunk, Hannah stood for a moment looking out over the Nile. The waters swirled darkly, wide and peaceful; a great silvered moon glowed in the southern sky, casting enticing shadows across the desert wilderness, gilding the shapes of the palm trees that edged the water. A sleepy bird called, and was quiet. Her calm restored, she slipped the green silk robe from her shoulders and, ignoring the muslin nightdress that lay very properly draped and ready over the chair – thanking as she did so the gods that had inspired her to leave the easily scandalized Mary in Cairo – she slid swiftly beneath the netting and into the bunk. In a pleasant ten minutes she was sound asleep.

*   *   *

She was woken by the splintering of glass.

She sat up, holding the cotton sheet to her shoulders, startled and disorientated.

Someone called, was answered, and fell to silence.

Hannah waited, listening.

From above her head came the sound of an uncertain footstep, a small, scrambling crash, a muttered curse.

She slipped from her bunk and reached for her robe.

It was dark on the passenger deck; the single lantern had burned low. In its dim light she saw the figure that leaned tensely, hands curled hard about the rail, head bowed; saw too the empty brandy bottle, and the glass lying shattered upon the table beside it.

'Harry?' She moved towards him, concerned. 'Harry – whatever's wrong?'

He appeared not to hear her. He neither turned nor moved.

She stepped further into the pale, deceptive light. 'Harry, what is it?'

In his clenched hand he held, crumpled, the letter that Fenella had brought.

She walked on bare, silent feet to his side. After a moment he turned his head to look at her. His black hair fell untidily across his forehead, the handsome face was bleak, and looked pale in the uncertain light, drawn by an emotion she could not in the shadows decipher. At first she took it for grief, then realized it could as well have been simple, black rage.

'What is it? What's the matter?'

'My mother,' he said. 'My mother is the matter.'

'Your – mother?' she repeated, and heard the stupid surprise in her own voice.

He turned on her. 'Yes, Hannah – my mother! I do have one, you know, as do most people. I wasn't washed up onto the beach at Brighton at high tide! Though by Christ I sometimes think I'd be better off if I had been!'

'Harry!'

He had flung away from her again, was leaning, elbows on the rails, glaring out across the water into the moonlit darkness.

Hannah waited for a long moment for him to speak, then

asked quietly, 'What's happened? She isn't –?' She stopped.

He did not move. 'Dead?' he asked, bitterly. 'Oh no. She isn't dead.'

Hannah was becoming more puzzled by the moment. She had already realized that despite the clarity of his speech Harry was well on the way to being very drunk indeed. 'What, then?'

He struggled with the words. 'She's – she's – oh, here!' With a sudden violent movement he thrust the letter into her hands. 'Read the bloody thing yourself. Where the hell's that other bottle?' He blundered across the deck to the small table beside the bookshelves.

Hannah took the paper, smoothed it, moved towards the lantern. The long silence that followed as she read the pleasant, serenely lucid words not once, not twice, but three times was broken only by the clink of glass upon bottle as Harry poured himself another half-tumbler of brandy.

At last she smoothed the letter, folded it very precisely, laid it upon the table and lifted her head to look at him.

He avoided her cool gaze.

'Your mother is getting married,' she said.

'Yes.'

'To a man of whom she is evidently extremely fond and who presumably loves her?'

He said nothing.

'And you are too spoiled, too possessive a child to be happy for her?' There was not the faintest trace of the usual sympathy or camaraderie in her voice or face.

The scathing words stung him. 'You don't understand!'

'No. I don't. And I don't think I ever could, so there seems little point in our discussing it.' She turned to leave.

Perversely, since his first reaction upon seeing her had been one of irritation, Harry put out a hand to stop her. 'Wait.'

She waited, but with obviously strained patience.

'You don't understand,' he said again, at last, well aware of and angry at the pathetic ineffectiveness of the childish words.

'Nothing you have said so far encourages me to understand.' It was said pleasantly enough, but he flinched a little, turning from her, reaching for the tumbler of brandy.

Hannah watched him dispassionately as he poured it down his throat. 'I do hope you aren't poisoning yourself,' she said. 'Abdo wasn't at all sure of the quality of that stuff. He said it was probably made from camel dung.'

'Abdo,' Harry said with sudden fierce clarity, 'can go hang.'

She shot him a look of pure dislike. She was at the stairs when he called her back. 'Hannah!' he hesitated. 'Please.'

For a moment she almost ignored the plea. Then with a small sigh she turned back. 'Harry, I really don't think you're in any fit state to talk tonight. Obviously you're upset and angry, though I can't for my life see why. Your mother has neither passed away nor is she ill. She hasn't squandered the family fortune and she hasn't disgraced the family name. After – ' she cast her mind back to the letter ' – after being a widow for the thirty-three years of your life, she has decided to marry an eminently respectable, kindly and apparently erudite man. All of this would seem to me – as it obviously seems to your mother – a cause rather for some small celebration than for – ' she allowed a moment's deliberation ' – rather than for what I can only describe as a childish display of pique. I simply can't imagine why this news should have upset you so. I have never once since I have met you heard any mention of your mother. You have, so I believe, been a soldier for many years, so it cannot be that you feel the jealousy that might be experienced by a son who lived at home? Why should you begrudge your mother her happiness?'

The line of Harry's jaw was grim. The anger – the utterly unexpected, savage fury – that had exploded within him at reading Mattie's news seethed in his belly, in his brandy-fuddled brain, drew the sinews of his hands to fists.

Hannah had tilted her head a little to look at him, but his face was in shadow. She saw, though, the tension that held him, knew the man well enough suddenly to wonder if this after all were not, despite her harsh words, something more than the mawkish and drunken outburst it appeared. 'I'm sorry,' she said, quietly, 'I had no right to say that and it really isn't any of my business. You no doubt have your reasons for feeling as you do. I can't help thinking it's a pity. Whatever lies between you and your mother that makes you wish her ill is nowhere evident in that letter. She loves you. It's clear in every line. She wants your blessing.' She laid a light hand upon his arm. 'Harry, of one thing I'm certain. In the end this bitterness, whatever its source, will harm no-one but you. Can you not let the past die and send her a word of happiness and approval?'

In the silence that followed, a felucca drifted like a ghost past the *Horus*, the tall, pale triangle of the sail glimmering in the darkness. Moments later the small waves of her wake slapped gently against the side of the dahabeeyah. In the reeds a bird twittered a sleepy complaint. Further up the bank the lights still glittered upon the steamer, and music drifted out across the water.

Harry said nothing. Hannah waited for what seemed a very long time, then, taking his silence as dismissal, once more turned to leave him.

Her bare foot was on the first step when she heard a small, choked sound from behind her. She turned her head.

Harry had hunched himself furiously against the tears that had so shockingly ambushed him. He stood where she had left him, leaning with his back against the rail. As she watched he bowed his face into his hands, shoulders shaking, though he made no other sound.

For the first time in her life Hannah Standish was utterly unnerved. Unlike most of her sex, she had seen men cry before; the bravest could be brought low by the torture of the surgeon's saw or the slow, gangrenous corruption of living flesh after a wound in battle. Nothing in her experience or upbringing, however, had prepared her for this, the sight of a man weeping in sheer emotional distress. She hovered for a moment, tempted to take the coward's way and pretend she had noticed nothing. She had taken another step down the stairs before she turned and walked swiftly back to him.

'Harry. Harry – what is it? What's distressing you so?'

He flung himself from her, fiercely. She saw the unmistakable gleam of tears on his face in the lantern light before the turn of his head hid them.

'Can't you tell me?' she asked, gently. 'Might – might it not help a little? To speak of it?'

Harry struggled for a moment in silence. Then, suddenly and savagely calmly, 'I can't speak of it,' he said, 'because I don't understand it myself. Had you asked me yesterday – this evening, even – what my reaction to such news might have been I would have said – would have believed – laughter! I don't understand myself why I'm so bitterly angry. So – so murderously – angry –' He ground the words out. Hannah saw the grim line of his jaw, the clenching of his muscles, and knew that he did not exaggerate. Helplessly she reached a hand towards his arm, but, half-afraid, hesitated and withdrew it before she touched him. He stood in rigid silence.

'It's – to do with your mother and her marriage,' she said finally, tentatively.

'Yes. It's to do with that.'

She shook her head helplessly. 'But Harry – why? *Why* are you so angry? What has your mother done that you find it so hard to wish her well?'

There was another long moment of struggle. 'I can't tell you,' he said, his voice almost inaudible, and then again, his head flung back as if in pain, '*I can't tell you!*'

Hannah was appalled and at the same time all but overcome with compassion at the anguished emotion. This was not the careless, carefree Harry Sherwood she had observed in Cairo and then come, as she thought, to know on the slow drift of the river in these past weeks. For the first time it occurred to her that he no less than she was not entirely the person he appeared to be. She stood irresolute, watching him. After his outburst he had quietened, taking a long breath, straightening his shoulders. His profile was flawlessly outlined by the pale light of the lantern behind it. As she stood watching him, studying the line of cheek and jaw, she was astonished to find that an almost painful surge of emotion – an emotion she was afraid to identify – had sharpened her heartbeat and caught her breath unevenly in her throat. Battling it fiercely, 'I hate to see you so unhappy,' she said softly, and hoped he did not hear, or at least would not understand, the sudden uncontrollable tremor in her voice.

He turned at last. 'I wish I could tell you. I wish I could

explain.' He was in command of himself again. His voice was quiet; there was an edge of something close to longing in it that disturbed her further.

'Couldn't you? Couldn't you try?'

There was only the smallest moment of hesitation before he shook his head a little, sharply. 'No. No, Hannah. It isn't possible. I'm sorry. Believe me – if I could tell anyone –' He stopped. He had bent his head and was studying her in the dim light, his lean face all at once intent. They were standing very close together, almost touching.

A tide of warmth, of sheer physical excitement, was rising in her; she had to exert all her willpower to resist an intemperate urge to reach a hand to his face. 'But – you will write to her? Send her your congratulations?' She was suddenly aware that beneath the silk robe she was naked. The fire crept from the pale, thin skin of her throat into her cheeks.

'Yes. I'll write.' His quiet voice was oddly abstracted. His dark eyes were still attentive upon her face, serious, oddly questing, as if he were discovering there something he had never seen before.

'I think it – quite charming – that she should have –' Hannah stopped, completely losing the fragile thread of her thought. As if drawn by a magnet, she took a step towards him. The music from the steamer had stopped, the distant talk and laughter had died. The strings of lanterns had been doused, and one by one the other lights were going out. The Nile night reclaimed its own; only the moon shimmered an enchanted path upon the moving waters. She stood utterly still as he reached for her, drew her to him, kissed her very gently. His lips were warm and dry and tasted not unpleasantly of brandy, his grip by contrast was rough, almost painful, upon her shoulders. For a moment she felt nothing, nothing but the surprise and pleasure that might be occasioned by an unexpected compliment or an unlooked-for gift. She stood within his hands like a child, docile, uncertain, her face turned up to his. Then, his lips still upon hers, he moved a little, stepping around her, so that she stood with her back to the rails, and felt the length of his body pressed against hers.

It was as if the world had exploded and disintegrated around her; all that was left was Harry, his hands upon her body, his lips upon hers. Hannah curled her arms about his neck, buried her fingers in the thick black hair, pressed her body against his, feeling the roughness of his clothes upon breasts and belly, the fine silk of her robe neither protection nor covering; she might as well have been naked. In that moment, quite unashamedly, she wished that she were. His arms tightened like a vice around her. The kiss was no longer gentle. Then, moments later, he let her go, very abruptly, and stepped back. They were both breathing heavily. 'Hannah! Oh, God, Hannah – I'm sorry!'

She shook her head. 'Don't be.' Her mouth felt bruised. Her gown had all but slipped from one shoulder. 'Harry, don't be.'

'I didn't mean – Hannah, I can't imagine what came over me.' It was no less than the simple truth. To Harry Sherwood, for the most part, the seduction of women came as easily and naturally as breathing; yet in these past days and weeks, as friendship had grown between them, it had never once occurred to him to think of Hannah in such a way. Tonight, however, angry and emotional, his senses blurred by brandy, by the velvet, exotic night and by the sudden discovery of an unexpected and eccentric beauty in that pale, spare-boned face with its wide clear eyes and impossible cloud of hair, it had seemed the most natural thing in the world to kiss her so. God in heaven, how had it come to this? Wasn't he in enough trouble already? 'Can you bring yourself to forgive me?'

Hannah's good sense had reasserted itself as smoothly as if it had never deserted her. She straightened her gown, tightening the belt, tying a neat knot. 'There's nothing to forgive.' She smiled a little, and again he wondered that he had never seen before the attraction of that vivid, intelligent face. 'It wasn't the most unpleasant thing to have happened to me by a long chalk.' The smile widened. 'And I did get the distinct impression that I kissed you back.'

Harry smiled at that, and her heart lurched. Firmly she resisted the urge to experiment further.

He reached for her hands. 'Hannah Standish, I truly believe I've never met another woman like you.'

'I most certainly hope not.' Gently she disentangled her hands, aware that until she composed herself – and despite appearances, she was far from being composed – every moment in his company was dangerous in the extreme. These alarming and newly awakened feelings notwithstanding, she had no intention in the world of becoming another scalp at Harry Sherwood's belt; the thought lifted her chin and stiffened her back a little. 'It's very late,' she said, 'and we've an early start in the morning.'

'Yes.'

'I'm sorry you were upset. I hope you feel a little better?'

'Yes.' Surprisingly, it was true.

She could not – absolutely could not – resist touching him one last time. Serenely she lifted her hands to his shoulders, raised herself a little onto her bare toes and kissed his cheek, very softly. 'Goodnight, Harry.'

'Goodnight.' Helplessly confused, he watched her walk into the darkness. She neither turned to look back, nor did she employ any wanton trick in her walk as so many women might have under the circumstances. She simply strode, as she always strode, away from him and disappeared down the stairs to the lower deck.

Once in her room Hannah stood for a moment leaning against the closed door, head tilted back, the fingers of one hand resting lightly upon her mouth. In thirty years of life she had never once behaved as she had tonight. In thirty years of life she had never once experienced that almost primeval surge of excitement, never glimpsed the fearful possibilities of fierce sexual attraction. For the briefest of moments she had understood as she never had before why women so often abandoned their pride and their prudence and gave themselves unconditionally into the perilous bondage of love – or, worse, of infatuation. She trembled still, half from the remembered excitement of that moment, half from pure terror at what might have happened; of how much of herself she might have surrendered.

One thing was absolutely certain; nothing must come of it. The very thought was absurd to the point of embarrassment. A combination of circumstances had arisen; it was well within her capabilities to ensure that such a thing never happened again.

She would have been relieved to know, as she slipped once more into her bunk to lie, restless and exasperatingly sleepless, staring into the glimmering darkness, that Harry on deck above her had come to the selfsame conclusion and, if anything, even more firmly.

It was ten days before Harry had the chance to follow up the information he had so unexpectedly picked up from Sheldon Rainsford, ten days of fair winds and exhilarating sailing, ten days in which the great river offered them vistas that ranged from green and Babylonic gardens along the eastern bank above Osyut to the strange angular ramparts of the desert mountains further south; from verdant, fertile fields and huddled mud-built villages that swarmed with life to vast and empty stretches of barren mud and rock and shimmering, sifting sand. In some places the river was encaged by sheer cliffs, their sunlit faces scarred by the dark, shadowy pockmarks of ancient rock tombs. In others the landscape stretched, flat and incandescent with heat, towards Arabia on the one side and Libya on the other, land and sky merging in the molten, metallic colours of a furnace. As they beat south the weather got hotter; days were spent for the most part on the cool, breezy deck or resting in cabins shaded by drawn blinds. The nights, however, were enchanting – warm as an English summer's day, lit by a moon that was indeed a cool, silver sister to the blazing sun, and that illuminated the exotic landscape in a pale glory of which Hannah, for one, never tired. She had made no fixed plans for this part of the journey, apart from a night spent in the small town of Girgeh, with its picturesque fallen mosque about which each year the changing floodwaters lapped and sucked, bringing it further to ruin, and a visit, much anticipated, to the great temple of Denderah. Two days beyond Denderah was Luxor – Thebes – the jewel of the Nile, where lay what must surely be the best-known and greatest tombs and ruins of the ancient world, and where they were planning to stay for most of the week.

Both Hannah and Harry kept to their own private resolutions. Neither by word nor by glance did either of them indicate that anything untoward had happened between them. Sometimes, Hannah found herself actually doubting her own memory; the incident had happened so quickly and in such a charged atmosphere that it had taken on something of the unreal quality of a dream. And yet for all their efforts something, undeniably, had changed. A certain comradeship had been growing between them for some time; now it was as if each had seen something in the other which until now had been hidden, and, far from making for embarrassment and awkwardness, as Hannah had at first feared, it had actually strengthened the friendship. They spent long hours together in easy silence upon the shaded passenger deck, Hannah drawing or painting, Harry sprawled upon a chair, sucking at his pipe, watching the ever-changing panorama of the riverbanks. They talked of the things they saw, and of some of the things they had done. Harry told of tiger shoots in India and of living with the proud desert dwellers of Morocco, Hannah of the wonders of Venice and Florence and of the six months she had spent in an apartment overlooking that artists' river, the Seine, in Paris. She spoke of her conventional parents and her understanding of their bemused and disapproving disappointment in their oddity of a daughter, of Leo and his kindness, of the years spent studying and later nursing under the redoubtable Miss Nightingale. Harry said nothing of his family and little of his personal past, and neither of them mentioned Mattie's letter or his reaction to it.

Another pleasure was their shared if inconsequential affection for the pretty, mercurial Laila. The child was for most of the time enchanting, her laughter as ready as a bird's song. She would swoop from one to the other, teasing and chattering, small and delicate hands moving expressively, blue eyes brilliant against the olive of her smooth skin. That she treated both the nurse who was utterly devoted to her and the crew who were openly in awe of her with less than care or courtesy was a fault for which her background was entirely to blame. By nature she was warm-hearted and impulsive, though her temper was capricious and she could be extremely autocratic. Brought up by a doting father to believe that the world about her existed almost entirely for her amusement and gratification, it said much for her strength of character that she remained a graceful, entertaining and likeable child, though when crossed she could be a termagant. When Harry went riding early one morning without her, she greeted his return with a torrent of furiously tearful reproaches and a well-aimed flower vase. An hour later she was all smiles and happy to help Hannah wind a skein of wool. For either of them to admire an item in a bazaar was for her to buy it on the spot and present it to them; yet when a button was lost from one of her favourite dresses she stormed about the dahabeeyah accusing any member of the crew she came across of having stolen it and threatening the most blood-thirsty of punishments. She treated Harry, to his amusement, as if she owned him, and admired and in some ways emulated Hannah, whilst clearly considering her an elderly lady of no physical charms. Laila was, after all, just fifteen years old, half Hannah's age, and had been beautiful from the moment of her birth. She had known from the age of three the effect her beauty could have on men of all ages. She had known, too, from the same age, how to get her own way. She had discovered, as Colonel Standish had suspected, before Hannah had ever known it that Harry had been chosen to accompany the *Horus* and had made her plans accordingly. She had not been in the least surprised that fate had fallen in so very conveniently with her own designs; it was to be expected. What neither Harry nor Hannah suspected was the depth of those designs.

Laila had first seen Harry Sherwood on her father's fortieth birthday. A picnic had been arranged with camel- and horse-racing. Harry, despite his damaged leg, had ridden for the garrison, mounted upon a stallion black as his own hair, fleet as the wind and vicious and unpredictable as a striking cobra. He had been in his element, and had won the admiration even of the reckless Bedouin against whom he rode. And Laila, wayward, headstrong, and of an age to fall headlong in love with as unsuitable a man as possible, had marked him for her own. Nothing that had happened since had made her change her mind; on the contrary, these past weeks had further confirmed it. That his attentions to her were light-hearted in the extreme, the courtesies of any man to a lovely and desirable girl, she could not see. She was used to the respect, in some cases the fear, accorded to her father by any man who came near her; of course Harry would be circumspect. He was a soldier, a man of no great means. It would not occur to him that he could approach the daughter of Ayman el Akad as a suitor. She lay in her bunk at night and dreamed of his gratitude and pleasure when they reached the Winter House and her father granted, as he was bound to grant, her dearest wish. It struck her as not in the least bizarre to think so; there had never been anything she had wanted that her father had not provided – why not this? She had long since determined to marry a European, as her father had – it was unthinkable to contemplate the thought of losing her freedom to an Egyptian husband who would expect her to adopt the veil and the all-concealing habarah – and had half expected to find herself parcelled off into one of the great merchant houses of London or Paris. But that was before Harry. Her father had enough money, he did not need more. And she wanted Harry as she had never wanted anything before, as he, quite obviously, wanted her. Nothing could be simpler. Her brother Mohammed, at present at school in England, would be required to make a dynastic marriage; such was the payment for the reward of an empire that would one day be bestowed upon him. But Laila saw no such restrictions upon herself. Harry loved her; even the woman that Hannah had dubbed 'Madam Mischief' had seen that, Laila was certain, remembering with smug satisfaction the venomous looks Fenella had directed at her. Her father would give her her heart's desire. He always had. And so she chattered and laughed and flirted and hugged her secret to herself, delighting in her beloved's ignorance of the bliss that lay ahead of them. Laila, in short, was a most dangerous of combinations: a child, naive, charming and greedy, and a woman, determined, blinded by infatuation and believing herself loved.

And Harry, watching for danger in one direction, entirely failed to perceive it creeping up upon him from another.

* * *

They sailed into Luxor, built picturesquely amongst the temples and the standing columns and pylons of the ancient city of Thebes, late in the afternoon, to the accompaniment of their own crew's enthusiastic drumming and singing. On the western bank two great sitting Colossi watched their coming with ravaged, mutilated faces. Their arrival was welcomed by the dipping flags and saluting guns of the dahabeeyahs already anchored along the bank – including, Hannah saw with pleasure, the *Ra* – and a long signal from the steam whistle of a less welcome sight, the steamer they had last seen at Osyut. It was with some small difficulty that she avoided looking at Harry to see his reaction, and with even more that she smothered an amused smile.

The first to come aboard the *Horus* – indeed he gave the impression of having been waiting eagerly upon the quay since dawn – was Ayman el Akad's representative in the town, a small, moustachioed man, dapper in the embroidered cloth coat called a gubbeh and a tasselled tarbush. His name was Ali abd Ela, he was honoured and delighted to welcome them to the wonders of Luxor and Thebes, and he bore with him a gift and a loving message for Laila from her father, and a large basket of fruit for the voyagers from himself and his staff. He also had an invitation to a reception to be held in two days' time in the House of the Waterbirds, on the west bank, owned by an English trader in antiquities, a Mr Charles Mansfield and his wife, who much enjoyed the company of their compatriots as they passed through the city. Many interesting people would be there, he assured them; even the Cook boat had delayed its departure so that its more important passengers might attend.

Hannah, with great care, looked anywhere but at Harry.

They accepted gifts, message and, perforce, invitation, with apparently equal pleasure. Already the ship was besieged; sellers of silks and sellers of antiquities, vendors of cheap beads and scarabs, donkeys and donkey-boys, guides, beggars and half-naked, screaming children had gathered along the bank and in a flock of small feluccas around them. Ali, quiet and deferential, bowed a little. 'You will excuse me?' Not awaiting a reply he turned, screeching like a turkey-cock. The small bodyguard who awaited him in military order upon the quay immediately drew short whips from their belts and proceeded to strike about them with indiscriminate savagery, driving the importuning crowd back.

'Oh, please!' Hannah began, shocked. Ali turned back, bowing a little, smiling unctuously. 'Don't worry, lady. All has been arranged. Today you rest. Tomorrow you see the temple and the ruins of ancient Thebes. The next day we take donkeys and go to El Karnak. All is arranged, lady, all is arranged. If you wish to ride to the Tombs of the Kings that, too, can be arranged.'

'I – thank you.' Bemused, Hannah nodded.

Laila was pinning the gift from her father, a small, jewelled brooch, upon the breast of her silk robe. 'Harry, would you help me, please? I can't fasten this.'

Harry bent to help her. Ali abd Ela watched, his face suddenly totally expressionless. Then he saluted. 'I leave you now. Please – anything you need, you simply ask. Ladies. Sir.' He bowed slightly to Hannah and Harry, deeper and with obsequious respect to Laila. 'Anything can be arranged. Anything.'

It was late afternoon before Harry could get away. He had mentioned his conversation with Sheldon Rainsford to no-one, not even to Abdo. Too many times before such information had led him on nothing but a wild goose chase; this time he would check it out himself first. Abdo could be brought in later if necessary. Hannah and Laila were aboard the *Ra* taking afternoon tea with the Rainsfords, most of the crew were ashore with the dragoman, resupplying the galley, or asleep in the shade of the lower deck. Harry settled his wide-brimmed hat upon his head, picked up the stick he still used to walk any distance and strolled unconcernedly, the very picture of the idle tourist, down the gangplank towards the eager crowd that, undeterred by Ali abd Ela's whips, had regathered on the bank.

'Here, Mister, here! Best donkey in Luxor! God save the Queen!'

'Donkey for Lord, here – donkey for King! Fastest donkey, Mister!'

335

'Scarabs, Sir – you want scarabs? Bring good luck.'

Harry waved them away, grabbed an urchin of nine or ten years. 'You know the Fountain of Lilies?'

The boy grinned, and the scabbed sore at the corner of his mouth cracked. 'I know, Effendi.'

'Good.' Harry felt in his pocket, tossed a coin. 'Take me there.' At sight of the money the begging children had surged forward again, shrieking at an earsplitting pitch. Harry tossed a few more coins into the crowd and hurried after his small guide as a murderous scramble ensued.

Luxor was not a very big town, nor was it any great commercial centre, its main attractions being its situation, surrounded as it was by a rich and fertile plain studded with palm groves, pastures and green, productive fields, and the access it gave to the ruins of one of the most famous cities of the ancient world. The boy led Harry through dusty streets to a narrow archway that gave onto the inevitable souk, though he was quick to see that there was nothing here to compare with the great bazaars of Cairo or Benisuef. Yet still there was plenty of life, even at this time in the afternoon. A string of camels, heavily loaded with some lush greenstuff, picked their disdainful way through the booths and stalls, groups of robed and turbaned men stood talking or squatted about the communal hookah upon the ground, involved in the ever-fascinating rounds of bargaining. Women swathed in the silk robe called the habarah paced past with beguiling dignity, dark eyes gleaming at the sight of a stranger, baskets and boxes balanced gracefully upon dark, draped heads, bare shapely feet firm and brown in the dust. Children and dogs, each as mischievous and undisciplined as the other, scavenged singly or in packs, tripping the unwary, stealing what they could, begging what they could not.

The boy turned out of the main thoroughfare and down an alley. The hubbub died behind them. Dust filtered through the air, gleaming in sunshine, swirling in shadow. The stench was suffocating. Harry resisted the urge to reach for his handkerchief.

'Here, Effendi. Fountain of Lilies.'

The fountain was set into a long, blank wall, two or three

storeys high, at a spot where one alleyway stood at an angle to another. Harry could see no obvious reason for the name; on the contrary, anything less lily-like he had rarely seen. Unusually in this country where the courteous provision of sweet water to a passing stranger was considered an essential duty, the trough was scummed and stinking, the flow of water a slimy trickle. Harry looked around, remembering the instructions Rainsford had given him. A short way down the second alley was a wrought-iron gate, leading to a courtyard. He reached into his pocket, tossed a coin to the lad. The boy grabbed it, shot him a single, curious look from bright, dark eyes and was gone, flitting like a ragged shadow around the corner, silent on bare feet.

Harry stood for a moment, rapidly reviewing the story he had invented to cover this visit; an uncle in England interested in importing Egyptian antiquities that were becoming so very fashionable at home – a chance recommendation from a dealer in Cairo – it was thin, but all he could manage. In Egypt, and especially in Luxor, one could be forgiven for imagining anyone in commerce to be either in or ready to join the lucrative business of exporting those artefacts for which Europeans were ready to pay so well. He brushed off his jacket, straightened his cuffs and walked briskly, stick clicking in time with his footsteps, to the gate.

It stood open, and the dirt courtyard beyond was empty.

Harry pulled the rusty bell chain. Distantly there came a cracked clatter, then silence.

Nothing happened.

'Hello?' He pushed through the gate and into the courtyard. The air was warm, the shadows as dark as the sun was brilliant. 'Hello, there? Anyone home?' In the quiet he heard the distant sounds of the market, the sudden trill of a songbird.

He walked to the only door in the yard, pushed it open and after only a moment's hesitation stepped through. He was standing in a warehouse, cool and cavernous. Carpets were everywhere, in rolls and in stacks, hanging from beams, draped over racks; the distinctive, pungent smell of them caught at his throat. After a moment his eyes adjusted to the gloom; the place was lit only by several long narrow windows high up in one wall. There was not the slightest sound. On quiet feet he began to explore.

There were thousands, possibly tens of thousands, of carpets and rugs, clear evidence of innocent and profitable trade. He poked about, squeezed between the stacks, searched through pile after pile only to find carpets and yet more carpets. If this place was used as a staging post for the smuggled guns it was hard to tell where they might be kept. Meticulously, yard by yard Harry searched, and found nothing. The air was chokingly stuffy. Sweat trickled uncomfortably beneath his shirt. He followed aisle after aisle. The sun, moving to the west, struck suddenly through the high windows, lighting the dust motes with gold. He was ready to give up and admit to yet another dead end when something caught his attention. He was standing in a wider aisle that led through the inevitable stacks of carpets; yet something was different. It took a moment for him to see what it was. Most of these carpet alleys ended in bare, white-washed wall, but at the end of this one a large and beautiful carpet hung, suspended from a wooden bar. He walked to it, drew it aside. It slid quietly; and in the wall that was revealed stood a door.

A locked door.

Harry put his shoulder to it. It budged not an inch. He looked around, could see nothing with which to force it. Frustrated, he shouldered it again, to absolutely no avail. With renewed energy he began to search; this time for something, anything, that might get him through that door. It took him ten precious minutes to find it: a long, jemmy-like piece of metal that was part of one of the racks upon which were draped a variety of prayer mats. He wrenched it free and returned to the door. Four or five minutes later the jamb splintered at last, and the door swung easily open. He straightened, sweating, the metal bar still in his hand, and found himself looking into a vast, low-ceilinged space, hot as an oven and dim as the shades of night. The only inlets for light or air were two tiny barred grilles set far apart and near the ceiling. There was a lingering stench upon the air that made his stomach roil uncomfortably.

He tossed his wide-brimmed hat aside, picked up his walking stick and stepped through the door, looking about him, a fierce mixture of anger and disgust welling in him like sickness as he took in his surroundings. There could be no doubt; the place was a slave-pen. At intervals of perhaps three or four feet around the walls hung heavy chains, three to each station, one holding an iron collar, the other two what were obviously metal wrist restraints. Other, longer chains, also with collars and handcuffs attached, were piled in heaps by the wall.

Sheldon Rainsford's words were clear in his brain: 'Find the slavers, and you've found your gun runners. They are one and the same.'

Irresistible, hostile rage was rising. It blurred his vision. He shook with it.

Harry lifted one of the neck fetters, weighing it in his hand; the dead, terrible weight of subjugation and bondage. With a sudden, convulsive movement he hurled it from him, caring nothing for the noise.

Had his father's people allowed themselves to be taken like this – dragged in chains – confined in airless holes like animals – caged, beaten, humiliated, stripped of their dignity, of their very identity?

Was this his heritage?

'No,' he said, aloud. And then again, 'No!'

About him was silence. Sweat dripped from his jaw, ran, stinging, into his eyes. He ran a tense hand through his damp hair, took a couple of long, slow breaths, forcing himself to be calm. Every moment of every day since Mattie had finally told him the brutal truth of his parentage, he had fought against the knowledge. In the darkest hours of the darkest nights he had felt it in his blood, like an ineradicable stain; humiliation, degradation, shame. Looking at these instruments of enslavement he felt not compassion, but an overwhelming rage, a fierce contempt; an echo, in his own heart, of dishonour.

He wiped the sweat from his forehead with the back of his hand, brought himself back to the purpose of the moment. 'Find the slavers and you've found your gun runners.' Was Rainsford right?

His eye fell upon something in the far corner of the room: a coffin-like box, its lid splintered and discarded beside it. He moved swiftly. The box was empty, the bottom split and broken as if its contents had been too heavy for it. Upon the discarded lid was stamped an emblem: a scarab, common enough, but set within a lozenge, and between its claws a device something like the ancient hieroglyphs he had seen in the tombs he had visited with Hannah. He saw it for only a moment, registering its unexpected familiarity before a sound behind him spun him on his heels. The men were almost upon him, knives raised. All three wore Arab robes, their faces dark in the darker shadows of their hoods. Harry flung himself sideways, saw the dull gleam of the blade that flickered close to his eye, felt the burning as its razor sharpness caught his cheekbone. Ignoring the sudden ominous stab of pain in his wounded leg, he rolled and came upright, spinning to face his attackers, in his hand the long blade that had been encased in his walking stick. The burlier of the three never even saw it; the weight of his own lunge impaled him. Harry stepped back quickly, whipping the stained blade free. The man grunted and dropped. The other two drew back, arms extended, the wicked curved knives weaving. Step by step Harry retreated to the wall, the long, slender sword flickering back and forth. One of his attackers danced forward, slashing, then back before Harry could reach him. He stumbled a little, pain shooting through his leg. Blood dripped from his chin. He saw the gleam of teeth in a dark face as the taller of his assailants smiled. In menacing quiet and with obvious purpose they began to move apart, one to the right, one to the left of him. The arc of the blade became wider and wider. The men moved closer, watching for an opening, waiting for the chance to rush him. There was no sound but the sound of their breathing. Harry shifted his weight from his damaged right leg. The blade flickered, warily, again. The man he threatened gestured with his knife, distracting him, and as he did so the other ducked within his guard and slashed at his sword arm. Harry brought the blade whistling round, missing the man's knife hand by an inch. As he did so, he saw movement. A tall, robed figure had slipped through the doorway. Harry flicked a glance, saw the raised arm, the quivering knife, flinched as the arm came down and the weapon flashed through the air, unerring as a bullet to its target. The smaller of his two assailants grunted, eyes wide. Blood flooded from his mouth. Harry stepped aside as, blindly, he groped, scratched at the wall with frantic fingers and slid to a bloody heap on the floor. There was a moment when all sound, all movement was suspended. Then the newcomer very calmly lifted his arm again, another slender throwing knife held between long dark fingers. Harry pushed himself away from the wall, sword point steady. With a roar his remaining attacker threw himself towards the door, shouldering the knife-thrower aside. They heard his blundering departure, the slam of the door.

'I think,' Abdo said, 'it would be wise to follow his example and leave. You can walk?'

'Yes.' As if to give the stiff word the lie, Harry took a step, stumbled and all but fell. In one swift movement the other man was beside him, catching his arm to support him. Harry shook it free. 'I'm all right. Abdo, what are you doing here?'

'Perhaps explanations should wait.' Coolly Abdo bent above the man he had killed and flicked back his hood. 'Do you know him?'

Harry brushed a hand against his cheek. It came away bright with blood. 'No.'

'This one?'

Harry was silent for a moment, as at least one explanation fell into place. 'This one, yes,' he said quietly, looking down into the dead face of Sheldon Rainsford's silent servant. 'So much for the deafening properties of running water.'

341

CHAPTER SEVENTEEN

'Hold still.' Hannah lifted Harry's chin with firm fingers. 'This is going to hurt a little, I'm afraid.'

Harry flinched as, with deft movements, she cleaned the cut on his face.

'I still think you should report this to the authorities – or at the very least to the Consul. To be set upon by robbers in broad daylight!'

'It was my own fault.' Gingerly Harry moved his head, flexed the muscles of his face. 'I went off on my own down a side alley – asking for trouble – ouch!'

'Hang on. Nearly done. We can't risk infection.' Brisk and competent, she finished her task. 'Now, let's have a look at that arm.'

Harry sat quietly under her ministrations. Abdo had gone into the town to telegraph to Cairo; reluctant as Harry was to risk having the colonel hand the case on to his professional intelligence men, still he had recognized the seriousness of the situation. Two men were dead. And although what little information Harry had managed to glean was mostly negative, there were Hannah and Laila to consider. The colonel had a right to know what had happened, and to decide what should be done. Harry hoped fervently, if a trifle optimistically, that Colonel Standish would agree that he should continue his investigations.

'There. Fortunately neither was too deep.' Hannah kept her voice cool and dispassionate. There was no need in the world for anyone to suspect the surge of horrified panic that had engulfed her at first sight of Harry's white, bloodied face, the fluttering of her heart now as she considered the might-have-beens. She studied his face, touched his cheek again, very lightly. 'There'll be something of a scar, I'm afraid.'

Harry shrugged, his eyes on the riverbank, watching for Abdo.

'How did you find me? How did you come to be there?' he had asked as he had followed the other man through a maze of windowless mud alleys to the riverbank. At Abdo's suggestion he had thrown the coarse, hooded robe of the bigger of his two assailants over his stained and dishevelled European clothes, and thus too hidden the bloody slash on his face.

Abdo had moved protectively closer as two men, talking volubly, came towards them and passed without a glance. 'I followed you.'

'Why?'

The glimmer of a smile flickered upon the black, handsome face. 'Was I not asked by Standish Bey to protect you? How can I do that if you roam alone? Unfortunately I lost you for a while in the bazaar. It was some time later that I found the boy who guided you to the fountain and – persuaded – him to tell me where he had taken you.'

'A bloody good job for me that you did.' Harry flicked a swift look at him. 'Where did you learn to throw a knife like that? Handy sort of trick!'

Again the smile. 'You'd like me to teach you?'

'That I would.'

They had walked on in silence for a moment. 'You saved my life,' Harry said, quietly, ashamed of his own awkwardness. 'Thank you.'

The other man shook his head. 'It's nothing.'

'Not to me it isn't.'

Eyes as dark as his own turned upon him. 'We have a long way to go yet, Captain Sherwood. Perhaps – who knows? – you'll get a chance to return the favour?' The words were spoken lightly, yet there was a certain grim purpose in them. 'These people – they aren't playing games, it seems.'

'When Colonel Standish hears what's happened he'll call us off, I should think.' There was regret in Harry's tone. 'He might even order us back to Cairo out of the way. There are the ladies to think of.'

Abdo said nothing.

'Bloody shame. I'd give my eye teeth to have another go

at those bastards.' He glanced again at his companion, remembered the nerveless calm with which he had beaten off the attack in the warehouse. Harry had been in enough tight corners to recognize true courage when he saw it. He'd known many a man lose his head under less harrowing circumstances. 'And I'll tell you one thing. When the chance comes there's no-one I'd rather have at my back.'

Abdo's quiet smile acknowledged the compliment.

They had reached the riverbank, disorientatingly normal after the events of the past hour, with its moored dahabeeyahs and feluccas, the stalls and booths of the ever-hopeful traders. A crowd of skinny children swarmed towards them, shrieking, thin arms outstretched. Harry stopped for a moment, turned to face the other man, thrust out his hand. 'I mean it. I owe you my life. And I thank you for it.'

For a moment so brief it was almost unnoticeable Abdo hesitated; for the first time since they had met Harry fancied that he was disconcerted. Then his well-shaped hand met Harry's, his grip dry and strong and, also for the first time, his smile was open and without guard.

'Here's Abdo,' Hannah said now, drying her hands.

The tall Nubian threaded his way along the quay, ignoring the clamour about him. Harry stood, left Hannah watching as he ran nimbly down the steps to the lower deck to greet him.

'Well?'

Abdo gravely handed him a printed wire. The five words were simplicity itself. 'Pursue with all vigour. Standish.'

Harry's eyes lifted to the other man's; simultaneously both smiled.

'Harry!' Laila leaned above them, calling down. 'Harry, where have you been? I've been looking for you for hours! I want to go riding. I want to go riding now!'

Hannah, to her own mildly amused surprise, found herself dressing for Mr and Mrs Charles Mansfield's reception with rather more care than usual. Against her own better judgement at the time, but on Mary's insistence, she had packed a pretty and rather fashionable promenade gown of pale blue and white striped silk with graceful leg o' mutton sleeves. The wasp waist and narrow skirt, sweeping to a small train behind, emphasized both her height and her slimness, whilst a foam of lace at breast and wrist softened nicely the almost boyish boniness of her figure. The ensemble was topped neatly with her favourite straw boater, ribboned and flowered to match the dress; about her hair she could do nothing, a problem with which after thirty years she had learned to live without too much despondency. At the end of her toilette she was relatively pleased with what little of herself she could see in the tiny mirror on her cabin wall. And if the corset and the ironbound boning that were necessary to achieve the fashionable shape restricted the breath and the layers of fussy petticoats hobbled her usual easy stride to a – she supposed – more ladylike pace, it was a price to be paid with a smile or not at all. She caught her own eye in the little mirror and could not resist laughing at her own foolishness.

Harry and Laila awaited her upon the deck, Harry looking like a well-dressed pirate in his immaculately pressed light suit, wide-brimmed Panama hat, and the vicious, slender line of the unhealed knife cut on his face. He would, she thought with sudden and disturbingly affectionate exasperation, cause even more hearts to flutter than usual with this newly acquired accessory. 'Every handsome man should have one,' she said approvingly, indicating the wound. 'Don't you think so, my dear?'

Laila clapped her hands. 'I think he looks like a brigand! Or St George, who's been scratched by the dragon!'

'Oh, come.' Hannah's eyes flicked with subversive amusement to Harry's face. 'That's a little far-fetched, isn't it?'

Laila laughed, pirouetted to Harry and took his arm. Quite unconsciously, in floating rose-pink silk and with a swathe of silken flowers in her raven hair, she put Hannah for all her unwonted exertions effortlessly in the shade – where, Hannah was ready to concede wryly, she belonged. So much for late-blooming vanity.

On the lower deck a small escort of sailors waited, baggy

trousers and shirts gleaming white, turbans of every hue tied rakishly about dark heads.

Hannah took Harry's other arm, very lightly. 'Are we ready? Then off we go.'

The House of the Waterbirds was set upon a rise of ground on the west bank of the river. The house stood within a grove of palms, was large and cool, and built about a series of courtyards in which water played and roofed colonnades threw welcome shade. The whitewashed walls were substantial, the marble floors shone smooth and beautiful. Doves perched and cooed upon the shallow, tiled roof and in the courtyard trees. It was furnished with restraint and in keeping with its setting: low divans and stools, vivid cushions and rugs, bright copper and silver, the European furniture plain and remarkably uncluttered. Greeted by their hosts and urged on into the shadowed interior to where silent-footed servants dispensed refreshing lemonade and tiny sweetmeats, Hannah exclaimed in pleasure. 'What a lovely house! Laila, don't you think it's beautiful?'

Laila flicked a lustrous glance disinterestedly about her. 'The Winter House is better. Harry, some lemonade, please.'

'You must see the garden; it is my wife's pride and joy.' Charles Mansfield had come up behind them, bluffly smiling. 'We're above the floods here, but have of course the advantage of the wonderful soil and the water. Mrs Mansfield is a passionate gardener –' he extended an arm to Laila, who ignored it and another to Hannah, who did not '– come, I'll introduce you to the other guests, and then later, perhaps, I could show you around?'

Hannah accepted the arm. 'How very kind.'

He led them through a courtyard towards an archway, from which issued the hum of conversation and laughter. Beyond the arch was a terrace, paved and shaded, that commanded a magnificent view of shining river and green, fertile plain, of the huddle of mud-coloured buildings that was Luxor and of the great spread of ancient temples and monuments that lay on both sides of the Nile, the remnants of ancient Thebes. Hannah gazed around. 'It's perfectly beautiful.' There were forty, per-

346

haps fifty people on the terrace already, mostly European. The non-Europeans were, she noted with no surprise, all men.

'We like it. Now, let me introduce you to Mr and Mrs Best – quite charming people from Epsom – ' he beamed at the plump little woman and her equally plump little husband ' – it is Epsom, isn't it? Mr and Mrs Best are on the Cook's steamer, you know.'

Hannah acknowledged the introduction. From the far side of the terrace Sibyl Rainsford's eyes had brightened at the sight of the newcomers and she waved. A little way from her a handsome couple stood, apparently absorbed in their own conversation; yet the woman's blue eyes flicked back and forth across the crowd as if looking for someone. They settled for a moment, dismissively upon Hannah, sharpened as they moved to Harry who, with Laila on his arm, was moving through the crowd behind her. Fenella Hampshire spoke a swift word to her companion, a tall, tanned, moustachioed man of about thirty, whose sleek brown head gleamed copper in the sun, laid a hand briefly on his arm, then turned and began to push through the crowd towards Harry. Hannah watched men's heads turn as she moved across the terrace. She passed within a foot of Hannah and did not even acknowledge her; yet Hannah, who could not for her life keep a derisive gleam from her eye as she watched the ill-mannered display, fancied that a little colour lifted in the lovely, pale face and flushed the soft expanse of exposed bosom as she passed.

'Why, Captain Sherwood,' Fenella called, her deep, husky voice pitched at a level to attract attention from every ear on the terrace, 'whatever happened to your pretty face? Did some poor benighted husband finally catch up with you?'

Hannah turned away, taking her host's arm, distracting him with a smile. 'Please, I'd love to see your garden. Would you show me?'

Harry had murmured something, angrily. Laila had drawn closer to him, clinging to his arm, looking up at Fenella with bright eyes and lifted chin, her very smile a provocation.

Hannah moved away. This was Harry's war. She wanted nothing of it. 'How absolutely charming.' The path from the terrace led through a perfect jungle of exotic plants to a small clearing in which a pool clothed in lilies glimmered in the sunshine. Beyond, through palms, the Nile glistened. Each turn of the path brought a new and artful surprise: an ancient statue, a pebbled pool, a tiny summerhouse, a brilliantly blooming bed of shrubs. They nodded and passed pleasantries with another couple who paced the paths. Above them the talk and laughter, which had abated a little, grew loud again. Hannah glanced up. Fenella Hampshire had rejoined her attentive companion, who leaned towards her, one hand possessively upon her bare arm. She shook it off with an impatient gesture, yet smiled her bright and glittering smile up into his face, and he, hastily, reached for a chair upon which she could settle, lovely as a butterfly in blue and silver. What fools men could be, Hannah found herself thinking tartly, when it came to a pretty face. She watched for a moment longer. Fenella's new swain was offering her lemonade, tempting her with a tiny cake. She took it, bit into it with shining teeth. Turned her head to look back onto the crowded terrace; and for a moment from her vantage point below Hannah glimpsed a flash of real hatred that hardened that pale, beautiful face and distorted it almost to ugliness. She did not have to follow the direction of the cold blue eyes to see at whom the look was directed. Hannah turned away. If anyone knew how to handle the dangers of a woman scorned it must surely be Harry Sherwood. And if he did not, why, it was certainly none of her business anyway. 'I'm sorry?' Her companion had asked a question and was waiting.

'I was suggesting tea – down in the colonnades there, do you see? Overlooking the river. It's the coolest place in the garden at this time of day.'

It was an hour or so later, after a pleasant interval spent with the Rainsfords and the MacDonalds, that Hannah noticed that Laila had disappeared. She stood on the terrace, scanning the thinning crowds. In the shade of the portico, Harry was deep in conversation with three or four other men. The Mansfields, who had proved such engaging hosts, were in another group seated about a fountain. Others, in couples or in larger groups, were scattered about the terrace, but there was no sign of Laila.

Nor of Fenella Hampshire.

The realization filled Hannah with unease. She looked again, more carefully. There could be no doubt; neither was there. Fenella's escort stood, ill at ease, with a middle-aged woman who talked animatedly at him whilst he too, Hannah noticed, was searching with his eyes for his missing partner.

Hannah strolled to the edge of the terrace. The sun was dipping in a magnificently blazing sky. She was hot now, sticky and tired, the train of her dress dragged behind her like some monstrous, heavy tail, holding her back. The corsets and bones that constricted her body had chafed her sore. All at once she wanted nothing but the cool deck of the dahabeeyah, her loose, unconventional clothing, their small, safe little brotherhood of discussion and laughter.

Far below her, upon one of the marble benches in the now-deserted colonnade where she had taken tea with Mr Mansfield, she saw them: silver and blue, and rose pink, fair head and dark, the prettiest of pictures, Fenella's straw hat with its decoration of dove's wings laid upon the bench beside her.

Hannah, unmindful of ceremony, lifted her skirts in both hands and hurried to the steps that led down to the path.

It took what seemed an age. At each turn of the path she glimpsed them; saw Laila's distraught attempt to rise, saw the strong, white hand that held her back. Saw, as she got closer, the expression of malice on the fair face as Madam Mischief did her worst. Hannah could not disguise her coming; as she saw them so she knew Fenella saw her. That she would arrive too late to prevent whatever devilment the other woman had in mind was obvious from the first. When, hot and breathless, she reached the end of the colonnade, it was to see Fenella Hampshire walking towards her, the setting sun gleaming upon the spun gold of her hair, no fold of her dress displaced, her charming hat swinging by its ribbons from her hand. Hannah watched her. As she approached she neither slowed nor quickened her even stride. Her smile was tranquil, the gleam in her eye spiteful. She nodded as she passed, as if acknowledging an acquaintance upon the promenade at Brighton. 'Good evening, Miss Standish.' And she was gone.

Laila sat as if struck to stone, the ivory tone of her skin paled to the colour of the marble upon which she rested.

Hannah sat beside her. Took the girl's cold hand in both of hers. 'Laila? Laila my dear, what is it?'

Laila shook her head.

'Laila – whatever she said – ignore it. She's a wicked, mischievous woman.'

'If you please,' Laila said, without looking at her, 'I should like to leave. Now.'

Hannah looked at her helplessly.

Laila stood. 'Now,' she repeated.

Harry was enjoying himself. The talk had turned to horses, and a small bottle of real Scotch whisky had appeared. 'Best little filly I ever saw,' one of his new acquaintances was saying, 'ran the legs off the rest – won by a mile and made me a fortune.'

Hannah touched his arm. 'Harry.'

He stepped reluctantly to one side, one ear still on the conversation. 'Yes?'

'It's Laila. She's –' Hannah hesitated '– she isn't feeling too well. I think I should take her back to the *Horus*.'

'Ah.' Harry's disappointment was as obvious as a boy's. 'Right – I'll say my goodbyes and join you –'

'No.' Hannah shook her head firmly. 'There's no need for that. We have the men to escort us back. You stay. We'll see you later.'

Harry made one more small effort. 'You're sure?'

'Of course I am. Stay as long as you like.'

His hesitation lasted only a moment longer. 'Right. If you need me send Abdo, or one of the crew.'

'I will.'

Laila awaited her at the front door, still silent, still with that frozen, stricken look of sickness upon her lovely face that caused the other departing guests to glance at her in curiosity. 'Is the young lady all right?' their hostess enquired anxiously.

'I must say she looks quite unwell. Are you certain she wouldn't like to stay? We have plenty of room.'

Hannah shook her head again. 'You're very kind but no, thank you. I can take care of her.'

Laila spoke not a word on the way back to the river. Nor for a long time did she speak once they were safe back aboard the *Horus*. At Hannah's suggestion, she changed into a cooler and more comfortable robe whilst Hannah did the same, and called for tea. When Laila reappeared on deck looking like a subdued child in rust-coloured silk, there were tear stains on her cheeks, and her eyes were red.

'Now,' Hannah said at last, settled beside her on a long, cushioned sofa and reaching for her hand, 'what did she say that was so very terrible? Tell me.'

Harry much enjoyed his evening. He had not realized how long a time it had been since he had last been in exclusively male company. With the rest of the guests gone and Mrs Mansfield, with much appreciated tact, retiring to her bed with a book, he, his host and two or three others sat on through the dazzling sunset emptying the bottle, talking war and politics, discussing the latest, wildest rumours about the true fate of General Gordon. It was fully dark by the time he returned, whistling softly as he walked to the dahabeeyah.

He saw as he came to the riverbank that the *Horus* was almost in darkness. Her mooring lights hung stem and stern, a lantern lit the gangplank and another burned on the upper passenger deck. The air had turned cooler and a faint breeze stirred the waters of the river, flapped the furled sails of the dahabeeyahs and feluccas that lay at anchor. He leaped lightly onto the plank, swung his way onto the boat, ran up the steps to the upper deck two at a time.

'Harry.'

Hannah's voice stopped him in his tracks. He peered into the darkness. She was sitting in a chair just out of the circle of lamplight. Her voice sounded strained. He took a step towards her. 'Hannah? Is that you? Is Laila all right?'

351

There was a moment's silence. Hannah took a breath he could hear. 'Harry, could you spare me a moment? I need to talk to you.'

Baffled but not overly concerned, he walked to where she sat and perched on the seat beside her, elbows on knees, hands loosely linked as he peered through the darkness at her. 'Well, of course. What is it?'

Since she had finally succumbed to Laila's hysterical pleading and seen her and her nurse safely escorted to the house of Ali abd Ela, Hannah had sat for hours anticipating this moment. She had examined and discarded a dozen ways to tell him what had happened. The longer she had turned it over in her mind, the more it had become clear to her; and the more she had come to understand what this might mean to Harry. Her anger at his own stupidity, which had set off this chain of events that could become a scandal that almost certainly would destroy him, had long since evaporated. Who knew what had driven him to betray his own secret, and to one so untrustworthy?

Hannah stood up, smoothing her gown with flat, nervous hands, turned from him to lean against one of the supports of the awning. She could not bear to watch his face as she spoke.

'Laila was not ill this afternoon.' Her voice was quiet and perfectly calm, she kept all emotion at bay as she spoke. 'She was – very upset. Mrs Hampshire had been extremely abusive to her.' She paused.

'She called me a little half-breed!' Laila had sobbed. 'She said the most awful things! Half-nigger, she said, touch of the tar-brush – filthy, she said I was filthy – a savage! And she was smiling, smiling all the time.' Hannah's lips tightened again with an almost uncontrollable fury. Not for the first time that evening she wished for a few quiet moments alone with Fenella Hampshire.

'Abusive?' she could hear the puzzlement, the beginnings of anger in Harry's tone. 'How, abusive?'

It was not in Hannah's nature to be anything but straightforward. 'She told her that your interest in Laila was based entirely upon what she chose to describe as Laila's "black blood". She said you could not mate with a respectable white woman

352

because – ' she took a breath, ' – because, she said, by your own admission to her you yourself are half black. She said – she said your father was a Negro slave. She used, needless to say, the most offensive language possible.' She turned to face his deadly silence. 'I'm sorry. But I had to tell you. You had to know. Harry, she's told Laila – she *enjoyed* telling her. She'll tell others. It's as certain as the day!'

He had not moved; seemed barely to be breathing. His face was blank with shock.

'Harry?' she asked, gently. 'It's true?' She had long since drawn her own conclusion; not even Fenella would dare to spread such calumny had it been ill-based.

For a long moment he neither moved nor spoke, then he raised bleak eyes to hers. 'That my father was a slave? Yes, it's true. But that I would ever dream of misusing a child's trust in such a way?'

'No! Harry, of course not! I never for one moment believed that you would.' For a second, faced with the terrible depth of his distress, her own hard-held control all but failed her. Yet she had learned in a hard school that to nurse a desperately wounded man one must keep a clear head and above all a cool and unemotional heart. 'Laila has gone to her father's agent's house,' she said, after a moment, when her voice once more was flawlessly calm. 'She insisted, I could not prevent it. She says she will not come back aboard the *Horus*. One can't blame her; she really is most terribly confused and distressed. She wants to leave Luxor tomorrow, overland for Aswan and the Winter House.'

He shook his head, blindly. 'She surely doesn't believe what that poisonous woman told her? She surely doesn't think that I would – ?' He stopped, dropped his face into his hands.

'She doesn't know what to believe. Harry, she has no defences against a woman like Fenella Hampshire.'

'I'll talk to her. I'll talk to her tomorrow – '

'I doubt she'll listen. If you have to tell her – and you do – that there was truth in what Fenella told her, then how is she to understand where to draw the line? She's a child – and it has to be said, charming as she is, a spoiled and self-centred child.

Listen.' Hannah moved to him at last, dropped to one knee on the deck before him, took his hand. 'Talk to her by all means, if she'll allow it. But if not, let her go. I'll go with her – she's in my charge, and I cannot do anything but see her safe into her father's care. We can take a couple of men from the crew, and anyway we'll be perfectly safe travelling by train. And while I'm with her, I'll talk to her; she'll listen, in the end she'll listen, I'm sure. And in the meanwhile –' She paused.

'And in the meanwhile,' he said, bleakly smiling, taking his hand from hers and standing abruptly, 'in the meanwhile my ghastly secret is out – or soon will be – and my career, such as it has been, in Her Britannic Majesty's bastard army is over.'

She said nothing. They both knew it to be the simple truth.

'Why?' she asked after a moment, coming to her feet beside him. 'Harry, in God's name! Why did you tell her?'

'I was drunk. And when I'm drunk I'm inclined to take risks. Haven't you noticed?' His voice was grimly self-derisive; he could not be blamed, she told herself, flinching, for the fact that another, more personal interpretation might be put on the words.

He walked to the rail, leaned on it. Again, painfully, she was reminded of that other night; and thinking of it, some small illumination suddenly lit the puzzle of Harry's reaction to his mother's letter. There were so many questions. So much she wanted to know.

'You'll take the dahabeeyah on to Aswan?' she asked. 'I can take Laila to her father's house and meet you there.'

Harry nodded. His face was drawn, the wound stood out, black against the bleached skin. With quiet movements she busied herself for a moment, came to him with a small glass, half full. She proffered it. 'Strictly medicinal.'

He took it without a word, tossed it back.

She walked back to the table, refilled the glass. Again he took it. Turned from her, looking into the night. The breeze fluttered the awning, lifted their hair, whispered in the rigging.

'When she told me – my mother – I couldn't – wouldn't! – believe it. I was eighteen years old. I was in love. I was a normal,

354

ordinary English boy, living a normal, ordinary English life. And then she told me.'

Hannah waited while he fought the battle for composure. 'What? What did she tell you?'

'That my father was a slave.' Suddenly his head went back. The hand holding the glass shook. 'Damn his soul to hell – my father was a slave!'

'How?' she asked, dismissing with calm practicality the desire to scream, to burst into useless tears. 'How did it happen?'

'What?' He turned his head blindly.

Relentlessly patient, she repeated, 'How did it happen?' She remembered the letter, the clear, intelligent, sensitive letter. She had sensed a kindred spirit. So much now had become clearer, so much more obscure. 'Harry – won't you tell me?'

'I don't know. I – don't remember.' Mattie's words of explanation he had heard through a merciless anger; he could barely recall them. He passed the back of his hand across his mouth. Each word was an effort. 'It was during the war – the American war – the man was brother to my fa– to my mother's husband. They were left alone – caught in Sherman's march to the sea –'

'So.' Hannah considered that. 'You're saying – your mother wasn't –' Even for a woman as strong-minded as she, the subject was so indelicate she could not bring herself to finish the sentence.

'Forced?' Harry threw back his head and laughed. She steeled herself against the sound. 'Oh no. Oh, absolutely not. She was at pains to point that out. She loved him, Hannah.' His voice dropped so low she could barely hear it, but the venom in it turned her blood cold. 'The bitch loved him,' he said.

'And why not?' Sudden anger burned. 'What are you saying? That the colour of a man's skin should make him an outcast? That the blood of such a man through no fault of his own stains his character, makes him less than human? That it is some sort of crime for a woman to love such a man?' Only then, looking into his face, did she realize what she was saying. Only then, in his face, did she see at last the barbarous pain he had suffered.

There was a very long moment's silence. 'No, Harry,' she said then, quietly, 'you're wrong. Entirely wrong.'

His smile was savage. 'You think so?'

'I know so.' Very deliberately she put her hands to his face, brought his lips to hers, kissed him as he, once, had kissed her. In that moment she cared nothing for what of herself she might be betraying; in that moment she would have given anything he asked.

He wrapped his arms about her, stood for a long while, head bowed, his cheek on her hair. When at last they stepped apart he was calmer. That she was not she took care to hide, taking refuge in short-term organization. 'So it's agreed?' she asked, briskly. 'I'll take Laila to her father – you and Abdo sail the *Horus* on to Aswan, and I'll meet you there.'

'Yes.' He had stepped away from her, self-absorbed, made no attempt to touch her, barely looked at her.

'What will you do?' she asked.

'I don't know. Resign my Commission, of course. Go back to the Legion, perhaps. No-one cares who you are there.'

She swallowed sharp, perhaps even bitter words; thus far she would go, but no further. Would Harry Sherwood ever learn, she wondered, that he was not the only one in the world with pride? The thought, if nothing else, served to clear her head and edge her voice with a dispassionate clarity. 'I still don't understand. All these years – and now this. Why did you tell her? Fenella Hampshire of all people? Drunk or sober, you must have known what a risk you were taking? Sooner or later only harm could have come of it.'

Harry took a moment to answer. The wind had risen further. The water slapped choppily at the side of the boat, the *Horus* shifted on the swell. 'I've known men go into battle for the first time, and discover terror,' he said at last, 'then again, and again, only to discover that the fear worsens, and the anticipation becomes even worse than the reality. It eats at them. The fear of death. The fear of mutilation. The fear of cowardice.'

She had stilled, was watching him, puzzled. 'You've known such fear?'

He shook his head. 'Not of battle, no. That isn't my devil,

thank God. We're all made differently. Different things frighten us, do they not?'

She said nothing, beginning to understand.

'I have known such men,' he continued thoughtfully after a moment, as if she had not interrupted, 'to throw themselves upon an enemy bayonet. To invite, at last, that which they most fear.'

The furled sail clapped above them. The pages of a magazine riffled open.

She was desperate to leave him; equally desperate to stay. 'Go to bed, Hannah,' he said. 'There is nothing you can do.'

She left him at the rail, looking into the windy night. The tears she kept at bay until at last she was alone.

Laila would not speak to Harry; nothing would persuade her. She was a hurt child, and like any hurt child she wanted to go home. There was no swaying her. A fruitless day was wasted before Harry accepted the inevitable and agreed to Hannah's plan. He still had a job to do, and now more than ever he wanted to do it well. With Hannah and Laila safely out of the way, he and Abdo would have a freer hand. Who knew, perhaps they would pick up the trail of the guns again; for certain he was, now, that guns had been stored in the slave warehouse. Sailing steadily and with no stops for sightseeing or socializing, they should reach Aswan in four or five days. Hannah would get there well before them; she would settle Laila in her father's house, and meet them when they arrived. Whatever mischief the mendacious Mrs Hampshire planned could not harm him until he got back to Cairo. Willy nilly then he supposed he would have to resign his Commission – before rather than after such action was requested of him; he would think no further than that.

The cool, windy weather held. The *Horus* made excellent time up the river. Both Abdo and the Reis seemed to accept without question Hannah's story that Laila was feeling unwell and had decided to take the quicker land route to the Winter House and the comforts and luxuries of home. For Harry these few days were far from unhappy; much as he had enjoyed the company of the women, there was something to be said for the Spartan male regime that now held sway on the dahabeeyah. There were no trips to temples and ruins, no polite tea-parties on the *Ra*, no requests for early stops and late starts, no endless demands upon his courtesy and his patience. He had time to think, time to come to terms with what had happened; time, even to convince himself that in the end all would be to the good. There were many places in the world where a man with Harry Sherwood's skills and reputation could sell his strong arm and his sword with no questions asked; there were lands unexplored and adventures still to be experienced; gold to be earned, if a man were not too fastidious. In the meantime, with the ladies safely out of the way and time on his hands, he took Abdo up on his offer of knife-throwing lessons, and watched himself with strange dispassion as, at first, he steeled himself against flinching from the touch of the other man's hand as he demonstrated the heft and hold of the knife, the closeness of his body as he stood behind him guiding his arm and his eye to the target. After two days he could send the blade whistling silently into a target a few inches wide; by the time Aswan hovered, shimmering, upon the horizon like a domed and minareted mirage, he could hit the exact spot almost every time. And meanwhile in those days an ease had grown between the two men that Harry would never have believed possible just a short time before. The shift in perception that he had to admit had begun with Hannah's withering anger at his attitude to Abdo, and had been reinforced when Abdo had saved his life at obvious risk to his own, was completed as they worked together helping to sail the dahabeeyah or honing and perfecting their expertise with the deadly throwing knives. And, as can so often happen, with that change came others, as important, as one room may lead onto another once the key to the door has been discovered. Looking back, Harry found himself uncomfortable with the recollection of his reaction to his mother's last letter; he would write, he told himself, not now, but soon, and wish her well. To his surprise the thought was a quite extraordinarily soothing one.

However, as he stood in the prow of the *Horus* beneath the graceful billow of sail, watching the city of Aswan move closer with each bend of the great river, five days after they had left Luxor, such domestic thoughts were far from his mind. For by then he had found the brooch, and an obstinate, unsettling unease made him glance up at the full sail, urging the dahabeeyah on, anxious to make landfall; anxious above all to see Hannah's wide, calm smile, hear the crisp and confident voice – to know that the wild suspicions that assailed him were as laughable as his good sense told him they were; to know that she was safe.

Harry had found the brooch the day before, wedged between the polished floorboards of the upper deck when he had bent to pick up a book. The thing had glittered at him as the dahabeeyah came about and the sun swept the deck. Prising it up with his fingernail, he had recognized it as the jewelled trinket he had helped Laila to pin to her robe on the day they had arrived at Luxor. A scarab, in gold, with extended claws that entrapped a carved hieroglyph . . .

He had looked at it for a long time; then swiftly dropped it in his pocket, spun on his heels and ran down the stairs that led to the sleeping quarters.

Laila's departure, as might be expected, had been chaotic. Many of her possessions were still in her small cabin, scattered like a child's discarded toys. He picked up a chased silver mirror; the scarab and its small mysterious sign was set upon the back. A hairbrush too carried the mark, and a tiny box that held a silken powder puff. The mark of Ayman el Akad, Laila's father.

The mark Harry had seen upon the broken lid of the box in the slave-pen at Luxor, where three men had tried to kill him.

CHAPTER EIGHTEEN

Harry well knew how unlikely it was that Hannah could possibly be on the quayside at Aswan awaiting them. However, as the *Horus* was deftly manoeuvred through the reefs, sandbanks and the busy river traffic and slipped into her mooring, still he hoped, and was disappointed when she was not. Nor, he quickly discovered, when he went ashore to make enquiries and to put the *Horus* on the governor's list to be taken up the cataracts two days hence, was she registered at either of the tourist hotels she had mentioned. No-one of their acquaintance, so far as Harry could see, had reached Aswan before them; the *Ra* was far behind and there were no other dahabeeyahs he recognized. Yet, he told himself, there was the possibility that she had met with old friends, or made some new acquaintance – or, he supposed, even more likely, that she had been invited to stay with Laila and her father at the Winter House for a couple of days. She could not have known exactly when the *Horus* would arrive. Wherever she was, sooner or later news would reach her, and she would come.

He got back to the *Horus* in the heat of mid-morning, finding to his surprise that Abdo meanwhile had gone ashore and not returned. With a patience that wore thinner with each hour and a growing concern that no attempt at rationalization could quell, he waited alone for Hannah, standing by the rail, watching the business of the thronged and noisy beach, upon which all sorts of commerce thrived, expecting at any moment to see the pale smiling face and the wiry red-gold mop coming towards him. But the morning wore on, and there was no sign. A camel train arrived to unload its bales onto a flat-bottomed cargo-boat, the usual swarms of donkey-boys and souvenir-sellers besieged the dahabeeyah, their wares different here from those he had seen further north. For Aswan was the gateway to Nubia, and the goods for sale here were of almost pagan workmanship: silver brooches and ivory bangles, great ostrich feathers, native spears, bows and arrows. He waved the eager, grasping hands away impatiently; and still there was neither sign nor news of Hannah.

Aswan was another baking stop for the crew of the dahabee-yah. Harry watched as the dragoman set off in search of flour, and the Reis hurried ashore to book a public oven. The day had begun overcast and uncomfortably hot. The lush green vegetation that edged the banks and clothed the great, bouldered Elephantine Island that here split the river into two channels before it plunged south into the cataracts hung limp and still. At last, in mid-afternoon, Harry could stand it no longer. On his exploration of the town that morning he had marked the existence of a stables behind the bazaar. He had also made enquiries as to the whereabouts of Ayman el Akad's Winter House, and had had pointed out to him the wide, stony, well-used track that led the four or five miles upstream through the granite heights of the Arabian bank to the valley where the house was situated. He would wait no longer; the logical likelihood was that Hannah was at the Winter House, perfectly well and safe. He would ride out and let her know that the *Horus* had arrived, her passage up the First Cataract to Philae – an experience he knew Hannah to be anticipating with some excitement – booked for the day after next. At the mere thought of physical action he felt more cheerful. A desert ride after the past few days cooped up on the *Horus* would do him good, and once the niggling worry of Hannah's whereabouts and safety had been settled, he could get back to the business of the guns and of his own future. The steamer on which Fenella was travelling had proceeded no further south than the barrier of Aswan and the cataracts, and had already turned back; it had passed them yesterday on its return voyage to Cairo. It would not be long before the woman Hannah had nicknamed so appropriately 'Madam Mischief' would be well placed to cause whatever mayhem she had decided upon. Oddly, he found the thought far less disturbing than he would previously have believed possible. The secret he had struggled for so long to conceal·was out, and there was nothing he could do about it. In some ways it was a relief – a shadow whose fearful threat had been dispersed by facing it in sunlight. There were other places than Egypt, other armies than the British, other ways of measuring self-esteem than by blood.

Harry strode up towards the town through the shifting kaleido-scope that was the traders' camp, where men of business of all ages, all colours, and many nationalities were settled amongst the bales of their merchandise awaiting transport north to the markets of Cairo and Alexandria. Small stone-built ovens, steaming kettles and the strong smell of coffee added to the feeling of a permanent settlement engendered by the energetic comings and goings, the lively groups of robed and turbaned merchants, the inevitable barefoot urchins, and the noisy packs of scavenging dogs. He kept an observant eye cocked, wondering if Abdo might not be somewhere here pursuing his business, but saw no sign of him. In the town he brushed aside the eager attentions of the camel-men anxious to persuade him to partake of the privilege of a ride into the desert upon a tasselled and obnoxious beast – a dubious pleasure which no self-respecting tourist was expected to avoid – and finally, after a few minutes' impatient haggling that left the stable owner aggrieved at the brevity of the ceremony but better off than he deserved to be, he was at last in the worn saddle and riding through the outskirts of the mud-built town that straggled along the shore. Here the rocks and whirlpools of the cataract replaced the wide, placid waters Harry had come to know. A dahabeeyah was being manoeuvred upstream; men stood gracefully balanced upon rocks above the vicious swirling of the waters, singing out to each other as the ropes were tossed from hand to hand, and the boat hauled on, difficult yard by difficult yard. Anxious as he was to push on, Harry could not resist for a moment reining in to watch. Slender and wiry, the men leaped from rock to rock, sure and lightfooted as deer, whilst the crew aboard the dahabeeyah laboured with oar and with sail, guiding the vessel through the waters whose peril was well illustrated by the wreckage everywhere, jammed between the granite boulders or cast upon the mud of the shore.

Harry urged his mount forward – he was a sorry beast, thin as a cat and long overdue an honourable retirement he would no doubt never be allowed to enjoy – still watching the fascinating activity. Then the trail he was following swung away from the river and into the narrow entrance of a hot, shadeless valley that ran straight as an arrow, rising slowly but steadily into the granite heights. Sand sifted against the raised, rocky trail, gave off a warmth that was stifling into air that was already all but unbreathable. The sky had cleared a little, though the sun was baleful still through a copper haze of clouds. High above a huge bird of prey wheeled, dipping below the valley edge, reappearing, soaring lazily. Harry narrowed his eyes against the shimmering heat, thinking he saw movement on the hillside, but as he reined in for a moment and scanned the granite cliffs all was still and quiet. He followed the clear track, the splayed footprints of camels, the smaller marks of man and horse, and the scuffed signs of a donkey train. The animal he rode was incapable of a speed much faster than the walking pace of a man; once or twice he found himself, despite the barb of urgency that still prickled at the back of his mind, having to force himself to stay awake as the animal plodded on with steady, swaying movement.

At the head of the valley, exactly as had been described to him, the trail wound on for perhaps a mile across a small rocky plateau before dropping down towards the valley of the Winter House. Here the temperature was higher than ever, the hypnotic regularity of his mount's gait an even more irresistible invitation to doze beneath the shade of the wide brim of his hat, to leave the animal to find its own way, as it was undoubtedly capable of doing.

The coming of the silent Bedouin horsemen as the track rounded a pile of boulders and revealed the stunning sight of the valley below took him entirely by surprise.

They sat, three of them, poised, dark-faced and watchful, swathed gracefully against the sun in immaculate robes of bleached white. Long, threatening rifles were cradled casually across one arm, their mounts were strong and swift-looking, standing like statues across the path. Jolted awake, and swinging his mount away from the human barrier, it did nothing for Harry's confidence to find three more ranged as calmly behind him. Cursing himself for being so easily caught, he steadied his horse and sat in silence, waiting.

No-one spoke. One of the three men ahead of him made an easy gesture. In a spray of sand and fine, tossing heads an escort was formed, and Harry found himself, willy nilly, and necessarily at a pace dictated by his scrawny mount, heading down towards the green vision below.

The house, vast, white and sprawling, nestled in gardens of palm and of flowering shrub; pools gleamed in courtyard and grove, lush greenery rambled about walls and framed arches and windows. Some distance from the house a tiny, palm-edged lake – obviously the source of the water used so lavishly upon the gardens – divided it from an ordered collection of long, low businesslike buildings, enclosed behind a high and substantial mud wall. More palms shaded an enclosure full of camels and donkeys, and beyond them smoke rose from a small encampment of the large and airy skin-draped tents of the Bedouin; the home, Harry could only assume, of his silent guard. There the lush green stopped, and the valley ended in a sloping cliff face studded with the inevitable, irregular openings of ancient rock tombs. The whole looked peaceful, prosperous and in these stark surroundings beautiful in the extreme. Harry found himself remembering Laila's casual, 'The Winter House is better,' and had to acknowledge it to be nothing but the truth.

The track, firm, easily negotiable and eminently defensible, wound down into the valley. Hedged in by his escort, stoically resisting the urge to curse himself and his ridiculous mount aloud and roundly, Harry descended it with as much dignity as he could muster. In the wide sweep of raked sand that fronted the house he dismounted, and a white-clad servant, as silent as the Bedouin, took the rein and led the horse away into the shade.

'This way.'

He followed the tall Bedouin through the open door and into the cool, magnificent interior. The entrance hall was amber and gold, and dominated by a golden figure of Anubis, the jackal-headed god. The walls were hung with silken prayer rugs, and there were shelves of jewelled artefacts – figurines, goblets, platters – that could only have come from plundered tombs.

Beyond the hall was a spacious room, very cool and comfortable, in which several large divans were set about low tables. Upon one of them reclined a slight man wearing a softly draped embroidered robe. His skin was smooth and olive-coloured, his eyes, his most striking feature, were heavy-lidded and lustrous. His sleek black hair lay smooth against a well-shaped skull. His expression, Harry noted with sinking heart, could not be described as welcoming.

'Captain Sherwood, I presume?'

'Yes, Sir.'

'I am Ayman el Akad.' Gracefully the man came to his feet. He was a full head shorter than Harry, yet his presence was such that the lack of inches was barely noticeable.

'A moment.' He clapped his hands sharply. Within a second a young man entered, bearing a tray upon which were tall glasses of lemonade, a pot of coffee and two small cups and a dish of dates. These laid quietly upon the table, the young man left, though not, Harry noticed, without a small, brightly enquiring glance in his direction.

'Please.' Courteously Laila's father waved a hand.

Harry took a glass of lemonade, perched upon the edge of a divan. The other man poured coffee, settled back, watching him. 'Your visit surprises me,' he said quietly, in perfect and absolutely accentless English, 'and I have to admit cannot be said to please me. In the story my daughter tells, you do not emerge very creditably.'

Harry sipped his lemonade, set the glass carefully down upon the table.

'I'm sorry that should be so, Sir,' he said, with equal care. 'The last thing that any of us wanted is that your daughter should have been distressed.'

'I entrusted her to your care – yours and Miss Standish's.

That the trip should have been so ill-managed – the dahabeeyah so uncomfortable, her quarters so cramped that she felt it necessary to cut short her stay with you, does not please me.'

Harry let out a small, relieved breath. It had occurred to him more than once to wonder what tale Hannah and Laila would concoct to explain their early arrival at the Winter House – for certainly the truth would not under any circumstances do, least of all from Laila's point of view. Hannah, it surely must have been, who had hit upon something so simple.

'I can only apologize, Sir,' he said, with what he hoped was a suitable show of contrition.

The man opposite nodded, coolly courteous. A slightly awkward silence fell. Harry sipped his lemonade then lifted his eyes to find his host still waiting, politely but with thinly concealed impatience. Waiting, he realized with a sudden and alarming premonition, for him, his apology delivered and accepted, to leave.

'Miss Standish –' he began, and as he asked knew with a sinking certainty the reply, '– she's here still?'

The surprise on the other man's face was answer enough. 'Miss Standish? Why, no. Why should she be here?'

'I – thought perhaps she might have stayed?' Harry was totally unprepared for the dismay the news engendered in him. He had been so very sure he would find Hannah safely settled here with Laila.

The sleek dark head shook. 'She came with my daughter, yes. But I have to say, sorry though I am to admit it, my feelings towards her were not perhaps as charitable as they might have been. Laila was obviously unhappy, and she had, after all, been in Miss Standish's care. The suggestion that she might remain here was not made.'

'When did she leave?' Harry's voice had taken on a dangerous edge. God in heaven, he had wasted a day upon this useless trip, whilst Hannah – what? Where was she? What could possibly have happened to her? He stood up.

Ayman el Akad came gracefully to his feet also. 'Two days since,' he said, mildly. 'She said something about friends in Aswan?'

Harry shook his head.

'I'm so sorry; I misunderstood. I assumed it was Miss Standish who had encouraged you to visit – to tender the courtesy of a personal apology.'

Harry found his hands were clenched. With care he relaxed them; with equal care he forced his numbed brain to reason. 'Please – might I speak to your daughter? She may have some idea –' He stopped as the other man lifted a sharp hand.

'I'm afraid that will not be possible.' There was no mistaking the iron chill beneath the icy politeness of the words. 'My daughter has made it quite clear that she does not wish to see or to speak to you or to Miss Standish again. I respect her wish; I expect you to do the same.'

Whatever else, Harry found himself thinking, Hannah's hopes of pacifying Laila appeared to have been comprehensively dashed. 'But –'

'No.' The word, though quiet, was adamant, and the lustrous eyes were markedly unfriendly. Harry was forced for a moment to wonder whether Laila after all had not confessed rather more than was comfortable to this formidable father of hers. He stood helpless. If Laila would not see him there was nothing he could do about it.

'I'm sorry,' el Akad said again. 'If your purpose in coming here was to seek out Miss Standish then I'm afraid you have had a wasted journey.' He clapped his hands again, sharply, twice. 'I'm sure you must be anxious to leave. You will, I am sure, find the adventurous Miss Standish safe somewhere in Aswan. I am certain she is very capable of looking after herself; she seemed to me a lady of very strong character.' The words were obviously not intended to sound anything like a compliment.

Harry heard movement behind him, glanced around to find himself once more hemmed in by the Bedouin who had escorted him from the plateau. His eyes flickered to the long, shining rifles they carried so negligently. 'Yes,' he said. 'I'm sure you're right.'

He allowed himself to be escorted outside where his sorry excuse for a mount awaited him. His host wished him a polite and less than cordial farewell. The red sun had moved to the stark cliff edges that were etched high against the burning sky, and shadows crept across the valley floor. A warm wind had sprung up, dusty, oddly stifling, carrying with it the merest trace of a fetid, unpleasant and unmistakable stench. In silence he swung himself into the creaking saddle, and in silence set off up the steeply winding path. The Bedouin rode behind him, watchfully. As they emerged from the ascent and onto the wide plateau, they reined in their horses and sat motionless, watching Harry, expressionless, as he rode away. For the first few hundred yards his back felt as exposed a target as a barn wall at a hundred paces. He knew from experience the range and accuracy of the long and lethal-looking French Berthier rifles with which they were so efficiently armed; nor did he doubt their ability to use them. He was glad when the flat, rocky plateau was behind him and the track began to dip down into the long, sloping valley that would take him eventually back to the river. He rode deep in uneasy thought and this time with no inclination in the world to sleep.

The movement he caught at the corner of his eye as he passed a stand of granite boulders had him rolling from the saddle and reaching beneath his coat in a single motion.

'Well done, Captain,' Abdo said, encouragingly. 'A couple of seconds faster and you might have made a contest of it.' His own knife was poised between long fingers, balanced and ready to throw. His tall frame was enveloped in a brown woollen robe, the hood thrown back to reveal the fine bones of his face and the gleam of his smile. A small, tasselled woollen saddle bag lay in the sand at his feet.

'Abdo! What in hell's name are you doing here?'

'Hunting,' the other said, briefly. 'As you are.'

Harry sheathed his knife, unsurprised to find his fingers a little less sure of themselves than they should be. These sudden appearances of Abdo's were unnerving. 'Any luck?' he was pleased to hear that his voice fairly matched the other's for coolness.

The smile gleamed again. 'A little. You?'

Harry reached for the reins, drew the animal into the shade

368

of the rocks. 'I found some brand new Berthier rifles in rather strange hands.'

'The Bedouin?'

Harry nodded.

'Ah.'

Harry waited for a moment, his patience precarious. 'Well? You've found something?'

'I've found Miss Standish. I hate to ask, Captain, but is this bag of bones truly the best you could do?'

Harry caught him by the arm, swung him, big as he was, to face him. 'Found her? Found her where?' Then, his eyes on the other man's face, he released his arm and stepped back. 'At the Winter House.' There was only the barest question in the words. 'She's at the Winter House?'

'Yes.'

'You've seen her?'

'From a distance.'

'She's at the Winter House,' Harry said again, as if to himself. 'And I'm the worst kind of fool. Yes, it was,' he added, absently, in answer to Abdo's question about the horse, 'unless I was ready to take a camel or a donkey.' He looked sharply back at Abdo 'You've seen her, you say? She's safe?'

'I said I'd seen her. I didn't say she was safe. I doubt that anyone within a hundred miles of Ayman el Akad is safe.' The words, spoken unemotionally, contained a terrible depth of bitterness.

'Don't riddle me, Abdo. Tell me, how do you know she's there?'

'I told you. I saw her. Walking in the garden, under guard, late this morning.' Abdo took the reins from him, led the horse into the shade of a rock, dropped the reins over the animal's head and tied them to a scrubby thorn. 'Come. It's easier to show you.' He glanced up at the sky. The wind was rising still, rags of clouds scudded from the south. Gritty sand lifted and swirled. He picked up the saddle bag, swung it with ease across his shoulder. 'Follow me.'

*   *   *

They approached this time not openly across the high and exposed track, but through the litter of rocks and boulders that edged the plateau and towards the cliff face with its pockmarks of rock tombs at the far end of the tiny valley. With the watchful Bedouin and their long rifles in mind, Harry was as ready as Abdo to go carefully, but yet there was an awful pressure of urgency in him, a desire to run, to launch himself screaming and barehanded down into the valley and upon those who held Hannah captive. It took all the calm and control acquired over fifteen years of soldiering to follow Abdo's oblique, roundabout route to the top of the valley, flitting from rock to rock, from shadow to shadow. At last they lay together, side by side and flat upon their bellies on a ridge above the gaping tomb mouths. A swift and stormy sunset had begun, the sky was alight with colour, and by contrast, the valley below was shadowed.

'Here, Captain.' Abdo reached into the saddle bag, and, eyes fixed upon the scene below, handed Harry a small pair of binoculars. 'The right-hand side of the building – around the court-yard with the rectangular pool. Look at the window on the outer wall.'

Harry fiddled impatiently with the glasses, swept the shadows, could find nothing, then more slowly quartered the area Abdo had pointed out.

Attached to the bars of a narrow window set into an otherwise blank whitewashed wall, something fluttered bravely, rippling and reflective in the half-light. A ribbon of some pale colour, streaming in the freshening breeze.

'Miss Standish is not without guile,' Abdo said, approvingly. 'Her signal caught my eye. I watched. And saw her when they allowed her to exercise in the courtyard.'

Harry had continued to sweep the compound with the glasses. Two men struggled across the sandy expanse towards one of the long, low buildings behind the mud wall. They carried two large steaming pots of what looked like animal mash. With no comment, Harry passed the glasses back to Abdo.

Abdo scanned the compound. 'Ayman el Akad feeds his other reluctant guests,' he said, softly.

'Is Hannah guarded?' Harry asked after a moment.

'Yes. On the courtyard side, where the door is. The window, as you see, is too high and too narrow to afford any thought of escape.'

'So.' Harry wriggled away from the edge and sat up. A gust of wind ballooned his shirt and stirred his hair. 'Here's a mess,' he said. 'The guns are there and the slaves are there.' He glanced at Abdo, who had also squirmed back from the edge and was sitting with his back propped against a rock. The Nubian nodded calmly. 'But,' Harry continued, 'with Hannah down there as well our hands are tied.' He ran a hand through his damp hair. 'We have to get her out. We have to get her out before we do anything else.'

As if by magic one of the slender, dangerous throwing knives had appeared in Abdo's hand. He smiled behind it, mildly. 'We'll do it,' he said softly, and the knife spun, flashing, in the air to be caught in his dark, steady fingers. 'In sh'Allah.'

The plan Abdo laid before him was simple and, as far as Harry could see, the best they could do in the circumstances. They had to work on the assumption that Hannah was in more or less immediate danger and they must act as swiftly as was possible. Abdo it was who said, with chill lack of emotion, 'He will send her with the slaves. There can be no other reason for the sparing of her life. If she is a prisoner it is because she saw or heard something that made her a danger to el Akad. If he believed her a danger he would not scruple to kill her. But his instincts are those of a merchant; an Arab merchant, a dealer in flesh. There are markets for a white skin, and for the strangeness of her hair, profitable markets. Why kill, when to sell would put silver in the coffers? But that, only, is while he is not threatened. First we must make her safe. Then we bring the soldiers. If the valley should be attacked, and Miss Standish should still be a prisoner, she would not survive the first few moments.'

The waiting was the worst.

It had been agreed that their best chance was to wait until well into the night, to wait for that time when sleep was deepest, and vigilance was least. To wait for the moment when, with luck, the rescue could be made with the minimum risk of the alarm being raised before morning.

They lay belly-down in silence on their ridge, watching the dying glories of the sunset, cursing the rising of the wind, the stinging sand, the fitfulness of the dying light.

Anxiety gnawed at Harry. What if tonight were the night the slavers came? What if they were forced to watch, helpless, as she was taken?

'Sleep,' Abdo said, and laid his head upon his arm.

Harry watched on.

It was perhaps half an hour past midnight, and the temperature had dropped like a stone before they moved. Abdo had already scouted the narrow path that wound between the gaping mouths of the rock tombs to the valley floor. In the fitful light of a moon that disappeared every now and again behind wind-driven rags of clouds, it was negotiable, with care.

'We should have started earlier,' Harry muttered as, painfully slowly, they inched their way down. Below them house and compound slumbered, lit only by the odd glow of a lantern. Nothing moved but the restless wind. A dog barked, and was quiet.

'Patience,' Abdo's voice was tranquil. 'The slavers won't come now before daylight. And by then Miss Standish will be safe and I will be on my way. Have faith. And watch where you are putting your feet.'

It was a long half-hour before they stood in the shadows at the foot of the cliff. Harry reached for one of his knives, and sensed Abdo's movement beside him as he did the same. 'Ready?'

'I'm ready.'

By good fortune the way down the cliff – more a sheep or goat track than a true path – lay between the Bedouin camp and the mud wall of the compound. In the camp a couple of dogs were yelping again, disturbed by the gusting wind. Beyond the compound the white walls of the Winter House gleamed through tossing branches. The noise and disturbance of the wind their ally, they slipped like shadows towards the house. Now that the action had begun all anxiety, all excitement had left Harry; cool and alert, he experienced an almost pleasurable frisson of anticipation. It was a feeling he recognized, a feeling he associated with the suspended moments before the sound of trumpet and of gunfire, of the savage shouts of men launched into battle.

The gate of the compound was guarded; two robed figures leaned, half asleep, in the shadows, sheltering from the wind, but they noticed nothing as Harry and Abdo, using the sheltering shadows, slipped past them.

They had made the simplest of plans, no words were necessary. At the corner of the house they split up, Abdo disappearing like a ghost into the darkness. Harry made his way around the outer wall to where the ribbon still fluttered bravely in the wind. The bars were within easy reach above him. He grasped them and hauled himself up.

A very small lamp burned in the room, which was furnished sparsely with chair and table and small divan. Upon the divan Hannah lay, fully clothed, her hair a dishevelled tangle about her face. A sudden surge of feeling that went far beyond simple relief jolted through him, taking him utterly by surprise. 'Hannah!' The word was a breath that mingled with the sound of the wind.

Hannah did not stir.

'Hannah! Wake up! Hannah!'

She started awake and sat up in one movement, hands raised to defend herself, mouth open to scream.

'Hannah, no! It's me – Harry – Hannah, don't make a noise – not a sound!' His voice was low and urgent. They had guessed this would be the danger – that Hannah, overwrought and frightened, unexpectedly roused, might herself give them away.

Her drawn face was white as paper, her eyes huge. She looked thinner than he remembered her. But her smile had not changed. 'Harry!' She sat stock still, looking up at him. Then 'Harry!' she whispered again, and jumped to her stockinged feet, moving swiftly across the room towards the window.

'Ssh!'

She nodded her understanding.

Harry's arms were failing him. He jerked his head towards the door of the room, mouthed Abdo's name twice.

Eyes still fixed upon him, she nodded again, quickly, turned to watch the door. Harry cautiously let himself back down to the ground, flexed his arms for a moment. When he hauled himself up again Hannah was sitting on the divan hastily pulling her boots on. The door rattled as the key was inserted in the lock. She cast a swift, anxious glance up at Harry, then faced the door, backed as far away as she could get, hands flat against the wall beside her.

The door swung inwards. Abdo's tall, robed figure all but filled the dark opening for a moment. Then he turned and bent to his burden. Blood darkened the white robe of the dead man he dragged through the door and pitched onto the divan. Harry saw Hannah clamp her lower teeth into her lip as she watched Abdo, with nerveless efficiency, arrange the corpse and cover it with a rug. Any small trick that might gain them precious time was worth trying.

Abdo looked up at the window and nodded. 'All's clear.'

Harry let himself down once more to the dusty ground, leaned against the wall and waited.

They slipped around the corner seconds later. For the briefest of moments Hannah clung to him, tense and trembling. He rested his cheek on her wild, wiry hair, his arms tight enough about her to stop her breath. Then she stepped back. 'What now?' Her whisper was calm. Her hand still held Harry's. The wind buffeted, the moon slid from behind a moving cloud and lit for a moment her white, composed face.

'We run like hell,' Harry said, encouragement in his voice. 'But quietly.' He turned.

She tugged at his hand. 'The road's that way.'

'I know where the road is,' he said. 'And so does everyone else. That's why we're going this way.'

It took them even longer to get back up the cliff to their chosen hiding place than it had to get down. With no questions and no complaints, badly hampered by her trailing skirts and tight, thin-soled boots, Hannah toiled with them. Abdo moved ahead like a shadow, turning to extend a firm helping hand when the path became narrow or extra steep. Harry brought up the rear, ears straining through the wind to listen for the shouts, the commotion, that would signal that the alarm had been raised; but the minutes passed, they climbed ever higher, and he heard nothing. They passed the eerie open mouths of the tombs, the wind whistling and echoing in their empty depths. After an hour they rested a while, Hannah dropping exhausted onto a rock, gasping for breath. A moment later she stood up and moved a little into the darkness.

'What are you doing?' Harry hissed.

'Mind your own business. And don't look,' she added repressively, rustling.

'I wouldn't see much if I did.' He could not keep amusement from his voice.

'Some might say that in my case that would be as true in broad daylight as in the dark!' There was more than a trace of the old subversive laughter in the words. 'Oh, goodness, that's better!' She rejoined them, a ghost in the darkness, holding something. 'Are these any use as a weapon, do you think? They've well-nigh killed me, but I don't see how they could be used against a Bedouin.'

'What are you talking about?'

'My corsets.'

That took Harry entirely by surprise.

'Don't choke!' she said, in only half-mocking alarm. 'Someone might hear you!'

They set off again, a little slower this time, as Abdo paused at the tomb entrances, looking for the one they had picked, and in which they had left the saddle bag.

'Here. This is the one.'

The entrance was narrow, having been blocked at some time by a rock fall. The shaft, illuminated by the swift flash from the precious torch Abdo had taken from the saddle bag, stretched back into the rock, chiselled square and sloping, the wall paintings faint and mysterious in the brief flicker of light.

The other two scrambled thankfully in after him, slipping and sliding on the debris. He turned on the torch again, shading it, and directing it down to the smooth rock of the floor. 'This way.'

They moved deeper. The passage widened into a room in which loomed a granite sarcophagus, intricately carved. 'How very charming,' Hannah said, dauntlessly cheerful. 'I like the furniture. Do we sit on it or under it?' Her voice, bravely pitched and with only the slightest quiver betraying it, echoed and was lost.

'Anywhere but in it,' Harry said. 'Our host has already bagged that spot.'

Abdo flicked a look at them both. Shook his head, as if at children. Neither noticed.

'Mind your manners, Captain Sherwood,' Hannah said severely. 'He probably likes it in there. At the very least I should think that after a couple of thousand years he's got rather used to it. It isn't fair to hurt his feelings.'

'Of course not.' Filthy, the neat and respectable suit in which he had set out that morning rumpled and torn as a tramp's, Harry executed a small salute in the direction of the tomb. 'My apologies.'

Hannah waited, as if listening. 'Well, that's all right,' she said. 'He accepts.'

'The English,' Abdo said, divesting himself of the dark woollen robe, handing the saddle bag to Harry, 'are surely the strangest tribe on the face of this earth.' He handed the robe to Hannah. 'You may find you need this. It's cold now. It will be colder around dawn.'

Hannah took it. 'Thank you.'

Abdo looked at Harry. 'You'll be safe enough here unless they have – '

'We'll be safe,' Harry interrupted, quickly.

Abdo shrugged.

'Just get back as fast as you can,' Harry said softly.

Abdo looked at him for a long moment. Inclined his head. 'I will,' he said. 'Allah be with you.'

'And with you.'

'I'm afraid,' Hannah said, as Abdo disappeared into darkness, 'that we have confused poor Abdo.'

Harry lifted the saddle bag, hefted it in his hand, shone the shaded torch into it. 'Serves him right,' he said, mildly, 'I'm beginning to feel that a bit of human weakness in the man wouldn't come amiss. Look at that. He's even thought to pack bread and cheese. The man's a bloody miracle worker.' He lifted his head, looking at her. A sudden silence fell. When he spoke again it was with abrupt and husky feeling. 'I am so very pleased to see you, Hannah.'

'And I you.' With no warning, all bravado had deserted her. Her eyes were huge and suddenly haunted in the dim light. 'Oh, Harry, I was so very frightened!' She was in his arms, her face hidden in his shoulder, her own shoulders shaking. He held her, fiercely, feeling the thin, strong body shaken by the sobs she had so long kept at bay, hearing in the incoherent words that mingled with the tears the terror she had until now refused to show.

'Hush now, hush my darling.' He rocked her, calming her as he might a distressed child. He laid his cheek upon her tangled hair. 'Hush now,' he said again, softly.

It took a some time for her to calm, longer still for him to let her go. Somehow, long after the sobs of terror and relief had died, long after the frightened flow of words had stopped, she stood within the circle of his arms, her face resting tiredly on his shoulder. His fingers had found her wet cheek, stroking, gentling, his face was still against her hair. She closed her eyes, willing the darkness and the danger away, feeling his nearness and his warmth, feeling above all the fierce and reassuring tenderness of his touch. She lifted her lips to his. The wind whistled eerily about the mouth of the tomb, the music of angels or of devils; if she could have done it she would have stopped time, there and then, and kept them embalmed in this moment, with no dangers to be braved, no decisions to be taken, no pride to stand between them.

'I love you, Harry Sherwood,' she said at last, softly, when his mouth lifted from hers. She raised a hand in the darkness to cover his lips. 'Don't say anything. There's no need. I don't expect you to love me. I can't even be certain that I want you to. I just don't want this night to pass without telling you, that's all. I've had little to do in the past two days but to think. I discovered –' she hesitated '– some regrets.'

Harry stood silent.

Hannah took her fingers away, kissed him again, long and lovingly. Then she stepped calmly from him. 'If – when – we get out of this I shall go home and I shall marry dear Leo, if he'll still have me. There are more ways to love than one. I'll make him a good wife, and a faithful one. But as long as I live I shall remember you. As long as I live some part of me will wish – that things might have been different.' She half turned from him. 'Now, tell me why we're here. Why did only you and Abdo come for me? I assumed that when you got my message you'd contact the garrison commander?'

His fingers caught her wrist. 'Hannah!'

'No.' Very firmly she shook herself free. 'Please understand, Harry. I know your feelings towards women – towards your own freedom. If I believed it a battle I could win, do you think I would not attempt it? I'm no Fenella Hampshire, Harry. I don't just want your bright eyes and your handsome body; I want your life. Your mind. Your friendship. Your trust. I want your love, your understanding. And I want your child.' She heard his quick breath. 'And since I know you aren't willing – aren't able – to give me those things, then I want nothing. I promise you that. I won't bother you. I'm no threat to your precious freedom, have no fear of that.' She stopped suddenly, sensing a change in him, her voice a little less composed than it had been. 'Harry?'

There was an extremely long silence. 'Well,' Harry said at last, very coolly, 'since in your usual sensible and lucid manner you seem to have worked all that out to your own satisfaction, perhaps we could get down to matters of more immediate importance? What message?'

She caught her breath as if he had slapped her. 'I – sent a message –' her voice gained strength in sudden anger '– I bribed a child, a boy, to carry a message to you –'

'When?'

Hannah thought for a moment. 'Two days ago.'

'We were still on the river. There was no message when we arrived.'

378

'How very exasperating.' Her voice was perfectly calm now, and as cold as his. She lifted a hand to her earlobe. 'They were quite my favourite earbobs, and it seemed I sacrificed them for nothing.'

He dug into the saddle bag, held out a chunk of bread and a piece of cheese. 'Here, you'd better eat this. What happened? Why did el Akad keep you prisoner?'

She took the food carefully, not touching his fingers. The story was quickly told; during its telling Harry kept his temper and his patience with a barely concealed effort.

Hannah had telegraphed the Winter House to tell Laila's father of their change of plan. His reaction she had found surprising; when they arrived by train in Aswan, an armed escort awaited Laila. Hannah was told firmly that her presence at the Winter House would not be welcome.

'And you still went?' Harry demanded.

'But of course I did! Laila is little more than a child – she was in my charge. I had promised to deliver her into her father's hands.' She laughed, suddenly and sharply, the sound devoid of all humour. 'I certainly did that, didn't I?'

'So you ignored el Akad's instructions and went with Laila to the Winter House?'

'Yes.'

'The Bedouin didn't try to stop you?'

He sensed her shrug in the gloom. 'They seemed a little – confused –'

'I can understand that.' His voice was grim.

She ignored the interruption. 'I don't believe they're used to a woman who argues with them; I simply told them that they'd got the message wrong. Then –' she paused, nibbled her lip for a moment '– then we arrived in the valley.'

'And?'

'And there was a lot of activity.'

'The slaves? Or the guns?'

'You know about it then? But how – if you didn't get my message?'

'I'll explain later. Go on.'

'It was the slaves. They were being driven into the pen as

379

we arrived. Shackled. Men, women and children – children! – shackled like animals! The drivers had whips! It was like something out of Dante's *Inferno*! Harry, slavery has been outlawed for a generation!'

'Which you no doubt explained to el Akad?' Harry suggested, a little wearily.

'Well, of course.'

'And found yourself – an unwilling guest.'

She was silent.

His exasperation boiled over. 'A situation entirely of your own making! Hannah, in God's name, I cannot understand why you can't behave like any other normal, rational woman!'

It was her turn for temper. 'Why should it be required that you should understand? What has it to do with you?'

'It appears to have landed me half-way up a cliff in the middle of nowhere with a helpless and recalcitrant woman and half the hounds of the Bedouin camp about to wake up and track –' He stopped.

'Recalcitrant I may be,' she said, crisply. 'Helpless I'm not. You think the dogs will track us?'

'It's a possibility. That's why we chose a tomb with a defendable entrance.'

'Well.' She bent to pick up Abdo's saddle bag. 'Much as I'd like to stand talking all night, perhaps we should set ourselves to defending it?'

Harry followed her back along the passage to the entrance. The moon had gone. The sky was black and as dense as velvet; stars glittered and were obscured by the scudding clouds. House and camp below were quiet.

'How long?' Hannah asked quietly. 'How long do you think we have before they discover I'm gone?'

Harry scanned the sky. 'Pray for dawn,' he said. 'Abdo should be back with help by then. And even if they find us –' he reached into the saddle bag, drew out a pair of pistols, laid them upon the heap of rubble that formed a natural barrier at the entrance '– we should be able to keep them off. For a while, anyway.' He hoped he sounded more confident than he actually felt.

Apparently he did. 'That's all right then,' Hannah said and

settled, in determined silence, to watch the valley below. Much later, she said into the obstinate quiet, a tremor of pain in her voice, 'Laila knew, I think. About the slaves. And the guns. She did nothing to save me. Nothing.'

Harry opted against the possibly debilitating effect of sympathy. 'Laila,' he said, blandly, 'young as she might be, is a woman. How can you possibly be surprised by anything she does – or does not – do?' and was rewarded by a snort of anger and a remarkably well-aimed stone.

With the faintest of smiles he settled himself back to his watch.

The alarm was raised just as the first rose and pearl-grey light of dawn was lifting in the eastern sky, etching the cliffs at the far end of the valley inkily against the pale drifts of colour. The valley below was still in darkness when a sudden shout roused Hannah from half-sleep and made Harry worm forward towards the edge. Within minutes, as the light grew stronger, the compound was ablaze with lanterns and alive with shouting men and barking dogs. At first the action was confused, with men running hither and thither with little apparent purpose. Then came the sound that Harry had most dreaded; the belling of hounds. It had been an odds-on chance that Ayman el Akad, with regular deliveries of slaves to his compound, would have hounds in his stables; it had been those odds that had influenced Harry to agree to Abdo's plan in the first place. It was by no means inconceivable that Abdo, travelling alone across the desert, could reach Aswan, and help, in a few hours. Hampered by Hannah, however valiant her efforts, there was no doubt that the three of them would have taken much longer, and, with hounds and mounted Bedouin on their trail, probably never reached it at all. Now all that they could hope for was that either the hounds would not find the trail up the cliff face, or that Abdo and the British Army arrived in time, before their hiding place was discovered. Harry narrowed his eyes, searching the path that led to the plateau; if Abdo had worked with his usual alarming efficiency, help could surely not be too far away?

They had a precious half-hour's grace before the hounds found the trail and set off, belling, across the compound towards the cliff bottom.

'Here they come,' Harry said, unnecessarily.

Hannah, the field glasses to her eyes, said nothing.

'At least they're all coming from the same direction – it doesn't seem to have occurred to anyone to go around the other way to cut off our escape to the top of the cliff. They probably don't realize we're up here. I'll get a couple of them before they know we're here.'

'Harry –'

'If worst comes to worst I want you to –'

'Harry!'

He turned at the urgency of her voice. Her face was the perfect picture of astonishment.

'What is it?'

In reply she handed him the glasses, and pointed. 'Over there. Look!'

He swept the opposite ridge, saw in the growing light the figures that flitted from rock to rock, from shadow to shadow, white-robed, dark-robed, some almost naked, all armed to the teeth. And amongst them a tall and unmistakable figure, robed too in white and armed with a long rifle and a curved, glinting blade that glittered barbarously as the first rays of the sun broke across the sky.

As they watched, puzzled and fascinated, the flood of attackers broke cover with a savage, ululating cry. The men below were taken utterly unawares. The group with the hounds broke and ran, back towards the compound, without even glancing upwards to where Harry and Hannah were hidden.

The tribesmen on the hillside, still screaming like demons, swept down upon the valley and its ill-prepared defenders.

'Well,' Hannah said, sitting down rather suddenly upon a convenient rock and looking in some surprise at the pistol she had picked up, as if she had no idea how it had come into her hand, 'whoever Abdo has brought to rescue us –' bewildered, she shook her bright, tangled head '– it certainly isn't the British Army!'

CHAPTER NINETEEN

It was slaughter. As they watched, wave after wave of yelling tribesmen swept down the hill and into the valley below in a murderous flood that carried all before it. Flesh and blood simply could not withstand such an onslaught. Abdo was everywhere, urging his men on, cutting through the fierce and formidable Bedouin who challenged him with the great curved blade that he wielded with lethal competence. To their credit, the compound's defenders very soon recovered from their shock and organized themselves into a semblance of brave defence; but they were overwhelmingly outnumbered, and the end was never in doubt. The tribesmen swarmed over the camp and the compound. The air was manic with screams, with the ululating cry of the attackers, the clattering, staccato sound of rifle fire. Bodies lay in heaps or sprawled alone, cut down where they stood, trampled bloodily by attacker and defender alike in desperate advance or even more desperate retreat. At last only the house stood untaken, though ringed around by the enemy, and a comparative quiet fell, broken only by the occasional shot.

In the compound the warehouse doors had been axed. Cases of weapons were dragged into the dawn sunlight, their contents brandished with yells and shouts of triumph by the tribesmen.

'He's coming,' Hannah said quietly. She was very pale, and had uttered not a word as she watched the brutal action beneath them. 'There. You see?' She pointed.

Abdo strode across the compound towards the foot of the cliff. He did not look up.

Harry, very carefully, laid down the revolver he had held in wary precaution all through the past minutes, and slipped from his leather belt two of the slim throwing knives Abdo had encouraged him to master. His face was grim.

Hannah stared. 'Harry – no!'

Harry ignored her. His eyes were steady and bright with anger as he watched Abdo toil up the path towards them.

Abdo must have known they were watching him, yet he did not stretch his measured stride, nor did he look up; he came calmly, and when he turned the corner of the path and stood before them his dark gaze was level and apparently unperturbed.

'Bastard,' Harry said, very quietly. 'Treacherous bastard.'

Beneath them the screams and yells of the victorious tribesmen were punctuated by rifle fire.

'Abdo – Laila's in the house,' Hannah said, rapidly. 'You won't let them harm her?'

His eyes still upon Harry, Abdo shook his head. 'I've given orders.'

'Orders,' Harry said savagely, weighing a knife in his hand. 'These barbarians take orders? From you?'

'Yes.' Abdo, Hannah suddenly saw, was unarmed; or at least he had laid aside the wicked blade with which he had carved such havoc in the compound below, and the long rifle was no longer in evidence.

'You're a thief and a liar,' Harry said, and the knife lifted a little. 'You are a betrayer of trust.'

Dark lids veiled dark eyes for a moment, but then the gaze was steady again. 'I came back for you,' Abdo said mildly. He did not add, 'And saved your skin a second time,' though the words hung between them, unacknowledged.

There were more shouts from below. The door of the second warehouse had been broken down; lines of men and women, still chained, were emerging, blinking and bewildered into the sun.

Harry's smile was bitter. 'No, you didn't. You came back for the guns. And for them.' He indicated with a contemptuous nod of his head the line of pathetic, shambling captives below.

'That's true, too.'

Harry had had time to add two and two together to produce a clear and devastating four. 'You're a Mahdist,' he said.

Abdo bowed his head once, and proudly.

'You pretended friendship, and allegiance. You're a traitor, I say.'

'Not to my own people. Captain, listen to me.' Suddenly the old Abdo was there – warm, magnetic, persuasive. 'This is my country – the British – the Europeans! – have no right to be here. The British don't even want to be here – you know it! Are we at the gates of London? Of Paris? Do we overrun the fields and the cities of England? No. All we ask is to be left alone in our own country and, if you refuse us that, we reserve the right to fight for our traditions, our religion and our freedom.'

'With treachery?' Harry's voice was fierce. 'A man fights in the field, with gun and with sword, and lives or dies by his belief.' He pointed the knife, his hand steady as rock.

'But what of guns and cannon ranged against knives and swords?' Abdo's defence was swift and fluent. 'How are my people to stand against rifles and field guns with nothing but bows and arrows and spears? Where is the valour in that, Captain? Where is the certainty, except of death? If they were your people – what would you do, Captain?'

Harry was silent.

'I have done what had to be done. You wanted to find the guns to prevent them from reaching my people; I wished only to ensure that they did, and if possible without further payment in flesh. Our roads ran parallel; the directions opposite. But we met, did we not? Somewhere along the roads – we met.'

'And you saved my life. Why don't you say it?'

'I would not,' Abdo said, simply.

'Why?' Harry asked. 'Why did you save me?'

Abdo shook his head. 'Captain Sherwood, you look for things too sharply defined, too black and white. All is not evil, or good. All is not right, or wrong.'

'It is your own people who operate the slave trade.' Hannah's quiet voice surprised them both, intent as they were upon one another. 'It is your own people who sell their sons and their daughters into captivity. It is the Arabs who are exchanging guns for captives. The Europeans outlawed slavery long ago.'

'And now turn a convenient blind eye to its existence,' Abdo said, bitterly.

Harry moved a little, restlessly. Beneath them there was a swift burst of rifle fire, then silence. 'If the British had known el Akad was running French guns in exchange for slaves, they would have stopped him,' he said.

Abdo lifted his head. 'For the guns, Captain,' he said softly. 'Not for the slaves. They have known for months that Ayman el Akad was involved in the slave trade. They counted it – ' he paused wryly ' – a native matter.'

'As – as Hannah points out – it is. That still doesn't excuse treachery.' Harry was dogged, the knife was still held at the ready.

'Neither,' Hannah said, watching him, 'does it explain why Abdo is here. Not, I assume, to hand us over to his bloodthirsty compatriots?'

Abdo shook his head.

'It would be easier,' Hannah suggested.

'Don't give him ideas,' Harry said.

'If I had wished you killed you would be dead by now.' The words were matter-of-fact.

It was self-evidently the truth. Harry gritted his teeth.

'And if you had wished me dead,' Abdo continued, his eyes on the knife Harry still held poised in his hand, 'you would, I think, have used that by now?'

'Are you sure of that?' Harry challenged him savagely.

Abdo spread his empty hands. 'One can never be sure of anything. Now, I must go. You remember where we left your horse?'

'I think so, yes.'

'There are two there, waiting; better horses than that crowbait of yours. Wait until we are gone, then leave. It will take you some time to reach Aswan, but you will be safe, I promise you. There will be no-one to follow you.'

'Laila – ' Hannah began.

'Will be safe. I promise.'

'I'll turn out the garrison,' Harry said. 'The minute I get to Aswan. Colonel Standish must have alerted the posts all along the river after my wire from Luxor – ' He stopped.

Abdo was shaking his head. 'I sent no wire from Luxor, Captain. I could not risk the Colonel recalling us.'

'So – the reply? Was a fake?'

The other man nodded.

'So. It doesn't matter anyway. The Lancers are at Aswan. They'll be on your trail as soon as we get to them.'

Abdo shrugged. 'Do as you will. They won't find us. The Nubian desert is a very big place, Captain Sherwood.'

'You forget one thing.'

'What's that?'

'I still have this.' Harry moved his hand a little and the knife glinted in the light.

'Use it, Captain. If you're going to.'

Hannah held her breath.

'Bastard!' Harry said, and the knife flew, gleaming, to bury itself in the sand at Abdo's feet. Harry turned sharply, to contemplate the compound below. The captives, released from their chains, milled uncertainly, lifting defensive hands, almost as afraid of their fierce saviours as they had been of their captors. 'Look at them!' he said, savagely. 'Animals! They're like animals! Why? Why do you care? What have they to do with you?'

Abdo moved to stand beside him. 'They are my brothers, Captain Sherwood,' he said. 'They are my brothers, and yours. Isn't that true? And should the strong stand aside while their weaker brethren are enslaved?'

Harry spun, eyes blazing in denial; but before he could speak there came the sudden and unmistakable crackle of rifle fire followed by the shrill call of a trumpet, not from the valley below but from the plateau over the opposite ridge. They all stilled, turning their heads towards the sound, like animals at the approach of hunters.

'Wh– what was that?' Hannah asked, unnecessarily.

Abdo had already gone, leaping down the narrow track, surefooted and swift, calling as he went.

Most of his men stood, confused, looking towards the source of the sound.

'There! Look!' Harry pointed. 'The Lancers! It's the bloody Lancers, God bless their shining buttons! How the hell did they get here?' The column had stopped on the edge of the plateau, their khaki uniforms and sun helmets making them all but invisible to the Dervishes below. Hannah saw the officer's arm raised. The trumpet shrilled again.

Hannah looked down to where Abdo, armed again with sword and rifle, was trying to organize his men, sending them with gesture and with shouted orders flying for cover. The slaves, some of them still chained, were huddled together, keening in fear. With a sweep of his arm Abdo sent men to shepherd them to safety in the grove of palms at the foot of the cliff. She heard sharp, businesslike orders, saw the men on the far ridge dismount and take aim at the milling tribesmen below; Abdo and his men were caught in the same trap that he had himself had sprung on el Akad and his Bedouin.

'Stop them! Harry, can't you stop them?' she cried urgently.

Harry shook his head.

'Fire!'

In the first withering volley men dropped like stones, as they ran for cover behind the mud walls of the compound. Hannah saw Abdo, tall and white-robed, a clear target, calmly directing his men. Again and again the long rifles of the Lancers spoke, and fresh blood spilled upon old in the compound below. The sun was high now, mercilessly bright and hot. Abdo was covering the confused retreat of the slaves, walking backwards, coolly aiming and firing up at the almost unseen enemy on the clifftop.

The Lancers were moving forward, inching down the hillside, each rank covered by disciplined fire from the next. Abdo retreated further, step by grim step.

Hannah was watching Abdo when the bullet took him. Harry turned at her sudden cry, his arm going about her as her hands flew to her mouth. Below them, Abdo staggered a couple of steps, dropped to one knee, his hands spread against the gaping wound in his chest. Bright blood spattered the white robe; and again, as a second bullet took him from behind and blasted him to the ground.

'Abdo,' Hannah said, very quietly, and briefly turned her head into Harry's shoulder, eyes closed against the terrible sight of death, and against the tears.

Over her bowed head, sombrely, Harry watched the fight as

it ebbed and flowed about the still, sprawled figure. Leaderless now, the tribesmen yet fought with a furious courage; but inch by inch, foot by disciplined foot the Lancers came on. And then, at last, the cavalry poured down the hillside, sweeping the last of resistance aside.

Hannah had pulled away from Harry, dashing the back of her hand briefly across her eyes. She looked pale and haggard, her face drawn, dirty and tearstained. Her skirts dragged in the dust and her hair was a bird's nest. He resisted the foolhardy urge to reach for her, to hold her, to shelter her from a world which he knew all too well, but of which, until today, she had surely lived in tranquil ignorance.

She turned, gathered her torn skirt in her hand.

'Where are you going?'

She hardly looked at him. 'Where do you think? Laila's down there somewhere. And Abdo –' She stopped.

'Hannah,' he said, 'Abdo is dead.'

'I know,' she said, undaunted. 'But I still have to see for myself.'

The soldiers were disarming and rounding up those Dervishes left standing. The occasional shot still rang out as some put up a last desperate fight or tried to escape. A couple broke and ran for the cliff path, and were cut down before they could reach it. An officer sat on a small, sturdy horse, watching order being brought to chaos. Harry pulled a crumpled handkerchief from his pocket, stepped to the path's edge, waving it in a sweep above his head. 'Hello there!' he called.

Several faces turned up towards them, in astonishment. Hannah stepped forward to join him.

The young officer shaded his eyes with his hand, then gestured. 'Come on down.' His words carried clearly in the hot air.

They scrambled down the stony track, aware of curiosity in the eyes that watched them. Once on the valley floor, Hannah walked directly to where Abdo's body lay, dropped to one knee beside it, reaching to turn the handsome head with its wide, staring eyes. Flies buzzed with stomach-turning persistence. She brushed them away, gently drew down the lids over the vacant eyes, sat back upon her heels, head bowed. Harry had followed her, and stood beside her, looking down. 'How did he know?' he asked, very low.

The words for a moment made no sense. She shook her head, not looking at him. 'Know what?

'"My brothers", he said, "and yours." How did he know?' There was an agonized depth of uncertainty in his voice.

Hannah closed her tired, burning eyes, tilted her head wearily back. 'Oh, Harry! You fool! He didn't know – of course he didn't know! And he wouldn't have cared if he had. Any more than I do!' Tears were running unchecked from the corners of her eyes, streaking her thin, dusty cheeks. 'Won't you ever understand? Must you always live in a cage of your own making?' She opened her eyes suddenly, looking directly up at him. Others were moving about them; the officer's horse stepped delicately around the bloodied heaps of bodies towards them. 'Did he truly save your life?'

'Yes.'

'And he is dead.' She watched him for a long moment, through tears. 'But there is a way to repay the debt that you owe him, even now. Isn't there?'

She saw in his face that he understood. Then he shook his head, fiercely. 'I can't. Hannah, I *can't*.'

She bowed her head for a moment, looking at Abdo's stiffening body. A tear dripped from her chin and marked her dusty blouse. 'No, of course not,' she said then, and stood, refusing his helping hand, her face steeled against him, her long mouth set. 'Of course not.'

'Hannah!'

'Would you be Captain Harry Sherwood?' The young officer's voice was light and pleasant, a voice to be heard on a summer's afternoon over the chink of tea cups in an English garden. They turned. The young man's lean, fair face was burned to gold by the desert sun, his blond moustache was bleached almost to white.

Harry came to attention, saluted, extended a hand. 'Of the Prince of Wales' Own.'

The young man leaned down to shake the proffered hand. 'Lieutenant Hubert Burrows, Sir. Of the Twenty-first. Glad to have found you in time.' He turned sharp blue eyes upon Hannah. 'Miss Hannah Standish?'

'Yes.' Hannah turned from Harry to the newcomer. 'How did you know?' Her voice was calm and crisp. Only her face showed the tell-tale traces of her tears.

'You sent a message. To Captain Sherwood here. It was delivered after Captain Sherwood had left Aswan, to your Reis, Hassan. He appears to be a man of unusual good sense. When Captain Sherwood did not return he brought the note to the garrison.'

There was a moment's silence. Every last vestige of blood appeared to have drained from Hannah's face. Harry stepped towards her. She drew back from him. 'My note?' she asked at last. 'That I sent with the child?'

'Yes.'

She swayed, very slightly. Harry, seeing her face, knew better than to attempt to touch her.

'Lieutenant, there is a child somewhere in the house – a girl.' She spoke quite clearly. 'Ayman el Akad's daughter Laila. May I look for her?'

'Not alone.' The lieutenant gave quick orders. A couple of troopers fell in beside Hannah. 'When you find her,' the young man's face was not unsympathetic, 'I'm afraid you'll have to tell her that her father is dead. We found his body.' He jerked his head towards the compound.

'I'll tell her.' Hannah spoke still with a cool control so at odds with her dishevelled appearance and haggard looks that Harry saw one trooper glance at another with raised brow and a rolling eye; a real schoolma'am we've got here, said the look.

'I'll come with you,' he said.

She shook her head, not looking at him. 'No. Laila won't want to see you. Of all people.' He could not believe the chill in her voice. She turned at last, and her face was a mask. 'At least let me find Laila. At least let me salvage something from this vicious mess.'

'It wasn't your fault,' he said.

'It was my message,' she said flatly. Her hands lifted to her earlobes; dropped to her side again. 'They were my pretty earbobs.' She smiled a small and bitter smile. 'It is Abdo's loss that I am not the kind of female that the world so admires. If I had collapsed in a suitably helpless heap and not made the pathetic attempt to save myself, he would have been with us still, would he not?' She saw his expression begin to change and shook her head, sharply and decisively, her hands raised against him. 'Don't try to help me, Harry. And I won't try to help you. That would seem the most sensible thing all round, don't you agree?' There was a small silence; when she spoke again her voice was softer, but no less clear. 'The Spanish say that hell is paved with good intentions. Did you know that? I never until now realized what it meant.'

She turned and strode, limp skirts dragging in the dust, towards the Winter House, followed by her escort. The lieutenant's horse moved a little, restlessly. He curbed it one-handed, looking after Hannah. 'A rather remarkable woman, I suspect?' There was the barest suggestion of a question in the words.

Harry did not reply.

Hannah found Laila huddled against a wall in a small room in the women's quarters of the house. Her nurse stood guard over her, ready to rend with her bare hands anyone who came near. When she saw Hannah, however, she burst into ready tears. 'It's all right, Fatma,' Hannah said, steadily, 'it's me. It's all over.' She approached the terrified child who, two days earlier, had been ready to see her sold into bondage. 'Laila – come now, my dear. It's me, Hannah.'

The Battle of Omdurman, in which some eight thousand British soldiers and seventeen thousand Egyptian and Sudanese troops faced over fifty thousand fanatical tribesmen in the blazingly hostile environment of the Sudanese desert, was fought on 2 September 1898, just seven months after Harry took stiff and formal leave of Hannah to return to Cairo, Hannah having opted to stay in the south to care for Laila until arrangements could be made for her brother to return to Egypt. It was ironic that, in the end, it was Hannah who observed the battle, having volunteered her services to the always hard-pressed army surgeons, whilst Harry, his Commission resigned, made his way north to Alexandria to take passage to Europe. Hannah it was who saw wave after wave of Dervishes, armed with bows and arrows, spears and swords, throw themselves against the well-armed, well-organized wall of British firepower. Courage there was on both sides; but courage could stand for nothing given the inequality of arms, and the tribesmen, despite their advantage of numbers, faced with rifles, machine guns and howitzers, were slaughtered as Abdo had foreseen. Though the defeat was not without honour – no man in Kitchener's army would forget the wild valour with which the Dervish forces, despite the odds, threw themselves over and again into the attack – in the end it was complete, and British pride and the British public were satisfied. Gordon and the defeat at Khartoum had at last been avenged. Hannah, labouring in the field hospital to help save the torn and bloodied bodies that were stretchered in, hour after hour, could only comfort herself with the knowledge that the single consignment of guns she had been unwittingly instrumental in preventing Abdo from capturing and delivering to his countrymen would certainly not have been enough to sway the battle, would simply, indeed, have been the cause of even more carnage; and that, had Abdo not died as he had, then he would almost certainly have been cut down here, just as uselessly, with his brothers.

She had had more than enough weary and lonely time since that awful day to remember, to grieve, to attempt to rationalize. And to regret.

She returned to Cairo a few days after the battle with a hospital train full of wounded. She busied herself for the whole of the trip, calm, cheerful and efficient, a popular figure with the injured men and officers for whom she so diligently cared. It was not too hard to ensure that she allowed herself scarcely a moment to gaze from the train windows at the moving vista of the Nile and its green, teeming banks, of the ancient sites and temples she had set out to visit with such excitement those long months before. Once or twice, despite herself, a scene caught her eye: a dahabeeyah, graceful sail belling, running carefree before the wind, a camel train winding its way across the vast sunlit spaces of the desert, the fallen columns of a great temple, the sand sifting about it. But each time she would turn away swiftly, distracting herself from her own pain by tending those about her whose sufferings were physical and could at least be eased.

Back in Cairo, and with her charges handed over to the military hospital, she made prompt arrangements to return to England. Harry had of course reported fully to her uncle the events in Aswan, before leaving. There had been no question of his remaining; Fenella Hampshire made no idle threats. By the time Harry had returned to Cairo, the story of his parentage was common knowledge. His last days in the garrison, Hannah gathered, had been far from uneventful, several of his erstwhile friends and comrades taking it unkindly that such an outrageous deceit should have been practised upon them.

'Landed young Archie Douglas in hospital with a broken arm and a face that looked as if it had been kicked by a camel!' the colonel complained. 'And Andy Carter fared no better – regimental boxing champion, and out of fighting for the next six months; that bounder Sherwood stamped on his hand! Always knew there was something wrong with that man – something not quite the thing, you know?'

'I have no doubt that whatever happened to Carter he most thoroughly deserved it,' Hannah said, caustically. 'Did it occur to anyone to enquire what he was trying to do when Harry chose to stamp on his hand? Knowing the man, I'd say Carter's lucky to have a hand left to mend. And if there's anything wrong with Harry Sherwood –' oh, the delight, the painful delight, simply in speaking the name aloud! '– and there is plenty wrong with him, I don't deny that, it isn't that his father was black, white or sky blue, nor that he was slave or free! It is rather that he accepts your terms and values instead of defying them and forging his own! In his own way he's as bad as you are! You disgust me. All of you.' It was said perfectly and blisteringly quietly, and it gave Hannah great pleasure to forbear from slamming the door behind her. But later, in the privacy of her room, it took the most stubborn marshalling of will not to scream, or to break something when she allowed herself to contemplate Harry's last harsh days in Cairo, spent as an outcast within an institution of which he had believed himself to be an accepted and integral part and which had been substitute home and family for fifteen years. For the briefest of moments she allowed herself to think of him; to remember his voice, his laughter, the turn of his head, the feel of his lips on hers, and to wonder where he was, what he was doing, but such self-indulgence was necessarily brief. She had long ago realized the danger of such thoughts to her own fragile equilibrium, and had perfected to an art her ability to shut them off, to drive them away with physical activity and a determined mind. It was, she thought a little ruefully as she set about the practical business of list-making and packing to return to England, what romanticists might term her heart that, for the first time in her life, refused to be taken in by such nonsense. For a moment her busy hands stilled, and she saw, as she had seen so often, Harry's face in the clear, harsh sunlight of a dusty, blood-drenched desert morning as he had stood looking down at Abdo's body and recognized the debt and its payment; and had known, of course – why wouldn't he? – so much better than she, exactly what she had been asking of him. 'I can't,' he had said. 'Hannah, I *can't!*'

She closed her eyes against a sudden, strange spasm of almost physical pain. Then, briskly, she reached for pen and paper. If she did not make a list of the things she would not require on the voyage, then the packing would be chaos of quite the worst kind.

The SS *Mauritius* was to leave Alexandria on 12 November, heading for the ports of northern France via Italy, Portugal and Spain. With a Mary so relieved to be leaving Egypt that she checked the time anxiously every half an hour, as if willing the minutes to pass, Hannah found herself comfortably ensconced in a reasonably sized cabin on the upper deck. They boarded the ship two days before she was due to leave and settled themselves into their quarters very quickly. Hannah, leaning on the rail outside the cabin and watching the bustle of the quay below, found herself now as eager to leave as was her maid. For the best part of her adult life she had longed to visit Egypt. From the moment she had set foot on Egyptian soil she had been fascinated by the place; but now the charm was gone. Every sight, every sound, every smell brought back a memory she would rather be rid of. The sight of a tall, graceful Nubian walking through the crowded bazaar stopped her heart and brought tears to her eyes. The sound of the muezzin, echoing through the dove-grey light of dawn over the sleeping city, brought back with perfect clarity the gentle movement of the dahabeeyah as she lay moored in the reedbeds of the Nile, the slap of the water, the call of the egrets, the sound of Harry's voice. No. The time for Egypt was done. Perhaps one day, when she was an old, old lady she would tell her wide-eyed grandchildren the improbable story of capture and imprisonment in a desert valley, of how a message entrusted to a small boy for the payment of a pretty pair of earbobs had prevented el Akad's guns from reaching the Dervishes, and had caused the death of an enemy who had been a friend. Perhaps. For now she wanted nothing but to leave. The *Mauritius* was to stop at Brindisi, and at Lisbon. She had never visited Portugal. It would make a very nice change.

'Miss Hannah?' Mary, round, pretty face faintly puzzled, had appeared at her elbow. In her hand she held a small, square envelope. 'I found this.' She held it out to Hannah.

'Found it? Found it where? What is it?'

'In the cabin. It's addressed to you.'

'Ah.' Hannah took it. 'Thank goodness we leave in a couple of hours. This is undoubtedly from someone's second cousin three times removed who would be delighted if we'd – ' She stopped. There was a very long silence. The paper trembled very slightly between her fingers.

'Miss Hannah? Is everything all right?'

'What? Oh, yes.' In a vague gesture Hannah put her fingertips to her forehead for a moment. 'Yes, everything is perfectly all right. Has the other trunk turned up?'

'Oh, yes, Miss – 'twas in the hold all the time.'

'Good. Oh, good.'

Mary peered at her. 'You sure you're all right, Miss?' she asked, perplexed.

'I'm quite well, Mary. Thank you.' Hannah stood for a long while after Mary had left, the note still in her hand. At last, with an effort far beyond that needed for such a simple movement, she pushed herself away from the rail, and turned towards the gangway that led down to the lower decks.

He was waiting where he had said he would be. He was shockingly thin, his skin yellowed, the lustrous dark eyes dull and deep-shadowed.

She joined him at the rail. This deck was much closer to the comings and goings of the quay. Men shouted, donkeys brayed, camels snorted, compulsively ill-natured, lines of patient porters trudged up and down the narrow gangplanks, loading supplies for the voyage.

'Hannah,' he said.

'Harry.'

'How are you?'

'Well, thank you. And you?' The stupid, stilted words echoed flatly in her brain.

He spread his long-fingered hands, smiled swiftly. Her heart turned. 'As you see.'

'You look,' she said, with charitable understatement, 'as if you haven't slept in a month.'

He shrugged. Where and when he had slept in these past months was not, as it happened, a subject he was happy to dwell upon.

'How did you find me?' she asked at last.

He shrugged again. 'Easily. I simply perused every passenger list of every ship that was leaving for Europe. Sooner or later you had to be here.'

'Ah.' She looked down at her hands, pretended great interest in a fierce and voluble argument that was taking place just beneath them. 'Might I ask why?'

There was a very long silence. 'I have a letter,' he said finally. 'I thought you might like – that is, I felt you ought – to see it.'

397

She turned in honest surprise. He held out an envelope, identical to that other that she had seen him hold that night on the *Horus*.

Hannah took it from him. Her eyes passed quickly over the first few sentences of guarded surprise and pleasure at hearing from him, then:

'You ask about your father,' Mattie had written in her clear, positive hand. 'I can only say, as I tried once before to tell you, that he was the bravest and kindest of men, and one who, in honour and with dignity, bore a cross that would crush most of us to the ground. The accident of race and of circumstance that oppressed and finally killed him was not of his making; it is his strength and his courage in overcoming it that you must understand and trust, and of which you should be proud. I have wished so very often to say to you that, if you must apportion blame, if you must hate, he of all people does not deserve your anger. He was the innocent. He the betrayed. If blame there is, then blame me, for I loved him, and was his death. Then I loved you, and in my fear of hurting you, I lied – and so, perhaps deservedly, I lost you. But Harry, no matter what society might think – and how evil is this hypocrisy that claims to champion the rights of all men but in fact condemns them for their race and their colour – his blood is no disgrace! He was a fine, intelligent man – as you are. His life was blighted by his parentage – as I fear, my dear, yours has been. But I say again, of all things, be proud of him. Now I shall seal this letter, and send it swiftly – for assuredly if I read it through it will be consigned, as have so many others, to the fire. My dear Rupert is sitting, watching me, his eyebrows quirked like question marks – the poor soul, as you may imagine, has much to bear – yet I must say that he manages, in charity, to pretend to contentment! Jake ate my best hat last week, wicked thing! Do you remember when he tore your best breeches to ribbons? How cross I was! I need not tell you, I think, how very much I long to see you. Until the day, I remain, your loving mother – '

Hannah slowly and meticulously folded the letter and handed it back to Harry. 'Jake?' she asked, her voice schooled to steadiness.

'My mother's dog. She calls them all Jake. She treats them as if they're all one animal. It can be a little disconcerting. The one who tore my breeches must be three or four back. I was – oh, eight years old, I'd say.'

'I see.' She looked intently out across the minarets and domes of the city. 'I very much like the sound of your mother,' she said, and then, a small piece of the puzzle clicking into place, 'You're travelling on the *Mauritius*?' Her voice showed no sign of emotion, she might have been addressing a new acquaintance met whilst strolling on the upper deck.

'Yes.'

'Why?'

He raised dark brows, half-smiling, refusing to rise to the bait. 'The ship's going to England, isn't it?'

'Eventually, yes.'

'Well, so am I.'

Hannah glanced at the letter. 'You're going home?'

'Yes. For a while, anyway.'

For the first time she allowed herself to look at him, steadily and long and without guard. 'I'm so very glad. It will be good for you, I think. And it will mean a very great deal to your mother.'

Harry shrugged slightly; his turn now to study the city as if it were the most interesting sight in the world. 'Perhaps.'

Hannah watched him. 'There's no perhaps. She loves you. She's always loved you. You know it.'

He held out for a moment longer, then his head ducked, a little tiredly. His hair had grown too long, it curled unkempt and dusty about his ears and neck. 'Yes. It's quite terrifying, isn't it, the capacity some women have for loving, through everything, a man who deserves it not at all?'

She lifted her head a little, sharply and warily.

He smiled then, his sudden, perilously beguiling smile as he turned to her. 'And then there are those who have more sense. Hannah – I'm sorry – I disappointed you.'

She shook her head.

'Oh, yes, I did. And I find that you made me face an uncomfortable fact: I disappoint myself. I know what you were saying; you wanted me to say, yes, I will repay Abdo by acknowledging, with pride, the blood and the heritage we share. A life for a life; it would be just. And for my father too, and my mother who loved him; it would be just. But –' he shook his head, the ravages of these last difficult and gracelessly self-indulgent months clear upon his face '– I can't,' he said as he had said before, 'Hannah – I can't.'

'I know. It was wrong to ask it of you.'

'Not yet. Not now. Perhaps not ever – I don't – what did you say?' His face was almost blank with surprise.

'I said, I know. I said, it was wrong to ask it of you.' She put an impatient hand to her face. 'Oh, goodness, wouldn't you think that a woman of my age could prevent herself from bursting into entirely unsuitable tears at peculiar moments?'

Harry had pushed himself away from the rail, was watching her intently, his face puzzled.

'I didn't know it then,' she continued, ignoring the tears, 'but I do now. I knew it, in fact, almost as soon as you left; but then it was too late. I knew I had lost you.' She almost laughed at that, and could not prevent the self-mockery. 'If I'd ever had you, that is, which I understand is doubtful. But one thing I did know: I'd angered you and lost your friendship, and it served me right –'

'Hannah – no!'

'Yes. I was wrong. I had absolutely no right to try to force you – to provoke you – into facing an emotional predicament that was completely personal. I had no right to attempt to impose on you my own thoughts and feelings. What has it to do with me? I'm glad that we've met again; it gives me a chance to do something I've been badly wanting to do; to apologize. What a self-righteous harridan you must have thought me!'

Harry regarded her for a long time and very thoughtfully. 'A self-righteous red-headed harridan, actually,' he said, at last.

'I can't help the red hair.'

'No.' He grinned again, swiftly. 'I know you can't. But you seem to have learned to live with it.' He smiled openly, finally, and with the old ease. 'Any tips you could pass on?'

The tears threatened her again. 'Oh, it's not difficult,' she said, lightly, 'you just ignore it and get on with something else.'

He appeared to think about that, nodded soberly. 'That sounds like good counsel. Do you have any more to offer?'

She shook her head.

He laughed outright at that, and gave her his arm. 'Penance, my dearest Hannah, doesn't become you at all! I'll lay a guinea that it won't last beyond the week!' She laid a repressive hand upon his arm, and he covered it with his, looking down at her. 'If it does I'll have to do something perfectly outrageous, to bring you to your senses.'

'Oh, dear. What a threat.'

Harry turned her to face him, suddenly sober. 'You told me, in Aswan, that you loved me.'

Hannah bent her head, deep colour lifting in her cheeks.

'Hannah, did you mean it?'

The sudden intensity in his voice brought her head back up, an odd defiance in the gesture. 'Harry Sherwood,' she said, her voice level, her colour still high, 'I may say things that are opinionated; I may say things that are ill-judged. But I never – never! – say things that I don't mean.'

'You said you loved me but that you were going to marry Leo.'

She sniffed in a far from ladylike fashion. 'Why, so I did.'

'Did you mean that?'

'When I said it?' she asked, carefully. 'Yes.'

'And now?'

She hesitated. 'I – don't know.'

'Well, that's a start.' He tucked her hand back into the crook of his arm, and began to stroll along the deck. 'Tell me, have you ever been known to change your mind?'

'Occasionally.'

A few more paces. Then, 'Lucky chap, Leo,' Harry said. 'I

wonder if he knows what a narrow shave he's had? But he'll be all right; no red-headed harridan for him. He can live the rest of his life in peace, fortunate chap.'

'Harry!'

He smiled benignly down at her. 'First stop Brindisi, I believe?' He put on a look of acute puzzlement. 'What does one do in Brindisi?'

'I've no idea. Harry –'

'Good. We can find out together. You speak Italian?'

'No.'

'Neither do I.' He stopped, took her fingers in his, brought them to his lips in a parody of flirtatious courtesy that had her snatching her hand away from him in exasperation. 'So I suppose that means we'll just have to spend the time talking to each other?'

CHAPTER TWENTY

'The last summer of the nineteenth century.' Mattie tossed a crust of bread onto the slow-moving waters of the river that ran along the western boundary of the garden of Coombe House. Several ducks piloted their swift way towards it, squabbled over it with noisy ill manners. 'What a very strange thought that is. It's quite hard to believe, isn't it? Here, you silly things – there's plenty more.' She tossed more crumbs onto the water, and more argument ensued.

Hannah, strolling beside her, nodded. Willows trailed long and graceful fingers in the river; in the depths beneath one of the trees, a fish jumped with a small splash. Earlier there had been a shower, but now the afternoon sun shone warm, and grass, flower and leaf glittered with diamond drops. The shaggy dog who trotted at Mattie's heels uttered a sudden gruff bark and dashed into a wet thicket.

'Jake! Come back here! Jake!'

The undergrowth rustled. Jake barked again, happily.

'One word from me,' Mattie said, with tranquil self-ridicule, 'and I'm afraid that animal does exactly as he wants.'

Hannah laughed. 'My mother used to say the same about me.'

Mattie slanted a smiling and observant glance at her. 'I'm not surprised.' She paused, and laughed a little. 'I hate to think what any mother might have said about me. I fear I always considered myself to be lucky never to have had one. Isn't that awful?'

The smile that Hannah returned was affectionate. Since these two had met there had been nothing but understanding between them. 'You don't mind?'

'Mind?'

'Me. And Harry. I'm well aware that I'm not every woman's idea of an ideal daughter-in-law.' It was Hannah's turn to sound wry; laughter gleamed in her eyes.

Mattie turned her head a little, smiling. 'It's not every woman's daughter-in-law who can also be counted a friend,' she said, softly. 'And certainly not every woman's daughter-in-law who is as brave as mine is!'

Hannah stopped for a moment, eyebrows raised in laughing question. They were of a height, these two, and not unlike in build. Mattie's thick silver hair was piled on top of her head in a coil that had suffered a little, as it often did, from her habit of gardening whilst walking; wisps had detached themselves and dropped softly about her face, a small twig sat like an ornament in the silver strands. She was dressed in a cotton shirt and serviceable brown skirt, which swung about her ankles as she walked and in no way inhibited her stride or prevented her from dropping frequently to her knees in the muddy flower beds.

'Brave? How − brave?' Hannah asked.

'Why, taking Harry on in the first place, of course! My dear, you must have been the very tower of courage to even have contemplated it!' Mattie smiled with the beguiling honesty that Hannah loved. 'He's mine, and I love him, but I'm well aware that he's not the easiest of men.'

'Perhaps,' Hannah said, turning to watch the ducks, the slight tightening of her fingers the only sign of tension. With a sudden breath she took the plunge. 'Perhaps fatherhood will change him? I hear it does happen?'

The silence was absolute.

Hannah waited for as long as she could bear, then faced the other woman.

Mattie was staring at her. She opened her mouth to speak, cleared her throat, tried again. 'Hannah! You − you're having a child?'

'Yes.'

'You know −?' Mattie stopped.

'Yes.'

'Oh, my dear girl. My dear, dear girl!' Mattie opened her arms, flung them about Hannah, hugging her, rocking her. 'What news, what wonderful news!'

'We waited until we were sure.' It was not entirely the truth, but in some ways close enough. Hannah's smile was suddenly brilliant. 'You missed the wedding. I thought you might like to plan the christening?' She and Harry had been married one stormy morning on the deck of the *Mauritius* as she battled across the Bay of Biscay; the place and the conditions, Hannah had often remarked since, a perfect omen for a union between chalk and cheese.

'When? When is the child due?'

'Next spring.' Hannah laughed as Jake bounded out from the bushes, wet and bedraggled, shaking himself boisterously all over them. 'As you said, a child of the twentieth century.'

Mattie took a breath. 'The twentieth century,' she repeated, and looked back at Hannah, suddenly sober. 'And what will it bring for him?' she asked.

Hannah shook her head, equally thoughtful. 'Who knows? Freedom, I hope. And understanding. Change, at any rate. Change for him and change for us.'

Mattie well understood the reference. 'You've been to more meetings?'

'Yes. Mattie, you should come! It isn't just women, you know – there are many men, well-educated, sensible men, who think that women should have the vote.'

'Perhaps I will.' Mattie raised a finger, 'But not for a while, young woman! Modern you may be, but child-bearing is no easier now than it was thirty years ago. You must be careful!'

Almost unconsciously Hannah's hand rested upon her still-flat stomach. 'Oh, I'll be careful. I promise.' She grinned. 'And the battle against stupidity and prejudice that the suffragists are fighting will take a lot longer than a few months. They won't miss me for a while. And then, who knows,' she tapped her stomach again, lightly, 'we might have a new recruit!'

'Two new recruits,' Mattie said. 'I think you're right. I ought to be there too. Why not? Why shouldn't the new century hold some excitement for us grannies?'

They resumed their walk, both for a moment absorbed in

their own thoughts. Across the lawns the old, ramshackle house, rambling and homely, basked in sunshine, its wet tiled roof gleaming. On the terrace two figures stood, Harry tall, slender, dark as a shadow, Rupert portly, happily dishevelled and puffing contentedly on his pipe. 'Harry's happy?' Mattie asked at last, softly.

Hannah was quiet for a moment. Then, 'Yes,' she said, and looked up with clear, honest eyes. 'With reservations.'

Harry had been furious when she told him; furious and frightened, and angry at himself for being so. It had taken all her skill, all her own firm and determined hopes, to calm him.

'It isn't certain that the blood will show.' Mattie's voice, not without effort, was crisp and sensible, the words blunt. 'It doesn't in Harry – well, I suppose if one knew, and looked for signs –' She stopped, then in a burst of unexpected fury clenched her hands and her jaw. 'Damn the world!' she said, very quietly. 'Damn this unfair, ignorant world!'

'Not all of it,' Hannah said, calmly. 'Not all of it is like that. And it will change. I know it will.'

Her mother-in-law stopped walking, turned to face her. Dark eyes held pale for a long moment, the one gaze sympathetic, but unconvinced, the other level and hopeful. 'Ah, Hannah,' was all Mattie said, a little sadly.

They began to walk again. Hannah slipped an arm into Mattie's. 'It will be all right.'

The other woman's mood lightened; she smiled warmly. 'Of course it will be. Of course.'

'Harry's making a great success of the stables – Mr Dodgeson said something about a partnership.'

'Really? Now that is good news. How strange to think of my poor, wild Harry a husband, a father, a respectable breeder of horseflesh.'

'His ambition is for the stables to be known for the best hunters in the south of England.'

Mattie crooked a graceless eyebrow. 'Is that all?'

'And providing he doesn't break his silly neck first, then I see no reason why he shouldn't do it. I've never seen a man ride more recklessly!' There was a tinge of wifely irritation in the words.

Mattie glanced at her. 'He has to do something recklessly, my dear.' Her smile took the edge from the words. 'It's the nature of the beast.'

Hannah laughed aloud, acknowledging a motherly half-rebuke. 'That's true.'

They turned back towards the house. Mattie stopped to dead-head a rose. Jake pushed off into the undergrowth again. Mattie pocketed her secateurs, shook her untidy head a little. 'A baby!' she said, softly. 'Gracious me! A baby!'

The men were waiting on the terrace. Hannah's heart gave the familiar yet still strange little lurch as Harry turned to her. Rupert heaved himself out of the wicker chair in which he had been sitting. 'Champagne,' he said, beaming. 'I hear there's cause for celebration!'

'Splendid idea.' Harry had come to Coombe House on that first, undoubtedly fraught occasion some months before determined to dislike his stepfather. Hannah smiled at the thought of it now; no-one could dislike Rupert. It simply was not possible. He was as wise, as kindly and as good-tempered as Mattie had described him; one might just as well try to dislike one's very favourite uncle. He would make a wonderful grandfather. She glanced at Harry. Please God, she prayed, make him the kind of father I know that he can be.

That one last battle had been the worst.

'Supposing –' he could not bring himself to voice the worst of his fears '– supposing something goes wrong?' he had said, appalled and shaking when she had told him her news. 'What will we do?'

'You mean supposing his skin is dark? His hair is curly? His features different from ours? We'll love him! That's what we'll do!' For all her understanding, Hannah had herself been furious. 'Harry, what chance has the child – any child! – if its own father is prejudiced against it?'

'I'm not! I'm not! It's just –' He had not been able to go on.

She had put her arms about him then, laid her face upon the thick black hair. 'I know. I know why you're frightened. But

407

Harry, you aren't eighteen years old now. And this is very nearly the twentieth century. Something's got to change. Why shouldn't we help that change? The child will be ours – yours and mine. The child will be beautiful and we'll love him. Or her. That's all that counts, isn't it, at least for now? We'll face everything else as it comes. We'll help him. He won't be alone. And if others care to think differently than we do, what does it matter? There'll be people to stand by us. People who know right from wrong. People who will love a man for what he is, not for what his father or his grandfather was. You've found that yourself already, you know it.'

It had taken time. For the first few weeks Harry had seemed unable fully to share her happiness, had resisted any attempt to speak about or to plan for the coming child; until the day they had watched a new-born foal, dazed, helpless, still wet from birth, stagger to its feet and nuzzle the warmth of its mother's teats. They had been standing in the hay-scented warmth of the stable. The little animal, all long, wobbly legs and huge eyes, stood trusting and quiet as the mare turned to lick it clean with a loving tongue. Hannah had felt all at once quite desperately alone, had fought the unexpected tears that burned in her eyes, turning a little from Harry so that he would not see. A moment later she had been taken by surprise to feel herself fiercely gathered into her husband's arms. She had felt the tears that had shaken him as the last, bitter pain had finally been washed away. The following day they had begun to discuss names, and at last he had agreed that they should tell Mattie and Rupert. To look at him now, Hannah thought, happiness rising as they lifted their glasses in a toast to the new life within her, no-one could doubt his pride and his pleasure. She exchanged a glance with Mattie, smiling affectionately at the glint of tears in the still-bright dark eyes.

'Weeping, Mattie dear?' Rupert put a huge arm about her shoulders. 'Can't have that, my dear; you can't drink Champagne when you're crying, you know. It makes the bubbles go up your nose.'

'Of course I'm not crying.' Mattie beamed about her. The tears spilled and ran down her cheeks. 'Why should I be crying?'

'Because Jake's digging a large hole in your best rose bed?' her son suggested, solemn-faced.

She rubbed her eyes, looked to where the huge dog, wet as a soaked rug, was doing just that. 'Well, he's got to have somewhere to bury his bone, now hasn't he?' she asked, mildly.

'That definitely decides it,' Hannah said.

'What? What does it decide?'

'Any little girl who has a grandmother as dotty as you deserves to be called after her. Don't you think?'

Harry grinned. Rupert, obviously already told of the idea, smiled at his wife with huge and quiet affection.

Mattie's expression was one of simple, speechless delight. 'You mean it? You'll call her after me?'

'If she's a she,' Hannah said, laughing. 'If not –' she hesitated, glanced at Harry and away '– if not, well, we haven't decided.'

There was an undeniably significant silence. Mattie, wisely, said nothing. Rupert, under no such delicate restraint, looked innocently from one to another. 'What are the choices?'

Hannah said nothing.

Harry finished his Champagne. 'Hannah,' he said, repressively, 'rather favours Joshua.'

Mattie caught her breath.

Hannah took another sip of her wine, set the glass down, turned composedly. 'I've always rather liked the name. But there's no need to take a decision yet. We've months to think about it.'

Harry's mouth set in a stubborn line.

'Time to go, my dear,' Hannah said. 'You wanted to be back for the evening gallop.'

Farewells taken, Mattie and Rupert stood watching the small dogcart bowl off down the uneven gravel drive towards the lane that led into Maidstone.

Rupert's voice was very gentle. 'And they all lived happily ever after,' he said.

'I hope so.' Mattie's voice was so quiet it was almost inaudible, and inevitable tears blurred it. 'Oh, God in heaven, I hope so!'

Rupert, very firmly, turned her to face him. 'There is more Champagne,' he said. 'I recommend it.'

'For celebration?' she asked, shakily. 'Or for the treatment of craven terror?'

'For either,' he said, equably. 'Or, of course, for both.' And quietly took her hand to lead her back into her garden.